FIRST BLOOD

FIRST BLOOD

BIRTH OF THE VAMPIRE

EDITED BY ASA MERRITT

an imprint of

ARC
MANOR
Rockville, Maryland

ISBN: 978-1-60450-481-1

Published by Phoenix Pick
an imprint of Arc Manor
P. O. Box 10339
Rockville, MD 20849-0339
www.ArcManor.com

CONTENTS

INTRODUCTION

ampires—humans or creatures that consume blood to survive—exist within ancient, deep wells of the human imagination. Nearly every culture in the world includes some version of them in their catalogue of myths, lore, and religion. However, this volume concerns not the vampires that haunted pre-modern or even pre-enlightenment man, but rather the vampires first depicted in literature. These works were generated by writers who spun vampire yarns with the knowledge that vampires are not real; they wrote about vampires without fear of being attacked, maimed, raped, killed, blood-drained, or made undead (with the exception of *Visum et Repertum,* a military report). However, although the writers of this collection knew vampires to be nonexistent, many (probably most) of their readers did not.

Our fascination with vampires originates from terror. These classical pieces of vampire literature were generated in a psychological landscape that gave far more legitimacy to evil and were read by a populace far more superstitious. I invite you, in the following pages, to give yourself over to such a mindset. The raucous ride with bloodsucking vampires through moments of insatiable hunger, perverse sex, murder, betrayal, and escape will be all the more thrilling.

Vampire literature originated in the mid-eighteenth century and ended with *Dracula,* the last piece in this collection. Given the saturation of contemporary culture with everything vampire, this may seem a fallacious claim. Yet as Oxford Professor Maud Ellmann brilliantly asserts, "Bram Stoker's achievement was to free vampires from literature and restore them to the realm of folklore" (Ellmann vii). The multiplicity of movies and books concerning vampires, as well as the vast cultural milieu with vampire themes, illustrates how diluted the vampire figure has become. Like the ghost or the dragon or the elf, the vampire is portrayed in an almost infinite number of ways. The literature in this collection toes a much stricter line: Every innovation within the tradition was taken extremely seriously. The modern history of graffiti provides a parallel. Initially tied intrinsically to the underground hip-hop and punk rock music scenes, the word *graffiti* is now an umbrella term used to describe everything from unsanctioned installation art to scrawled expletives, making it impossible to pin down in a few sentences. The same holds true for the word *vampire*.

Yet the pieces in this collection are incredibly relevant to understanding today's vampire. As broad as the genre has become, it did have a foundation, and you are about to explore it. You will see the vampires in the following works become increasingly human. They graduate from ruthless bloodsucking beasts of folklore to medieval lovers to urbane gentlemen. Any exposure to the most popular twenty-first century vampires reveals that this trajectory hasn't stopped. Classical vampire literature has also cemented core themes of vampire art such as transgression, religion, sex, and moral ambiguity. In addition to themes, nearly all the common vampire traits and "rules" emerge in these works for the first time.

This book is divided into three parts. The first contains one report and three poems translated from German as well as a ballad poem that Samuel Coleridge wrote. The second presents two English novellas and excerpts from a serial novel. The final part consists of Bram Stoker's seminal novel, *Dracula*. The provided introductions discuss central themes, trends, and developments. Be aware that the tales and poems that follow are exciting pieces of literature outside their importance to the vampire genre. I strongly encourage you to read each of them prior to reading the introductions provided. These narratives derive much of their power from shock and suspense; to deprive yourself of that would be a disservice. The ballads "William and Helen" and "Christabel" are best experienced if read aloud.

PART I: A GERMAN DUSK

*V*ampire literature began in Germany, where the first pieces of vampire poetry and fiction were written. Early German works inspired and informed all vampire literature that followed. No fewer than four pieces of this collection are translated from German; without these works, the vampires we know today—the characters of TV shows, films, and popular fiction—would never have come to be. Why Germany? Why not England? After all, *Dracula*, the most influential piece of vampire literature, was written in English. Why not Eastern Europe, where superstition surrounding vampires was embraced more than anywhere else in the world? No simple answer exists, but analysis of the geopolitical, literary, and cultural trends that dominated Germany during the eighteenth century helps illuminate the question.

Military and geopolitical engagements placed Germans, including German scientists and philosophers, in proximity to the heartland of vampire superstition—namely, Hungary and the Balkans. This was the result of one chapter of the centuries-long Ottoman-Hapsburg wars. Between 1716 and 1718, Austrian forces won a series of key victories that gave them control of the region. After the military conflict ceased, Austria maintained a political and military presence. Consequently, the Austrians quickly became involved with local issues, one being the hysteria around so-called vampires.

The first piece in this collection, *Visum et Repertum* (Seen and Discovered)—the only non-fiction text—captures both the local fears and superstitions regarding vampires as well as the response of the occupying forces. You will read how respected officials deemed vampires to be real. It is easy to imagine how sensationally such news would be received. While the native population of Hungary experienced vampire hysteria, Germans—seemingly safe in their more "civilized" enclave—experienced a scientific hysteria of their own. Could it be possible? Could vampires exist? Academics, scientists, scholars, and adventurers set an Eastern course to answer the question. The steady flow of their detailed, compelling reports that returned from such expeditions elevated "the vampire question" to a prominent place in the German public consciousness. The general public read of fangs and blood in the newspapers, discussed the magical properties of garlic, and speculated about the desires of the undead. It's no wonder that the nation's greatest imaginations soon turned their efforts to the topic as well.

The emergence of the vampire anticipated the soon-to-be prevailing fictional style, Gothic. Characterized by classical settings, mystery, dread, terror, mysticism, madness, and darkness, Gothic fiction held an important place in Western literature throughout the late eighteenth century and into the nineteenth during the golden years of Romantic poets such as Keats, Coleridge, Byron, and Shelley. Its stock characters include rakes, cripples, demons, maidens, and conjurers. The Gothic movement, an offshoot of Romanticism, rejected the hyper-rational, scientific notions of the Enlightenment in favor of emotional expressiveness and connection to forces beyond the scope of human civilization. The three German poems that follow *Visum et Repertum* in this collection are situated squarely within this literary landscape. Each poem summons images of nightmarish medieval settings and contains overtures and references to the less rational, more mysterious attitude of the ancient world. However, it is important to note that, although the following poems conform to the Gothic style, they do embrace one central tenet of the Age of Reason: the rejection of Christianity as a source of truth. This decision went on to play a crucial role in vampire fiction.

In addition to the introduction of Gothic Romanticism, a second literary movement emerged as these early vampire poems were being composed: German nationalism. Many eighteenth-century German thinkers sought to develop a literary tradition and literary canon in Germany that rivaled those of the English and French. One leader of this movement was Johann Gottfried Herder, a philosopher and writer whose ideas informed the work of luminaries such as Immanuel Kant and Goethe. Herder insisted that Germany was amiss in not developing a strong national literature—that German writers had too long worked in the shadow of writers from other Western nations. Accordingly, he insisted on acknowledgement of the "Volk"—that is, "the people of Germany"—as the heart of the German national identity. He published numerous collections of German folk tales in hopes of eliciting commitment to German themes from the nation's writers. "Lenore," Bürger's poem in this collection, was fashioned with Herder's ideals in mind. Herder similarly inspired Goethe, who went on to write "The Bride of Corinth."

To the contemporary English-speaking reader, the following German works present the most challenges. They are poems, translated, and very old. Nevertheless, their importance in the development of the genre cannot be overstated, and the fight through the sometimes cumbersome vocabulary and syntax is certainly worth the insight you will acquire into the history of vampire literature.

VISUM ET REPERTUM[1]

1732

VARIOUS AUSTRIAN OFFICIALS

*V*isum et Repertum, a military report first published in 1732, provides an example of the kind of texts arriving from the East that informed and inspired the first forays into vampire literature. Written in German, the report details official findings of the case of Arnold Paole, a former Serbian soldier believed to be a vampire. The report leaves no doubt that Europeans' fascination with vampires stemmed not simply from ancient folklore, but from contemporary accounts. To understand the origins of the literary vampire, it is important to study these latter accounts. It wasn't until the masses encountered the vampire in print—that is, in mainstream publications—that the figure was taken seriously enough to garner the attention of the most creative imaginations of the day. This is partly explained by the sheer magnitude of the audience such reports reached. Frayling, as quoted by Senf, stated that:

> This unusually detailed report caused a sensation: at the annual Leipzig fair, in 1732, a cheap version of the Arnold Paole story became an instant best-seller; on March 3rd, the *Dutch Gleaner* (which was very popular in Versailles court circles) ran a detailed and suitably embellished account... Some English periodicals, including the *London Journal* and the *Gentleman's Magazine*, immediately cobbled together translations or adaptations, which appeared from March to May 1732...Augustin Calmet anthologized all these articles in his full-length *Treatise* (Senf 25).

In addition to its appeal to a broad readership, the report, ironically, also lured writers with its objective, factual tone. It reads as soberly as a medical diagnosis and concludes—with the stamp of the Hapsburg Monarchy— that vampires are real. This seed of concrete belief, planted in thousands of literate households across Europe, paved the way for innumerable fictitious

---

1 Seen and Discovered (Latin).

15

opportunities. The process was not unlike the fictionalizing of the "Orient" by French and British novelists following the initial contact their respective countries made with the Middle East. In that case, the barely known, exotic, and mysterious lands of Egypt and Persia provided writers with a blank canvas—a world to color and perceive and enliven by their own reckoning. News of the vampire, continually evolving and always sensational, was forged into being a similar vessel for fiction: a character as vast and rich as the East, whose sole defining trait was an appetite for blood.

VISUM ET REPERTUM

*Q*fter it had been reported that in the village of Medvegia the so-called vampires had killed some people by sucking their blood, I was, by high degree of a local Honorable Supreme Command, sent there to investigate the matter thoroughly along with officers detailed for that purpose and two subordinate medical officers, and therefore carried out and heard the present inquiry in the company of the captain of the Stallath Company of haiduks,[2] Gorschiz Hadnack, the standard-bearer and the oldest haiduk of the village, as follows: who unanimously recount that about five years ago a local haiduk by the name of Arnold Paole broke his neck in a fall from a haywagon. This man had during his lifetime often revealed that, near Gossowa in Turkish Serbia, he had been troubled by a vampire, wherefore he had eaten from the earth of the vampire's grave and had smeared himself with the vampire's blood, in order to be free from the velation he had suffered.

In 20 or 30 days after his death some people complained that they were being bothered by this same Arnod Paole; and in fact four people were killed by him. In order to end this evil, they dug up this Arnold Paole 40 days after his death - this on the advice of a soldier, who had been present at such events before; and they found that he was quite complete and undecayed, and that fresh blood had flowed from his eyes, nose, mouth, and ears; that the shirt, the covering, and the coffin were completely bloody; that the old nails on his hands and feet, along with the skin, had fallen off, and that new ones had grown; and since they saw from this that he was a true vampire, they drove a stake through his heart, according to their custom, whereby he gave an audible groan and bled copiously, Thereupon they burned the body the same day to ashes and threw these into the grave.

---

2 Mercenary.

These people say further that all those who were tormented and killed by the vampire must themselves become vampires.

Therefore they disinterred the above-mentioned four people in the same way. Then they also add that this Arnod Paole attacked not only the people but also the cattle, and sucked out their blood. And since the people used the flesh of such cattle, it appears that some vampires are again present here, inasmuch as, in a period of three months, 17 young and old people died, among them some who, with no previous illness, died in two or at the most three days. In addition, the haiduk Jowiza reports that his step-daughter, by name of Stanacka, lay down to sleep 15 days ago, fresh and healthy, but at midnight she started up out of her sleep with a terrible cry, fearful and trembling, and complained that she had been throttled by the son of a haiduk by the name of Milloe, who had died nine weeks earlier, whereupon she had experienced a great pain in the chest and became worse hour by hour, until finally she died on the third day. At this we went the same afternoon to the graveyard, along with the often-mentioned oldest haiduks of the village, in order to cause the suspicious graves to be opened and to examine the bodies in them, whereby, after all of them had been dissected, there was found:

1. A woman by the name of Stana, 20 years old, who had died in childbirth two months ago, after a three-day illness, and who had herself said, before her death, she had painted herself with the blood of a vampire, wherefore both she and her child - which had died right after birth and because of a careless burial had been half eaten by the dogs- must also become vampires. She was quite complete and undecayed. After the opening of the body there was found in the cavitate pectoris a quantity of fresh extravascular blood. The vessels of the arteries and veins, like the ventriculis ortis, were not, as is usual, filled with coagulated blood, and the whole viscera, that is, the lung, liver, stomach, spleen, and intestines were quite fresh as they would be in a healthy person.

The uterus was however quite enlarged and very inflamed externally, for the placenta and lochia had remained in place, wherefore the same was in complete putredine. The skin on her hands and feet, along with the old nails, fell away on their own, but on the other hand completely new nails were evident, along with a fresh and vivid skin.

2. There was a woman by the name of Miliza (60 years old), who had died after a three-month sickness and had been buried 90-some days earlier. In the chest much liquid blood was found; and the other viscera were, like those mentioned before, in a good condition. During her dissection, all the haiduks who were standing around marveled greatly at her plumpness and perfect body, uniformly stating that they had known the woman well, from

her youth, and that she had; throughout her life, looked and been very lean and dried up, and they emphasized that she had come to this surprising plumpness in the grave. They also said that it was she who started the vampires this time, because she had eaten of the flesh of those sheep that had been killed by the previous vampires.

3. There was an eight-day-old child which had lain in the grave for 90 days and was similarly in a condition of vampirism.

4. The son of a haiduk, 16 years old, was dug up, having lain in the earth for nine weeks, after he had died from a three-day illness, and was found like the other vampires.

5. Joachim, also the son of a haiduk, 17 years old; had died after a three-day illness. He had been buried eight weeks and four days and, on being dissected; was found in similar condition.

6. A woman by the name of Ruscha who had died after a ten-day illness and had been buried six weeks previous, in whom there was much fresh blood not only in the chest but also in fundo ventriculi. The same showed itself in her child, which was 18 days old and had died five weeks previously.

7. No less did a girl ten years of age, who had died two months previously, find herself in the above-mentioned condition, quite complete and undecayed; and had much fresh blood in her chest.

8. They caused the wife of the Hadnack to be dug up, along with her child. She had died seven weeks previously, her child - who was eight weeks old- 21 days previously, and it was found that both mother and child were completely decomposed, although earth and grave were like those of the vampires lying nearby.

9. A servant of the local corporal of the haiduks, by the name of Rhade, 21 years old, died after a three-month-long illness, and after a five week burial was found completely decomposed.

10. The wife of the local bariactar, along with her child, having died five weeks previously, were also completely decomposed.

11. With Stanche, a local haiduk, 60 years old; who had died six weeks previously, I noticed a profuse liquid blood, like the others, in the chest and stomach. The entire body was in the oft-named condition of vampirism.

12. Milloe, a haiduk, 25 years old; who had lain for six weeks in the earth, also was found in the condition of vampirism mentioned.

13. Stanoika, the wife of a haiduk, 20 years old, died after a three-day illness and had been buried 18 days previously. In the dissection I found that she

was in her countenance quite red and of a vivid color, and, as was mentioned above, she had been throttled, at midnight, by Milloe, the son of the haiduk, and there was also to be seen, on the right side under the ear, a bloodshot blue mark, the length of a finger. As she was being taken out of the grave, a quantity of fresh blood flowed from her nose. With the dissection I found; as mentioned often already, a regular fragrant fresh bleeding, not only in the chest cavity, but also in ventriculo cordis. All the viscera found themselves in a completely good and healthy condition. The hypodermis of the entire body, along with the fresh nails of hands and feet, was as though completely fresh.

After the examination had taken place, the heads of the vampires were cut off by the local gypsies and burned along with the bodies, and then the ashes were thrown into the river Morava. The decomposed bodies, however, were laid back into their own graves. Which I attest along with those assistant medical officers provided for me. Actum ut supra:[3]

L.S. Johannes Fluchinger, Regimental Medical Officer of the Foot Regiment of the Honorable B. Furstenbusch.

L.S. J.H. Siegel, Medical Officer of the Honorable Morall Regiment. .S. Johann Friedrich Baumgarten, Medical Officer of the Foot Regiment of the Honorable B. Furstenbusch.

Undersigned attest herewith that all which the Regimental Medical Officer of the Foot Regiment of the Honorable B. Furstenbusch has observed in the matter of vampires—along with both medical officers who signed with him—is in every way truthful and has been undertaken, observed, and examined in our own presence. In confirmation thereof is our signature in our own hand, of our making, Belgrade, January 26, 1732.

L.S. Buttener, Lieutenant Colonel of the Honorable Alexandrian Regiment.

L.S. J.H. von Lindenfels, Officer of the Honorable Alexandrian Regiment.

---

3 On the stated date (Latin). In reference to the signatures.

THE VAMPIRE

1748

HEINRICH AUGUST OSSENFELDER

ree of scientific jargon, academic debate, and field anecdotes of Hapsburg soldiers, "The Vampire" by Heinrich Ossenfelder *imagines* a
vampire. The poem is nothing short of the missing link in vampire
literature. Prior to its publication, the public sated its fascination with the
undead through folklore (in the oral tradition) and non-fiction exclusively.
After its publication, other poets and eventually novelists began to enlist
the deep well of vampire lore to explore themes of transgression, religion,
and sex. The fact that "The Vampire" was published in a scientific journal alongside an article about vampire reports in Eastern Europe illustrates
how quietly this evolution began. Just as humankind's missing link gave us
upright posture and opposable thumbs, "The Vampire" generated signature
tropes of vampire literature.

The poem tells a story of unrequited love. A young woman's religious
piety, "Unbending, fast and firm," fends off the advances of the poem's
speaker, who is, in fact, a vampire. Her refusal leads the speaker to announce that he will visit her during the night, rape her, and kill her (more
or less simultaneously). In a mere twenty-two lines, Ossenfelder introduces
numerous hallmarks of vampire literature. The "young maiden's" name is
Christine—a direct reference to Christianity. We see here for the first time
vampires symbolically representing the threat of superstition to Christianity. The poem's final two lines, "Compared with such instruction / What are
a mother's charms," suggest that the vampire is not only a threat, but he may
also represent a better alternative. In addition, the references to Hungary in
lines six and seven set the precedent for situating vampire stories in Central
and Eastern Europe—one that will be honored in the majority of works in
this anthology.

Most significantly, the poem portrays the vampire as a dangerous figure,
yet undeniably erotic. His sexual aims will be achieved, and his prowess

will cause his victim to "tremble." Lines such as, "For thus shall I be kissing / And death's threshold thou' it be crossing" suggest that the vampire will lead Christine to orgasm, despite the fact that he is penetrating her by force. The poem's brazen ending invites the reader to imagine sex without the constraints of a moral code. This invitation to sexually transgress emerges in one form or another in every work in this volume. Despite history's general direction of increased sexual liberation and openness, this invitation still holds massive appeal.

THE VAMPIRE

My dear young maiden clingeth
Unbending. fast and firm
To all the long-held teaching
Of a mother ever true;
As in vampires unmortal
Folk on the Theyse's[4] portal
Heyduck-like[5] do believe.
But my Christine thou dost dally,
And wilt my loving parry
Till I myself avenging
To a vampire's health a-drinking
Him toast in pale tockay[6].

And as softly thou art sleeping
To thee shall I come creeping
And thy life's blood drain away.
And so shalt thou be trembling
For thus shall I be kissing
And death's threshold thou' it be crossing
With fear, in my cold arms.
And last shall I thee question
Compared to such instruction
What are a mother's charms?

---

4 River in Hungary
5 Official of the Hungarian Court.
6 Type of wine.

WILLIAM AND HELEN

(AN ADAPTION OF "LENORE" (1773)
BY GOTTFRIED AUGUST BÜRGER)

1794

SIR WALTER SCOTT

Selecting a translation of Gottfried August Bürger's "Lenore" proved one of the more difficult tasks in the creation of this anthology. Many satisfactory translations exist, each with their particular strengths: Some possess superior diction, others grammatical fluidity, etc. I have selected Sir Walter Scott's rendition, entitled "William and Helen," because of its robust, exhilarating pace. Lenore's story is primarily the story of a single blistering ride through the night atop a dynamo of a horse, and "William and Helen" similarly blisters as a poem. Spirited readings of gothic ballads in front of private and semi-public audiences frequently occurred during the early nineteenth century as a popular form of entertainment. In fact, Scott learned of "Lenore" through such a reading. After learning the poem's basic premise from a friend who had heard it read in Edinburgh, Scott sought his own copy in German and began translating in earnest. If you enjoy this poem, be sure to read other translations. In respect to the other fine poets who poured their efforts into "Lenore," it must be stated that Scott's version does fail in places where others succeed. For example, the horrifying images of ghosts and the cemetery depicted in the end of the poem scratch and claw off the page in Taylor's and Rossetti's translations whereas in Scott's they merely suffice. Such are the challenges of translation.

"Lenore" relates a tale of young love gone wrong. A young woman (Lenore in most versions, Helen in Scott's version) patiently waits for her husband-to-be, William, to return from war. However, he does not arrive with the train of returning soldiers, but instead dramatically appears to her that night riding a horse. Upon seeing him, Helen is overcome with joy, and the two of them set off on a breakneck ride to their "bridal bed," which lies at some location William will not disclose. Gradually, Helen's elation subsides as the nature and endpoint of the horse ride becomes increasingly unclear and frightening. Yet William ignores her entreaties for answers and continues on. The poem ends in a terrifying churchyard and cemetery, where "shriek and cry whiz round" and "unhallow'd ghosts were heard." Dismounting from his horse, William's corporeal form transforms to "a ghastly skeleton." He descends into a grave, leaving Helen alone at the mercy of the spirits that surround her.

In charting the development of the vampire in literature, "Lenore" may seem an odd selection as the poem neither depicts an actual vampire nor alludes to one. Nevertheless, writers of vampire literature who followed Bürger appropriated many aspects of the poem's central narrative—most notably, that a character returns from the dead to claim the life of a loved one. Another reason why "Lenore" belongs in the canon of classical vampire literature is its numerous similarities to Ossenfelder's "The Vampire," which, as previously established, is the grandfather of all vampire literature. Both poems hinge on a tainted romantic arrangement that is destructive yet inevitable as, in both cases, the male vampire figure has undeniable sexual power. "Lenore" and the "The Vampire" also similarly represent resistance to each respective vampire in the form of a mother figure. The mothers condemn the objects of their daughters' desire. In doing so, both Christine's mother and the mother of Helen offer religious admonishments. In "Lenore," the mother enlists another argument: that the lover in question has been unfaithful. This adds yet another ripple in the vampire's irresistibility. Despite his moral failings, the vampire maintains his allure.

Finally, any discussion of "Lenore" is not complete without mentioning its most famous line: *"Denn die Toten reiten schnell"* (For the dead travel fast). Regrettably, Scott doesn't use this phrase, but its succinct potency lives on in numerous vampire books and films that followed "Lenore," including a direct reference in *Dracula*.

WILLIAM AND HELEN

I.

From heavy dreams fair Helen rose,
And eyed the dawning red:
"Alas, my love, thou tarriest long!
O art thou false or dead?"—

II.

With gallant Fred'rick's princely power
He sought the bold Crusade;
But not a word from Judah's wars[7]
Told Helen how he sped.

III.

With Paynim and with Saracen[8]
At length a truce was made,
And every knight return'd to dry
The tears his love had shed.

IV.

Our gallant host was homeward bound
With many a song of joy;
Green waved the laurel in each plume,
The badge of victory.

V.

And old and young, and sire and son,
To meet them crowd the way,
With shouts, and mirth, and melody,
The debt of love to pay.

VI.

Full many a maid her true-love met,
And sobb'd in his embrace,
And flutt'ring joy in tears and smiles
Array'd full many a face.

VII.

Nor joy nor smile for Helen sad
She sought the host in vain;
For none could tell her William's fate,
In faithless, or if slain.

---

7 The Third Crusade.
8 *Paynim* and *Saracen* were terms used to describe non-Christian, indigenous peoples of the Holy Land.

VIII.

The martial band is past and gone;
She rends her raven hair,
And in distraction's bitter mood
She weeps with wild despair.

IX.

"O rise, my child," her mother said,
"Nor sorrow thus in vain;
A perjured lover's fleeting heart
No tears recall again."—

X.

"O mother, what is gone, is gone,
What's lost for ever lorn:
Death, death alone can comfort me;
O had I ne'er been born!

XI.

"O break, my heart, — O break at once!
Drink my life-blood, Despair!
No joy remains on earth for me,
For me in Heaven no share."—

XII.

"O enter not in judgement, Lord!"
The pious mother prays;
"Impute not guilt to thy frail child!
She knows not what she says.

XIII.

"O say thy pater noster,[9] child,
O turn to God and grace!
His will, that turn'd thy bliss to bale,
Can change thy bale to bliss."—

XIV.

"O mother, mother, what is bliss?

9 Our Father (Latin). First two words of the Lord's Prayer: "Our Father, who art in heaven..."

O mother, what is bale?
My William's love was heaven on earth,
Without it earth is hell.

XV.

"Why should I pray to ruthless Heaven,
Since my loved William's slain?
I only pray'd for William's sake,
And all my prayers were vain."—

XVI.

"O take the sacrament, my child,
And check these tears that flow;
By resignation's humble prayer,
O hallow'd be thy woe!"—

XVII.

"No sacrament can quench this fire,
Or slake this scorching pain;
No sacrament can bid the dead
Arise and live again.

XVIII.

"O break, my heart, — O break at once!
Be thou my God, Despair!
Heaven's heaviest blow has fallen on me,
And vain each fruitless prayer."—

XIX.

"O enter not in judgement, Lord,
With thy frail child of clay!
She knows not what her tongue has spoke;
Impute it not, I pray!

XX.

"Forbear, my child, this desperate woe,
And turn to God and grace;
Well can devotion's heavenly glow
Convert thy bale to bliss."—

XXI.

"O mother, mother, what is bliss?
O mother, what is bale?
Without my William what were heaven,
Or with him what were hell?"—

XXII.

Wild she arraigns the eternal doom,
Upbraids each sacred power,
Till, spent, she sought her silent room,
All in the lonely tower.

XXIII.

She beat her breast, she wrung her hands,
Till sun and day were o'er,
And through the glimmering lattice shone
The twinkling of the star.

XXIV.

Then, crash! the heavy drawbridge fell
That o'er the moat was hung;
And, clatter! clatter! on its boards
The hoof of courser[10] rung.

XXV.

The clank of echoing steel was heard
As off the rider bounded;
And slowly on the winding stair
A heavy footstep sounded.

XXVI.

And hark! and hark! a knock — Tap! tap!
A rustling stifled noise;—
Door-latch and tinkling staples ring;—
At length a whispering voice.

XXVII.

"Awake, awake, arise, my love!

---

10 Swift or spirited horse.

How, Helen, dost thou fare?
Wak'st thou, or sleep'st? laugh'st thou or weep'st?
Hast thought on me, my fair?"—

XXVIII.

"My love! my love! — so late by night!—
I waked, I wept for thee:
Much have I borne since dawn of morn;
Where, William, couldst thou be?"—

XXIX.

"We saddle late — from Hungary
I rode since darkness fell;
And to its bourne[11] we both return
Before the matin-bell."[12]—

XXX.

"O rest this night within my arms,
And warm thee in their fold!
Chill howls through hawthorn bush the wind:—
My love is deadly cold."—

XXXI.

"Let the wind howl through hawthorn bush!
This night we must away;
The steed is wight,[13] the spur is bright;
I cannot stay till day.

XXXII.

"Busk, busk, and boune![14] Thou mount'st behind
Upon my black barb steed:
O'er stock and stile, a hundred miles,
We haste to bridal bed."—

---

11 Boundary.
12 Call to morning prayer.
13 Valiant.
14 *Busk* and *boune*: 'prepare oneself,' and 'get ready,' respectively (Scottish).

XXXIII.

"To-night — to-night a hundred miles!—
O dearest William, stay!
The bell strikes twelve — dark, dismal hour!
O wait, my love, till day!"—

XXXIV.

"Look here, look here — the moon shines clear—
Full fast I ween we ride;
Mount and away! for ere the day
We reach our bridal bed.

XXXV.

"The black barb snorts, the bridle rings;
Haste, busk, and boune, and seat thee!
The feast is made, the chamber spread,
The bridal guests await thee."—

XXXVI.

Strong love prevail'd: She busks, she bounes,
She mounts barb behind,
And round her darling William's waist
Her lily arms she twined.

XXXVII.

And, hurry! hurry! off they rode,
As fast as fast might be;
Spurn'd from the courser's thundering heels
The flashing pebbles flee.

XXXVIII.

And on the right, and on the left,
Ere they could snatch a view,
Fast, fast each mountain, mead, and plain,
And cot, and castle, flew.

XXXIX.

"Sit fast — dost fear? — The moon shines clear —
Fleet goes my barb — keep hold!

Fear'st thou?" — "O no!" she faintly said;
"But why so stern and cold?

XL.

"What yonder rings? what yonder sings?
Why shrieks the owlet grey?"—
"'Tis death-bells' clang, 'tis funeral song,
The body to the clay.

XLI.

"With song and clang, at morrow's dawn,
Ye may inter the dead:
To-night I ride with my young bride,
To deck our bridal bed.

XLII.

"Come with thy choir, thou coffin'd guest,
To swell our nuptial song!
Come, priest, to bless our marriage feast!
Come all, come all along!"—

XLIII.

Ceased clang and song; down sunk the bier;
The shrouded corpse arose:
And, hurry! hurry! all the train
The thundering steed pursues.

XLIV.

And, forward! forward! on they go;
High snorts the straining steed;
Thick pants the rider's labouring breath,
As headlong on they speed.

XLV.

"O William, why this savage haste?
And where thy bridal bed?"—
"'Tis distant far, low, damp, and chill,
And narrow, trustless maid."—

XLVI.

"No room for me?" — "Enough for both;—
Speed, speed, my barb, thy course!"
O'er thundering bridge, through boiling surge
He drove the furious horse.

XLVII.

Tramp! tramp! along the land they rode,
Splash! splash! along the sea;
The scourge[15] is wight,[16] the spur is bright,
The flashing pebbles flee.

XLVIII.

Fled past on right and left how fast
Each forest, grove, and bower!
On right and left fled past how fast
Each city, town, and tower!

XLIX.

"Dost fear? dost fear? The moon shines clear,
Dost fear to ride with me?—
Hurrah! hurrah! the dead can ride!"—
"O William, let them be!—

L.

"See there, see there! What yonder swings
And creaks 'mid whistling rain?"—
"Gibbet[17] and steel, th' accursed wheel;[18]
A murderer in his chain.—

LI.

"Hollo! thou felon, follow here:
To bridal bed we ride;
And thou shalt prance a fetter dance
Before me and my bride."—

---

15 Whip.
16 Nimble.
17 Gallows where executed were left to hang.
18 Torture device.

LII.

And, hurry! hurry! clash, clash, clash!
The wasted form descends;
And fleet as wind through hazel bush
The wild career attends.

LIII.

Tramp! tramp! along the land they rode,
Splash! splash! along the sea;
The scourge is red, the spur drops blood,
The flashing pebbles flee.

LIV.

How fled what moonshine faintly show'd!
How fled what darkness hid!
How fled the earth beneath their feet,
The heaven above their head!

LV.

"Dost fear? dost fear? The moon shines clear,
And well the dead can ride;
Does faithful Helen fear for them?"—
"O leave in peace the dead!"—

LVI.

"Barb! Barb! methinks I hear the cock;
The sand will soon be run:
Barb! Barb! I smell the morning air;
The race is wellnigh done."

LVII.

Tramp! tramp! along the land they rode;
Splash! splash! along the sea;
The scourge is red, the spur drops blood,
The flashing pebbles flee.

LVIII.

"Hurrah! hurrah! well ride the dead;
The bride, the bridge is come;

And soon we reach the bridal bed,
For, Helen, here's my home."—

LIX.

Reluctant on its rusty hinge
Revolved an iron door,
And by the pale moon's setting beam
Were seen a church and tower.

LX.

With many a shriek and cry whiz round
The birds of midnight, scared;
And rustling like autumnal leaves
Unhallow'd ghosts were heard.

LXI.

O'er many a tomb and tombstones pale
He spurr'd the fiery horse,
Till sudden at an open grave
He check'd the wondrous course.

LXII.

The falling gauntlet quits the rein,
Down drops the casque of steel,
The cuirass leaves his shrinking side,
The spur his gory heel.

LXIII.

The eyes desert the naked skull,
The mould'ring flesh the bone,
Till Helen's lily arms entwine
A ghastly skeleton.

LXIV.

The furious barb snorts fire and foam,
And, with a fearful bound,
Dissolves at once in empty air,
And leaves her on the ground.

LXV.

Half seen by fits, by fits half heard,
Pale spectres flit along,
Wheel round the maid in dismal dance,
And howl the funeral song;

LXVI.

"E'en when the heart's with anguish cleft,
Revere the doom of Heaven,
Her soul is from her body reft;
Her spirit be forgiven!"

THE BRIDE OF CORINTH

1797

JOHANN WOLFGANG VON GOETHE

"The Bride of Corinth," by Goethe, was the first piece of vampire literature written by one of the greats. Bürger and Ossenfelder were certainly respected writers of their time, but incomparable to Goethe, who wielded a great deal of literary power and influence from an early age. Accordingly, Goethe's "The Bride of Corinth" influenced the genre in a way similar to *"Visum et Repertum"*: Readership expanded, and the vampire figure grew within the public consciousness. By writing an entire ballad about a vampire, Goethe effectively approved vampires as a legitimate and important topic of literature. That fact alone warrants the poem's place in this collection, but its role in the history of vampire literature extends far beyond its popularity. The poem addresses central themes explored by its predecessors and lays track for many developments that follow.

More so than "The Vampire" or "Lenore," "The Bride of Corinth" places the conflict between Christianity and old-world religion front and center. A young man sets out to find the girl he's destined to marry per an agreement made long ago between their fathers. However, when he arrives at the home of his bride-to-be, he discovers that the family has converted to Christianity, rendering marriage impossible. In fact, the young girl has been forced to become a nun. Despite this, the object of his love elects to ignore the religious stipulations her mother has imposed (as before, the mother is the agent of the Christian agenda) and returns the man's affections. Like its predecessors, the poem asserts that Christianity is unable to repress love—specifically, love buttressed by faith in the heathen belief system.

This assertion is key to understanding why we love vampire literature. Although struggles with religious identity may not dominate today's readership, everyone can relate to the experience of being emotionally imprisoned by some external force. Whether it be society's condemnation of homosexuality, pressure to improve one's financial standing, or a mother tyrannically enforcing a

35

curfew, we all seek ways in which to pursue our dreams and desires unfettered. The vampire is capable of this freedom. It is inherent in her nature, and by reading about her we both vicariously experience her freedom and are encouraged to pursue the life we want to live. In other words, because the vampire is emboldened, she emboldens us. She is the hero of the disempowered.

However, as in life, the virtue of the vampire is not untainted. The young woman in "The Bride of Corinth" transgresses out of love, but not solely. She also is driven to the man by necessity, for in Goethe's story, she must take his life to survive. Somewhat confusedly, the poem reveals that the girl is dead, that her forced conversion led to not just a spiritual death, but a literal one, and that this death has led to her status as a vampire. Forced to come back from the grave, the bride's actions develop and expand the notion, established in "Lenore," of an individual returning from death to destroy her lover. This rule that vampires must continue to attack to survive went on to become a defining characteristic of vampires—one that remains today. The pursuit of one's desires comes with a destructive price.

Goethe began numerous other stock vampire tropes that are still consistently employed. The vampire in "The Bride of Corinth" exists in typical human form, but with physical alterations. She has "chilly blood, / But no heart is beating in her breast." A lock of hair as a gift for a vampire appears in this poem for the first time, as does the rule that vampires cannot eat regular food: "she drank of nought but blood-red wine. / For to taste the bread / There before them spread, / Nought he spoke could make the maid incline." Little did Goethe know that each of these details would generate entire plotlines for subsequent vampire series.

"The Bride of Corinth" is the last German work of this anthology. What began as scientific and military reports about supernatural creatures became by the turn of the nineteenth century a full-fledged genre for German writers to explore. Ossenfelder's "The Vampire" was a compact imaginative bomb that introduced literature to a new character; "Lenore" presented a love story gone horrifically awry; and finally, "The Bride of Corinth" provided writers with a fully formed model of the vampire character to reject, embrace, or evolve.

THE BRIDE OF CORINTH

Once a stranger youth to Corinth came,
Who in Athens lived, but hoped that he
From a certain townsman there might claim,
As his father's friend, kind courtesy.

Son and daughter, they
Had been wont to say
Should thereafter bride and bridegroom be.

But can he that boon so highly prized,
Save tis dearly bought, now hope to get?
They are Christians and have been baptized,
He and all of his are heathens yet.
For a newborn creed,
Like some loathsome weed,
Love and truth to root out oft will threat.

Father, daughter, all had gone to rest,
And the mother only watches late;
She receives with courtesy the guest,
And conducts him to the room of state.
Wine and food are brought,
Ere by him besought

Bidding him good night. she leaves him straight.

But he feels no relish now, in truth,
For the dainties so profusely spread;
Meat and drink forgets the wearied youth,
And, still dress'd, he lays him on the bed.
Scarce are closed his eyes,
When a form in-hies[19]
Through the open door with silent tread.

By his glimmering lamp discerns he now
How, in veil and garment white array'd,
With a black and gold band round her brow,
Glides into the room a bashful maid.
But she, at his sight,
Lifts her hand so white,
And appears as though full sore afraid.

---

19 Enters quickly.

"Am I," cries she, "such a stranger here,
That the guest's approach they could not name?
Ah, they keep me in my cloister drear,
Well nigh feel I vanquish'd by my shame.
On thy soft couch now
Slumber calmly thou!
"I'll return as swiftly as I came."

"Stay, thou fairest maiden!" cries the boy,
Starting from his couch with eager haste:
"Here are Ceres', Bacchus'[20] gifts of joy;
Amor bringest thou, with beauty grac'd!
Thou art pale with fear!
Loved one let us here
Prove the raptures the Immortals taste."

"Draw not nigh, O Youth! afar remain!
Rapture now can never smile on me;
For the fatal step, alas! is ta'en,
Through my mother's sick-bed phantasy.
Cured, she made this oath:
'Youth and nature both
Shall henceforth to Heav'n devoted be.'

From the house, so silent now, are driven
All the gods who reign'd supreme of yore;
One Invisible now rules in heaven,
On the cross a Saviour they adore.
Victims slay they here,
Neither lamb nor steer,
But the altars reek with human gore.

And he lists[21], and ev'ry word he weighs,
While his eager soul drinks in each sound:
"Can it be that now before my gaze
Stands my loved one on this silent ground? Pledge to me thy troth!
Through our father's oath:
With Heav'ns blessing will our love be crown'd."

---

20 Ceres and Bacchus were Roman gods of food and drink
21 Listens.

"Kindly youth, I never can be thine!
'Tis my sister they intend for thee.
When I in the silent cloister pine,
Ah, within her arms remember me!
Thee alone I love,
While love's pangs I prove
Soon the earth will veil my misery."

"No! for by this glowing flame I swear,
Hymen[22] hath himself propitious shown:
Let us to my fathers house repair,
And thou'lt find that joy is not yet flown,
Sweetest, here then stay,
And without delay
Hold we now our wedding feast alone!"

Then exchange they tokens of their truth;
She gives him a golden chain to wear,
And a silver chalice would the youth
Give her in return of beauty rare.
"That is not for me;
Yet I beg of thee,
One lock only give me of thy hair."

Now the ghostly hour of midnight knell'd,
And she seem'd right joyous at the sign;
To her pallid lips the cup she held,
But she drank of nought but blood-red wine.
For to taste the bread
There before them spread,
Nought he spoke could make the maid incline.

To the youth the goblet then she brought,—
He too quaff'd with eager joy the bowl.
Love to crown the silent feast he sought,
Ah! full love-sick was the stripling's soul.
From his prayer she shrinks,
Till at length he sinks
On the bed and weeps without control.

---

22 Greek god of marriage.

39

And she comes, and lays her near the boy:
"How I grieve to see thee sorrowing so!
If thou think'st to clasp my form with joy,
Thou must learn this secret sad to know;
Yes! the maid, whom thou
Call'st thy loved one now,
Is as cold as ice, though white as snow."

Then he clasps her madly in his arm,
While love's youthful might pervades his frame:
"Thou might'st hope, when with me, to grow warm.
E'en if from the grave thy spirit came!
Breath for breath, and kiss!
Overflow of bliss!
Dost not thou, like me, feel passion's flame?"

Love still closer rivets now their lips,
Tears they mingle with their rapture blest,
From his mouth the flame she wildly sips,
Each is with the other's thought possess'd.
His hot ardour's flood
Warms her chilly blood,
But no heart is beating in her breast.

In her care to see that nought went wrong,
Now the mother happen'd to draw near;
t the door long hearkens she, full long,
Wond'ring at the sounds that greet her ear.
Tones of joy and sadness,
And love's blissful madness,
As of bride and bridegroom they appear.

From the door she will not now remove
'Till she gains full certainty of this;
And with anger hears she vows of love,
Soft caressing words of mutual bliss.
"Hush! the cock's loud strain!
But thou'lt come again,
When the night returns!"—then kiss on kiss.

Then her wrath the mother cannot hold,
But unfastens straight the lock with ease
"In this house are girls become so bold,
As to seek e'en strangers' lusts to please?"
By her lamp's clear glow
Looks she in,—and oh!
Sight of horror!—'tis her child she sees.

Fain the youth would, in his first alarm,
With the veil that o'er her had been spread,
With the carpet, shield his love from harm;
But she casts them from her, void of dread,
And with spirit's strength,
In its spectre length,
Lifts her figure slowly from the bed.

"Mother! mother!"—Thus her wan lips say:
"May not I one night of rapture share?
From the warm couch am I chased away?
Do I waken only to despair?
It contents not thee
To have driven me
An untimely shroud of death to wear?

"But from out my coffin's prison-bounds
By a wond'rous fate I'm forced to rove,
While the blessings and the chaunting sounds
That your priests delight in, useless prove.
Water, salt, are vain
Fervent youth to chain,
Ah, e'en Earth can never cool down love!

"When that infant vow of love was spoken,
Venus'[23] radiant temple smiled on both.
Mother! thou that promise since hast broken,
Fetter'd by a strange, deceitful oath.
Gods, though, hearken ne'er,
Should a mother swear
To deny her daughter's plighted troth.

---

23 Roman goddess of love.

From my grave to wander I am forc'd,
Still to seek The Good's long-sever'd link,
Still to love the bridegroom I have lost,
And the life-blood of his heart to drink;
When his race is run,
I must hasten on,
And the young must 'neath my vengeance sink.

"Beauteous youth! no longer mayst thou live;
Here must shrivel up thy form so fair;
Did not I to thee a token give,
Taking in return this lock of hair?
View it to thy sorrow!
Grey thou'lt be to-morrow,
Only to grow brown again when there.

"Mother, to this final prayer give ear!
Let a funeral pile be straightway dress'd;
Open then my cell so sad and drear,
That the flames may give the lovers rest!
When ascends the fire
From the glowing pyre,
To the gods of old we'll hasten, blest."

CHRISTABEL

PART I, 1797. PART II, 1800.
SAMUEL TAYLOR COLERIDGE

Following close on the heels of the Germans, Coleridge wrote "Christabel." Although written in English, the poem belongs in Part I of this anthology for a variety of reasons. First, it is a poem—specifically, a ballad poem—not a work of fiction. Therefore, stylistically "Christabel" mirrors "The Bride of Corinth" and "William and Helen" far more closely than the works that follow it. In addition, the tone of "Christabel" is of the Gothic school celebrated by Goethe and Bürger. As we shall see, the fiction of Part II remains loyal in many regard to Gothic tropes, yet each of these pieces take their action to the present day whereas the characters and places of "Christabel" are clearly from a more ancient era.

Published in 1816, "Christabel" is the first major piece of vampire literature composed in the English language. Intended by Coleridge to be ultimately five parts, he only wrote two, and these two he wrote three years apart from one another. Supposedly, the unfinished parts would reveal the vampire theme more overtly. Two potential predecessors of "Christabel" deserve mention. The first is "Thalaba the Destroyer" by Robert Southey (written after "Christabel," but published before), which obliquely references a vampire. The second is Lord Byron's "The Giaour," whose vampire figure features more prominently than in "Thalaba" yet still remains peripheral to the poem's primary narrative and themes. Although the word *vampire* does not appear anywhere in the lines of "Christabel," thanks to tremendous twentieth-century scholarship, it's clear that Coleridge approached the lengthy poem with vampire lore as the central inspiration. The most important proponent of this position was Arthur Nethercot, whose book *The Road to Tryerniaine* exhaustively compares the poem's content to Coleridge's source material. Nethercot went on to publish an additional article comparing "Christabel" to LeFanu's *Carmilla* (in Part II), establishing undeniable connections between the two works. James Twitchell is also responsible for establishing "Christabel" as an example of vampire fiction

"Christabel" expands many of the themes established by the German poems. Most notably, an unsealed marriage emerges as an important plot point. Like Helen in "William and Helen" and the young woman in "Bride of Corinth," Christabel has a "lover that's far away." However, in this poem, the lover never comes back. Instead, a new love interest takes his place in the form of Geraldine. As noted, the unions of the partners in "William and Helen" and "Bride of Corinth" are transgressive acts because they defy the authority of family and God. The union in "Christabel" is transgressive for this reason as well as others: She is committing infidelity. Furthermore, her lover is (initially) a woman. When Christabel says, "Sure I have sinned! Now in heaven be praised if all be well!" she may be expressing guilt for all three of these transgressions. The ambiguity of Christabel's feelings toward Geraldine makes determining the source of her regret difficult. She's clearly taken with Geraldine's beauty and radiance, yet she simultaneously rejects her. This dichotomy can be read in multiple ways. Christabel, ashamed of herself, may be manufacturing hatred for the source of her shame, or she may be aware of Geraldine's spurious nature and simply trying to eject her from the castle before she does more damage. "Christabel's" multitude of possible interpretations helps explain the poem's longevity despite its unfinished status.

As an essential stepping stone, "Christabel" stands as the best representative of the transition between the German and English conceptions of the literary vampire. Coleridge, like Goethe, was a household name among the educated class of England. Consequently, the publication of this poem primed the British readership for Polidori, Rymer, and LeFanu, who would go on to write the first English vampire fiction. The poem introduced many new vampire characteristics, such as a relationship to moonlight, aversion to thresholds, and mistrust of animals. Most importantly, Geraldine's femininity informed the genre's erotic tradition. Indeed, "Christabel" was the first instance in which a vampire figure's sexual acts are carried out without the use of brute force.

CHRISTABEL PART I (1797)

'Tis the middle of night by the castle clock
And the owls have awakened the crowing cock;
Tu-whit!- Tu-whoo!

And hark, again! the crowing cock,
How drowsily it crew.

Sir Leoline, the Baron rich,
Hath a toothless mastiff, which
From her kennel beneath the rock
Maketh answer to the clock,
Four for the quarters, and twelve for the hour;
Ever and aye, by shine and shower,
Sixteen short howls, not over loud;
Some say, she sees my lady's shroud.

Is the night chilly and dark?
The night is chilly, but not dark.
The thin grey cloud is spread on high,
It covers but not hides the sky.
The moon is behind, and at the full;
And yet she looks both small and dull.
The night is chill, the cloud is grey:
'T is a month before the month of May,
And the Spring comes slowly up this way.

The lovely lady, Christabel,
Whom her father loves so well,
What makes her in the wood so late,
A furlong from the castle gate?
She had dreams all yesternight
Of her own betrothed knight;
And she in the midnight wood will pray
For the weal[24] of her lover that's far away.

She stole along, she nothing spoke,
The sighs she heaved were soft and low,
And naught was green upon the oak,
But moss and rarest mistletoe:
She kneels beneath the huge oak tree,
And in silence prayeth she.

The lady sprang up suddenly,
The lovely lady, Christabel!

24 Well-being.

It moaned as near, as near can be,
But what it is she cannot tell.-
On the other side it seems to be,
Of the huge, broad-breasted, old oak tree.

The night is chill; the forest bare;
Is it the wind that moaneth bleak?
There is not wind enough in the air
To move away the ringlet curl
From the lovely lady's cheek-
There is not wind enough to twirl
The one red leaf, the last of its clan,
That dances as often as dance it can,
Hanging so light, and hanging so high,
On the topmost twig that looks up at the sky.

Hush, beating heart of Christabel!
Jesu[25], Maria, shield her well!
She folded her arms beneath her cloak,
And stole to the other side of the oak.
        What sees she there?

There she sees a damsel bright,
Dressed in a silken robe of white,
That shadowy in the moonlight shone:
The neck that made that white robe wan,
Her stately neck, and arms were bare;
Her blue-veined feet unsandaled were;
And wildly glittered here and there
The gems entangled in her hair.
I guess, 't was frightful there to see
A lady so richly clad as she—
Beautiful exceedingly!

'Mary mother, save me now!'
Said Christabel, 'and who art thou?'

The lady strange made answer meet,
And her voice was faint and sweet:—
        'Have pity on my sore distress,

_____
25 Jesus; vocative form.

I scarce can speak for weariness:
Stretch forth thy hand, and have no fear!'
Said Christabel, 'How camest thou here?'
And the lady, whose voice was faint and sweet,
Did thus pursue her answer meet:—

'My sire is of a noble line,
And my name is Geraldine:
Five warriors seized me yestermorn,
Me, even me, a maid forlorn:
They choked my cries with force and fright,
And tied me on a palfrey[26] white.
The palfrey was as fleet as wind,
And they rode furiously behind.
They spurred amain, their steeds were white:
And once we crossed the shade of night.
As sure as Heaven shall rescue me,
I have no thought what men they be;
Nor do I know how long it is
(For I have lain entranced, I wis[27])
Since one, the tallest of the five,
Took me from the palfrey's back,
A weary woman, scarce alive.
Some muttered words his comrades spoke:
He placed me underneath this oak;
He swore they would return with haste;
Whither they went I cannot tell-
I thought I heard, some minutes past,
Sounds as of a castle bell.
Stretch forth thy hand,' thus ended she,
'And help a wretched maid to flee.'

Then Christabel stretched forth her hand,
And comforted fair Geraldine:
'O well, bright dame, may you command
The service of Sir Leoline;
And gladly our stout chivalry
Will he send forth, and friends withal,
To guide and guard you safe and free

26 Riding horse.
27 Know.

47

Home to your noble father's hall.'

She rose: and forth with steps they passed
That strove to be, and were not, fast.
Her gracious stars the lady blest,
And thus spake on sweet Christabel:
'All our household are at rest,
The hall is silent as the cell;
Sir Leoline is weak in health,
And may not well awakened be,
But we will move as if in stealth;
And I beseech your courtesy,
This night, to share your couch with me.'

They crossed the moat, and Christabel
Took the key that fitted well;
A little door she opened straight,
All in the middle of the gate;
The gate that was ironed within and without,
Where an army in battle array had marched out.
The lady sank, belike through pain,
And Christabel with might and main
Lifted her up, a weary weight,
Over the threshold of the gate:
Then the lady rose again,
And moved, as she were not in pain.

So, free from danger, free from fear,
They crossed the court: right glad they were.
And Christabel devoutly cried
To the Lady by her side;
'Praise we the Virgin all divine,
Who hath rescued thee from thy distress!'
'Alas, alas!' said Geraldine,
'I cannot speak for weariness.'
So, free from danger, free from fear,
They crossed the court: right glad they were.

Outside her kennel the mastiff old

Lay fast asleep, in moonshine cold.
The mastiff old did not awake,
Yet she an angry moan did make.
And what can ail the mastiff bitch?
Never till now she uttered yell
Beneath the eye of Christabel.
Perhaps it is the owlet's scritch:
For what can aid the mastiff bitch?

They passed the hall, that echoes still,
Pass as lightly as you will.
The brands[28] were flat, the brands were dying,
Amid their own white ashes lying;
But when the lady passed, there came
A tongue of light, a fit of flame;
And Christabel saw the lady's eye,
And nothing else saw she thereby,
Save the boss of the shield of Sir Leoline tall,
Which hung in a murky old niche in the wall.
'O softly tread,' said Christabel,
'My father seldom sleepeth well.'

Sweet Christabel her feet doth bare,
And, jealous of the listening air,
They steal their way from stair to stair,
Now in glimmer, and now in gloom,
And now they pass the Baron's room,
As still as death, with stifled breath!
And now have reached her chamber door;
And now doth Geraldine press down
The rushes of the chamber floor.

The moon shines dim in the open air,
And not a moonbeam enters here.
But they without its light can see
The chamber carved so curiously,
Carved with figures strange and sweet,
All made out of the carver's brain,
For a lady's chamber meet:
The lamp with twofold silver chain

28 Pieces of partially burnt wood.

49

Is fastened to an angel's feet.

The silver lamp burns dead and dim;
But Christabel the lamp will trim.
She trimmed the lamp, and made it bright,
And left it swinging to and fro,
While Geraldine, in wretched plight,
Sank down upon the floor below.

'O weary lady, Geraldine,
I pray you, drink this cordial wine!
It is a wine of virtuous powers;
My mother made it of wild flowers.'

'And will your mother pity me,
Who am a maiden most forlorn?'
Christabel answered- 'Woe is me!
She died the hour that I was born.
I have heard the grey-haired friar tell,
How on her death-bed she did say,
That she should hear the castle-bell
Strike twelve upon my wedding-day.
O mother dear! that thou wert here!'
'I would,' said Geraldine, 'she were!'

But soon, with altered voice, said she—
'Off, wandering mother! Peak and pine!²⁹
I have power to bid thee flee.'
Alas! what ails poor Geraldine?
Why stares she with unsettled eye?
Can she the bodiless dead espy?
And why with hollow voice cries she,
'Off, woman, off! this hour is mine—
Though thou her guardian spirit be,
Off, woman. off! 't is given to me.'

Then Christabel knelt by the lady's side,
And raised to heaven her eyes so blue—
'Alas!' said she, 'this ghastly ride—
Dear lady! it hath wildered you!'

---

29 *Peak and pink*: Grow sickly and lose flesh (as through grief).

The lady wiped her moist cold brow,
And faintly said, "'Tis over now!'

Again the wild-flower wine she drank:
Her fair large eyes 'gan glitter bright,
And from the floor, whereon she sank,
The lofty lady stood upright:
She was most beautiful to see,
Like a lady of a far countree.

And thus the lofty lady spake—
'All they, who live in the upper sky,
Do love you, holy Christabel!
And you love them, and for their sake,
And for the good which me befell,
Even I in my degree will try,
Fair maiden, to requite you well.
But now unrobe yourself; for I
Must pray, ere yet in bed I lie.'

Quoth Christabel, 'So let it be!'
And as the lady bade, did she.
Her gentle limbs did she undress
And lay down in her loveliness.

But through her brain, of weal and woe,
So many thoughts moved to and fro,
That vain it were her lids to close;
So half-way from the bed she rose,
And on her elbow did recline.
To look at the lady Geraldine.

Beneath the lamp the lady bowed,
And slowly rolled her eyes around;
Then drawing in her breath aloud,
Like one that shuddered, she unbound
The cincture from beneath her breast:
Her silken robe, and inner vest,
Dropped to her feet, and full in view,
Behold! her bosom and half her side—
A sight to dream of, not to tell!

O shield her! shield sweet Christabel!

Yet Geraldine nor speaks nor stirs:
Ah! what a stricken look was hers!
Deep from within she seems half-way
To lift some weight with sick assay,
And eyes the maid and seeks delay;
Then suddenly, as one defied,
Collects herself in scorn and pride,
And lay down by the maiden's side!—
And in her arms the maid she took,
      Ah, well-a-day!
And with low voice and doleful look
These words did say:
'In the touch of this bosom there worketh a spell,
Which is lord of thy utterance, Christabel!
Thou knowest to-night, and wilt know to-morrow,
This mark of my shame, this seal of my sorrow;
But vainly thou warrest[30],
For this is alone in
Thy power to declare,
That in the dim forest
Thou heard'st a low moaning,
And found'st a bright lady, surpassingly fair:
And didst bring her home with thee, in love and in charity,
To shield her and shelter her from the damp air.'

It was a lovely sight to see
The lady Christabel, when she
Was praying at the old oak tree.
Amid the jagged shadows
Of mossy leafless boughs,
Kneeling in the moonlight,
To make her gentle vows;
Her slender palms together prest,
Heaving sometimes on her breast;
Her face resigned to bliss or bale—
Her face, oh, call it fair not pale,
And both blue eyes more bright than clear.
Each about to have a tear.

---

30 Fight.

With open eyes (ah, woe is me!)
Asleep, and dreaming fearfully,
Fearfully dreaming, yet, I wis,
Dreaming that alone, which is—
O sorrow and shame! Can this be she,
The lady, who knelt at the old oak tree?
And lo! the worker of these harms,
That holds the maiden in her arms,
Seems to slumber still and mild,
As a mother with her child.

A star hath set, a star hath risen,
O Geraldine! since arms of thine
Have been the lovely lady's prison.
O Geraldine! one hour was thine—
Thou'st had thy will! By tarn and rill[31],
The night-birds all that hour were still.
But now they are jubilant anew,
From cliff and tower, tu-whoo! tu-whoo!
Tu-whoo! tu-whoo! from wood and fell!

And see! the lady Christabel
Gathers herself from out her trance;
Her limbs relax, her countenance
Grows sad and soft; the smooth thin lids
Close o'er her eyes; and tears she sheds—
Large tears that leave the lashes bright!
And oft the while she seems to smile
As infants at a sudden light!
Yea, she doth smile, and she doth weep,
Like a youthful hermitess,
Beauteous in a wilderness,
Who, praying always, prays in sleep.
And, if she move unquietly,
Perchance, 't is but the blood so free
Comes back and tingles in her feet.
No doubt, she hath a vision sweet.
What if her guardian spirit 't were,
What if she knew her mother near?

---

31 *Tarn and rill*: Lake and river.

But this she knows, in joys and woes,
That saints will aid if men will call:
For the blue sky bends over all.

CHRISTABEL PART II (1800)

Each matin[32] bell, the Baron saith,
Knells us back to a world of death.
These words Sir Leoline first said,
When he rose and found his lady dead:
These words Sir Leoline will say
Many a morn to his dying day!

And hence the custom and law began
That still at dawn the sacristan[33],
Who duly pulls the heavy bell,
Five and forty beads must tell
Between each stroke—a warning knell,
Which not a soul can choose but hear
From Bratha Head to Wyndermere[34].
Saith Bracy the bard, 'So let it knell!
And let the drowsy sacristan
Still count as slowly as he can!'
There is no lack of such, I ween,
As well fill up the space between.
In Langdale Pike and Witch's Lair,
And Dungeon-ghyll so foully rent,
With ropes of rock and bells of air
Three sinful sextons' ghosts are pent,
Who all give back, one after t' other,
The death-note to their living brother;
And oft too, by the knell offended,
Just as their one! two! three! is ended,
The devil mocks the doleful tale
With a merry peal from Borrowdale.

---

32 Morning prayer service.
33 Sexton.
34 All the places and geographical locales of part two are near the border of historic English counties Cumberland and Westmoreland. Coleridge lived in this area from 1800-1804.

The air is still! through mist and cloud
That merry peal comes ringing loud;
And Geraldine shakes off her dread,
And rises lightly from the bed;
Puts on her silken vestments white,
And tricks her hair in lovely plight[35],
And nothing doubting of her spell
Awakens the lady Christabel.
'Sleep you, sweet lady Christabel?
I trust that you have rested well.'

And Christabel awoke and spied
The same who lay down by her side—
O rather say, the same whom she
Raised up beneath the old oak tree!
Nay, fairer yet! and yet more fair!
For she belike hath drunken deep
Of all the blessedness of sleep!
And while she spake, her looks, her air,
Such gentle thankfulness declare,
That (so it seemed) her girded vests
Grew tight beneath her heaving breasts.
'Sure I have sinned!' said Christabel,
'Now heaven be praised if all be well!'
And in low faltering tones, yet sweet,
Did she the lofty lady greet
With such perplexity of mind
As dreams too lively leave behind.

So quickly she rose, and quickly arrayed
Her maiden limbs, and having prayed
That He, who on the cross did groan,
Might wash away her sins unknown,
She forthwith led fair Geraldine
To meet her sire, Sir Leoline.
The lovely maid and the lady tall
Are pacing both into the hall,
And pacing on through page and groom,
Enter the Baron's presence-room.

---

35 Neutral or positive condition (Archaic).

The Baron rose, and while he prest
His gentle daughter to his breast,
With cheerful wonder in his eyes
The lady Geraldine espies,
And gave such welcome to the same,
As might beseem so bright a dame!

But when he heard the lady's tale,
And when she told her father's name,
Why waxed Sir Leoline so pale,
Murmuring o'er the name again,
Lord Roland de Vaux of Tryermaine[36]?
Alas! they had been friends in youth;
But whispering tongues can poison truth;
And constancy lives in realms above;
And life is thorny; and youth is vain;
And to be wroth with one we love
Doth work like madness in the brain.
And thus it chanced, as I divine,
With Roland and Sir Leoline.
Each spake words of high disdain
And insult to his heart's best brother:
They parted- ne'er to meet again!
But never either found another
To free the hollow heart from paining—
They stood aloof, the scars remaining,
Like cliffs which had been rent asunder;
A dreary sea now flows between.
But neither heat, nor frost, nor thunder,
Shall wholly do away, I ween,
The marks of that which once hath been.
Sir Leoline, a moment's space,
Stood gazing on the damsel's face:
And the youthful Lord of Tryermaine
Came back upon his heart again.

O then the Baron forgot his age,
His noble heart swelled high with rage;
He swore by the wounds in Jesu's side
He would proclaim it far and wide,

---

36 Lord Roland was a noble of Cumberland.

With trump and solemn heraldry,
That they, who thus had wronged the dame
Were base as spotted infamy!
'And if they dare deny the same,
My herald shall appoint a week,
And let the recreant traitors seek
My tourney court- that there and then
I may dislodge their reptile souls
From the bodies and forms of men!'
He spake: his eye in lightning rolls!
For the lady was ruthlessly seized; and he kenned[37]
In the beautiful lady the child of his friend!

And now the tears were on his face,
And fondly in his arms he took
Fair Geraldine who met the embrace,
Prolonging it with joyous look.
Which when she viewed, a vision fell
Upon the soul of Christabel,
The vision of fear, the touch and pain!
She shrunk and shuddered, and saw again—
(Ah, woe is me! Was it for thee,
Thou gentle maid! such sights to see?)
Again she saw that bosom old,
Again she felt that bosom cold,
And drew in her breath with a hissing sound:
Whereat the Knight turned wildly round,
And nothing saw, but his own sweet maid
With eyes upraised, as one that prayed.

The touch, the sight, had passed away,
And in its stead that vision blest,
Which comforted her after-rest,
While in the lady's arms she lay,
Had put a rapture in her breast,
And on her lips and o'er her eyes
Spread smiles like light!
With new surprise,
'What ails then my beloved child?'
The Baron said- His daughter mild

---

37 Perceived.

Made answer, 'All will yet be well!'
I ween, she had no power to tell
Aught else: so mighty was the spell.

Yet he who saw this Geraldine,
Had deemed her sure a thing divine.
Such sorrow with such grace she blended,
As if she feared she had offended
Sweet Christabel, that gentle maid!
And with such lowly tones she prayed
She might be sent without delay
Home to her father's mansion.
'Nay!
Nay, by my soul!' said Leoline.
'Ho! Bracy the bard, the charge be thine!
Go thou, with music sweet and loud,
And take two steeds with trappings proud,
And take the youth whom thou lov'st best
To bear thy harp, and learn thy song,
And clothe you both in solemn vest,
And over the mountains haste along,
Lest wandering folk, that are abroad,
Detain you on the valley road.

'And when he has crossed the Irthing flood,
My merry bard! he hastes, he hastes
Up Knorren Moor, through Halegarth Wood,
And reaches soon that castle good
Which stands and threatens Scotland's wastes.

'Bard Bracy! bard Bracy! your horses are fleet,
Ye must ride up the hall, your music so sweet,
More loud than your horses' echoing feet!
And loud and loud to Lord Roland call,
Thy daughter is safe in Langdale hall[38]!
Thy beautiful daughter is safe and free—
Sir Leoline greets thee thus through me.
He bids thee come without delay
With all thy numerous array;
And take thy lovely daughter home:

---

38 Supposed castle of medieval Cumberland.

And he will meet thee on the way
With all his numerous array
White with their panting palfreys' foam:
And, by mine honor! I will say,
That I repent me of the day
When I spake words of fierce disdain
To Roland de Vaux of Tryermaine!—
—For since that evil hour hath flown,
Many a summer's sun hath shone;
Yet ne'er found I a friend again
Like Roland de Vaux of Tryermaine.'

The lady fell, and clasped his knees,
Her face upraised, her eyes o'erflowing;
And Bracy replied, with faltering voice,
His gracious hail on all bestowing;
'Thy words, thou sire of Christabel,
Are sweeter than my harp can tell;
Yet might I gain a boon of thee,
This day my journey should not be,
So strange a dream hath come to me;
That I had vowed with music loud
To clear yon wood from thing unblest,
Warned by a vision in my rest!
For in my sleep I saw that dove,
That gentle bird, whom thou dost love,
And call'st by thy own daughter's name—
Sir Leoline! I saw the same,
Fluttering, and uttering fearful moan,
Among the green herbs in the forest alone.
Which when I saw and when I heard,
I wondered what might ail the bird;
For nothing near it could I see,
Save the grass and herbs underneath the old tree.
And in my dream methought I went
To search out what might there be found;
And what the sweet bird's trouble meant,
That thus lay fluttering on the ground.
I went and peered, and could descry
No cause for her distressful cry;
But yet for her dear lady's sake

I stooped, methought, the dove to take,
When lo! I saw a bright green snake
Coiled around its wings and neck.
Green as the herbs on which it couched,
Close by the dove's its head it crouched;
And with the dove it heaves and stirs,
Swelling its neck as she swelled hers!
I woke; it was the midnight hour,
The clock was echoing in the tower;
But though my slumber was gone by,
This dream it would not pass away—
It seems to live upon my eye!
And thence I vowed this self-same day
With music strong and saintly song
To wander through the forest bare,
Lest aught unholy loiter there.'

Thus Bracy said: the Baron, the while,
Half-listening heard him with a smile;
Then turned to Lady Geraldine,
His eyes made up of wonder and love;
And said in courtly accents fine,
'Sweet maid, Lord Roland's beauteous dove,
With arms more strong than harp or song,
Thy sire and I will crush the snake!'
He kissed her forehead as he spake,
And Geraldine in maiden wise
Casting down her large bright eyes,
With blushing cheek and courtesy fine
She turned her from Sir Leoline;
Softly gathering up her train,
That o'er her right arm fell again;
And folded her arms across her chest,
And couched her head upon her breast,
And looked askance at Christabel—
Jesu, Maria, shield her well!

A snake's small eye blinks dull and shy,
And the lady's eyes they shrunk in her head,
Each shrunk up to a serpent's eye,
And with somewhat of malice, and more of dread,

At Christabel she looked askance!—
One moment—and the sight was fled!
But Christabel in dizzy trance
Stumbling on the unsteady ground
Shuddered aloud, with a hissing sound;
And Geraldine again turned round,
And like a thing that sought relief,
Full of wonder and full of grief,
She rolled her large bright eyes divine
Wildly on Sir Leoline.

The maid, alas! her thoughts are gone,
She nothing sees—no sight but one!
The maid, devoid of guile and sin,
I know not how, in fearful wise,
So deeply had she drunken in
That look, those shrunken serpent eyes,
That all her features were resigned
To this sole image in her mind:
And passively did imitate
That look of dull and treacherous hate!
And thus she stood, in dizzy trance,
Still picturing that look askance
With forced unconscious sympathy
Full before her father's view—
As far as such a look could be
In eyes so innocent and blue!

And when the trance was o'er, the maid
Paused awhile, and inly prayed:
Then falling at the Baron's feet,
'By my mother's soul do I entreat
That thou this woman send away!'
She said: and more she could not say;
For what she knew she could not tell,
O'er-mastered by the mighty spell.
Why is thy cheek so wan and wild,
Sir Leoline? Thy only child
Lies at thy feet, thy joy, thy pride.
So fair, so innocent, so mild;
The same, for whom thy lady died!

O by the pangs of her dear mother
Think thou no evil of thy child!
For her, and thee, and for no other,
She prayed the moment ere she died:
Prayed that the babe for whom she died,
Might prove her dear lord's joy and pride!
That prayer her deadly pangs beguiled,
Sir Leoline!
And wouldst thou wrong thy only child,
Her child and thine?

Within the Baron's heart and brain
If thoughts, like these, had any share,
They only swelled his rage and pain,
And did but work confusion there.
His heart was cleft with pain and rage,
His cheeks they quivered, his eyes were wild,
Dishonored thus in his old age;
Dishonored by his only child,
And all his hospitality
To the insulted daughter of his friend
By more than woman's jealousy
Brought thus to a disgraceful end—
He rolled his eye with stern regard
Upon the gentle minstrel bard,
And said in tones abrupt, austere—
'Why, Bracy! dost thou loiter here?
I bade thee hence!' The bard obeyed;
And turning from his own sweet maid,
The aged knight, Sir Leoline,
Led forth the lady Geraldine!

THE CONCLUSION TO PART II

A little child, a limber elf,
Singing, dancing to itself,
A fairy thing with red round cheeks,
That always finds, and never seeks,
Makes such a vision to the sight
As fills a father's eyes with light;
And pleasures flow in so thick and fast

Upon his heart, that he at last
Must needs express his love's excess
With words of unmeant bitterness.
Perhaps 'tis pretty[39] to force together
Thoughts so all unlike each other;
To mutter and mock a broken charm,
To dally with wrong that does no harm.
Perhaps 'tis tender too and pretty
At each wild word to feel within
A sweet recoil of love and pity.
And what, if in a world of sin
(O sorrow and shame should this be true!)
Such giddiness of heart and brain
Comes seldom save from rage and pain,
So talks as it's most used to do.

---

39 Brave (Archaic).

PART II: THE CROSSING

$\mathcal{I}$f Part I of this volume portrayed the seeds of an entire genre, Part II depicts a critical period of refinement. The following three works set crucial precedents about what it means to be a vampire: the rules, the desires, the behavior. These pieces also codified vampire themes—among others, transgression, eroticism, and moral ambiguity. More so than the poems that precede these works, as well as *Dracula* that follows, *The Vampire* by Polidori, *Varney the Vampire* by Rymer, and *Carmilla* by LeFanu defined modern vampire literature.

This "great leap" can be best understood by tracking British literary history. During the late eighteenth and early nineteenth centuries, Romantic poets dominated British literature. Reacting to the Enlightenment and Industrial Revolution, Coleridge, Keats, Wordsworth, Southey, and Byron forged an aesthetic that emphasized beauty, nature, and individual emotional experience. However, by the 1820s, fiction supplanted poetry as the dominant mode of literature and reigned as such for the duration of the Victorian era. The shift from poetry to fiction helped engender an increased English focus on psychological themes. Ballads, which placed a premium on action and plot, were replaced by novels, novellas, and short stories— forms that invite omniscient commentary on a character's inner thoughts, motivations, and feelings.

This shift led to the most profound innovation in the history of vampire literature: the portrayal of vampires who understand and possess complex elements of human psychology. Although the vampire figures of Part I are certainly not raving, animalistic, blood-sucking beasts, their familiarity with the spectrum of human experience pales in comparison to the likes of Lord Ruthven, Varney, and Carmilla. In every respect, these latter vampires are more advanced. Their acts of violence are more nuanced and complex, their methods of capture more sophisticated, and their ability to function in the world of men more adroit. These vampires are of a breed whose felicity with people's feelings makes them irresistibly fascinating.

Endowing vampires with human psychology is most evident in *Varney*, in which Rymer repeatedly uses his authorial license to disclose Varney's thoughts and emotions. Given that *The Vampyre* and *Carmilla* are first-person narratives, Polidori and LeFanu don't have that luxury. Nevertheless, they each establish their vampire's understanding of human psychology through their narrators Laura and Aubrey, who express how the vampires make *them* feel. The breadth of emotions each experiences on account of their vampire companions can only be explained by acknowledging that the respective vampires are well aware of how their behavior affects the feelings of others.

It's important to note that, in addition to the rise of fiction over poetry, the emergence of Realism was also responsible for the shift to psychologically advanced vampires. Less concerned with romance and idealism, writers like George Eliot sought to explore everyday life and the impact of social conditions. Polidori, Rymer, and LeFanu incorporated these themes into their works. Accordingly, the pieces included in Part II all take place in contemporary, not medieval, times. The characters are no longer classical archetypes, but everyday people. *The Vampyre*, *Varney*, and *Carmilla* all include moments that illustrate how both writers and readers of the time were interested in very practical matters, such as money and class. This inclusion of Realism was critical, but the writers of Part II did not fail to honor the tradition within which they were working; indeed, they maintained many of the themes and tropes of Gothic fiction descended from early German Romanticism. The vampire, being a pseudo-mythical (pseudo because belief of their existence was still maintained by many) creature that inhabits the night and threatens the safety of society, emerged as an ideal figure to straddle Gothic and Realist modes.

The trajectory of vampires increasingly expressing and understanding human psychology remains in place today. Although the genre is peppered with exceptions, vampires continue to mature—both emotionally and ethically—in their representations in literature. I would argue that their enduring viability as fictional characters lies in their relation to humanity (whether embodying it or manipulating it). The writers of this section are responsible for starting this trend. If it weren't for them, an anthology such as this would not include the word *literature* so frequently. Instead, vampire tales would exist exclusively in the realm of "genre fiction." This is not to denigrate popular, entertainment-driven fiction. I am only suggesting that if it weren't for Polidori, Rymer, and LeFanu, the purview of the vampire figure in today's culture would be significantly smaller.

The gradual evolution we see in the following pages did not occur fluidly. Movement towards humanesque vampires came in fits and starts. We witness the following English authors wrestling to forge new ground within an established literary vampire tradition. At times, their vampires exhibit shocking tenderness; in other instances, they behave no less bestially than their folkloric ancestors. Yet these growing pains are simply evidence that vampire literature was finally moving into adulthood.

THE VAMPYRE: A TALE

1819

JOHN WILLIAM POLIDORI

The Vampyre came into being as part of what must be the most influential episode of ghost story swapping of all time. It started when a terrible storm held the traveling Lord Byron and John William Polidori (at the time, Byron's physician) captive at the Villa Diodati near Lake Geneva in Switzerland. Literary luminaries Percy Bysshe Shelley, Mary Wollstonecraft Shelley, and Claire Clairmont joined them, and the creative group quickly found themselves reading and writing fantastic tales as a means to wait out the rain. Over the course of those few days, the seeds were planted that would spawn not only Polidori's *The Vampyre*, but also Mary Shelley's *Frankenstein*.

The rough plotline for *The Vampyre* was actually Byron's. He presented a "Fragment of a Novel" as his ghost story; only later did Polidori elect to transform Byron's initial spark of inspiration into a full novella. Although there is no issue of plagiarism, the authorship of *The Vampyre* was initially misrepresented. Fortuitously for the story's success, the *New Monthly Magazine* attributed *The Vampyre* to Byron when it published the work without Polidori's permission. This created a mess for Byron and Polidori, yet it resulted in the story's immediate widespread circulation. Goethe, upon reading the story, declared it Byron's best work, which only further fueled its popularity. However, even without a Byron byline, *The Vampyre* deserves praise and discussion. The story was a critical step in the construction of the literary vampire.

The first striking factor in *The Vampyre* is that it contains an introduction. Written by staff writers of the *New Monthly*, the introduction is a survey—meant in every way to be taken seriously—of earlier depictions of vampires. It discusses the Arnold Paole case, Far Eastern ideas about vampires as represented in an excerpt of Byron's "The Giaour," as well as Southey's poem "Thalaba the Destroyer." That the editors had the impulse to include such a discussion demonstrates how the vampire figure still remained a relatively recent object of fascination; the literary and historical (not folkloric) tradition was so young that the subject still required clarification. A salient point in the introduction is the brief explanation of how one becomes a vampire: "In many parts of Greece it is considered as a sort of punishment after death, for some heinous crime committed whilst in existence, that the deceased is not only doomed to vampyrise, but compelled to confine his infernal visitations solely to those beings he loved most while upon earth—those to whom he was bound by ties of kindred and affection." Although such theories flourish in folklore, this is the first such example in literature. The notion that living an eternal life of evil is a consequence of committing a crime went on to become an important factor in the development of the vampire.

As a narrative, *The Vampyre* is a potboiler. Lord Ruthven is not overtly established as a vampire until midway through the story, and Polidori deftly keeps key details concealed while gradually building dread and suspense. The story hinges around Lord Ruthven's interactions with three young women, as perceived by the naive protagonist Aubrey. The first woman is an unnamed virgin in Rome, the second is a girl named Ianthe with whom Aubrey falls in love while in Greece, and the third is Aubrey's sister. Whereas Polidori implies that the first dies at Ruthven's hands, there's no question the second two do. Aware of Ruthven's weak moral compass and despite warnings about the man who arrives from home, Aubrey doesn't pin Ruthven for the first two crimes until the final few pages of *The Vampyre*. Having realized that Ruthven killed his lover and seeks his sister next, Aubrey desperately tries to prevent catastrophe. Whether Aubrey will succeed or fail rivets the reader until the novella's final page.

Numerous character traits associated with today's vampire emerge in *The Vampyre*. One of the most important is the vampire's status as an aristocrat. Like Varney, Carmilla, and Lord Dracula that follow, Lord Ruthven belongs to the upper circles of society and possesses aristocratic lineage. In addition, Polidori links the moon and vampires, establishing the notion (that will ultimately become essential to Varney) that the moon is a rejuvenating force. Most importantly, Lord Ruthven cements erotic prowess as an intrinsic characteristic of the vampire.

Contrasting how this last trait manifests itself in *The Vampyre* to how it appears in Ossenfelder's "The Vampire" and "William and Helen" reveals how Polidori crafts a far more human creature. The female victims in the earlier poems clearly feel some kind of undeniable attraction to the vampire figure at hand, yet their ultimate end happens simultaneously to something very akin to rape. The scene of Ianthe's murder indicates that Lord Ruthven has not entirely lost the savagery of his predecessors (which include all the vampires of folklore); however, his pursuits of the virgin in Rome as well as Miss Aubrey are characterized by seduction rather than force—a critical development among vampires. With Miss Aubrey, Lord Ruthven is patient. He courts her for months and employs the "serpent's art" to win her favor. The prize is no longer simply the consumption of blood, but also the chase—a chase that, unlike the spontaneous, breezy nature of today's courtship process, is driven by sadistic tendencies.

However monstrously it manifests itself in Lord Ruthven, cruelty *is* a human trait, and it distinguishes him from earlier vampires. His victims are not the only ones to experience it. Anyone who receives his financial charity is soon cast into ruin. He destroys reputations, undermining even the most confident. Senf correctly identifies Ruthven as a "moral parasite," and his cruelty is often masked under the guise of other fundamentally human emotions, such as generosity and kindness. After Ianthe's death, Ruthven consoles a scared Aubrey: "But Lord Ruthven, by his kind words…and still more by the attention, anxiety, and care which he showed, soon reconciled him to his presence." Like any despicable human, Lord Ruthven manipulates others for personal gain. This humanesque behavior corresponds with the characters of Gothic fiction. Morrison insightfully writes:

The significance of Polidori's momentous transformations of the figure of the vampire from bestial ghoul to glamorous aristocrat cannot be grasped fully without recognizing that his Lord Ruthven is really the conventional rakehell or libertine with a few vampiric attributes grafted onto him…for Polidori the 'vampire story' is conceived as a variant upon the moral tale, a tale designed principally as a *warning*—here, against the fascinating power of the libertinism represented by his employer Byron.

Thus, the vampire emerged as a figure complex enough to be a metaphor for a specific subset of society. In Morrison's view, Lord Ruthven is essentially more human than vampire. This blurring is what makes the contemporary vampire riveting.

Polidori wrote *The Vampyre* a mere two and a half decades after the ballads of Coleridge and Goethe, making an enormous contribution to the genre. Only Ossenfelder, the creator of the genre, holds a more important role in the evolution of classical vampire literature. *Dracula*, as will be discussed, certainly had more *influence* on later filmmakers and writers, but it was Polidori who fundamentally changed the literary vampire from a creature of the night to a man (or woman very soon) who walks among us.

THE VAMPYRE: A TALE

INTRODUCTION[40]

*T*he superstition upon which this tale is founded is very general in the East. Among the Arabians it appears to be common: it did not, however, extend itself to the Greeks until after the establishment of Christianity; and it has only assumed its present form since the division of the Latin and Greek churches; at which time, the idea becoming prevalent, that a Latin body could not corrupt if buried in their territory, it gradually increased, and formed the subject of many wonderful stories, still extant, of the dead rising from their graves, and feeding upon the blood of the young and beautiful. In the West it spread, with some slight variation, all over Hungary, Poland, Austria, and Lorraine, where the belief existed, that vampyres nightly imbibed a certain portion of the blood of their victims, who became emaciated, lost their strength, and speedily died of consumptions; whilst these human blood-suckers fattened—and their veins became distended to such a state of repletion, as to cause the blood to flow from all the passages of their bodies, and even from the very pores of their skins.

In the London Journal, of March, 1732, is a curious, and, of course, credible account of a particular case of vampyrism, which is stated to have occurred at Madreyga, in Hungary. It appears, that upon an examination of the commander-in-chief and magistrates of the place, they positively and unanimously affirmed, that, about five years before, a certain Heyduke, named Arnold Paul, had been heard to say, that, at Cassovia, on the frontiers of the Turkish Servia, he had been tormented by a vampyre, but had found a way to rid himself of the evil, by eating some of the earth out of the vampyre's grave, and rubbing himself with his blood. This precaution, however, did not prevent him from becoming a vampyre[41] himself; for, about twenty or thirty days after his death and burial, many persons complained of having been tormented by him, and a deposition was made, that four persons had been deprived of life by his attacks. To prevent further mischief,

40 Written by the staff writers of the New Monthly, the journal that first published The Vampyre
41 Polidori's footnote: "The universal belief is, that a person sucked by a vampyre becomes a vampyre himself, and sucks in his turn."

the inhabitants having consulted their Hadagni,[42] took up the body, and found it (as is supposed to be usual in cases of vampyrism) fresh, and entirely free from corruption, and emitting at the mouth, nose, and ears, pure and florid blood. Proof having been thus obtained, they resorted to the accustomed remedy. A stake was driven entirely through the heart and body of Arnold Paul, at which he is reported to have cried out as dreadfully as if he had been alive. This done, they cut off his head, burned his body, and threw the ashes into his grave. The same measures were adopted with the corses of those persons who had previously died from vampyrism, lest they should, in their turn, become agents upon others who survived them.

This monstrous rodomontade is here related, because it seems better adapted to illustrate the subject of the present observations than any other instance which could be adduced. In many parts of Greece it is considered as a sort of punishment after death, for some heinous crime committed whilst in existence, that the deceased is not only doomed to vampyrise, but compelled to confine his infernal visitations solely to those beings he loved most while upon earth—those to whom he was bound by ties of kindred and affection—a supposition alluded to in the "Giaour."[43]

> But first on earth, as Vampyre sent,
> Thy corse shall from its tomb be rent;
> Then ghastly haunt the native place,
> And suck the blood of all thy race;
> There from thy daughter, sister, wife,
> At midnight drain the stream of life;
> Yet loathe the banquet which perforce
> Must feed thy livid living corse,
> Thy victims, ere they yet expire,
> Shall know the demon for their sire;
> As cursing thee, thou cursing them,
> Thy flowers are withered on the stem.
> But one that for thy crime must fall,
> The youngest, best beloved of all,
> Shall bless thee with a father's name—
> That word shall wrap thy heart in flame!
> Yet thou must end thy task and mark
> Her cheek's last tinge—her eye's last spark,
> And the last glassy glance must view
> Which freezes o'er its lifeless blue;

---

42 Polidori's footnote: "Chief Bailiff."
43 "The Giaour" is a poem by Lord Byron.

Then with unhallowed hand shall tear
The tresses of her yellow hair,
Of which, in life a lock when shorn
Affection's fondest pledge was worn—
But now is borne away by thee
Memorial of thine agony!
Yet with thine own best blood shall drip;
Thy gnashing tooth, and haggard lip;
Then stalking to thy sullen grave,
Go—and with Gouls and Afrits rave,
Till these in horror shrink away
From spectre more accursed than they.

Mr. Southey has also introduced in his wild but beautiful poem of "Thalaba," the vampyre corse of the Arabian maid Oneiza, who is represented as having returned from the grave for the purpose of tormenting him she best loved whilst in existence. But this cannot be supposed to have resulted from the sinfulness of her life, she being pourtrayed throughout the whole of the tale as a complete type of purity and innocence. The veracious Tournefort gives a long account in his travels of several astonishing cases of vampyrism, to which he pretends to have been an eyewitness; and Calmet, in his great work upon this subject, besides a variety of anecdotes, and traditionary narratives illustrative of its effects, has put forth some learned dissertations, tending to prove it to be a classical, as well as barbarian error.

Many curious and interesting notices on this singularly horrible superstition might be added; though the present may suffice for the limits of a note, necessarily devoted to explanation, and which may now be concluded by merely remarking, that though the term Vampyre is the one in most general acceptation, there are several others synonimous with it, made use of in various parts of the world: as Vroucolocha, Vardoulacha, Goul, Broucoloka, etc.

THE VAMPYRE.

It happened that in the midst of the dissipations attendant upon a London winter, there appeared at the various parties of the leaders of the ton a nobleman, more remarkable for his singularities, than his rank. He gazed upon the mirth around him, as if he could not participate therein. Apparently, the light laughter of the fair only attracted his attention, that he might by a look quell it, and throw fear into those breasts where thoughtlessness reigned. Those who felt this sensation of awe, could not explain whence it arose: some attributed it to the dead grey eye, which, fixing upon the object's face, did not seem to penetrate, and at one glance to pierce through to the inward workings of the heart; but fell upon the cheek with a leaden ray that weighed upon the skin it could not pass. His peculiarities caused him to be invited to every house; all wished to see him, and those who had been accustomed to violent excitement, and now felt the weight of ennui, were pleased at having something in their presence capable of engaging their attention. In spite of the deadly hue of his face, which never gained a warmer tint, either from the blush of modesty, or from the strong emotion of passion, though its form and outline were beautiful, many of the female hunters after notoriety attempted to win his attentions, and gain, at least, some marks of what they might term affection: Lady Mercer, who had been the mockery of every monster shewn in drawing-rooms since her marriage, threw herself in his way, and did all but put on the dress of a mountebank, to attract his notice:—though in vain:—when she stood before him, though his eyes were apparently fixed upon her's, still it seemed as if they were unperceived;—even her unappalled impudence was baffled, and she left the field. But though the common adultress could not influence even the guidance of his eyes, it was not that the female sex was indifferent to him: yet such was the apparent caution with which he spoke to the virtuous wife and innocent daughter, that few knew he ever addressed himself to females. He had, however, the reputation of a winning tongue; and whether it was that it even overcame the dread of his singular character, or that they were moved by his apparent hatred of vice, he was as often among those females who form the boast of their sex from their domestic virtues, as among those who sully it by their vices.

About the same time, there came to London a young gentleman of the name of Aubrey: he was an orphan left with an only sister in the possession of great wealth, by parents who died while he was yet in childhood. Left also to himself by guardians, who thought it their duty merely to take care of his fortune, while they relinquished the more important charge of his mind to the care of mercenary subalterns,[44] he cultivated more his imagination than his judgment. He had, hence, that high romantic feeling of honour and candour, which daily ruins so many milliners' apprentices. He believed all to sympathise with virtue, and thought that vice was thrown in by Providence merely for the picturesque effect of the scene, as we see in romances: he thought that the misery of a cottage merely consisted in the vesting of clothes, which were as warm, but which were better adapted to the painter's eye by their irregular folds and various coloured patches. He

44 Junior officer.

thought, in fine, that the dreams of poets were the realities of life. He was handsome, frank, and rich: for these reasons, upon his entering into the gay circles, many mothers surrounded him, striving which should describe with least truth their languishing or romping favourites: the daughters at the same time, by their brightening countenances when he approached, and by their sparkling eyes, when he opened his lips, soon led him into false notions of his talents and his merit. Attached as he was to the romance of his solitary hours, he was startled at finding, that, except in the tallow and wax candles that flickered, not from the presence of a ghost, but from want of snuffing, there was no foundation in real life for any of that congeries of pleasing pictures and descriptions contained in those volumes, from which he had formed his study. Finding, however, some compensation in his gratified vanity, he was about to relinquish his dreams, when the extraordinary being we have above described, crossed him in his career.

He watched him; and the very impossibility of forming an idea of the character of a man entirely absorbed in himself, who gave few other signs of his observation of external objects, than the tacit assent to their existence, implied by the avoidance of their contact: allowing his imagination to picture every thing that flattered its propensity to extravagant ideas, he soon formed this object into the hero of a romance, and determined to observe the offspring of his fancy, rather than the person before him. He became acquainted with him, paid him attentions, and so far advanced upon his notice, that his presence was always recognised. He gradually learnt that Lord Ruthven's affairs were embarrassed, and soon found, from the notes of preparation in —— Street, that he was about to travel. Desirous of gaining some information respecting this singular character, who, till now, had only whetted his curiosity, he hinted to his guardians, that it was time for him to perform the tour, which for many generations has been thought necessary to enable the young to take some rapid steps in the career of vice towards putting themselves upon an equality with the aged, and not allowing them to appear as if fallen from the skies, whenever scandalous intrigues are mentioned as the subjects of pleasantry or of praise, according to the degree of skill shewn in carrying them on. They consented: and Aubrey immediately mentioning his intentions to Lord Ruthven, was surprised to receive from him a proposal to join him. Flattered by such a mark of esteem from him, who, apparently, had nothing in common with other men, he gladly accepted it, and in a few days they had passed the circling waters.

Hitherto, Aubrey had had no opportunity of studying Lord Ruthven's character, and now he found, that, though many more of his actions were exposed to his view, the results offered different conclusions from the apparent motives to his conduct. His companion was profuse in his liberality;—the idle, the vagabond, and the beggar, received from his hand more than enough to relieve their immediate wants. But Aubrey could not avoid remarking, that it was not upon the virtuous, reduced to indigence by the misfortunes attendant even upon virtue, that he bestowed his alms;—these were sent from the door with hardly suppressed sneers; but when the profligate came to ask something, not to relieve his wants, but to allow him to wallow in his lust, or to sink him still deeper in his iniquity, he was sent away with rich charity. This was, however, attributed by him to the greater importunity of the vicious, which generally prevails over the retiring bashfulness of the virtuous indigent. There was one circumstance about the charity of his Lordship, which was still more impressed upon his mind: all those upon whom it was bestowed, inevitably found that there was a curse upon it, for they were all either led to the scaffold, or sunk to the lowest and the most abject misery. At Brussels and other towns through which they passed, Aubrey was surprized at the apparent eagerness with which his companion sought for the centres of all fashionable vice; there he entered into all the spirit of the faro[45] table: he betted, and always gambled with success, except where the known sharper was his antagonist, and then he lost even more than he gained; but it was always with the same unchanging face, with which he generally watched the society around: it was not, however, so when he encountered the rash youthful novice, or the luckless father of a numerous family; then his very wish seemed fortune's law—this apparent abstractedness of mind was laid aside, and his eyes sparkled with more fire than that of the cat whilst dallying with the half-dead mouse. In every town, he left the formerly affluent youth, torn from the circle he adorned, cursing, in the solitude of a dungeon, the fate that had drawn him within the reach of this fiend; whilst many a father sat frantic, amidst the speaking looks of mute hungry children, without a single farthing of his late immense wealth, wherewith to buy even sufficient to satisfy their present craving. Yet he took no money from the gambling table; but immediately lost, to the ruiner of many, the last gilder he had just snatched from the convulsive grasp of the innocent: this might but be the result of a certain degree of knowledge, which was not, however, capable of combating the cunning of the more experienced. Aubrey often wished to represent this to his friend, and beg him to resign that charity and pleasure which proved the ruin of all, and did not tend to his own profit;—but he delayed it—for each day he hoped his friend would give him some opportunity of speaking frankly and openly to him; however, this never occurred. Lord Ruthven in his carriage, and amidst the various wild and rich scenes of nature, was always the same: his eye spoke less than his lip; and though Aubrey was near the object of his curiosity,

45 Casino card game.

he obtained no greater gratification from it than the constant excitement of vainly wishing to break that mystery, which to his exalted imagination began to assume the appearance of something supernatural.

They soon arrived at Rome, and Aubrey for a time lost sight of his companion; he left him in daily attendance upon the morning circle of an Italian countess, whilst he went in search of the memorials of another almost deserted city. Whilst he was thus engaged, letters arrived from England, which he opened with eager impatience; the first was from his sister, breathing nothing but affection; the others were from his guardians, the latter astonished him; if it had before entered into his imagination that there was an evil power resident in his companion, these seemed to give him sufficient reason for the belief. His guardians insisted upon his immediately leaving his friend, and urged, that his character was dreadfully vicious, for that the possession of irresistible powers of seduction, rendered his licentious habits more dangerous to society. It had been discovered, that his contempt for the adultress had not originated in hatred of her character; but that he had required, to enhance his gratification, that his victim, the partner of his guilt, should be hurled from the pinnacle of unsullied virtue, down to the lowest abyss of infamy and degradation: in fine, that all those females whom he had sought, apparently on account of their virtue, had, since his departure, thrown even the mask aside, and had not scrupled to expose the whole deformity of their vices to the public gaze.

Aubrey determined upon leaving one, whose character had not yet shown a single bright point on which to rest the eye. He resolved to invent some plausible pretext for abandoning him altogether, purposing, in the mean while, to watch him more closely, and to let no slight circumstances pass by unnoticed. He entered into the same circle, and soon perceived, that his Lordship was endeavouring to work upon the inexperience of the daughter of the lady whose house he chiefly frequented. In Italy, it is seldom that an unmarried female is met with in society; he was therefore obliged to carry on his plans in secret; but Aubrey's eye followed him in all his windings, and soon discovered that an assignation had been appointed, which would most likely end in the ruin of an innocent, though thoughtless girl. Losing no time, he entered the apartment of Lord Ruthven, and abruptly asked him his intentions with respect to the lady, informing him at the same time that he was aware of his being about to meet her that very night. Lord Ruthven answered, that his intentions were such as he supposed all would have upon such an occasion; and upon being pressed whether he intended to marry her, merely laughed. Aubrey retired; and, immediately writing a note, to say, that from that moment he must decline accompanying his Lordship in the remainder of their proposed tour, he ordered his servant to seek other apartments, and calling upon the mother of the lady, informed her of all he knew, not only with regard to her daughter, but also concerning the character of his Lordship. The assignation was prevented. Lord Ruthven next day merely sent his servant to notify his complete assent to a separation; but did not hint any suspicion of his plans having been foiled by Aubrey's interposition.

Having left Rome, Aubrey directed his steps towards Greece, and crossing the Peninsula, soon found himself at Athens. He then fixed his residence in the house of a Greek; and soon occupied himself in tracing the faded records of ancient glory upon monuments that apparently, ashamed of chronicling the deeds of freemen only before slaves, had hidden themselves beneath the sheltering soil or many coloured lichen. Under the same roof as himself, existed a being, so beautiful and delicate, that she might have formed the model for a painter, wishing; to pourtray on canvass the promised hope of the faithful in Mahomet's paradise,[46] save that her eyes spoke too much mind for any one to think she could belong to those who had no souls. As she danced upon the plain, or tripped along the mountain's side, one would have thought the gazelle a poor type of her beauties; for who would have exchanged her eye, apparently the eye of animated nature, for that sleepy luxurious look of the animal suited but to the taste of an epicure. The light step of Ianthe often accompanied Aubrey in his search after antiquities, and often would the unconscious girl, engaged in the pursuit of a Kashmere butterfly, show the whole beauty of her form, floating as it were upon the wind, to the eager gaze of him, who forgot the letters he had just decyphered upon an almost effaced tablet, in the contemplation of her sylph-[47]like figure. Often would her tresses falling, as she flitted around, exhibit in the sun's ray such delicately brilliant and swiftly fading hues, its might well excuse the forgetfulness of the antiquary, who let escape from his mind the very object he had before thought of vital importance to the proper interpretation of a passage in Pausanias.[48] But why attempt to describe charms which all feel, but none can appreciate?—It was innocence, youth, and beauty, unaffected by crowded drawing-rooms and stifling balls. Whilst he drew those remains of which lie wished to preserve a memorial for his future hours, she would stand by, and watch the magic effects of his pencil, in tracing the scenes of her native place; she would then describe to him the circling dance upon the open plain, would paint, to him in all the glowing colours of youthful memory, the marriage pomp she remembered viewing in her infancy; and then, turning to subjects that had evidently

---

46 The Koran states that virgin women are among the rewards of the afterlife.
47 Fairy, or spirit of the air.
48 Ancient Greek geographer.

made a greater impression upon her mind, would tell him all the super-natural tales of her nurse. Her earnestness and apparent belief of what she narrated, excited the interest even of Aubrey; and often as she told him the tale of the living vampyre, who had passed years amidst his friends, and dearest ties, forced every year, by feeding upon the life of a lovely female to prolong his existence for the ensuing months, his blood would run cold, whilst he attempted to laugh her out of such idle and horrible fantasies; but Ianthe cited to him the names of old men, who had at last detected one living among themselves, after several of their near relatives and children had been found marked with the stamp of the fiend's appetite; and when she found him so incredulous, she begged of him to believe her, for it had been, remarked, that those who had dared to question their existence, always had some proof given, which obliged them, with grief and heartbreaking, to confess it was true. She detailed to him the traditional appearance of these monsters, and his horror was increased, by hearing a pretty accurate description of Lord Ruthven; he, however, still persisted in persuading her, that there could be no truth in her fears, though at the same time he wondered at the many coincidences which had all tended to excite a belief in the supernatural power of Lord Ruthven.

Aubrey began to attach himself more and more to Ianthe; her innocence, so contrasted with all the affected virtues of the women among whom he had sought for his vision of romance, won his heart; and while he ridiculed the idea of a young man of English habits, marrying an uneducated Greek girl, still he found himself more and more attached to the almost fairy form before him. He would tear himself at times from her, and, forming a plan for some antiquarian research, he would depart, determined not to return until his object was attained; but he always found it impossible to fix his attention upon the ruins around him, whilst in his mind he retained an image that seemed alone the rightful possessor of his thoughts. Ianthe was unconscious of his love, and was ever the same frank infantile being he had first known. She always seemed to part from him with reluctance; but it was because she had no longer any one with whom she could visit her favourite haunts, whilst her guardian was occupied in sketching or uncovering some fragment which had yet escaped the destructive hand of time. She had appealed to her parents on the subject of Vampyres, and they both, with several present, affirmed their existence, pale with horror at the very name. Soon after, Aubrey determined to proceed upon one of his excursions, which was to detain him for a few hours; when they heard the name of the place, they all at once begged of him not to return at night, as he must necessarily pass through a wood, where no Greek would ever remain, after the day had closed, upon any consideration. They described it as the resort of

THE VAMPYRE: A TALE

the vampyres in their nocturnal orgies, and denounced the most heavy evils as impending upon him who dared to cross their path. Aubrey made light of their representations, and tried to laugh them out of the idea; but when he saw them shudder at his daring thus to mock a superior, infernal power, the very name of which apparently made their blood freeze, he was silent.

Next morning Aubrey set off upon his excursion unattended; he was surprised to observe the melancholy face of his host, and was concerned to find that his words, mocking the belief of those horrible fiends, had inspired them with such terror. When he was about to depart, Ianthe came to the side of his horse, and earnestly begged of him to return, ere night allowed the power of these beings to be put in action;—he promised. He was, however, so occupied in his research, that he did not perceive that day-light would soon end, and that in the horizon there was one of those specks which, in the warmer climates, so rapidly gather into a tremendous mass, and pour all their rage upon the devoted country.—He at last, however, mounted his horse, determined to make up by speed for his delay: but it was too late. Twilight, in these southern climates, is almost unknown; immediately the sun sets, night begins: and ere he had advanced far, the power of the storm was above—its echoing thunders had scarcely an interval of rest—its thick heavy rain forced its way through the canopying foliage, whilst the blue forked lightning seemed to fall and radiate at his very feet. Suddenly his horse took fright, and he was carried with dreadful rapidity through the entangled forest. The animal at last, through fatigue, stopped, and he found, by the glare of lightning, that he was in the neighbourhood of a hovel that hardly lifted itself up from the masses of dead leaves and brushwood which surrounded it. Dismounting, he approached, hoping to find some one to guide him to the town, or at least trusting to obtain shelter from the pelting of the storm. As he approached, the thunders, for a moment silent, allowed him to hear the dreadful shrieks of a woman mingling with the stifled, exultant mockery of a laugh, continued in one almost unbroken sound;—he was startled: but, roused by the thunder which again rolled over his head, he, with a sudden effort, forced open the door of the hut. He found himself in utter darkness: the sound, however, guided him. He was apparently unperceived; for, though he called, still the sounds continued, and no notice was taken of him. He found himself in contact with some one, whom he immediately seized; when a voice cried, "Again baffled!" to which a loud laugh succeeded; and he felt himself grappled by one whose strength seemed superhuman: determined to sell[49] his life as dearly as he could, he struggled; but it was in vain: he was lifted from his feet and hurled with enormous force against the ground:—his enemy threw

49 Value (Archaic).

himself upon him, and kneeling upon his breast, had placed his hands upon his throat—when the glare of many torches penetrating through the hole that gave light in the day, disturbed him;—he instantly rose, and, leaving his prey, rushed through the door, and in a moment the crashing of the brandies, as he broke through the wood, was no longer heard. The storm was now still; and Aubrey, incapable of moving, was soon heard by those without. They entered; the light of their torches fell upon the mud walls, and the thatch loaded on every individual straw with heavy flakes of soot. At the desire of Aubrey they searched for her who had attracted him by her cries; he was again left in darkness; but what was his horror, when the light of the torches once more burst upon him, to perceive the airy form of his fair conductress brought in a lifeless corse. He shut his eyes, hoping that it was but a vision arising from his disturbed imagination; but he again saw the same form, when he unclosed them, stretched by his side. There was no colour upon her cheek, not even upon her lip; yet there was a stillness about her face that seemed almost as attaching as the life that once dwelt there:—upon her neck and breast was blood, and upon her throat were the marks of teeth having opened the vein:—to this the men pointed, crying, simultaneously struck with horror, "A Vampyre! a Vampyre!" A litter was quickly formed, and Aubrey was laid by the side of her who had lately been to him the object of so many bright and fairy visions, now fallen with the flower of life that had died within her. He knew not what his thoughts were—his mind was benumbed and seemed to shun reflection, and take refuge in vacancy—he held almost unconsciously in his hand a naked dagger of a particular construction, which had been found in the hut. They were soon met by different parties who had been engaged in the search of her whom a mother had missed. Their lamentable cries, as they approached the city, forewarned the parents of some dreadful catastrophe. —To describe their grief would be impossible; but when they ascertained the cause of their child's death, they looked at Aubrey, and pointed to the corse. They were inconsolable; both died broken-hearted.

Aubrey being put to bed was seized with a most violent fever, and was often delirious; in these intervals he would call upon Lord Ruthven and upon Ianthe—by some unaccountable combination he seemed to beg of his former companion to spare the being he loved. At other times he would imprecate maledictions upon his head, and curse him as her destroyer. Lord Ruthven, chanced at this time to arrive at Athens, and, from whatever motive, upon hearing of the state of Aubrey, immediately placed himself in the same house, and became his constant attendant. When the latter recovered from his delirium, he was horrified and startled at the sight of him whose image he had now combined with that of a Vampyre; but Lord Ruthven, by his kind words, implying almost repentance for the fault that had caused their separation, and still more by the attention, anxiety, and care which he showed, soon reconciled him to his presence. His lordship seemed quite changed; he no longer appeared that apathetic being who had so astonished Aubrey; but as soon as his convalescence began to be rapid, he again gradually retired into the same state of mind, and Aubrey perceived no difference from the former man, except that at times he was surprised to meet his gaze fixed intently upon him, with a smile of malicious exultation playing upon his lips: he knew not why, but this smile haunted him. During the last stage of the invalid's recovery, Lord Ruthven was apparently engaged in watching the tideless waves raised by the cooling breeze, or in marking the progress of those orbs, circling, like our world, the moveless sun;—indeed, he appeared to wish to avoid the eyes of all.

Aubrey's mind, by this shock, was much weakened, and that elasticity of spirit which had once so distinguished him now seemed to have fled for ever. He was now as much a lover of solitude and silence as Lord Ruthven; but much as he wished for solitude, his mind could not find it in the neighbourhood of Athens; if he sought it amidst the ruins he had formerly frequented, Ianthe's form stood by his side—if he sought it in the woods, her light step would appear wandering amidst the underwood, in quest of the modest violet; then suddenly turning round, would show, to his wild imagination, her pale face and wounded throat, with a meek smile upon her lips. He determined to fly scenes, every feature of which created such bitter associations in his mind. He proposed to Lord Ruthven, to whom he held himself bound by the tender care he had taken of him during his illness, that they should visit those parts of Greece neither had yet seen. They travelled in every direction, and sought every spot to which a recollection could be attached: but though they thus hastened from place to place, yet they seemed not to heed what they gazed upon. They heard much of robbers, but they gradually began to slight these reports, which they imagined were only the invention of individuals, whose interest it was to excite the generosity of those whom they defended from pretended dangers. In consequence of thus neglecting the advice of the inhabitants, on one occasion they travelled with only a few guards, more to serve as guides than as a defence. Upon entering, however, a narrow defile, at the bottom of which was the bed of a torrent, with large masses of rock brought down from the neighbouring precipices, they had reason to repent their negligence; for scarcely were the whole of the party engaged in the narrow pass, when they were startled by the whistling of bullets close to their heads, and by the echoed report of several guns. In an instant their guards had left them, and, placing themselves behind rocks, had begun to fire in the direction whence the report came.

Lord Ruthven and Aubrey, imitating their example, retired for a moment behind the sheltering turn of the defile: but ashamed of being thus detained by a foe, who with insulting shouts bade them advance, and being exposed to unresisting slaughter, if any of the robbers should climb above and take them in the rear, they determined at once to rush forward in search of the enemy. Hardly had they lost the shelter of the rock, when Lord Ruthven received a shot in the shoulder, which brought him to the ground. Aubrey hastened to his assistance; and, no longer heeding the contest or his own peril, was soon surprised by seeing the robbers' faces around him—his guards having, upon Lord Ruthven's being wounded, immediately thrown up their arms and surrendered.

By promises of great reward, Aubrey soon induced them to convey his wounded friend to a neighbouring cabin; and having agreed upon a ransom, he was no more disturbed by their presence—they being content merely to guard the entrance till their comrade should return with the promised sum, for which he had an order. Lord Ruthven's strength rapidly decreased; in two days mortification ensued, and death seemed advancing with hasty steps. His conduct and appearance had not changed; he seemed as unconscious of pain as he had been of the objects about him: but towards the close of the last evening, his mind became apparently uneasy, and his eye often fixed upon Aubrey, who was induced to offer his assistance with more than usual earnestness—"Assist me! you may save me—you may do more than that—I mean not my life, I heed the death of my existence as little as that of the passing day; but you may save my honour, your friend's honour."—"How? tell me how? I would do any thing," replied Aubrey.—" I need but little—my life ebbs apace—I cannot explain the whole—but if you would conceal all you know of me, my honour were free from stain in the world's mouth—and if my death were unknown for some time in England—I—I—but life."—"It shall not be known."—"Swear!" cried the dying man, raising himself with exultant violence, "Swear by all your soul reveres, by all your nature fears, swear that, for a year and a day you will not impart your knowledge of my crimes or death to any living being in any way, whatever may happen, or whatever you may see. "—His eyes seemed bursting from their sockets: "I swear!" said Aubrey; he sunk laughing upon his pillow, and breathed no more.

Aubrey retired to rest, but did not sleep; the many circumstances attending his acquaintance with this man rose upon his mind, and he knew not why; when he remembered his oath a cold shivering came over him, as if from the presentiment of something horrible awaiting him. Rising early in the morning, he was about to enter the hovel in which he had left the corpse, when a robber met him, and informed him that it was no longer there, having been conveyed by himself and comrades, upon his retiring, to the pinnacle of a neighbouring mount, according to a promise they had given his lordship, that it should be exposed to the first cold ray of the moon that rose after his death. Aubrey astonished, and taking several of the men, determined to go and bury it upon the spot where it lay. But, when he had mounted to the summit he found no trace of either the corpse or the clothes, though the robbers swore they pointed out the identical rock: on which they had laid the body. For a time his mind was bewildered in conjectures, but he at last returned, convinced that they had buried the corpse for the sake of the clothes.

Weary of a country in which he had met with such terrible misfortunes, and in which all apparently conspired to heighten that superstitious melancholy that had seized upon his mind, he resolved to leave it, and soon arrived at Smyrna. While waiting for a vessel to convey him to Otranto, or to Naples, he occupied himself in arranging those effects he had with him belonging to Lord Ruthven. Amongst other things there was a case containing several weapons of offence, more or less adapted to ensure the death of the victim. There were several daggers and ataghans.[50] Whilst turning them over, and examining their curious forms, what was his surprise at finding a sheath apparently ornamented in the same style as the dagger discovered in the fatal hut—he shuddered—hastening to gain further proof, he found the weapon, and his horror may be imagined when he discovered that it fitted, though peculiarly shaped, the sheath he held in his hand. His eyes seemed to need no further certainty—they seemed gazing to be bound to the dagger; yet still he wished to disbelieve; but the particular form, the same varying tints upon the haft and sheath were alike in splendour on both, and left no room for doubt; there were also drops of blood on each.

He left Smyrna, and on his way home, at Rome, his first inquiries were concerning the lady he had attempted to snatch from Lord Ruthven's seductive arts. Her parents were in distress, their fortune ruined, and she had not been heard of since the departure of his lordship. Aubrey's mind became almost broken under so many repeated horrors; he was afraid that this lady had fallen a victim to the destroyer of Ianthe. He became morose and silent; and his only occupation consisted in urging the speed of the postilions,[51] as if he were going to save the life of some one he held dear. He arrived at Calais; a breeze, which seemed obedient to his will, soon wafted him to the English shores; and he hastened to the mansion of his fathers, and there, for a moment, appeared to lose, in the embraces and caresses of his sister, all memory of the past. If she before, by her infantine caresses, had gained his

50 Turkish sabers.
51 Carriage drivers.

affection, now that the woman began to appear, she was still more attaching as a companion.

Miss Aubrey had not that winning grace which gains the gaze and applause of the drawing-room assemblies. There was none of that light brilliancy which only exists in the heated atmosphere of a crowded apartment. Her blue eye was never lit up by the levity of the mind beneath. There was a melancholy charm about it which did not seem to arise from misfortune, but from some feeling within, that appeared to indicate a soul conscious of a brighter realm. Her step was not that light footing, which strays where'er a butterfly or a colour may attract—it was sedate and pensive. When alone, her face was never brightened by the smile of joy; but when her brother breathed to her his affection, and would in her presence forget those griefs she knew destroyed his rest, who would have exchanged her smile for that of the voluptuary? It seemed as if those eyes,—that face were then playing in the light of their own native sphere. She was yet only eighteen, and had not been presented to the world, it having been thought by her guardians more fit that her presentation should be delayed until her brother's return from the continent, when he might be her protector. It was now, therefore, resolved that the next drawing-room, which was fast approaching, should be the epoch of her entry into the "busy scene." Aubrey would rather have remained in the mansion of his fathers, and fed upon the melancholy which overpowered him. He could not fed interest about the frivolities of fashionable strangers, when his mind had been so torn by the events he had witnessed; but he determined to sacrifice his own comfort to the protection of his sister. They soon arrived in town, and prepared for the next day, which had been announced as a drawing-room.

The crowd was excessive—a drawing-room had not been held for a long time, and all who were anxious to bask in the smile of royalty, hastened thither. Aubrey was there with his sister. While he was standing in a corner by himself, heedless of all around him, engaged in the remembrance that the first time he had seen Lord Ruthven was in that very place—he felt himself suddenly seized by the arm, and a voice he recognized too well, sounded in his ear—"Remember your oath." He had hardly courage to turn, fearful of seeing a spectre that would blast him, when he perceived, at a little distance, the same figure which had attracted his notice on this spot upon his first entry into society. He gazed till his limbs almost refusing to bear their weight, he was obliged to take the arm of a friend, and forcing a passage through the crowd, he threw himself into his carriage, and was driven home. He paced the room with hurried steps, and fixed his hands upon his head, as if he were afraid his thoughts were bursting from his brain. Lord Ruthven again before him—circumstances started up in dreadful array—the dagger—his oath.—He roused himself, he could not believe it possible—the dead rise again!—He thought his imagination had conjured up the image, his mind was resting upon. It was impossible that it could be real—he determined, therefore, to go again into society; for though he attempted to ask concerning Lord Ruthven, the name hung upon his lips, and he could not succeed in gaining information. He went a few nights after with his sister to the assembly of a near relation. Leaving her under the protection of a matron, he retired into a recess, and there gave himself up to his own devouring thoughts. Perceiving, at last, that many were leaving, he roused himself, and entering another room, found his sister surrounded by several, apparently in earnest conversation; he attempted to pass and get near her, when one, whom he requested to move, turned round, and revealed to him those features he most abhorred. He sprang forward, seized his sister's arm, and, with hurried step, forced her towards the street: at the door he found himself impeded by the crowd of servants who were waiting for their lords; and while he was engaged in passing them, he again heard that voice whisper close to him—"Remember your oath!"—He did not dare to turn, but, hurrying his sister, soon reached home.

Aubrey became almost distracted. If before his mind had been absorbed by one subject, how much more completely was it engrossed, now that the certainty of the monster's living again pressed upon his thoughts. His sister's attentions were now unheeded, and it was in vain that she intreated him to explain to her what had caused his abrupt conduct. He only uttered a few words, and those terrified her. The more he thought, the more he was bewildered. His oath startled him;—was he then to allow this monster to roam, bearing ruin upon his breath, amidst all he held dear, and not avert its progress? His very sister might have been touched by him. But even if he were to break his oath, and disclose his suspicions, who would believe him? He thought of employing his own hand to free the world from such a wretch; but death, he remembered, had been already mocked. For days he remained in this state; shut up in his room, he saw no one, and eat only when his sister came, who, with eyes streaming with tears, besought him, for her sake, to support nature. At last, no longer capable of bearing stillness and solitude, he left his house, roamed from street to street, anxious to fly that image which haunted him. His dress became neglected, and he wandered, as often exposed to the noon-day sun as to the midnight damps. He was no longer to be recognized; at first he returned with the evening to the house; but at last he laid him down to rest wherever fatigue overtook him. His sister, anxious for his safety, employed people to follow him; but they were soon distanced by him who fled from a pursuer swifter than any—from thought. His conduct, however, suddenly changed. Struck with the idea that he left by his absence the whole of his friends, with a fiend amongst them, of whose presence they were unconscious, he determined to enter again into society, and watch him closely, anxious to forewarn, in spite of his oath, all whom Lord Ruthven approached with intimacy. But when he entered into a room, his haggard and suspicious looks were so striking, his inward shudderings so visible, that his sister was at last obliged to beg of him to abstain from seeking, for her sake, a society which affected him so strongly. When, however, remonstrance proved unavailing, the guardians thought proper to interpose, and, fearing that his mind was becoming alienated, they thought it high time to resume again that trust which had been before imposed upon them by Aubrey's parents.

Desirous of saving him from the injuries and sufferings he had daily encountered in his wanderings, and of preventing him from exposing to the general eye those marks of what they considered folly, they engaged a physician to reside in the house, and take constant care of him. He hardly appeared to notice it, so completely was his mind absorbed by one terrible subject. His incoherence became at last so great, that he was confined to his chamber. There he would often lie for days, incapable of being roused. He had become emaciated, his eyes had attained a glassy lustre;—the only sign of affection and recollection remaining displayed itself upon the entry of his sister; then he would sometimes start, and, seizing her hands, with looks that severely afflicted her, he would desire her not to touch him. "Oh, do not touch him—if your love for me is aught, do not go near him!" When, however, she inquired to whom he referred, his only answer was, "True! true!" and again he sank into a state, whence not even she could rouse him. This lasted many months: gradually, however, as the year was passing, his incoherences became less frequent, and his mind threw off a portion of its gloom, whilst his guardians observed, that several times in the day he would count upon his fingers a definite number, and then smile.

The time had nearly elapsed, when, upon the last day of the year, one of his guardians entering his room, began to converse with his physician upon the melancholy circumstance of Aubrey's being in so awful a situation, when his sister was going next day to be married. Instantly Aubrey's attention was attracted; he asked anxiously to whom. Glad of this mark of returning intellect, of which they feared he had been deprived, they mentioned the name of the Earl of Marsden. Thinking this was a young Earl whom he had met with in society, Aubrey seemed pleased, and astonished them still more by his expressing his intention to be present at the nuptials, and desiring to see his sister. They answered not, but in a few minutes his sister was with him. He was apparently again capable of being affected by the influence of her lovely smile; for he pressed her to his breast, and kissed her cheek, wet with tears, flowing at the thought of her brother's being once more alive to the feelings of affection. He began to speak with all his wonted warmth, and to congratulate her upon her marriage with a person so distinguished for rank and every accomplishment; when he suddenly perceived a locket upon her breast; opening it, what was his surprise at beholding the features of the monster who had so long influenced his life. He seized the portrait in a paroxysm of rage, and trampled it under foot. Upon her asking him why he thus destroyed the resemblance of her future husband, he looked as if he did not understand her—then seizing her hands, and gazing on her with a frantic expression of countenance, he bade her swear that she would never wed this monster, for he—— But he could not advance—it seemed as if that voice again bade him remember his oath—he turned suddenly round, thinking Lord Ruthven was near him but saw no one. In the meantime the guardians and physician, who had heard the whole, and thought this was but a return of his disorder, entered, and forcing him from Miss Aubrey, desired her to leave him. He fell upon his knees to them, he implored, he begged of them to delay but for one day. They, attributing this to the insanity they imagined had taken possession of his mind, endeavoured to pacify him, and retired.

Lord Ruthven had called the morning after the drawing-room, and had been refused with every one else. When he heard of Aubrey's ill health, he readily understood himself to be the cause of it; but when he learned that he was deemed insane, his exultation and pleasure could hardly be concealed from those among whom he had gained this information. He hastened to the house of his former companion, and, by constant attendance, and the pretence of great affection for the brother and interest in his fate, he gradually won the ear of Miss Aubrey. Who could resist his power? His tongue had dangers and toils to recount—could speak of himself as of an individual having no sympathy with any being on the crowded earth, save with her to whom he addressed himself;—could tell how, since he knew her, his existence, had begun to seem worthy of preservation, if it were merely that he might listen to her soothing accents;—in fine, he knew so well how to use the serpent's art, or such was the will of fate, that he gained her affections. The title of the elder branch falling at length to him, lie obtained an important embassy, which served as an excuse for hastening the marriage, (in spite of her brother's deranged state,) which was to take place the very day before his departure for the continent.

Aubrey, when he was left by the physician and his guardians, attempted to bribe the servants, but in vain. He asked for pen and paper; it was given him; he wrote a letter to his sister, conjuring her, as she valued her own happiness, her own honour, and the honour of those now in the grave, who once held her in their arms as their hope and the hope of their house, to delay but for a few hours that marriage, on which he denounced the most heavy curses. The servants promised they would deliver it; but giving it to the physician, he thought it better not to harass any more the mind of Miss Aubrey by, what he considered, the ravings of a maniac. Night passed on without rest to the busy inmates of the house; and Aubrey heard, with a horror that may more easily be conceived than described, the notes of busy preparation. Morning came, and the sound of carriages broke upon his ear. Aubrey grew almost frantic. The curiosity of the servants at last overcame their vigilance, they gradually stole away, leaving him in the custody of an helpless old woman. He seized the opportunity, with one bound was out of the room, and in a moment found himself in the apartment where all were nearly assembled. Lord Ruthven was the first to perceive him: lie immediately approached, and, taking his arm by force, hurried him from the room, speechless with rage. When on the staircase, Lord Ruthven whispered in his ear—"Remember your oath, and know, if not my bride to day, your sister is dishonoured. Women are frail!" So saying, he pushed him towards his attendants, who, roused by the old woman, had come in search of him. Aubrey could no longer support himself; his rage not finding vent, had broken a blood-vessel, and he was conveyed to bed. This was not mentioned to his sister, who was not present when he entered, as the physician was afraid of agitating her. The marriage was solemnized, and the bride and bridegroom left London.

Aubrey's weakness increased; the effusion of blood produced symptoms of the near approach of death. He desired his sister's guardians might be called, and when the midnight hour had struck, he related composedly what the reader has perused—he died immediately after.

The guardians hastened to protect Miss Aubrey; but when they arrived, it was too late. Lord Ruthven had disappeared, and Aubrey's sister had glutted the thirst of a VAMPYRE!

VARNEY THE VAMPIRE: OR, THE FEAST OF BLOOD

1847

JAMES MALCOLM RYMER

*T*hanks to the enthusiasm of devoted vampire fans across the globe, scholars have recently unearthed and republished all 800+ pages of *Varney the Vampire*, one of the most widely read penny dreadful serial fiction sagas of the nineteenth century. Printed on cheap pamphlets, the serial introduced the potency of a vampire narrative to the masses on an unprecedented scale.

While Varney left an indelible stamp on the vampire genre, the text deserves special attention simply due to its scale and imaginative scope. James Malcolm Rymer, the author of the series (only recently has the question of authorship been answered conclusively), committed himself so absolutely to the character Varney and the worlds he inhabited that he was able to maintain the serial's popularity for two years. Rymer had a loyal following, and the expectations his readership placed upon him anticipated the relationships contemporary popular fiction masters such as King and Rice share with their readers.

The haphazard, shoddy publishing standards that produced dreadfuls like *Varney* are partly responsible for scholars relegating them to footnotes. The publishing process was characterized by the absence of any editorial review whatsoever. Chapters never underwent rewrites or were even proofread. Indeed, historical accounts of Rymer indicate that he churned out each installment only hours before each issue went to press. Accordingly, the original text of *Varney* is an absolute mess. Typographical, grammatical, and formatting errors riddle nearly every page, and sometimes words are even printed upside down. The manuscript acquired for this project came with the majority of errors fixed. I've left the remaining ones to try in some small way to recreate the experience of reading a penny dreadful. Publishing in the nineteenth century possessed a free-for-all, egalitarian quality that today only exists on the Internet. Its battiness, inconsistency, and disregard for precision help make *Varney* the fascinating piece of writing that it is.

As for narrative method, Rymer focuses almost exclusively on plot. Short sentences, rapid-fire dialogue, chase scenes, and high drama are present in nearly every chapter. I've included the first four chapters to provide a sample of this style. During the infrequent moments when Rymer does withdraw from the story to discuss character and plot in a more meditative, reflective tone, he reveals central themes in a matter-of-fact manner. Chapters 20, 33, and 40 were selected for this reason, as they provide a glimpse into the interior life of Varney. It is during these pockets of prose that one witnesses the development of the vampire figure.

Varney is one of the first vampires to exhibit positive human traits. Lord Ruthven presented a figure who possesses human cruelty and even has the ability to imitate generosity and kindness. However, ultimately, if Ruthven were human, he would be deemed a sociopath. Varney, on the other hand, is capable of feeling guilt. Chapter 33 demonstrates such emotional self-awareness. Skulking around Bannerwith Hall, Varney can only be described as melancholic and introspective. Not only does his behavior indicate this, Rymer announces it: "A strong emotion seemed to come over him, such as no one could have supposed would for one moment have possessed the frame of one so apparently unconnected with all human sympathies" (XXXIII). Yet this sentiment does not last. By the end of the chapter, Varney is once again "diabolical" and declares, "I have no right to count myself in the great muster-roll of humanity."

We witness a similar and even more poignant pattern in Chapter 34. Flora and Varney engage in an extended conversation (an innovation in and of itself) during which Varney speaks at length about his feelings and his conflicting feelings about being a vampire:

"Flora," he said, "it is not that I am so enamored of an existence to be prolonged only by such frightful means, which induces me to become a terror to you or to others. Believe me, that if my victims, those whom my insatiable thirst for blood make wretched, suffer much, I, the vampyre, am not without my moments of unutterable agony. But it is a mysterious law of our nature, that as the period approaches when the exhausted energies of life require a new support from the warm, gushing fountain of another's veins, the strong desire to live grows upon us, until, in a paroxysm of wild insanity, which will recognize no obstacles, human or divine, we seek a victim" (Chapter 34).

Yet by the end of the chapter, Varney once again returns to his typical violent state.

These incongruous representations of Varney are partly a product of Rymer's general inconsistency, but also a product of the still adolescent conception of the literary vampire. As discussed in the introduction to this section, nineteenth-century writers of vampire fiction sought to stay true to the vampire of the German poets and the creatures of folklore while simultaneously reinventing the vampire as a figure with ethical and moral dimensions. Rymer wrestles with this dilemma for almost 900 pages.

Other, less overt characteristics also make Varney a more human character than his predecessors. For example, things besides the need for blood often motivate his behavior. Various sub-plots include Varney running after money, fortune, and social advancement. The young women he assaults are just one genus of his victims. In this regard, Varney—like Lord Ruthven—is complex enough to be a metaphor for a social predator. Perhaps even more notably, Varney emerges as a human figure because he is often no less brutal and cruel than the humans he encounters. If Varney is vile, so are the citizens with whom he interacts. Chapter 40 brings this reality to the fore, when an angry mob stampedes through town looking for Varney. The mob is described as wielding "flails, scythes, sickles, bludgeons, etc...and it was with concentrated rage that they now pressed onward." The inhumanity of the mob is emphasized by certain humane exceptions. One woman urges the mob to "drive a stake through him...it's the humanest way," while another man "shrank with horror from seeing even such a creature as Varney sacrificed at the shrine of popular resentment, and murdered by an infuriated populace." Setting the saga of *Varney* in the present day, like *The Vampyre*, advances the agenda of social realist fiction, further leaving behind Gothic settings and tropes. Giving Varney free reign within a contemporary, urban world familiar to Rymer's readership establishes him as a vampire of the people. Like Lord Ruthven, Varney possesses not only superhuman physical traits, but also sophisticated social skills.

Herr, who edited the most recent publication of *Varney*, rigorously defends the saga's literary merit. Due to the haphazard quality of the text, cliché-driven plots, and numerous cases of crass misogyny, critics have reason for their disdain. Nevertheless, Herr is correct in pronouncing Varney a critical figure in the development of vampire literature. Although the plotlines of the epic-length serial often become repetitive, Varney's character evolves in a way that humans evolve. Rymer sets the precedent for a vampire that is emotionally complex and who faces human challenges. A good example is how Varney is jealous of Charles Holland, Laura's love interest. Most importantly, Varney is the sole vampire in this anthology who is a *moral* being—not necessarily a good being, but one for which good exists. Having a conscience is perhaps the most human of human traits, and Varney is the progenitor of this development. The presence of a conscience is reinforced when in the novel's conclusion it is revealed that Varney (whose original, human name was Mortimer) was forced to become a vampire after he killed his own son. In the case of Varney, his emotional pain is a product of his own actions—a relationship that is at the core of ethics.

In addition to trailblazing the road to a more human vampire, *Varney* refines many other central vampire themes. Varney was the first vampire with fangs, the first to leave puncture marks on his victims, and the first with superhuman hypnotic powers and strength. In addition, Varney expanded the erotic element of the vampire figure. His victims are not simply assaulted in the night, but rather seduced, entranced by his sexual mystique. "There was a wonderful fascination in the manner now of Varney. His voice sounded like music itself. His words flowed from his tongue, each gently and properly accented, with all the charm of eloquence" (Chapter XX). As in *The Vampyre*, marriage plays an important role in the relationship between the vampire and his victim. Both Lord Ruthven and Varney frequently marry their targets before initiating a physical attack, which suggests the vampire's needs are not strictly physiological, but also psychological. We witness in this heightened eroticism a vampire endowed with sources of power that are definitively human in nature. Reading about the exploits of creatures with superhuman speed and immeasurable strength certainly has fantastic appeal, yet watching the deliberate and precise destruction of a delicate female psyche (a theme rightly eviscerated by feminist scholarship) titillates in a far more interesting way. As readers, we experience both the thrill of total conquest and the terror of personal annihilation—emotional experiences that the majority of us fortunately never encounter.

VARNEY THE VAMPIRE: OR, THE FEAST OF BLOOD (SELECTED CHAPTERS)

PREFACE

*T*he unprecedented success of the romance of "Varney the Vampyre," leaves the Author but little to say further, than that he accepts that success and its results as gratefully as it is possible for any one to do popular favours.

A belief in the existence of Vampyres first took its rise in Norway and Sweden, from whence it rapidly spread to more southern regions, taking a firm hold of the imaginations of the more credulous portion of mankind.

The following romance is collected from seemingly the most authentic sources, and the Author must leave the question of credibility entirely to his readers, not even thinking that he his peculiarly called upon to express his own opinion upon the subject.

Nothing has been omitted in the life of the unhappy Varney, which could tend to throw a light upon his most extraordinary career, and the fact of his death just as it is here related, made a great noise at the time through Europe and is to be found in the public prints for the year 1713.

With these few observations, the Author and Publisher, are well content to leave the work in the hands of a public, which has stamped it with an approbation far exceeding their most sanguine expectations, and which is calculated to act as the strongest possible incentive to the production of other works, which in a like, or perchance a still further degree may be deserving of public patronage and support.

To the whole of the Metropolitan Press for their laudatory notices, the Author is peculiarly obliged.

London Sep. 1847

CHAPTER I.

—"How graves give up their dead.
And how the night air hideous grows
With shrieks!"

MIDNIGHT.—THE HAIL-STORM.—THE DREADFUL
VISITOR.—THE VAMPYRE.

The solemn tones of an old cathedral clock have announced midnight—the air is thick and heavy—a strange, death like stillness pervades all nature. Like the ominous calm which precedes some more than usually terrific outbreak of the elements, they seem to have paused even in their ordinary fluctuations, to gather a terrific strength for the great effort. A faint peal of thunder now comes from far off. Like a signal gun for the battle of the winds to begin, it appeared to awaken them from their lethargy, and one awful, warring hurricane swept over a whole city, producing more devastation in the four or five minutes it lasted, than would a half century of ordinary phenomena.

It was as if some giant had blown upon some toy town, and scattered many of the buildings before the hot blast of his terrific breath; for as suddenly as that blast of wind had come did it cease, and all was as still and calm as before.

Sleepers awakened, and thought that what they had heard must be the confused chimera of a dream. They trembled and turned to sleep again.

All is still—still as the very grave. Not a sound breaks the magic of repose. What is that—a strange, pattering noise, as of a million of fairy feet? It is hail—yes, a hail-storm has burst over the city. Leaves are dashed from the trees, mingled with small boughs; windows that lie most opposed to the direct fury of the pelting particles of ice are broken, and the rapt repose that before was so remarkable in its intensity, is exchanged for a noise which, in its accumulation, drowns every cry of surprise or consternation which here and there arose from persons who found their houses invaded by the storm.

Now and then, too, there would come a sudden gust of wind that in its strength, as it blew laterally, would, for a moment, hold millions of the hailstones suspended in mid air, but it was only to dash them with redoubled force in some new direction, where more mischief was to be done.

Oh, how the storm raged! Hail—rain—wind. It was, in very truth, an awful night.

There is an antique chamber in an ancient house. Curious and quaint carvings adorn the walls, and the large chimney-piece is a curiosity of itself. The ceiling is low, and a large bay window, from roof to floor, looks to the west. The window is latticed, and filled with curiously painted glass and rich stained pieces, which send in a strange, yet beautiful light, when sun or moon shines into the apartment. There is but one portrait in that room, although the walls seem panelled for the express purpose of containing a series of pictures. That portrait is of a young man, with a pale face, a stately brow, and a strange expression about the eyes, which no one cared to look on twice.

There is a stately bed in that chamber, of carved walnut-wood is it made, rich in design and elaborate in execution; one of those works of art which owe their existence to the Elizabethan era. It is hung with heavy silken and damask furnishing; nodding feathers are at its corners—covered with dust are they, and they lend a funereal aspect to the room. The floor is of polished oak.

God! how the hail dashes on the old bay window! Like an occasional discharge of mimic musketry, it comes clashing, beating, and cracking upon the small panes; but they resist it—their small size saves them; the wind, the hail, the rain, expend their fury in vain.

The bed in that old chamber is occupied. A creature formed in all fashions of loveliness lies in a half sleep upon that ancient couch—a girl young and beautiful as a spring morning. Her long hair has escaped from its confinement and streams over the blackened coverings of the bedstead; she has been restless in her sleep, for the clothing of the bed is in much confusion. One arm is over her head, the other hangs nearly off the side of the bed near to which she lies. A neck and bosom that would have formed a study for the rarest sculptor that ever Providence gave genius to, were half disclosed. She moaned slightly in her sleep, and once or twice the lips moved as if in prayer—at least one might judge so, for the name of Him who suffered for all came once faintly from them.

She has endured much fatigue, and the storm does not awaken her; but it can disturb the slumbers it does not possess the power to destroy entirely. The turmoil of the elements wakes the senses, although it cannot entirely break the repose they have lapsed into.

Oh, what a world of witchery was in that mouth, slightly parted, and exhibiting within the pearly teeth that glistened even in the faint light that came from that bay window. How sweetly the long silken eyelashes lay upon the cheek. Now she moves, and one shoulder is entirely visible—whiter, fairer than the spotless clothing of the bed on which she lies, is the smooth skin of that fair creature, just budding into womanhood, and in that transition state which presents to us all the charms of the girl—almost of the child, with the more matured beauty and gentleness of advancing years.

Was that lightning? Yes—an awful, vivid, terrifying flash—then a roaring peal of thunder, as if a thousand mountains were rolling one over the other in the blue vault of Heaven! Who sleeps now in that ancient city? Not one living soul. The dread trumpet of eternity could not more effectually have awakened any one.

The hail continues. The wind continues. The uproar of the elements seems at its height. Now she awakens—that beautiful girl on the antique bed; she opens those eyes of celestial blue, and a faint cry of alarm bursts from her lips. At least it is a cry which, amid the noise and turmoil without, sounds but faint and weak. She sits upon the bed and presses her hands upon her eyes. Heavens! what a wild torrent of wind, and rain, and hail! The thunder likewise seems intent upon awakening sufficient echoes to last until the next flash of forked lightning should again produce the wild concussion of the air. She murmurs a prayer—a prayer for those she loves best; the names of those dear to her gentle heart come from her lips; she weeps and prays; she thinks then of what devastation the storm must surely produce, and to the great God of Heaven she prays for all living things. Another flash—a wild, blue, bewildering flash of lightning streams across that bay window, for an instant bringing out every colour in it with terrible distinctness. A shriek bursts from the lips of the young girl, and then, with eyes fixed upon that window, which, in another moment, is all darkness, and with such an expression of terror upon her face as it had never before known, she trembled, and the perspiration of intense fear stood upon her brow.

"What—what was it?" she gasped; "real, or a delusion? Oh, God, what was it? A figure tall and gaunt, endeavouring from the outside to unclasp the window. I saw it. That flash of lightning revealed it to me. It stood the whole length of the window."

There was a lull of the wind. The hail was not falling so thickly—moreover, it now fell, what there was of it, straight, and yet a strange clattering sound came upon the glass of that long window. It could not be a delusion—she is awake, and she hears it. What can produce it? Another flash of lightning—another shriek—there could be now no delusion.

A tall figure is standing on the ledge immediately outside the long window. It is its finger-nails upon the glass that produces the sound so like the hail, now that the hail has ceased. Intense fear paralysed the limbs of that beautiful girl. That one shriek is all she can utter—with hands clasped, a face of marble, a heart beating so wildly in her bosom, that each moment it seems as if it would break its confines, eyes distended and fixed upon the window, she waits, froze with horror. The pattering and clattering of the nails continue. No word is spoken, and now she fancies she can trace the darker form of that figure against the window, and she can see the long arms moving to and fro, feeling for some mode of entrance. What strange light is that which now gradually creeps up into the air? red and terrible—brighter and brighter it grows. The lightning has set fire to a mill, and the reflection of the rapidly consuming building falls upon that long window. There can be no mistake. The figure is there, still feeling for an entrance, and clattering against the glass with its long nails, that appear as if the growth of many years had been untouched. She tries to scream again but a choking sensation comes over her, and she cannot. It is too dreadful—she tries to move—each limb seems weighed down by tons of lead—she can but in a hoarse faint whisper cry,—

"Help—help—help—help!"

And that one word she repeats like a person in a dream. The red glare of the fire continues. It throws up the tall gaunt figure in hideous relief against the long window. It shows, too, upon the one portrait that is in the chamber, and that portrait appears to fix its eyes upon the attempting intruder, while the flickering light from the fire makes it look fearfully life-like. A small pane of glass is broken, and the form from without introduces a long gaunt hand, which seems utterly destitute of flesh. The fastening is removed, and one-half of the window, which opens like folding doors, is swung wide open upon its hinges.

And yet now she could not scream—she could not move. "Help!—help!—help!" was all she could say. But, oh, that look of terror that sat upon her face, it was dreadful—a look to haunt the memory for a lifetime—a look to obtrude itself upon the happiest moments, and turn them to bitterness.

The figure turns half round, and the light falls upon the face. It is perfectly white—perfectly bloodless. The eyes look like polished tin; the lips are drawn back, and the principal feature next to those dreadful eyes is the teeth—the fearful looking teeth—projecting like those of some wild animal, hideously, glaringly white, and fang-like. It approaches the bed with a strange, gliding movement. It clashes together the long nails that literally appear to hang from the finger ends. No sound comes from its lips. Is she going mad—that young and beautiful girl exposed to so much terror? she has drawn up all her limbs; she cannot even now say help. The power of articulation is gone, but the power of movement has returned to her; she can draw herself slowly along to the other side of the bed from that towards which the hideous appearance is coming.

But her eyes are fascinated. The glance of a serpent could not have produced a greater effect upon her than did the fixed gaze of those awful, metallic-looking eyes that were bent on her face. Crouching down so that the gigantic height was lost, and the horrible, protruding, white face was the most prominent object, came on the figure. What was it?—what did it want there?—what made it look so hideous—so unlike an inhabitant of the earth, and yet to be on it?

Now she has got to the verge of the bed, and the figure pauses. It seemed as if when it paused she lost the power to proceed. The clothing of the bed was now clutched in her hands with unconscious power. She drew her breath short and thick. Her bosom heaves, and her limbs tremble, yet she cannot withdraw her eyes from that marble-looking face. He holds her with his glittering eye.

The storm has ceased—all is still. The winds are hushed; the church clock proclaims the hour of one: a hissing sound comes from the throat of the hideous being, and he raises his long, gaunt arms—the lips move. He advances. The girl places one small foot from the bed on to the floor. She is unconsciously dragging the clothing with her. The door of the room is in that direction—can she reach it? Has she power to walk?—can she withdraw her eyes from the face of the intruder, and so break the hideous charm? God of Heaven! is it real, or some dream so like reality as to nearly overturn the judgment for ever?

The figure has paused again, and half on the bed and half out of it that young girl lies trembling. Her long hair streams across the entire width of the bed. As she has slowly moved along she has left it streaming across the pillows. The pause lasted about a minute—oh, what an age of agony. That minute was, indeed, enough for madness to do its full work in.

With a sudden rush that could not be foreseen—with a strange howling cry that was enough to awaken terror in every breast, the figure seized the long tresses of her hair, and twining them round his bony hands he held her to the bed. Then she screamed—Heaven granted her then power to scream. Shriek followed shriek in rapid succession. The bed-clothes fell in a heap by the side of the bed—she was dragged by her long silken hair completely on to it again. Her beautifully rounded limbs quivered with the agony of her soul. The glassy, horrible eyes of the figure ran over that angelic form with a hideous satisfaction—horrible profanation. He drags her head to the bed's edge. He forces it back by the long hair still entwined in his grasp. With a plunge he seizes her neck in his fang-like teeth—a gush of blood, and a hideous sucking noise follows. *The girl has swooned, and the vampyre is at his hideous repast!*

CHAPTER II.

THE ALARM.—THE PISTOL SHOT.—THE PURSUIT AND ITS CONSEQUENCES.

*L*ights flashed about the building, and various room doors opened; voices called one to the other. There was an universal stir and commotion among the inhabitants.

"Did you hear a scream, Harry?" asked a young man, half-dressed, as he walked into the chamber of another about his own age.

"I did—where was it?"

"God knows. I dressed myself directly."

"All is still now."

"Yes; but unless I was dreaming there was a scream."

"We could not both dream there was. Where did you think it came from?"

"It burst so suddenly upon my ears that I cannot say."

There was a tap now at the door of the room where these young men were, and a female voice said,—

"For God's sake, get up!"

"We are up," said both the young men, appearing.

"Did you hear anything?"

"Yes, a scream."

"Oh, search the house—search the house; where did it come from—can you tell?"

"Indeed we cannot, mother."

Another person now joined the party. He was a man of middle age, and, as he came up to them, he said,—

"Good God! what is the matter?"

Scarcely had the words passed his lips, than such a rapid succession of shrieks came upon their ears, that they felt absolutely stunned by them. The elderly lady, whom one of the young men had called mother, fainted, and would have fallen to the floor of the corridor in which they all stood, had she not been promptly supported by the last comer, who himself staggered, as those piercing cries came upon the night air. He, however, was the first to recover, for the young men seemed paralysed.

"Henry," he cried, "for God's sake support your mother. Can you doubt that these cries come from Flora's room?"

The young man mechanically supported his mother, and then the man who had just spoken darted back to his own bed-room, from whence he returned in a moment with a pair of pistols, and shouting,—

"Follow me, who can!" he bounded across the corridor in the direction of the antique apartment, from whence the cries proceeded, but which were now hushed.

That house was built for strength, and the doors were all of oak, and of considerable thickness. Unhappily, they had fastenings within, so that when the man reached the chamber of her who so much required help, he was helpless, for the door was fast.

"Flora! Flora!" he cried; "Flora, speak!"

All was still.

"Good God!" he added; "we must force the door."

"I hear a strange noise within," said the young man, who trembled violently.

"And so do I. What does it sound like?"

"I scarcely know; but it nearest resembles some animal eating, or sucking some liquid."

"What on earth can it be? Have you no weapon that will force the door? I shall go mad if I am kept here."

"I have," said the young man. "Wait here a moment."

He ran down the staircase, and presently returned with a small, but powerful, iron crow-bar.

"This will do," he said.

"It will, it will.—Give it to me."

"Has she not spoken?"

"Not a word. My mind misgives me that something very dreadful must have happened to her."

"And that odd noise!"

"Still goes on. Somehow, it curdles the very blood in my veins to hear it."

The man took the crow-bar, and with some difficulty succeeded in introducing it between the door and the side of the wall—still it required great strength to move it, but it did move, with a harsh, crackling sound.

"Push it!" cried he who was using the bar, "push the door at the same time."

The younger man did so. For a few moments the massive door resisted. Then, suddenly, something gave way with a loud snap—it was a part of the lock,—and the door at once swung wide open.

How true it is that we measure time by the events which happen within a given space of it, rather than by its actual duration.

To those who were engaged in forcing open the door of the antique chamber, where slept the young girl whom they named Flora, each moment was swelled into an hour of agony; but, in reality, from the first moment of the alarm to that when the loud cracking noise heralded the destruction of the fastenings of the door, there had elapsed but very few minutes indeed.

"It opens—it opens," cried the young man.

"Another moment," said the stranger, as he still plied the crowbar—"another moment, and we shall have free ingress to the chamber. Be patient."

This stranger's name was Marchdale; and even as he spoke, he succeeded in throwing the massive door wide open, and clearing the passage to the chamber.

To rush in with a light in his hand was the work of a moment to the young man named Henry; but the very rapid progress he made into the apartment prevented him from observing accurately what it contained, for the wind that came in from the open window caught the flame of the candle, and although it did not actually extinguish it, it blew it so much on one side, that it was comparatively useless as a light.

"Flora—Flora!" he cried.

Then with a sudden bound something dashed from off the bed. The concussion against him was so sudden and so utterly unexpected, as well as so tremendously violent, that he was thrown down, and, in his fall, the light was fairly extinguished.

All was darkness, save a dull, reddish kind of light that now and then, from the nearly consumed mill in the immediate vicinity, came into the room. But by that light, dim, uncertain, and flickering as it was, some one was seen to make for the window.

Henry, although nearly stunned by his fall, saw a figure, gigantic in height, which nearly reached from the floor to the ceiling. The other young man, George, saw it, and Mr. Marchdale likewise saw it, as did the lady who had spoken to the two young men in the corridor when first the screams of the young girl awakened alarm in the breasts of all the inhabitants of that house.

The figure was about to pass out at the window which led to a kind of balcony, from whence there was an easy descent to a garden.

Before it passed out they each and all caught a glance of the side-face, and they saw that the lower part of it and the lips were dabbled in blood. They saw, too, one of those fearful-looking, shining, metallic eyes which presented so terrible an appearance of unearthly ferocity.

No wonder that for a moment a panic seized them all, which paralysed any exertions they might otherwise have made to detain that hideous form.

But Mr. Marchdale was a man of mature years; he had seen much of life, both in this and in foreign lands; and he, although astonished to the extent of being frightened, was much more likely to recover sooner than his younger companions, which, indeed, he did, and acted promptly enough.

"Don't rise, Henry," he cried. "Lie still."

Almost at the moment he uttered these words, he fired at the figure, which then occupied the window, as if it were a gigantic figure set in a frame.

The report was tremendous in that chamber, for the pistol was no toy weapon, but one made for actual service, and of sufficient length and bore of barrel to carry destruction along with the bullets that came from it.

"If that has missed its aim," said Mr. Marchdale, "I'll never pull a trigger again."

As he spoke he dashed forward, and made a clutch at the figure he felt convinced he had shot.

The tall form turned upon him, and when he got a full view of the face, which he did at that moment, from the opportune circumstance of the lady returning at the instant with a light she had been to her own chamber to procure, even he, Marchdale, with all his courage, and that was great, and all his nervous energy, recoiled a step or two, and uttered the exclamation of, "Great God!"

That face was one never to be forgotten. It was hideously flushed with colour—the colour of fresh blood; the eyes had a savage and remarkable lustre; whereas, before, they had looked like polished tin—they now wore a ten times brighter aspect, and flashes of light seemed to dart from them. The mouth was open, as if, from the natural formation of the countenance, the lips receded much from the large canine looking teeth.

A strange howling noise came from the throat of this monstrous figure, and it seemed upon the point of rushing upon Mr. Marchdale. Suddenly, then, as if some impulse had seized upon it, it uttered a wild and terrible shrieking kind of laugh; and then turning, dashed through the window, and in one instant disappeared from before the eyes of those who felt nearly annihilated by its fearful presence.

"God help us!" ejaculated Henry.

Mr. Marchdale drew a long breath, and then, giving a stamp on the floor, as if to recover himself from the state of agitation into which even he was thrown, he cried,—

"Be it what or who it may, I'll follow it"

"No—no—do not," cried the lady.

"I must, I will. Let who will come with me—I follow that dreadful form."

As he spoke, he took the road it took, and dashed through the window into the balcony.

"And we, too, George," exclaimed Henry; "we will follow Mr. Marchdale. This dreadful affair concerns us more nearly than it does him."

The lady who was the mother of these young men, and of the beautiful girl who had been so awfully visited, screamed aloud, and implored of them to stay. But the voice of Mr. Marchdale was heard exclaiming aloud,—

"I see it—I see it; it makes for the wall."

They hesitated no longer, but at once rushed into the balcony, and from thence dropped into the garden.

The mother approached the bed-side of the insensible, perhaps the murdered girl; she saw her, to all appearance, weltering in blood, and, overcome by her emotions, she fainted on the floor of the room.

When the two young men reached the garden, they found it much lighter than might have been fairly expected; for not only was the morning rapidly approaching, but the mill was still burning, and those mingled lights made almost every object plainly visible, except when deep shadows were thrown from some gigantic trees that had stood for centuries in that sweetly wooded spot. They heard the voice of Mr. Marchdale, as he cried,—

"There—there—towards the wall. There—there—God! how it bounds along."

The young men hastily dashed through a thicket in the direction from whence his voice sounded, and then they found him looking wild and terrified, and with something in his hand which looked like a portion of clothing.

"Which way, which way?" they both cried in a breath.

He leant heavily on the arm of George, as he pointed along a vista of trees, and said in a low voice,—

"God help us all. It is not human. Look there—look there—do you not see it?"

They looked in the direction he indicated. At the end of this vista was the wall of the garden. At that point it was full twelve feet in height, and as they looked, they saw the hideous, monstrous form they had traced from the chamber of their sister, making frantic efforts to clear the obstacle.

Then they saw it bound from the ground to the top of the wall, which it very nearly reached, and then each time it fell back again into the garden with such a dull, heavy sound, that the earth seemed to shake again with the concussion. They trembled—well indeed they might, and for some minutes they watched the figure making its fruitless efforts to leave the place.

"What—what is it?" whispered Henry, in hoarse accents. "God, what can it possibly be?"

"I know not," replied Mr. Marchdale. "I did seize it. It was cold and clammy like a corpse. It cannot be human."

"Not human?"

"Look at it now. It will surely escape now."

"No, no—we will not be terrified thus—there is Heaven above us. Come on, and, for dear Flora's sake, let us make an effort yet to seize this bold intruder."

"Take this pistol," said Marchdale. "It is the fellow of the one I fired. Try its efficacy."

"He will be gone," exclaimed Henry, as at this moment, after many repeated attempts and fearful falls, the figure reached the top of the wall, and then hung by its long arms a moment or two, previous to dragging itself completely up.

The idea of the appearance, be it what it might, entirely escaping, seemed to nerve again Mr. Marchdale, and he, as well as the two young men, ran forward towards the wall. They got so close to the figure before it sprang down on the outer side of the wall, that to miss killing it with the bullet from the pistol was a matter of utter impossibility, unless wilfully.

Henry had the weapon, and he pointed it full at the tall form with a steady aim. He pulled the trigger—the explosion followed, and that the bullet did its office there could be no manner of doubt, for the figure gave a howling shriek, and fell headlong from the wall on the outside.

"I have shot him," cried Henry, "I have shot him."

CHAPTER III.

THE DISAPPEARANCE OF THE BODY.—FLORA'S RECOVERY AND MADNESS.—THE OFFER OF ASSISTANCE FROM SIR FRANCIS VARNEY.

"He is human!" cried Henry; "I have surely killed him."

"It would seem so," said Mr. Marchdale. "Let us now hurry round to the outside of the wall, and see where he lies."

This was at once agreed to, and the whole three of them made what expedition they could towards a gate which led into a paddock, across which they hurried, and soon found themselves clear of the garden wall, so that they could make way towards where they fully expected to find the body of him who had worn so unearthly an aspect, but who it would be an excessive relief to find was human.

So hurried was the progress they made, that it was scarcely possible to exchange many words as they went; a kind of breathless anxiety was upon them, and in the speed they disregarded every obstacle, which would, at any other time, have probably prevented them from taking the direct road they sought.

It was difficult on the outside of the wall to say exactly which was the precise spot which it might be supposed the body had fallen on; but, by following the wall in its entire length, surely they would come upon it.

They did so; but, to their surprise, they got from its commencement to its further extremity without finding any dead body, or even any symptoms of one having lain there.

At some parts close to the wall there grew a kind of heath, and, consequently, the traces of blood would be lost among it, if it so happened that at the precise spot at which the strange being had seemed to topple over, such vegetation had existed. This was to be ascertained; but now, after traversing the whole length of the wall twice, they came to a halt, and looked wonderingly in each other's faces.

"There is nothing here," said Harry.

"Nothing," added his brother.

"It could not have been a delusion," at length said Mr. Marchdale, with a shudder.

"A delusion?" exclaimed the brother! "That is not possible; we all saw it."

"Then what terrible explanation can we give?"

"By heavens! I know not," exclaimed Henry. "This adventure surpasses all belief, and but for the great interest we have in it, I should regard it with a world of curiosity."

"It is too dreadful," said George; "for God's sake, Henry, let us return to ascertain if poor Flora is killed."

"My senses," said Henry, "were all so much absorbed in gazing at that horrible form, that I never once looked towards her further than to see that she was, to appearance, dead. God help her! poor—poor, beautiful Flora. This is, indeed, a sad, sad fate for you to come to. Flora—Flora—"

"Do not weep, Henry," said George. "Rather let us now hasten home, where we may find that tears are premature. She may yet be living and restored to us."

"And," said Mr. Marchdale, "she may be able to give us some account of this dreadful visitation."

"True—true," exclaimed Henry; "we will hasten home."

They now turned their steps homeward, and as they went they much blamed themselves for all leaving home together, and with terror pictured what might occur in their absence to those who were now totally unprotected.

"It was a rash impulse of us all to come in pursuit of this dreadful figure," remarked Mr. Marchdale; "but do not torment yourself, Henry. There may be no reason for your fears."

At the pace they went, they very soon reached the ancient house, and when they came in sight of it, they saw lights flashing from the windows, and the shadows of faces moving to and fro, indicating that the whole household was up, and in a state of alarm.

Henry, after some trouble, got the hall door opened by a terrified servant, who was trembling so much that she could scarcely hold the light she had with her.

"Speak at once, Martha," said Henry. "Is Flora living?"

"Yes; but—"

"Enough—enough! Thank God she lives; where is she now?"

"In her own room, Master Henry. Oh, dear—oh, dear, what will become of us all?"

Henry rushed up the staircase, followed by George and Mr. Marchdale, nor paused he once until he reached the room of his sister.

"Mother," he said, before he crossed the threshold, "are you here?"

"I am, my dear—I am. Come in, pray come in, and speak to poor Flora."

"Come in, Mr. Marchdale," said Henry—"come in; we make no stranger of you."

They all then entered the room.

Several lights had been now brought into that antique chamber, and, in addition to the mother of the beautiful girl who had been so fearfully visited, there were two female domestics, who appeared to be in the greatest possible fright, for they could render no assistance whatever to anybody.

The tears were streaming down the mother's face, and the moment she saw Mr. Marchdale, she clung to his arm, evidently unconscious of what she was about, and exclaimed,—

"Oh, what is this that has happened—what is this? Tell me, Marchdale! Robert Marchdale, you whom I have known even from my childhood, you will not deceive me. Tell me the meaning of all this?"

"I cannot," he said, in a tone of much emotion. "As God is my judge, I am as much puzzled and amazed at the scene that has taken place here to-night as you can be."

The mother wrung her hands and wept.

"It was the storm that first awakened me," added Marchdale; "and then I heard a scream."

The brothers tremblingly approached the bed. Flora was placed in a sitting, half-reclining posture, propped up by pillows. She was quite insensible, and her face was fearfully pale; while that she breathed at all could be but very faintly seen. On some of her clothing, about the neck, were spots of blood, and she looked more like one who had suffered some long and grievous illness, than a young girl in the prime of life and in the most robust health, as she had been on the day previous to the strange scene we have recorded.

"Does she sleep?" said Henry, as a tear fell from his eyes upon her pallid cheek.

"No," replied Mr. Marchdale. "This is a swoon, from which we must recover her."

Active measures were now adopted to restore the languid circulation, and, after persevering in them for some time, they had the satisfaction of seeing her open her eyes.

Her first act upon consciousness returning, however, was to utter a loud shriek, and it was not until Henry implored her to look around her, and see that she was surrounded by none but friendly faces, that she would venture again to open her eyes, and look timidly from one to the other. Then she shuddered, and burst into tears as she said,—

"Oh, Heaven, have mercy upon me—Heaven, have mercy upon me, and save me from that dreadful form."

"There is no one here, Flora," said Mr. Marchdale, "but those who love you, and who, in defence of you, if needs were would lay down their lives."

"Oh, God! Oh, God!"

"You have been terrified. But tell us distinctly what has happened? You are quite safe now."

She trembled so violently that Mr. Marchdale recommended that some stimulant should be given to her, and she was persuaded, although not without considerable difficulty, to swallow a small portion of some wine from a cup. There could be no doubt but that the stimulating effect of the wine was beneficial, for a slight accession of colour visited her cheeks, and she spoke in a firmer tone as she said,—

"Do not leave me. Oh, do not leave me, any of you. I shall die if left alone now. Oh, save me—save me. That horrible form! That fearful face!"

"Tell us how it happened, dear Flora?" said Henry.

"Or would you rather endeavour to get some sleep first?" suggested Mr. Marchdale.

"No—no—no," she said, "I do not think I shall ever sleep again."

"Say not so; you will be more composed in a few hours, and then you can tell us what has occurred."

"I will tell you now. I will tell you now."

She placed her hands over her face for a moment, as if to collect her scattered, thoughts, and then she added,—

"I was awakened by the storm, and I saw that terrible apparition at the window. I think I screamed, but I could not fly. Oh, God! I could not fly. It came—it seized me by the hair. I know no more. I know no more."

She passed her hand across her neck several times, and Mr. Marchdale said, in an anxious voice,—

"You seem, Flora, to have hurt your neck—there is a wound."

"A wound!" said the mother, and she brought a light close to the bed, where all saw on the side of Flora's neck a small punctured wound; or, rather two, for there was one a little distance from the other.

It was from these wounds the blood had come which was observable upon her night clothing.

"How came these wounds?" said Henry.

"I do not know," she replied. "I feel very faint and weak, as if I had almost bled to death."

"You cannot have done so, dear Flora, for there are not above half-a-dozen spots of blood to be seen at all."

Mr. Marchdale leaned against the carved head of the bed for support, and he uttered a deep groan. All eyes were turned upon him, and Henry said, in a voice of the most anxious inquiry,—

"You have something to say, Mr. Marchdale, which will throw some light upon this affair."

"No, no, no, nothing!" cried Mr. Marchdale, rousing himself at once from the appearance of depression that had come over him. "I have nothing to say, but that I think Flora had better get some sleep if she can."

"No sleep-no sleep for me," again screamed Flora. "Dare I be alone to sleep?"

"But you shall not be alone, dear Flora," said Henry. "I will sit by your bedside and watch you."

She took his hand in both hers, and while the tears chased each other down her cheeks, she said,—

"Promise me, Henry, by all your hopes of Heaven, you will not leave me."

"I promise!"

She gently laid herself down, with a deep sigh, and closed her eyes.

"She is weak, and will sleep long," said Mr. Marchdale.

"You sigh," said Henry. "Some fearful thoughts, I feel certain, oppress your heart."

"Hush-hush!" said Mr. Marchdale, as he pointed to Flora. "Hush! not here—not here."

"I understand," said Henry.

"Let her sleep."

There was a silence of some few minutes duration. Flora had dropped into a deep slumber. That silence was first broken by George, who said,—

"Mr. Marchdale, look at that portrait."

He pointed to the portrait in the frame to which we have alluded, and the moment Marchdale looked at it he sunk into a chair as he exclaimed,—

"Gracious Heaven, how like!"

"It is—it is," said Henry. "Those eyes—"

"And see the contour of the countenance, and the strange shape of the mouth."

"Exact—exact."

"That picture shall be moved from here. The sight of it is at once sufficient to awaken all her former terrors in poor Flora's brain if she should chance to awaken and cast her eyes suddenly upon it."

"And is it so like him who came here?" said the mother.

"It is the very man himself," said Mr. Marchdale. "I have not been in this house long enough to ask any of you whose portrait that may be?"

"It is," said Henry, "the portrait of Sir Runnagate Bannerworth, an ancestor of ours, who first, by his vices, gave the great blow to the family prosperity."

"Indeed. How long ago?"

"About ninety years."

"Ninety years. 'Tis a long while—ninety years."

"You muse upon it."

"No, no. I do wish, and yet I dread—"

"What?"

"To say something to you all. But not here—not here. We will hold a consultation on this matter to-morrow. Not now—not now."

"The daylight is coming quickly on," said Henry; "I shall keep my sacred promise of not moving from this room until Flora awakens; but there can be no occasion for the detention of any of you. One is sufficient here. Go all of you, and endeavour to procure what rest you can."

"I will fetch you my powder-flask and bullets," said Mr. Marchdale; "and you can, if you please, reload the pistols. In about two hours more it will be broad daylight."

This arrangement was adopted. Henry did reload the pistols, and placed them on a table by the side of the bed, ready for immediate action, and then, as Flora was sleeping soundly, all left the room but himself.

Mrs. Bannerworth was the last to do so. She would have remained, but for the earnest solicitation of Henry, that she would endeavour to get some sleep to make up for her broken night's repose, and she was indeed so broken down by her alarm on Flora's account, that she had not power to resist, but with tears flowing from her eyes, she sought her own chamber.

And now the calmness of the night resumed its sway in that evil-fated mansion; and although no one really slept but Flora, all were still. Busy thought kept every one else wakeful. It was a mockery to lie down at all, and Henry, full of strange and painful feelings as he was, preferred his present position to the anxiety and apprehension on Flora's account which he knew he should feel if she were not within the sphere of his own observation, and she slept as soundly as some gentle infant tired of its playmates and its sports.

CHAPTER IV.

THE MORNING.—THE CONSULTATION.—THE FEARFUL SUGGESTION.

What wonderfully different impressions and feelings, with regard to the same circumstances, come across the mind in the broad, clear, and beautiful light of day to what haunt the imagination, and often render the judgment almost incapable of action, when the heavy shadow of night is upon all things.

There must be a downright physical reason for this effect—it is so remarkable and so universal. It seems that the sun's rays so completely alter and modify the constitution of the atmosphere, that it produces, as we inhale it, a wonderfully different effect upon the nerves of the human subject.

We can account for this phenomenon in no other way. Perhaps never in his life had he, Henry Bannerworth, felt so strongly this transition of feeling as he now felt it, when the beautiful daylight gradually dawned upon him, as he kept his lonely watch by the bedside of his slumbering sister.

That watch had been a perfectly undisturbed one. Not the least sight or sound of any intrusion had reached his senses. All had been as still as the very grave.

And yet while the night lasted, and he was more indebted to the rays of the candle, which he had placed upon a shelf, for the power to distinguish objects than to the light of the morning, a thousand uneasy and strange sensations had found a home in his agitated bosom.

He looked so many times at the portrait which was in the panel that at length he felt an undefined sensation of terror creep over him whenever he took his eyes off it.

He tried to keep himself from looking at it, but he found it vain, so he adopted what, perhaps, was certainly the wisest, best plan, namely, to look at it continually.

He shifted his chair so that he could gaze upon it without any effort, and he placed the candle so that a faint light was thrown upon it, and there he sat, a prey to many conflicting and uncomfortable feelings, until the daylight began to make the candle flame look dull and sickly.

Solution for the events of the night he could find none. He racked his imagination in vain to find some means, however vague, of endeavouring to account for what occurred, and still he was at fault. All was to him wrapped in the gloom of the most profound mystery.

And how strangely, too, the eyes of that portrait appeared to look upon him—as if instinct with life, and as if the head to which they belonged was busy in endeavouring to find out the secret communings of his soul. It was wonderfully well executed that portrait; so life-like, that the very features seemed to move as you gazed upon them.

"It shall be removed," said Henry. "I would remove it now, but that it seems absolutely painted on the panel, and I should awake Flora in any attempt to do so."

He arose and ascertained that such was the case, and that it would require a workman, with proper tools adapted to the job, to remove the portrait.

"True," he said, "I might now destroy it, but it is a pity to obscure a work of such rare art as this is; I should blame myself if I were. It shall be removed to some other room of the house, however."

Then, all of a sudden, it struck Henry how foolish it would be to remove the portrait from the wall of a room which, in all likelihood, after that night, would be uninhabited; for it was not probable that Flora would choose again to inhabit a chamber in which she had gone through so much terror.

"It can be left where it is," he said, "and we can fasten up, if we please, even the very door of this room, so that no one need trouble themselves any further about it."

The morning was now coming fast, and just as Henry thought he would partially draw a blind across the window, in order to shield from the direct rays of the sun the eyes of Flora, she awoke.

"Help—help!" she cried, and Henry was by her side in a moment.

"You are safe, Flora—you are safe," he said.

"Where is it now?" she said.

"What—what, dear Flora?"

"The dreadful apparition. Oh, what have I done to be made thus perpetually miserable?"

"Think no more of it, Flora."

"I must think. My brain is on fire! A million of strange eyes seem gazing on me."

"Great Heaven! she raves," said Henry.

"Hark—hark—hark! He comes on the wings of the storm. Oh, it is most horrible—horrible!"

Henry rang the bell, but not sufficiently loudly to create any alarm. The sound reached the waking ear of the mother, who in a few moments was in the room.

"She has awakened," said Henry, "and has spoken, but she seems to me to wander in her discourse. For God's sake, soothe her, and try to bring her mind round to its usual state."

"I will, Henry—I will."

"And I think, mother, if you were to get her out of this room, and into some other chamber as far removed from this one as possible, it would tend to withdraw her mind from what has occurred."

"Yes; it shall be done. Oh, Henry, what was it—what do you think it was?"

"I am lost in a sea of wild conjecture. I can form no conclusion; where is Mr. Marchdale?"

"I believe in his chamber."

"Then I will go and consult with him."

Henry proceeded at once to the chamber, which was, as he knew, occupied by Mr. Marchdale; and as he crossed the corridor, he could not but pause a moment to glance from a window at the face of nature.

As is often the case, the terrific storm of the preceding evening had cleared the air, and rendered it deliciously invigorating and life-like. The weather had been dull, and there had been for some days a certain heaviness in the atmosphere, which was now entirely removed.

The morning sun was shining with uncommon brilliancy, birds were singing in every tree and on every bush; so pleasant, so spirit-stirring, health-giving a morning, seldom had he seen. And the effect upon his spirits was great, although not altogether what it might have been, had all gone on as it usually was in the habit of doing at that house. The ordinary little casualties of evil fortune had certainly from time to time, in the shape of illness, and one thing or another, attacked the family of the Bannerworths in common with every other family, but here suddenly had arisen a something at once terrible and inexplicable.

115

He found Mr. Marchdale up and dressed, and apparently in deep and anxious thought. The moment he saw Henry, he said,—

"Flora is awake, I presume."

"Yes, but her mind appears to be much disturbed."

"From bodily weakness, I dare say."

"But why should she be bodily weak? she was strong and well, ay, as well as she could ever be in all her life. The glow of youth and health was on her cheeks. Is it possible that, in the course of one night, she should become bodily weak to such an extent?"

"Henry," said Mr. Marchdale, sadly, "sit down. I am not, as you know, a superstitious man."

"You certainly are not."

"And yet, I never in all my life was so absolutely staggered as I have been by the occurrences of to-night."

"Say on."

"There is a frightful, a hideous solution of them; one which every consideration will tend to add strength to, one which I tremble to name now, although, yesterday, at this hour, I should have laughed it to scorn."

"Indeed!"

"Yes, it is so. Tell no one that which I am about to say to you. Let the dreadful suggestion remain with ourselves alone, Henry Bannerworth."

"I—I am lost in wonder."

"You promise me?"

"What—what?"

"That you will not repeat my opinion to any one."

"I do."

"On your honour."

"On my honour, I promise."

Mr. Marchdale rose, and proceeding to the door, he looked out to see that there were no listeners near. Having ascertained then that they were quite alone, he returned, and drawing a chair close to that on which Henry sat, he said,—

"Henry, have you never heard of a strange and dreadful superstition which, in some countries, is extremely rife, by which it is supposed that there are beings who never die."

"Never die!"

"Never. In a word, Henry, have you never heard of—of—I dread to pronounce the word."

"Speak it. God of Heaven! let me hear it."

"A *vampyre*!"

Henry sprung to his feet. His whole frame quivered with emotion; the drops of perspiration stood upon his brow, as, in, a strange, hoarse voice, he repeated the words,—

"A vampyre!"

"Even so; one who has to renew a dreadful existence by human blood—one who lives on for ever, and must keep up such a fearful existence upon human gore—one who eats not and drinks not as other men—a vampyre."

Henry dropped into his seat, and uttered a deep groan of the most exquisite anguish.

"I could echo that groan," said Marchdale, "but that I am so thoroughly bewildered I know not what to think."

"Good God—good God!"

"Do not too readily yield belief in so dreadful a supposition, I pray you."

"Yield belief!" exclaimed Henry, as he rose, and lifted up one of his hands above his head. "No; by Heaven, and the great God of all, who there rules, I will not easily believe aught so awful and so monstrous."

"I applaud your sentiment, Henry; not willingly would I deliver up myself to so frightful a belief—it is too horrible. I merely have told you of that which you saw was on my mind. You have surely before heard of such things."

"I have—I have."

"I much marvel, then, that the supposition did not occur to you, Henry."

"It did not—it did not, Marchdale. It—it was too dreadful, I suppose, to find a home in my heart. Oh! Flora, Flora, if this horrible idea should once occur to you, reason cannot, I am quite sure, uphold you against it."

"Let no one presume to insinuate it to her, Henry. I would not have it mentioned to her for worlds."

"Nor I—nor I. Good God! I shudder at the very thought—the mere possibility; but there is no possibility, there can be none. I will not believe it."

"Nor I."

"No; by Heaven's justice, goodness, grace, and mercy, I will not believe it."

"'Tis well sworn, Henry; and now, discarding the supposition that Flora has been visited by a vampyre, let us seriously set about endeavouring, if we can, to account for what has happened in this house."

"I—I cannot now."

"Nay, let us examine the matter; if we can find any natural explanation, let us cling to it, Henry, as the sheet-anchor of our very souls."

"Do you think. You are fertile in expedients. Do you think, Marchdale; and, for Heaven's sake, and for the sake of our own peace, find out some other way of accounting for what has happened, than the hideous one you have suggested."

"And yet my pistol bullets hurt him not; he has left the tokens of his presence on the neck of Flora."

"Peace, oh! peace. Do not, I pray you, accumulate reasons why I should receive such a dismal, awful superstition. Oh, do not, Marchdale, as you love me!"

"You know that my attachment to you," said Marchdale, "is sincere; and yet, Heaven help us!"

His voice was broken by grief as he spoke, and he turned aside his head to hide the bursting tears that would, despite all his efforts, show themselves in his eyes.

"Marchdale," added Henry, after a pause of some moments' duration, "I will sit up to-night with my sister."

"Do—do!"

"Think you there is a chance it may come again?"

"I cannot—I dare not speculate upon the coming of so dreadful a visitor, Henry; but I will hold watch with you most willingly."

"You will, Marchdale?"

"My hand upon it. Come what dangers may, I will share them with you, Henry."

"A thousand thanks. Say nothing, then, to George of what we have been talking about. He is of a highly susceptible nature, and the very idea of such a thing would kill him."

"I will; be mute. Remove your sister to some other chamber, let me beg of you, Henry; the one she now inhabits will always be suggestive of horrible thoughts."

"I will; and that dreadful-looking portrait, with its perfect likeness to him who came last night."

"Perfect indeed. Do you intend to remove it?"

"I do not. I thought of doing so; but it is actually on the panel in the wall, and I would not willingly destroy it, and it may as well remain where it is in that chamber, which I can readily now believe will become henceforward a deserted one in this house."

"It may well become such."

"Who comes here? I hear a step."

There was a tip at the door at this moment, and George made his appearance in answer to the summons to come in. He looked pale and ill; his face betrayed how much he had mentally suffered during that night, and almost directly he got into the bed-chamber he said,—

I shall, I am sure, be censured by you both for what I am going to say; but I cannot help saying it, nevertheless, for to keep it to myself would destroy me."

"Good God, George! what is it?" said Mr. Marchdale.

"Speak it out!" said Henry.

"I have been thinking of what has occurred here, and the result of that thought has been one of the wildest suppositions that ever I thought I should have to entertain. Have you never heard of a vampyre?"

Henry sighed deeply, and Marchdale was silent.

"I say a vampyre," added George, with much excitement in his manner. "It is a fearful, a horrible supposition; but our poor, dear Flora has been visited by a vampyre, and I shall go completely mad!"

He sat down, and covering his face with his hands, he wept bitterly and abundantly.

"George," said Henry, when he saw that the frantic grief had in some measure abated—"be calm, George, and endeavour to listen to me."

"I hear, Henry."

"Well, then, do not suppose that you are the only one in this house to whom so dreadful a superstition has occurred."

"Not the only one?"

"No; it has occurred to Mr. Marchdale also."

"Gracious Heaven!"

"He mentioned it to me; but we have both agreed to repudiate it with horror."

"To—repudiate—it?"

"Yes, George."

"And yet—and yet—"

"Hush, hush! I know what you would say. You would tell us that our repudiation of it cannot affect the fact. Of that we are aware; but yet will we disbelieve that which a belief in would be enough to drive us mad."

"What do you intend to do?"

"To keep this supposition to ourselves, in the first place; to guard it most zealously from the ears of Flora."

"Do you think she has ever heard of vampyres?"

"I never heard her mention that in all her reading she had gathered even a hint of such a fearful superstition. If she has, we must be guided by circumstances, and do the best we can."

"Pray Heaven she may not!"

"Amen to that prayer, George," said Henry. "Mr. Marchdale and I intend to keep watch over Flora to-night."

"May not I join you?"

"Your health, dear George, will not permit you to engage in such matters. Do you seek your natural repose, and leave it to us to do the best we can in this most fearful and terrible emergency."

"As you please, brother, and as you please, Mr. Marchdale. I know I am a frail reed, and my belief is that this affair will kill me quite. The truth is, I am horrified—utterly and frightfully horrified. Like my poor, dear sister, I do not believe I shall ever sleep again."

"Do not fancy that, George," said Marchdale. "You very much add to the uneasiness which must be your poor mother's portion, by allowing this circumstance to so much affect you. You well know her affection for you all, and let me therefore, as a very old friend of hers, entreat you to wear as cheerful an aspect as you can in her presence."

"For once in my life," said George, sadly, "I will; to my dear mother, endeavour to play the hypocrite."

"Do so," said Henry. "The motive will sanction any such deceit as that, George, be assured."

The day wore on, and Poor Flora remained in a very precarious situation. It was not until mid-day that Henry made up his mind he would call in a medical gentleman to her, and then he rode to the neighbouring market-town, where he knew an extremely intelligent practitioner resided. This gentleman Henry resolved upon, under a promise of secrecy, makings confidant of; but, long before he reached him, he found he might well dispense with the promise of secrecy.

He had never thought, so engaged had he been with other matters, that the servants were cognizant of the whole affair, and that from them he had no expectation of being able to keep the whole story in all its details. Of course such an opportunity for tale-bearing and gossiping was not likely to be lost; and while Henry was thinking over how he had better act in the matter, the news that Flora Bannerworth had been visited in the night by a vampyre—for the servants named the visitation such at once—was spreading all over the county.

As he rode along, Henry met a gentleman on horseback who belonged to the county, and who, reining in his steed, said to him,

"Good morning, Mr. Bannerworth."

"Good morning," responded Henry, and he would have ridden on, but the gentleman added,—

"Excuse me for interrupting you, sir; but what is the strange story that is in everybody's mouth about a vampyre?"

Henry nearly fell off his horse, he was so much astonished, and, wheeling the animal around, he said,—

"In everybody's mouth!"

"Yes; I have heard it from at least a dozen persons."

"You surprise me."

"It is untrue? Of course I am not so absurd as really to believe about the vampyre; but is there no foundation at all for it? We generally find that at the bottom of these common reports there is a something around which, as a nucleus, the whole has formed."

"My sister is unwell."

"Ah, and that's all. It really is too bad, now."

"We had a visitor last night."

"A thief, I suppose?"

"Yes, yes—I believe a thief. I do believe it was a thief, and she was terrified."

"Of course, and upon such a thing is grafted a story of a vampyre, and the marks of his teeth being in her neck, and all the circumstantial particulars."

"Yes, yes."

"Good morning, Mr. Bannerworth."

Henry bade the gentleman good morning, and much vexed at the publicity which the affair had already obtained, he set spurs to his horse, determined that he would speak to no one else upon so uncomfortable a theme. Several attempts were made to stop him, but he only waved his hand and trotted on, nor did he pause in his speed till he reached the door of Mr. Chillingworth, the medical man whom he intended to consult.

Henry knew that at such a time he would be at home, which was the case, and he was soon closeted with the man of drugs. Henry begged his patient hearing, which being accorded, he related to him at full length what had happened, not omitting, to the best of his remembrance, any one particular. When he had concluded his narration, the doctor shifted his position several times, and then said,—

"That's all?"

"Yes—and enough too."

"More than enough, I should say, my young friend. You astonish me."

"Can you form any supposition, sir, on the subject?"

"Not just now. What is your own idea?"

"I cannot be said to have one about it. It is too absurd to tell you that my brother George is impressed with a belief a vampyre has visited the house."

"I never in all my life heard a more circumstantial narrative in favour of so hideous a superstition."

"Well, but you cannot believe—"

"Believe what?"

"That the dead can come to life again, and by such a process keep up vitality."

"Do you take me for a fool?"

"Certainly not."

"Then why do you ask me such questions?"

"But the glaring facts of the case."

"I don't care if they were ten times more glaring, I won't believe it. I would rather believe you were all mad, the whole family of you—that at the full of the moon you all were a little cracked."

"And so would I."

"You go home now, and I will call and see your sister in the course of two hours. Something may turn up yet, to throw some new light upon this strange subject."

With this understanding Henry went home, and he took care to ride as fast as before, in order to avoid questions, so that he got back to his old ancestral home without going through the disagreeable ordeal of having to explain to any one what had disturbed the peace of it.

When Henry reached his home, he found that the evening was rapidly coming on, and before he could permit himself to think upon any other subject, he inquired how his terrified sister had passed the hours during his absence.

He found that but little improvement had taken place in her, and that she had occasionally slept, but to awaken and speak incoherently, as if the shock she had received had had some serious affect upon her nerves. He repaired at once to her room, and, finding that she was awake, he leaned over her, and spoke tenderly to her.

"Flora," he said, "dear Flora, you are better now?"

"Harry, is that you?"

"Yes, dear."

"Oh, tell me what has happened?"

"Have you not a recollection, Flora?"

"Yes, yes, Henry; but what was it? They none of them will tell me what it was, Henry."

"Be calm, dear. No doubt some attempt to rob the house."

"Think you so?"

"Yes; the bay window was peculiarly adapted for such a purpose; but now that you are removed here to this room, you will be able to rest in peace."

"I shall die of terror, Henry. Even now those eyes are glaring on me so hidiously. Oh, it is fearful—it is very fearful, Henry. Do you not pity me, and no one will promise to remain with me at night."

"Indeed, Flora, you are mistaken, for I intend to sit by your bedside armed, and so preserve you from all harm."

She clutched his hand eagerly, as she said,—

"You will, Henry. You will, and not think it too much trouble, dear Henry."

"It can be no trouble, Flora."

"Then I shall rest in peace, for I know that the dreadful vampyre cannot come to me when you are by–"

"The what, Flora!"

"The vampyre, Henry. It was a vampyre."

"Good God, who told you so?"

"No one. I have read of them in the book of travels in Norway, which Mr. Marchdale lent us all."

"Alas, alas!" groaned Henry. "Discard, I pray you, such a thought from your mind."

"Can we discard thoughts. What power have we but from that mind, which is ourselves?"

"True, true."

"Hark, what noise is that? I thought I heard a noise. Henry, when you go, ring for some one first. Was there not a noise?"

"The accidental shutting of some door, dear."

"Was it that?"

"It was."

"Then I am relieved. Henry, I sometimes fancy I am in the tomb, and that some one is feasting on my flesh. They do say, too, that those who in life have been bled by a vampyre, become themselves vampyres, and have the same horrible taste for blood as those before them. Is it not horrible?"

"You only vex yourself by such thoughts, Flora. Mr. Chillingworth is coming to see you."

"Can he minister to a mind diseased?"

"But yours is not, Flora. Your mind is healthful, and so, although his power extends not so far, we will thank Heaven, dear Flora, that you need it not."

She sighed deeply, as she said,—

"Heaven help me! I know not, Henry. The dreadful being held on by my hair. I must have it all taken off. I tried to get away, but it dragged me back—a brutal thing it was. Oh, then at that moment, Henry, I felt as if something strange took place in my brain, and that I was going mad! I saw those glazed eyes close to, mine—I felt a hot, pestiferous breath upon my face—help—help!"

"Hush! my Flora, hush! Look at me."

"I am calm again. It fixed its teeth in my throat. Did I faint away?"

"You did, dear; but let me pray you to refer all this to imagination; or at least the greater part of it."

"But you saw it."

"Yes—"

"All saw it."

"We all saw some man—a housebreaker—It must have been some housebreaker. What more easy, you know, dear Flora, than to assume some such disguise?"

"Was anything stolen?"

"Not that I know of; but there was an alarm, you know."

Flora shook her head, as she said, in a low voice,—

"That which came here was more than mortal. Oh, Henry, if it had but killed me, now I had been happy; but I cannot live—I hear it breathing now."

"Talk of something else, dear Flora," said the much distressed Henry; "you will make yourself much worse, if you indulge yourself in these strange fancies."

"Oh, that they were but fancies!"

"They are, believe me."

"There is a strange confusion in my brain, and sleep comes over me suddenly, when I least expect it. Henry, Henry, what I was, I shall never, never be again."

"Say not so. All this will pass away like a dream, and leave so faint a trace upon your memory, that the time will come when you will wonder it ever made so deep an impression on your mind."

"You utter these words, Henry," she said, "but they do not come from your heart. Ah, no, no, no! Who comes?"

The door was opened by Mrs. Bannerworth, who said,—

"It is only me, my dear. Henry, here is Dr. Chillingworth in the dining-room."

Henry turned to Flora, saying,—

"You will see him, dear Flora? You know Mr. Chillingworth well."

"Yes, Henry, yes, I will see him, or whoever you please."

"Shew Mr. Chillingworth up," said Henry to the servant.

In a few moments the medical man was in the room, and he at once approached the bedside to speak to Flora, upon whose pale countenance he looked with evident interest, while at the same time it seemed mingled with a painful feeling—at least so his own face indicated.

"Well, Miss Bannerworth," he said, "what is all this I hear about an ugly dream you have had?"

"A dream?" said Flora, as she fixed her beautiful eyes on his face.

"Yes, as I understand."

She shuddered, and was silent.

"Was it not a dream, then?" added Mr. Chillingworth.

She wrung her hands, and in a voice of extreme anguish and pathos, said,—

"Would it were a dream—would it were a dream! Oh, if any one could but convince me it was a dream!"

"Well, will you tell me what it was?"

"Yes, sir, it was a vampyre."

Mr. Chillingworth glanced at Henry, as he said, in reply to Flora's words,—

"I suppose that is, after all, another name, Flora, for the nightmare?"

"No—no—no!"

"Do you really, then, persist in believing anything so absurd, Miss Bannerworth?"

"What can I say to the evidence of my own senses?" she replied. "I saw it, Henry saw it, George saw, Mr. Marchdale, my mother—all saw it. We could not all be at the same time the victims of the same delusion."

"How faintly you speak."

"I am very faint and ill."

"Indeed. What wound is that on your neck?"

A wild expression came over the face of Flora; a spasmodic action of the muscles, accompanied with a shuddering, as if a sudden chill had come over the whole mass of blood took place, and she said,—

"It is the mark left by the teeth of the vampyre."

The smile was a forced one upon the face of Mr. Chillingworth.

"Draw up the blind of the window, Mr. Henry," he said, "and let me examine this puncture to which your sister attaches so extraordinary a meaning."

The blind was drawn up, and a strong light was thrown into the room. For full two minutes Mr. Chillingworth attentively examined the two small wounds in the neck of Flora. He took a powerful magnifying glass from his pocket, and looked at them through it, and after his examination was concluded, he said,—

"They are very trifling wounds, indeed."

"But how inflicted?" said Henry.

"By some insect, I should say, which probably—it being the season for many insects—has flown in at the window"

"I know the motive," said Flora "which prompts all these suggestions it is a kind one, and I ought to be the last to quarrel with it; but what I have seen, nothing can make me believe I saw not, unless I am, as once or twice I have thought myself, really mad."

"How do you now feel in general health?"

"Far from well; and a strange drowsiness at times creeps over me. Even now I feel it."

She sunk back on the pillows as she spoke and closed her eyes with a deep sigh.

Mr. Chillingworth beckoned Henry to come with him from the room, but the latter had promised that he would remain with Flora; and as Mrs. Bannerworth had left the chamber because she was unable to control her feelings, he rang the bell, and requested that his mother would come.

She did so, and then Henry went down stairs along with the medical man, whose opinion he was certainly eager to be now made acquainted with.

As soon as they were alone in an old-fashioned room which was called the oak closet, Henry turned to Mr. Chillingworth, and said,—

"What, now, is your candid opinion, sir? You have seen my sister, and those strange indubitable evidences of something wrong."

"I have; and to tell you candidly the truth, Mr. Henry, I am sorely perplexed."

"I thought you would be."

"It is not often that a medical man likes to say so much, nor is it, indeed, often prudent that he should do so, but in this case I own I am much puzzled. It is contrary to all my notions upon all such subjects."

"Those wounds, what do you think of them?"

"I know not what to think. I am completely puzzled as regards them."

"But, but do they not really bear the appearance of being bites?"

"They really do."

"And so far, then, they are actually in favour of the dreadful supposition which poor Flora entertains."

"So far they certainly are. I have no doubt in the world of their being bites; but we not must jump to a conclusion that the teeth which inflicted them were human. It is a strange case, and one which I feel assured must give you all much uneasiness, as, indeed, it gave me; but, as I said before, I will not let my judgment give in to the fearful and degrading superstition which all the circumstances connected with this strange story would seem to justify."

"It is a degrading superstition."

"To my mind your sister seems to be labouring under the effect of some narcotic."

"Indeed!"

"Yes; unless she really has lost a quantity of blood, which loss has decreased the heart's action sufficiently to produce the languor under which she now evidently labours."

"Oh, that I could believe the former supposition, but I am confident she has taken no narcotic; she could not even do so by mistake, for there is no drug of the sort in the house. Besides, she is not heedless by any means. I am quite convinced she has not done so."

"Then I am fairly puzzled, my young friend, and I can only say that I would freely have given half of what I am worth to see that figure you saw last night."

"What would you have done?"

"I would not have lost sight of it for the world's wealth."

"You would have felt your blood freeze with horror. The face was terrible."

"And yet let it lead me where it liked I would have followed it."

"I wish you had been here."

"I wish to Heaven I had. If I though there was the least chance of another visit I would come and wait with patience every night for a month."

"I cannot say," replied Henry. "I am going to sit up to-night with my sister, and I believe, our friend Mr. Marchdale will share my watch with me."

Mr. Chillingworth appeared to be for a few moments lost in thought, and then suddenly rousing himself, as if he found it either impossible to come to any rational conclusion upon the subject, or had arrived at one which he chose to keep to himself, he said,—

"Well, well, we must leave the matter at present as it stands. Time may accomplish something towards its development, but at present so palpable a mystery I never came across, or a matter in which human calculation was so completely foiled."

"Nor I—nor I."

"I will send you some medicines, such as I think will be of service to Flora, and depend upon seeing me by ten o'clock to-morrow morning."

"You have, of course, heard something," said Henry to the doctor, as he was pulling on his gloves, "about vampyres."

"I certainly have, and I understand that in some countries, particularly Norway and Sweden, the superstition is a very common one."

"And in the Levant."

"Yes. The ghouls of the Mahometans are of the same description of beings. All that I have heard of the European vampyre has made it a being which can be killed, but is restored to life again by the rays of a full moon falling on the body."

"Yes, yes, I have heard as much."

"And that the hideous repast of blood has to be taken very frequently, and that if the vampyre gets it not he wastes away, presenting the appearance of one in the last stage of a consumption, and visibly, so to speak, dying."

"That is what I have understood."

"To-night, do you know, Mr. Bannerworth, is the full of the moon."

Henry started.

"If now you had succeeded in killing—. Pshaw, what am I saying. I believe I am getting foolish, and that the horrible superstition is beginning to fasten itself upon me as well as upon all of you. How strangely the fancy will wage war with the judgment in such a way as this."

"The full of the moon," repeated Henry, as he glanced towards the window, "and the night is near at hand."

"Banish these thoughts from your mind," said the doctor, "or else, my young friend, you will make yourself decidedly ill. Good evening to you, for it is evening. I shall see you to-morrow morning."

Mr. Chillingworth appeared now to be anxious to go, and Henry no longer opposed his departure; but when he was gone a sense of great loneliness came over him.

"To-night," he repeated, "is the full of the moon. How strange that this dreadful adventure should have taken place just the night before. 'Tis very strange. Let me see—let me see."

He took from the shelves of a book case the work which Flora had mentioned, entitled, "Travels in Norway," in which work he found some account of the popular belief in vampyres.

He opened the work at random, and then some of the leaves turned over of themselves to a particular place, as the leaves of a book will frequently do when it has been kept open a length of time at that part, and the binding stretched there more than anywhere else. There was a note at the bottom of one of the pages at this part of the book, and Henry read as follows:—

"With regard to these vampyres, it is believed by those who are inclined to give credence to so dreadful a superstition, that they always endeavour to make their feast of blood, for the revival of their bodily powers, on some evening immediately preceding a full moon, because if any accident befal them, such as being shot, or otherwise killed or wounded, they can recover by lying down somewhere where the full moon's rays will fall upon them."

Henry let the book drop from his hands with a groan and a shudder.

CHAPTER XX.

THE DREADFUL MISTAKE.—THE TERRIFIC INTERVIEW IN THE CHAMBER.—THE ATTACK OF THE VAMPYRE.

The footstep which Flora, upon the close of the tale she had been reading, heard approaching her apartment, came rapidly along the corridor.

"It is Henry, returned to conduct me to an interview with Charles's uncle," she said. "I wonder, now, what manner of man he is. He should in some respects resemble Charles; and if he do so, I shall bestow upon him some affection for that alone."

Tap—tap came upon the chamber door. Flora was not at all alarmed now, as she had been when Henry brought her the manuscript. From some strange action of the nervous system, she felt quite confident, and resolved to brave everything. But then she felt quite sure that it was Henry, and before the knocking had taken her by surprise.

"Come in," she said, in a cheerful voice. "Come in."

The door opened with wonderful swiftness—a figure stepped into the room, and then closed it as rapidly, and stood against it. Flora tried to scream, but her tongue refused its office; a confused whirl of sensations passed through her brain—she trembled, and an icy coldness came over her. It was Sir Francis Varney, the vampyre!

He had drawn up his tall, gaunt frame to its full height, and crossed his arms upon his breast; there was a hideous smile upon his sallow countenance, and his voice was deep and sepulchral, as he said,—

"Flora Bannerworth, hear that which I have to say, and hear it calmly. You need have nothing to fear. Make an alarm—scream, or shout for help, and, by the hell beneath us, you are lost!"

There was a death-like, cold, passionless manner about the utterance of these words, as if they were spoken mechanically, and came from no human lips.

Flora heard them, and yet scarcely comprehended them; she stepped slowly back till she reached a chair, and there she held for support. The only part of the address of Varney that thoroughly reached her ears, was that if she gave any alarm some dreadful consequences were to ensue. But it was not on account of these words that she really gave no alarm; it was because she was utterly unable to do so.

"Answer me," said Varney. "Promise that you will hear that which I have to say. In so promising you commit yourself to no evil, and you shall hear that which shall give you much peace."

It was in vain she tried to speak; her lips moved, but she uttered no sound.

"You are terrified," said Varney, "and yet I know not why. I do not come to do you harm, although harm have you done me. Girl, I come to rescue you from a thraldom of the soul under which you now labour."

There was a pause of some moments' duration, and then, faintly, Flora managed to say,—

"Help! help! Oh, help me, Heaven!"

Varney made a gesture of impatience, as he said,—

"Heaven works no special matters now. Flora Bannerworth, if you have as much intellect as your nobility and beauty would warrant the world in supposing, you will listen to me."

"I—I hear," said Flora, as she still, dragging the chair with her, increased the distance between them.

"'Tis well. You are now more composed."

She fixed her eyes upon the face of Varney with a shudder. There could be no mistake. It was the same which, with the strange, glassy looking eyes, had glared upon her on that awful night of the storm when she was visited by the vampyre. And Varney returned that gaze unflinchingly There was a hideous and strange contortion of his face now as he said,—

"You are beautiful. The most cunning statuary might well model some rare work of art from those rounded limbs, that were surely made to bewitch the gazer. Your skin rivals the driven snow—what a face of loveliness, and what a form of enchantment."

She did not speak, but a thought came across her mind, which at once crimsoned her cheek—she knew she had fainted on the first visit of the vampyre, and now he, with a hideous reverence, praised beauties which he might have cast his demoniac eyes over at such a time.

"You understand me," he said. "Well, let that pass. I am something allied to humanity yet."

"Speak your errand," gasped Flora, "or come what may, I scream for help to those who will not be slow to render it."

"I know it."

"You know I will scream?"

"No; you will hear me. I know they would not be slow to tender help to you, but you will not call for it; I will present to you no necessity."

"Say on—say on."

"You perceive I do not attempt to approach you; my errand is one of peace."

"Peace from you! Horrible being, if you be really what even now my appalled imagination shrinks from naming you, would not even to you absolute annihilation be a blessing?"

"Peace, peace. I came not here to talk on such a subject. I must be brief, Flora Bannerworth, for time presses. I do not hate you. Wherefore should I? You are young, and you are beautiful, and you bear a name which should command, and does command, some portion of my best regard."

"There is a portrait," said Flora, "in this house."

"No more—no more. I know what you would say."

"It is yours."

"The house, and all within, I covet," he said, uneasily. "Let that suffice. I have quarrelled with your brother—I have quarrelled with one who just now fancies he loves you."

"Charles Holland loves me truly."

"It does not suit me now to dispute that point with you. I have the means of knowing more of the secrets of the human heart than common men. I tell you, Flora Bannerworth, that he who talks to you of love, loves you not but with the fleeting fancy of a boy; and there is one who hides deep in his heart a world of passion, one who has never spoken to you of love, and yet who loves you with a love as far surpassing the evanescent fancy of this boy Holland, as does the mighty ocean the most placid lake that ever basked in idleness beneath a summer's sun."

There was a wonderful fascination in the manner now of Varney. His voice sounded like music itself. His words flowed from his tongue, each gently and properly accented, with all the charm of eloquence.

Despite her trembling horror of that man—despite her fearful opinion, which might be said to amount to a conviction of what he really was, Flora felt an irresistible wish to hear him speak on. Ay, despite too, the ungrateful theme to her heart which he had now chosen as the subject of his discourse, she felt her fear of him gradually dissipating, and now when he made a pause, she said,—

"You are much mistaken. On the constancy and truth of Charles Holland, I would stake my life."

"No doubt, no doubt."

"Have you spoken now that which you had to say?"

"No, no. I tell you I covet this place, I would purchase it, but having with your bad-tempered brothers quarrelled, they will hold no further converse with me."

"And well they may refuse."

"Be, that as it may, sweet lady, I come to you to be my mediator. In the shadow of the future I can see many events which are to come."

"Indeed."

"It is so. Borrowing some wisdom from the past, and some from resources I would not detail to you, I know that if I have inflicted much misery upon you, I can spare you much more. Your brother or your lover will challenge me."

"Oh, no, no."

"I say such will happen, and I can kill either. My skill as well as my strength is superhuman."

"Mercy! mercy!" gasped Flora. "I will spare either or both on a condition."

"What fearful condition?"

"It is not a fearful one. Your terrors go far before the fact. All I wish, maiden, of you is to induce these imperious brothers of yours to sell or let the Hall to me."

"Is that all?"

"It is. I ask no more, and, in return, I promise you not only that I will not fight with them, but that you shall never see me again. Rest securely, maiden, you will be undisturbed by me."

"Oh, God! that were indeed an assurance worth the striving for," said Flora.

"It is one you may have. But—"

"Oh, I knew—my heart told me there was yet some fearful condition to come."

"You are wrong again. I only ask of you that you keep this meeting a secret."

"No, no, no—I cannot."

"Nay, what so easy?"

"I will not; I have no secrets from those I love."

"Indeed, you will find soon the expediency of a few at least; but if you will not, I cannot urge it longer. Do as your wayward woman's nature prompts you."

There was a slight, but a very slight, tone of aggravation in these words, and the manner in which they were uttered.

As he spoke, he moved from the door towards the window, which opened into a kitchen garden. Flora shrunk as far from him as possible, and for a few moments they regarded each other in silence.

"Young blood," said Varney, "mantles in your veins."

She shuddered with terror.

"Be mindful of the condition I have proposed to you. I covet Banner-worth Hall."

"I—I hear."

"And I must have it. I will have it, although my path to it be through a sea of blood. You understand me, maiden? Repeat what has passed between us or not, as you please. I say, beware of me, if you keep not the condition I have proposed."

"Heaven knows that this place is becoming daily more hateful to us all," said Flora.

"Indeed!"

"You well might know so much. It is no sacrifice to urge it now. I will urge my brother."

"Thanks—a thousand thanks. You may not live to regret even having made a friend of Varney—"

"The vampyre!" said Flora.

He advanced towards her a step, and she involuntarily uttered a scream of terror.

In an instant his hand clasped her waist with the power of an iron vice; she felt hit hot breath flushing on her cheek. Her senses reeled, and she found herself sinking. She gathered all her breath and all her energies into one piercing shriek, and then she fell to the floor. There was a sudden crash of broken glass, and then all was still.

CHAPTER XXXIII.

THE STRANGE INTERVIEW.—THE CHASE THROUGH THE HALL.

It was with the most melancholy aspect that anything human could well bear, that Sir Francis Varney took his lonely walk, although perhaps in saying so much, probably we are instituting a comparison which circumstances scarcely empower us to do; for who shall say that that singular man, around whom a very atmosphere of mystery seemed to be perpetually increasing, was human?

Averse as we are to believe in the supernatural, or even to invest humanity with any preternatural powers, the more than singular facts and circumstances surrounding the existence and the acts of that man bring to the mind a kind of shuddering conviction, that if he be indeed really mortal he still must possess some powers beyond ordinary mortality, and be walking the earth for some unhallowed purposes, such as ordinary men with the ordinary attributes of human nature can scarcely guess at.

Silently and alone he took his way through that beautiful tract of country, comprehending such picturesque charms of hill and dale which lay between his home and Bannerworth Hall. He was evidently intent upon reaching the latter place by the shortest possible route, and in the darkness of that night, for the moon had not yet risen, he showed no slight acquaintance with the intricacies of that locality, that he was at all enabled to pursue so undeviatingly a tract as that which he took.

He muttered frequently to himself low, indistinct words as he went, and chiefly did they seem to have reference to that strange interview he had so recently had with one who, from some combination of circumstances scarcely to be guessed at, evidently exercised a powerful control over him, and was enabled to make a demand upon his pecuniary resources of rather startling magnitude.

And yet, from a stray word or two, which were pronounced more distinctly, he did not seem to be thinking in anger over that interview; but it would appear that it rather had recalled to his remembrance circumstances of a painful and a degrading nature, which time had not been able entirely to obliterate from his recollection.

"Yes, yes," he said, as he paused upon the margin of the wood, to the confines of which he, or what seemed to be he, had once been chased by Marchdale and the Bannerworths—"yes, the very sight of that man recalls all the frightful pageantry of a horrible tragedy, which I can never—never forget. Never can it escape my memory, as a horrible, a terrific fact; but it is the sight of this man alone that can recall all its fearful minutiae to my mind, and paint to my imagination, in the most vivid colours, every, the least particular connected with that time of agony. These periodical visits much affect me. For months I dread them, and for months I am but slowly recovering from the shocks they give me. 'But once more,' he says—'but once more,' and then we shall not meet again. Well, well; perchance before that time arrives, I may be able to possess myself of those resources which will enable me to forestall his visit, and so at least free myself from the pang of expecting him."

He paused at the margin of the wood, and glanced in the direction of Bannerworth Hall. By the dim light which yet showed from out the light sky, he could discern the ancient gable ends, and turret-like windows; he could see the well laid out gardens, and the grove of stately firs that shaded it from the northern blasts, and, as he gazed, a strong emotion seemed to come over him, such as no one could have supposed would for one moment have possessed the frame of one so apparently unconnected with all human sympathies.

"I know this spot well," he said, "and my appearance here on that eventful occasion, when the dread of my approach induced a crime only second to murder itself, was on such a night as this, when all was so still and calm around, and when he who, at the merest shadow of my presence, rather chose to rush on death than be assured it was myself. Curses on the circumstances that so foiled me! I should have been most wealthy. I should have possessed the means of commanding the adulation of those who now hold me but cheaply; but still the time may come. I have a hope yet, and that greatness which I have ever panted for, that magician-like power over my kind, which the possession of ample means alone can give, may yet be mine."

Wrapping his cloak more closely around him, he strode forward with that long, noiseless step which was peculiar to him. Mechanically he appeared to avoid those obstacles of hedge and ditch which impeded his pathway. Surely be had come that road often, or he would not so easily have pursued his way. And now he stood by the edge of a plantation which in some measure protected from trespassers the more private gardens of the Hall, and there he paused, as if a feeling of irresolution had come over him, or it might be, as indeed it seemed from his subsequent conduct, that he had come without any fixed intention, or if with a fixed intention, without any regular plan of carrying it into effect.

Did he again dream of intruding into any of the chambers of that mansion, with the ghastly aspect of that terrible creation with which, in the minds of its inhabitants, he seemed to be but too closely identified? He was pale, attenuated, and trembled. Could it be that so soon it had become necessary to renew the life-blood in his veins in the awful manner which it is supposed the vampyre brood are compelled to protract their miserable existence?

It might be so, and that he was even now reflecting upon how once more he could kindle the fire of madness in the brain of that beautiful girl, who he had already made so irretrievably wretched.

He leant against an aged tree, and his strange, lustrous-looking eyes seemed to collect every wandering scintillation of light that was around, and to shine with preternatural intensity.

"I must, I will," he said, "be master of Bannerworth Hall. It must come to that. I have set an existence upon its possession, and I will have it; and then, if with my own hands I displace it brick by brick and stone by stone, I will discover that hidden secret which no one but myself now dreams of. It shall be done by force or fraud, by love or by despair, I care not which; the end shall sanctify all means. Ay, even if I wade through blood to my desire, I say it shall be done."

There was a holy and a still calmness about the night much at variance with the storm of angry passion that appeared to be momentarily gathering power in the breast of that fearful man. Not the least sound came from Bannerworth Hall, and it was only occasionally that from afar off on the night air there came the bark of some watchdog, or the low of distant cattle. All else was mute save when the deep sepulchral tones of that man, if man he was, gave an impulse to the soft air around him.

With a strolling movement as if he were careless if he proceeded in that direction or not, he still went onward toward the house, and now he stood by that little summer-house once so sweet and so dear a retreat, in which the heart-stricken Flora had held her interview with him whom she loved with a devotion unknown to meaner minds.

This spot scarcely commanded any view of the house, for so enclosed was it among evergreens and blooming flowers, that it seemed like a very wilderness of nature, upon which, with liberal hand, she had showered down in wild luxuriance her wildest floral beauties.

In and around that spot the night air was loaded with sweets. The mingled perfume of many flowers made that place seem a very paradise. But oh, how sadly at variance with that beauty and contentedness of nature was he who stood amidst such beauty! All incapable as he was of appreciating its tenderness, or of gathering the faintest moral from its glory.

"Why am I here?" he said. "Here, without fixed design or stability of purpose, like some miser who has hidden his own hoards so deeply within the bowels of the earth he cannot hope that he shall ever again be able to bring them to the light of day. I hover around this spot which I feel—which I know—contains my treasure, though I cannot lay my hands upon it, or exult in its glistening beauty."

Even as he spoke he cowered down like some guilty thing, for he heard a faint footstep upon the garden path. So light, so fragile was the step, that, in the light of day, the very hum of summer insects would have drowned the noise; but he heard it, that man of crime—of unholy and awful impulses. He heard it, and he shrunk down among the shrubs and flowers till he was hidden completely from observation amid a world of fragrant essences.

Was it some one stealthily in that place even as he was, unwelcome or unknown? or was it one who had observed him intrude upon the privacy of those now unhappy precincts, and who was coming to deal upon him that death which, vampyre though he might be, he was yet susceptible of from mortal hands?

The footstep advanced, and lower down he shrunk until his coward-heart beat against the very earth itself. He knew that he was unarmed, a circumstance rare with him, and only to be accounted for by the disturbance of his mind consequent upon the visit of that strange man to his house, whose presence had awakened so many conflicting emotions.

Nearer and nearer still came that light footstep, and his deep-seated fears would not let him perceive that it was not the step of caution or of treachery, but owed its lightness to the natural grace and freedom of movement of its owner.

The moon must have arisen, although obscured by clouds, through which it cast but a dim radiance, for the night had certainly grown lighter; so that although there were no strong shadows cast, a more diffused brightness was about all things, and their outlines looked not so dancing, and confused the one with the other.

He strained his eyes in the direction whence the sounds proceeded, and then his fears for his personal safety vanished, for he saw it was a female form that was slowly advancing towards him.

His first impulse was to rise, for with the transient glimpse he got of it, he knew that it must be Flora Bannerworth; but a second thought, probably one of intense curiosity to know what could possibly have brought her to such a spot at such a time, restrained him, and he was quiet. But if the surprise of Sir Francis Varney was great to see Flora Bannerworth at such a time in such a place, we have no doubt, that with the knowledge which our readers have of her, their astonishment would more than fully equal his; and when we come to consider, that since that eventful period when the sanctity of her chamber had been so violated by that fearful midnight visitant, it must appear somewhat strange that she could gather courage sufficient to wander forth alone at such an hour.

Had she no dread of meeting that unearthly being? Did the possibility that she might fall into his ruthless grasp, not come across her mind with a shuddering consciousness of its probability? Had she no reflection that each step she took, was taking her further and further from those who would aid her in all extremities? It would seem not, for she walked onward, unheeding, and apparently unthinking of the presence, possible or probable, of that bane of her existence.

But let us look at her again. How strange and spectral-like she moves along; there seems no speculation in her countenance, but with a strange and gliding step, she walks like some dim shadow of the past in that ancient garden. She is very pale, and on her brow there is the stamp of suffering; her dress is a morning robe, she holds it lightly round her, and thus she moves forward towards that summer-house which probably to her was sanctified by having witnessed those vows of pure affection, which came from the lips of Charles Holland, about whose fate there now hung so great a mystery.

Has madness really seized upon the brain of that beautiful girl? Has the strong intellect really sunk beneath the oppressions to which it has been subjected? Does she now walk forth with a disordered intellect, the queen of some fantastic realm, viewing the material world with eyes that are not of earth; shunning perhaps that which she should have sought, and, perchance, in her frenzy, seeking that which in a happier frame of mind she would have shunned.

Such might have been the impression of any one who had looked upon her for a moment, and who knew the disastrous scenes through which she had so recently passed; but we can spare our readers the pangs of such a supposition. We have bespoken their love for Flora Bannerworth, and we are certain that she has it; therefore would we spare them, even for a few brief moments, from imagining that cruel destiny had done its worst, and that the fine and beautiful spirit we have so much commended had lost its power of rational reflection. No; thank Heaven, such is not the case. Flora

Bannerworth is not mad, but under the strong influence of some eccentric dream, which has pictured to her mind images which have no home but in the airy realms of imagination. She has wandered forth from her chamber to that sacred spot where she had met him she loved, and heard the noblest declaration of truth and constancy that ever flowed from human lips.

Yes, she is sleeping; but, with a precision such as the somnambulist so strangely exerts, she trod the well-known paths slowly, but surely, toward that summer's bower, where her dreams had not told her lay crouching that most hideous spectre of her imagination, Sir Francis Varney. He who stood between her and her heart's best joy; he who had destroyed all hope of happiness, and who had converted her dearest affections into only so many causes of greater disquietude than the blessings they should have been to her.

Oh! could she have imagined but for one moment that he was there, with what an eagerness of terror would she have flown back again to the shelter of those walls, where at least was to be found some protection from the fearful vampyre's embrace, and where she would be within hail of friendly hearts, who would stand boldly between her and every thought of harm.

But she knew it not, and onwards she went until the very hem of her garment touched the face of Sir Francis Varney.

And he was terrified—he dared not move—he dared not speak! The idea that she had died, and that this was her spirit, come to wreak some terrible vengeance upon him, for a time possessed him, and so paralysed with fear was he, that he could neither move nor speak.

It had been well if, during that trance of indecision in which his coward heart placed him, Flora had left the place, and again sought her home; but unhappily such an impulse came not over her; she sat upon that rustic seat, where she had reposed when Charles had clasped her to his heart, and through her very dream the remembrance of that pure affection came across her, and in the tenderest and most melodious accents, she said,—

"Charles! Charles! and do you love me still? No—no; you have not forsaken me. Save me, save me from the vampyre!"

She shuddered, and Sir Francis Varney heard her weeping.

"Fool that I am," he muttered, "to be so terrified. She sleeps. This is one of the phases which a disordered imagination oft puts on. She sleeps, and perchance this may be an opportunity of further increasing the dread of my visitation, which shall make Bannerworth Hall far too terrible a dwelling-place for her; and well I know, if she goes, they will all go. It will become a deserted house, and that is what I want. A house, too, with such an evil reputation, that none but myself, who have created that reputation, will venture within its walls:—a house, which superstition will point out as the abode of evil spirits;—a house, as it were, by general opinion, ceded to the vampyre. Yes, it shall be my own; fit dwelling-place for a while for me. I have sworn it shall be mine, and I will keep my oath, little such as I have to do with vows."

He rose, and moved slowly to the narrow entrance of the summer-house; a movement he could make, without at all disturbing Flora, for the rustic seat, on which she sat, was at its further extremity. And there he stood, the upper part of his gaunt and hideous form clearly defined upon the now much lighter sky, so that if Flora Bannerworth had not been in that trance of sleep in which she really was, one glance upward would let her see the hideous companion she had, in that once much-loved spot—a spot hitherto sacred to the best and noblest feelings, but now doomed for ever to be associated with that terrific spectre of despair.

But she was in no state to see so terrible a sight. Her hands were over her face, and she was weeping still.

"Surely, he loves me," she whispered; "he has said he loved me, and he does not speak in vain. He loves me still, and I shall again look upon his face, a Heaven to me! Charles! Charles! you will come again? Surely, they sin against the divinity of love, who would tell me that you love me not!"

"Ha!" muttered Varney, "this passion is her first, and takes a strong hold on her young heart—she loves him—but what are human affections to me? I have no right to count myself in the great muster-roll of humanity. I look not like an inhabitant of the earth, and yet am on it. I love no one, expect no love from any one, but I will make humanity a slave to me; and the lip-service of them who hate me in their hearts, shall be as pleasant jingling music to my ear, as if it were quite sincere! I will speak to this girl; she is not mad—perchance she may be."

There was a diabolical look of concentrated hatred upon Varney's face, as he now advanced two paces towards the beautiful Flora.

CHAPTER XL.

THE POPULAR RIOT.—SIR FRANCIS VARNEY'S DANGER.—THE SUGGESTION AND ITS RESULTS.

Such, then, were the circumstances which at once altered the whole aspect of the affairs, and, from private and domestic causes of very deep annoyance, led to public results of a character which seemed likely to involve the whole country-side in the greatest possible confusion.

But while we blame Mr. Chillingworth for being so indiscreet as to communicate the secret of such a person as Varney the vampyre to his wife, we trust in a short time to be enabled to show that he made as much reparation as it was possible to make for the mischief he had unintentionally committed. And now as he struggled onward—apparently onward—first and foremost among the rioters, he was really doing all in his power to quell that tumult which superstition and dread had raised.

Human nature truly delights in the marvellous, and in proportion as a knowledge of the natural phenomena of nature is restricted, and unbridled imagination allowed to give the rein to fathomless conjecture, we shall find an eagerness likewise to believe the marvellous to be the truth.

That dim and uncertain condition concerning vampyres, originating probably as it had done in Germany, had spread itself slowly, but insidiously, throughout the whole of the civilized world.

In no country and in no clime is there not something which bears a kind of family relationship to the veritable vampyre of which Sir Francis Varney appeared to be so choice a specimen.

The *ghoul* of eastern nations is but the same being, altered to suit habits and localities; and the *sema* of the Scandinavians is but the vampyre of a more primitive race, and a personification of that morbid imagination which has once fancied the probability of the dead walking again among the living, with all the frightful insignia of corruption and the grave about them.

Although not popular in England, still there had been tales told of such midnight visitants, so that Mrs. Chillingworth, when she had imparted the information which she had obtained, had already some rough material to work upon in the minds of her auditors, and therefore there was no great difficulty in very soon establishing the fact.

Under such circumstances, ignorant people always do what they have heard has been done by some one else before them and in an incredibly short space of time the propriety of catching Sir Francis Varney, depriving him of his vampyre-like existence, and driving a stake through his body, became not at all a questionable proposition.

Alas, poor Mr. Chillingworth! as well might he have attempted King Canute's task of stemming the waves of the ocean as that of attempting to stop the crowd from proceeding to Sir Francis Varney's house.

His very presence was a sort of confirmation of the whole affair. In vain he gesticulated, in vain he begged and prayed that they would go back, and in vain he declared that full and ample justice should be done upon the vampyre, provided popular clamour spared him, and he was left to more deliberate judgment.

Those who were foremost in the throng paid no attention to these remonstrances while those who were more distant heard them not, and, for all they knew, he might be urging the crowd on to violence, instead of deprecating it.

Thus, then, this disorderly rabble soon reached the house of Sir Francis Varney and loudly demanded of his terrified servant where he was to be found.

The knocking at the Hall door was prodigious, and, with a laudable desire, doubtless, of saving time, the moment one was done amusing himself with the ponderous knocker, another seized it; so that until the door was flung open by some of the bewildered and terrified men, there was no cessation whatever of the furious demands for admittance.

"Varney the vampyre—Varney the vampyre!" cried a hundred voices. "Death to the vampyre! Where is he? Bring him out. Varney the vampyre!"

The servants were too terrified to speak for some moments, as they saw such a tumultuous assemblage seeking their master, while so singular a name was applied to him. At length, one more bold than the rest contrived to stammer out,—

"My good people, Sir Francis Varney is not at home. He took an early breakfast, and has been out nearly an hour."

The mob paused a moment in indecision, and then one of the foremost cried,—

"Who'd suppose they'd own he was at home? He's hiding somewhere of course; let's pull him out."

"Ah, pull him out—pull him out!" cried many voices. A rush was made into the hall and in a very few minutes its chambers were ransacked, and all its hidden places carefully searched, with the hope of discovering the hidden form of Sir Francis Varney.

The servants felt that, with their inefficient strength, to oppose the proceedings of an assemblage which seemed to be unchecked by all sort of law or reason, would be madness; they therefore only looked on, with wonder and dismay, satisfied certainly in their own minds that Sir Francis would not be found, and indulging in much conjecture as to what would be the result of such violent and unexpected proceedings.

Mr. Chillingworth hoped that time was being gained, and that some sort of indication of what was going on would reach the unhappy object of popular detestation sufficiently early to enable him to provide for his own safety.

He knew he was breaking his own engagement to be present at the duel between Henry Bannerworth and Sir Francis Varney, and, as that thought recurred to him, he dreaded that his professional services might be required on one side or the other; for he knew, or fancied he knew, that mutual hatred dictated the contest; and he thought that if ever a duel had taken place which was likely to be attended with some disastrous result, that was surely the one.

But how could he leave, watched and surrounded as he was by an infuriated multitude—how could he hope but that his footsteps would be dogged, or that the slightest attempt of his to convey a warning to Sir Francis Varney, would not be the means of bringing down upon his head the very danger he sought to shield him from.

In this state of uncertainty, then, did our medical man remain, a prey to the bitterest reflections, and full of the direst apprehensions, without having the slightest power of himself to alter so disastrous a train of circumstances.

Dissatisfied with their non-success, the crowd twice searched the house of Sir Francis Varney, from the attics to the basement; and then, and not till then, did they begin reluctantly to believe that the servants must have spoken the truth.

"He's in the town somewhere," cried one. "Let's go back to the town."

It is strange how suddenly any mob will obey any impulse, and this perfectly groundless supposition was sufficient to turn their steps back again in the direction whence they came, and they had actually, in a straggling sort of column, reached halfway towards the town, when they encountered a boy, whose professional pursuit consisted in tending sheep very early of a morning, and who at once informed them that he had seen Sir Francis Varney in the wood, half way between Bannerworth Hall and his own home.

This event at once turned the whole tide again, and with renewed clamours, carrying Mr. Chillingworth along with them, they now rapidly neared the real spot, where, probably, had they turned a little earlier, they would have viewed the object of their suspicion and hatred.

But, as we have already recorded, the advancing throng was seen by the parties on the ground, where the duel could scarcely have been said to have been fought; and then had Sir Francis Varney dashed into the wood, which was so opportunely at hand to afford him a shelter from his enemies, and from the intricacies of which—well acquainted with them as he doubtless was,—he had every chance of eluding their pursuit.

The whole affair was a great surprise to Henry and his friends, when they saw such a string of people advancing, with such shouts and imprecations; they could not, for the life of them, imagine what could have excited such a turn out among the ordinarily industrious and quiet inhabitants of a town, remarkable rather for the quietude and steadiness of its population, than for any violent outbreaks of popular feeling.

"What can Mr. Chillingworth be about," said Henry, "to bring such a mob here? has he taken leave of his senses?"

"Nay," said Marchdale; "look again; he seems to be trying to keep them back, although ineffectually, for they will not be stayed."

"D——e," said the admiral, "here's a gang of pirates; we shall be boarded and carried before we know where we are, Jack."

"Ay ay, sir," said Jack.

"And is that all you've got to say, you lubber, when you see your admiral in danger? You'd better go and make terms with the enemy at once."

"Really, this is serious," said Henry; "they shout for Varney. Can Mr. Chillingworth have been so mad as to adopt this means of stopping the duel?"

"Impossible," said Marchdale; "if that had been his intention, he could have done so quietly, through the medium of the civil authorities."

"Hang me!" exclaimed the admiral, "if there are any civil authorities; they talk of smashing somebody. What do they say, Jack? I don't hear quite so well as I used."

"You always was a little deaf," said Jack.

"What?"

"A little deaf, I say."

"Why, you lubberly lying swab, how dare you say so?"

"Because you was."

"You slave-going scoundrel!"

"For Heaven's sake, do not quarrel at such a time as this!" said Henry; "we shall be surrounded in a moment. Come, Mr. Marchdale, let you and I visit these people, and ascertain what it is that has so much excited their indignation."

"Agreed," said Marchdale; and they both stepped forward at a rapid pace, to meet the advancing throng.

The crowd which had now approached to within a short distance of the expectant little party, was of a most motley description, and its appearance, under many circumstances, would cause considerable risibility. Men and women were mixed indiscriminately together, and in the shouting, the latter, if such a thing were possible, exceeded the former, both in discordance and energy.

Every individual composing that mob carried some weapon calculated for defence, such as flails, scythes, sickles, bludgeons, &c., and this mode of arming caused them to wear a most formidable appearance; while the passion that superstition had called up was strongly depicted in their inflamed features. Their fury, too, had been excited by their disappointment, and it was with concentrated rage that they now pressed onward.

The calm and steady advance of Henry and Mr. Marchdale to meet the advancing throng, seemed to have the effect of retarding their progress a little, and they came to a parley at a hedge, which separated them from the meadow in which the duel had been fought.

"You seem to be advancing towards us," said Henry. "Do you seek me or any of my friends; and if so, upon what errand? Mr. Chillingworth, for Heaven's sake, explain what is the cause of all this assault. You seem to be at the head of it."

"Seem to be," said Mr. Chillingworth, "without being so. You are not sought, nor any of your friends?"

"Who, then?"

"Sir Francis Varney," was the immediate reply.

"Indeed! and what has he done to excite popular indignation? of private wrong I can accuse him; but I desire no crowd to take up my cause, or to avenge my quarrels."

"Mr. Bannerworth, it has become known, through my indiscretion, that Sir Frances Varney is suspected of being a vampyre."

"Is this so?"

"Hurrah!" shouted the mob. "Down with the vampyre! hurrah! where is he? Down with him!"

"Drive a stake through him," said a woman; "it's the only way, and the humanest. You've only to take a hedge stake and sharpen it a bit at one end, and char it a little in the fire so as there mayt'n't be no splinters to hurt, and then poke it through his stomach."

The mob gave a great shout at this humane piece of advice, and it was some time before Henry could make himself heard at all, even to those who were nearest to him.

When he did succeed in so doing, he cried, with a loud voice,—

"Hear me, all of you. It is quite needless for me to inquire how you became possessed of the information that a dreadful suspicion hangs over the person of Sir Francis Varney; but if, in consequence of hearing such news, you fancy this public demonstration will be agreeable to me, or likely to relieve those who are nearest or dearest to me from the state of misery and apprehension into which they have fallen, you are much mistaken."

"Hear him, hear him!" cried Mr. Marchdale; "he speaks both wisdom and truth."

"If anything," pursued Henry, "could add to the annoyance of vexation and misery we have suffered, it would assuredly be the being made subjects of every-day gossip, and every-day clamour."

"You hear him?" said Mr. Marchdale.

"Yes, we does," said a man; "but we comes out to catch a vampyre, for all that."

"Oh, to be sure," said the humane woman; "nobody's feelings is nothing to us. Are we to be woke up in the night with vampyres sucking our bloods while we've got a stake in the country?"

"Hurrah!" shouted everybody. "Down with the vampyre! where is he?"

"You are wrong. I assure you, you are all wrong," said Mr. Chillingworth, imploringly; "there is no vampyre here, you see. Sir Francis Varney has not only escaped, but he will take the law of all of you."

This was an argument which appeared to stagger a few, but the bolder spirits pushed them on, and a suggestion to search the wood having been made by some one who was more cunning than his neighbours, that measure was at once proceeded with, and executed in a systematic manner, which made those who knew it to be the hiding-place of Sir Francis Varney tremble for his safety.

It was with a strange mixture of feeling that Henry Bannerworth waited the result of the search for the man who but a few minutes before had been opposed to him in a contest of life or death.

The destruction of Sir Francis Varney would certainly have been an effectual means of preventing him from continuing to be the incubus he then was upon the Bannerworth family; and yet the generous nature of Henry shrank with horror from seeing even such a creature as Varney sacrificed at the shrine of popular resentment, and murdered by an infuriated populace.

He felt as great an interest in the escape of the vampyre as if some great advantage to himself bad been contingent upon such an event; and, although he spoke not a word, while the echoes of the little wood were all awakened by the clamorous manner in which the mob searched for their victim, his feelings could be well read upon his countenance.

The admiral, too, without possessing probably the fine feelings of Henry Bannerworth, took an unusually sympathetic interest in the fate of the vampyre; and, after placing himself in various attitudes of intense excitement, he exclaimed,—

"D—n it, Jack, I do hope, after all, the vampyre will get the better of them. It's like a whole flotilla attacking one vessel—a lubberly proceeding at the best, and I'll be hanged if I like it. I should like to pour in a broadside into those fellows, just to let them see it wasn't a proper English mode of fighting. Shouldn't you, Jack?"

"Ay, ay, sir, I should."

"Shiver me, if I see an opportunity, if I don't let some of those rascals know what's what."

Scarcely had these words escaped the lips of the old admiral than there arose a loud shout from the interior of the wood. It was a shout of success, and seemed at the very least to herald the capture of the unfortunate Varney.

"By Heaven!" exclaimed Henry, "they have him."

"God forbid!" said Mr. Marchdale; "this grows too serious."

"Bear a hand, Jack," said the admiral: "we'll have a fight for it yet; they sha'n't murder even a vampyre in cold blood. Load the pistols and send a flying shot or two among the rascals, the moment they appear."

"No, no," said Henry; "no more violence, at least there has been enough—there has been enough."

Even as he spoke there came rushing from among the trees, at the corner of the wood, the figure of a man. There needed but one glance to assure them who it was. Sir Francis Varney had been seen, and was flying before those implacable foes who had sought his life.

He had divested himself of his huge cloak, as well as of his low slouched hat, and, with a speed which nothing but the most absolute desperation could have enabled him to exert, he rushed onward, beating down before him every obstacle, and bounding over the meadows at a rate that, if he could have continued it for any length of time, would have set pursuit at defiance.

"Bravo!" shouted the admiral, "a stern chase is a long chase, and I wish them joy of it—d——e, Jack, did you ever see anybody get along like that?"

"Ay, ay, sir."

"You never did, you scoundrel."

"Yes, I did."

"When and where?"

"When you ran away off the sound."

The admiral turned nearly blue with anger, but Jack looked perfectly imperturbable, as he added,—

"You know you ran away after the French frigates who wouldn't stay to fight you."

"Ah! that indeed. There he goes, putting on every stitch of canvass, I'll be bound."

"And there they come," said Jack, as he pointed to the corner of the wood, and some of the more active of the vampyre's pursuers showed themselves.

It would appear as if the vampyre had been started from some hiding-place in the interior of the wood, and had then thought it expedient altogether to leave that retreat, and make his way to some more secure one across the open country, where there would be more obstacles to his discovery than perseverance could overcome. Probably, then, among the brushwood and trees, for a few moments he had been again lost sight of, until those who were closest upon his track had emerged from among the dense foliage, and saw him scouring across the country at such headlong speed. These were but few, and in their extreme anxiety themselves to capture Varney, whose precipate and terrified flight brought a firm conviction to their minds of his being a vampyre, they did not stop to get much of a reinforcement, but plunged on like greyhounds in his track.

"Jack," said the admiral, "this won't do. Look at that great lubberly fellow with the queer smock-frock."

"Never saw such a figure-head in my life," said Jack.

"Stop him."

"Ay, ay, sir."

The man was coming on at a prodigious rate, and Jack, with all the deliberation in the world, advanced to meet him; and when they got sufficiently close together, that in a few moments they must encounter each other, Jack made himself into as small a bundle as possible, and presented his shoulder to the advancing countryman in such a way, that he flew off it at a tangent, as if he had run against a brick wall, and after rolling head over heels for some distance, safely deposited himself in a ditch, where he disappeared completely for a few moments from all human observation.

"Don't say I hit you," said Jack. "Curse yer, what did yer run against me for? Sarves you right. Lubbers as don't know how to steer, in course runs agin things."

"Bravo," said the admiral; "there's another of them."

The pursuers of Varney the vampyre, however, now came too thick and fast to be so easily disposed of, and as soon as his figure could be seen coursing over the meadows, and springing over road and ditch with an agility almost frightful to look upon, the whole rabble rout was in pursuit of him.

By this time, the man who had fallen into the ditch had succeeded in making his appearance in the visible world again, and as he crawled up the bank, looking a thing of mire and mud, Jack walked up to him with all the carelessness in the world, and said to him,—

"Any luck, old chap?"

"Oh, murder!" said the man, "what do you mean? who are you? where am I? what's the matter? Old Muster Fowler, the fat crowner, will set upon me now."

"Have you caught anything?" said Jack.

"Caught anything?"

"Yes; you've been in for eels, haven't you?"

"D—n!"

"Well, it is odd to me, as some people can't go a fishing without getting out of temper. Have it your own way; I won't interfere with you;" and away Jack walked.

The man cleared the mud out of his eyes, as well as he could, and looked after him with a powerful suspicion that in Jack he saw the very cause of his mortal mishap: but, somehow or other, his immersion in the not over limpid stream had wonderfully cooled his courage, and casting one despairing look upon his begrimed apparel, and another at the last of the stragglers who were pursuing Sir Francis Varney across the fields, he thought it prudent to get home as fast he could, and get rid of the disagreeable results of an adventure which had turned out for him anything but auspicious or pleasant.

Mr. Chillingworth, as though by a sort of impulse to be present in case Sir Francis Varney should really be run down and with a hope of saving him from personal violence, had followed the foremost of the rioters in the wood, found it now quite impossible for him to carry on such a chase as that which was being undertaken across the fields after Sir Francis Varney.

His person was unfortunately but ill qualified for the continuance of such a pursuit, and, although with the greatest reluctance, he at last felt himself compelled to give it up.

In making his way through the intricacies of the wood, he had been seriously incommoded by the thick undergrowth, and he had accidentally encountered several miry pools, with which he had involuntarily made a closer acquaintance than was at all conducive either to his personal appearance or comfort. The doctor's temper, though, generally speaking, one of the most even, was at last affected by his mishaps, and he could not restrain from an execration upon his want of prudence in letting his wife have a knowledge of a secret that was not his own, and the producing an unlooked for circumstance, the termination of which might be of a most disastrous nature.

Tired, therefore, and nearly exhausted by the exertions he had already taken, he emerged now alone from the wood, and near the spot where stood Henry Bannerworth and his friends in consultation.

The jaded look of the surgeon was quite sufficient indication of the trouble and turmoil he had gone through, and some expressions of sympathy for his condition were dropped by Henry, to whom he replied,—

"Nay, my young friend, I deserve it all. I have nothing but my own indiscretion to thank for all the turmoil and tumult that has arisen this morning."

"But to what possible cause can we attribute such an outrage?"

"Reproach me as much as you will, I deserve it. A man may prate of his own secrets if he like, but he should be careful of those of other people. I trusted yours to another, and am properly punished."

"Enough," said Henry; "we'll say no more of that, Mr. Chillingworth. What is done cannot be undone, and we had better spend our time in reflection of how to make the best of what is, than in useless lamentation over its causes. What is to be done?"

"Nay, I know not. Have you fought the duel?"

"Yes; and, as you perceive, harmlessly."

"Thank Heaven for that."

"Nay, I had my fire, which Sir Francis Varney refused to return; so the affair had just ended, when the sound of approaching tumult came upon our ears."

"What a strange mixture," exclaimed Marchdale, "of feelings and passions this Varney appears to be. At one moment acting with the apparent greatest malignity; and another, seeming to have awakened in his mind a romantic generosity which knows no bounds. I cannot understand him."

"Nor I, indeed," said Henry; "but yet I somehow tremble for his fate, and I seem to feel that something ought to be done to save him from the fearful consequences of popular feeling. Let us hasten to the town, and procure what assistance we may: but a few persons, well organised and properly armed, will achieve wonders against a desultory and ill-appointed multitude. There may be a chance of saving him, yet, from the imminent danger which surrounds him."

"That's proper," cried the admiral. "I don't like to see anybody run down. A fair fight's another thing. Yard arm and yard arm—stink pots and pipkins—broadside to broadside—and throw in your bodies, if you like, on the lee quarter; but don't do anything shabby. What do you think of it, Jack?"

"Why, I means to say as how if Varney only keeps on sail as he's been doing, that the devil himself wouldn't catch him in a gale."

"And yet," said Henry, "it is our duty to do the best we can. Let us at once to the town, and summons all the assistance in our power. Come on—come on!"

His friends needed no further urging, but, at a brisk pace, they all proceeded by the nearest footpaths towards the town.

It puzzled his pursuers to think in what possible direction Sir Francis Varney expected to find sustenance or succour, when they saw how curiously he took his flight across the meadows. Instead of endeavouring, by any circuitous path, to seek the shelter of his own house, or to throw himself upon the care of the authorities of the town, who must, to the extent of their power, have protected him, he struck across the fields, apparently without aim or purpose, seemingly intent upon nothing but to distance his pursuers in a long chase, which might possibly tire them, or it might not, according to their or his powers of endurance.

We say this seemed to be the case, but it was not so in reality. Sir Francis Varney had a deeper purpose, and it was scarcely to be supposed that a man of his subtle genius, and, apparently, far-seeing and reflecting intellect, could have so far overlooked the many dangers of his position as not to be fully prepared for some such contingency as that which had just now occurred.

Holding, as he did, so strange a place in society—living among men, and yet possessing so few attributes in common with humanity—he must all along have felt the possibility of drawing upon himself popular violence.

He could not wholly rely upon the secrecy of the Bannerworth family, much as they might well be supposed to shrink from giving publicity to circumstances of so fearfully strange and perilous a nature as those which had occurred amongst them. The merest accident might, at any moment, make him the town's talk. The overhearing of a few chance words by some gossiping domestic—some ebullition of anger or annoyance by some member of the family—or a communication from some friend who had been treated with confidence—might, at any time, awaken around him some such a storm as that which now raged at his heels.

Varney the vampire must have calculated this. He must have felt the possibility of such a state of things; and, as a matter of course, politicly provided himself with some place of refuge.

After about twenty minutes of hard chasing across the fields, there could be no doubt of his intentions. He had such a place of refuge; and, strange a one as it might appear, he sped towards it in as direct a line as ever a well-sped arrow flew towards its mark.

That place of refuge, to the surprise of every one, appeared to be the ancient ruin, of which we have before spoken, and which was so well known to every inhabitant of the county.

Truly, it seemed like some act of mere desperation for Sir Francis Varney to hope there to hide himself. There remained within, of what had once been a stately pile, but a few grey crumbling walls, which the hunted have would have passed unheeded, knowing that not for one instant could he have baffled his pursuers by seeking so inefficient a refuge.

And those who followed hard and fast upon the track of Sir Francis Varney felt so sure of their game, when they saw whither he was speeding, that they relaxed in their haste considerably, calling loudly to each other that the vampire was caught at last, for he could be easily surrounded among the old ruins, and dragged from amongst its moss-grown walls.

In another moment, with a wild dash and a cry of exultation, he sprang out of sight, behind an angle, formed by what had been at one time one of the principal supports of the ancient structure.

Then, as if there was still something so dangerous about him, that only ·
by a great number of hands could he be hoped to be secured, the infuriated peasantry gathered in a dense circle around what they considered his
temporary place of refuge, and as the sun, which had now climbed above
the tree tops, and dispersed, in a great measure, many of the heavy clouds
of morning, shone down upon the excited group, they might have been supposed there assembled to perform some superstitious rite, which time had
hallowed as an association of the crumbling ruin around which they stood.

By the time the whole of the stragglers, who had persisted in the chase,
had come up, there might have been about fifty or sixty resolute men, each
intent upon securing the person of one whom they felt, while in existence,
would continue to be a terror to all the weaker and dearer portions of their
domestic circles.

There was a pause of several minutes. Those who had come the fleetest
were gathering breath, and those who had come up last were looking to
their more forward companions for some information as to what had occurred before their arrival.

All was profoundly still within the ruin, and then suddenly, as if by common consent, there arose from every throat a loud shout of "Down with the
vampyre! down with the vampyre!"

The echoes of that shout died away, and then all was still as before, while
a superstitious feeling crept over even the boldest. It would almost seem as
if they had expected some kind of response from Sir Francis Varney to the
shout of defiance with which they had just greeted him; but the very calmness, repose, and absolute quiet of the ruin, and all about it, alarmed them,
and they looked the one at the other as if the adventure after all were not
one of the pleasantest description, and might not fall out so happily as they
had expected.

Yet what danger could there be? there were they, more than half a hundred stout, strong men, to cope with one; they felt convinced that he was
completely in their power; they knew the ruins could not hide him, and that
five minutes time given to the task, would suffice to explore every nook and
corner of them.

And yet they hesitated, while an unknown terror shook their nerves, and
seemingly from the very fact that they had run down their game successfully, they dreaded to secure the trophy of the chase.

One bold spirit was wanting; and, if it was not a bold one that spoke at
length, he might be complimented as being comparatively such. It was one
who had not been foremost in the chase, perchance from want of physical
power, who now stood forward, and exclaimed,—

"What are you waiting for, now? You can have him when you like. If you want your wives and children to sleep quietly in their beds, you will secure the vampyre. Come on—we all know he's here—why do you hesitate? Do you expect me to go alone and drag him out by the ears?"

Any voice would have sufficed to break the spell which bound them. This did so; and, with one accord, and yells of imprecation, they rushed forward and plunged among the old walls of the ruin.

Less time than we have before remarked would have enabled any one to explore the tottering fabric sufficient to bring a conviction to their minds that, after all, there might have been some mistake about the matter, and Sir Francis Varney was not quite caught yet.

It was astonishing how the fact of not finding him in a moment, again roused all their angry feelings against him, and dispelled every feeling of superstitious awe with which he had been surrounded; rage gave place to the sort of shuddering horror with which they had before contemplated his immediate destruction, when they had believed him to be virtually within their very grasp.

Over and over again the ruins were searched—hastily and impatiently by some, carefully and deliberately by others, until there could be no doubt upon the mind of every one individual, that somehow or somewhere within the shadow of those walls, Sir Francis Varney had disappeared most mysteriously.

Then it would have been a strange sight for any indifferent spectator to have seen how they shrunk, one by one, out of the shadow of those ruins; each seeming to be afraid that the vampyre, in some mysterious manner, would catch him if he happened to be the last within their sombre influence; and, when they had all collected in the bright, open space, some little distance beyond, they looked at each other and at the ruins, with dubious expressions of countenance, each, no doubt, wishing that each would suggest something of a consolatory or practicable character.

"What's to be done, now?" said one.

"Ah! that's it," said another, sententiously. "I'll be hanged if I know."

"He's given us the slip," remarked a third.

"But he can't have given us the slip," said one man, who was particularly famous for a dogmatical spirit of argumentation; "how is it possible? he must be here, and I say he is here."

"Find him, then," cried several at once.

"Oh! that's nothing to do with the argument; he's here, whether we find him or not."

One very cunning fellow laid his finger on his nose, and beckoned to a comrade to retire some paces, where he delivered himself of the following very oracular sentiment:—

"My good friend, you must know Sir Francis Varney is here or he isn't."

"Agreed, agreed."

"Well, if he isn't here it's no use troubling our heads any more about him; but, otherwise, it's quite another thing, and, upon the whole, I must say, that I rather think he is."

All looked at him, for it was evident he was big with some suggestion. After a pause, he resumed,—

"Now, my good friends, I propose that we all appear to give it up, and to go away; but that some one of us shall remain and hide among the ruins for some time, to watch, in case the vampyre makes his appearance from some hole or corner that we haven't found out."

"Oh, capital!" said everybody.

"Then you all agree to that?"

"Yes, yes."

"Very good; that's the only way to nick him. Now, we'll pretend to give it up; let's all of us talk loud about going home."

They did all talk loud about going home; they swore that it was not worth the trouble of catching him, that they gave it up as a bad job; that he might go to the deuce in any way he liked, for all they cared; and then they all walked off in a body, when, the man who had made the suggestion, suddenly cried,—

"Hilloa! hilloa!—stop! stop! you know one of us is to wait?"

"Oh, ay; yes, yes, yes!" said everybody, and still they moved on.

"But really, you know, what's the use of this? who's to wait?"

That was, indeed, a knotty question, which induced a serious consultation, ending in their all, with one accord, pitching upon the author of the suggestion, as by far the best person to hide in the ruins and catch the vampyre.

They then all set off at full speed; but the cunning fellow, who certainly had not the slightest idea of so practically carrying out his own suggestion, scampered off after them with a speed that soon brought him in the midst of the throng again, and so, with fear in their looks, and all the evidences of fatigue about them, they reached the town to spread fresh and more exaggerated accounts of the mysterious conduct of Varney the vampyre.

CARMILLA

1872

J. SHERIDAN LE FANU

By the time J. Sheridan LeFanu wrote *Carmilla* in 1872, enough vampire literature had been produced that LeFanu was writing within an established genre. This turning point invariably occurs in the development of any subgenre. Enough words get written about any one theme and writers no longer can create without keeping in mind how their contribution fits within the tradition. LeFanu was aware of this and, in many regards, closely followed precedents established by Polidori and Rymer. Some of these precedents are prosaic. Carmilla, like Lord Ruthven and Varney, is an aristocrat. *Carmilla* also takes place in Eastern Europe, the established home of vampire narratives. However, the most important trend LeFanu continues is increasing the proximity of the vampire figure to both human society and human psychology.

More than any vampire before her, Carmilla functions at ease in human society. Although exceptional in certain ways, she looks, speaks, and behaves like a normal person. Her status as a vampire is not revealed until late in the story; until that moment, she appears hardly more unusual than a strange girl who sleeps late and has homoerotic tendencies. Unlike Lord Ruthven, who has a bad reputation, or Varney, who is consistently the outcast, Carmilla is never an object of public ridicule until the novella's conclusion. No one suspects her wicked core.

LeFanu's careful treatment of his novella's setting also illustrates Carmilla's capacity for integration. This is not immediately apparent because, like *The Vampyre*, *Carmilla* maintains many characteristics of Gothic fiction, whose tropes typically separate characters from contemporary society. Laura, Carmilla's victim, lives alone with her family in a remote castle tucked away in the woods in Styria, part of Austria. She lives in a world of sylvan woods and ancient ruins, in a culture that includes hunchback apothecaries (a lovely example of a Gothic character). Yet within this world of mythic overtones, LeFanu still pays special attention to the kind of realistic details that distinguish Part II of this anthology from Part I. These details emerge in the discussions and depictions of money and class. The story opens with a discussion of how the East is far more affordable than England and how it's possible to live well on a very small income. Later, General Spielsdorf, a secondary character whose niece also falls victim to Carmilla, retells the evening of revelry that ultimately led to her demise. The description of aristocratic excess recalls those of Jay Gatsby's parties:

> There was such a display of fireworks as Paris itself had never witnessed. And such music—music, you know is my weakness—such ravishing music!…As you wandered through these fantastically illuminated grounds, the moon-lighted chateau throwing a rosy light from its long rows of windows, you would suddenly hear these ravishing voices stealing from the silence of some grove, or rising from boats upon the lake (Chapter XI).

However, this description is immediately followed by Spielsdorf acknowledging that the world of the beautiful and damned is not his own. "It was a very aristocratic assembly. I was myself almost the only 'nobody' present."

Identity and class are themes that characterize Victorian social realism, and LeFanu adroitly situates his fantastic tale in a world attuned to these issues. As Senf writes, "LeFanu generally manipulates his source materials to stress the ordinary rather than the exceptional" (Senf 49). This artful fusion of Gothic and Realist styles makes Carmilla a vampire figure who has her roots in folklore and superstition, but who also exists in a very real, very human, contemporary world.

Although Carmilla is notable for her increased ability to function within human society, she truly departs from her vampire ancestors in her sophisticated adoption of human sexuality—a development fundamentally linked to the fact she is a female vampire. Many argue that government and law exist to mitigate man's base and aggressive tendencies—namely, to quell inevitable war. If one gives credence to this line of thought, then Lord Ruthven, Varney, and certainly the male vampires who precede them represent this inherent masculine quality of humans. Carmilla, on the other hand, is not driven by an intrinsic desire to destroy. She does ultimately kill humans by drinking their blood, yet her "attacks" in *Carmilla* are presented in the vocabulary of love. Her tools are neither strength nor speed, but rather affection and sex. Polidori and Rymer, by increasing the prominence of the "romantic chase," made rudimentary inroads in this thematic development, but ultimately their vampires were sexual monsters. LeFanu is so self-assured in his erotic prose that he makes Polidori and Rymer seem like adolescents who know nothing of the bedroom other than dirty anecdotes passed down from older brothers. Compare the following passage from *Carmilla* to the one below it from *Varney* to see the extremity of difference in the way these writers treat sex:

> Sometimes after an hour of apathy, my strange and beautiful companion would take my hand and hold it with a fond pressure, renewed again and again; blushing softly, gazing in my face with languid and burning eyes, and breathing so fast that her dress rose and fell with the tumultuous respiration. It was like the ardour of a lover; it embarrassed me; it was hateful and yet overpowering; and with gloating eyes she drew me to her, and her hot lips traveled along my cheek in kisses; and she would whisper, almost in sobs, "You are mine, you *shall* be mine, and you and I are one for ever." Then she had thrown herself back in her chair, with her small hands over her eyes, leaving me trembling (Chapter IV).

To Rymer's:

> The bed-clothes fell in a heap by the side of the bed—she was dragged by her long silken hair completely on to it again. Her beautifully rounded limbs quivered with the agony of her soul. The glassy, horrible eyes of the figure ran over that angelic form with a hideous satisfaction—horrible profanation. He drags her head to the bed's edge. He forces it back by the long hair still entwined in his grasp. With a plunge he seizes her neck in his fang-like teeth—a gush of blood, and a hideous sucking noise follows. *The girl has swooned, and the vampyre is at his hideous repast!* (Chapter I).

The relationship between Laura and Carmilla, a fascinating inversion of the traditional male vampire/female victim arrangement, is not strictly sexual; it is also characterized by a unique intimacy, adding another shade of humanity to the literary vampire. Varney and Lord Ruthven, as well as Dracula who follows, are also selective in the gender of their victims, but for these male vampires, their relationship with their victims is only superficially emotional. The case can be made that Varney does develop relationships with his victims, but simply because he sometimes feels remorse and Flora sometimes feels pity does not mean that the two of them share an emotional *connection*. The connection between Carmilla and Laura is love, which makes Carmilla's true nature all the more heartbreaking. The connection is so strong that, despite knowing that Carmilla is nothing short of a mass murderer, Laura confesses in the novella's final lines that her memory of Carmilla is "ambiguous…sometimes the playful, languid, beautiful girl…Often from a reverie I have started, fancying I heard the light step of Carmilla at the drawing room door" (Chapter XVI). *Carmilla's* lesbian content not only served as a literary fodder for the then-burgeoning women's rights movement, but also invites transgression—an established theme of vampire literature. The invited transgression is not just sexual, but also ethical. Laura's lingering desire is execrable. How could one hold feelings for such a monster? Yet what we feel and what we know is "right" do not always align. Stories like *Carmilla* serve as an important reminder that such conflicted emotions are a normal part of the human condition.

Carmilla is also important to the canon because it raises Christianity, a recurring theme in vampire literature, from dormancy. Recall that in the poems of Part I, Christianity played the important role of the antagonist to the vampire force. Recall also that Christianity proved to be an ineffective resistance. Although not clearly stated, it is certainly implied that Ossenfelder's vampire triumphs over the "long-held teachings." Likewise, Christianity fails to keep Helen away from her betrothed in "William and Helen." "Bride of Corinth," Goethe's poem that focuses on the battle between Christianity and the old world religions, similarly shows religion's ineffectiveness in stopping a vampire.

Carmilla witnesses a reversal of this—a reversal that will become even more pronounced in *Dracula*. The moment occurs when Laura and Carmilla happen across a funeral procession for a young woman. The mourners are singing hymns, and Laura joins them. Carmilla's response—the first such response of the novella—is unexpected and vicious. She not only loathes the music, but it also physically affects her: "Her face underwent a change that alarmed and even terrified me for a moment. It darkened, and became horribly livid; her teeth and hands were clenched, and she frowned and compressed her lips..." (Chapter IV).

A complete explanation of why Christianity went from an ineffective to an effective stay against vampires is a task that requires an in-depth analysis of religious history that is beyond the scope of this anthology. However, generally speaking, writers' treatment of religion in literature follows society's general disposition toward religion at the time of publication. The early German poems in this collection were written during the Age of Reason, when Christianity was no longer considered an absolute source of truth. In the same vein, England experienced religious revivalism during the nineteenth century. Regardless of a particular historical moment, the vampire has emerged as a figure through which questions of faith and religions can be explored. This capability of vampire literature remains today.

Not only does *Carmilla* assert that religion is a viable way to fight evil, but the novella also warns that strictly scientific methods are ineffective. General Spielsdorf loses his niece to Carmilla well before she begins to pursue Laura. In response to Laura's father's skepticism, he says: "You believe in nothing but what consists with your own prejudices and illusions. I remember when I was like you, but I have learned better" (Chapter X). Throughout the story, Laura's father is dismissive of any mention of the supernatural. As such, LeFanu seems to be suggesting that Rationalism has the same dogmatic risks as Fundamentalism.

CARMILLA

PROLOGUE

Upon a paper attached to the Narrative which follows, Doctor Hesselius has written a rather elaborate note, which he accompanies with a reference to his Essay on the strange subject which the MS. illuminates.

This mysterious subject he treats, in that Essay, with his usual learning and acumen, and with remarkable directness and condensation. It will form but one volume of the series of that extraordinary man's collected papers.

As I publish the case, in this volume, simply to interest the "laity," I shall forestall the intelligent lady, who relates it, in nothing; and after due consideration, I have determined, therefore, to abstain from presenting any precis of the learned Doctor's reasoning, or extract from his statement on a subject which he describes as "involving, not improbably, some of the profoundest arcana of our dual existence, and its intermediates."

I was anxious on discovering this paper, to reopen the correspondence commenced by Doctor Hesselius, so many years before, with a person so clever and careful as his informant seems to have been. Much to my regret, however, I found that she had died in the interval.

She, probably, could have added little to the Narrative which she communicates in the following pages, with, so far as I can pronounce, such conscientious particularity.

I. AN EARLY FRIGHT

*I*n Styria[52], we, though by no means magnificent people, inhabit a castle, or schloss. A small income, in that part of the world, goes a great way. Eight or nine hundred a year does wonders. Scantily enough ours

---

52 Region of Austria.

would have answered among wealthy people at home. My father is English, and I bear an English name, although I never saw England. But here, in this lonely and primitive place, where everything is so marvelously cheap, I really don't see how ever so much more money would at all materially add to our comforts, or even luxuries.

My father was in the Austrian service, and retired upon a pension and his patrimony, and purchased this feudal residence, and the small estate on which it stands, a bargain.

Nothing can be more picturesque or solitary. It stands on a slight eminence in a forest. The road, very old and narrow, passes in front of its drawbridge, never raised in my time, and its moat, stocked with perch, and sailed over by many swans, and floating on its surface white fleets of water lilies.

Over all this the schloss shows its many-windowed front; its towers, and its Gothic chapel.

The forest opens in an irregular and very picturesque glade before its gate, and at the right a steep Gothic bridge carries the road over a stream that winds in deep shadow through the wood. I have said that this is a very lonely place. Judge whether I say truth. Looking from the hall door towards the road, the forest in which our castle stands extends fifteen miles to the right, and twelve to the left. The nearest inhabited village is about seven of your English miles to the left. The nearest inhabited schloss of any historic associations, is that of old General Spielsdorf, nearly twenty miles away to the right.

I have said "the nearest inhabited village," because there is, only three miles westward, that is to say in the direction of General Spielsdorf's schloss, a ruined village, with its quaint little church, now roofless, in the aisle of which are the moldering tombs of the proud family of Karnstein, now extinct, who once owned the equally desolate chateau which, in the thick of the forest, overlooks the silent ruins of the town.

Respecting the cause of the desertion of this striking and melancholy spot, there is a legend which I shall relate to you another time.

I must tell you now, how very small is the party who constitute the inhabitants of our castle. I don't include servants, or those dependents who occupy rooms in the buildings attached to the schloss. Listen, and wonder! My father, who is the kindest man on earth, but growing old; and I, at the date of my story, only nineteen. Eight years have passed since then.

I and my father constituted the family at the schloss. My mother, a Styrian lady, died in my infancy, but I had a good-natured governess, who had been with me from, I might almost say, my infancy. I could not remember the time when her fat, benignant face was not a familiar picture in my memory.

This was Madame Perrodon, a native of Berne, whose care and good nature now in part supplied to me the loss of my mother, whom I do not even remember, so early I lost her. She made a third at our little dinner party. There was a fourth, Mademoiselle De Lafontaine, a lady such as you term, I believe, a "finishing governess." She spoke French and German, Madame Perrodon French and broken English, to which my father and I added English, which, partly to prevent its becoming a lost language among us, and partly from patriotic motives, we spoke every day. The consequence was a Babel[53], at which strangers used to laugh, and which I shall make no attempt to reproduce in this narrative. And there were two or three young lady friends besides, pretty nearly of my own age, who were occasional visitors, for longer or shorter terms; and these visits I sometimes returned.

These were our regular social resources; but of course there were chance visits from "neighbors" of only five or six leagues distance. My life was, notwithstanding, rather a solitary one, I can assure you.

My gouvernantes had just so much control over me as you might conjecture such sage persons would have in the case of a rather spoiled girl, whose only parent allowed her pretty nearly her own way in everything.

The first occurrence in my existence, which produced a terrible impression upon my mind, which, in fact, never has been effaced, was one of the very earliest incidents of my life which I can recollect. Some people will think it so trifling that it should not be recorded here. You will see, however, by-and-by, why I mention it. The nursery, as it was called, though I had it all to myself, was a large room in the upper story of the castle, with a steep oak roof. I can't have been more than six years old, when one night I awoke, and looking round the room from my bed, failed to see the nursery maid. Neither was my nurse there; and I thought myself alone. I was not frightened, for I was one of those happy children who are studiously kept in ignorance of ghost stories, of fairy tales, and of all such lore as makes us cover up our heads when the door cracks suddenly, or the flicker of an expiring candle makes the shadow of a bedpost dance upon the wall, nearer to our faces. I was vexed and insulted at finding myself, as I conceived, neglected, and I began to whimper, preparatory to a hearty bout of roaring; when to my surprise, I saw a solemn, but very pretty face looking at me from the side of the bed. It was that of a young lady who was kneeling, with her hands under the coverlet. I looked at her with a kind of pleased wonder, and ceased whimpering. She caressed me with her hands, and lay down beside me on the bed,

---

53 Babel was a tower in the bible that was never completed due to language barriers stemming from numerous languages.

and drew me towards her, smiling; I felt immediately delightfully soothed, and fell asleep again. I was wakened by a sensation as if two needles ran into my breast very deep at the same moment, and I cried loudly. The lady started back, with her eyes fixed on me, and then slipped down upon the floor, and, as I thought, hid herself under the bed.

I was now for the first time frightened, and I yelled with all my might and main. Nurse, nursery maid, housekeeper, all came running in, and hearing my story, they made light of it, soothing me all they could meanwhile. But, child as I was, I could perceive that their faces were pale with an unwonted look of anxiety, and I saw them look under the bed, and about the room, and peep under tables and pluck open cupboards; and the housekeeper whispered to the nurse: "Lay your hand along that hollow in the bed; someone did lie there, so sure as you did not; the place is still warm."

I remember the nursery maid petting me, and all three examining my chest, where I told them I felt the puncture, and pronouncing that there was no sign visible that any such thing had happened to me.

The housekeeper and the two other servants who were in charge of the nursery, remained sitting up all night; and from that time a servant always sat up in the nursery until I was about fourteen.

I was very nervous for a long time after this. A doctor was called in, he was pallid and elderly. How well I remember his long saturnine face, slightly pitted with smallpox, and his chestnut wig. For a good while, every second day, he came and gave me medicine, which of course I hated.

The morning after I saw this apparition I was in a state of terror, and could not bear to be left alone, daylight though it was, for a moment.

I remember my father coming up and standing at the bedside, and talking cheerfully, and asking the nurse a number of questions, and laughing very heartily at one of the answers; and patting me on the shoulder, and kissing me, and telling me not to be frightened, that it was nothing but a dream and could not hurt me.

But I was not comforted, for I knew the visit of the strange woman was not a dream; and I was awfully frightened.

I was a little consoled by the nursery maid's assuring me that it was she who had come and looked at me, and lain down beside me in the bed, and that I must have been half-dreaming not to have known her face. But this, though supported by the nurse, did not quite satisfy me.

I remembered, in the course of that day, a venerable old man, in a black cassock, coming into the room with the nurse and housekeeper, and talking a little to them, and very kindly to me; his face was very sweet and gentle, and he told me they were going to pray, and joined my hands together, and desired me to say, softly, while they were praying, "Lord hear all good prayers for us, for Jesus' sake." I think these were the very words, for I often repeated them to myself, and my nurse used for years to make me say them in my prayers.

I remembered so well the thoughtful sweet face of that white-haired old man, in his black cassock, as he stood in that rude, lofty, brown room, with the clumsy furniture of a fashion three hundred years old about him, and the scanty light entering its shadowy atmosphere through the small lattice. He kneeled, and the three women with him, and he prayed aloud with an earnest quavering voice for, what appeared to me, a long time. I forget all my life preceding that event, and for some time after it is all obscure also, but the scenes I have just described stand out vivid as the isolated pictures of the phantasmagoria surrounded by darkness.

II. A GUEST

Gam now going to tell you something so strange that it will require all your faith in my veracity to believe my story. It is not only true, nevertheless, but truth of which I have been an eyewitness.

It was a sweet summer evening, and my father asked me, as he sometimes did, to take a little ramble with him along that beautiful forest vista which I have mentioned as lying in front of the schloss.

"General Spielsdorf cannot come to us so soon as I had hoped," said my father, as we pursued our walk.

He was to have paid us a visit of some weeks, and we had expected his arrival next day. He was to have brought with him a young lady, his niece and ward, Mademoiselle Rheinfeldt, whom I had never seen, but whom I had heard described as a very charming girl, and in whose society I had promised myself many happy days. I was more disappointed than a young lady living in a town, or a bustling neighborhood can possibly imagine. This visit, and the new acquaintance it promised, had furnished my day dream for many weeks.

"And how soon does he come?" I asked.

"Not till autumn. Not for two months, I dare say," he answered. "And I am very glad now, dear, that you never knew Mademoiselle Rheinfeldt."

"And why?" I asked, both mortified and curious.

"Because the poor young lady is dead," he replied. "I quite forgot I had not told you, but you were not in the room when I received the General's letter this evening."

I was very much shocked. General Spielsdorf had mentioned in his first letter, six or seven weeks before, that she was not so well as he would wish her, but there was nothing to suggest the remotest suspicion of danger.

"Here is the General's letter," he said, handing it to me. "I am afraid he is in great affliction; the letter appears to me to have been written very nearly in distraction."

We sat down on a rude bench, under a group of magnificent lime trees. The sun was setting with all its melancholy splendor behind the sylvan horizon, and the stream that flows beside our home, and passes under the steep old bridge I have mentioned, wound through many a group of noble trees, almost at our feet, reflecting in its current the fading crimson of the sky. General Spielsdorf's letter was so extraordinary, so vehement, and in some places so self-contradictory, that I read it twice over—the second time aloud to my father—and was still unable to account for it, except by supposing that grief had unsettled his mind.

It said "I have lost my darling daughter, for as such I loved her. During the last days of dear Bertha's illness I was not able to write to you.

"Before then I had no idea of her danger. I have lost her, and now learn all, too late. She died in the peace of innocence, and in the glorious hope of a blessed futurity. The fiend who betrayed our infatuated hospitality has done it all. I thought I was receiving into my house innocence, gaiety, a charming companion for my lost Bertha. Heavens! what a fool have I been!

"I thank God my child died without a suspicion of the cause of her sufferings. She is gone without so much as conjecturing the nature of her illness, and the accursed passion of the agent of all this misery. I devote my remaining days to tracking and extinguishing a monster. I am told I may hope to accomplish my righteous and merciful purpose. At present there is scarcely a gleam of light to guide me. I curse my conceited incredulity, my despicable affectation of superiority, my blindness, my obstinacy—all—too late. I cannot write or talk collectedly now. I am distracted. So soon as I shall have a little recovered, I mean to devote myself for a time to enquiry, which may possibly lead me as far as Vienna. Some time in the autumn, two months hence, or earlier if I live, I will see you—that is, if you permit me; I will then tell you all that I scarce dare put upon paper now. Farewell. Pray for me, dear friend."

In these terms ended this strange letter. Though I had never seen Bertha Rheinfeldt my eyes filled with tears at the sudden intelligence; I was startled, as well as profoundly disappointed.

The sun had now set, and it was twilight by the time I had returned the General's letter to my father.

It was a soft clear evening, and we loitered, speculating upon the possible meanings of the violent and incoherent sentences which I had just been reading. We had nearly a mile to walk before reaching the road that passes the schloss in front, and by that time the moon was shining brilliantly. At the drawbridge we met Madame Perrodon and Mademoiselle De Lafontaine, who had come out, without their bonnets, to enjoy the exquisite moonlight.

We heard their voices gabbling in animated dialogue as we approached. We joined them at the drawbridge, and turned about to admire with them the beautiful scene.

The glade through which we had just walked lay before us. At our left the narrow road wound away under clumps of lordly trees, and was lost to sight amid the thickening forest. At the right the same road crosses the steep and picturesque bridge, near which stands a ruined tower which once guarded that pass; and beyond the bridge an abrupt eminence rises, covered with trees, and showing in the shadows some grey ivy-clustered rocks.

Over the sward and low grounds a thin film of mist was stealing like smoke, marking the distances with a transparent veil; and here and there we could see the river faintly flashing in the moonlight.

No softer, sweeter scene could be imagined. The news I had just heard made it melancholy; but nothing could disturb its character of profound serenity, and the enchanted glory and vagueness of the prospect.

My father, who enjoyed the picturesque, and I, stood looking in silence over the expanse beneath us. The two good governesses, standing a little way behind us, discoursed upon the scene, and were eloquent upon the moon.

Madame Perrodon was fat, middle-aged, and romantic, and talked and sighed poetically. Mademoiselle De Lafontaine—in right of her father who was a German, assumed to be psychological, metaphysical, and something of a mystic—now declared that when the moon shone with a light so intense it was well known that it indicated a special spiritual activity. The effect of the full moon in such a state of brilliancy was manifold. It acted on dreams, it acted on lunacy, it acted on nervous people, it had marvelous physical influences connected with life. Mademoiselle related that her cousin, who was mate of a merchant ship, having taken a nap on deck on such a night, lying on his back, with his face full in the light on the moon, had wakened, after a dream of an old woman clawing him by the cheek, with his features horribly drawn to one side; and his countenance had never quite recovered its equilibrium.

"The moon, this night," she said, "is full of idyllic and magnetic influence—and see, when you look behind you at the front of the schloss how all its windows flash and twinkle with that silvery splendor, as if unseen hands had lighted up the rooms to receive fairy guests."

There are indolent styles of the spirits in which, indisposed to talk our-selves, the talk of others is pleasant to our listless ears; and I gazed on, pleased with the tinkle of the ladies' conversation.

"I have got into one of my moping moods tonight," said my father, after a silence, and quoting Shakespeare, whom, by way of keeping up our English, he used to read aloud, he said:

"'In truth I know not why I am so sad. It wearies me: you say it wearies you; But how I got it—came by it.'"[54]

"I forget the rest. But I feel as if some great misfortune were hanging over us. I suppose the poor General's afflicted letter has had something to do with it."

At this moment the unwonted sound of carriage wheels and many hoofs upon the road, arrested our attention.

They seemed to be approaching from the high ground overlooking the bridge, and very soon the equipage emerged from that point. Two horsemen first crossed the bridge, then came a carriage drawn by four horses, and two men rode behind.

It seemed to be the traveling carriage of a person of rank; and we were all immediately absorbed in watching that very unusual spectacle. It be-came, in a few moments, greatly more interesting, for just as the carriage had passed the summit of the steep bridge, one of the leaders, taking fright, communicated his panic to the rest, and after a plunge or two, the whole team broke into a wild gallop together, and dashing between the horsemen who rode in front, came thundering along the road towards us with the speed of a hurricane.

The excitement of the scene was made more painful by the clear, long-drawn screams of a female voice from the carriage window.

We all advanced in curiosity and horror; me rather in silence, the rest with various ejaculations of terror.

Our suspense did not last long. Just before you reach the castle draw-bridge, on the route they were coming, there stands by the roadside a magnificent lime tree, on the other stands an ancient stone cross, at sight of which the horses, now going at a pace that was perfectly frightful, swerved so as to bring the wheel over the projecting roots of the tree.

I knew what was coming. I covered my eyes, unable to see it out, and turned my head away; at the same moment I heard a cry from my lady friends, who had gone on a little.

---

54 *Merchant of Venice*, Act I, scene i.

Curiosity opened my eyes, and I saw a scene of utter confusion. Two of the horses were on the ground, the carriage lay upon its side with two wheels in the air; the men were busy removing the traces, and a lady with a commanding air and figure had got out, and stood with clasped hands, raising the handkerchief that was in them every now and then to her eyes.

Through the carriage door was now lifted a young lady, who appeared to be lifeless. My dear old father was already beside the elder lady, with his hat in his hand, evidently tendering his aid and the resources of his schloss. The lady did not appear to hear him, or to have eyes for anything but the slender girl who was being placed against the slope of the bank.

I approached; the young lady was apparently stunned, but she was certainly not dead. My father, who piqued himself on being something of a physician, had just had his fingers on her wrist and assured the lady, who declared herself her mother, that her pulse, though faint and irregular, was undoubtedly still distinguishable. The lady clasped her hands and looked upward, as if in a momentary transport of gratitude; but immediately she broke out again in that theatrical way which is, I believe, natural to some people.

She was what is called a fine looking woman for her time of life, and must have been handsome; she was tall, but not thin, and dressed in black velvet, and looked rather pale, but with a proud and commanding countenance, though now agitated strangely.

"Who was ever being so born to calamity?" I heard her say, with clasped hands, as I came up. "Here am I, on a journey of life and death, in prosecuting which to lose an hour is possibly to lose all. My child will not have recovered sufficiently to resume her route for who can say how long. I must leave her: I cannot, dare not, delay. How far on, sir, can you tell, is the nearest village? I must leave her there; and shall not see my darling, or even hear of her till my return, three months hence."

I plucked my father by the coat, and whispered earnestly in his ear: "Oh! papa, pray ask her to let her stay with us—it would be so delightful. Do, pray."

"If Madame will entrust her child to the care of my daughter, and of her good gouvernante, Madame Perrodon, and permit her to remain as our guest, under my charge, until her return, it will confer a distinction and an obligation upon us, and we shall treat her with all the care and devotion which so sacred a trust deserves."

"I cannot do that, sir, it would be to task your kindness and chivalry too cruelly," said the lady, distractedly.

"It would, on the contrary, be to confer on us a very great kindness at the moment when we most need it. My daughter has just been disappointed by a cruel misfortune, in a visit from which she had long anticipated a great deal of happiness. If you confide this young lady to our care it will be her best consolation. The nearest village on your route is distant, and affords no such inn as you could think of placing your daughter at; you cannot allow her to continue her journey for any considerable distance without danger. If, as you say, you cannot suspend your journey, you must part with her tonight, and nowhere could you do so with more honest assurances of care and tenderness than here."

There was something in this lady's air and appearance so distinguished and even imposing, and in her manner so engaging, as to impress one, quite apart from the dignity of her equipage, with a conviction that she was a person of consequence.

By this time the carriage was replaced in its upright position, and the horses, quite tractable, in the traces again.

The lady threw on her daughter a glance which I fancied was not quite so affectionate as one might have anticipated from the beginning of the scene; then she beckoned slightly to my father, and withdrew two or three steps with him out of hearing; and talked to him with a fixed and stern countenance, not at all like that with which she had hitherto spoken.

I was filled with wonder that my father did not seem to perceive the change, and also unspeakably curious to learn what it could be that she was speaking, almost in his ear, with so much earnestness and rapidity.

Two or three minutes at most I think she remained thus employed, then she turned, and a few steps brought her to where her daughter lay, supported by Madame Perrodon. She kneeled beside her for a moment and whispered, as Madame supposed, a little benediction in her ear; then hastily kissing her she stepped into her carriage, the door was closed, the footmen in stately liveries jumped up behind, the outriders spurred on, the postilions cracked their whips, the horses plunged and broke suddenly into a furious canter that threatened soon again to become a gallop, and the carriage whirled away, followed at the same rapid pace by the two horsemen in the rear.

III. WE COMPARE NOTES

We followed the cortege with our eyes until it was swiftly lost to sight in the misty wood; and the very sound of the hoofs and the wheels died away in the silent night air.

Nothing remained to assure us that the adventure had not been an illusion of a moment but the young lady, who just at that moment opened her eyes. I could not see, for her face was turned from me, but she raised her head, evidently looking about her, and I heard a very sweet voice ask complainingly, "Where is mamma?"

Our good Madame Perrodon answered tenderly, and added some comfortable assurances.

I then heard her ask:

"Where am I? What is this place?" and after that she said, "I don't see the carriage; and Matska, where is she?"

Madame answered all her questions in so far as she understood them; and gradually the young lady remembered how the misadventure came about, and was glad to hear that no one in, or in attendance on, the carriage was hurt; and on learning that her mamma had left her here, till her return in about three months, she wept.

I was going to add my consolations to those of Madame Perrodon when Mademoiselle De Lafontaine placed her hand upon my arm, saying:

"Don't approach, one at a time is as much as she can at present converse with; a very little excitement would possibly overpower her now."

As soon as she is comfortably in bed, I thought, I will run up to her room and see her.

My father in the meantime had sent a servant on horseback for the physician, who lived about two leagues away; and a bedroom was being prepared for the young lady's reception.

The stranger now rose, and leaning on Madame's arm, walked slowly over the drawbridge and into the castle gate.

In the hall, servants waited to receive her, and she was conducted forthwith to her room. The room we usually sat in as our drawing room is long, having four windows, that looked over the moat and drawbridge, upon the forest scene I have just described.

It is furnished in old carved oak, with large carved cabinets, and the chairs are cushioned with crimson Utrecht velvet. The walls are covered with tapestry, and surrounded with great gold frames, the figures being as large as life, in ancient and very curious costume, and the subjects represented are hunting, hawking, and generally festive. It is not too stately to be extremely comfortable; and here we had our tea, for with his usual patriotic leanings he insisted that the national beverage should make its appearance regularly with our coffee and chocolate.

We sat here this night, and with candles lighted, were talking over the adventure of the evening.

Madame Perrodon and Mademoiselle De Lafontaine were both of our party. The young stranger had hardly lain down in her bed when she sank into a deep sleep; and those ladies had left her in the care of a servant.

"How do you like our guest?" I asked, as soon as Madame entered. "Tell me all about her?"

"I like her extremely," answered Madame, "she is, I almost think, the prettiest creature I ever saw; about your age, and so gentle and nice."

"She is absolutely beautiful," threw in Mademoiselle, who had peeped for a moment into the stranger's room.

"And such a sweet voice!" added Madame Perrodon.

"Did you remark a woman in the carriage, after it was set up again, who did not get out," inquired Mademoiselle, "but only looked from the window?"

"No, we had not seen her."

Then she described a hideous black woman, with a sort of colored turban on her head, and who was gazing all the time from the carriage window, nodding and grinning derisively towards the ladies, with gleaming eyes and large white eyeballs, and her teeth set as if in fury.

"Did you remark what an ill-looking pack of men the servants were?" asked Madame.

"Yes," said my father, who had just come in, "ugly, hang-dog[55] looking fellows as ever I beheld in my life. I hope they mayn't rob the poor lady in the forest. They are clever rogues, however; they got everything to rights in a minute."

"I dare say they are worn out with too long traveling," said Madame.

"Besides looking wicked, their faces were so strangely lean, and dark, and sullen. I am very curious, I own; but I dare say the young lady will tell you all about it tomorrow, if she is sufficiently recovered."

"I don't think she will," said my father, with a mysterious smile, and a little nod of his head, as if he knew more about it than he cared to tell us.

This made us all the more inquisitive as to what had passed between him and the lady in the black velvet, in the brief but earnest interview that had immediately preceded her departure.

We were scarcely alone, when I entreated him to tell me. He did not need much pressing.

"There is no particular reason why I should not tell you. She expressed a reluctance to trouble us with the care of her daughter, saying she was in delicate health, and nervous, but not subject to any kind of seizure—she volunteered that—nor to any illusion; being, in fact, perfectly sane."

"How very odd to say all that!" I interpolated. "It was so unnecessary."

"At all events it was said," he laughed, "and as you wish to know all that passed, which was indeed very little, I tell you. She then said, 'I am making a long journey of vital importance—she emphasized the word—rapid and secret; I shall return for my child in three months; in the meantime, she will

55 Dejected.

be silent as to who we are, whence we come, and whither we are traveling.'
That is all she said. She spoke very pure French. When she said the word
'secret,' she paused for a few seconds, looking sternly, her eyes fixed on mine.
I fancy she makes a great point of that. You saw how quickly she was gone.
I hope I have not done a very foolish thing, in taking charge of the young
lady."

For my part, I was delighted. I was longing to see and talk to her; and
only waiting till the doctor should give me leave. You, who live in towns,
can have no idea how great an event the introduction of a new friend is, in
such a solitude as surrounded us.

The doctor did not arrive till nearly one o'clock; but I could no more have
gone to my bed and slept, than I could have overtaken, on foot, the carriage
in which the princess in black velvet had driven away.

When the physician came down to the drawing room, it was to report
very favorably upon his patient. She was now sitting up, her pulse quite
regular, apparently perfectly well. She had sustained no injury, and the little
shock to her nerves had passed away quite harmlessly. There could be no
harm certainly in my seeing her, if we both wished it; and, with this permission I sent, forthwith, to know whether she would allow me to visit her for
a few minutes in her room.

The servant returned immediately to say that she desired nothing more.

You may be sure I was not long in availing myself of this permission.

Our visitor lay in one of the handsomest rooms in the schloss. It was,
perhaps, a little stately. There was a somber piece of tapestry opposite the
foot of the bed, representing Cleopatra with the asps to her bosom;[56] and
other solemn classic scenes were displayed, a little faded, upon the other
walls. But there was gold carving, and rich and varied color enough in the
other decorations of the room, to more than redeem the gloom of the old
tapestry.

There were candles at the bedside. She was sitting up; her slender pretty
figure enveloped in the soft silk dressing gown, embroidered with flowers,
and lined with thick quilted silk, which her mother had thrown over her
feet as she lay upon the ground.

What was it that, as I reached the bedside and had just begun my little
greeting, struck me dumb in a moment, and made me recoil a step or two
from before her? I will tell you.

I saw the very face which had visited me in my childhood at night, which
remained so fixed in my memory, and on which I had for so many years so
often ruminated with horror, when no one suspected of what I was thinking.

---

56 Cleopatra is said to have committed suicide by allowing an asp to bite her.

It was pretty, even beautiful; and when I first beheld it, wore the same melancholy expression.

But this almost instantly lighted into a strange fixed smile of recognition.

There was a silence of fully a minute, and then at length she spoke; I could not.

"How wonderful!" she exclaimed. "Twelve years ago, I saw your face in a dream, and it has haunted me ever since."

"Wonderful indeed!" I repeated, overcoming with an effort the horror that had for a time suspended my utterances. "Twelve years ago, in vision or reality, I certainly saw you. I could not forget your face. It has remained before my eyes ever since."

Her smile had softened. Whatever I had fancied strange in it, was gone, and it and her dimpling cheeks were now delightfully pretty and intelligent.

I felt reassured, and continued more in the vein which hospitality indicated, to bid her welcome, and to tell her how much pleasure her accidental arrival had given us all, and especially what a happiness it was to me.

I took her hand as I spoke. I was a little shy, as lonely people are, but the situation made me eloquent, and even bold. She pressed my hand, she laid hers upon it, and her eyes glowed, as, looking hastily into mine, she smiled again, and blushed.

She answered my welcome very prettily. I sat down beside her, still wondering; and she said:

"I must tell you my vision about you; it is so very strange that you and I should have had, each of the other so vivid a dream, that each should have seen, I you and you me, looking as we do now, when of course we both were mere children. I was a child, about six years old, and I awoke from a confused and troubled dream, and found myself in a room, unlike my nursery, wainscoted clumsily in some dark wood, and with cupboards and bedsteads, and chairs, and benches placed about it. The beds were, I thought, all empty, and the room itself without anyone but myself in it; and I, after looking about me for some time, and admiring especially an iron candlestick with two branches, which I should certainly know again, crept under one of the beds to reach the window; but as I got from under the bed, I heard someone crying; and looking up, while I was still upon my knees, I saw you—most assuredly you—as I see you now; a beautiful young lady, with golden hair and large blue eyes, and lips—your lips—you as you are here.

"Your looks won me; I climbed on the bed and put my arms about you, and I think we both fell asleep. I was aroused by a scream; you were sitting up screaming. I was frightened, and slipped down upon the ground, and, it seemed to me, lost consciousness for a moment; and when I came to myself, I was again in my nursery at home. Your face I have never forgotten since.

I could not be misled by mere resemblance. You are the lady whom I saw then."

It was now my turn to relate my corresponding vision, which I did, to the undisguised wonder of my new acquaintance.

"I don't know which should be most afraid of the other," she said, again smiling—"If you were less pretty I think I should be very much afraid of you, but being as you are, and you and I both so young, I feel only that I have made your acquaintance twelve years ago, and have already a right to your intimacy; at all events it does seem as if we were destined, from our earliest childhood, to be friends. I wonder whether you feel as strangely drawn towards me as I do to you; I have never had a friend—shall I find one now?" She sighed, and her fine dark eyes gazed passionately on me.

Now the truth is, I felt rather unaccountably towards the beautiful stranger. I did feel, as she said, "drawn towards her," but there was also something of repulsion. In this ambiguous feeling, however, the sense of attraction immensely prevailed. She interested and won me; she was so beautiful and so indescribably engaging.

I perceived now something of languor and exhaustion stealing over her, and hastened to bid her good night.

"The doctor thinks," I added, "that you ought to have a maid to sit up with you tonight; one of ours is waiting, and you will find her a very useful and quiet creature."

"How kind of you, but I could not sleep, I never could with an attendant in the room. I shan't require any assistance—and, shall I confess my weakness, I am haunted with a terror of robbers. Our house was robbed once, and two servants murdered, so I always lock my door. It has become a habit—and you look so kind I know you will forgive me. I see there is a key in the lock."

She held me close in her pretty arms for a moment and whispered in my ear, "Good night, darling, it is very hard to part with you, but good night; tomorrow, but not early, I shall see you again."

She sank back on the pillow with a sigh, and her fine eyes followed me with a fond and melancholy gaze, and she murmured again "Good night, dear friend."

Young people like, and even love, on impulse. I was flattered by the evident, though as yet undeserved, fondness she showed me. I liked the confidence with which she at once received me. She was determined that we should be very near friends.

Next day came and we met again. I was delighted with my companion; that is to say, in many respects.

Her looks lost nothing in daylight—she was certainly the most beautiful creature I had ever seen, and the unpleasant remembrance of the face presented in my early dream, had lost the effect of the first unexpected recognition.

She confessed that she had experienced a similar shock on seeing me, and precisely the same faint antipathy that had mingled with my admiration of her. We now laughed together over our momentary horrors.

IV. HER HABITS—A SAUNTER

I told you that I was charmed with her in most particulars.

There were some that did not please me so well.

She was above the middle height of women. I shall begin by describing her.

She was slender, and wonderfully graceful. Except that her movements were languid—very languid—indeed, there was nothing in her appearance to indicate an invalid. Her complexion was rich and brilliant; her features were small and beautifully formed; her eyes large, dark, and lustrous; her hair was quite wonderful, I never saw hair so magnificently thick and long when it was down about her shoulders; I have often placed my hands under it, and laughed with wonder at its weight. It was exquisitely fine and soft, and in color a rich very dark brown, with something of gold. I loved to let it down, tumbling with its own weight, as, in her room, she lay back in her chair talking in her sweet low voice, I used to fold and braid it, and spread it out and play with it. Heavens! If I had but known all!

I said there were particulars which did not please me. I have told you that her confidence won me the first night I saw her; but I found that she exercised with respect to herself, her mother, her history, everything in fact connected with her life, plans, and people, an ever wakeful reserve. I dare say I was unreasonable, perhaps I was wrong; I dare say I ought to have respected the solemn injunction laid upon my father by the stately lady in black velvet. But curiosity is a restless and unscrupulous passion, and no one girl can endure, with patience, that hers should be baffled by another. What harm could it do anyone to tell me what I so ardently desired to know? Had she no trust in my good sense or honor? Why would she not believe me when I assured her, so solemnly, that I would not divulge one syllable of what she told me to any mortal breathing.

There was a coldness, it seemed to me, beyond her years, in her smiling melancholy persistent refusal to afford me the least ray of light.

I cannot say we quarreled upon this point, for she would not quarrel upon any. It was, of course, very unfair of me to press her, very ill-bred, but I really could not help it; and I might just as well have let it alone.

What she did tell me amounted, in my unconscionable estimation—to nothing.

It was all summed up in three very vague disclosures:

First—Her name was Carmilla.

Second—Her family was very ancient and noble.

Third—Her home lay in the direction of the west.

She would not tell me the name of her family, nor their armorial bearings, nor the name of their estate, nor even that of the country they lived in.

You are not to suppose that I worried her incessantly on these subjects. I watched opportunity, and rather insinuated than urged my inquiries. Once or twice, indeed, I did attack her more directly. But no matter what my tactics, utter failure was invariably the result. Reproaches and caresses were all lost upon her. But I must add this, that her evasion was conducted with so pretty a melancholy and deprecation, with so many, and even passionate declarations of her liking for me, and trust in my honor, and with so many promises that I should at last know all, that I could not find it in my heart long to be offended with her.

She used to place her pretty arms about my neck, draw me to her, and laying her cheek to mine, murmur with her lips near my ear, "Dearest, your little heart is wounded; think me not cruel because I obey the irresistible law of my strength and weakness; if your dear heart is wounded, my wild heart bleeds with yours. In the rapture of my enormous humiliation I live in your warm life, and you shall die—die, sweetly die—into mine. I cannot help it; as I draw near to you, you, in your turn, will draw near to others, and learn the rapture of that cruelty, which yet is love; so, for a while, seek to know no more of me and mine, but trust me with all your loving spirit."

And when she had spoken such a rhapsody, she would press me more closely in her trembling embrace, and her lips in soft kisses gently glow upon my cheek.

Her agitations and her language were unintelligible to me.

From these foolish embraces, which were not of very frequent occurrence, I must allow, I used to wish to extricate myself; but my energies seemed to fail me. Her murmured words sounded like a lullaby in my ear, and soothed my resistance into a trance, from which I only seemed to recover myself when she withdrew her arms.

In these mysterious moods I did not like her. I experienced a strange tumultuous excitement that was pleasurable, ever and anon, mingled with a vague sense of fear and disgust. I had no distinct thoughts about her while such scenes lasted, but I was conscious of a love growing into adoration, and also of abhorrence. This I know is paradox, but I can make no other attempt to explain the feeling.

I now write, after an interval of more than ten years, with a trembling hand, with a confused and horrible recollection of certain occurrences and situations, in the ordeal through which I was unconsciously passing; though with a vivid and very sharp remembrance of the main current of my story.

But, I suspect, in all lives there are certain emotional scenes, those in which our passions have been most wildly and terribly roused, that are of all others the most vaguely and dimly remembered.

Sometimes after an hour of apathy, my strange and beautiful companion would take my hand and hold it with a fond pressure, renewed again and again; blushing softly, gazing in my face with languid and burning eyes, and breathing so fast that her dress rose and fell with the tumultuous respiration. It was like the ardor of a lover; it embarrassed me; it was hateful and yet over-powering; and with gloating eyes she drew me to her, and her hot lips traveled along my cheek in kisses; and she would whisper, almost in sobs, "You are mine, you shall be mine, you and I are one for ever." Then she had thrown herself back in her chair, with her small hands over her eyes, leaving me trembling.

"Are we related," I used to ask; "what can you mean by all this? I remind you perhaps of someone whom you love; but you must not, I hate it; I don't know you—I don't know myself when you look so and talk so."

She used to sigh at my vehemence, then turn away and drop my hand.

Respecting these very extraordinary manifestations I strove in vain to form any satisfactory theory—I could not refer them to affectation or trick. It was unmistakably the momentary breaking out of suppressed instinct and emotion. Was she, notwithstanding her mother's volunteered denial, subject to brief visitations of insanity; or was there here a disguise and a romance? I had read in old storybooks of such things. What if a boyish lover had found his way into the house, and sought to prosecute his suit in masquerade, with the assistance of a clever old adventuress. But there were many things against this hypothesis, highly interesting as it was to my vanity.

I could boast of no little attentions such as masculine gallantry delights to offer. Between these passionate moments there were long intervals of commonplace, of gaiety, of brooding melancholy, during which, except that I detected her eyes so full of melancholy fire, following me, at times I might have been as nothing to her. Except in these brief periods of mysterious excitement her ways were girlish; and there was always a languor about her, quite incompatible with a masculine system in a state of health.

In some respects her habits were odd. Perhaps not so singular in the opinion of a town lady like you, as they appeared to us rustic people. She used to come down very late, generally not till one o'clock, she would then take a cup of chocolate, but eat nothing; we then went out for a walk, which was a mere saunter, and she seemed, almost immediately, exhausted, and either returned to the schloss or sat on one of the benches that were placed, here and there, among the trees. This was a bodily languor in which her mind did not sympathize. She was always an animated talker, and very intelligent.

She sometimes alluded for a moment to her own home, or mentioned an adventure or situation, or an early recollection, which indicated a people of strange manners, and described customs of which we knew nothing. I gathered from these chance hints that her native country was much more remote than I had at first fancied.

As we sat thus one afternoon under the trees a funeral passed us by. It was that of a pretty young girl, whom I had often seen, the daughter of one of the rangers of the forest. The poor man was walking behind the coffin of his darling; she was his only child, and he looked quite heartbroken.

Peasants walking two-and-two came behind, they were singing a funeral hymn.

I rose to mark my respect as they passed, and joined in the hymn they were very sweetly singing.

My companion shook me a little roughly, and I turned surprised.

She said brusquely, "Don't you perceive how discordant that is?"

"I think it very sweet, on the contrary," I answered, vexed at the interruption, and very uncomfortable, lest the people who composed the little procession should observe and resent what was passing.

I resumed, therefore, instantly, and was again interrupted. "You pierce my ears," said Carmilla, almost angrily, and stopping her ears with her tiny fingers. "Besides, how can you tell that your religion and mine are the same; your forms wound me, and I hate funerals. What a fuss! Why you must die—everyone must die; and all are happier when they do. Come home."

"My father has gone on with the clergyman to the churchyard. I thought you knew she was to be buried today."

"She? I don't trouble my head about peasants. I don't know who she is," answered Carmilla, with a flash from her fine eyes.

"She is the poor girl who fancied she saw a ghost a fortnight ago, and has been dying ever since, till yesterday, when she expired."

"Tell me nothing about ghosts. I shan't sleep tonight if you do."

"I hope there is no plague or fever coming; all this looks very like it," I continued. "The swineherd's young wife died only a week ago, and she thought something seized her by the throat as she lay in her bed, and nearly strangled her. Papa says such horrible fancies do accompany some forms of fever. She was quite well the day before. She sank afterwards, and died before a week."

"Well, her funeral is over, I hope, and her hymn sung; and our ears shan't be tortured with that discord and jargon. It has made me nervous. Sit down here, beside me; sit close; hold my hand; press it hard-hard-harder."

We had moved a little back, and had come to another seat.

She sat down. Her face underwent a change that alarmed and even terrified me for a moment. It darkened, and became horribly livid; her teeth and hands were clenched, and she frowned and compressed her lips, while she stared down upon the ground at her feet, and trembled all over with a continued shudder as irrepressible as ague. All her energies seemed strained to suppress a fit, with which she was then breathlessly tugging; and at length a low convulsive cry of suffering broke from her, and gradually the hysteria subsided. "There! That comes of strangling people with hymns!" she said at last. "Hold me, hold me still. It is passing away."

And so gradually it did; and perhaps to dissipate the somber impression which the spectacle had left upon me, she became unusually animated and chatty; and so we got home.

This was the first time I had seen her exhibit any definable symptoms of that delicacy of health which her mother had spoken of. It was the first time, also, I had seen her exhibit anything like temper.

Both passed away like a summer cloud; and never but once afterwards did I witness on her part a momentary sign of anger. I will tell you how it happened.

She and I were looking out of one of the long drawing room windows, when there entered the courtyard, over the drawbridge, a figure of a wanderer whom I knew very well. He used to visit the schloss generally twice a year.

It was the figure of a hunchback, with the sharp lean features that generally accompany deformity. He wore a pointed black beard, and he was smiling from ear to ear, showing his white fangs. He was dressed in buff, black, and scarlet, and crossed with more straps and belts than I could count, from which hung all manner of things. Behind, he carried a magic lantern, and two boxes, which I well knew, in one of which was a salamander, and in the other a mandrake. These monsters used to make my father laugh. They were compounded of parts of monkeys, parrots, squirrels, fish, and hedgehogs, dried and stitched together with great neatness and startling effect. He had a fiddle, a box of conjuring apparatus, a pair of foils and masks attached to his belt, several other mysterious cases dangling about him, and a black staff with copper ferrules in his hand. His companion was a rough spare dog, that followed at his heels, but stopped short, suspiciously at the drawbridge, and in a little while began to howl dismally.

In the meantime, the mountebank, standing in the midst of the court-yard, raised his grotesque hat, and made us a very ceremonious bow, paying his compliments very volubly in execrable French, and German not much better.

Then, disengaging his fiddle, he began to scrape a lively air to which he sang with a merry discord, dancing with ludicrous airs and activity, that made me laugh, in spite of the dog's howling.

Then he advanced to the window with many smiles and salutations, and his hat in his left hand, his fiddle under his arm, and with a fluency that never took breath, he gabbled a long advertisement of all his accomplishments, and the resources of the various arts which he placed at our service, and the curiosities and entertainments which it was in his power, at our bidding, to display.

"Will your ladyships be pleased to buy an amulet against the oupire[57], which is going like the wolf, I hear, through these woods," he said dropping his hat on the pavement. "They are dying of it right and left and here is a charm that never fails; only pinned to the pillow, and you may laugh in his face."

These charms consisted of oblong slips of vellum, with cabalistic ciphers and diagrams upon them.

Carmilla instantly purchased one, and so did I.

He was looking up, and we were smiling down upon him, amused; at least, I can answer for myself. His piercing black eye, as he looked up in our faces, seemed to detect something that fixed for a moment his curiosity. In an instant he unrolled a leather case, full of all manner of odd little steel instruments.

"See here, my lady," he said, displaying it, and addressing me, "I profess, among other things less useful, the art of dentistry. Plague take the dog!" he interpolated. "Silence, beast! He howls so that your ladyships can scarcely hear a word. Your noble friend, the young lady at your right, has the sharpest tooth,—long, thin, pointed, like an awl, like a needle; ha, ha! With my sharp and long sight, as I look up, I have seen it distinctly; now if it happens to hurt the young lady, and I think it must, here am I, here are my file, my punch, my nippers; I will make it round and blunt, if her ladyship pleases; no longer the tooth of a fish, but of a beautiful young lady as she is. Hey? Is the young lady displeased? Have I been too bold? Have I offended her?"

---

57 Vampire of Polish folklore.

The young lady, indeed, looked very angry as she drew back from the window.

"How dares that mountebank insult us so? Where is your father? I shall demand redress from him. My father would have had the wretch tied up to the pump, and flogged with a cart whip, and burnt to the bones with the cattle brand!"

She retired from the window a step or two, and sat down, and had hardly lost sight of the offender, when her wrath subsided as suddenly as it had risen, and she gradually recovered her usual tone, and seemed to forget the little hunchback and his follies.

My father was out of spirits that evening. On coming in he told us that there had been another case very similar to the two fatal ones which had lately occurred. The sister of a young peasant on his estate, only a mile away, was very ill, had been, as she described it, attacked very nearly in the same way, and was now slowly but steadily sinking.

"All this," said my father, "is strictly referable to natural causes. These poor people infect one another with their superstitions, and so repeat in imagination the images of terror that have infested their neighbors."

"But that very circumstance frightens one horribly," said Carmilla.

"How so?" inquired my father.

"I am so afraid of fancying I see such things; I think it would be as bad as reality."

"We are in God's hands: nothing can happen without his permission, and all will end well for those who love him. He is our faithful creator; He has made us all, and will take care of us."

"Creator! Nature!" said the young lady in answer to my gentle father. "And this disease that invades the country is natural. Nature. All things proceed from Nature—don't they? All things in the heaven, in the earth, and under the earth, act and live as Nature ordains? I think so."

"The doctor said he would come here today," said my father, after a silence. "I want to know what he thinks about it, and what he thinks we had better do."

"Doctors never did me any good," said Carmilla.

"Then you have been ill?" I asked.

"More ill than ever you were," she answered.

"Long ago?"

"Yes, a long time. I suffered from this very illness; but I forget all but my pain and weakness, and they were not so bad as are suffered in other diseases."

"You were very young then?"

"I dare say, let us talk no more of it. You would not wound a friend?"

She looked languidly in my eyes, and passed her arm round my waist lovingly, and led me out of the room. My father was busy over some papers near the window.

"Why does your papa like to frighten us?" said the pretty girl with a sigh and a little shudder.

"He doesn't, dear Carmilla, it is the very furthest thing from his mind."

"Are you afraid, dearest?"

"I should be very much if I fancied there was any real danger of my being attacked as those poor people were."

"You are afraid to die?"

"Yes, every one is."

"But to die as lovers may—to die together, so that they may live together.

"Girls are caterpillars while they live in the world, to be finally butterflies when the summer comes; but in the meantime there are grubs and larvae, don't you see—each with their peculiar propensities, necessities and structure. So says Monsieur Buffon, in his big book, in the next room."

Later in the day the doctor came, and was closeted with papa for some time.

He was a skilful man, of sixty and upwards, he wore powder, and shaved his pale face as smooth as a pumpkin. He and papa emerged from the room together, and I heard papa laugh, and say as they came out:

"Well, I do wonder at a wise man like you. What do you say to hippogriffs and dragons?"

The doctor was smiling, and made answer, shaking his head—

"Nevertheless life and death are mysterious states, and we know little of the resources of either."

And so they walked on, and I heard no more. I did not then know what the doctor had been broaching, but I think I guess it now.

V. A WONDERFUL LIKENESS

This evening there arrived from Gratz the grave, dark-faced son of the picture cleaner, with a horse and cart laden with two large packing cases, having many pictures in each. It was a journey of ten leagues, and whenever a messenger arrived at the schloss from our little capital of Gratz, we used to crowd about him in the hall, to hear the news.

This arrival created in our secluded quarters quite a sensation. The cases remained in the hall, and the messenger was taken charge of by the servants till he had eaten his supper. Then with assistants, and armed with hammer, ripping chisel, and turnscrew, he met us in the hall, where we had assembled to witness the unpacking of the cases.

Carmilla sat looking listlessly on, while one after the other the old pictures, nearly all portraits, which had undergone the process of renovation, were brought to light. My mother was of an old Hungarian family, and most of these pictures, which were about to be restored to their places, had come to us through her.

My father had a list in his hand, from which he read, as the artist rummaged out the corresponding numbers. I don't know that the pictures were very good, but they were, undoubtedly, very old, and some of them very curious also. They had, for the most part, the merit of being now seen by me, I may say, for the first time; for the smoke and dust of time had all but obliterated them.

"There is a picture that I have not seen yet," said my father. "In one corner, at the top of it, is the name, as well as I could read, 'Marcia Karnstein,' and the date '1698'; and I am curious to see how it has turned out."

I remembered it; it was a small picture, about a foot and a half high, and nearly square, without a frame; but it was so blackened by age that I could not make it out.

The artist now produced it, with evident pride. It was quite beautiful; it was startling; it seemed to live. It was the effigy of Carmilla!

"Carmilla, dear, here is an absolute miracle. Here you are, living, smiling, ready to speak, in this picture. Isn't it beautiful, Papa? And see, even the little mole on her throat."

My father laughed, and said "Certainly it is a wonderful likeness," but he looked away, and to my surprise seemed but little struck by it, and went on talking to the picture cleaner, who was also something of an artist, and discoursed with intelligence about the portraits or other works, which his art had just brought into light and color, while I was more and more lost in wonder the more I looked at the picture.

"Will you let me hang this picture in my room, papa?" I asked.

"Certainly, dear," said he, smiling, "I'm very glad you think it so like. It must be prettier even than I thought it, if it is."

The young lady did not acknowledge this pretty speech, did not seem to hear it. She was leaning back in her seat, her fine eyes under their long lashes gazing on me in contemplation, and she smiled in a kind of rapture.

"And now you can read quite plainly the name that is written in the corner. It is not Marcia; it looks as if it was done in gold. The name is Mircalla, Countess Karnstein, and this is a little coronet over and underneath A.D. 1698. I am descended from the Karnsteins; that is, mamma was."

"Ah!" said the lady, languidly, "so am I, I think, a very long descent, very ancient. Are there any Karnsteins living now?"

"None who bear the name, I believe. The family were ruined, I believe, in some civil wars, long ago, but the ruins of the castle are only about three miles away."

"How interesting!" she said, languidly. "But see what beautiful moonlight!" She glanced through the hall door, which stood a little open. "Suppose you take a little ramble round the court, and look down at the road and river."

"It is so like the night you came to us," I said.

She sighed; smiling.

She rose, and each with her arm about the other's waist, we walked out upon the pavement.

In silence, slowly we walked down to the drawbridge, where the beautiful landscape opened before us.

"And so you were thinking of the night I came here?" she almost whispered.

"Are you glad I came?"

"Delighted, dear Carmilla," I answered.

"And you asked for the picture you think like me, to hang in your room," she murmured with a sigh, as she drew her arm closer about my waist, and let her pretty head sink upon my shoulder. "How romantic you are, Carmilla," I said. "Whenever you tell me your story, it will be made up chiefly of some one great romance."

She kissed me silently.

"I am sure, Carmilla, you have been in love; that there is, at this moment, an affair of the heart going on."

"I have been in love with no one, and never shall," she whispered, "unless it should be with you."

How beautiful she looked in the moonlight!

Shy and strange was the look with which she quickly hid her face in my neck and hair, with tumultuous sighs, that seemed almost to sob, and pressed in mine a hand that trembled.

Her soft cheek was glowing against mine. "Darling, darling," she murmured, "I live in you; and you would die for me, I love you so."

I started from her.

She was gazing on me with eyes from which all fire, all meaning had flown, and a face colorless and apathetic.

"Is there a chill in the air, dear?" she said drowsily. "I almost shiver; have I been dreaming? Let us come in. Come; come; come in."

"You look ill, Carmilla; a little faint. You certainly must take some wine," I said.

"Yes. I will. I'm better now. I shall be quite well in a few minutes. Yes, do give me a little wine," answered Carmilla, as we approached the door.

"Let us look again for a moment; it is the last time, perhaps, I shall see the moonlight with you."

"How do you feel now, dear Carmilla? Are you really better?" I asked.

I was beginning to take alarm, lest she should have been stricken with the strange epidemic that they said had invaded the country about us.

"Papa would be grieved beyond measure," I added, "if he thought you were ever so little ill, without immediately letting us know. We have a very skilful doctor near us, the physician who was with papa today."

"I'm sure he is. I know how kind you all are; but, dear child, I am quite well again. There is nothing ever wrong with me, but a little weakness.

"People say I am languid; I am incapable of exertion; I can scarcely walk as far as a child of three years old: and every now and then the little strength I have falters, and I become as you have just seen me. But after all I am very easily set up again; in a moment I am perfectly myself. See how I have recovered."

So, indeed, she had; and she and I talked a great deal, and very animated she was; and the remainder of that evening passed without any recurrence of what I called her infatuations. I mean her crazy talk and looks, which embarrassed, and even frightened me.

But there occurred that night an event which gave my thoughts quite a new turn, and seemed to startle even Carmilla's languid nature into momentary energy.

VI. A VERY STRANGE AGONY

When we got into the drawing room, and had sat down to our coffee and chocolate, although Carmilla did not take any, she seemed quite herself again, and Madame, and Mademoiselle De Lafontaine, joined us, and made a little card party, in the course of which papa came in for what he called his "dish of tea."

When the game was over he sat down beside Carmilla on the sofa, and asked her, a little anxiously, whether she had heard from her mother since her arrival.

She answered "No."

He then asked whether she knew where a letter would reach her at present.

"I cannot tell," she answered ambiguously, "but I have been thinking of leaving you; you have been already too hospitable and too kind to me. I have given you an infinity of trouble, and I should wish to take a carriage tomorrow, and post in pursuit of her; I know where I shall ultimately find her, although I dare not yet tell you."

"But you must not dream of any such thing," exclaimed my father, to my great relief. "We can't afford to lose you so, and I won't consent to your leaving us, except under the care of your mother, who was so good as to consent to your remaining with us till she should herself return. I should be quite happy if I knew that you heard from her: but this evening the accounts of the progress of the mysterious disease that has invaded our neighborhood, grow even more alarming; and my beautiful guest, I do feel the responsibility, unaided by advice from your mother, very much. But I shall do my best; and one thing is certain, that you must not think of leaving us without her distinct direction to that effect. We should suffer too much in parting from you to consent to it easily."

"Thank you, sir, a thousand times for your hospitality," she answered, smiling bashfully. "You have all been too kind to me; I have seldom been so happy in all my life before, as in your beautiful chateau, under your care, and in the society of your dear daughter."

So he gallantly, in his old-fashioned way, kissed her hand, smiling and pleased at her little speech.

I accompanied Carmilla as usual to her room, and sat and chatted with her while she was preparing for bed.

"Do you think," I said at length, "that you will ever confide fully in me?"

She turned round smiling, but made no answer, only continued to smile on me.

"You won't answer that?" I said. "You can't answer pleasantly; I ought not to have asked you."

"You were quite right to ask me that, or anything. You do not know how dear you are to me, or you could not think any confidence too great to look for. But I am under vows, no nun half so awfully, and I dare not tell my story yet, even to you. The time is very near when you shall know everything. You will think me cruel, very selfish, but love is always selfish; the more ardent the more selfish. How jealous I am you cannot know. You must come with me, loving me, to death; or else hate me and still come with me, and hating me through death and after. There is no such word as indifference in my apathetic nature."

"Now, Carmilla, you are going to talk your wild nonsense again," I said hastily.

"Not I, silly little fool as I am, and full of whims and fancies; for your sake I'll talk like a sage. Were you ever at a ball?"

"No; how you do run on. What is it like? How charming it must be."

"I almost forget, it is years ago."

I laughed.

"You are not so old. Your first ball can hardly be forgotten yet."

"I remember everything about it—with an effort. I see it all, as divers see what is going on above them, through a medium, dense, rippling, but transparent. There occurred that night what has confused the picture, and made its colours faint. I was all but assassinated in my bed, wounded here," she touched her breast, "and never was the same since."

"Were you near dying?"

"Yes, very—a cruel love—strange love, that would have taken my life. Love will have its sacrifices. No sacrifice without blood. Let us go to sleep now; I feel so lazy. How can I get up just now and lock my door?"

She was lying with her tiny hands buried in her rich wavy hair, under her cheek, her little head upon the pillow, and her glittering eyes followed me wherever I moved, with a kind of shy smile that I could not decipher.

I bid her good night, and crept from the room with an uncomfortable sensation.

I often wondered whether our pretty guest ever said her prayers. I certainly had never seen her upon her knees. In the morning she never came down until long after our family prayers were over, and at night she never left the drawing room to attend our brief evening prayers in the hall.

If it had not been that it had casually come out in one of our careless talks that she had been baptised, I should have doubted her being a Christian. Religion was a subject on which I had never heard her speak a word. If I had known the world better, this particular neglect or antipathy would not have so much surprised me.

The precautions of nervous people are infectious, and persons of a like temperament are pretty sure, after a time, to imitate them. I had adopted Carmilla's habit of locking her bedroom door, having taken into my head all her whimsical alarms about midnight invaders and prowling assassins. I had also adopted her precaution of making a brief search through her room, to satisfy herself that no lurking assassin or robber was "ensconced."

These wise measures taken, I got into my bed and fell asleep. A light was burning in my room. This was an old habit, of very early date, and which nothing could have tempted me to dispense with.

Thus fortified I might take my rest in peace. But dreams come through stone walls, light up dark rooms, or darken light ones, and their persons make their exits and their entrances as they please, and laugh at locksmiths.

I had a dream that night that was the beginning of a very strange agony. I cannot call it a nightmare, for I was quite conscious of being asleep.

But I was equally conscious of being in my room, and lying in bed, precisely as I actually was. I saw, or fancied I saw, the room and its furniture just as I had seen it last, except that it was very dark, and I saw something moving round the foot of the bed, which at first I could not accurately distinguish. But I soon saw that it was a sooty-black animal that resembled a monstrous cat. It appeared to me about four or five feet long for it measured fully the length of the hearthrug as it passed over it; and it continued to-ing and fro-ing with the lithe, sinister restlessness of a beast in a cage. I could not cry out, although as you may suppose, I was terrified. Its pace was growing faster, and the room rapidly darker and darker, and at length so dark that I could no longer see anything of it but its eyes. I felt it spring lightly on the bed. The two broad eyes approached my face, and suddenly I felt a stinging pain as if two large needles darted, an inch or two apart, deep into my breast. I waked with a scream. The room was lighted by the candle that burnt there all through the night, and I saw a female figure standing at the foot of the bed, a little at the right side. It was in a dark loose dress, and its hair was down and covered its shoulders. A block of stone could not have been more still. There was not the slightest stir of respiration. As I stared at it, the figure appeared to have changed its place, and was now nearer the door; then, close to it, the door opened, and it passed out.

I was now relieved, and able to breathe and move. My first thought was that Carmilla had been playing me a trick, and that I had forgotten to secure my door. I hastened to it, and found it locked as usual on the inside. I was afraid to open it—I was horrified. I sprang into my bed and covered my head up in the bedclothes, and lay there more dead than alive till morning.

VII. DESCENDING

*I*t would be vain my attempting to tell you the horror with which, even now, I recall the occurrence of that night. It was no such transitory terror as a dream leaves behind it. It seemed to deepen by time, and communicated itself to the room and the very furniture that had encompassed the apparition.

I could not bear next day to be alone for a moment. I should have told papa, but for two opposite reasons. At one time I thought he would laugh at my story, and I could not bear its being treated as a jest; and at another I thought he might fancy that I had been attacked by the mysterious complaint which had invaded our neighborhood. I had myself no misgiving of the kind, and as he had been rather an invalid for some time, I was afraid of alarming him.

I was comfortable enough with my good-natured companions, Madame Perrodon, and the vivacious Mademoiselle Lafontaine. They both perceived that I was out of spirits and nervous, and at length I told them what lay so heavy at my heart.

Mademoiselle laughed, but I fancied that Madame Perrodon looked anxious.

"By-the-by," said Mademoiselle, laughing, "the long lime tree walk, behind Carmilla's bedroom window, is haunted!"

"Nonsense!" exclaimed Madame, who probably thought the theme rather inopportune, "and who tells that story, my dear?"

"Martin says that he came up twice, when the old yard gate was being repaired, before sunrise, and twice saw the same female figure walking down the lime tree avenue."

"So he well might, as long as there are cows to milk in the river fields," said Madame.

"I daresay; but Martin chooses to be frightened, and never did I see fool more frightened."

"You must not say a word about it to Carmilla, because she can see down that walk from her room window," I interposed, "and she is, if possible, a greater coward than I."

Carmilla came down rather later than usual that day.

"I was so frightened last night," she said, so soon as were together, "and I am sure I should have seen something dreadful if it had not been for that charm I bought from the poor little hunchback whom I called such hard names. I had a dream of something black coming round my bed, and I awoke in a perfect horror, and I really thought, for some seconds, I saw a dark figure near the chimney-piece, but I felt under my pillow for my charm, and the moment my fingers touched it, the figure disappeared, and I felt quite certain, only that I had it by me, that something frightful would have made its appearance, and, perhaps, throttled me, as it did those poor people we heard of.

"Well, listen to me," I began, and recounted my adventure, at the recital of which she appeared horrified.

"And had you the charm near you?" she asked, earnestly.

"No, I had dropped it into a china vase in the drawing room, but I shall certainly take it with me tonight, as you have so much faith in it."

At this distance of time I cannot tell you, or even understand, how I overcame my horror so effectually as to lie alone in my room that night. I remember distinctly that I pinned the charm to my pillow. I fell asleep almost immediately, and slept even more soundly than usual all night.

Next night I passed as well. My sleep was delightfully deep and dreamless.

But I wakened with a sense of lassitude and melancholy, which, however, did not exceed a degree that was almost luxurious.

"Well, I told you so," said Carmilla, when I described my quiet sleep, "I had such delightful sleep myself last night; I pinned the charm to the breast of my nightdress. It was too far away the night before. I am quite sure it was all fancy, except the dreams. I used to think that evil spirits made dreams, but our doctor told me it is no such thing. Only a fever passing by, or some other malady, as they often do, he said, knocks at the door, and not being able to get in, passes on, with that alarm."

"And what do you think the charm is?" said I.

"It has been fumigated or immersed in some drug, and is an antidote against the malaria," she answered.

"Then it acts only on the body?"

"Certainly; you don't suppose that evil spirits are frightened by bits of ribbon, or the perfumes of a druggist's shop? No, these complaints, wandering in the air, begin by trying the nerves, and so infect the brain, but before they can seize upon you, the antidote repels them. That I am sure is what the charm has done for us. It is nothing magical, it is simply natural."

I should have been happier if I could have quite agreed with Carmilla, but I did my best, and the impression was a little losing its force.

For some nights I slept profoundly; but still every morning I felt the same lassitude, and a languor weighed upon me all day. I felt myself a changed girl. A strange melancholy was stealing over me, a melancholy that I would not have interrupted. Dim thoughts of death began to open, and an idea that I was slowly sinking took gentle, and, somehow, not unwelcome, possession of me. If it was sad, the tone of mind which this induced was also sweet.

Whatever it might be, my soul acquiesced in it.

I would not admit that I was ill, I would not consent to tell my papa, or to have the doctor sent for.

Carmilla became more devoted to me than ever, and her strange paroxysms of languid adoration more frequent. She used to gloat on me with increasing ardor the more my strength and spirits waned. This always shocked me like a momentary glare of insanity.

Without knowing it, I was now in a pretty advanced stage of the strangest illness under which mortal ever suffered. There was an unaccountable fascination in its earlier symptoms that more than reconciled me to the incapacitating effect of that stage of the malady. This fascination increased for a time, until it reached a certain point, when gradually a sense of the horrible mingled itself with it, deepening, as you shall hear, until it discolored and perverted the whole state of my life.

The first change I experienced was rather agreeable. It was very near the turning point from which began the descent of Avernus[58].

Certain vague and strange sensations visited me in my sleep. The prevailing one was of that pleasant, peculiar cold thrill which we feel in bathing, when we move against the current of a river. This was soon accompanied by dreams that seemed interminable, and were so vague that I could never recollect their scenery and persons, or any one connected portion of their action. But they left an awful impression, and a sense of exhaustion, as if I had passed through a long period of great mental exertion and danger.

After all these dreams there remained on waking a remembrance of having been in a place very nearly dark, and of having spoken to people whom I could not see; and especially of one clear voice, of a female's, very deep, that spoke as if at a distance, slowly, and producing always the same sensation of indescribable solemnity and fear. Sometimes there came a sensation as if a hand was drawn softly along my cheek and neck. Sometimes it was as if warm lips kissed me, and longer and longer and more lovingly as they reached my throat, but there the caress fixed itself. My heart beat faster, my breathing rose and fell rapidly and full drawn; a sobbing, that rose into a sense of strangulation, supervened, and turned into a dreadful convulsion, in which my senses left me and I became unconscious.

It was now three weeks since the commencement of this unaccountable state.

My sufferings had, during the last week, told upon my appearance. I had grown pale, my eyes were dilated and darkened underneath, and the languor which I had long felt began to display itself in my countenance.

My father asked me often whether I was ill; but, with an obstinacy which now seems to me unaccountable, I persisted in assuring him that I was quite well.

In a sense this was true. I had no pain, I could complain of no bodily derangement. My complaint seemed to be one of the imagination, or the nerves, and, horrible as my sufferings were, I kept them, with a morbid reserve, very nearly to myself.

It could not be that terrible complaint which the peasants called the oupire, for I had now been suffering for three weeks, and they were seldom ill for much more than three days, when death put an end to their miseries.

Carmilla complained of dreams and feverish sensations, but by no means of so alarming a kind as mine. I say that mine were extremely alarming. Had I been capable of comprehending my condition, I would have invoked aid and advice on my knees. The narcotic of an unsuspected influence was acting upon me, and my perceptions were benumbed.

---

58 Lake near Naples, Italy, thought to be the entrance to Hell.

I am going to tell you now of a dream that led immediately to an odd discovery.

One night, instead of the voice I was accustomed to hear in the dark, I heard one, sweet and tender, and at the same time terrible, which said, "Your mother warns you to beware of the assassin." At the same time a light unexpectedly sprang up, and I saw Carmilla, standing, near the foot of my bed, in her white nightdress, bathed, from her chin to her feet, in one great stain of blood.

I wakened with a shriek, possessed with the one idea that Carmilla was being murdered. I remember springing from my bed, and my next recollection is that of standing on the lobby, crying for help.

Madame and Mademoiselle came scurrying out of their rooms in alarm; a lamp burned always on the lobby, and seeing me, they soon learned the cause of my terror.

I insisted on our knocking at Carmilla's door. Our knocking was unanswered.

It soon became a pounding and an uproar. We shrieked her name, but all was vain.

We all grew frightened, for the door was locked. We hurried back, in panic, to my room. There we rang the bell long and furiously. If my father's room had been at that side of the house, we would have called him up at once to our aid. But, alas! he was quite out of hearing, and to reach him involved an excursion for which we none of us had courage.

Servants, however, soon came running up the stairs; I had got on my dressing gown and slippers meanwhile, and my companions were already similarly furnished. Recognizing the voices of the servants on the lobby, we sallied out together; and having renewed, as fruitlessly, our summons at Carmilla's door, I ordered the men to force the lock. They did so, and we stood, holding our lights aloft, in the doorway, and so stared into the room.

We called her by name; but there was still no reply. We looked round the room. Everything was undisturbed. It was exactly in the state in which I had left it on bidding her good night. But Carmilla was gone.

VIII. SEARCH

*Q*t sight of the room, perfectly undisturbed except for our violent entrance, we began to cool a little, and soon recovered our senses sufficiently to dismiss the men. It had struck Mademoiselle that possibly Carmilla had been wakened by the uproar at her door, and in her first panic had jumped from her bed, and hid herself in a press, or behind a curtain, from which she could not, of course, emerge until the majordomo and his myrmidons had withdrawn. We now recommenced our search, and began to call her name again.

It was all to no purpose. Our perplexity and agitation increased. We examined the windows, but they were secured. I implored of Carmilla, if she had concealed herself, to play this cruel trick no longer—to come out and to end our anxieties. It was all useless. I was by this time convinced that she was not in the room, nor in the dressing room, the door of which was still locked on this side. She could not have passed it. I was utterly puzzled. Had Carmilla discovered one of those secret passages which the old housekeeper said were known to exist in the schloss, although the tradition of their exact situation had been lost? A little time would, no doubt, explain all—utterly perplexed as, for the present, we were.

It was past four o'clock, and I preferred passing the remaining hours of darkness in Madame's room. Daylight brought no solution of the difficulty.

The whole household, with my father at its head, was in a state of agitation next morning. Every part of the chateau was searched. The grounds were explored. No trace of the missing lady could be discovered. The stream was about to be dragged; my father was in distraction; what a tale to have to tell the poor girl's mother on her return. I, too, was almost beside myself, though my grief was quite of a different kind.

The morning was passed in alarm and excitement. It was now one o'clock, and still no tidings. I ran up to Carmilla's room, and found her standing at her dressing table. I was astounded. I could not believe my eyes. She beckoned me to her with her pretty finger, in silence. Her face expressed extreme fear.

I ran to her in an ecstasy of joy; I kissed and embraced her again and again. I ran to the bell and rang it vehemently, to bring others to the spot who might at once relieve my father's anxiety.

"Dear Carmilla, what has become of you all this time? We have been in agonies of anxiety about you," I exclaimed. "Where have you been? How did you come back?"

"Last night has been a night of wonders," she said.

"For mercy's sake, explain all you can."

"It was past two last night," she said, "when I went to sleep as usual in my bed, with my doors locked, that of the dressing room, and that opening upon the gallery. My sleep was uninterrupted, and, so far as I know, dreamless; but I woke just now on the sofa in the dressing room there, and I found the door between the rooms open, and the other door forced. How could all this have happened without my being wakened? It must have been accompanied with a great deal of noise, and I am particularly easily wakened; and how could I have been carried out of my bed without my sleep having been interrupted, I whom the slightest stir startles?"

By this time, Madame, Mademoiselle, my father, and a number of the servants were in the room. Carmilla was, of course, overwhelmed with inquiries, congratulations, and welcomes. She had but one story to tell, and seemed the least able of all the party to suggest any way of accounting for what had happened.

My father took a turn up and down the room, thinking. I saw Carmilla's eye follow him for a moment with a sly, dark glance.

When my father had sent the servants away, Mademoiselle having gone in search of a little bottle of valerian and salvolatile, and there being no one now in the room with Carmilla, except my father, Madame, and myself, he came to her thoughtfully, took her hand very kindly, led her to the sofa, and sat down beside her.

"Will you forgive me, my dear, if I risk a conjecture, and ask a question?"

"Who can have a better right?" she said. "Ask what you please, and I will tell you everything. But my story is simply one of bewilderment and darkness. I know absolutely nothing. Put any question you please, but you know, of course, the limitations mamma has placed me under."

"Perfectly, my dear child. I need not approach the topics on which she desires our silence. Now, the marvel of last night consists in your having been removed from your bed and your room, without being wakened, and this removal having occurred apparently while the windows were still secured, and the two doors locked upon the inside. I will tell you my theory and ask you a question."

Carmilla was leaning on her hand dejectedly; Madame and I were listening breathlessly.

"Now, my question is this. Have you ever been suspected of walking in your sleep?"

"Never, since I was very young indeed."

"But you did walk in your sleep when you were young?"

"Yes; I know I did. I have been told so often by my old nurse."

My father smiled and nodded.

"Well, what has happened is this. You got up in your sleep, unlocked the door, not leaving the key, as usual, in the lock, but taking it out and locking it on the outside; you again took the key out, and carried it away with you to some one of the five-and-twenty rooms on this floor, or perhaps upstairs or downstairs. There are so many rooms and closets, so much heavy furniture, and such accumulations of lumber, that it would require a week to search this old house thoroughly. Do you see, now, what I mean?"

"I do, but not all," she answered.

"And how, papa, do you account for her finding herself on the sofa in the dressing room, which we had searched so carefully?"

"She came there after you had searched it, still in her sleep, and at last awoke spontaneously, and was as much surprised to find herself where she was as any one else. I wish all mysteries were as easily and innocently explained as yours, Carmilla," he said, laughing. "And so we may congratulate ourselves on the certainty that the most natural explanation of the occurrence is one that involves no drugging, no tampering with locks, no burglars, or poisoners, or witches—nothing that need alarm Carmilla, or anyone else, for our safety."

Carmilla was looking charmingly. Nothing could be more beautiful than her tints. Her beauty was, I think, enhanced by that graceful languor that was peculiar to her. I think my father was silently contrasting her looks with mine, for he said:

"I wish my poor Laura was looking more like herself"; and he sighed.

So our alarms were happily ended, and Carmilla restored to her friends.

IX. THE DOCTOR

*A*s Carmilla would not hear of an attendant sleeping in her room, my father arranged that a servant should sleep outside her door, so that she would not attempt to make another such excursion without being arrested at her own door.

That night passed quietly; and next morning early, the doctor, whom my father had sent for without telling me a word about it, arrived to see me.

Madame accompanied me to the library; and there the grave little doctor, with white hair and spectacles, whom I mentioned before, was waiting to receive me.

I told him my story, and as I proceeded he grew graver and graver.

We were standing, he and I, in the recess of one of the windows, facing one another. When my statement was over, he leaned with his shoulders against the wall, and with his eyes fixed on me earnestly, with an interest in which was a dash of horror.

After a minute's reflection, he asked Madame if he could see my father.

He was sent for accordingly, and as he entered, smiling, he said:

"I dare say, doctor, you are going to tell me that I am an old fool for having brought you here; I hope I am."

But his smile faded into shadow as the doctor, with a very grave face, beckoned him to him.

He and the doctor talked for some time in the same recess where I had just conferred with the physician. It seemed an earnest and argumentative conversation. The room is very large, and I and Madame stood together, burning with curiosity, at the farther end. Not a word could we hear, however, for they spoke in a very low tone, and the deep recess of the window quite concealed the doctor from view, and very nearly my father, whose foot, arm, and shoulder only could we see; and the voices were, I suppose, all the less audible for the sort of closet which the thick wall and window formed.

After a time my father's face looked into the room; it was pale, thoughtful, and, I fancied, agitated.

"Laura, dear, come here for a moment. Madame, we shan't trouble you, the doctor says, at present."

Accordingly I approached, for the first time a little alarmed; for, although I felt very weak, I did not feel ill; and strength, one always fancies, is a thing that may be picked up when we please.

My father held out his hand to me, as I drew near, but he was looking at the doctor, and he said:

"It certainly is very odd; I don't understand it quite. Laura, come here, dear; now attend to Doctor Spielsberg, and recollect yourself."

"You mentioned a sensation like that of two needles piercing the skin, somewhere about your neck, on the night when you experienced your first horrible dream. Is there still any soreness?"

"None at all," I answered.

"Can you indicate with your finger about the point at which you think this occurred?"

"Very little below my throat—here," I answered.

I wore a morning dress, which covered the place I pointed to.

"Now you can satisfy yourself," said the doctor. "You won't mind your papa's lowering your dress a very little. It is necessary, to detect a symptom of the complaint under which you have been suffering."

I acquiesced. It was only an inch or two below the edge of my collar.

"God bless me!—so it is," exclaimed my father, growing pale.

"You see it now with your own eyes," said the doctor, with a gloomy triumph.

"What is it?" I exclaimed, beginning to be frightened.

"Nothing, my dear young lady, but a small blue spot, about the size of the tip of your little finger; and now," he continued, turning to papa, "the question is what is best to be done?"

"Is there any danger?" I urged, in great trepidation.

"I trust not, my dear," answered the doctor. "I don't see why you should not recover. I don't see why you should not begin immediately to get better. That is the point at which the sense of strangulation begins?"

"Yes," I answered.

"And—recollect as well as you can—the same point was a kind of center of that thrill which you described just now, like the current of a cold stream running against you?"

"It may have been; I think it was."

"Ay, you see?" he added, turning to my father. "Shall I say a word to Madame?"

"Certainly," said my father.

He called Madame to him, and said:

"I find my young friend here far from well. It won't be of any great consequence, I hope; but it will be necessary that some steps be taken, which I will explain by-and-by; but in the meantime, Madame, you will be so good as not to let Miss Laura be alone for one moment. That is the only direction I need give for the present. It is indispensable."

"We may rely upon your kindness, Madame, I know," added my father.

Madame satisfied him eagerly.

"And you, dear Laura, I know you will observe the doctor's direction."

"I shall have to ask your opinion upon another patient, whose symptoms slightly resemble those of my daughter, that have just been detailed to you—very much milder in degree, but I believe quite of the same sort. She is a young lady—our guest; but as you say you will be passing this way again this evening, you can't do better than take your supper here, and you can then see her. She does not come down till the afternoon."

"I thank you," said the doctor. "I shall be with you, then, at about seven this evening."

And then they repeated their directions to me and to Madame, and with this parting charge my father left us, and walked out with the doctor; and I saw them pacing together up and down between the road and the moat, on the grassy platform in front of the castle, evidently absorbed in earnest conversation.

The doctor did not return. I saw him mount his horse there, take his leave, and ride away eastward through the forest.

Nearly at the same time I saw the man arrive from Dranfield with the letters, and dismount and hand the bag to my father.

In the meantime, Madame and I were both busy, lost in conjecture as to the reasons of the singular and earnest direction which the doctor and my father had concurred in imposing. Madame, as she afterwards told me, was afraid the doctor apprehended a sudden seizure, and that, without prompt assistance, I might either lose my life in a fit, or at least be seriously hurt.

The interpretation did not strike me; and I fancied, perhaps luckily for my nerves, that the arrangement was prescribed simply to secure a companion, who would prevent my taking too much exercise, or eating unripe fruit, or doing any of the fifty foolish things to which young people are supposed to be prone.

About half an hour after my father came in—he had a letter in his hand—and said:

"This letter had been delayed; it is from General Spielsdorf. He might have been here yesterday, he may not come till tomorrow or he may be here today."

He put the open letter into my hand; but he did not look pleased, as he used when a guest, especially one so much loved as the General, was coming.

On the contrary, he looked as if he wished him at the bottom of the Red Sea. There was plainly something on his mind which he did not choose to divulge.

"Papa, darling, will you tell me this?" said I, suddenly laying my hand on his arm, and looking, I am sure, imploringly in his face.

"Perhaps," he answered, smoothing my hair caressingly over my eyes.

"Does the doctor think me very ill?"

"No, dear; he thinks, if right steps are taken, you will be quite well again, at least, on the high road to a complete recovery, in a day or two," he answered, a little dryly. "I wish our good friend, the General, had chosen any other time; that is, I wish you had been perfectly well to receive him."

"But do tell me, papa," I insisted, "what does he think is the matter with me?"

"Nothing; you must not plague me with questions," he answered, with more irritation than I ever remember him to have displayed before; and seeing that I looked wounded, I suppose, he kissed me, and added, "You shall know all about it in a day or two; that is, all that I know. In the meantime you are not to trouble your head about it."

He turned and left the room, but came back before I had done wondering and puzzling over the oddity of all this; it was merely to say that he was going to Karnstein, and had ordered the carriage to be ready at twelve, and that I and Madame should accompany him; he was going to see the priest who lived near those picturesque grounds, upon business, and as Carmilla had never seen them, she could follow, when she came down, with Mademoiselle, who would bring materials for what you call a picnic, which might be laid for us in the ruined castle.

At twelve o'clock, accordingly, I was ready, and not long after, my father, Madame and I set out upon our projected drive.

Passing the drawbridge we turn to the right, and follow the road over the steep Gothic bridge, westward, to reach the deserted village and ruined castle of Karnstein.

No sylvan drive can be fancied prettier. The ground breaks into gentle hills and hollows, all clothed with beautiful wood, totally destitute of the comparative formality which artificial planting and early culture and pruning impart.

The irregularities of the ground often lead the road out of its course, and cause it to wind beautifully round the sides of broken hollows and the steeper sides of the hills, among varieties of ground almost inexhaustible.

Turning one of these points, we suddenly encountered our old friend, the General, riding towards us, attended by a mounted servant. His portmanteaus[59] were following in a hired wagon, such as we term a cart.

The General dismounted as we pulled up, and, after the usual greetings, was easily persuaded to accept the vacant seat in the carriage and send his horse on with his servant to the schloss.

X. BEREAVED

It was about ten months since we had last seen him: but that time had sufficed to make an alteration of years in his appearance. He had grown thinner; something of gloom and anxiety had taken the place of that cordial serenity which used to characterize his features. His dark blue eyes, always penetrating, now gleamed with a sterner light from under his shaggy grey eyebrows. It was not such a change as grief alone usually induces, and angrier passions seemed to have had their share in bringing it about.

We had not long resumed our drive, when the General began to talk, with his usual soldierly directness, of the bereavement, as he termed it, which he had sustained in the death of his beloved niece and ward; and he then broke out in a tone of intense bitterness and fury, inveighing against the "hellish arts" to which she had fallen a victim, and expressing, with more exasperation than piety, his wonder that Heaven should tolerate so monstrous an indulgence of the lusts and malignity of hell.

---

59 Traveling bag.

My father, who saw at once that something very extraordinary had befallen, asked him, if not too painful to him, to detail the circumstances which he thought justified the strong terms in which he expressed himself.

"I should tell you all with pleasure," said the General, "but you would not believe me."

"Why should I not?" he asked.

"Because," he answered testily, "you believe in nothing but what consists with your own prejudices and illusions. I remember when I was like you, but I have learned better."

"Try me," said my father; "I am not such a dogmatist as you suppose. Besides which, I very well know that you generally require proof for what you believe, and am, therefore, very strongly predisposed to respect your conclusions."

"You are right in supposing that I have not been led lightly into a belief in the marvelous—for what I have experienced is marvelous—and I have been forced by extraordinary evidence to credit that which ran counter, diametrically, to all my theories. I have been made the dupe of a preternatural conspiracy."

Notwithstanding his professions of confidence in the General's penetration, I saw my father, at this point, glance at the General, with, as I thought, a marked suspicion of his sanity.

The General did not see it, luckily. He was looking gloomily and curiously into the glades and vistas of the woods that were opening before us.

"You are going to the Ruins of Karnstein?" he said. "Yes, it is a lucky coincidence; do you know I was going to ask you to bring me there to inspect them. I have a special object in exploring. There is a ruined chapel, ain't there, with a great many tombs of that extinct family?"

"So there are—highly interesting," said my father. "I hope you are thinking of claiming the title and estates?"

My father said this gaily, but the General did not recollect the laugh, or even the smile, which courtesy exacts for a friend's joke; on the contrary, he looked grave and even fierce, ruminating on a matter that stirred his anger and horror.

"Something very different," he said, gruffly. "I mean to unearth some of those fine people. I hope, by God's blessing, to accomplish a pious sacrilege here, which will relieve our earth of certain monsters, and enable honest people to sleep in their beds without being assailed by murderers. I have strange things to tell you, my dear friend, such as I myself would have scouted as incredible a few months since."

My father looked at him again, but this time not with a glance of suspicion—with an eye, rather, of keen intelligence and alarm.

"The house of Karnstein," he said, "has been long extinct: a hundred years at least. My dear wife was maternally descended from the Karnsteins. But the name and title have long ceased to exist. The castle is a ruin; the very village is deserted; it is fifty years since the smoke of a chimney was seen there; not a roof left."

"Quite true. I have heard a great deal about that since I last saw you; a great deal that will astonish you. But I had better relate everything in the order in which it occurred," said the General. "You saw my dear ward—my child, I may call her. No creature could have been more beautiful, and only three months ago none more blooming."

"Yes, poor thing! when I saw her last she certainly was quite lovely," said my father. "I was grieved and shocked more than I can tell you, my dear friend; I knew what a blow it was to you."

He took the General's hand, and they exchanged a kind pressure. Tears gathered in the old soldier's eyes. He did not seek to conceal them. He said:

"We have been very old friends; I knew you would feel for me, childless as I am. She had become an object of very near interest to me, and repaid my care by an affection that cheered my home and made my life happy. That is all gone. The years that remain to me on earth may not be very long; but by God's mercy I hope to accomplish a service to mankind before I die, and to subserve the vengeance of Heaven upon the fiends who have murdered my poor child in the spring of her hopes and beauty!"

"You said, just now, that you intended relating everything as it occurred," said my father. "Pray do; I assure you that it is not mere curiosity that prompts me."

By this time we had reached the point at which the Drunstall road, by which the General had come, diverges from the road which we were traveling to Karnstein.

"How far is it to the ruins?" inquired the General, looking anxiously forward.

"About half a league," answered my father. "Pray let us hear the story you were so good as to promise."

XI. THE STORY

"With all my heart," said the General, with an effort; and after a short pause in which to arrange his subject, he commenced one of the strangest narratives I ever heard.

"My dear child was looking forward with great pleasure to the visit you had been so good as to arrange for her to your charming daughter." Here he made me a gallant but melancholy bow. "In the meantime we had an invitation to my old friend the Count Carlsfeld, whose schloss is about six leagues to the other side of Karnstein. It was to attend the series of fetes which, you remember, were given by him in honor of his illustrious visitor, the Grand Duke Charles."

"Yes; and very splendid, I believe, they were," said my father.

"Princely! But then his hospitalities are quite regal. He has Aladdin's lamp. The night from which my sorrow dates was devoted to a magnificent masquerade. The grounds were thrown open, the trees hung with colored lamps. There was such a display of fireworks as Paris itself had never witnessed. And such music—music, you know, is my weakness—such ravishing music! The finest instrumental band, perhaps, in the world, and the finest singers who could be collected from all the great operas in Europe. As you wandered through these fantastically illuminated grounds, the moon-lighted chateau throwing a rosy light from its long rows of windows, you would suddenly hear these ravishing voices stealing from the silence of some grove, or rising from boats upon the lake. I felt myself, as I looked and listened, carried back into the romance and poetry of my early youth.

"When the fireworks were ended, and the ball beginning, we returned to the noble suite of rooms that were thrown open to the dancers. A masked ball, you know, is a beautiful sight; but so brilliant a spectacle of the kind I never saw before.

"It was a very aristocratic assembly. I was myself almost the only 'nobody' present.

"My dear child was looking quite beautiful. She wore no mask. Her excitement and delight added an unspeakable charm to her features, always lovely. I remarked a young lady, dressed magnificently, but wearing a mask, who appeared to me to be observing my ward with extraordinary interest. I had seen her, earlier in the evening, in the great hall, and again, for a few minutes, walking near us, on the terrace under the castle windows, similarly employed. A lady, also masked, richly and gravely dressed, and with a stately air, like a person of rank, accompanied her as a chaperon.

"Had the young lady not worn a mask, I could, of course, have been much more certain upon the question whether she was really watching my poor darling.

"I am now well assured that she was.

"We were now in one of the salons. My poor dear child had been dancing, and was resting a little in one of the chairs near the door; I was standing near. The two ladies I have mentioned had approached and the younger took the chair next my ward; while her companion stood beside me, and for a little time addressed herself, in a low tone, to her charge.

"Availing herself of the privilege of her mask, she turned to me, and in the tone of an old friend, and calling me by my name, opened a conversation with me, which piqued my curiosity a good deal. She referred to many scenes where she had met me—at Court, and at distinguished houses. She alluded to little incidents which I had long ceased to think of, but which, I found, had only lain in abeyance in my memory, for they instantly started into life at her touch.

"I became more and more curious to ascertain who she was, every moment. She parried my attempts to discover very adroitly and pleasantly. The knowledge she showed of many passages in my life seemed to me all but unaccountable; and she appeared to take a not unnatural pleasure in foiling my curiosity, and in seeing me flounder in my eager perplexity, from one conjecture to another.

"In the meantime the young lady, whom her mother called by the odd name of Millarca, when she once or twice addressed her, had, with the same ease and grace, got into conversation with my ward.

"She introduced herself by saying that her mother was a very old acquaintance of mine. She spoke of the agreeable audacity which a mask rendered practicable; she talked like a friend; she admired her dress, and insinuated very prettily her admiration of her beauty. She amused her with laughing criticisms upon the people who crowded the ballroom, and laughed at my poor child's fun. She was very witty and lively when she pleased, and after a time they had grown very good friends, and the young stranger lowered her mask, displaying a remarkably beautiful face. I had never seen it before, neither had my dear child. But though it was new to us, the features were so engaging, as well as lovely, that it was impossible not to feel the attraction powerfully. My poor girl did so. I never saw anyone more taken with another at first sight, unless, indeed, it was the stranger herself, who seemed quite to have lost her heart to her.

"In the meantime, availing myself of the license of a masquerade, I put not a few questions to the elder lady.

"'You have puzzled me utterly,' I said, laughing. 'Is that not enough? Won't you, now, consent to stand on equal terms, and do me the kindness to remove your mask?'

"'Can any request be more unreasonable?' she replied. 'Ask a lady to yield an advantage! Beside, how do you know you should recognize me? Years make changes.'

"'As you see,' I said, with a bow, and, I suppose, a rather melancholy little laugh.

"'As philosophers tell us,' she said; 'and how do you know that a sight of my face would help you?'

"'I should take chance for that,' I answered. 'It is vain trying to make yourself out an old woman; your figure betrays you.'

"'Years, nevertheless, have passed since I saw you, rather since you saw me, for that is what I am considering. Millarca, there, is my daughter; I cannot then be young, even in the opinion of people whom time has taught to be indulgent, and I may not like to be compared with what you remember me. You have no mask to remove. You can offer me nothing in exchange.'

"'My petition is to your pity, to remove it.'

"'And mine to yours, to let it stay where it is,' she replied.

"'Well, then, at least you will tell me whether you are French or German; you speak both languages so perfectly.'

"'I don't think I shall tell you that, General; you intend a surprise, and are meditating the particular point of attack.'

"'At all events, you won't deny this,' I said, 'that being honored by your permission to converse, I ought to know how to address you. Shall I say Madame la Comtesse?'

"She laughed, and she would, no doubt, have met me with another evasion—if, indeed, I can treat any occurrence in an interview every circumstance of which was prearranged, as I now believe, with the profoundest cunning, as liable to be modified by accident.

"'As to that,' she began; but she was interrupted, almost as she opened her lips, by a gentleman, dressed in black, who looked particularly elegant and distinguished, with this drawback, that his face was the most deadly pale I ever saw, except in death. He was in no masquerade—in the plain evening dress of a gentleman; and he said, without a smile, but with a courtly and unusually low bow:—

"'Will Madame la Comtesse permit me to say a very few words which may interest her?'

"The lady turned quickly to him, and touched her lip in token of silence; she then said to me, 'Keep my place for me, General; I shall return when I have said a few words.'

"And with this injunction, playfully given, she walked a little aside with the gentleman in black, and talked for some minutes, apparently very earnestly. They then walked away slowly together in the crowd, and I lost them for some minutes.

"I spent the interval in cudgeling my brains for a conjecture as to the identity of the lady who seemed to remember me so kindly, and I was thinking of turning about and joining in the conversation between my pretty ward and the Countess's daughter, and trying whether, by the time she returned, I might not have a surprise in store for her, by having her name, title, chateau, and estates at my fingers' ends. But at this moment she returned, accompanied by the pale man in black, who said:

"'I shall return and inform Madame la Comtesse when her carriage is at the door.'

"He withdrew with a bow."

XII. A PETITION

"'Then we are to lose Madame la Comtesse, but I hope only for a few hours,' I said, with a low bow.

"'It may be that only, or it may be a few weeks. It was very unlucky his speaking to me just now as he did. Do you now know me?'

"I assured her I did not.

"'You shall know me,' she said, 'but not at present. We are older and better friends than, perhaps, you suspect. I cannot yet declare myself. I shall in three weeks pass your beautiful schloss, about which I have been making enquiries. I shall then look in upon you for an hour or two, and renew a friendship which I never think of without a thousand pleasant recollections. This moment a piece of news has reached me like a thunderbolt. I must set out now, and travel by a devious route, nearly a hundred miles, with all the dispatch I can possibly make. My perplexities multiply. I am only deterred by the compulsory reserve I practice as to my name from making a very singular request of you. My poor child has not quite recovered her strength. Her horse fell with her, at a hunt which she had ridden out to witness, her nerves have not yet recovered the shock, and our physician says that she must on no account exert herself for some time to come. We came here, in consequence, by very easy stages—hardly six leagues a day. I must now travel day and night, on a mission of life and death—a mission the critical and momentous nature of which I shall be able to explain to you when we meet, as I hope we shall, in a few weeks, without the necessity of any concealment.'

"She went on to make her petition, and it was in the tone of a person from whom such a request amounted to conferring, rather than seeking a favor.

"This was only in manner, and, as it seemed, quite unconsciously. Than the terms in which it was expressed, nothing could be more deprecatory. It was simply that I would consent to take charge of her daughter during her absence.

"This was, all things considered, a strange, not to say, an audacious request. She in some sort disarmed me, by stating and admitting everything that could be urged against it, and throwing herself entirely upon my chivalry. At the same moment, by a fatality that seems to have predetermined all that happened, my poor child came to my side, and, in an undertone, besought me to invite her new friend, Millarca, to pay us a visit. She had just been sounding her, and thought, if her mamma would allow her, she would like it extremely.

"At another time I should have told her to wait a little, until, at least, we knew who they were. But I had not a moment to think in. The two ladies assailed me together, and I must confess the refined and beautiful face of the young lady, about which there was something extremely engaging, as well as the elegance and fire of high birth, determined me; and, quite overpowered, I submitted, and undertook, too easily, the care of the young lady, whom her mother called Millarca.

"The Countess beckoned to her daughter, who listened with grave attention while she told her, in general terms, how suddenly and peremptorily she had been summoned, and also of the arrangement she had made for her under my care, adding that I was one of her earliest and most valued friends.

"I made, of course, such speeches as the case seemed to call for, and found myself, on reflection, in a position which I did not half like.

"The gentleman in black returned, and very ceremoniously conducted the lady from the room.

"The demeanor of this gentleman was such as to impress me with the conviction that the Countess was a lady of very much more importance than her modest title alone might have led me to assume.

"Her last charge to me was that no attempt was to be made to learn more about her than I might have already guessed, until her return. Our distinguished host, whose guest she was, knew her reasons.

"'But here,' she said, 'neither I nor my daughter could safely remain for more than a day. I removed my mask imprudently for a moment, about an hour ago, and, too late, I fancied you saw me. So I resolved to seek an opportunity of talking a little to you. Had I found that you had seen me, I would have thrown myself on your high sense of honor to keep my secret some weeks. As it is, I am satisfied that you did not see me; but if you now suspect, or, on reflection, should suspect, who I am, I commit myself, in like manner, entirely to your honor. My daughter will observe the same secrecy, and I well know that you will, from time to time, remind her, lest she should thoughtlessly disclose it.'

"She whispered a few words to her daughter, kissed her hurriedly twice, and went away, accompanied by the pale gentleman in black, and disappeared in the crowd.

"'In the next room,' said Millarca, 'there is a window that looks upon the hall door. I should like to see the last of mamma, and to kiss my hand to her.'

"We assented, of course, and accompanied her to the window. We looked out, and saw a handsome old-fashioned carriage, with a troop of couriers and footmen. We saw the slim figure of the pale gentleman in black, as he held a thick velvet cloak, and placed it about her shoulders and threw the hood over her head. She nodded to him, and just touched his hand with hers. He bowed low repeatedly as the door closed, and the carriage began to move.

"'She is gone,' said Millarca, with a sigh.

"'She is gone,' I repeated to myself, for the first time—in the hurried moments that had elapsed since my consent—reflecting upon the folly of my act.

"'She did not look up,' said the young lady, plaintively.

"'The Countess had taken off her mask, perhaps, and did not care to show her face,' I said; 'and she could not know that you were in the window.'

"She sighed, and looked in my face. She was so beautiful that I relented. I was sorry I had for a moment repented of my hospitality, and I determined to make her amends for the unavowed churlishness of my reception.

"The young lady, replacing her mask, joined my ward in persuading me to return to the grounds, where the concert was soon to be renewed. We did so, and walked up and down the terrace that lies under the castle windows.

"Millarca became very intimate with us, and amused us with lively descriptions and stories of most of the great people whom we saw upon the terrace. I liked her more and more every minute. Her gossip without being ill-natured, was extremely diverting to me, who had been so long out of the great world. I thought what life she would give to our sometimes lonely evenings at home.

"This ball was not over until the morning sun had almost reached the horizon. It pleased the Grand Duke to dance till then, so loyal people could not go away, or think of bed.

"We had just got through a crowded saloon, when my ward asked me what had become of Millarca. I thought she had been by her side, and she fancied she was by mine. The fact was, we had lost her.

"All my efforts to find her were vain. I feared that she had mistaken, in the confusion of a momentary separation from us, other people for her new friends, and had, possibly, pursued and lost them in the extensive grounds which were thrown open to us.

"Now, in its full force, I recognized a new folly in my having undertaken the charge of a young lady without so much as knowing her name; and fettered as I was by promises, of the reasons for imposing which I knew nothing, I could not even point my inquiries by saying that the missing young lady was the daughter of the Countess who had taken her departure a few hours before.

"Morning broke. It was clear daylight before I gave up my search. It was not till near two o'clock next day that we heard anything of my missing charge.

"At about that time a servant knocked at my niece's door, to say that he had been earnestly requested by a young lady, who appeared to be in great distress, to make out where she could find the General Baron Spielsdorf and the young lady his daughter, in whose charge she had been left by her mother.

"There could be no doubt, notwithstanding the slight inaccuracy, that our young friend had turned up; and so she had. Would to heaven we had lost her!

"She told my poor child a story to account for her having failed to recover us for so long. Very late, she said, she had got to the housekeeper's bedroom in despair of finding us, and had then fallen into a deep sleep which, long as it was, had hardly sufficed to recruit her strength after the fatigues of the ball.

"That day Millarca came home with us. I was only too happy, after all, to have secured so charming a companion for my dear girl."

XIII. THE WOODMAN

"There soon, however, appeared some drawbacks. In the first place, Millarca complained of extreme languor—the weakness that remained after her late illness—and she never emerged from her room till the afternoon was pretty far advanced. In the next place, it was accidentally discovered, although she always locked her door on the inside, and never disturbed the key from its place till she admitted the maid to assist at her toilet, that she was undoubtedly sometimes absent from her room in the very early morning, and at various times later in the day, before she wished it to be understood that she was stirring. She was repeatedly seen from the windows of the schloss, in the first faint grey of the morning, walking through the trees, in an easterly direction, and looking like a person in a trance. This convinced me that she walked in her sleep. But this hypothesis did not solve the puzzle. How did she pass out from her room, leaving the door locked on the inside? How did she escape from the house without unbarring door or window?

"In the midst of my perplexities, an anxiety of a far more urgent kind presented itself.

"My dear child began to lose her looks and health, and that in a manner so mysterious, and even horrible, that I became thoroughly frightened.

"She was at first visited by appalling dreams; then, as she fancied, by a specter, sometimes resembling Millarca, sometimes in the shape of a beast, indistinctly seen, walking round the foot of her bed, from side to side.

"Lastly came sensations. One, not unpleasant, but very peculiar, she said, resembled the flow of an icy stream against her breast. At a later time, she felt something like a pair of large needles pierce her, a little below the throat, with a very sharp pain. A few nights after, followed a gradual and convulsive sense of strangulation; then came unconsciousness."

I could hear distinctly every word the kind old General was saying, because by this time we were driving upon the short grass that spreads on either side of the road as you approach the roofless village which had not shown the smoke of a chimney for more than half a century.

You may guess how strangely I felt as I heard my own symptoms so exactly described in those which had been experienced by the poor girl who, but for the catastrophe which followed, would have been at that moment a visitor at my father's chateau. You may suppose, also, how I felt as I heard him detail habits and mysterious peculiarities which were, in fact, those of our beautiful guest, Carmilla!

A vista opened in the forest; we were on a sudden under the chimneys and gables of the ruined village, and the towers and battlements of the dismantled castle, round which gigantic trees are grouped, overhung us from a slight eminence.

In a frightened dream I got down from the carriage, and in silence, for we had each abundant matter for thinking; we soon mounted the ascent, and were among the spacious chambers, winding stairs, and dark corridors of the castle.

"And this was once the palatial residence of the Karnsteins!" said the old General at length, as from a great window he looked out across the village, and saw the wide, undulating expanse of forest. "It was a bad family, and here its bloodstained annals were written," he continued. "It is hard that they should, after death, continue to plague the human race with their atrocious lusts. That is the chapel of the Karnsteins, down there."

He pointed down to the grey walls of the Gothic building partly visible through the foliage, a little way down the steep. "And I hear the axe of a woodman," he added, "busy among the trees that surround it; he possibly may give us the information of which I am in search, and point out the grave of Mircalla, Countess of Karnstein. These rustics preserve the local traditions of great families, whose stories die out among the rich and titled so soon as the families themselves become extinct."

"We have a portrait, at home, of Mircalla, the Countess Karnstein; should you like to see it?" asked my father.

"Time enough, dear friend," replied the General. "I believe that I have seen the original; and one motive which has led me to you earlier than I at first intended, was to explore the chapel which we are now approaching."

"What! see the Countess Mircalla," exclaimed my father; "why, she has been dead more than a century!"

"Not so dead as you fancy, I am told," answered the General.

"I confess, General, you puzzle me utterly," replied my father, looking at him, I fancied, for a moment with a return of the suspicion I detected before. But although there was anger and detestation, at times, in the old General's manner, there was nothing flighty.

"There remains to me," he said, as we passed under the heavy arch of the Gothic church—for its dimensions would have justified its being so styled—"but one object which can interest me during the few years that remain to me on earth, and that is to wreak on her the vengeance which, I thank God, may still be accomplished by a mortal arm."

"What vengeance can you mean?" asked my father, in increasing amazement.

"I mean, to decapitate the monster," he answered, with a fierce flush, and a stamp that echoed mournfully through the hollow ruin, and his clenched hand was at the same moment raised, as if it grasped the handle of an axe, while he shook it ferociously in the air.

"What?" exclaimed my father, more than ever bewildered.

"To strike her head off."

"Cut her head off!"

"Aye, with a hatchet, with a spade, or with anything that can cleave through her murderous throat. You shall hear," he answered, trembling with rage. And hurrying forward he said:

"That beam will answer for a seat; your dear child is fatigued; let her be seated, and I will, in a few sentences, close my dreadful story."

The squared block of wood, which lay on the grass-grown pavement of the chapel, formed a bench on which I was very glad to seat myself, and in the meantime the General called to the woodman, who had been removing some boughs which leaned upon the old walls; and, axe in hand, the hardy old fellow stood before us.

He could not tell us anything of these monuments; but there was an old man, he said, a ranger of this forest, at present sojourning in the house of the priest, about two miles away, who could point out every monument of the old Karnstein family; and, for a trifle, he undertook to bring him back with him, if we would lend him one of our horses, in little more than half an hour.

"Have you been long employed about this forest?" asked my father of the old man.

"I have been a woodman here," he answered in his patois, "under the forester, all my days; so has my father before me, and so on, as many generations as I can count up. I could show you the very house in the village here, in which my ancestors lived."

"How came the village to be deserted?" asked the General.

"It was troubled by revenants, sir; several were tracked to their graves, there detected by the usual tests, and extinguished in the usual way, by decapitation, by the stake, and by burning; but not until many of the villagers were killed.

"But after all these proceedings according to law," he continued—"so many graves opened, and so many vampires deprived of their horrible animation—the village was not relieved. But a Moravian nobleman, who happened to be traveling this way, heard how matters were, and being skilled—as many people are in his country—in such affairs, he offered to deliver the village from its tormentor. He did so thus: There being a bright moon that night, he ascended, shortly after sunset, the towers of the chapel here, from whence he could distinctly see the churchyard beneath him; you can see it from that window. From this point he watched until he saw the vampire come out of his grave, and place near it the linen clothes in which he had been folded, and then glide away towards the village to plague its inhabitants.

"The stranger, having seen all this, came down from the steeple, took the linen wrappings of the vampire, and carried them up to the top of the tower, which he again mounted. When the vampire returned from his prowlings and missed his clothes, he cried furiously to the Moravian, whom he saw at the summit of the tower, and who, in reply, beckoned him to ascend and take them. Whereupon the vampire, accepting his invitation, began to climb the steeple, and so soon as he had reached the battlements, the Moravian, with a stroke of his sword, clove his skull in twain, hurling him down to the churchyard, whither, descending by the winding stairs, the stranger followed and cut his head off, and next day delivered it and the body to the villagers, who duly impaled and burnt them.

"This Moravian nobleman had authority from the then head of the family to remove the tomb of Mircalla, Countess Karnstein, which he did effectually, so that in a little while its site was quite forgotten."

"Can you point out where it stood?" asked the General, eagerly.

The forester shook his head, and smiled.

"Not a soul living could tell you that now," he said; "besides, they say her body was removed; but no one is sure of that either."

Having thus spoken, as time pressed, he dropped his axe and departed, leaving us to hear the remainder of the General's strange story.

XIV. THE MEETING

"My beloved child," he resumed, "was now growing rapidly worse. The physician who attended her had failed to produce the slightest impression on her disease, for such I then supposed it to be. He saw my alarm, and suggested a consultation. I called in an abler physician, from Gratz.

"Several days elapsed before he arrived. He was a good and pious, as well as a learned man. Having seen my poor ward together, they withdrew to my library to confer and discuss. I, from the adjoining room, where I awaited their summons, heard these two gentlemen's voices raised in something sharper than a strictly philosophical discussion. I knocked at the door and entered. I found the old physician from Gratz maintaining his theory. His rival was combating it with undisguised ridicule, accompanied with bursts of laughter. This unseemly manifestation subsided and the altercation ended on my entrance.

"'Sir,' said my first physician, 'my learned brother seems to think that you want a conjuror, and not a doctor.'

"'Pardon me,' said the old physician from Gratz, looking displeased, 'I shall state my own view of the case in my own way another time. I grieve, Monsieur le General, that by my skill and science I can be of no use. Before I go I shall do myself the honor to suggest something to you.'

"He seemed thoughtful, and sat down at a table and began to write.

"Profoundly disappointed, I made my bow, and as I turned to go, the other doctor pointed over his shoulder to his companion who was writing, and then, with a shrug, significantly touched his forehead.

"This consultation, then, left me precisely where I was. I walked out into the grounds, all but distracted. The doctor from Gratz, in ten or fifteen minutes, overtook me. He apologized for having followed me, but said that he could not conscientiously take his leave without a few words more. He told me that he could not be mistaken; no natural disease exhibited the same symptoms; and that death was already very near. There remained, however, a day, or possibly two, of life. If the fatal seizure were at once arrested, with great care and skill her strength might possibly return. But all hung now upon the confines of the irrevocable. One more assault might extinguish the last spark of vitality which is, every moment, ready to die.

"'And what is the nature of the seizure you speak of?' I entreated.

"'I have stated all fully in this note, which I place in your hands upon the distinct condition that you send for the nearest clergyman, and open my letter in his presence, and on no account read it till he is with you; you would despise it else, and it is a matter of life and death. Should the priest fail you, then, indeed, you may read it.'

"He asked me, before taking his leave finally, whether I would wish to see a man curiously learned upon the very subject, which, after I had read his letter, would probably interest me above all others, and he urged me earnestly to invite him to visit him there; and so took his leave.

"The ecclesiastic was absent, and I read the letter by myself. At another time, or in another case, it might have excited my ridicule. But into what quackeries will not people rush for a last chance, where all accustomed means have failed, and the life of a beloved object is at stake?

"Nothing, you will say, could be more absurd than the learned man's letter.

"It was monstrous enough to have consigned him to a madhouse. He said that the patient was suffering from the visits of a vampire! The punctures which she described as having occurred near the throat, were, he insisted, the insertion of those two long, thin, and sharp teeth which, it is well known, are peculiar to vampires; and there could be no doubt, he added, as to the well-defined presence of the small livid mark which all concurred in describing as that induced by the demon's lips, and every symptom described by the sufferer was in exact conformity with those recorded in every case of a similar visitation.

"Being myself wholly skeptical as to the existence of any such portent as the vampire, the supernatural theory of the good doctor furnished, in my opinion, but another instance of learning and intelligence oddly associated with some one hallucination. I was so miserable, however, that, rather than try nothing, I acted upon the instructions of the letter.

"I concealed myself in the dark dressing room, that opened upon the poor patient's room, in which a candle was burning, and watched there till she was fast asleep. I stood at the door, peeping through the small crevice, my sword laid on the table beside me, as my directions prescribed, until, a little after one, I saw a large black object, very ill-defined, crawl, as it seemed to me, over the foot of the bed, and swiftly spread itself up to the poor girl's throat, where it swelled, in a moment, into a great, palpitating mass.

"For a few moments I had stood petrified. I now sprang forward, with my sword in my hand. The black creature suddenly contracted towards the foot of the bed, glided over it, and, standing on the floor about a yard below the foot of the bed, with a glare of skulking ferocity and horror fixed on me, I saw Millarca. Speculating I know not what, I struck at her instantly with my sword; but I saw her standing near the door, unscathed. Horrified, I pursued, and struck again. She was gone; and my sword flew to shivers against the door.

"I can't describe to you all that passed on that horrible night. The whole house was up and stirring. The specter Millarca was gone. But her victim was sinking fast, and before the morning dawned, she died."

The old General was agitated. We did not speak to him. My father walked to some little distance, and began reading the inscriptions on the tombstones; and thus occupied, he strolled into the door of a side chapel to prosecute his researches. The General leaned against the wall, dried his eyes, and sighed heavily. I was relieved on hearing the voices of Carmilla and Madame, who were at that moment approaching. The voices died away.

In this solitude, having just listened to so strange a story, connected, as it was, with the great and titled dead, whose monuments were moldering among the dust and ivy round us, and every incident of which bore so awfully upon my own mysterious case—in this haunted spot, darkened by the towering foliage that rose on every side, dense and high above its noiseless walls—a horror began to steal over me, and my heart sank as I thought that my friends were, after all, not about to enter and disturb this triste and ominous scene.

The old General's eyes were fixed on the ground, as he leaned with his hand upon the basement of a shattered monument.

Under a narrow, arched doorway, surmounted by one of those demoniacal grotesques in which the cynical and ghastly fancy of old Gothic carving delights, I saw very gladly the beautiful face and figure of Carmilla enter the shadowy chapel.

I was just about to rise and speak, and nodded smiling, in answer to her peculiarly engaging smile; when with a cry, the old man by my side caught up the woodman's hatchet, and started forward. On seeing him a brutalized change came over her features. It was an instantaneous and horrible transformation, as she made a crouching step backwards. Before I could utter a scream, he struck at her with all his force, but she dived under his blow, and unscathed, caught him in her tiny grasp by the wrist. He struggled for a moment to release his arm, but his hand opened, the axe fell to the ground, and the girl was gone.

He staggered against the wall. His grey hair stood upon his head, and a moisture shone over his face, as if he were at the point of death.

The frightful scene had passed in a moment. The first thing I recollect after, is Madame standing before me, and impatiently repeating again and again, the question, "Where is Mademoiselle Carmilla?"

I answered at length, "I don't know—I can't tell—she went there," and I pointed to the door through which Madame had just entered; "only a minute or two since."

"But I have been standing there, in the passage, ever since Mademoiselle Carmilla entered; and she did not return."

She then began to call "Carmilla," through every door and passage and from the windows, but no answer came.

"She called herself Carmilla?" asked the General, still agitated.

"Carmilla, yes," I answered.

"Aye," he said; "that is Millarca. That is the same person who long ago was called Mircalla, Countess Karnstein. Depart from this accursed ground, my poor child, as quickly as you can. Drive to the clergyman's house, and stay there till we come. Begone! May you never behold Carmilla more; you will not find her here."

XV. ORDEAL AND EXECUTION

*A*s he spoke one of the strangest looking men I ever beheld entered the chapel at the door through which Carmilla had made her entrance and her exit. He was tall, narrow-chested, stooping, with high shoulders, and dressed in black. His face was brown and dried in with deep furrows; he wore an oddly-shaped hat with a broad leaf. His hair, long and grizzled, hung on his shoulders. He wore a pair of gold spectacles, and walked slowly, with an odd shambling gait, with his face sometimes turned up to the sky, and sometimes bowed down towards the ground, seemed to wear a perpetual smile; his long thin arms were swinging, and his lank hands, in old black gloves ever so much too wide for them, waving and gesticulating in utter abstraction.

"The very man!" exclaimed the General, advancing with manifest delight. "My dear Baron, how happy I am to see you, I had no hope of meeting you so soon." He signed to my father, who had by this time returned, and leading the fantastic old gentleman, whom he called the Baron to meet him. He introduced him formally, and they at once entered into earnest conversation. The stranger took a roll of paper from his pocket, and spread it on the worn surface of a tomb that stood by. He had a pencil case in his fingers, with which he traced imaginary lines from point to point on the paper, which from their often glancing from it, together, at certain points of the building, I concluded to be a plan of the chapel. He accompanied, what I may term, his lecture, with occasional readings from a dirty little book, whose yellow leaves were closely written over.

They sauntered together down the side aisle, opposite to the spot where I was standing, conversing as they went; then they began measuring distances by paces, and finally they all stood together, facing a piece of the sidewall, which they began to examine with great minuteness; pulling off the ivy that clung over it, and rapping the plaster with the ends of their sticks, scraping here, and knocking there. At length they ascertained the existence of a broad marble tablet, with letters carved in relief upon it.

With the assistance of the woodman, who soon returned, a monumental inscription, and carved escutcheon, were disclosed. They proved to be those of the long lost monument of Mircalla, Countess Karnstein.

The old General, though not I fear given to the praying mood, raised his hands and eyes to heaven, in mute thanksgiving for some moments.

"Tomorrow," I heard him say; "the commissioner will be here, and the Inquisition will be held according to law."

Then turning to the old man with the gold spectacles, whom I have described, he shook him warmly by both hands and said:

"Baron, how can I thank you? How can we all thank you? You will have delivered this region from a plague that has scourged its inhabitants for more than a century. The horrible enemy, thank God, is at last tracked."

My father led the stranger aside, and the General followed. I know that he had led them out of hearing, that he might relate my case, and I saw them glance often quickly at me, as the discussion proceeded.

My father came to me, kissed me again and again, and leading me from the chapel, said:

"It is time to return, but before we go home, we must add to our party the good priest, who lives but a little way from this; and persuade him to accompany us to the schloss."

In this quest we were successful: and I was glad, being unspeakably fatigued when we reached home. But my satisfaction was changed to dismay, on discovering that there were no tidings of Carmilla. Of the scene that had occurred in the ruined chapel, no explanation was offered to me, and it was clear that it was a secret which my father for the present determined to keep from me.

The sinister absence of Carmilla made the remembrance of the scene more horrible to me. The arrangements for the night were singular. Two servants, and Madame were to sit up in my room that night; and the ecclesiastic with my father kept watch in the adjoining dressing room.

The priest had performed certain solemn rites that night, the purport of which I did not understand any more than I comprehended the reason of this extraordinary precaution taken for my safety during sleep.

I saw all clearly a few days later.

The disappearance of Carmilla was followed by the discontinuance of my nightly sufferings.

You have heard, no doubt, of the appalling superstition that prevails in Upper and Lower Styria, in Moravia, Silesia, in Turkish Serbia, in Poland, even in Russia; the superstition, so we must call it, of the Vampire.

If human testimony, taken with every care and solemnity, judicially, before commissions innumerable, each consisting of many members, all chosen for integrity and intelligence, and constituting reports more voluminous perhaps than exist upon any one other class of cases, is worth anything, it is difficult to deny, or even to doubt the existence of such a phenomenon as the Vampire.

For my part I have heard no theory by which to explain what I myself have witnessed and experienced, other than that supplied by the ancient and well-attested belief of the country.

The next day the formal proceedings took place in the Chapel of Karnstein.

The grave of the Countess Mircalla was opened; and the General and my father recognized each his perfidious and beautiful guest, in the face now disclosed to view. The features, though a hundred and fifty years had passed since her funeral, were tinted with the warmth of life. Her eyes were open; no cadaverous smell exhaled from the coffin. The two medical men, one officially present, the other on the part of the promoter of the inquiry, attested the marvelous fact that there was a faint but appreciable respiration, and a corresponding action of the heart. The limbs were perfectly flexible, the flesh elastic; and the leaden coffin floated with blood, in which to a depth of seven inches, the body lay immersed.

Here then, were all the admitted signs and proofs of vampirism. The body, therefore, in accordance with the ancient practice, was raised, and a sharp stake driven through the heart of the vampire, who uttered a piercing shriek at the moment, in all respects such as might escape from a living person in the last agony. Then the head was struck off, and a torrent of blood flowed from the severed neck. The body and head was next placed on a pile of wood, and reduced to ashes, which were thrown upon the river and borne away, and that territory has never since been plagued by the visits of a vampire.

My father has a copy of the report of the Imperial Commission, with the signatures of all who were present at these proceedings, attached in verification of the statement. It is from this official paper that I have summarized my account of this last shocking scene.

XVI. CONCLUSION

$\mathcal{I}$ write all this you suppose with composure. But far from it; I cannot think of it without agitation. Nothing but your earnest desire so repeatedly expressed, could have induced me to sit down to a task that has unstrung my nerves for months to come, and reinduced a shadow of the unspeakable horror which years after my deliverance continued to make my days and nights dreadful, and solitude insupportably terrific.

Let me add a word or two about that quaint Baron Vordenburg, to whose curious lore we were indebted for the discovery of the Countess Mircalla's grave.

He had taken up his abode in Gratz, where, living upon a mere pittance, which was all that remained to him of the once princely estates of his family, in Upper Styria, he devoted himself to the minute and laborious investigation of the marvelously authenticated tradition of Vampirism. He had at his fingers' ends all the great and little works upon the subject.

"Magia Posthuma," "Phlegon de Mirabilibus," "Augustinus de cura pro Mortuis," "Philosophicae et Christianae Cogitationes de Vampiris," by John Christofer Herenberg; and a thousand others, among which I remember only a few of those which he lent to my father. He had a voluminous digest of all the judicial cases, from which he had extracted a system of principles that appear to govern—some always, and others occasionally only—the condition of the vampire. I may mention, in passing, that the deadly pallor attributed to that sort of revenants, is a mere melodramatic fiction. They present, in the grave, and when they show themselves in human society, the appearance of healthy life. When disclosed to light in their coffins, they exhibit all the symptoms that are enumerated as those which proved the vampire-life of the long-dead Countess Karnstein.

How they escape from their graves and return to them for certain hours every day, without displacing the clay or leaving any trace of disturbance in the state of the coffin or the cerements, has always been admitted to be utterly inexplicable. The amphibious existence of the vampire is sustained by daily renewed slumber in the grave. Its horrible lust for living blood supplies the vigor of its waking existence. The vampire is prone to be fascinated with an engrossing vehemence, resembling the passion of love, by particular persons. In pursuit of these it will exercise inexhaustible patience and stratagem, for access to a particular object may be obstructed in a hundred ways. It will never desist until it has satiated its passion, and drained the very life of its coveted victim. But it will, in these cases, husband and protract its murderous enjoyment with the refinement of an epicure, and heighten it by the gradual approaches of an artful courtship. In these cases it seems to yearn for something like sympathy and consent. In ordinary ones it goes direct to its object, overpowers with violence, and strangles and exhausts often at a single feast.

The vampire is, apparently, subject, in certain situations, to special conditions. In the particular instance of which I have given you a relation, Mircalla seemed to be limited to a name which, if not her real one, should at least reproduce, without the omission or addition of a single letter, those, as we say, anagrammatically, which compose it.

Carmilla did this; so did Millarca.

My father related to the Baron Vordenburg, who remained with us for two or three weeks after the expulsion of Carmilla, the story about the Moravian nobleman and the vampire at Karnstein churchyard, and then he asked the Baron how he had discovered the exact position of the long-concealed tomb of the Countess Mircalla? The Baron's grotesque features puckered up into a mysterious smile; he looked down, still smiling on his worn spectacle case and fumbled with it. Then looking up, he said:

"I have many journals, and other papers, written by that remarkable man; the most curious among them is one treating of the visit of which you speak, to Karnstein. The tradition, of course, discolors and distorts a little. He might have been termed a Moravian nobleman, for he had changed his abode to that territory, and was, beside, a noble. But he was, in truth, a native of Upper Styria. It is enough to say that in very early youth he had been a passionate and favored lover of the beautiful Mircalla, Countess Karnstein. Her early death plunged him into inconsolable grief. It is the nature of vampires to increase and multiply, but according to an ascertained and ghostly law.

"Assume, at starting, a territory perfectly free from that pest. How does it begin, and how does it multiply itself? I will tell you. A person, more or less wicked, puts an end to himself. A suicide, under certain circumstances, becomes a vampire. That specter visits living people in their slumbers; they die, and almost invariably, in the grave, develop into vampires. This happened in the case of the beautiful Mircalla, who was haunted by one of those demons.

My ancestor, Vordenburg, whose title I still bear, soon discovered this, and in the course of the studies to which he devoted himself, learned a great deal more.

"Among other things, he concluded that suspicion of vampirism would probably fall, sooner or later, upon the dead Countess, who in life had been his idol. He conceived a horror, be she what she might, of her remains being profaned by the outrage of a posthumous execution. He has left a curious paper to prove that the vampire, on its expulsion from its amphibious existence, is projected into a far more horrible life; and he resolved to save his once beloved Mircalla from this.

"He adopted the stratagem of a journey here, a pretended removal of her remains, and a real obliteration of her monument. When age had stolen upon him, and from the vale of years, he looked back on the scenes he was leaving, he considered, in a different spirit, what he had done, and a horror took possession of him. He made the tracings and notes which have guided me to the very spot, and drew up a confession of the deception that he had practiced. If he had intended any further action in this matter, death prevented him; and the hand of a remote descendant has, too late for many, directed the pursuit to the lair of the beast."

We talked a little more, and among other things he said was this:

"One sign of the vampire is the power of the hand. The slender hand of Mircalla closed like a vice of steel on the General's wrist when he raised the hatchet to strike. But its power is not confined to its grasp; it leaves a numbness in the limb it seizes, which is slowly, if ever, recovered from."

The following Spring my father took me a tour through Italy. We remained away for more than a year. It was long before the terror of recent events subsided; and to this hour the image of Carmilla returns to memory with ambiguous alternations—sometimes the playful, languid, beautiful girl; sometimes the writhing fiend I saw in the ruined church; and often from a reverie I have started, fancying I heard the light step of Carmilla at the drawing room door.

PART III: DRACULA: THE VAMPIRE UNLEASHED

DRACULA

1897

BRAM STOKER

For most readers born before 1980, some representation of Dracula—whether it be a film, book, or costume—was likely their first encounter with a vampire. Every introduction of the more than one hundred published English versions of *Dracula* asserts the book's enormous influence—not just on vampire literature and art, but across the cultural spectrum. Even the most hyperbolic expressions of this idea are warranted. *Dracula* really did change everything, and the ubiquity of the vampire in today's contemporary culture can be directly linked to Bram Stoker's classic novel of horror and suspense. Since the 1970s, scholars have pummeled *Dracula* with every conceivable weapon of analysis and literary theory. The book has been read through imperialist, Marxist, and feminist lenses, just to name the most recognizable. However, this essay will focus on how *Dracula* fits within the tradition of vampire literature.

More than five times longer than any other work in this anthology (except *Varney*, which is exempt due to its episodic nature), *Dracula* plumbs certain themes far deeper than its predecessors simply due to its length alone. The number of protagonists Stoker elects to employ allows treatment of themes by multiple characters, not just one or two. The drawn-out single plot allows motifs to be developed slowly and complexly. Consequently, the novel possesses a layered quality hitherto unprecedented in the genre. The reader of vampire fiction spends more time adventuring through a vampire saga alongside Van Helsing and Harker than they ever have before.

Stoker earns this commitment by developing a plot strong enough to hold our attention for three hundred or so pages. At its core, *Dracula* is a potboiler: a horror story designed to entrance and titillate. Every page is written with the next page in mind; Stoker knew that he had to keep things exciting for a readership that sated itself with sensationalist penny dreadfuls.

So, like any master of suspense, Stoker was careful about what information he revealed and when. A short story called "Dracula's Guest,"[60] published after Stoker's death, was in fact the original first chapter of *Dracula*. In it, Harker comes across a tomb of a vampire on his way to Dracula's castle. Stoker decided to cut this chapter from the final draft. Instead of indulging in blatant foreshadowing, Stoker deftly employs subtler means of creating dread. For example, when Harker rides on a carriage toward an intersection where a "representative" of Count Dracula (later we learn it is Dracula himself) picks him up, the peasants riding with him shudder in fear as darkness nears. Something wicked this way comes, but Stoker elects to keep us in the proverbial dark as well. The mini-sagas—the fight for Lucy's life, the chase of Dracula through Transylvania—all have very high stakes. If they don't get her blood in time, Lucy will die. If they don't catch Dracula, he'll one day return to England and destroy civilization. We, as readers, become invested in the protagonists' quests. Keeping the stakes unabashedly high, Stoker maintains a clutch on us until the novel's final pages. Since he's got his hook in so deep, he has the freedom to explore important themes of vampire literature.

As previously discussed, *Carmilla* reestablished Christianity as a tool to combat vampires. This trend continues in *Dracula*, where it constitutes a central and constant motif. Influenced by the religious revivalism of the nineteenth century, Stoker creates a monster extremely susceptible to Christian iconography. Crucifixes, crosses, and communion wafers appear repeatedly as tools to ward off the monster, and they are always effective. The Lord is continually invoked for protection and guidance, and as the novel progresses the characters appear to recognize that without God they may not succeed. Van Helsing declares that he and his comrades are "ministers of God's own wish" (Chapter 24).

The increased focus and affirmation of Christianity correlate with the theme initiated by Polidori and LeFanu—namely, that the skills and attitude of modernity may not provide solutions to all problems. In *The Vampyre*, Aubrey laughs off the warnings of the Greek peasants. Similarly, Carmilla's father does not take the notion of a vampire seriously until the very end. In *Dracula*, only traditional, non-Western medical knowledge is capable of defeating the monster. Van Helsing refrains from disclosing to Harker the reasons behind his unusual treatments in fear that Harker will think him insane and cease to trust his medical capabilities. In this regard, *Dracula* critiques modernity and further depicts the insecurity many contemporary readers had about it. The fear expressed by the novel's protagonists is generated not only from the visceral fear of a monster, but also a subtler fear

---

60   The story indirectly thanks LeFanu and Bürger for their contributions to the genre.

of the unknown and seemingly unknowable. Senf writes: "Harker's fright indicates that on one metaphorical level Dracula represents a kind of reverse imperialism, this time with the primitive trying to colonize the civilized world" (Senf 59). Typewriters and phonographs—and all the other new-fangled tools of the nineteenth century—prove inadequate as well as fall under threat. In their attempts to defeat Dracula (whether Stoker intended it or not), Van Helsing, Harker, Quincy Morris, John Seward, and Arthur Holmwood almost seem comical—a humor that, although not present in *Dracula*'s predecessors, stems from a similar notion that modern man lacks the tools necessary to defeat otherworldly threats.

Another important precedent that *Dracula* follows is setting the action in contemporary times and society. Although the novel starts in the majestic mountains of Eastern Europe, it quickly moves to bustling London. Like Varney, Lord Ruthven, and Carmilla, Dracula is a creature that manages to fit in well enough with society that he can operate undetected. For example, a workman who helped him load boxes of earth into his London apartment recalled him to be the "strongest chap I ever struck, an' him a old feller, with a white moustache, one that thin you would think he couldn't throw a shadder" (Chapter 20). Certainly unusual, Dracula's presence is hardly alarming. In fact, Dracula's original purpose in inviting Harker out to his castle was so that he could learn the customs of English people. The previously quoted incident indicates he learned them quite sufficiently.

This facsimile of human life that Dracula leads is not just appearances. Like his Part II predecessors, Dracula has an acute understanding of human psychology. Like Carmilla and Lord Ruthven, Dracula is not revealed to be a vampire until well into the novel, forcing the reader to consider him a man before he's a monster. Conflating these two conceptions of Dracula engenders a tendency to view the monster through a human lens and judge him by traditional ethical standards. Dracula's similarity to the stock rake character, in his appearance and predatory nature, further connects him to the world of humans.

His understanding of human psychology manifests itself most clearly in the first part of the book, when he plays host to Harker. In addition to being well acquainted with typical host duties such as providing meals and a room, Dracula understands complicated human behavioral norms. For example, when conversing about Dracula's impending trip, he says: "Now here let me say frankly, lest you should think it strange that I have sought the services of one so far off from London instead of some one resident there, that my motive was that no local interest might be served save my wish only, and as one of London residence might, perhaps, have some purpose of himself or friend to serve, I went thus afield to seek my agent" (Chapter 3).

However, this level of sophistication does not last. After Chapter 4, Dracula's encounters with people (except those related by a third party) are almost exclusively wordless. His interactions are varied enough to allow him to function as a social metaphor (in the tradition of Varney and Lord Ruthven), but his behavior is more characteristic of the monstrous vampires of folklore than the integrated vampires of Part II. Stoker's endowment of Dracula with extraordinary supernatural powers (the ability to scale walls like a lizard or transform into a bat or dog) further separates him from the humanesque figures of Carmilla, Varney, and Lord Ruthven. In this sense, *Dracula* can be seen as a regression. Far less nuanced than Carmilla and Varney (Lord Ruthven is about on par), Dracula is not a substantively important character. His primary function is to provide Stoker's protagonists with an antagonist.

The novel's epistolary style reinforces this configuration. Dracula's absence from the narrative allows each protagonist to project his or her own, individual fears onto him. Van Helsing sees him as a threat to Christian civilization. Harker, ashamed of his attraction to the three ghost-like female vampires he discovers in Dracula's castle, sees Dracula as a threat to his faithfulness. All the men fear Dracula not only as a killer, but also as a threat to the oppressive system of gender roles that characterized Victorian society. Stoker's simplistic depiction of Mina as a paragon of feminine virtue cements this idea: Dracula has chosen her to be his victim; thus, she requires rescuing not only because she's an innocent human being, but also because she represents the model of women whom the men of the novel are invested in preserving. Dracula's successful destruction of Lucy can be read as punishment for operating outside her specified role. Early in the novel she says, "Why can't they let a girl marry three men, or as many as want her, and save all this trouble?" (Chapter 5). For Stoker, such scandalous statements do not go unnoticed.

The prudish, claustrophobic attitude toward sex that permeates the novel speaks volumes about the historical moment of *Dracula*'s publication, but reverses the trend established by the Part II works of sexualizing vampire literature. In some sense, *Dracula* is all about sex. Nevertheless, its consistent omission is not for the sake of subtlety. Rather, it is evidence of an author who could not write about sex confidently or comfortably. An essay Stoker wrote years later that encouraged censorship of salacious material confirms this. However, resistance to sexual material does not make *Dracula* weak literature. Stoker's sexual frustration and confusion were not uncommon; nor are they uncommon today. Although earlier pieces in this collection more effectively pursue the possibilities of sexual transgression, no piece compares with *Dracula*'s articulation of the oppression that must be transgressed. The stifled lust that lurks under Stoker's words remains compelling today.

DRACULA

BRAM STOKER

CONTENTS (DRACULA)

✄ CHAPTER 1 ☙
JONATHAN HARKER'S JOURNAL

3 May. Bistritz.—Left Munich at 8:35 P.M., on 1st May, arriving at Vienna early next morning; should have arrived at 6:46, but train was an hour late. Buda-Pesth seems a wonderful place, from the glimpse which I got of it from the train and the little I could walk through the streets. I feared to go very far from the station, as we had arrived late and would start as near the correct time as possible.

The impression I had was that we were leaving the West and entering the East; the most western of splendid bridges over the Danube, which is here of noble width and depth, took us among the traditions of Turkish rule.

We left in pretty good time, and came after nightfall to Klausenburgh. Here I stopped for the night at the Hotel Royale. I had for dinner, or rather supper, a chicken done up some way with red pepper, which was very good but thirsty. (*Mem.* get recipe for Mina.) I asked the waiter, and he said it was called "paprika hendl," and that, as it was a national dish, I should be able to get it anywhere along the Carpathians.

I found my smattering of German very useful here, indeed, I don't know how I should be able to get on without it.

Having had some time at my disposal when in London, I had visited the British Museum, and made search among the books and maps in the library regarding Transylvania; it had struck me that some foreknowledge of the country could hardly fail to have some importance in dealing with a nobleman of that country.

I find that the district he named is in the extreme east of the country, just on the borders of three states, Transylvania, Moldavia, and Bukovina, in the midst of the Carpathian mountains; one of the wildest and least known portions of Europe.

I was not able to light on any map or work giving the exact locality of the Castle Dracula, as there are no maps of this country as yet to compare with our own Ordnance Survey Maps; but I found that Bistritz, the post town named by Count Dracula, is a fairly well-known place. I shall enter here some of my notes, as they may refresh my memory when I talk over my travels with Mina.

In the population of Transylvania there are four distinct nationalities: Saxons in the South, and mixed with them the Wallachs, who are the descendants of the Dacians; Magyars in the West, and Szekelys in the East and North. I am going among the latter, who claim to be descended from Attila and the Huns. This may be so, for when the Magyars conquered the country in the eleventh century they found the Huns settled in it.

I read that every known superstition in the world is gathered into the horseshoe of the Carpathians, as if it were the centre of some sort of imaginative whirlpool; if so my stay may be very interesting. (*Mem.*, I must ask the Count all about them.)

I did not sleep well, though my bed was comfortable enough, for I had all sorts of queer dreams. There was a dog howling all night under my window, which may have had something to do with it; or it may have been the paprika, for I had to drink up all the water in my carafe, and was still thirsty. Towards morning I slept and was wakened by the continuous knocking at my door, so I guess I must have been sleeping soundly then.

I had for breakfast more paprika, and a sort of porridge of maize flour which they said was "mamaliga", and egg-plant stuffed with forcemeat[61], a very excellent dish, which they call "impletata". (*Mem.*, get recipe for this also.)

I had to hurry breakfast, for the train started a little before eight, or rather it ought to have done so, for after rushing to the station at 7:30 I had to sit in the carriage for more than an hour before we began to move.

It seems to me that the further east you go the more unpunctual are the trains. What ought they to be in China?

All day long we seemed to dawdle through a country which was full of beauty of every kind. Sometimes we saw little towns or castles on the top of steep hills such as we see in old missals; sometimes we ran by rivers and streams which seemed from the wide stony margin on each side of them to be subject to great floods. It takes a lot of water, and running strong, to sweep the outside edge of a river clear.

At every station there were groups of people, sometimes crowds, and in all sorts of attire. Some of them were just like the peasants at home or those I saw coming through France and Germany, with short jackets, and round hats, and home-made trousers; but others were very picturesque.

The women looked pretty, except when you got near them, but they were very clumsy about the waist. They had all full white sleeves of some kind or other, and most of them had big belts with a lot of strips of something

---

61 Ground meat or fish.

fluttering from them like the dresses in a ballet, but of course there were petticoats under them.

The strangest figures we saw were the Slovaks, who were more barbarian than the rest, with their big cow-boy hats, great baggy dirty-white trousers, white linen shirts, and enormous heavy leather belts, nearly a foot wide, all studded over with brass nails. They wore high boots, with their trousers tucked into them, and had long black hair and heavy black moustaches. They are very picturesque, but do not look prepossessing. On the stage they would be set down at once as some old Oriental band of brigands. They are, however, I am told, very harmless and rather wanting in natural self-assertion.

It was on the dark side of twilight when we got to Bistritz, which is a very interesting old place. Being practically on the frontier—for the Borgo Pass leads from it into Bukovina—it has had a very stormy existence, and it certainly shows marks of it. Fifty years ago a series of great fires took place, which made terrible havoc on five separate occasions. At the very beginning of the seventeenth century it underwent a siege of three weeks and lost 13,000 people, the casualties of war proper being assisted by famine and disease.

Count Dracula had directed me to go to the Golden Krone Hotel, which I found, to my great delight, to be thoroughly old-fashioned, for of course I wanted to see all I could of the ways of the country.

I was evidently expected, for when I got near the door I faced a cheery-looking elderly woman in the usual peasant dress—white undergarment with a long double apron, front, and back, of coloured stuff fitting almost too tight for modesty. When I came close she bowed and said, "The Herr Englishman?"

"Yes," I said, "Jonathan Harker."

She smiled, and gave some message to an elderly man in white shirt-sleeves, who had followed her to the door.

He went, but immediately returned with a letter:

> "My friend.—Welcome to the Carpathians. I am anxiously expecting you. Sleep well tonight. At three tomorrow the diligence will start for Bukovina; a place on it is kept for you. At the Borgo Pass my carriage will await you and will bring you to me. I trust that your journey from London has been a happy one, and that you will enjoy your stay in my beautiful land.
>
> —*Your friend,*
>
> *Dracula.*"

4 May—I found that my landlord had got a letter from the Count, directing him to secure the best place on the coach for me; but on making inquiries as to details he seemed somewhat reticent, and pretended that he could not understand my German.

This could not be true, because up to then he had understood it perfectly; at least, he answered my questions exactly as if he did.

He and his wife, the old lady who had received me, looked at each other in a frightened sort of way. He mumbled out that the money had been sent in a letter, and that was all he knew. When I asked him if he knew Count Dracula, and could tell me anything of his castle, both he and his wife crossed themselves, and, saying that they knew nothing at all, simply refused to speak further. It was so near the time of starting that I had no time to ask anyone else, for it was all very mysterious and not by any means comforting.

Just before I was leaving, the old lady came up to my room and said in a hysterical way: "Must you go? Oh! Young Herr, must you go?" She was in such an excited state that she seemed to have lost her grip of what German she knew, and mixed it all up with some other language which I did not know at all. I was just able to follow her by asking many questions. When I told her that I must go at once, and that I was engaged on important business, she asked again:

"Do you know what day it is?" I answered that it was the fourth of May. She shook her head as she said again:

"Oh, yes! I know that! I know that, but do you know what day it is?"

On my saying that I did not understand, she went on:

"It is the eve of St. George's Day. Do you not know that tonight, when the clock strikes midnight, all the evil things in the world will have full sway? Do you know where you are going, and what you are going to?" She was in such evident distress that I tried to comfort her, but without effect. Finally, she went down on her knees and implored me not to go; at least to wait a day or two before starting.

It was all very ridiculous but I did not feel comfortable. However, there was business to be done, and I could allow nothing to interfere with it.

I tried to raise her up, and said, as gravely as I could, that I thanked her, but my duty was imperative, and that I must go.

She then rose and dried her eyes, and taking a crucifix from her neck offered it to me.

I did not know what to do, for, as an English Churchman, I have been taught to regard such things as in some measure idolatrous, and yet it seemed so ungracious to refuse an old lady meaning so well and in such a state of mind.

She saw, I suppose, the doubt in my face, for she put the rosary round my neck and said, "For your mother's sake," and went out of the room.

I am writing up this part of the diary whilst I am waiting for the coach, which is, of course, late; and the crucifix is still round my neck.

Whether it is the old lady's fear, or the many ghostly traditions of this place, or the crucifix itself, I do not know, but I am not feeling nearly as easy in my mind as usual.

If this book should ever reach Mina before I do, let it bring my goodbye. Here comes the coach!

5 May. The Castle.—The grey of the morning has passed, and the sun is high over the distant horizon, which seems jagged, whether with trees or hills I know not, for it is so far off that big things and little are mixed.

I am not sleepy, and, as I am not to be called till I awake, naturally I write till sleep comes.

There are many odd things to put down, and, lest who reads them may fancy that I dined too well before I left Bistritz, let me put down my dinner exactly.

I dined on what they called "robber steak"—bits of bacon, onion, and beef, seasoned with red pepper, and strung on sticks, and roasted over the fire, in simple style of the London cat's meat!

The wine was Golden Mediasch, which produces a queer sting on the tongue, which is, however, not disagreeable.

I had only a couple of glasses of this, and nothing else.

When I got on the coach, the driver had not taken his seat, and I saw him talking to the landlady.

They were evidently talking of me, for every now and then they looked at me, and some of the people who were sitting on the bench outside the door—came and listened, and then looked at me, most of them pityingly. I could hear a lot of words often repeated, queer words, for there were many nationalities in the crowd, so I quietly got my polyglot dictionary from my bag and looked them out.

I must say they were not cheering to me, for amongst them were "Ordog"—Satan, "Pokol"—hell, "stregoica"—witch, "vrolok" and "vlko-slak"—both mean the same thing, one being Slovak and the other Servian for something that is either werewolf or vampire. (*Mem.*, I must ask the Count about these superstitions.)

When we started, the crowd round the inn door, which had by this time swelled to a considerable size, all made the sign of the cross and pointed two fingers towards me.

With some difficulty, I got a fellow passenger to tell me what they meant. He would not answer at first, but on learning that I was English, he explained that it was a charm or guard against the evil eye.

This was not very pleasant for me, just starting for an unknown place to meet an unknown man. But everyone seemed so kind-hearted, and so sorrowful, and so sympathetic that I could not but be touched.

I shall never forget the last glimpse which I had of the inn yard and its crowd of picturesque figures, all crossing themselves, as they stood round the wide archway, with its background of rich foliage of oleander and orange trees in green tubs clustered in the centre of the yard.

Then our driver, whose wide linen drawers covered the whole front of the boxseat,—"gotza" they call them—cracked his big whip over his four small horses, which ran abreast, and we set off on our journey.

I soon lost sight and recollection of ghostly fears in the beauty of the scene as we drove along, although had I known the language, or rather languages, which my fellow-passengers were speaking, I might not have been able to throw them off so easily. Before us lay a green sloping land full of forests and woods, with here and there steep hills, crowned with clumps of trees or with farmhouses, the blank gable end to the road. There was everywhere a bewildering mass of fruit blossom—apple, plum, pear, cherry. And as we drove by I could see the green grass under the trees spangled with the fallen petals. In and out amongst these green hills of what they call here the "Mittel Land" ran the road, losing itself as it swept round the grassy curve, or was shut out by the straggling ends of pine woods, which here and there ran down the hillsides like tongues of flame. The road was rugged, but still we seemed to fly over it with a feverish haste. I could not understand then what the haste meant, but the driver was evidently bent on losing no time in reaching Borgo Prund. I was told that this road is in summertime excellent, but that it had not yet been put in order after the winter snows. In this respect it is different from the general run of roads in the Carpathians, for it is an old tradition that they are not to be kept in too good order. Of old the Hospadars would not repair them, lest the Turk should think that they were preparing to bring in foreign troops, and so hasten the war which was always really at loading point.

Beyond the green swelling hills of the Mittel Land rose mighty slopes of forest up to the lofty steeps of the Carpathians themselves. Right and left of us they towered, with the afternoon sun falling full upon them and bringing out all the glorious colours of this beautiful range, deep blue and purple in the shadows of the peaks, green and brown where grass and rock mingled, and an endless perspective of jagged rock and pointed crags, till these were themselves lost in the distance, where the snowy peaks rose grandly. Here and there seemed mighty rifts in the mountains, through which, as the sun began to sink, we saw now and again the white gleam of falling water. One of my companions touched my arm as we swept round the base of a hill and opened up the lofty, snow-covered peak of a mountain, which seemed, as we wound on our serpentine way, to be right before us.

"Look! Isten szek!"—"God's seat!"—and he crossed himself reverently.

As we wound on our endless way, and the sun sank lower and lower behind us, the shadows of the evening began to creep round us. This was emphasized by the fact that the snowy mountain-top still held the sunset, and seemed to glow out with a delicate cool pink. Here and there we passed Cszeks and slovaks, all in picturesque attire, but I noticed that goitre was painfully prevalent. By the roadside were many crosses, and as we swept by, my companions all crossed themselves. Here and there was a peasant man or woman kneeling before a shrine, who did not even turn round as we approached, but seemed in the self-surrender of devotion to have neither eyes nor ears for the outer world. There were many things new to me. For instance, hay-ricks in the trees, and here and there very beautiful masses of weeping birch, their white stems shining like silver through the delicate green of the leaves.

Now and again we passed a leiter-wagon—the ordinary peasant's cart—with its long, snakelike vertebra, calculated to suit the inequalities of the road. On this were sure to be seated quite a group of homecoming peasants, the Cszeks with their white, and the Slovaks with their coloured sheepskins, the latter carrying lance-fashion their long staves, with axe at end. As the evening fell it began to get very cold, and the growing twilight seemed to merge into one dark mistiness the gloom of the trees, oak, beech, and pine, though in the valleys which ran deep between the spurs of the hills, as we ascended through the Pass, the dark firs stood out here and there against the background of late-lying snow. Sometimes, as the road was cut through the pine woods that seemed in the darkness to be closing down upon us, great masses of greyness which here and there bestrewed the trees, produced a peculiarly weird and solemn effect, which carried on the thoughts and grim fancies engendered earlier in the evening, when the falling sunset threw into strange relief the ghost-like clouds which amongst the Carpathians seem to wind ceaselessly through the valleys. Sometimes the hills were so steep that, despite our driver's haste, the horses could only go slowly. I wished to get down and walk up them, as we do at home, but the driver would not hear of it. "No, no," he said. "You must not walk here. The dogs are too fierce." And then he added, with what he evidently meant for grim pleasantry—for he looked round to catch the approving smile of the rest—

"And you may have enough of such matters before you go to sleep." The only stop he would make was a moment's pause to light his lamps.

When it grew dark there seemed to be some excitement amongst the passengers, and they kept speaking to him, one after the other, as though urging him to further speed. He lashed the horses unmercifully with his long whip, and with wild cries of encouragement urged them on to further exertions. Then through the darkness I could see a sort of patch of grey light ahead of us, as though there were a cleft in the hills. The excitement of the passengers grew greater. The crazy coach rocked on its great leather springs, and swayed like a boat tossed on a stormy sea. I had to hold on. The road grew more level, and we appeared to fly along. Then the mountains seemed to come nearer to us on each side and to frown down upon us. We were entering on the Borgo Pass. One by one several of the passengers offered me gifts, which they pressed upon me with an earnestness which would take no denial. These were certainly of an odd and varied kind, but each was given in simple good faith, with a kindly word, and a blessing, and that same strange mixture of fear-meaning movements which I had seen outside the hotel at Bistritz—the sign of the cross and the guard against the evil eye. Then, as we flew along, the driver leaned forward, and on each side the passengers, craning over the edge of the coach, peered eagerly into the darkness. It was evident that something very exciting was either happening or expected, but though I asked each passenger, no one would give me the slightest explanation. This state of excitement kept on for some little time. And at last we saw before us the Pass opening out on the eastern side. There were dark, rolling clouds overhead, and in the air the heavy, oppressive sense of thunder. It seemed as though the mountain range had separated two atmospheres, and that now we had got into the thunderous one. I was now myself looking out for the conveyance which was to take me to the Count. Each moment I expected to see the glare of lamps through the blackness, but all was dark. The only light was the flickering rays of our own lamps, in which the steam from our hard-driven horses rose in a white cloud. We could see now the sandy road lying white before us, but there was on it no sign of a vehicle. The passengers drew back with a sigh of gladness, which seemed to mock my own disappointment. I was already thinking what I had best do, when the driver, looking at his watch, said to the others something which I could hardly hear, it was spoken so quietly and in so low a tone, I thought it was "An hour less than the time." Then turning to me, he spoke in German worse than my own.

"There is no carriage here. The Herr is not expected after all. He will now come on to Bukovina, and return tomorrow or the next day, better the next day." Whilst he was speaking the horses began to neigh and snort and plunge wildly, so that the driver had to hold them up. Then, amongst a chorus of screams from the peasants and a universal crossing of themselves, a caleche, with four horses, drove up behind us, overtook us, and drew up beside the coach. I could see from the flash of our lamps as the rays fell on them, that the horses were coal-black and splendid animals. They were driven by a tall man, with a long brown beard and a great black hat, which seemed to hide his face from us. I could only see the gleam of a pair of very bright eyes, which seemed red in the lamplight, as he turned to us.

He said to the driver, "You are early tonight, my friend."

The man stammered in reply, "The English Herr was in a hurry."

To which the stranger replied, "That is why, I suppose, you wished him to go on to Bukovina. You cannot deceive me, my friend. I know too much, and my horses are swift."

As he spoke he smiled, and the lamplight fell on a hard-looking mouth, with very red lips and sharp-looking teeth, as white as ivory. One of my companions whispered to another the line from Burger's "Lenore".

"Denn die Todten reiten Schnell." ("For the dead travel fast.")

The strange driver evidently heard the words, for he looked up with a gleaming smile. The passenger turned his face away, at the same time putting out his two fingers and crossing himself. "Give me the Herr's luggage," said the driver, and with exceeding alacrity my bags were handed out and put in the caleche. Then I descended from the side of the coach, as the caleche was close alongside, the driver helping me with a hand which caught my arm in a grip of steel. His strength must have been prodigious.

Without a word he shook his reins, the horses turned, and we swept into the darkness of the pass. As I looked back I saw the steam from the horses of the coach by the light of the lamps, and projected against it the figures of my late companions crossing themselves. Then the driver cracked his whip and called to his horses, and off they swept on their way to Bukovina. As they sank into the darkness I felt a strange chill, and a lonely feeling come over me. But a cloak was thrown over my shoulders, and a rug across my knees, and the driver said in excellent German—"The night is chill, mein Herr, and my master the Count bade me take all care of you. There is a flask of slivovitz (the plum brandy of the country) underneath the seat, if you should require it."

I did not take any, but it was a comfort to know it was there all the same. I felt a little strangely, and not a little frightened. I think had there been any alternative I should have taken it, instead of prosecuting that unknown night journey. The carriage went at a hard pace straight along, then we made a complete turn and went along another straight road. It seemed to me that we were simply going over and over the same ground again, and so I took note of some salient point, and found that this was so. I would have liked to have asked the driver what this all meant, but I really feared to do so, for I thought that, placed as I was, any protest would have had no effect in case there had been an intention to delay.

By-and-by, however, as I was curious to know how time was passing, I struck a match, and by its flame looked at my watch. It was within a few minutes of midnight. This gave me a sort of shock, for I suppose the general superstition about midnight was increased by my recent experiences. I waited with a sick feeling of suspense.

Then a dog began to howl somewhere in a farmhouse far down the road, a long, agonized wailing, as if from fear. The sound was taken up by another dog, and then another and another, till, borne on the wind which now sighed softly through the Pass, a wild howling began, which seemed to come from all over the country, as far as the imagination could grasp it through the gloom of the night.

At the first howl the horses began to strain and rear, but the driver spoke to them soothingly, and they quieted down, but shivered and sweated as though after a runaway from sudden fright. Then, far off in the distance, from the mountains on each side of us began a louder and a sharper howling, that of wolves, which affected both the horses and myself in the same way. For I was minded to jump from the caleche and run, whilst they reared again and plunged madly, so that the driver had to use all his great strength to keep them from bolting. In a few minutes, however, my own ears got accustomed to the sound, and the horses so far became quiet that the driver was able to descend and to stand before them.

He petted and soothed them, and whispered something in their ears, as I have heard of horse-tamers doing, and with extraordinary effect, for under his caresses they became quite manageable again, though they still trembled. The driver again took his seat, and shaking his reins, started off at a great pace. This time, after going to the far side of the Pass, he suddenly turned down a narrow roadway which ran sharply to the right.

Soon we were hemmed in with trees, which in places arched right over the roadway till we passed as through a tunnel. And again great frowning rocks guarded us boldly on either side. Though we were in shelter, we could hear the rising wind, for it moaned and whistled through the rocks, and the branches of the trees crashed together as we swept along. It grew colder and colder still, and fine, powdery snow began to fall, so that soon we and all around us were covered with a white blanket. The keen wind still carried the howling of the dogs, though this grew fainter as we went on our way. The baying of the wolves sounded nearer and nearer, as though they were closing round on us from every side. I grew dreadfully afraid, and the horses shared my fear. The driver, however, was not in the least disturbed. He kept turning his head to left and right, but I could not see anything through the darkness.

Suddenly, away on our left I saw a faint flickering blue flame[62]. The driver saw it at the same moment. He at once checked the horses, and, jumping to the ground, disappeared into the darkness. I did not know what to do, the less as the howling of the wolves grew closer. But while I wondered, the driver suddenly appeared again, and without a word took his seat, and we resumed our journey. I think I must have fallen asleep and kept dreaming of the incident, for it seemed to be repeated endlessly, and now looking back, it is like a sort of awful nightmare. Once the flame appeared so near the road, that even in the darkness around us I could watch the driver's motions. He went rapidly to where the blue flame arose, it must have been very faint, for it did not seem to illumine the place around it at all, and gathering a few stones, formed them into some device.

Once there appeared a strange optical effect. When he stood between me and the flame he did not obstruct it, for I could see its ghostly flicker all the same. This startled me, but as the effect was only momentary, I took it that my eyes deceived me straining through the darkness. Then for a time there were no blue flames, and we sped onwards through the gloom, with the howling of the wolves around us, as though they were following in a moving circle.

At last there came a time when the driver went further afield than he had yet gone, and during his absence, the horses began to tremble worse than ever and to snort and scream with fright. I could not see any cause for it, for the howling of the wolves had ceased altogether. But just then the moon, sailing through the black clouds, appeared behind the jagged crest of a bee-tling, pine-clad rock, and by its light I saw around us a ring of wolves, with white teeth and lolling red tongues, with long, sinewy limbs and shaggy hair. They were a hundred times more terrible in the grim silence which held them than even when they howled. For myself, I felt a sort of paralysis of fear. It is only when a man feels himself face to face with such horrors that he can understand their true import.

All at once the wolves began to howl as though the moonlight had had some peculiar effect on them. The horses jumped about and reared, and looked helplessly round with eyes that rolled in a way painful to see. But the living ring of terror encompassed them on every side, and they had perforce to remain within it. I called to the coachman to come, for it seemed to me that our only chance was to try to break out through the ring and to aid his

---

62 Medieval folklore links blue flame with St. George, a Christian knight and dragon slayer.

approach, I shouted and beat the side of the caleche, hoping by the noise to scare the wolves from the side, so as to give him a chance of reaching the trap. How he came there, I know not, but I heard his voice raised in a tone of imperious command, and looking towards the sound, saw him stand in the roadway. As he swept his long arms, as though brushing aside some impalpable obstacle, the wolves fell back and back further still. Just then a heavy cloud passed across the face of the moon, so that we were again in darkness.

When I could see again the driver was climbing into the caleche, and the wolves disappeared. This was all so strange and uncanny that a dreadful fear came upon me, and I was afraid to speak or move. The time seemed interminable as we swept on our way, now in almost complete darkness, for the rolling clouds obscured the moon.

We kept on ascending, with occasional periods of quick descent, but in the main always ascending. Suddenly, I became conscious of the fact that the driver was in the act of pulling up the horses in the courtyard of a vast ruined castle, from whose tall black windows came no ray of light, and whose broken battlements showed a jagged line against the sky.

✑ CHAPTER 2 ✒
JONATHAN HARKER'S JOURNAL CONTINUED

5 May.—I must have been asleep, for certainly if I had been fully awake I must have noticed the approach of such a remarkable place. In the gloom the courtyard looked of considerable size, and as several dark ways led from it under great round arches, it perhaps seemed bigger than it really is. I have not yet been able to see it by daylight.

When the caleche stopped, the driver jumped down and held out his hand to assist me to alight. Again I could not but notice his prodigious strength. His hand actually seemed like a steel vice that could have crushed mine if he had chosen. Then he took my traps, and placed them on the ground beside me as I stood close to a great door, old and studded with large iron nails, and set in a projecting doorway of massive stone. I could see even in the dim light that the stone was massively carved, but that the carving had been much worn by time and weather. As I stood, the driver jumped again into his seat and shook the reins. The horses started forward, and trap and all disappeared down one of the dark openings.

I stood in silence where I was, for I did not know what to do. Of bell or knocker there was no sign. Through these frowning walls and dark window openings it was not likely that my voice could penetrate. The time I waited seemed endless, and I felt doubts and fears crowding upon me. What sort of place had I come to, and among what kind of people? What sort of grim adventure was it on which I had embarked? Was this a customary incident in the life of a solicitor's clerk sent out to explain the purchase of a London estate to a foreigner? Solicitor's clerk! Mina would not like that. Solicitor, for just before leaving London I got word that my examination was success-ful, and I am now a full-blown solicitor! I began to rub my eyes and pinch myself to see if I were awake. It all seemed like a horrible nightmare to me, and I expected that I should suddenly awake, and find myself at home, with the dawn struggling in through the windows, as I had now and again felt in the morning after a day of overwork. But my flesh answered the pinching test, and my eyes were not to be deceived. I was indeed awake and among the Carpathians. All I could do now was to be patient, and to wait the com-ing of morning.

Just as I had come to this conclusion I heard a heavy step approaching behind the great door, and saw through the chinks the gleam of a coming light. Then there was the sound of rattling chains and the clanking of mas-sive bolts drawn back. A key was turned with the loud grating noise of long disuse, and the great door swung back.

Within, stood a tall old man, clean shaven save for a long white mous-tache, and clad in black from head to foot, without a single speck of colour about him anywhere. He held in his hand an antique silver lamp, in which the flame burned without a chimney or globe of any kind, throwing long quivering shadows as it flickered in the draught of the open door. The old man motioned me in with his right hand with a courtly gesture, saying in excellent English, but with a strange intonation.

"Welcome to my house! Enter freely and of your own free will!" He made no motion of stepping to meet me, but stood like a statue, as though his gesture of welcome had fixed him into stone. The instant, however, that I had stepped over the threshold, he moved impulsively forward, and holding out his hand grasped mine with a strength which made me wince, an effect which was not lessened by the fact that it seemed cold as ice, more like the hand of a dead than a living man. Again he said,

"Welcome to my house! Enter freely. Go safely, and leave something of the happiness you bring!" The strength of the handshake was so much akin to that which I had noticed in the driver, whose face I had not seen, that for a moment I doubted if it were not the same person to whom I was speaking. So to make sure, I said interrogatively, "Count Dracula?"

He bowed in a courtly way as he replied, "I am Dracula, and I bid you welcome, Mr. Harker, to my house. Come in, the night air is chill, and you must need to eat and rest." As he was speaking, he put the lamp on a bracket on the wall, and stepping out, took my luggage. He had carried it in before I could forestall him. I protested, but he insisted.

"Nay, sir, you are my guest. It is late, and my people are not available. Let me see to your comfort myself." He insisted on carrying my traps along the passage, and then up a great winding stair, and along another great passage, on whose stone floor our steps rang heavily. At the end of this he threw open a heavy door, and I rejoiced to see within a well-lit room in which a table was spread for supper, and on whose mighty hearth a great fire of logs, freshly replenished, flamed and flared.

The Count halted, putting down my bags, closed the door, and crossing the room, opened another door, which led into a small octagonal room lit by a single lamp, and seemingly without a window of any sort. Passing through this, he opened another door, and motioned me to enter. It was a welcome sight. For here was a great bedroom well lighted and warmed with another log fire, also added to but lately, for the top logs were fresh, which sent a hollow roar up the wide chimney. The Count himself left my luggage inside and withdrew, saying, before he closed the door.

"You will need, after your journey, to refresh yourself by making your toilet. I trust you will find all you wish. When you are ready, come into the other room, where you will find your supper prepared."

The light and warmth and the Count's courteous welcome seemed to have dissipated all my doubts and fears. Having then reached my normal state, I discovered that I was half famished with hunger. So making a hasty toilet, I went into the other room.

I found supper already laid out. My host, who stood on one side of the great fireplace, leaning against the stonework, made a graceful wave of his hand to the table, and said,

"I pray you, be seated and sup how you please. You will I trust, excuse me that I do not join you, but I have dined already, and I do not sup."

I handed to him the sealed letter which Mr. Hawkins had entrusted to me. He opened it and read it gravely. Then, with a charming smile, he handed it to me to read. One passage of it, at least, gave me a thrill of pleasure.

"I must regret that an attack of gout, from which malady I am a constant sufferer, forbids absolutely any travelling on my part for some time to come. But I am happy to say I can send a sufficient substitute, one in whom I have every possible confidence. He is a young man, full of energy and talent in his own way, and of a very faithful disposition. He is discreet and silent, and has grown into manhood in my service. He shall be ready to attend on you when you will during his stay, and shall take your instructions in all matters."

The count himself came forward and took off the cover of a dish, and I fell to at once on an excellent roast chicken. This, with some cheese and a salad and a bottle of old tokay[63], of which I had two glasses, was my supper. During the time I was eating it the Count asked me many questions as to my journey, and I told him by degrees all I had experienced.

By this time I had finished my supper, and by my host's desire had drawn up a chair by the fire and begun to smoke a cigar which he offered me, at the same time excusing himself that he did not smoke. I had now an opportunity of observing him, and found him of a very marked physiognomy.

His face was a strong, a very strong, aquiline, with high bridge of the thin nose and peculiarly arched nostrils, with lofty domed forehead, and hair growing scantily round the temples but profusely elsewhere. His eyebrows were very massive, almost meeting over the nose, and with bushy hair that seemed to curl in its own profusion. The mouth, so far as I could see it under the heavy moustache, was fixed and rather cruel-looking, with peculiarly sharp white teeth. These protruded over the lips, whose remarkable ruddiness showed astonishing vitality in a man of his years. For the rest, his ears were pale, and at the tops extremely pointed. The chin was broad and strong, and the cheeks firm though thin. The general effect was one of extraordinary pallor.

Hitherto I had noticed the backs of his hands as they lay on his knees in the firelight, and they had seemed rather white and fine. But seeing them now close to me, I could not but notice that they were rather coarse, broad, with squat fingers. Strange to say, there were hairs in the centre of the palm. The nails were long and fine, and cut to a sharp point. As the Count leaned over me and his hands touched me, I could not repress a shudder. It may have been that his breath was rank, but a horrible feeling of nausea came over me, which, do what I would, I could not conceal.

The Count, evidently noticing it, drew back. And with a grim sort of smile, which showed more than he had yet done his protuberant teeth, sat himself down again on his own side of the fireplace. We were both silent for a while, and as I looked towards the window I saw the first dim streak of the coming dawn. There seemed a strange stillness over everything. But as I listened, I heard as if from down below in the valley the howling of many wolves. The Count's eyes gleamed, and he said.

"Listen to them, the children of the night. What music they make!" Seeing, I suppose, some expression in my face strange to him, he added, "Ah,

63 Hungarian wine.

sir, you dwellers in the city cannot enter into the feelings of the hunter."
Then he rose and said.

"But you must be tired. Your bedroom is all ready, and tomorrow you
shall sleep as late as you will. I have to be away till the afternoon, so sleep
well and dream well!" With a courteous bow, he opened for me himself the
door to the octagonal room, and I entered my bedroom.

I am all in a sea of wonders. I doubt. I fear. I think strange things, which
I dare not confess to my own soul. God keep me, if only for the sake of
those dear to me!

7 May.—It is again early morning, but I have rested and enjoyed the last
twenty-four hours. I slept till late in the day, and awoke of my own accord.
When I had dressed myself I went into the room where we had supped, and
found a cold breakfast laid out, with coffee kept hot by the pot being placed
on the hearth. There was a card on the table, on which was written—"I have
to be absent for a while. Do not wait for me. D." I set to and enjoyed a hearty
meal. When I had done, I looked for a bell, so that I might let the servants
know I had finished, but I could not find one. There are certainly odd de-
ficiencies in the house, considering the extraordinary evidences of wealth
which are round me. The table service is of gold, and so beautifully wrought
that it must be of immense value. The curtains and upholstery of the chairs
and sofas and the hangings of my bed are of the costliest and most beautiful
fabrics, and must have been of fabulous value when they were made, for they
are centuries old, though in excellent order. I saw something like them in
Hampton Court, but they were worn and frayed and moth-eaten. But still
in none of the rooms is there a mirror. There is not even a toilet glass on my
table, and I had to get the little shaving glass from my bag before I could either shave or brush my hair. I have not yet seen a servant anywhere, or heard
a sound near the castle except the howling of wolves. Some time after I had
finished my meal, I do not know whether to call it breakfast or dinner, for it
was between five and six o'clock when I had it, I looked about for something
to read, for I did not like to go about the castle until I had asked the Count's
permission. There was absolutely nothing in the room, book, newspaper, or
even writing materials, so I opened another door in the room and found a
sort of library. The door opposite mine I tried, but found locked.

In the library I found, to my great delight, a vast number of English
books, whole shelves full of them, and bound volumes of magazines and
newspapers. A table in the centre was littered with English magazines and
newspapers, though none of them were of very recent date. The books were
of the most varied kind, history, geography, politics, political economy, bot-
any, geology, law, all relating to England and English life and customs and

manners. There were even such books of reference as the London Directory, the "Red" and "Blue" books, Whitaker's Almanac, the Army and Navy Lists, and it somehow gladdened my heart to see it, the Law List.

Whilst I was looking at the books, the door opened, and the Count entered. He saluted me in a hearty way, and hoped that I had had a good night's rest. Then he went on.

"I am glad you found your way in here, for I am sure there is much that will interest you. These companions," and he laid his hand on some of the books, "have been good friends to me, and for some years past, ever since I had the idea of going to London, have given me many, many hours of pleasure. Through them I have come to know your great England, and to know her is to love her. I long to go through the crowded streets of your mighty London, to be in the midst of the whirl and rush of humanity, to share its life, its change, its death, and all that makes it what it is. But alas! As yet I only know your tongue through books. To you, my friend, I look that I know it to speak."

"But, Count," I said, "You know and speak English thoroughly!" He bowed gravely.

"I thank you, my friend, for your all too-flattering estimate, but yet I fear that I am but a little way on the road I would travel. True, I know the grammar and the words, but yet I know not how to speak them."

"Indeed," I said, "You speak excellently."

"Not so," he answered. "Well, I know that, did I move and speak in your London, none there are who would not know me for a stranger. That is not enough for me. Here I am noble. I am a *Boyar*[64]. The common people know me, and I am master. But a stranger in a strange land, he is no one. Men know him not, and to know not is to care not for. I am content if I am like the rest, so that no man stops if he sees me, or pauses in his speaking if he hears my words, 'Ha, ha! A stranger!' I have been so long master that I would be master still, or at least that none other should be master of me. You come to me not alone as agent of my friend Peter Hawkins, of Exeter, to tell me all about my new estate in London. You shall, I trust, rest here with me a while, so that by our talking I may learn the English intonation. And I would that you tell me when I make error, even of the smallest, in my speaking. I am sorry that I had to be away so long today, but you will, I know forgive one who has so many important affairs in hand."

Of course I said all I could about being willing, and asked if I might come into that room when I chose. He answered, "Yes, certainly," and added.

"You may go anywhere you wish in the castle, except where the doors are locked, where of course you will not wish to go. There is reason that

---

64 Nobleman.

all things are as they are, and did you see with my eyes and know with my knowledge, you would perhaps better understand." I said I was sure of this, and then he went on.

"We are in Transylvania, and Transylvania is not England. Our ways are not your ways, and there shall be to you many strange things. Nay, from what you have told me of your experiences already, you know something of what strange things there may be."

This led to much conversation, and as it was evident that he wanted to talk, if only for talking's sake, I asked him many questions regarding things that had already happened to me or come within my notice. Sometimes he sheered off the subject, or turned the conversation by pretending not to understand, but generally he answered all I asked most frankly. Then as time went on, and I had got somewhat bolder, I asked him of some of the strange things of the preceding night, as for instance, why the coachman went to the places where he had seen the blue flames. He then explained to me that it was commonly believed that on a certain night of the year, last night, in fact, when all evil spirits are supposed to have unchecked sway, a blue flame is seen over any place where treasure has been concealed.

"That treasure has been hidden," he went on, "in the region through which you came last night, there can be but little doubt. For it was the ground fought over for centuries by the Wallachian, the Saxon, and the Turk. Why, there is hardly a foot of soil in all this region that has not been enriched by the blood of men, patriots or invaders. In the old days there were stirring times, when the Austrian and the Hungarian came up in hordes, and the patriots went out to meet them, men and women, the aged and the children too, and waited their coming on the rocks above the passes, that they might sweep destruction on them with their artificial avalanches. When the invader was triumphant he found but little, for whatever there was had been sheltered in the friendly soil."

"But how," said I, "can it have remained so long undiscovered, when there is a sure index to it if men will but take the trouble to look?" The Count smiled, and as his lips ran back over his gums, the long, sharp, canine teeth showed out strangely. He answered:

"Because your peasant is at heart a coward and a fool! Those flames only appear on one night, and on that night no man of this land will, if he can help it, stir without his doors. And, dear sir, even if he did he would not know what to do. Why, even the peasant that you tell me of who marked the place of the flame would not know where to look in daylight even for his own work. Even you would not, I dare be sworn, be able to find these places again?"

"There you are right," I said. "I know no more than the dead where even to look for them." Then we drifted into other matters.

"Come," he said at last, "tell me of London and of the house which you have procured for me." With an apology for my remissness, I went into my own room to get the papers from my bag. Whilst I was placing them in order I heard a rattling of china and silver in the next room, and as I passed through, noticed that the table had been cleared and the lamp lit, for it was by this time deep into the dark. The lamps were also lit in the study or library, and I found the Count lying on the sofa, reading, of all things in the world, an English Bradshaw's Guide. When I came in he cleared the books and papers from the table, and with him I went into plans and deeds and figures of all sorts. He was interested in everything, and asked me a myriad questions about the place and its surroundings. He clearly had studied beforehand all he could get on the subject of the neighbourhood, for he evidently at the end knew very much more than I did. When I remarked this, he answered.

"Well, but, my friend, is it not needful that I should? When I go there I shall be all alone, and my friend Harker Jonathan, nay, pardon me. I fall into my country's habit of putting your patronymic first, my friend Jonathan Harker will not be by my side to correct and aid me. He will be in Exeter, miles away, probably working at papers of the law with my other friend, Peter Hawkins. So!"

We went thoroughly into the business of the purchase of the estate at Purfleet. When I had told him the facts and got his signature to the necessary papers, and had written a letter with them ready to post to Mr. Hawkins, he began to ask me how I had come across so suitable a place. I read to him the notes which I had made at the time, and which I inscribe here.

"At Purfleet, on a byroad, I came across just such a place as seemed to be required, and where was displayed a dilapidated notice that the place was for sale. It was surrounded by a high wall, of ancient structure, built of heavy stones, and has not been repaired for a large number of years. The closed gates are of heavy old oak and iron, all eaten with rust.

"The estate is called Carfax, no doubt a corruption of the old *Quatre Face*, as the house is four sided, agreeing with the cardinal points of the compass. It contains in all some twenty acres, quite surrounded by the solid stone wall above mentioned. There are many trees on it, which make it in places gloomy, and there is a deep, dark-looking pond or small lake, evidently fed by some springs, as the water is clear and flows away in a fair-sized stream. The house is very large and of all periods back, I should say, to mediaeval times, for one part is of stone immensely thick, with only a few windows high up and heavily barred with iron. It looks like part of a keep, and is close to an old chapel or church. I could not enter it, as I had not the key of the door leading to it from the house, but I have taken with my Kodak views of it from various points. The house had been added to, but in a very straggling way, and I can only guess at the amount of ground it covers, which must be very great. There are but few houses close at hand, one being a very large house only recently added to and formed into a private lunatic asylum. It is not, however, visible from the grounds."

When I had finished, he said, "I am glad that it is old and big. I myself am of an old family, and to live in a new house would kill me. A house cannot be made habitable in a day, and after all, how few days go to make up a century. I rejoice also that there is a chapel of old times. We Transylvanian nobles love not to think that our bones may lie amongst the common dead. I seek not gaiety nor mirth, not the bright voluptuousness of much sunshine and sparkling waters which please the young and gay. I am no longer young, and my heart, through weary years of mourning over the dead, is not attuned to mirth. Moreover, the walls of my castle are broken. The shadows are many, and the wind breathes cold through the broken battlements and casements. I love the shade and the shadow, and would be alone with my thoughts when I may." Somehow his words and his look did not seem to accord, or else it was that his cast of face made his smile look malignant and saturnine.

Presently, with an excuse, he left me, asking me to pull my papers together. He was some little time away, and I began to look at some of the books around me. One was an atlas, which I found opened naturally to England, as if that map had been much used. On looking at it I found in certain places little rings marked, and on examining these I noticed that one was near London on the east side, manifestly where his new estate was situated. The other two were Exeter, and Whitby on the Yorkshire coast.

It was the better part of an hour when the Count returned. "Aha!" he said. "Still at your books? Good! But you must not work always. Come! I am informed that your supper is ready." He took my arm, and we went into the next room, where I found an excellent supper ready on the table. The Count again excused himself, as he had dined out on his being away from home. But he sat as on the previous night, and chatted whilst I ate. After supper I smoked, as on the last evening, and the Count stayed with me, chatting and asking questions on every conceivable subject, hour after hour. I felt that it was getting very late indeed, but I did not say anything, for I felt under obligation to meet my host's wishes in every way. I was not sleepy, as the long sleep yesterday had fortified me, but I could not help experiencing that chill which comes over one at the coming of the dawn, which is like, in its way, the turn of the tide. They say that people who are near death die generally at the change to dawn or at the turn of the tide. Anyone who has when tired, and tied as it were to his post, experienced this change in the atmosphere can well believe it. All at once we heard the crow of the cock coming up with preternatural shrillness through the clear morning air.

Count Dracula, jumping to his feet, said, "Why there is the morning again! How remiss I am to let you stay up so long. You must make your conversation regarding my dear new country of England less interesting, so that I may not forget how time flies by us," and with a courtly bow, he quickly left me.

I went into my room and drew the curtains, but there was little to notice. My window opened into the courtyard, all I could see was the warm grey of quickening sky. So I pulled the curtains again, and have written of this day.

8 May.—I began to fear as I wrote in this book that I was getting too diffuse. But now I am glad that I went into detail from the first, for there is something so strange about this place and all in it that I cannot but feel uneasy. I wish I were safe out of it, or that I had never come. It may be that this strange night existence is telling on me, but would that that were all! If there were any one to talk to I could bear it, but there is no one. I have only the Count to speak with, and he—I fear I am myself the only living soul within the place. Let me be prosaic so far as facts can be. It will help me to bear up, and imagination must not run riot with me. If it does I am lost. Let me say at once how I stand, or seem to.

I only slept a few hours when I went to bed, and feeling that I could not sleep any more, got up. I had hung my shaving glass by the window, and was just beginning to shave. Suddenly I felt a hand on my shoulder, and heard the Count's voice saying to me, "Good morning." I started, for it amazed me that I had not seen him, since the reflection of the glass covered the whole room behind me. In starting I had cut myself slightly, but did not notice it at the moment. Having answered the Count's salutation, I turned to the glass again to see how I had been mistaken. This time there could be no error, for the man was close to me, and I could see him over my shoulder. But there was no reflection of him in the mirror! The whole room behind me was displayed, but there was no sign of a man in it, except myself.

This was startling, and coming on the top of so many strange things, was beginning to increase that vague feeling of uneasiness which I always have when the Count is near. But at the instant I saw that the cut had bled a little, and the blood was trickling over my chin. I laid down the razor, turning as I did so half round to look for some sticking plaster. When the Count saw my face, his eyes blazed with a sort of demoniac fury, and he suddenly made a grab at my throat. I drew away and his hand touched the string of beads which held the crucifix. It made an instant change in him, for the fury passed so quickly that I could hardly believe that it was ever there.

"Take care," he said, "take care how you cut yourself. It is more dangerous that you think in this country." Then seizing the shaving glass, he went on, "And this is the wretched thing that has done the mischief. It is a foul bauble of man's vanity. Away with it!" And opening the window with one wrench of his terrible hand, he flung out the glass, which was shattered into a thousand pieces on the stones of the courtyard far below. Then he withdrew without a word. It is very annoying, for I do not see how I am to shave, unless in my watch-case or the bottom of the shaving pot, which is fortunately of metal.

When I went into the dining room, breakfast was prepared, but I could not find the Count anywhere. So I breakfasted alone. It is strange that as yet I have not seen the Count eat or drink. He must be a very peculiar man! After breakfast I did a little exploring in the castle. I went out on the stairs, and found a room looking towards the South.

The view was magnificent, and from where I stood there was every opportunity of seeing it. The castle is on the very edge of a terrific precipice. A stone falling from the window would fall a thousand feet without touching anything! As far as the eye can reach is a sea of green tree tops, with occasionally a deep rift where there is a chasm. Here and there are silver threads where the rivers wind in deep gorges through the forests.

But I am not in heart to describe beauty, for when I had seen the view I explored further. Doors, doors, doors everywhere, and all locked and bolted. In no place save from the windows in the castle walls is there an available exit. The castle is a veritable prison, and I am a prisoner!

℘ CHAPTER 3 ℭ

JONATHAN HARKER'S JOURNAL CONTINUED

When I found that I was a prisoner a sort of wild feeling came over me. I rushed up and down the stairs, trying every door and peering out of every window I could find, but after a little the conviction of my helplessness overpowered all other feelings. When I look back after a few hours I think I must have been mad for the time, for I behaved much as a rat does in a trap. When, however, the conviction had come to me that I was helpless I sat down quietly, as quietly as I have ever done anything in my life, and began to think over what was best to be done. I am thinking still, and as yet have come to no definite conclusion. Of one thing only am I certain. That it is no use making my ideas known to the Count. He knows well that I am imprisoned, and as he has done it himself, and has doubtless his own motives for it, he would only deceive me if I trusted him fully with the facts. So far as I can see, my only plan will be to keep my knowledge and my fears to myself, and my eyes open. I am, I know, either being deceived, like a baby, by my own fears, or else I am in desperate straits, and if the latter be so, I need, and shall need, all my brains to get through.

I had hardly come to this conclusion when I heard the great door below shut, and knew that the Count had returned. He did not come at once into the library, so I went cautiously to my own room and found him making the bed. This was odd, but only confirmed what I had all along thought, that there are no servants in the house. When later I saw him through the chink of the hinges of the door laying the table in the dining room, I was assured of it. For if he does himself all these menial offices, surely it is proof that there is no one else in the castle, it must have been the Count himself who was the driver of the coach that brought me here. This is a terrible thought, for if so, what does it mean that he could control the wolves, as he did, by only holding up his hand for silence? How was it that all the people at Bistritz and on the coach had some terrible fear for me? What meant the giving of the crucifix, of the garlic, of the wild rose, of the mountain ash?

Bless that good, good woman who hung the crucifix round my neck! For it is a comfort and a strength to me whenever I touch it. It is odd that a thing which I have been taught to regard with disfavour and as idolatrous should in a time of loneliness and trouble be of help. Is it that there is something in the essence of the thing itself, or that it is a medium, a tangible help, in conveying memories of sympathy and comfort? Some time, if it may be, I must examine this matter and try to make up my mind about it. In the meantime I must find out all I can about Count Dracula, as it may help me to understand. Tonight he may talk of himself, if I turn the conversation that way. I must be very careful, however, not to awake his suspicion.

Midnight.—I have had a long talk with the Count. I asked him a few questions on Transylvania history, and he warmed up to the subject wonderfully. In his speaking of things and people, and especially of battles, he spoke as if he had been present at them all. This he afterwards explained by saying that to a *Boyar* the pride of his house and name is his own pride, that their glory is his glory, that their fate is his fate. Whenever he spoke of his house he always said "we", and spoke almost in the plural, like a king speaking. I wish I could put down all he said exactly as he said it, for to me it was most fascinating. It seemed to have in it a whole history of the country. He grew excited as he spoke, and walked about the room pulling his great white moustache and grasping anything on which he laid his hands as though he would crush it by main strength. One thing he said which I shall put down as nearly as I can, for it tells in its way the story of his race.

"We Szekelys have a right to be proud, for in our veins flows the blood of many brave races who fought as the lion fights, for lordship. Here, in the whirlpool of European races, the Ugric tribe bore down from Iceland the fighting spirit which Thor and Wodin gave them, which their Berserkers[65] displayed to such fell intent on the seaboards of Europe, aye, and of Asia and Africa too, till the peoples thought that the werewolves themselves had come. Here, too, when they came, they found the Huns, whose war-like fury had swept the earth like a living flame, till the dying peoples held that in their veins ran the blood of those old witches, who, expelled from Scythia had mated with the devils in the desert. Fools, fools! What devil or what witch was ever so great as Attila, whose blood is in these veins?" He held up his arms. "Is it a wonder that we were a conquering race, that we were proud, that when the Magyar, the Lombard, the Avar, the Bulgar, or the Turk poured his thousands on our frontiers, we drove them back? Is it strange that when Arpad and his legions swept through the Hungarian fatherland he found us here when he reached the frontier, that the Honfo-glalas was completed there? And when the Hungarian flood swept eastward, the Szekelys were claimed as kindred by the victorious Magyars, and to us for centuries was trusted the guarding of the frontier of Turkeyland. Aye, and more than that, endless duty of the frontier guard, for as the Turks say, 'water sleeps, and the enemy is sleepless.' Who more gladly than we throughout the Four Nations received the 'bloody sword,' or at its warlike call flocked quicker to the standard of the King? When was redeemed that great shame of my nation, the shame of Cassova, when the flags of the Wallach and the Magyar went down beneath the Crescent? Who was it but one of my own race who as Voivode[66] crossed the Danube and beat the Turk on his own ground? This was a Dracula indeed! Woe was it that his own unworthy brother, when he had fallen, sold his people to the Turk and brought the shame of slavery on them! Was it not this Dracula, indeed, who inspired that other of his race who in a later age again and again brought his forces over the great river into Turkeyland, who, when he was beaten back, came again, and again, though he had to come alone from the bloody field where his troops were being slaughtered, since he knew that he alone could ultimately triumph! They said that he thought only of himself. Bah! What good are peasants without a leader? Where ends the war without a

---

65 Norse warriors.
66 Prince.

brain and heart to conduct it? Again, when, after the battle of Mohacs, we threw off the Hungarian yoke, we of the Dracula blood were amongst their leaders, for our spirit would not brook that we were not free. Ah, young sir, the Szekelys, and the Dracula as their heart's blood, their brains, and their swords, can boast a record that mushroom growths like the Hapsburgs and the Romanoffs can never reach. The warlike days are over. Blood is too precious a thing in these days of dishonourable peace, and the glories of the great races are as a tale that is told."

It was by this time close on morning, and we went to bed. (*Mem.*, this diary seems horribly like the beginning of the "Arabian Nights," for everything has to break off at cockcrow, or like the ghost of Hamlet's father.)

12 May.—Let me begin with facts, bare, meager facts, verified by books and figures, and of which there can be no doubt. I must not confuse them with experiences which will have to rest on my own observation, or my memory of them. Last evening when the Count came from his room he began by asking me questions on legal matters and on the doing of certain kinds of business. I had spent the day wearily over books, and, simply to keep my mind occupied, went over some of the matters I had been examined in at Lincoln's Inn. There was a certain method in the Count's inquiries, so I shall try to put them down in sequence. The knowledge may somehow or some time be useful to me.

First, he asked if a man in England might have two solicitors or more. I told him he might have a dozen if he wished, but that it would not be wise to have more than one solicitor engaged in one transaction, as only one could act at a time, and that to change would be certain to militate against his interest. He seemed thoroughly to understand, and went on to ask if there would be any practical difficulty in having one man to attend, say, to banking, and another to look after shipping, in case local help were needed in a place far from the home of the banking solicitor. I asked to explain more fully, so that I might not by any chance mislead him, so he said,

"I shall illustrate. Your friend and mine, Mr. Peter Hawkins, from under the shadow of your beautiful cathedral at Exeter, which is far from London, buys for me through your good self my place at London. Good! Now here let me say frankly, lest you should think it strange that I have sought the services of one so far off from London instead of some one resident there, that my motive was that no local interest might be served save my wish only, and as one of London residence might, perhaps, have some purpose of himself or friend to serve, I went thus afield to seek my agent, whose labours should be only to my interest. Now, suppose I, who have much of affairs, wish to ship goods, say, to Newcastle, or Durham, or Harwich, or

Dover, might it not be that it could with more ease be done by consigning to one in these ports?"

I answered that certainly it would be most easy, but that we solicitors had a system of agency one for the other, so that local work could be done locally on instruction from any solicitor, so that the client, simply placing himself in the hands of one man, could have his wishes carried out by him without further trouble.

"But," said he, "I could be at liberty to direct myself. Is it not so?"

"Of course," I replied, and "Such is often done by men of business, who do not like the whole of their affairs to be known by any one person."

"Good!" he said, and then went on to ask about the means of making consignments and the forms to be gone through, and of all sorts of difficulties which might arise, but by forethought could be guarded against. I explained all these things to him to the best of my ability, and he certainly left me under the impression that he would have made a wonderful solicitor, for there was nothing that he did not think of or foresee. For a man who was never in the country, and who did not evidently do much in the way of business, his knowledge and acumen were wonderful. When he had satisfied himself on these points of which he had spoken, and I had verified all as well as I could by the books available, he suddenly stood up and said, "Have you written since your first letter to our friend Mr. Peter Hawkins, or to any other?"

It was with some bitterness in my heart that I answered that I had not, that as yet I had not seen any opportunity of sending letters to anybody.

"Then write now, my young friend," he said, laying a heavy hand on my shoulder, "write to our friend and to any other, and say, if it will please you, that you shall stay with me until a month from now."

"Do you wish me to stay so long?" I asked, for my heart grew cold at the thought.

"I desire it much, nay I will take no refusal. When your master, employer, what you will, engaged that someone should come on his behalf, it was understood that my needs only were to be consulted. I have not stinted. Is it not so?"

What could I do but bow acceptance? It was Mr. Hawkins' interest, not mine, and I had to think of him, not myself, and besides, while Count Dracula was speaking, there was that in his eyes and in his bearing which made me remember that I was a prisoner, and that if I wished it I could have no choice. The Count saw his victory in my bow, and his mastery in the trouble of my face, for he began at once to use them, but in his own smooth, resistless way.

"I pray you, my good young friend, that you will not discourse of things other than business in your letters. It will doubtless please your friends to know that you are well, and that you look forward to getting home to them. Is it not so?" As he spoke he handed me three sheets of note paper and three envelopes. They were all of the thinnest foreign post, and looking at them, then at him, and noticing his quiet smile, with the sharp, canine teeth lying over the red underlip, I understood as well as if he had spoken that I should be more careful what I wrote, for he would be able to read it. So I determined to write only formal notes now, but to write fully to Mr. Hawkins in secret, and also to Mina, for to her I could write shorthand, which would puzzle the Count, if he did see it. When I had written my two letters I sat quiet, reading a book whilst the Count wrote several notes, referring as he wrote them to some books on his table. Then he took up my two and placed them with his own, and put by his writing materials, after which, the instant the door had closed behind him, I leaned over and looked at the letters, which were face down on the table. I felt no compunction in doing so for under the circumstances I felt that I should protect myself in every way I could.

One of the letters was directed to Samuel F. Billington, No. 7, The Crescent, Whitby, another to Herr Leutner, Varna. The third was to Coutts & Co., London, and the fourth to Herren Klopstock & Billreuth, bankers, Buda Pesth. The second and fourth were unsealed. I was just about to look at them when I saw the door handle move. I sank back in my seat, having just had time to resume my book before the Count, holding still another letter in his hand, entered the room. He took up the letters on the table and stamped them carefully, and then turning to me, said,

"I trust you will forgive me, but I have much work to do in private this evening. You will, I hope, find all things as you wish." At the door he turned, and after a moment's pause said, "Let me advise you, my dear young friend. Nay, let me warn you with all seriousness, that should you leave these rooms you will not by any chance go to sleep in any other part of the castle. It is old, and has many memories, and there are bad dreams for those who sleep unwisely. Be warned! Should sleep now or ever overcome you, or be like to do, then haste to your own chamber or to these rooms, for your rest will then be safe. But if you be not careful in this respect, then," He finished his speech in a gruesome way, for he motioned with his hands as if he were washing them. I quite understood. My only doubt was as to whether any dream could be more terrible than the unnatural, horrible net of gloom and mystery which seemed closing around me.

Later.—I endorse the last words written, but this time there is no doubt in question. I shall not fear to sleep in any place where he is not. I have placed the crucifix over the head of my bed, I imagine that my rest is thus freer from dreams, and there it shall remain.

When he left me I went to my room. After a little while, not hearing any sound, I came out and went up the stone stair to where I could look out towards the South. There was some sense of freedom in the vast expanse, inaccessible though it was to me, as compared with the narrow darkness of the courtyard. Looking out on this, I felt that I was indeed in prison, and I seemed to want a breath of fresh air, though it were of the night. I am beginning to feel this nocturnal existence tell on me. It is destroying my nerve. I start at my own shadow, and am full of all sorts of horrible imaginings. God knows that there is ground for my terrible fear in this accursed place! I looked out over the beautiful expanse, bathed in soft yellow moonlight till it was almost as light as day. In the soft light the distant hills became melted, and the shadows in the valleys and gorges of velvety blackness. The mere beauty seemed to cheer me. There was peace and comfort in every breath I drew. As I leaned from the window my eye was caught by something moving a storey below me, and somewhat to my left, where I imagined, from the order of the rooms, that the windows of the Count's own room would look out. The window at which I stood was tall and deep, stone-mullioned, and though weatherworn, was still complete. But it was evidently many a day since the case had been there. I drew back behind the stonework, and looked carefully out.

What I saw was the Count's head coming out from the window. I did not see the face, but I knew the man by the neck and the movement of his back and arms. In any case I could not mistake the hands which I had had some many opportunities of studying. I was at first interested and somewhat amused, for it is wonderful how small a matter will interest and amuse a man when he is a prisoner. But my very feelings changed to repulsion and terror when I saw the whole man slowly emerge from the window and begin to crawl down the castle wall over the dreadful abyss, face down with his cloak spreading out around him like great wings. At first I could not believe my eyes. I thought it was some trick of the moonlight, some weird effect of shadow, but I kept looking, and it could be no delusion. I saw the fingers and toes grasp the corners of the stones, worn clear of the mortar by the stress of years, and by thus using every projection and inequality move downwards with considerable speed, just as a lizard moves along a wall.

What manner of man is this, or what manner of creature, is it in the semblance of man? I feel the dread of this horrible place overpowering me. I am in fear, in awful fear, and there is no escape for me. I am encompassed about with terrors that I dare not think of.

15 May.—Once more I have seen the count go out in his lizard fashion. He moved downwards in a sidelong way, some hundred feet down, and a good deal to the left. He vanished into some hole or window. When his head had disappeared, I leaned out to try and see more, but without avail. The distance was too great to allow a proper angle of sight. I knew he had left the castle now, and thought to use the opportunity to explore more than I had dared to do as yet. I went back to the room, and taking a lamp, tried all the doors. They were all locked, as I had expected, and the locks were comparatively new. But I went down the stone stairs to the hall where I had entered originally. I found I could pull back the bolts easily enough and unhook the great chains. But the door was locked, and the key was gone! That key must be in the Count's room. I must watch should his door be unlocked, so that I may get it and escape. I went on to make a thorough examination of the various stairs and passages, and to try the doors that opened from them. One or two small rooms near the hall were open, but there was nothing to see in them except old furniture, dusty with age and moth-eaten. At last, however, I found one door at the top of the stairway which, though it seemed locked, gave a little under pressure. I tried it harder, and found that it was not really locked, but that the resistance came from the fact that the hinges had fallen somewhat, and the heavy door rested on the floor. Here was an opportunity which I might not have again, so I exerted myself, and with many efforts forced it back so that I could enter. I was now in a wing of the castle further to the right than the rooms I knew and a storey lower down. From the windows I could see that the suite of rooms lay along to the south of the castle, the windows of the end room looking out both west and south. On the latter side, as well as to the former, there was a great precipice. The castle was built on the corner of a great rock, so that on three sides it was quite impregnable, and great windows were placed here where sling, or bow, or culverin[67] could not reach, and consequently light and comfort, impossible to a position which had to be guarded, were secured. To the west was a great valley, and then, rising far away, great jagged mountain fastnesses, rising peak on peak, the sheer rock studded with mountain ash and thorn, whose roots clung in cracks and crevices and crannies of the stone. This was evidently the portion of the castle occupied by the ladies in bygone days, for the furniture had more an air of comfort than any I had seen.

The windows were curtainless, and the yellow moonlight, flooding in through the diamond panes, enabled one to see even colours, whilst it softened the wealth of dust which lay over all and disguised in some measure the ravages of time and moth. My lamp seemed to be of little effect in the brilliant moonlight, but I was glad to have it with me, for there was a dread

67 Cannon.

loneliness in the place which chilled my heart and made my nerves tremble. Still, it was better than living alone in the rooms which I had come to hate from the presence of the Count, and after trying a little to school my nerves, I found a soft quietude come over me. Here I am, sitting at a little oak table where in old times possibly some fair lady sat to pen, with much thought and many blushes, her ill-spelt love letter, and writing in my diary in shorthand all that has happened since I closed it last. It is the nineteenth century up-to-date with a vengeance. And yet, unless my senses deceive me, the old centuries had, and have, powers of their own which mere "modernity" cannot kill.

Later: The morning of 16 May.—God preserve my sanity, for to this I am reduced. Safety and the assurance of safety are things of the past. Whilst I live on here there is but one thing to hope for, that I may not go mad, if, indeed, I be not mad already. If I be sane, then surely it is maddening to think that of all the foul things that lurk in this hateful place the Count is the least dreadful to me, that to him alone I can look for safety, even though this be only whilst I can serve his purpose. Great God! Merciful God, let me be calm, for out of that way lies madness indeed. I begin to get new lights on certain things which have puzzled me. Up to now I never quite knew what Shakespeare meant when he made Hamlet say:—

> "My tablets! Quick, my tablets!
> 'Tis meet that I put it down," etc.,

For now, feeling as though my own brain were unhinged or as if the shock had come which must end in its undoing, I turn to my diary for repose. The habit of entering accurately must help to soothe me.

The Count's mysterious warning frightened me at the time. It frightens me more not when I think of it, for in the future he has a fearful hold upon me. I shall fear to doubt what he may say!

When I had written in my diary and had fortunately replaced the book and pen in my pocket I felt sleepy. The Count's warning came into my mind, but I took pleasure in disobeying it. The sense of sleep was upon me, and with it the obstinacy which sleep brings as outrider. The soft moonlight soothed, and the wide expanse without gave a sense of freedom which refreshed me. I determined not to return tonight to the gloom-haunted rooms, but to sleep here, where, of old, ladies had sat and sung and lived sweet lives whilst their gentle breasts were sad for their menfolk away in the midst of remorseless wars. I drew a great couch out of its place near the corner, so that as I lay, I could look at the lovely view to east and south, and unthinking of and uncaring for the dust, composed myself for sleep. I suppose I must have fallen asleep. I hope so, but I fear, for all that followed was startlingly real, so real that now sitting here in the broad, full sunlight of the morning, I cannot in the least believe that it was all sleep.

I was not alone. The room was the same, unchanged in any way since I came into it. I could see along the floor, in the brilliant moonlight, my own footsteps marked where I had disturbed the long accumulation of dust. In the moonlight opposite me were three young women, ladies by their dress and manner. I thought at the time that I must be dreaming when I saw them, they threw no shadow on the floor. They came close to me, and looked at me for some time, and then whispered together. Two were dark, and had high aquiline noses, like the Count, and great dark, piercing eyes, that seemed to be almost red when contrasted with the pale yellow moon. The other was fair, as fair as can be, with great masses of golden hair and eyes like pale sapphires. I seemed somehow to know her face, and to know it in connection with some dreamy fear, but I could not recollect at the moment how or where. All three had brilliant white teeth that shone like pearls against the ruby of their voluptuous lips. There was something about them that made me uneasy, some longing and at the same time some deadly fear. I felt in my heart a wicked, burning desire that they would kiss me with those red lips. It is not good to note this down, lest some day it should meet Mina's eyes and cause her pain, but it is the truth. They whispered together, and then they all three laughed, such a silvery, musical laugh, but as hard as though the sound never could have come through the softness of human lips. It was like the intolerable, tingling sweetness of waterglasses when played on by a cunning hand. The fair girl shook her head coquettishly, and the other two urged her on.

One said, "Go on! You are first, and we shall follow. Yours is the right to begin."

The other added, "He is young and strong. There are kisses for us all."

I lay quiet, looking out from under my eyelashes in an agony of delightful anticipation. The fair girl advanced and bent over me till I could feel the movement of her breath upon me. Sweet it was in one sense, honey-sweet, and sent the same tingling through the nerves as her voice, but with a bitter underlying the sweet, a bitter offensiveness, as one smells in blood.

I was afraid to raise my eyelids, but looked out and saw perfectly under the lashes. The girl went on her knees, and bent over me, simply gloating. There was a deliberate voluptuousness which was both thrilling and repulsive, and as she arched her neck she actually licked her lips like an animal, till I could see in the moonlight the moisture shining on the scarlet lips and on the red tongue as it lapped the white sharp teeth. Lower and lower went her head as the lips went below the range of my mouth and chin and seemed to fasten on my throat. Then she paused, and I could hear the churning sound of her tongue as it licked her teeth and lips, and I could feel the hot breath on my neck. Then the skin of my throat began to tingle as one's flesh does when the hand that is to tickle it approaches nearer, nearer. I could feel the soft, shivering touch of the lips on the super sensitive skin of my throat, and the hard dents of two sharp teeth, just touching and pausing there. I closed my eyes in languorous ecstasy and waited, waited with beating heart.

But at that instant, another sensation swept through me as quick as lightning. I was conscious of the presence of the Count, and of his being as if lapped in a storm of fury. As my eyes opened involuntarily I saw his strong hand grasp the slender neck of the fair woman and with giant's power draw it back, the blue eyes transformed with fury, the white teeth champing with rage, and the fair cheeks blazing red with passion. But the Count! Never did I imagine such wrath and fury, even to the demons of the pit. His eyes were positively blazing. The red light in them was lurid, as if the flames of hell fire blazed behind them. His face was deathly pale, and the lines of it were hard like drawn wires. The thick eyebrows that met over the nose now seemed like a heaving bar of white-hot metal. With a fierce sweep of his arm, he hurled the woman from him, and then motioned to the others, as though he were beating them back. It was the same imperious gesture that I had seen used to the wolves. In a voice which, though low and almost in a whisper seemed to cut through the air and then ring in the room he said,

"How dare you touch him, any of you? How dare you cast eyes on him when I had forbidden it? Back, I tell you all! This man belongs to me! Beware how you meddle with him, or you'll have to deal with me."

The fair girl, with a laugh of ribald coquetry, turned to answer him. "You yourself never loved. You never love!" On this the other women joined, and such a mirthless, hard, soulless laughter rang through the room that it almost made me faint to hear. It seemed like the pleasure of fiends.

Then the Count turned, after looking at my face attentively, and said in a soft whisper, "Yes, I too can love. You yourselves can tell it from the past. Is it not so? Well, now I promise you that when I am done with him you shall kiss him at your will. Now go! Go! I must awaken him, for there is work to be done."

"Are we to have nothing tonight?" said one of them, with a low laugh, as she pointed to the bag which he had thrown upon the floor, and which moved as though there were some living thing within it. For answer he nodded his head. One of the women jumped forward and opened it. If my ears did not deceive me there was a gasp and a low wail, as of a half smothered child. The women closed round, whilst I was aghast with horror. But as I looked, they disappeared, and with them the dreadful bag. There was no door near them, and they could not have passed me without my noticing. They simply seemed to fade into the rays of the moonlight and pass out through the window, for I could see outside the dim, shadowy forms for a moment before they entirely faded away.

Then the horror overcame me, and I sank down unconscious.

ஒ CHAPTER 4 ஓ
JONATHAN HARKER'S JOURNAL CONTINUED

J awoke in my own bed. If it be that I had not dreamt, the Count must have carried me here. I tried to satisfy myself on the subject, but could not arrive at any unquestionable result. To be sure, there were certain small evidences, such as that my clothes were folded and laid by in a manner which was not my habit. My watch was still unwound, and I am rigorously accustomed to wind it the last thing before going to bed, and many such details. But these things are no proof, for they may have been evidences that my mind was not as usual, and, for some cause or another, I had certainly been much upset. I must watch for proof. Of one thing I am glad. If it was that the Count carried me here and undressed me, he must have been hurried in his task, for my pockets are intact. I am sure this diary would have been a mystery to him which he would not have brooked. He would have taken or destroyed it. As I look round this room, although it has been to me so full of fear, it is now a sort of sanctuary, for nothing can be more dreadful than those awful women, who were, who are, waiting to suck my blood.

18 May.—I have been down to look at that room again in daylight, for I *must* know the truth. When I got to the doorway at the top of the stairs I found it closed. It had been so forcibly driven against the jamb that part of the woodwork was splintered. I could see that the bolt of the lock had not been shot, but the door is fastened from the inside. I fear it was no dream, and must act on this surmise.

19 May.—I am surely in the toils[68]. Last night the Count asked me in the suavest tones to write three letters, one saying that my work here was nearly done, and that I should start for home within a few days, another that I was starting on the next morning from the time of the letter, and the third that I had left the castle and arrived at Bistritz. I would fain have rebelled, but felt that in the present state of things it would be madness to quarrel openly with the Count whilst I am so absolutely in his power. And to refuse would be to excite his suspicion and to arouse his anger. He knows that I

---

68 Like a trapped animal.

know too much, and that I must not live, lest I be dangerous to him. My only chance is to prolong my opportunities. Something may occur which will give me a chance to escape. I saw in his eyes something of that gathering wrath which was manifest when he hurled that fair woman from him. He explained to me that posts were few and uncertain, and that my writing now would ensure ease of mind to my friends. And he assured me with so much impressiveness that he would countermand the later letters, which would be held over at Bistritz until due time in case chance would admit of my prolonging my stay, that to oppose him would have been to create new suspicion. I therefore pretended to fall in with his views, and asked him what dates I should put on the letters.

He calculated a minute, and then said, "The first should be June 12, the second June 19, and the third June 29."

I know now the span of my life. God help me!

28 May.—There is a chance of escape, or at any rate of being able to send word home. A band of Szgany have come to the castle, and are encamped in the courtyard. These are gipsies. I have notes of them in my book. They are peculiar to this part of the world, though allied to the ordinary gipsies all the world over. There are thousands of them in Hungary and Transylvania, who are almost outside all law. They attach themselves as a rule to some great noble or *boyar*, and call themselves by his name. They are fearless and without religion, save superstition, and they talk only their own varieties of the Romany tongue.

I shall write some letters home, and shall try to get them to have them posted. I have already spoken to them through my window to begin acquaintanceship. They took their hats off and made obeisance and many signs, which however, I could not understand any more than I could their spoken language . . .

I have written the letters. Mina's is in shorthand, and I simply ask Mr. Hawkins to communicate with her. To her I have explained my situation, but without the horrors which I may only surmise. It would shock and frighten her to death were I to expose my heart to her. Should the letters not carry, then the Count shall not yet know my secret or the extent of my knowledge. . . .

I have given the letters. I threw them through the bars of my window with a gold piece, and made what signs I could to have them posted. The man who took them pressed them to his heart and bowed, and then put them in his cap. I could do no more. I stole back to the study, and began to read. As the Count did not come in, I have written here . . .

The Count has come. He sat down beside me, and said in his smooth-est voice as he opened two letters, "The Szgany has given me these, of which, though I know not whence they come, I shall, of course, take care. See!"—He must have looked at it.—"One is from you, and to my friend Peter Hawkins. The other,"—here he caught sight of the strange symbols as he opened the envelope, and the dark look came into his face, and his eyes blazed wickedly,—"The other is a vile thing, an outrage upon friend-ship and hospitality! It is not signed. Well! So it cannot matter to us." And he calmly held letter and envelope in the flame of the lamp till they were consumed.

Then he went on, "The letter to Hawkins, that I shall, of course send on, since it is yours. Your letters are sacred to me. Your pardon, my friend, that unknowingly I did break the seal. Will you not cover it again?" He held out the letter to me, and with a courteous bow handed me a clean envelope.

I could only redirect it and hand it to him in silence. When he went out of the room I could hear the key turn softly. A minute later I went over and tried it, and the door was locked.

When, an hour or two after, the Count came quietly into the room, his coming awakened me, for I had gone to sleep on the sofa. He was very cour-teous and very cheery in his manner, and seeing that I had been sleeping, he said, "So, my friend, you are tired? Get to bed. There is the surest rest. I may not have the pleasure of talk tonight, since there are many labours to me, but you will sleep, I pray."

I passed to my room and went to bed, and, strange to say, slept without dreaming. Despair has its own calms.

31 May.—This morning when I woke I thought I would provide myself with some papers and envelopes from my bag and keep them in my pocket, so that I might write in case I should get an opportunity, but again a surprise, again a shock!

Every scrap of paper was gone, and with it all my notes, my memoranda, relating to railways and travel, my letter of credit, in fact all that might be useful to me were I once outside the castle. I sat and pondered awhile, and then some thought occurred to me, and I made search of my portmanteau and in the wardrobe where I had placed my clothes.

The suit in which I had travelled was gone, and also my overcoat and rug. I could find no trace of them anywhere. This looked like some new scheme of villainy . . .

17 June.—This morning, as I was sitting on the edge of my bed cudgelling my brains, I heard without a crackling of whips and pounding and scraping of horses' feet up the rocky path beyond the courtyard. With joy I hurried to the window, and saw drive into the yard two great leiter-wagons, each drawn by eight sturdy horses, and at the head of each pair a Slovak, with his wide hat, great nail-studded belt, dirty sheepskin, and high boots. They had also their long staves in hand. I ran to the door, intending to descend and try and join them through the main hall, as I thought that way might be opened for them. Again a shock, my door was fastened on the outside.

Then I ran to the window and cried to them. They looked up at me stupidly and pointed, but just then the "hetman"[69] of the Szgany came out, and seeing them pointing to my window, said something, at which they laughed.

Henceforth no effort of mine, no piteous cry or agonized entreaty, would make them even look at me. They resolutely turned away. The leiter-wagons contained great, square boxes, with handles of thick rope. These were evidently empty by the ease with which the Slovaks handled them, and by their resonance as they were roughly moved.

When they were all unloaded and packed in a great heap in one corner of the yard, the Slovaks were given some money by the Szgany, and spitting on it for luck, lazily went each to his horse's head. Shortly afterwards, I heard the crackling of their whips die away in the distance.

24 June.—Last night the Count left me early, and locked himself into his own room. As soon as I dared I ran up the winding stair, and looked out of the window, which opened South. I thought I would watch for the Count, for there is something going on. The Szgany are quartered somewhere in the castle and are doing work of some kind. I know it, for now and then, I hear a far-away muffled sound as of mattock and spade, and, whatever it is, it must be the end of some ruthless villainy.

I had been at the window somewhat less than half an hour, when I saw something coming out of the Count's window. I drew back and watched carefully, and saw the whole man emerge. It was a new shock to me to find that he had on the suit of clothes which I had worn whilst travelling here, and slung over his shoulder the terrible bag which I had seen the women take away. There could be no doubt as to his quest, and in my garb, too! This, then, is his new scheme of evil, that he will allow others to see me, as they think, so that he may both leave evidence that I have been seen in the towns or villages posting my own letters, and that any wickedness which he may do shall by the local people be attributed to me.

It makes me rage to think that this can go on, and whilst I am shut up here, a veritable prisoner, but without that protection of the law which is even a criminal's right and consolation.

---

69 Commander.

I thought I would watch for the Count's return, and for a long time sat doggedly at the window. Then I began to notice that there were some quaint little specks floating in the rays of the moonlight. They were like the tiniest grains of dust, and they whirled round and gathered in clusters in a nebulous sort of way. I watched them with a sense of soothing, and a sort of calm stole over me. I leaned back in the embrasure in a more comfortable position, so that I could enjoy more fully the aerial gambolling.

Something made me start up, a low, piteous howling of dogs somewhere far below in the valley, which was hidden from my sight. Louder it seemed to ring in my ears, and the floating moats of dust to take new shapes to the sound as they danced in the moonlight. I felt myself struggling to awake to some call of my instincts. Nay, my very soul was struggling, and my half-remembered sensibilities were striving to answer the call. I was becoming hypnotised!

Quicker and quicker danced the dust. The moonbeams seemed to quiver as they went by me into the mass of gloom beyond. More and more they gathered till they seemed to take dim phantom shapes. And then I started, broad awake and in full possession of my senses, and ran screaming from the place.

The phantom shapes, which were becoming gradually materialised from the moonbeams, were those three ghostly women to whom I was doomed.

I fled, and felt somewhat safer in my own room, where there was no moonlight, and where the lamp was burning brightly.

When a couple of hours had passed I heard something stirring in the Count's room, something like a sharp wail quickly suppressed. And then there was silence, deep, awful silence, which chilled me. With a beating heart, I tried the door, but I was locked in my prison, and could do nothing. I sat down and simply cried.

As I sat I heard a sound in the courtyard without, the agonised cry of a woman. I rushed to the window, and throwing it up, peered between the bars.

There, indeed, was a woman with dishevelled hair, holding her hands over her heart as one distressed with running. She was leaning against the corner of the gateway. When she saw my face at the window she threw herself forward, and shouted in a voice laden with menace, "Monster, give me my child!"

She threw herself on her knees, and raising up her hands, cried the same words in tones which wrung my heart. Then she tore her hair and beat her breast, and abandoned herself to all the violences of extravagant emotion. Finally, she threw herself forward, and though I could not see her, I could hear the beating of her naked hands against the door.

Somewhere high overhead, probably on the tower, I heard the voice of the Count calling in his harsh, metallic whisper. His call seemed to be answered from far and wide by the howling of wolves. Before many minutes had passed a pack of them poured, like a pent-up dam when liberated, through the wide entrance into the courtyard.

There was no cry from the woman, and the howling of the wolves was but short. Before long they streamed away singly, licking their lips.

I could not pity her, for I knew now what had become of her child, and she was better dead.

What shall I do? What can I do? How can I escape from this dreadful thing of night, gloom, and fear?

25 June.—No man knows till he has suffered from the night how sweet and dear to his heart and eye the morning can be. When the sun grew so high this morning that it struck the top of the great gateway opposite my window, the high spot which it touched seemed to me as if the dove from the ark had lighted there. My fear fell from me as if it had been a vaporous garment which dissolved in the warmth.

I must take action of some sort whilst the courage of the day is upon me. Last night one of my post-dated letters went to post, the first of that fatal series which is to blot out the very traces of my existence from the earth.

Let me not think of it. Action!

It has always been at night-time that I have been molested or threatened, or in some way in danger or in fear. I have not yet seen the Count in the daylight. Can it be that he sleeps when others wake, that he may be awake whilst they sleep? If I could only get into his room! But there is no possible way. The door is always locked, no way for me.

Yes, there is a way, if one dares to take it. Where his body has gone why may not another body go? I have seen him myself crawl from his window. Why should not I imitate him, and go in by his window? The chances are desperate, but my need is more desperate still. I shall risk it. At the worst it can only be death, and a man's death is not a calf's, and the dreaded Hereafter may still be open to me. God help me in my task! Goodbye, Mina, if I fail. Goodbye, my faithful friend and second father. Goodbye, all, and last of all Mina!

Same day, later.—I have made the effort, and God helping me, have come safely back to this room. I must put down every detail in order. I went whilst my courage was fresh straight to the window on the south side, and at once got outside on this side. The stones are big and roughly cut, and the mortar has by process of time been washed away between them. I took off my boots, and ventured out on the desperate way. I looked down once, so as to make sure that a sudden glimpse of the awful depth would not overcome me, but after that kept my eyes away from it. I know pretty well the direction and distance of the Count's window, and made for it as well as I could, having regard to the opportunities available. I did not feel dizzy, I suppose I was too excited, and the time seemed ridiculously short till I found myself standing on the window sill and trying to raise up the sash. I was filled with agitation, however, when I bent down and slid feet foremost in through the window. Then I looked around for the Count, but with surprise and gladness, made a discovery. The room was empty! It was barely furnished with odd things, which seemed to have never been used.

The furniture was something the same style as that in the south rooms, and was covered with dust. I looked for the key, but it was not in the lock, and I could not find it anywhere. The only thing I found was a great heap of gold in one corner, gold of all kinds, Roman, and British, and Austrian, and Hungarian, and Greek and Turkish money, covered with a film of dust, as though it had lain long in the ground. None of it that I noticed was less than three hundred years old. There were also chains and ornaments, some jewelled, but all of them old and stained.

At one corner of the room was a heavy door. I tried it, for, since I could not find the key of the room or the key of the outer door, which was the main object of my search, I must make further examination, or all my efforts would be in vain. It was open, and led through a stone passage to a circular stairway, which went steeply down.

I descended, minding carefully where I went for the stairs were dark, being only lit by loopholes in the heavy masonry. At the bottom there was a dark, tunnel-like passage, through which came a deathly, sickly odour, the odour of old earth newly turned. As I went through the passage the smell grew closer and heavier. At last I pulled open a heavy door which stood ajar, and found myself in an old ruined chapel, which had evidently been used as a graveyard. The roof was broken, and in two places were steps leading to vaults, but the ground had recently been dug over, and the earth placed in great wooden boxes, manifestly those which had been brought by the Slovaks.

There was nobody about, and I made a search over every inch of the ground, so as not to lose a chance. I went down even into the vaults, where the dim light struggled, although to do so was a dread to my very soul. Into two of these I went, but saw nothing except fragments of old coffins and piles of dust. In the third, however, I made a discovery.

There, in one of the great boxes, of which there were fifty in all, on a pile of newly dug earth, lay the Count! He was either dead or asleep. I could not say which, for eyes were open and stony, but without the glassiness of death, and the cheeks had the warmth of life through all their pallor. The lips were as red as ever. But there was no sign of movement, no pulse, no breath, no beating of the heart.

I bent over him, and tried to find any sign of life, but in vain. He could not have lain there long, for the earthy smell would have passed away in a few hours. By the side of the box was its cover, pierced with holes here and there. I thought he might have the keys on him, but when I went to search I saw the dead eyes, and in them dead though they were, such a look of hate, though unconscious of me or my presence, that I fled from the place, and leaving the Count's room by the window, crawled again up the castle wall. Regaining my room, I threw myself panting upon the bed and tried to think.

29 June.—Today is the date of my last letter, and the Count has taken steps to prove that it was genuine, for again I saw him leave the castle by the same window, and in my clothes. As he went down the wall, lizard fashion, I wished I had a gun or some lethal weapon, that I might destroy him. But I fear that no weapon wrought along by man's hand would have any effect on him. I dared not wait to see him return, for I feared to see those weird sisters. I came back to the library, and read there till I fell asleep.

I was awakened by the Count, who looked at me as grimly as a man could look as he said, "Tomorrow, my friend, we must part. You return to your beautiful England, I to some work which may have such an end that we may never meet. Your letter home has been despatched. Tomorrow I shall not be here, but all shall be ready for your journey. In the morning come the Szgany, who have some labours of their own here, and also come some Slovaks. When they have gone, my carriage shall come for you, and shall bear you to the Borgo Pass to meet the diligence from Bukovina to Bistritz. But I am in hopes that I shall see more of you at Castle Dracula."

I suspected him, and determined to test his sincerity. Sincerity! It seems like a profanation of the word to write it in connection with such a monster, so I asked him point-blank, "Why may I not go tonight?"

"Because, dear sir, my coachman and horses are away on a mission."

"But I would walk with pleasure. I want to get away at once."

He smiled, such a soft, smooth, diabolical smile that I knew there was some trick behind his smoothness. He said, "And your baggage?"

"I do not care about it. I can send for it some other time."

The Count stood up, and said, with a sweet courtesy which made me rub my eyes, it seemed so real, "You English have a saying which is close to my heart, for its spirit is that which rules our *boyars*, 'Welcome the coming, speed the parting guest.' Come with me, my dear young friend. Not an hour shall you wait in my house against your will, though sad am I at your going, and that you so suddenly desire it. Come!" With a stately gravity, he, with the lamp, preceded me down the stairs and along the hall. Suddenly he stopped. "Hark!"

Close at hand came the howling of many wolves. It was almost as if the sound sprang up at the rising of his hand, just as the music of a great orchestra seems to leap under the baton of the conductor. After a pause of a moment, he proceeded, in his stately way, to the door, drew back the ponderous bolts, unhooked the heavy chains, and began to draw it open.

To my intense astonishment I saw that it was unlocked. Suspiciously, I looked all round, but could see no key of any kind.

As the door began to open, the howling of the wolves without grew louder and angrier. Their red jaws, with champing teeth, and their blunt-clawed feet as they leaped, came in through the opening door. I knew than that to struggle at the moment against the Count was useless. With such allies as these at his command, I could do nothing.

But still the door continued slowly to open, and only the Count's body stood in the gap. Suddenly it struck me that this might be the moment and means of my doom. I was to be given to the wolves, and at my own instigation. There was a diabolical wickedness in the idea great enough for the Count, and as the last chance I cried out, "Shut the door! I shall wait till morning." And I covered my face with my hands to hide my tears of bitter disappointment.

With one sweep of his powerful arm, the Count threw the door shut, and the great bolts clanged and echoed through the hall as they shot back into their places.

In silence we returned to the library, and after a minute or two I went to my own room. The last I saw of Count Dracula was his kissing his hand to me, with a red light of triumph in his eyes, and with a smile that Judas in hell might be proud of.

When I was in my room and about to lie down, I thought I heard a whispering at my door. I went to it softly and listened. Unless my ears deceived me, I heard the voice of the Count.

"Back! Back to your own place! Your time is not yet come. Wait! Have patience! Tonight is mine. Tomorrow night is yours!"

There was a low, sweet ripple of laughter, and in a rage I threw open the door, and saw without the three terrible women licking their lips. As I appeared, they all joined in a horrible laugh, and ran away.

I came back to my room and threw myself on my knees. It is then so near the end? Tomorrow! Tomorrow! Lord, help me, and those to whom I am dear!

30 June.—These may be the last words I ever write in this diary. I slept till just before the dawn, and when I woke threw myself on my knees, for I determined that if Death came he should find me ready.

At last I felt that subtle change in the air, and knew that the morning had come. Then came the welcome cockcrow, and I felt that I was safe. With a glad heart, I opened the door and ran down the hall. I had seen that the door was unlocked, and now escape was before me. With hands that trembled with eagerness, I unhooked the chains and threw back the massive bolts.

But the door would not move. Despair seized me. I pulled and pulled at the door, and shook it till, massive as it was, it rattled in its casement. I could see the bolt shot. It had been locked after I left the Count.

Then a wild desire took me to obtain the key at any risk, and I determined then and there to scale the wall again, and gain the Count's room. He might kill me, but death now seemed the happier choice of evils. Without a pause I rushed up to the east window, and scrambled down the wall, as before, into the Count's room. It was empty, but that was as I expected. I could not see a key anywhere, but the heap of gold remained. I went through the door in the corner and down the winding stair and along the dark passage to the old chapel. I knew now well enough where to find the monster I sought.

The great box was in the same place, close against the wall, but the lid was laid on it, not fastened down, but with the nails ready in their places to be hammered home.

I knew I must reach the body for the key, so I raised the lid, and laid it back against the wall. And then I saw something which filled my very soul with horror. There lay the Count, but looking as if his youth had been half restored. For the white hair and moustache were changed to dark iron-grey. The cheeks were fuller, and the white skin seemed ruby-red underneath. The mouth was redder than ever, for on the lips were gouts of fresh blood, which trickled from the corners of the mouth and ran down over the chin and neck. Even the deep, burning eyes seemed set amongst swollen flesh, for the lids and pouches underneath were bloated. It seemed as if the whole awful creature were simply gorged with blood. He lay like a filthy leech, exhausted with his repletion.

I shuddered as I bent over to touch him, and every sense in me revolted at the contact, but I had to search, or I was lost. The coming night might see my own body a banquet in a similar war to those horrid three. I felt all over the body, but no sign could I find of the key. Then I stopped and looked at the Count. There was a mocking smile on the bloated face which seemed to drive me mad. This was the being I was helping to transfer to London, where, perhaps, for centuries to come he might, amongst its teeming millions, satiate his lust for blood, and create a new and ever-widening circle of semi-demons to batten on the helpless.

The very thought drove me mad. A terrible desire came upon me to rid the world of such a monster. There was no lethal weapon at hand, but I seized a shovel which the workmen had been using to fill the cases, and lifting it high, struck, with the edge downward, at the hateful face. But as I did so the head turned, and the eyes fell upon me, with all their blaze of basilisk horror. The sight seemed to paralyze me, and the shovel turned in my hand and glanced from the face, merely making a deep gash above the forehead. The shovel fell from my hand across the box, and as I pulled it away the flange of the blade caught the edge of the lid which fell over again, and hid the horrid thing from my sight. The last glimpse I had was of the bloated face, blood-stained and fixed with a grin of malice which would have held its own in the nethermost hell.

I thought and thought what should be my next move, but my brain seemed on fire, and I waited with a despairing feeling growing over me. As I waited I heard in the distance a gipsy song sung by merry voices coming closer, and through their song the rolling of heavy wheels and the cracking of whips. The Szgany and the Slovaks of whom the Count had spoken were coming. With a last look around and at the box which contained the vile body, I ran from the place and gained the Count's room, determined to rush out at the moment the door should be opened. With strained ears, I listened, and heard downstairs the grinding of the key in the great lock and the falling back of the heavy door. There must have been some other means of entry, or some one had a key for one of the locked doors.

Then there came the sound of many feet tramping and dying away in some passage which sent up a clanging echo. I turned to run down again towards the vault, where I might find the new entrance, but at the moment there seemed to come a violent puff of wind, and the door to the winding stair blew to with a shock that set the dust from the lintels flying. When I ran to push it open, I found that it was hopelessly fast. I was again a prisoner, and the net of doom was closing round me more closely.

As I write there is in the passage below a sound of many tramping feet and the crash of weights being set down heavily, doubtless the boxes, with their freight of earth. There was a sound of hammering. It is the box being nailed down. Now I can hear the heavy feet tramping again along the hall, with many other idle feet coming behind them.

The door is shut, the chains rattle. There is a grinding of the key in the lock. I can hear the key withdrawn, then another door opens and shuts. I hear the creaking of lock and bolt.

Hark! In the courtyard and down the rocky way the roll of heavy wheels, the crack of whips, and the chorus of the Szgany as they pass into the distance.

I am alone in the castle with those horrible women. Faugh! Mina is a woman, and there is nought in common. They are devils of the Pit!

I shall not remain alone with them. I shall try to scale the castle wall farther than I have yet attempted. I shall take some of the gold with me, lest I want it later. I may find a way from this dreadful place.

And then away for home! Away to the quickest and nearest train! Away from the cursed spot, from this cursed land, where the devil and his children still walk with earthly feet!

At least God's mercy is better than that of those monsters, and the precipice is steep and high. At its foot a man may sleep, as a man. Goodbye, all. Mina!

ᔄ CHAPTER 5 ᔂ

LETTER FROM MISS MINA MURRAY TO MISS LUCY WESTENRA

9 May.

My dearest Lucy,

Forgive my long delay in writing, but I have been simply overwhelmed with work. The life of an assistant schoolmistress is sometimes trying. I am longing to be with you, and by the sea, where we can talk together freely and build our castles in the air. I have been working very hard lately, because I want to keep up with Jonathan's studies, and I have been practicing shorthand very assiduously. When we are married I shall be able to be useful to Jonathan, and if I can stenograph well enough I can take down what he wants to say in this way and write it out for him on the typewriter, at which also I am practicing very hard.

He and I sometimes write letters in shorthand, and he is keeping a stenographic journal of his travels abroad. When I am with you I shall keep a diary in the same way. I don't mean one of those two-pages-to-the-week-with-Sunday-squeezed- in-a-corner diaries, but a sort of journal which I can write in whenever I feel inclined.

I do not suppose there will be much of interest to other people, but it is not intended for them. I may show it to Jonathan some day if there is in it anything worth sharing, but it is really an exercise book. I shall try to do what I see lady journalists do, interviewing and writing descriptions and trying to remember conversations. I am told that, with a little practice, one can remember all that goes on or that one hears said during a day.

However, we shall see. I will tell you of my little plans when we meet. I have just had a few hurried lines from Jonathan from Transylvania. He is well, and will be returning in about a week. I am longing to hear all his news. It must be nice to see strange countries. I wonder if we, I mean Jonathan and I, shall ever see them together. There is the ten o'clock bell ringing. Goodbye.

Your loving

Mina

Tell me all the news when you write. You have not told me anything for a long time. I hear rumours, and especially of a tall, handsome, curly-haired man???

LETTER, LUCY WESTENRA TO MINA MURRAY

17, Chatham Street
Wednesday

My dearest Mina,

I must say you tax me very unfairly with being a bad correspondent. I wrote you *twice* since we parted, and your last letter was only your *second*. Besides, I have nothing to tell you. There is really nothing to interest you.

Town is very pleasant just now, and we go a great deal to picture-galleries and for walks and rides in the park. As to the tall, curly-haired man, I suppose it was the one who was with me at the last Pop. Someone has evidently been telling tales.

That was Mr. Holmwood. He often comes to see us, and he and Mamma get on very well together, they have so many things to talk about in common.

We met some time ago a man that would just *do for you*, if you were not already engaged to Jonathan. He is an excellent *parti*[70], being handsome, well off, and of good birth. He is a doctor and really clever. Just fancy! He is only nine-and twenty, and he has an immense lunatic asylum all under his own care. Mr. Holmwood introduced him to me, and he called here to see us, and often comes now. I think he is one of the most resolute men I ever saw, and yet the most calm. He seems absolutely imperturbable. I can fancy what a wonderful power he must have over his patients. He has a curious habit of looking one straight in the face, as if trying to read one's thoughts. He tries this on very much with me, but I flatter myself he has got a tough nut to crack. I know that from my glass.

Do you ever try to read your own face? *I do*, and I can tell you it is not a bad study, and gives you more trouble than you can well fancy if you have never tried it.

He says that I afford him a curious psychological study, and I humbly think I do. I do not, as you know, take sufficient interest in dress to be able to describe the new fashions. Dress is a bore. That is slang again, but never mind. Arthur says that every day.

There, it is all out, Mina, we have told all our secrets to each other since we were children. We have slept together and eaten together, and laughed and cried together, and now, though I have spoken, I would like to speak more. Oh, Mina, couldn't you guess? I love him. I am blushing as I write, for although I *think* he loves me, he has not told me so in words. But, oh, Mina, I love him. I love him! There, that does me good.

I wish I were with you, dear, sitting by the fire undressing, as we used to sit, and I would try to tell you what I feel. I do not know how I am writing this even to you. I am afraid to stop, or I should tear up the letter, and I don't want to stop, for I *do so* want to tell you all.

---

70 Candidate for marriage.

Let me hear from you *at once*, and tell me all that you think about it. Mina, pray for my happiness.

Lucy

P.S.—I need not tell you this is a secret. Goodnight again. L.

LETTER, LUCY WESTENRA TO MINA MURRAY

24 May

My dearest Mina,

Thanks, and thanks, and thanks again for your sweet letter. It was so nice to be able to tell you and to have your sympathy.

My dear, it never rains but it pours. How true the old proverbs are. Here am I, who shall be twenty in September, and yet I never had a proposal till today, not a real proposal, and today I had three. Just fancy! THREE proposals in one day! Isn't it awful! I feel sorry, really and truly sorry, for two of the poor fellows. Oh, Mina, I am so happy that I don't know what to do with myself. And three proposals! But, for goodness' sake, don't tell any of the girls, or they would be getting all sorts of extravagant ideas, and imagining themselves injured and slighted if in their very first day at home they did not get six at least. Some girls are so vain! You and I, Mina dear, who are engaged and are going to settle down soon soberly into old married women, can despise vanity. Well, I must tell you about the three, but you must keep it a secret, dear, from *every one* except, of course, Jonathan. You will tell him, because I would, if I were in your place, certainly tell Arthur. A woman ought to tell her husband everything. Don't you think so, dear? And I must be fair. Men like women, certainly their wives, to be quite as fair as they are. And women, I am afraid, are not always quite as fair as they should be.

Well, my dear, number One came just before lunch. I told you of him, Dr. John Seward, the lunatic asylum man, with the strong jaw and the good forehead. He was very cool outwardly, but was nervous all the same. He had evidently been schooling himself as to all sorts of little things, and remembered them, but he almost managed to sit down on his silk hat, which men don't generally do when they are cool, and then when he wanted to appear at ease he kept playing with a lancet in a way that made me nearly scream. He spoke to me, Mina, very straightforwardly. He told me how dear I was to him, though he had known me so little, and what his life would be with me to help and cheer him. He was going to tell me how unhappy he would be if I did not care for him, but when he saw me cry he said he was a brute and would not add to my present trouble. Then he broke off and asked if I could love him in time, and when I shook my head his hands trembled, and then with some hesitation he asked me if I cared already for any one else. He put it very nicely, saying that he did not want to wring my confidence from me, but only to know, because if a woman's heart was free a man might have hope. And then, Mina, I felt a sort of duty to tell him that there was some one. I only told him that much, and then he stood up, and he looked very strong and very grave as he took both my hands in his and said he hoped I would be happy, and that If I ever wanted a friend I must count him one of my best.

Oh, Mina dear, I can't help crying, and you must excuse this letter being all blotted. Being proposed to is all very nice and all that sort of thing, but it isn't at all a happy thing when you have to see a poor fellow, whom you know loves you honestly, going away and looking all broken hearted, and to know that, no matter what he may say at the moment, you are passing out of his life. My dear, I must stop here at present, I feel so miserable, though I am so happy.

Evening.

Arthur has just gone, and I feel in better spirits than when I left off, so I can go on telling you about the day.

Well, my dear, number Two came after lunch. He is such a nice fellow, an American from Texas, and he looks so young and so fresh that it seems almost impossible that he has been to so many places and has such adventures. I sympathize with poor Desdemona when she had such a stream poured in her ear, even by a black man. I suppose that we women are such cowards that we think a man will save us from fears, and we marry him. I know now what I would do if I were a man and wanted to make a girl love me. No, I don't, for there was Mr. Morris telling us his stories, and Arthur never told any, and yet . . .

My dear, I am somewhat previous. Mr. Quincy P. Morris found me alone. It seems that a man always does find a girl alone. No, he doesn't, for Arthur tried twice to *make* a chance, and I helping him all I could, I am not ashamed to say it now. I must tell you beforehand that Mr. Morris doesn't always speak slang, that is to say, he never does so to strangers or before them, for he is really well educated and has exquisite manners, but he found out that it amused me to hear him talk American slang, and whenever I was present, and there was no one to be shocked, he said such funny things. I am afraid, my dear, he has to invent it all, for it fits exactly into whatever else he has to say. But this is a way slang has. I do not know myself if I shall ever speak slang. I do not know if Arthur likes it, as I have never heard him use any as yet.

Well, Mr. Morris sat down beside me and looked as happy and jolly as he could, but I could see all the same that he was very nervous. He took my hand in his, and said ever so sweetly . . .

"Miss Lucy, I know I ain't good enough to regulate the fixin's of your little shoes, but I guess if you wait till you find a man that is you will go join them seven young women with the lamps when you quit. Won't you just hitch up alongside of me and let us go down the long road together, driving in double harness?"

Well, he did look so good humoured and so jolly that it didn't seem half so hard to refuse him as it did poor Dr. Seward. So I said, as lightly as I could, that I did not know anything of hitching, and that I wasn't broken to harness at all yet. Then he said that he had spoken in a light manner, and he hoped that if he had made a mistake in doing so on so grave, so momentous, and occasion for him, I would forgive him. He really did look serious when he was saying it, and I couldn't help feeling a sort of exultation that he was number Two in one day. And then, my dear, before I could say a word he began pouring out a perfect torrent of love-making, laying his very heart and soul at my feet. He looked so earnest over it that I shall never again think that a man must be playful always, and never earnest, because he is merry at times. I suppose he saw something in my face which checked him, for he suddenly stopped, and said with a sort of manly fervour that I could have loved him for if I had been free . . .

"Lucy, you are an honest hearted girl, I know. I should not be here speaking to you as I am now if I did not believe you clean grit, right through to the very depths of your soul. Tell me, like one good fellow to another, is there any one else that you care for? And if there is I'll never trouble you a hair's breadth again, but will be, if you will let me, a very faithful friend."

My dear Mina, why are men so noble when we women are so little worthy of them? Here was I almost making fun of this great hearted, true gentleman. I burst into tears, I am afraid, my dear, you will think this a very sloppy letter in more ways than one, and I really felt very badly.

Why can't they let a girl marry three men, or as many as want her, and save all this trouble? But this is heresy, and I must not say it. I am glad to say that, though I was crying, I was able to look into Mr. Morris' brave eyes, and I told him out straight . . .

"Yes, there is some one I love, though he has not told me yet that he even loves me." I was right to speak to him so frankly, for quite a light came into his face, and he put out both his hands and took mine, I think I put them into his, and said in a hearty way . . .

"That's my brave girl. It's better worth being late for a chance of winning you than being in time for any other girl in the world. Don't cry, my dear. If it's for me, I'm a hard nut to crack, and I take it standing up. If that other fellow doesn't know his happiness, well, he'd better look for it soon, or he'll have to deal with me. Little girl, your honesty and pluck have made me a friend, and that's rarer than a lover, it's more selfish anyhow. My dear, I'm going to have a pretty lonely walk between this and Kingdom Come. Won't you give me one kiss? It'll be something to keep off the darkness now and then. You can, you know, if you like, for that other good fellow, or you could not love him, hasn't spoken yet."

That quite won me, Mina, for it *was* brave and sweet of him, and noble too, to a rival, wasn't it? And he so sad, so I leant over and kissed him.

He stood up with my two hands in his, and as he looked down into my face, I am afraid I was blushing very much, he said, "Little girl, I hold your hand, and you've kissed me, and if these things don't make us friends nothing ever will. Thank you for your sweet honesty to me, and goodbye."

He wrung my hand, and taking up his hat, went straight out of the room without looking back, without a tear or a quiver or a pause, and I am crying like a baby.

Oh, why must a man like that be made unhappy when there are lots of girls about who would worship the very ground he trod on? I know I would if I were free, only I don't want to be free. My dear, this quite upset me, and I feel I cannot write of happiness just at once, after telling you of it, and I don't wish to tell of the number Three until it can be all happy. Ever your loving . . .

Lucy

P.S.—Oh, about number Three, I needn't tell you of number Three, need I? Besides, it was all so confused. It seemed only a moment from his coming into the room till both his arms were round me, and he was kissing me. I am very, very happy, and I don't know what I have done to deserve it. I must only try in the future to show that I am not ungrateful to God for all His goodness to me in sending to me such a lover, such a husband, and such a friend.

Goodbye.

DR. SEWARD'S DIARY
(KEPT IN PHONOGRAPH)

25 May.—Ebb tide in appetite today. Cannot eat, cannot rest, so diary instead. Since my rebuff of yesterday I have a sort of empty feeling. Nothing in the world seems of sufficient importance to be worth the doing. As I knew that the only cure for this sort of thing was work, I went amongst the patients. I picked out one who has afforded me a study of much interest. He is so quaint that I am determined to understand him as well as I can. Today I seemed to get nearer than ever before to the heart of his mystery.

I questioned him more fully than I had ever done, with a view to making myself master of the facts of his hallucination. In my manner of doing it there was, I now see, something of cruelty. I seemed to wish to keep him to the point of his madness, a thing which I avoid with the patients as I would the mouth of hell.

(*Mem.*, Under what circumstances would I not avoid the pit of hell?) *Omnia Romae venalia sunt.*[71] Hell has its price! verb. sap.[72] If there be anything behind this instinct it will be valuable to trace it afterwards *accurately*, so I had better commence to do so, therefore . . .

R. M, Renfield, age 59. Sanguine temperament, great physical strength, morbidly excitable, periods of gloom, ending in some fixed idea which I cannot make out. I presume that the sanguine temperament itself and the disturbing influence end in a mentally-accomplished finish, a possibly dangerous man, probably dangerous if unselfish. In selfish men caution is as secure an armour for their foes as for themselves. What I think of on this point is, when self is the fixed point the centripetal force is balanced with the centrifugal. When duty, a cause, etc., is the fixed point, the latter force is paramount, and only accident or a series of accidents can balance it.

LETTER, QUINCEY P. MORRIS TO HON. ARTHUR HOLMOOD

25 May.

My dear Art,

We've told yarns by the campfire in the prairies, and dressed one another's wounds after trying a landing at the Marquesas, and drunk healths on the shore of Titicaca. There are more yarns to be told, and other wounds to be healed, and another health to be drunk. Won't you let this be at my campfire tomorrow night? I have no hesitation in asking you, as I know a certain lady is engaged to a certain dinner party, and that you are free. There will only be one other, our old pal at the Korea, Jack Seward. He's coming, too, and we both want to mingle our weeps over the wine cup, and to drink a health with all our hearts to the happiest man in all the wide world, who has won the noblest heart that God has made and best worth winning. We promise you a hearty welcome, and a loving greeting, and a health as true as your own right hand. We shall both swear to leave you at home if you drink too deep to a certain pair of eyes. Come!

Yours, as ever and always,

Quincey P. Morris

71 All Romans are venal (Latin).
72 Short for, *verbum sapienti sat est*: A word is sufficient to a wise man (Latin).

TELEGRAM FROM ARTHUR HOLMWOOD
TO QUINCEY P. MORRIS

26 May

Count me in every time. I bear messages which will make both your ears tingle.

Art

❧ CHAPTER 6 ☙
MINA MURRAY'S JOURNAL

24 July. Whitby.—Lucy met me at the station, looking sweeter and lovelier than ever, and we drove up to the house at the Crescent in which they have rooms. This is a lovely place. The little river, the Esk, runs through a deep valley, which broadens out as it comes near the harbour. A great viaduct runs across, with high piers, through which the view seems somehow further away than it really is. The valley is beautifully green, and it is so steep that when you are on the high land on either side you look right across it, unless you are near enough to see down. The houses of the old town—the side away from us, are all red-roofed, and seem piled up one over the other anyhow, like the pictures we see of Nuremberg. Right over the town is the ruin of Whitby Abbey, which was sacked by the Danes, and which is the scene of part of "Marmion," where the girl was built up in the wall. It is a most noble ruin, of immense size, and full of beautiful and romantic bits. There is a legend that a white lady is seen in one of the windows. Between it and the town there is another church, the parish one, round which is a big graveyard, all full of tombstones. This is to my mind the nicest spot in Whitby, for it lies right over the town, and has a full view of the harbour and all up the bay to where the headland called Kettleness stretches out into the sea. It descends so steeply over the harbour that part of the bank has fallen away, and some of the graves have been destroyed.

In one place part of the stonework of the graves stretches out over the sandy pathway far below. There are walks, with seats beside them, through the churchyard, and people go and sit there all day long looking at the beautiful view and enjoying the breeze.

I shall come and sit here often myself and work. Indeed, I am writing now, with my book on my knee, and listening to the talk of three old men who are sitting beside me. They seem to do nothing all day but sit here and talk.

The harbour lies below me, with, on the far side, one long granite wall stretching out into the sea, with a curve outwards at the end of it, in the middle of which is a lighthouse. A heavy seawall runs along outside of it. On the near side, the seawall makes an elbow crooked inversely, and its end too has a lighthouse. Between the two piers there is a narrow opening into the harbour, which then suddenly widens.

It is nice at high water, but when the tide is out it shoals away to nothing, and there is merely the stream of the Esk, running between banks of sand, with rocks here and there. Outside the harbour on this side there rises for about half a mile a great reef, the sharp of which runs straight out from behind the south lighthouse. At the end of it is a buoy with a bell, which swings in bad weather, and sends in a mournful sound on the wind.

They have a legend here that when a ship is lost bells are heard out at sea. I must ask the old man about this. He is coming this way . . .

He is a funny old man. He must be awfully old, for his face is gnarled and twisted like the bark of a tree. He tells me that he is nearly a hundred, and that he was a sailor in the Greenland fishing fleet when Waterloo was fought. He is, I am afraid, a very sceptical person, for when I asked him about the bells at sea and the White Lady at the abbey he said very brusquely,

"I wouldn't fash masel'[73] about them, miss. Them things be all wore out. Mind, I don't say that they never was, but I do say that they wasn't in my time. They be all very well for comers and trippers, an' the like, but not for a nice young lady like you. Them feet-folks[74] from York and Leeds that be always eatin' cured herrin's and drinkin' tea an' lookin' out to buy cheap jet would creed aught. I wonder masel' who'd be bothered tellin' lies to them, even the newspapers, which is full of fool-talk."

I thought he would be a good person to learn interesting things from, so I asked him if he would mind telling me something about the whale fishing in the old days. He was just settling himself to begin when the clock struck six, whereupon he laboured to get up, and said,

"I must gang ageeanwards home now, miss. My grand-daughter doesn't like to be kept waitin' when the tea is ready, for it takes me time to crammle aboon the grees,[75] for there be a many of 'em, and miss, I lack belly-timber[76] sairly by the clock."

73 Whitby dialect for 'fuss myself.' Stoker relied on *A Glossary of Words Used in the Neighbourhood of Whitby* by F. K. Robinson.
74 Derogatory slang for those who travel by foot instead of by carriage.
75 Hobble down the stairs.
76 Food.

He hobbled away, and I could see him hurrying, as well as he could, down the steps. The steps are a great feature on the place. They lead from the town to the church, there are hundreds of them, I do not know how many, and they wind up in a delicate curve. The slope is so gentle that a horse could easily walk up and down them.

I think they must originally have had something to do with the abbey. I shall go home too. Lucy went out, visiting with her mother, and as they were only duty calls, I did not go.

1 August.—I came up here an hour ago with Lucy, and we had a most interesting talk with my old friend and the two others who always come and join him. He is evidently the Sir Oracle of them, and I should think must have been in his time a most dictatorial person.

He will not admit anything, and down faces everybody. If he can't out-argue them he bullies them, and then takes their silence for agreement with his views.

Lucy was looking sweetly pretty in her white lawn frock. She has got a beautiful colour since she has been here.

I noticed that the old men did not lose any time in coming and sitting near her when we sat down. She is so sweet with old people, I think they all fell in love with her on the spot. Even my old man succumbed and did not contradict her, but gave me double share instead. I got him on the subject of the legends, and he went off at once into a sort of sermon. I must try to remember it and put it down.

"It be all fool-talk, lock, stock, and barrel, that's what it be and nowt else. These bans an' wafts an' boh-ghosts an' bar-guests an' bogles an' all anent them is only fit to set bairns an' dizzy women a'belderin'.[77] They be nowt but air-blebs.[78] They, an' all grims an' signs an' warnin's, be all invented by parsons an' illsome berk-bodies[79] an' railway touters to skeer an' scunner hafflin's,[80] an' to get folks to do somethin' that they don't other incline to. It makes me ireful to think o' them. Why, it's them that, not content with printin' lies on paper an' preachin' them out of pulpits, does want to be cuttin' them on the tombstones. Look here all around you in what airt ye will. All them steans, holdin' up their heads as well as they can out of their pride, is acant, simply tumblin' down with the weight o' the lies wrote on them, 'Here lies the body' or 'Sacred to the memory' wrote on all of them, an' yet in nigh half of them there bean't no bodies at all, an' the memories of them bean't cared a pinch of snuff about, much less sacred. Lies all of

77 Curses and ghosts and apparitions and harbingers of death and hobgoblins and all concerning them is only fit to set children and half-witted women a-crying.
78 Bubbles.
79 Learned people.
80 Scare half-wits.

them, nothin' but lies of one kind or another! My gog, but it'll be a quare scowderment[81] at the Day of Judgment when they come tumblin' up in their death-sarks, all jouped together an' trying' to drag their tombsteans with them to prove how good they was, some of them trimmlin' an' dithering, with their hands that dozzened an' slippery from lyin' in the sea that they can't even keep their gurp o' them."

I could see from the old fellow's self-satisfied air and the way in which he looked round for the approval of his cronies that he was "showing off," so I put in a word to keep him going.

"Oh, Mr. Swales, you can't be serious. Surely these tombstones are not all wrong?"

"Yabblins![82] There may be a poorish few not wrong, savin' where they make out the people too good, for there be folk that do think a balm-bowl be like the sea, if only it be their own. The whole thing be only lies. Now look you here. You come here a stranger, an' you see this kirkgarth."

I nodded, for I thought it better to assent, though I did not quite understand his dialect. I knew it had something to do with the church.

He went on, "And you consate that all these steans be aboon folk that be haped here, snod an' snog?" I assented again. "Then that be just where the lie comes in. Why, there be scores of these laybeds that be toom as old Dun's 'baccabox on Friday night."

He nudged one of his companions, and they all laughed. "And, my gog! How could they be otherwise? Look at that one, the aftest abaft the bier-bank, read it!"

I went over and read, "Edward Spencelagh, master mariner, murdered by pirates off the coast of Andres, April, 1854, age 30." When I came back Mr. Swales went on,

"Who brought him home, I wonder, to hap him here? Murdered off the coast of Andres! An' you consated his body lay under! Why, I could name ye a dozen whose bones lie in the Greenland seas above," he pointed northwards, "or where the currants may have drifted them. There be the steans around ye. Ye can, with your young eyes, read the small print of the lies from here. This Braithwaite Lowery, I knew his father, lost in the *Lively* off Greenland in '20, or Andrew Woodhouse, drowned in the same seas in 1777, or John Paxton, drowned off Cape Farewell a year later, or old John Rawlings, whose grandfather sailed with me, drowned in the Gulf of Finland in '50. Do ye think that all these men will have to make a rush to Whitby when the trumpet sounds? I have me antherums aboot it![83] I tell ye that when they

---

81 Queer commotion.
82 Possibly.
83 I doubt it!

got here they'd be jommlin' and jostlin' one another that way that it 'ud be like a fight up on the ice in the old days, when we'd be at one another from daylight to dark, an' tryin' to tie up our cuts by the aurora borealis." This was evidently local pleasantry, for the old man cackled over it, and his cronies joined in with gusto.

"But," I said, "surely you are not quite correct, for you start on the assumption that all the poor people, or their spirits, will have to take their tombstones with them on the Day of Judgment. Do you think that will be really necessary?"

"Well, what else be they tombstones for? Answer me that, miss!"

"To please their relatives, I suppose."

"To please their relatives, you suppose!" This he said with intense scorn. "How will it pleasure their relatives to know that lies is wrote over them, and that everybody in the place knows that they be lies?"

He pointed to a stone at our feet which had been laid down as a slab, on which the seat was rested, close to the edge of the cliff. "Read the lies on that thruff-stone," he said.

The letters were upside down to me from where I sat, but Lucy was more opposite to them, so she leant over and read, "Sacred to the memory of George Canon, who died, in the hope of a glorious resurrection, on July 29, 1873, falling from the rocks at Kettleness. This tomb was erected by his sorrowing mother to her dearly beloved son. 'He was the only son of his mother, and she was a widow.' Really, Mr. Swales, I don't see anything very funny in that!" She spoke her comment very gravely and somewhat severely.

"Ye don't see aught funny! Ha-ha! But that's because ye don't gawm[84] the sorrowin' mother was a hell-cat that hated him because he was acrewk'd, a regular lamiter[85] he was, an' he hated her so that he committed suicide in order that she mightn't get an insurance she put on his life. He blew nigh the top of his head off with an old musket that they had for scarin' crows with. 'Twarn't for crows then, for it brought the clegs and the dowps[86] to him. That's the way he fell off the rocks. And, as to hopes of a glorious resurrection, I've often heard him say masel' that he hoped he'd go to hell, for his mother was so pious that she'd be sure to go to heaven, an' he didn't want to addle where she was. Now isn't that stean at any rate," he hammered it with his stick as he spoke, "a pack of lies? And won't it make Gabriel keckle when Geordie comes pantin' ut the grees with the tompstean balanced on his hump, and asks to be took as evidence!"

---

84 Know.
85 Cripple.
86 Horse flies and carrion.

I did not know what to say, but Lucy turned the conversation as she said, rising up, "Oh, why did you tell us of this? It is my favourite seat, and I cannot leave it, and now I find I must go on sitting over the grave of a suicide."

"That won't harm ye, my pretty, an' it may make poor Geordie gladsome to have so trim a lass sittin' on his lap. That won't hurt ye. Why, I've sat here off an' on for nigh twenty years past, an' it hasn't done me no harm. Don't ye fash about them as lies under ye, or that doesn' lie there either! It'll be time for ye to be getting scart when ye see the tombsteans all run away with, and the place as bare as a stubble-field. There's the clock, and I must gang. My service to ye, ladies!" And off he hobbled.

Lucy and I sat awhile, and it was all so beautiful before us that we took hands as we sat, and she told me all over again about Arthur and their coming marriage. That made me just a little heart-sick, for I haven't heard from Jonathan for a whole month.

The same day .—I came up here alone, for I am very sad. There was no letter for me. I hope there cannot be anything the matter with Jonathan. The clock has just struck nine. I see the lights scattered all over the town, sometimes in rows where the streets are, and sometimes singly. They run right up the Esk and die away in the curve of the valley. To my left the view is cut off by a black line of roof of the old house next to the abbey. The sheep and lambs are bleating in the fields away behind me, and there is a clatter of donkeys' hoofs up the paved road below. The band on the pier is playing a harsh waltz in good time, and further along the quay there is a Salvation Army meeting in a back street. Neither of the bands hears the other, but up here I hear and see them both. I wonder where Jonathan is and if he is thinking of me! I wish he were here.

DR. SEWARD'S DIARY

5 June.—The case of Renfield grows more interesting the more I get to understand the man. He has certain qualities very largely developed, selfishness, secrecy, and purpose.

I wish I could get at what is the object of the latter. He seems to have some settled scheme of his own, but what it is I do not know. His redeeming quality is a love of animals, though, indeed, he has such curious turns in it that I sometimes imagine he is only abnormally cruel. His pets are of odd sorts.

Just now his hobby is catching flies. He has at present such a quantity that I have had myself to expostulate. To my astonishment, he did not break out into a fury, as I expected, but took the matter in simple seriousness. He thought for a moment, and then said, "May I have three days? I shall clear them away." Of course, I said that would do. I must watch him.

18 June.—He has turned his mind now to spiders, and has got several very big fellows in a box. He keeps feeding them his flies, and the number of the latter is becoming sensibly diminished, although he has used half his food in attracting more flies from outside to his room.

1 July.—His spiders are now becoming as great a nuisance as his flies, and today I told him that he must get rid of them.

He looked very sad at this, so I said that he must some of them, at all events. He cheerfully acquiesced in this, and I gave him the same time as before for reduction.

He disgusted me much while with him, for when a horrid blowfly, bloated with some carrion food, buzzed into the room, he caught it, held it exultantly for a few moments between his finger and thumb, and before I knew what he was going to do, put it in his mouth and ate it.

I scolded him for it, but he argued quietly that it was very good and very wholesome, that it was life, strong life, and gave life to him. This gave me an idea, or the rudiment of one. I must watch how he gets rid of his spiders.

He has evidently some deep problem in his mind, for he keeps a little notebook in which he is always jotting down something. Whole pages of it are filled with masses of figures, generally single numbers added up in batches, and then the totals added in batches again, as though he were fo-cussing some account, as the auditors put it.

8 July.—There is a method in his madness, and the rudimentary idea in my mind is growing. It will be a whole idea soon, and then, oh, unconscious cerebration, you will have to give the wall to your conscious brother.

I kept away from my friend for a few days, so that I might notice if there were any change. Things remain as they were except that he has parted with some of his pets and got a new one.

He has managed to get a sparrow, and has already partially tamed it. His means of taming is simple, for already the spiders have diminished. Those that do remain, however, are well fed, for he still brings in the flies by tempting them with his food.

19 July—We are progressing. My friend has now a whole colony of sparrows, and his flies and spiders are almost obliterated. When I came in he ran to me and said he wanted to ask me a great favour, a very, very great favour. And as he spoke, he fawned on me like a dog.

I asked him what it was, and he said, with a sort of rapture in his voice and bearing, "A kitten, a nice, little, sleek playful kitten, that I can play with, and teach, and feed, and feed, and feed!"

I was not unprepared for this request, for I had noticed how his pets went on increasing in size and vivacity, but I did not care that his pretty family of tame sparrows should be wiped out in the same manner as the flies and spiders. So I said I would see about it, and asked him if he would not rather have a cat than a kitten.

His eagerness betrayed him as he answered, "Oh, yes, I would like a cat! I only asked for a kitten lest you should refuse me a cat. No one would refuse me a kitten, would they?"

I shook my head, and said that at present I feared it would not be possible, but that I would see about it. His face fell, and I could see a warning of danger in it, for there was a sudden fierce, sidelong look which meant killing. The man is an undeveloped homicidal maniac. I shall test him with his present craving and see how it will work out, then I shall know more.

10 pm.—I have visited him again and found him sitting in a corner brooding. When I came in he threw himself on his knees before me and implored me to let him have a cat, that his salvation depended upon it.

I was firm, however, and told him that he could not have it, whereupon he went without a word, and sat down, gnawing his fingers, in the corner where I had found him. I shall see him in the morning early.

20 July.—Visited Renfield very early, before attendant went his rounds. Found him up and humming a tune. He was spreading out his sugar, which he had saved, in the window, and was manifestly beginning his fly catching again, and beginning it cheerfully and with a good grace.

I looked around for his birds, and not seeing them, asked him where they were. He replied, without turning round, that they had all flown away. There were a few feathers about the room and on his pillow a drop of blood. I said nothing, but went and told the keeper to report to me if there were anything odd about him during the day.

11 am.—The attendant has just been to see me to say that Renfield has been very sick and has disgorged a whole lot of feathers. "My belief is, doctor," he said, "that he has eaten his birds, and that he just took and ate them raw!"

11 pm.—I gave Renfield a strong opiate tonight, enough to make even him sleep, and took away his pocketbook to look at it. The thought that has been buzzing about my brain lately is complete, and the theory proved.

My homicidal maniac is of a peculiar kind. I shall have to invent a new classification for him, and call him a zoophagous (life-eating) maniac. What he desires is to absorb as many lives as he can, and he has laid himself out to achieve it in a cumulative way. He gave many flies to one spider and many spiders to one bird, and then wanted a cat to eat the many birds. What would have been his later steps?

It would almost be worth while to complete the experiment. It might be done if there were only a sufficient cause. Men sneered at vivisection, and yet look at its results today! Why not advance science in its most difficult and vital aspect, the knowledge of the brain?

Had I even the secret of one such mind, did I hold the key to the fancy of even one lunatic, I might advance my own branch of science to a pitch compared with which Burdon-Sanderson's physiology or Ferrier's brain knowledge would be as nothing. If only there were a sufficient cause! I must not think too much of this, or I may be tempted. A good cause might turn the scale with me, for may not I too be of an exceptional brain, congenitally?

How well the man reasoned. Lunatics always do within their own scope. I wonder at how many lives he values a man, or if at only one. He has closed the account most accurately, and today begun a new record. How many of us begin a new record with each day of our lives?

To me it seems only yesterday that my whole life ended with my new hope, and that truly I began a new record. So it shall be until the Great Recorder sums me up and closes my ledger account with a balance to profit or loss.

Oh, Lucy, Lucy, I cannot be angry with you, nor can I be angry with my friend whose happiness is yours, but I must only wait on hopeless and work. Work! Work!

If I could have as strong a cause as my poor mad friend there, a good, unselfish cause to make me work, that would be indeed happiness.

MINA MURRAY'S JOURNAL

26 July.—I am anxious, and it soothes me to express myself here. It is like whispering to one's self and listening at the same time. And there is also something about the shorthand symbols that makes it different from writing. I am unhappy about Lucy and about Jonathan. I had not heard from Jonathan for some time, and was very concerned, but yesterday dear Mr. Hawkins, who is always so kind, sent me a letter from him. I had written asking him if he had heard, and he said the enclosed had just been received. It is only a line dated from Castle Dracula, and says that he is just starting for home. That is not like Jonathan. I do not understand it, and it makes me uneasy.

Then, too, Lucy, although she is so well, has lately taken to her old habit of walking in her sleep. Her mother has spoken to me about it, and we have decided that I am to lock the door of our room every night.

Mrs. Westenra has got an idea that sleep-walkers always go out on roofs of houses and along the edges of cliffs and then get suddenly wakened and fall over with a despairing cry that echoes all over the place.

Poor dear, she is naturally anxious about Lucy, and she tells me that her husband, Lucy's father, had the same habit, that he would get up in the night and dress himself and go out, if he were not stopped.

Lucy is to be married in the autumn, and she is already planning out her dresses and how her house is to be arranged. I sympathise with her, for I do the same, only Jonathan and I will start in life in a very simple way, and shall have to try to make both ends meet.

Mr. Holmwood, he is the Hon. Arthur Holmwood, only son of Lord Godalming, is coming up here very shortly, as soon as he can leave town, for his father is not very well, and I think dear Lucy is counting the moments till he comes.

She wants to take him up in the seat on the churchyard cliff and show him the beauty of Whitby. I daresay it is the waiting which disturbs her. She will be all right when he arrives.

27 July.—No news from Jonathan. I am getting quite uneasy about him, though why I should I do not know, but I do wish that he would write, if it were only a single line.

Lucy walks more than ever, and each night I am awakened by her moving about the room. Fortunately, the weather is so hot that she cannot get cold. But still, the anxiety and the perpetually being awakened is beginning to tell on me, and I am getting nervous and wakeful myself. Thank God, Lucy's health keeps up. Mr. Holmwood has been suddenly called to Ring to see his father, who has been taken seriously ill. Lucy frets at the postponement of seeing him, but it does not touch her looks. She is a trifle stouter, and her cheeks are a lovely rose-pink. She has lost the anemic look which she had. I pray it will all last.

3 August.—Another week gone by, and no news from Jonathan, not even to Mr. Hawkins, from whom I have heard. Oh, I do hope he is not ill. He surely would have written. I look at that last letter of his, but somehow it does not satisfy me. It does not read like him, and yet it is his writing. There is no mistake of that.

Lucy has not walked much in her sleep the last week, but there is an odd concentration about her which I do not understand, even in her sleep she seems to be watching me. She tries the door, and finding it locked, goes about the room searching for the key.

6 August.—Another three days, and no news. This suspense is getting dreadful. If I only knew where to write to or where to go to, I should feel easier. But no one has heard a word of Jonathan since that last letter. I must only pray to God for patience.

Lucy is more excitable than ever, but is otherwise well. Last night was very threatening, and the fishermen say that we are in for a storm. I must try to watch it and learn the weather signs.

Today is a grey day, and the sun as I write is hidden in thick clouds, high over Kettleness. Everything is grey except the green grass, which seems like emerald amongst it, grey earthy rock, grey clouds, tinged with the sunburst at the far edge, hang over the grey sea, into which the sandpoints stretch like grey figures. The sea is tumbling in over the shallows and the sandy flats with a roar, muffled in the sea-mists drifting inland. The horizon is lost in a grey mist. All vastness, the clouds are piled up like giant rocks, and there is a 'brool'[87] over the sea that sounds like some passage of doom. Dark figures are on the beach here and there, sometimes half shrouded in the mist, and seem 'men like trees walking'. The fishing boats are racing for home, and rise and dip in the ground swell as they sweep into the harbour, bending to the scuppers[88]. Here comes old Mr. Swales. He is making straight for me, and I can see, by the way he lifts his hat, that he wants to talk.

I have been quite touched by the change in the poor old man. When he sat down beside me, he said in a very gentle way, "I want to say something to you, miss."

I could see he was not at ease, so I took his poor old wrinkled hand in mine and asked him to speak fully.

So he said, leaving his hand in mine, "I'm afraid, my deary, that I must have shocked you by all the wicked things I've been sayin' about the dead, and such like, for weeks past, but I didn't mean them, and I want ye to remember that when I'm gone. We aud folks that be daffled, and with one foot abaft the krok-hooal,[89] don't altogether like to think of it, and we don't want to feel scart of it, and that's why I've took to makin' light of it, so that I'd cheer up my own heart a bit. But, Lord love ye, miss, I ain't afraid of dyin', not a bit, only I don't want to die if I can help it. My time must be <u>nigh at hand n</u>ow, for I be aud, and a hundred years is too much for any

87 A deep, murmuring sound.
88 Opening on a ship's deck that lets excess water escape.
89 Grave.

man to expect. And I'm so nigh it that the Aud Man is already whettin' his scythe. Ye see, I can't get out o' the habit of caffin'[90] about it all at once. The chafts[91] will wag as they be used to. Some day soon the Angel of Death will sound his trumpet for me. But don't ye dooal an' greet, my deary!"—for he saw that I was crying—"if he should come this very night I'd not refuse to answer his call. For life be, after all, only a waitin' for somethin' else than what we're doin', and death be all that we can rightly depend on. But I'm content, for it's comin' to me, my deary, and comin' quick. It may be comin' while we be lookin' and wonderin'. Maybe it's in that wind out over the sea that's bringin' with it loss and wreck, and sore distress, and sad hearts. Look! Look!" he cried suddenly. "There's something in that wind and in the hoast beyont that sounds, and looks, and tastes, and smells like death. It's in the air. I feel it comin'. Lord, make me answer cheerful, when my call comes!" He held up his arms devoutly, and raised his hat. His mouth moved as though he were praying. After a few minutes' silence, he got up, shook hands with me, and blessed me, and said goodbye, and hobbled off. It all touched me, and upset me very much.

I was glad when the coastguard came along, with his spyglass under his arm. He stopped to talk with me, as he always does, but all the time kept looking at a strange ship.

"I can't make her out," he said. "She's a Russian, by the look of her. But she's knocking about in the queerest way. She doesn't know her mind a bit. She seems to see the storm coming, but can't decide whether to run up north in the open, or to put in here. Look there again! She is steered mighty strangely, for she doesn't mind the hand on the wheel, changes about with every puff of wind. We'll hear more of her before this time tomorrow."

෨ CHAPTER 7 ෴

CUTTING FROM "THE DAILYGRAPH", 8 AUGUST
(PASTED IN MINA MURRAY'S JOURNAL)

From a correspondent.

Whitby.

One of the greatest and suddenest storms on record has just been experienced here, with results both strange and unique. The weather

90 Chafing.
91 Jaws.

had been somewhat sultry, but not to any degree uncommon in the month of August. Saturday evening was as fine as was ever known, and the great body of holiday-makers laid out yesterday for visits to Mulgrave Woods, Robin Hood's Bay, Rig Mill, Runswick, Staithes, and the various trips in the neighborhood of Whitby. The steamers *Emma* and *Scarborough* made trips up and down the coast, and there was an unusual amount of 'tripping' both to and from Whitby. The day was unusually fine till the afternoon, when some of the gossips who frequent the East Cliff churchyard, and from the commanding eminence watch the wide sweep of sea visible to the north and east, called attention to a sudden show of 'mares tails' high in the sky to the northwest. The wind was then blowing from the south-west in the mild degree which in barometrical language is ranked 'No. 2, light breeze.'

The coastguard on duty at once made report, and one old fisherman, who for more than half a century has kept watch on weather signs from the East Cliff, foretold in an emphatic manner the coming of a sudden storm. The approach of sunset was so very beautiful, so grand in its masses of splendidly coloured clouds, that there was quite an assemblage on the walk along the cliff in the old church-yard to enjoy the beauty. Before the sun dipped below the black mass of Kettleness, standing boldly athwart the western sky, its downward way was marked by myriad clouds of every sunset colour, flame, purple, pink, green, violet, and all the tints of gold, with here and there masses not large, but of seemingly absolute blackness, in all sorts of shapes, as well outlined as colossal silhouettes. The ex-perience was not lost on the painters, and doubtless some of the sketches of the 'Prelude to the Great Storm' will grace the R. A and R. I. walls in May next.

More than one captain made up his mind then and there that his 'cobble' or his 'mule', as they term the different classes of boats, would remain in the harbour till the storm had passed. The wind fell away entirely during the evening, and at midnight there was a dead calm, a sultry heat, and that prevailing intensity which, on the approach of thunder, affects persons of a sensitive nature.

There were but few lights in sight at sea, for even the coasting steam-ers, which usually hug the shore so closely, kept well to seaward, and but few fishing boats were in sight. The only sail noticeable was a foreign schooner with all sails set, which was seemingly going westwards. The foolhardiness or ignorance of her officers was a prolific theme for comment whilst she remained in sight, and efforts were made to signal her to reduce sail in the face of her danger. Before the night shut down she was seen with sails idly flapping as she gently rolled on the undulating swell of the sea.

"As idle as a painted ship upon a painted ocean."

Shortly before ten o'clock the stillness of the air grew quite oppressive, and the silence was so marked that the bleating of a sheep inland or the barking of a dog in the town was distinctly heard, and the band on the pier, with its lively French air, was like a dischord in the great harmony of nature's silence. A little after midnight came a strange sound from over the sea, and high overhead the air began to carry a strange, faint, hollow booming.

Then without warning the tempest broke. With a rapidity which, at the time, seemed incredible, and even afterwards is impossible to realize, the whole aspect of nature at once became convulsed. The waves rose in growing fury, each over-topping its fellow, till in a very few minutes the lately glassy sea was like a roaring and devouring monster. White-crested waves beat madly on the level sands and rushed up the shelving cliffs. Others broke over the piers, and with their spume swept the lanthorns of the lighthouses which rise from the end of either pier of Whitby Harbour.

The wind roared like thunder, and blew with such force that it was with difficulty that even strong men kept their feet, or clung with grim clasp to the iron stanchions. It was found necessary to clear the entire pier from the mass of onlookers, or else the fatalities of the night would have increased manifold. To add to the difficulties and dangers of the time, masses of sea-fog came drifting inland. White, wet clouds, which swept by in ghostly fashion, so dank and damp and cold that it needed but little effort of imagination to think that the spirits of those lost at sea were touching their living brethren with the clammy hands of death, and many a one shuddered as the wreaths of sea-mist swept by.

At times the mist cleared, and the sea for some distance could be seen in the glare of the lightning, which came thick and fast, followed by such peals of thunder that the whole sky overhead seemed trembling under the shock of the footsteps of the storm.

Some of the scenes thus revealed were of immeasurable grandeur and of absorbing interest. The sea, running mountains high, threw skywards with each wave mighty masses of white foam, which the tempest seemed to snatch at and whirl away into space. Here and there a fishing boat, with a rag of sail, running madly for shelter before the blast, now and again the white wings of a storm-tossed seabird. On the summit of the East Cliff the new searchlight was ready for experiment, but had not yet been tried. The officers in charge of it got it into working order, and in the pauses of onrushing mist swept with it the surface of the sea. Once or twice its service was most effective, as when a fishing boat, with gunwale under water, rushed into the harbour, able, by the guidance of the sheltering light, to avoid the danger of dashing against the piers. As each boat achieved the safety of the port there was a shout of joy from the mass of people on the shore, a shout which for a moment seemed to cleave the gale and was then swept away in its rush.

Before long the searchlight discovered some distance away a schooner with all sails set, apparently the same vessel which had been noticed earlier in the evening. The wind had by this time backed to the east, and there was a shudder amongst the watchers on the cliff as they realized the terrible danger in which she now was.

Between her and the port lay the great flat reef on which so many good ships have from time to time suffered, and, with the wind blowing from its present quarter, it would be quite impossible that she should fetch the entrance of the harbour.

It was now nearly the hour of high tide, but the waves were so great that in their troughs the shallows of the shore were almost visible, and the schooner, with all sails set, was rushing with such speed that, in the words of one old salt, "she must fetch up somewhere, if it was only in hell". Then came another rush of sea-fog, greater than any hitherto, a mass of dank mist, which seemed to close on all things like a grey pall, and left available to men only the organ of hearing, for the roar of the tempest, and the crash of the thunder, and the booming of the mighty billows came through the damp oblivion even louder than before. The rays of the searchlight were kept fixed on the harbour mouth across the East Pier, where the shock was expected, and men waited breathless.

The wind suddenly shifted to the northeast, and the remnant of the sea fog melted in the blast. And then, *mirabile dictu*,[92] between the piers, leaping from wave to wave as it rushed at headlong speed, swept the strange schooner before the blast, with all sail set, and gained the safety of the harbour. The searchlight followed her, and a shudder ran through all who saw her, for lashed to the helm was a corpse, with drooping head, which swung horribly to and fro at each motion of the ship. No other form could be seen on the deck at all.

A great awe came on all as they realised that the ship, as if by a miracle, had found the harbour, unsteered save by the hand of a dead man! However, all took place more quickly than it takes to write these words. The schooner paused not, but rushing across the harbour, pitched herself on that accumulation of sand and gravel washed by many tides and many storms into the southeast corner of the pier jutting under the East Cliff, known locally as Tate Hill Pier.

There was of course a considerable concussion as the vessel drove up on the sand heap. Every spar, rope, and stay was strained, and some of the 'top-hammer' came crashing down. But, strangest of all, the very instant the shore was touched, an immense dog sprang up on deck from below, as if shot up by the concussion, and running forward, jumped from the bow on the sand.

Making straight for the steep cliff, where the churchyard hangs over the laneway to the East Pier so steeply that some of the flat tombstones, thruffsteans or through-stones, as they call them in Whitby vernacular, actually project over where the sustaining cliff has fallen away, it disappeared in the darkness, which seemed intensified just beyond the focus of the searchlight.

It so happened that there was no one at the moment on Tate Hill Pier, as all those whose houses are in close proximity were either in bed or were out on the heights above. Thus the coastguard on duty on the eastern side of the harbour, who at once ran down to the little pier, was the first to climb aboard. The men working the searchlight, after scouring the entrance of the harbour without seeing anything, then turned the light on the derelict and kept it there. The coastguard ran aft, and when he came beside the wheel, bent over to examine it, and recoiled at once as though under some

---

92 Wonderful to relate (Latin).

sudden emotion. This seemed to pique general curiosity, and quite a number of people began to run.

It is a good way round from the West Cliff by the Draw-bridge to Tate Hill Pier, but your correspondent is a fairly good runner, and came well ahead of the crowd. When I arrived, however, I found already assembled on the pier a crowd, whom the coastguard and police refused to allow to come on board. By the courtesy of the chief boatman, I was, as your correspondent, permitted to climb on deck, and was one of a small group who saw the dead seaman whilst actually lashed to the wheel.

It was no wonder that the coastguard was surprised, or even awed, for not often can such a sight have been seen. The man was simply fastened by his hands, tied one over the other, to a spoke of the wheel. Between the inner hand and the wood was a crucifix, the set of beads on which it was fastened being around both wrists and wheel, and all kept fast by the binding cords. The poor fellow may have been seated at one time, but the flapping and buffeting of the sails had worked through the rudder of the wheel and had dragged him to and fro, so that the cords with which he was tied had cut the flesh to the bone.

Accurate note was made of the state of things, and a doctor, Surgeon J. M. Caffyn, of 33, East Elliot Place, who came immediately after me, declared, after making examination, that the man must have been dead for quite two days.

In his pocket was a bottle, carefully corked, empty save for a little roll of paper, which proved to be the addendum to the log.

The coastguard said the man must have tied up his own hands, fastening the knots with his teeth. The fact that a coastguard was the first on board may save some complications later on, in the Admiralty Court, for coastguards cannot claim the salvage which is the right of the first civilian entering on a derelict. Already, however, the legal tongues are wagging, and one young law student is loudly asserting that the rights of the owner are already completely sacrificed, his property being held in contravention of the statues of mortmain, since the tiller, as emblemship, if not proof, of delegated possession, is held in a dead hand.

It is needless to say that the dead steersman has been reverently removed from the place where he held his honourable watch and ward till death, a steadfastness as noble as that of the young Casabianca, and placed in the mortuary to await inquest.

Already the sudden storm is passing, and its fierceness is abating. Crowds are scattering backward, and the sky is beginning to redden over the Yorkshire wolds[93].

I shall send, in time for your next issue, further details of the derelict ship which found her way so miraculously into harbour in the storm.

Whitby.

9 August.—The sequel to the strange arrival of the derelict in the storm last night is almost more startling than the thing itself. It turns out that the schooner is Russian from Varna, and is called the *Demeter.* She is almost entirely in ballast of silver sand, with only a small amount of cargo, a number of great wooden boxes filled with mould.

This cargo was consigned to a Whitby solicitor, Mr. S.F. Billington, of 7, The Crescent, who this morning went aboard and took formal possession of the goods consigned to him.

The Russian consul, too, acting for the charter-party, took formal possession of the ship, and paid all harbour dues, etc.

Nothing is talked about here today except the strange coincidence. The officials of the Board of Trade have been most exacting in seeing that every compliance has been made with existing regulations. As the matter is to be a 'nine days wonder', they are evidently determined that there shall be no cause of other complaint.

A good deal of interest was abroad concerning the dog which landed when the ship struck, and more than a few of the members of the S.P.C.A., which is very strong in Whitby, have tried to befriend the animal. To the general disappointment, however, it was not to be found. It seems to have disappeared entirely from the town. It may be that it was frightened and made its way on to the moors, where it is still hiding in terror.

---

93 Open, elevated stretches of land.

There are some who look with dread on such a possibility, lest later on it should in itself become a danger, for it is evidently a fierce brute. Early this morning a large dog, a half-bred mastiff belonging to a coal merchant close to Tate Hill Pier, was found dead in the roadway opposite its master's yard. It had been fighting, and manifestly had had a savage opponent, for its throat was torn away, and its belly was slit open as if with a savage claw.

Later.—By the kindness of the Board of Trade inspector, I have been permitted to look over the log book of the *Demeter*, which was in order up to within three days, but contained nothing of special interest except as to facts of missing men. The greatest interest, however, is with regard to the paper found in the bottle, which was today produced at the inquest. And a more strange narrative than the two between them unfold it has not been my lot to come across.

As there is no motive for concealment, I am permitted to use them, and accordingly send you a transcript, simply omitting technical details of seamanship and supercargo. It almost seems as though the captain had been seized with some kind of mania before he had got well into blue water, and that this had developed persistently throughout the voyage. Of course my statement must be taken *cum grano*,[94] since I am writing from the dictation of a clerk of the Russian consul, who kindly translated for me, time being short.

LOG OF THE "DEMETER"
Varna to Whitby

Written 18 July, things so strange happening, that I shall keep accurate note henceforth till we land.

On 6 July we finished taking in cargo, silver sand and boxes of earth. At noon set sail. East wind, fresh. Crew, five hands . . . two mates, cook, and myself, (captain).

On 11 July at dawn entered Bosphorus. Boarded by Turkish Customs officers. Backsheesh.[95] All correct. Under way at 4 p.m.

On 12 July through Dardanelles. More Customs officers and flagboat of guarding squadron. Backsheesh again. Work of officers thorough, but quick. Want us off soon. At dark passed into Archipelago.

94 Short for, *Cum grano solis*: Take with a grain of salt (Latin).
95 Bribe or tip money.

On 13 July passed Cape Matapan. Crew dissatisfied about something. Seemed scared, but would not speak out.

On 14 July was somewhat anxious about crew. Men all steady fellows, who sailed with me before. Mate could not make out what was wrong. They only told him there was *something*, and crossed themselves. Mate lost temper with one of them that day and struck him. Expected fierce quarrel, but all was quiet.

On 16 July mate reported in the morning that one of the crew, Petrofsky, was missing. Could not account for it. Took larboard watch eight bells last night, was relieved by Amramoff, but did not go to bunk. Men more downcast than ever. All said they expected something of the kind, but would not say more than there was *something* aboard. Mate getting very impatient with them. Feared some trouble ahead.

On 17 July, yesterday, one of the men, Olgaren, came to my cabin, and in an awestruck way confided to me that he thought there was a strange man aboard the ship. He said that in his watch he had been sheltering behind the deckhouse, as there was a rain storm, when he saw a tall, thin man, who was not like any of the crew, come up the companionway, and go along the deck forward and disappear. He followed cautiously, but when he got to bows found no one, and the hatchways were all closed. He was in a panic of superstitious fear, and I am afraid the panic may spread. To allay it, I shall today search the entire ship carefully from stem to stern.

Later in the day I got together the whole crew, and told them, as they evidently thought there was some one in the ship, we would search from stem to stern. First mate angry, said it was folly, and to yield to such foolish ideas would demoralise the men, said he would engage to keep them out of trouble with the handspike. I let him take the helm, while the rest began a thorough search, all keeping abreast, with lanterns. We left no corner unsearched. As there were only the big wooden boxes, there were no odd corners where a man could hide. Men much relieved when search over, and went back to work cheerfully. First mate scowled, but said nothing.

22 July.—Rough weather last three days, and all hands busy with sails, no time to be frightened. Men seem to have forgotten their dread. Mate cheerful again, and all on good terms. Praised men for work in bad weather. Passed Gibraltar and out through Straits. All well.

24 July.—There seems some doom over this ship. Already a hand short, and entering the Bay of Biscay with wild weather ahead, and yet last night another man lost, disappeared. Like the first, he came off his watch and was not seen again. Men all in a panic of fear, sent a round robin, asking to have double watch, as they fear to be alone. Mate angry. Fear there will be some trouble, as either he or the men will do some violence.

28 July.—Four days in hell, knocking about in a sort of maelstrom, and the wind a tempest. No sleep for any one. Men all worn out. Hardly know how to set a watch, since no one fit to go on. Second mate volunteered to steer and watch, and let men snatch a few hours sleep. Wind abating, seas still terrific, but feel them less, as ship is steadier.

29 July.—Another tragedy. Had single watch tonight, as crew too tired to double. When morning watch came on deck could find no one except steersman. Raised outcry, and all came on deck. Thorough search, but no one found. Are now without second mate, and crew in a panic. Mate and I agreed to go armed henceforth and wait for any sign of cause.

30 July.—Last night. Rejoiced we are nearing England. Weather fine, all sails set. Retired worn out, slept soundly, awakened by mate telling me that both man of watch and steersman missing. Only self and mate and two hands left to work ship.

1 August.—Two days of fog, and not a sail sighted. Had hoped when in the English Channel to be able to signal for help or get in somewhere. Not having power to work sails, have to run before wind. Dare not lower, as could not raise them again. We seem to be drifting to some terrible doom. Mate now more demoralised than either of men. His stronger nature seems to have worked inwardly against himself. Men are beyond fear, working stolidly and patiently, with minds made up to worst. They are Russian, he Roumanian.

2 August, midnight.—Woke up from few minutes sleep by hearing a cry, seemingly outside my port. Could see nothing in fog. Rushed on deck, and ran against mate. Tells me he heard cry and ran, but no sign of man on watch. One more gone. Lord, help us! Mate says we must be past Straits of Dover, as in a moment of fog lifting he saw North Foreland, just as he heard the man cry out. If so we are now off in the North Sea, and only God can guide us in the fog, which seems to move with us, and God seems to have deserted us.

3 August.—At midnight I went to relieve the man at the wheel and when I got to it found no one there. The wind was steady, and as we ran before it there was no yawing. I dared not leave it, so shouted for the mate. After a few seconds, he rushed up on deck in his flannels. He looked wild-eyed and haggard, and I greatly fear his reason has given way. He came close to me and whispered hoarsely, with his mouth to my ear, as though fearing the very air might hear. "It is here. I know it now. On the watch last night I saw It, like a man, tall and thin, and ghastly pale. It was in the bows, and looking out. I crept behind It, and gave it my knife, but the knife went through It, empty as the air." And as he spoke he took the knife and drove it savagely into space. Then he went on, "But It is here, and I'll find It. It is in the hold, perhaps in one of those boxes. I'll unscrew them one by one and see. You work the helm." And with a warning look and his finger on his lip, he went below. There was springing up a choppy wind, and I could not leave the helm. I saw him come out on deck again with a tool chest and lantern, and go down the forward hatchway. He is mad, stark, raving mad, and it's no use my trying to stop him. He can't hurt those big boxes, they are invoiced as clay, and to pull them about is as harmless a thing as he can do. So here I stay and mind the helm, and write these notes. I can only trust in God and wait till the fog clears. Then, if I can't steer to any harbour with the wind that is, I shall cut down sails, and lie by, and signal for help . . .

It is nearly all over now. Just as I was beginning to hope that the mate would come out calmer, for I heard him knocking away at something in the hold, and work is good for him, there came up the hatchway a sudden, startled scream, which made my blood run cold, and up on the deck he came as if shot from a gun, a raging madman, with his eyes rolling and his face convulsed with fear. "Save me! Save me!" he cried, and then looked round on the blanket of fog. His horror turned to despair, and in a steady voice he said, "You had better come too, captain, before it is too late. *He* is there! I know the secret now. The sea will save me from Him, and it is all that is left!" Before I could say a word, or move forward to seize him, he sprang on the bulwark and deliberately threw himself into the sea. I suppose I know the secret too, now. It was this madman who had got rid of the men one by one, and now he has followed them himself. God help me! How am I to account for all these horrors when I get to port? *When* I get to port! Will that ever be?

4 August.—Still fog, which the sunrise cannot pierce, I know there is sunrise because I am a sailor, why else I know not. I dared not go below, I dared not leave the helm, so here all night I stayed, and in the dimness of the night I saw it, Him! God, forgive me, but the mate was right to jump overboard. It was better to die like a man. To die like a sailor in blue water, no man can object. But I am captain, and I must not leave my ship. But I shall baffle this fiend or monster, for I shall tie my hands to the wheel when my strength begins to fail, and along with them I shall tie that which He, It, dare not touch. And then, come good wind or foul, I shall save my soul, and my honour as a captain. I am growing weaker, and the night is coming on. If He can look me in the face again, I may not have time to act. . . If we are wrecked, mayhap this bottle may be found, and those who find it may understand. If not . . . well, then all men shall know that I have been true to my trust. God and the Blessed Virgin and the Saints help a poor ignorant soul trying to do his duty . . .

Of course the verdict was an open one. There is no evidence to adduce, and whether or not the man himself committed the murders there is now none to say. The folk here hold almost universally that the captain is simply a hero, and he is to be given a public funeral. Already it is arranged that his body is to be taken with a train of boats up the Esk for a piece and then brought back to Tate Hill Pier and up the abbey steps, for he is to be buried in the churchyard on the cliff. The owners of more than a hundred boats have already given in their names as wishing to follow him to the grave.

No trace has ever been found of the great dog, at which there is much mourning, for, with public opinion in its present state, he would, I believe, be adopted by the town. Tomorrow will see the funeral, and so will end this one more 'mystery of the sea'.

MINA MURRAY'S JOURNAL

8 August.—Lucy was very restless all night, and I too, could not sleep. The storm was fearful, and as it boomed loudly among the chimney pots, it made me shudder. When a sharp puff came it seemed to be like a distant gun. Strangely enough, Lucy did not wake, but she got up twice and dressed herself. Fortunately, each time I awoke in time and managed to undress her without waking her, and got her back to bed. It is a very strange thing, this sleep-walking, for as soon as her will is thwarted in any physical way, her intention, if there be any, disappears, and she yields herself almost exactly to the routine of her life.

Early in the morning we both got up and went down to the harbour to see if anything had happened in the night. There were very few people about, and though the sun was bright, and the air clear and fresh, the big, grim-looking waves, that seemed dark themselves because the foam that topped them was like snow, forced themselves in through the mouth of the harbour, like a bullying man going through a crowd. Somehow I felt glad that Jonathan was not on the sea last night, but on land. But, oh, is he on land or sea? Where is he, and how? I am getting fearfully anxious about him. If I only knew what to do, and could do anything!

10 August.—The funeral of the poor sea captain today was most touching. Every boat in the harbour seemed to be there, and the coffin was carried by captains all the way from Tate Hill Pier up to the churchyard. Lucy came with me, and we went early to our old seat, whilst the cortege of boats went up the river to the Viaduct and came down again. We had a lovely view, and saw the procession nearly all the way. The poor fellow was laid to rest near our seat so that we stood on it, when the time came and saw everything.

Poor Lucy seemed much upset. She was restless and uneasy all the time, and I cannot but think that her dreaming at night is telling on her. She is quite odd in one thing. She will not admit to me that there is any cause for restlessness, or if there be, she does not understand it herself.

There is an additional cause in that poor Mr. Swales was found dead this morning on our seat, his neck being broken. He had evidently, as the doctor said, fallen back in the seat in some sort of fright, for there was a look of fear and horror on his face that the men said made them shudder. Poor dear old man!

Lucy is so sweet and sensitive that she feels influences more acutely than other people do. Just now she was quite upset by a little thing which I did not much heed, though I am myself very fond of animals.

One of the men who came up here often to look for the boats was followed by his dog. The dog is always with him. They are both quiet persons, and I never saw the man angry, nor heard the dog bark. During the service the dog would not come to its master, who was on the seat with us, but kept a few yards off, barking and howling. Its master spoke to it gently, and then harshly, and then angrily. But it would neither come nor cease to make a noise. It was in a fury, with its eyes savage, and all its hair bristling out like a cat's tail when puss is on the war path.

Finally the man too got angry, and jumped down and kicked the dog, and then took it by the scruff of the neck and half dragged and half threw it on the tombstone on which the seat is fixed. The moment it touched the stone the poor thing began to tremble. It did not try to get away, but crouched down, quivering and cowering, and was in such a pitiable state of terror that I tried, though without effect, to comfort it.

Lucy was full of pity, too, but she did not attempt to touch the dog, but looked at it in an agonised sort of way. I greatly fear that she is of too super sensitive a nature to go through the world without trouble. She will be dreaming of this tonight, I am sure. The whole agglomeration of things, the ship steered into port by a dead man, his attitude, tied to the wheel with a crucifix and beads, the touching funeral, the dog, now furious and now in terror, will all afford material for her dreams.

I think it will be best for her to go to bed tired out physically, so I shall take her for a long walk by the cliffs to Robin Hood's Bay and back. She ought not to have much inclination for sleep-walking then.

∞ CHAPTER 8 ∞
MINA MURRAY'S JOURNAL

Same day, 11 o'clock P.M.—Oh, but I am tired! If it were not that I had made my diary a duty I should not open it tonight. We had a lovely walk. Lucy, after a while, was in gay spirits, owing, I think, to some dear cows who came nosing towards us in a field close to the lighthouse, and frightened the wits out of us. I believe we forgot everything, except of course, personal fear, and it seemed to wipe the slate clean and give us a fresh start. We had a capital 'severe tea' at Robin Hood's Bay in a sweet little old-fashioned inn, with a bow window right over the seaweed-covered rocks of the strand. I believe we should have shocked the 'New Woman' with our appetites. Men are more tolerant, bless them! Then we walked home with some, or rather many, stoppages to rest, and with our hearts full of a constant dread of wild bulls.

Lucy was really tired, and we intended to creep off to bed as soon as we could. The young curate came in, however, and Mrs. Westenra asked him to stay for supper. Lucy and I had both a fight for it with the dusty miller. I know it was a hard fight on my part, and I am quite heroic. I think that some day the bishops must get together and see about breeding up a new class of curates, who don't take supper, no matter how hard they may be pressed to, and who will know when girls are tired.

Lucy is asleep and breathing softly. She has more colour in her cheeks than usual, and looks, oh so sweet. If Mr. Holmwood fell in love with her seeing her only in the drawing room, I wonder what he would say if he saw her now. Some of the 'New Women' writers will some day start an idea that men and women should be allowed to see each other asleep before proposing or accepting. But I suppose the 'New Woman' won't condescend in future to accept. She will do the proposing herself. And a nice job she will make of it too! There's some consolation in that. I am so happy tonight, because dear Lucy seems better. I really believe she has turned the corner, and that we are over her troubles with dreaming. I should be quite happy if I only knew if Jonathan . . . God bless and keep him.

11 August.—Diary again. No sleep now, so I may as well write. I am too agitated to sleep. We have had such an adventure, such an agonizing experience. I fell asleep as soon as I had closed my diary. . . . Suddenly I became broad awake, and sat up, with a horrible sense of fear upon me, and of some feeling of emptiness around me. The room was dark, so I could not see Lucy's bed. I stole across and felt for her. The bed was empty. I lit a match and found that she was not in the room. The door was shut, but not locked, as I had left it. I feared to wake her mother, who has been more than usually ill lately, so threw on some clothes and got ready to look for her. As I was leaving the room it struck me that the clothes she wore might give me some clue to her dreaming intention. Dressing-gown would mean house, dress outside. Dressing-gown and dress were both in their places. "Thank God," I said to myself, "she cannot be far, as she is only in her nightdress."

I ran downstairs and looked in the sitting room. Not there! Then I looked in all the other rooms of the house, with an ever-growing fear chilling my heart. Finally, I came to the hall door and found it open. It was not wide open, but the catch of the lock had not caught. The people of the house are careful to lock the door every night, so I feared that Lucy must have gone out as she was. There was no time to think of what might happen. A vague over-mastering fear obscured all details.

I took a big, heavy shawl and ran out. The clock was striking one as I was in the Crescent, and there was not a soul in sight. I ran along the North Terrace, but could see no sign of the white figure which I expected. At the edge of the West Cliff above the pier I looked across the harbour to the East Cliff, in the hope or fear, I don't know which, of seeing Lucy in our favourite seat.

There was a bright full moon, with heavy black, driving clouds, which threw the whole scene into a fleeting diorama of light and shade as they sailed across. For a moment or two I could see nothing, as the shadow of a cloud obscured St. Mary's Church and all around it. Then as the cloud passed I could see the ruins of the abbey coming into view, and as the edge of a narrow band of light as sharp as a sword-cut moved along, the church and churchyard became gradually visible. Whatever my expectation was, it was not disappointed, for there, on our favourite seat, the silver light of the moon struck a half-reclining figure, snowy white. The coming of the cloud was too quick for me to see much, for shadow shut down on light almost immediately, but it seemed to me as though something dark stood behind the seat where the white figure shone, and bent over it. What it was, whether man or beast, I could not tell.

I did not wait to catch another glance, but flew down the steep steps to the pier and along by the fish-market to the bridge, which was the only way to reach the East Cliff. The town seemed as dead, for not a soul did I see. I rejoiced that it was so, for I wanted no witness of poor Lucy's condition. The time and distance seemed endless, and my knees trembled and my breath came laboured as I toiled up the endless steps to the abbey. I must have gone fast, and yet it seemed to me as if my feet were weighted with lead, and as though every joint in my body were rusty.

When I got almost to the top I could see the seat and the white figure, for I was now close enough to distinguish it even through the spells of shadow. There was undoubtedly something, long and black, bending over the half-reclining white figure. I called in fright, "Lucy! Lucy!" and something raised a head, and from where I was I could see a white face and red, gleaming eyes.

Lucy did not answer, and I ran on to the entrance of the churchyard. As I entered, the church was between me and the seat, and for a minute or so I lost sight of her. When I came in view again the cloud had passed, and the moonlight struck so brilliantly that I could see Lucy half reclining with her head lying over the back of the seat. She was quite alone, and there was not a sign of any living thing about.

When I bent over her I could see that she was still asleep. Her lips were parted, and she was breathing, not softly as usual with her, but in long, heavy gasps, as though striving to get her lungs full at every breath. As I came close, she put up her hand in her sleep and pulled the collar of her nightdress close around her, as though she felt the cold. I flung the warm shawl over her, and drew the edges tight around her neck, for I dreaded lest she should get some deadly chill from the night air, unclad as she was. I feared to wake her all at once, so, in order to have my hands free to help her, I fastened the shawl at her throat with a big safety pin. But I must have been clumsy in my anxiety and pinched or pricked her with it, for by-and-by, when her breathing became quieter, she put her hand to her throat again and moaned. When I had her carefully wrapped up I put my shoes on her feet, and then began very gently to wake her.

At first she did not respond, but gradually she became more and more uneasy in her sleep, moaning and sighing occasionally. At last, as time was passing fast, and for many other reasons, I wished to get her home at once, I shook her forcibly, till finally she opened her eyes and awoke. She did not seem surprised to see me, as, of course, she did not realize all at once where she was.

Lucy always wakes prettily, and even at such a time, when her body must have been chilled with cold, and her mind somewhat appalled at waking unclad in a churchyard at night, she did not lose her grace. She trembled a little, and clung to me. When I told her to come at once with me home, she rose without a word, with the obedience of a child. As we passed along, the gravel hurt my feet, and Lucy noticed me wince. She stopped and wanted to insist upon my taking my shoes, but I would not. However, when we got to the pathway outside the churchyard, where there was a puddle of water, remaining from the storm, I daubed my feet with mud, using each foot in turn on the other, so that as we went home, no one, in case we should meet any one, should notice my bare feet.

Fortune favoured us, and we got home without meeting a soul. Once we saw a man, who seemed not quite sober, passing along a street in front of us. But we hid in a door till he had disappeared up an opening such as there are here, steep little closes, or 'wynds', as they call them in Scotland. My heart beat so loud all the time sometimes I thought I should faint. I was filled with anxiety about Lucy, not only for her health, lest she should suffer from the exposure, but for her reputation in case the story should get wind. When we got in, and had washed our feet, and had said a prayer of thankfulness together, I tucked her into bed. Before falling asleep she asked, even implored, me not to say a word to any one, even her mother, about her sleep-walking adventure.

I hesitated at first, to promise, but on thinking of the state of her mother's health, and how the knowledge of such a thing would fret her, and think too, of how such a story might become distorted, nay, infallibly would, in case it should leak out, I thought it wiser to do so. I hope I did right. I have locked the door, and the key is tied to my wrist, so perhaps I shall not be again disturbed. Lucy is sleeping soundly. The reflex of the dawn is high and far over the sea . . .

Same day, noon.—All goes well. Lucy slept till I woke her and seemed not to have even changed her side. The adventure of the night does not seem to have harmed her, on the contrary, it has benefited her, for she looks better this morning than she has done for weeks. I was sorry to notice that my clumsiness with the safety-pin hurt her. Indeed, it might have been serious, for the skin of her throat was pierced. I must have pinched up a piece of loose skin and have transfixed it, for there are two little red points like pin-pricks, and on the band of her nightdress was a drop of blood. When I apologised and was concerned about it, she laughed and petted me, and said she did not even feel it. Fortunately it cannot leave a scar, as it is so tiny.

Same day, night.—We passed a happy day. The air was clear, and the sun bright, and there was a cool breeze. We took our lunch to Mulgrave Woods, Mrs. Westenra driving by the road and Lucy and I walking by the cliff-path and joining her at the gate. I felt a little sad myself, for I could not but feel how *absolutely* happy it would have been had Jonathan been with me. But there! I must only be patient. In the evening we strolled in the Casino Terrace, and heard some good music by Spohr and Mackenzie, and went to bed early. Lucy seems more restful than she has been for some time, and fell asleep at once. I shall lock the door and secure the key the same as before, though I do not expect any trouble tonight.

12 August.—My expectations were wrong, for twice during the night I was wakened by Lucy trying to get out. She seemed, even in her sleep, to be a little impatient at finding the door shut, and went back to bed under a sort of protest. I woke with the dawn, and heard the birds chirping outside of the window. Lucy woke, too, and I was glad to see, was even better than on the previous morning. All her old gaiety of manner seemed to have come back, and she came and snuggled in beside me and told me all about Arthur. I told her how anxious I was about Jonathan, and then she tried to comfort me. Well, she succeeded somewhat, for, though sympathy can't alter facts, it can make them more bearable.

13 August.—Another quiet day, and to bed with the key on my wrist as before. Again I awoke in the night, and found Lucy sitting up in bed, still asleep, pointing to the window. I got up quietly, and pulling aside the blind, looked out. It was brilliant moonlight, and the soft effect of the light over the sea and sky, merged together in one great silent mystery, was beautiful beyond words. Between me and the moonlight flitted a great bat, coming and going in great whirling circles. Once or twice it came quite close, but was, I suppose, frightened at seeing me, and flitted away across the harbour towards the abbey. When I came back from the window Lucy had lain down again, and was sleeping peacefully. She did not stir again all night.

14 August.—On the East Cliff, reading and writing all day. Lucy seems to have become as much in love with the spot as I am, and it is hard to get her away from it when it is time to come home for lunch or tea or dinner. This afternoon she made a funny remark. We were coming home for dinner, and had come to the top of the steps up from the West Pier and stopped to look at the view, as we generally do. The setting sun, low down in the sky, was just dropping behind Kettleness. The red light was thrown over on the East Cliff and the old abbey, and seemed to bathe everything in a beautiful rosy glow. We were silent for a while, and suddenly Lucy murmured as if to herself . . .

"His red eyes again! They are just the same." It was such an odd expression, coming *apropos* of nothing, that it quite startled me. I slewed round a little, so as to see Lucy well without seeming to stare at her, and saw that she was in a half dreamy state, with an odd look on her face that I could not quite make out, so I said nothing, but followed her eyes. She appeared to be looking over at our own seat, whereon was a dark figure seated alone. I was quite a little startled myself, for it seemed for an instant as if the stranger had great eyes like burning flames, but a second look dispelled the illusion. The red sunlight was shining on the windows of St. Mary's Church behind our seat, and as the sun dipped there was just sufficient change in the refraction and reflection to make it appear as if the light moved. I called Lucy's attention to the peculiar effect, and she became herself with a start, but she looked sad all the same. It may have been that she was thinking of that terrible night up there. We never refer to it, so I said nothing, and we went home to dinner. Lucy had a headache and went early to bed. I saw her asleep, and went out for a little stroll myself.

I walked along the cliffs to the westward, and was full of sweet sadness, for I was thinking of Jonathan. When coming home, it was then bright moonlight, so bright that, though the front of our part of the Crescent was in shadow, everything could be well seen, I threw a glance up at our window, and saw Lucy's head leaning out. I opened my handkerchief and waved it. She did not notice or make any movement whatever. Just then, the moonlight crept round an angle of the building, and the light fell on the window. There distinctly was Lucy with her head lying up against the side of the window sill and her eyes shut. She was fast asleep, and by her, seated on the window sill, was something that looked like a good-sized bird. I was afraid she might get a chill, so I ran upstairs, but as I came into the room she was moving back to her bed, fast asleep, and breathing heavily. She was holding her hand to her throat, as though to protect if from the cold.

I did not wake her, but tucked her up warmly. I have taken care that the door is locked and the window securely fastened.

She looks so sweet as she sleeps, but she is paler than is her wont, and there is a drawn, haggard look under her eyes which I do not like. I fear she is fretting about something. I wish I could find out what it is.

15 August.—Rose later than usual. Lucy was languid and tired, and slept on after we had been called. We had a happy surprise at breakfast. Arthur's father is better, and wants the marriage to come off soon. Lucy is full of quiet joy, and her mother is glad and sorry at once. Later on in the day she told me the cause. She is grieved to lose Lucy as her very own, but she is rejoiced that she is soon to have some one to protect her. Poor dear, sweet lady! She confided to me that she has got her death warrant. She has not told Lucy, and made me promise secrecy. Her doctor told her that within a few months, at most, she must die, for her heart is weakening. At any time, even now, a sudden shock would be almost sure to kill her. Ah, we were wise to keep from her the affair of the dreadful night of Lucy's sleep-walking.

17 August.—No diary for two whole days. I have not had the heart to write. Some sort of shadowy pall seems to be coming over our happiness. No news from Jonathan, and Lucy seems to be growing weaker, whilst her mother's hours are numbering to a close. I do not understand Lucy's fading away as she is doing. She eats well and sleeps well, and enjoys the fresh air, but all the time the roses in her cheeks are fading, and she gets weaker and more languid day by day. At night I hear her gasping as if for air.

I keep the key of our door always fastened to my wrist at night, but she gets up and walks about the room, and sits at the open window. Last night I found her leaning out when I woke up, and when I tried to wake her I could not.

She was in a faint. When I managed to restore her, she was weak as water, and cried silently between long, painful struggles for breath. When I asked her how she came to be at the window she shook her head and turned away.

I trust her feeling ill may not be from that unlucky prick of the safety-pin. I looked at her throat just now as she lay asleep, and the tiny wounds seem not to have healed. They are still open, and, if anything, larger than before, and the edges of them are faintly white. They are like little white dots with red centres. Unless they heal within a day or two, I shall insist on the doctor seeing about them.

LETTER, SAMUEL F. BILLINGTON & SON, SOLICITORS WHITBY, TO MESSRS. CARTER, PATERSON & CO., LONDON.

17 August

"*Dear Sirs,*—

Herewith please receive invoice of goods sent by Great Northern Railway. Same are to be delivered at Carfax, near Purfleet, immediately on receipt at goods station King's Cross. The house is at present empty, but enclosed please find keys, all of which are labelled.

"You will please deposit the boxes, fifty in number, which form the consignment, in the partially ruined building forming part of the house and marked 'A' on rough diagrams enclosed. Your agent will easily recognize the locality, as it is the ancient chapel of the mansion. The goods leave by the train at 9:30 tonight, and will be due at King's Cross at 4:30 tomorrow afternoon. As our client wishes the delivery made as soon as possible, we shall be obliged by your having teams ready at King's Cross at the time named and forthwith conveying the goods to destination. In order to obviate any delays possible through any routine requirements as to payment in your departments, we enclose cheque herewith for ten pounds, receipt of which please acknowledge. Should the charge be less than this amount, you can return balance, if greater, we shall at once send cheque for difference on hearing from you. You are to leave the keys on coming away in the main hall of the house, where the proprietor may get them on his entering the house by means of his duplicate key.

"Pray do not take us as exceeding the bounds of business courtesy in pressing you in all ways to use the utmost expedition.

"We are, dear Sirs, Faithfully yours,

Samuel F. Billington & Son"

LETTER, MESSRS. CARTER, PATERSON & CO., LONDON, TO MESSRS. BILLINGTON & SON, WHITBY.

21 August.

"Dear Sirs,—

We beg to acknowledge 10 pounds received and to return cheque of £1, 17s, 9d, amount of overplus, as shown in receipted account herewith. Goods are delivered in exact accordance with instructions, and keys left in parcel in main hall, as directed.

"We are, dear Sirs, Yours respectfully, Pro

Carter, Paterson & Co."

MINA MURRAY'S JOURNAL.

18 August.—I am happy today, and write sitting on the seat in the church-yard. Lucy is ever so much better. Last night she slept well all night, and did not disturb me once.

The roses seem coming back already to her cheeks, though she is still sadly pale and wan-looking. If she were in any way anemic I could under-stand it, but she is not. She is in gay spirits and full of life and cheerfulness. All the morbid reticence seems to have passed from her, and she has just reminded me, as if I needed any reminding, of that night, and that it was here, on this very seat, I found her asleep.

As she told me she tapped playfully with the heel of her boot on the stone slab and said,

"My poor little feet didn't make much noise then! I daresay poor old Mr. Swales would have told me that it was because I didn't want to wake up Geordie."

As she was in such a communicative humour, I asked her if she had dreamed at all that night.

Before she answered, that sweet, puckered look came into her forehead, which Arthur, I call him Arthur from her habit, says he loves, and indeed, I don't wonder that he does. Then she went on in a half-dreaming kind of way, as if trying to recall it to herself.

"I didn't quite dream, but it all seemed to be real. I only wanted to be here in this spot. I don't know why, for I was afraid of something, I don't know what. I remember, though I suppose I was asleep, passing through the streets and over the bridge. A fish leaped as I went by, and I leaned over to look at it, and I heard a lot of dogs howling. The whole town seemed as if it must be full of dogs all howling at once, as I went up the steps. Then I had a vague memory of something long and dark with red eyes, just as we saw in the sunset, and something very sweet and very bitter all around me at once. And then I seemed sinking into deep green water, and there was a singing in my ears, as I have heard there is to drowning men, and then everything seemed passing away from me. My soul seemed to go out from my body and float about the air. I seem to remember that once the West Lighthouse was right under me, and then there was a sort of agonizing feeling, as if I were in an earthquake, and I came back and found you shaking my body. I saw you do it before I felt you."

Then she began to laugh. It seemed a little uncanny to me, and I listened to her breathlessly. I did not quite like it, and thought it better not to keep her mind on the subject, so we drifted on to another subject, and Lucy was like her old self again. When we got home the fresh breeze had braced her up, and her pale cheeks were really more rosy. Her mother rejoiced when she saw her, and we all spent a very happy evening together.

19 August.—Joy, joy, joy! Although not all joy. At last, news of Jonathan. The dear fellow has been ill, that is why he did not write. I am not afraid to think it or to say it, now that I know. Mr. Hawkins sent me on the letter, and wrote himself, oh so kindly. I am to leave in the morning and go over to Jonathan, and to help to nurse him if necessary, and to bring him home. Mr. Hawkins says it would not be a bad thing if we were to be married out there. I have cried over the good Sister's letter till I can feel it wet against my bosom, where it lies. It is of Jonathan, and must be near my heart, for he is in my heart. My journey is all mapped out, and my luggage ready. I am only taking one change of dress. Lucy will bring my trunk to London and keep it till I send for it, for it may be that . . . I must write no more. I must keep it to say to Jonathan, my husband. The letter that he has seen and touched must comfort me till we meet.

LETTER, SISTER AGATHA, HOSPITAL OF ST. JOSEPH AND STE. MARY BUDA-PESTH, TO MISS WILLHELMINA MURRAY

12 August,

"Dear Madam.

"I write by desire of Mr. Jonathan Harker, who is himself not strong enough to write, though progressing well, thanks to God and St. Joseph and Ste. Mary. He has been under our care for nearly six weeks, suffering from a violent brain fever. He wishes me to convey his love, and to say that by this post I write for him to Mr. Peter Hawkins, Exeter, to say, with his dutiful respects, that he is sorry for his delay, and that all of his work is completed. He will require some few weeks' rest in our sanatorium in the hills, but will then return. He wishes me to say that he has not sufficient money with him, and that he would like to pay for his staying here, so that others who need shall not be wanting for help.

"Believe me,

"Yours, with sympathy and all blessings.

Sister Agatha

"P.S.—My patient being asleep, I open this to let you know something more. He has told me all about you, and that you are shortly to be his wife. All blessings to you both! He has had some fearful shock, so says our doctor, and in his delirium his ravings have been dreadful, of wolves and poison and blood, of ghosts and demons, and I fear to say of what. Be careful of him always that there may be nothing to excite him of this kind for a long time to come. The traces of such an illness as his do not lightly die away. We should have written long ago, but we knew nothing of his friends, and there was nothing on him, nothing that anyone could understand. He came in the train from Klausenburg, and the guard was told by the station master there that he rushed into the station shouting for a ticket for home. Seeing from his violent demeanour that he was English, they gave him a ticket for the furthest station on the way thither that the train reached.

"Be assured that he is well cared for. He has won all hearts by his sweetness and gentleness. He is truly getting on well, and I have no doubt will in a few weeks be all himself. But be careful of him for safety's sake. There are, I pray God and St. Joseph and Ste. Mary, many, many, happy years for you both."

DR. SEWARD'S DIARY

19 August.—Strange and sudden change in Renfield last night. About eight o'clock he began to get excited and sniff about as a dog does when setting. The attendant was struck by his manner, and knowing my interest in him, encouraged him to talk. He is usually respectful to the attendant and at times servile, but tonight, the man tells me, he was quite haughty. Would not condescend to talk with him at all.

All he would say was, "I don't want to talk to you. You don't count now. The master is at hand."

The attendant thinks it is some sudden form of religious mania which has seized him. If so, we must look out for squalls, for a strong man with homicidal and religious mania at once might be dangerous. The combination is a dreadful one.

At nine o'clock I visited him myself. His attitude to me was the same as that to the attendant. In his sublime self-feeling the difference between myself and the attendant seemed to him as nothing. It looks like religious mania, and he will soon think that he himself is God.

These infinitesimal distinctions between man and man are too paltry for an Omnipotent Being. How these madmen give themselves away! The real God taketh heed lest a sparrow fall. But the God created from human vanity sees no difference between an eagle and a sparrow. Oh, if men only knew!

For half an hour or more Renfield kept getting excited in greater and greater degree. I did not pretend to be watching him, but I kept strict observation all the same. All at once that shifty look came into his eyes which we always see when a madman has seized an idea, and with it the shifty movement of the head and back which asylum attendants come to know so well. He became quite quiet, and went and sat on the edge of his bed resignedly, and looked into space with lack-luster eyes.

I thought I would find out if his apathy were real or only assumed, and tried to lead him to talk of his pets, a theme which had never failed to excite his attention.

At first he made no reply, but at length said testily, "Bother them all! I don't care a pin about them."

"What?" I said. "You don't mean to tell me you don't care about spiders?" (Spiders at present are his hobby and the notebook is filling up with columns of small figures.)

To this he answered enigmatically, "The Bride maidens rejoice the eyes that wait the coming of the bride. But when the bride draweth nigh, then the maidens shine not to the eyes that are filled."

He would not explain himself, but remained obstinately seated on his bed all the time I remained with him.

I am weary tonight and low in spirits. I cannot but think of Lucy, and how different things might have been. If I don't sleep at once, chloral, the modern Morpheus! $C_2 HCl_3 O$. H_2O! I must be careful not to let it grow into a habit. No, I shall take none tonight! I have thought of Lucy, and I shall not dishonour her by mixing the two. If need be, tonight shall be sleepless.

Later.—Glad I made the resolution, gladder that I kept to it. I had lain tossing about, and had heard the clock strike only twice, when the night watchman came to me, sent up from the ward, to say that Renfield had escaped. I threw on my clothes and ran down at once. My patient is too dangerous a person to be roaming about. Those ideas of his might work out dangerously with strangers.

The attendant was waiting for me. He said he had seen him not ten minutes before, seemingly asleep in his bed, when he had looked through the observation trap in the door. His attention was called by the sound of the window being wrenched out. He ran back and saw his feet disappear through the window, and had at once sent up for me. He was only in his night gear, and cannot be far off.

The attendant thought it would be more useful to watch where he should go than to follow him, as he might lose sight of him whilst getting out of the building by the door. He is a bulky man, and couldn't get through the window.

I am thin, so, with his aid, I got out, but feet foremost, and as we were only a few feet above ground landed unhurt.

The attendant told me the patient had gone to the left, and had taken a straight line, so I ran as quickly as I could. As I got through the belt of trees I saw a white figure scale the high wall which separates our grounds from those of the deserted house.

I ran back at once, told the watchman to get three or four men immediately and follow me into the grounds of Carfax, in case our friend might be dangerous. I got a ladder myself, and crossing the wall, dropped down on the other side. I could see Renfield's figure just disappearing behind the angle of the house, so I ran after him. On the far side of the house I found him pressed close against the old iron-bound oak door of the chapel.

He was talking, apparently to some one, but I was afraid to go near enough to hear what he was saying, lest I might frighten him, and he should run off.

Chasing an errant swarm of bees is nothing to following a naked lunatic, when the fit of escaping is upon him! After a few minutes, however, I could see that he did not take note of anything around him, and so ventured to draw nearer to him, the more so as my men had now crossed the wall and were closing him in. I heard him say . . .

"I am here to do your bidding, Master. I am your slave, and you will reward me, for I shall be faithful. I have worshipped you long and afar off.

Now that you are near, I await your commands, and you will not pass me by, will you, dear Master, in your distribution of good things?"

He *is* a selfish old beggar anyhow. He thinks of the loaves and fishes even when he believes his is in a real Presence. His manias make a startling combination. When we closed in on him he fought like a tiger. He is immensely strong, for he was more like a wild beast than a man.

I never saw a lunatic in such a paroxysm of rage before, and I hope I shall not again. It is a mercy that we have found out his strength and his danger in good time. With strength and determination like his, he might have done wild work before he was caged.

He is safe now, at any rate. Jack Sheppard himself couldn't get free from the strait waistcoat that keeps him restrained, and he's chained to the wall in the padded room.

His cries are at times awful, but the silences that follow are more deadly still, for he means murder in every turn and movement.

Just now he spoke coherent words for the first time. "I shall be patient, Master. It is coming, coming, coming!"

So I took the hint, and came too. I was too excited to sleep, but this diary has quieted me, and I feel I shall get some sleep tonight.

ꙮ CHAPTER 9 ଔ
LETTER, MINA HARKER TO LUCY WESTENRA

Buda-Pesth, 24 August.

"My dearest Lucy,

"I know you will be anxious to hear all that has happened since we parted at the railway station at Whitby.

"Well, my dear, I got to Hull all right, and caught the boat to Hamburg, and then the train on here. I feel that I can hardly recall anything of the journey, except that I knew I was coming to Jonathan, and that as I should have to do some nursing, I had better get all the sleep I could. I found my dear one, oh, so thin and pale and weak-looking. All the resolution has gone out of his dear eyes, and that quiet dignity which I told you was in his face has vanished. He is only a wreck of himself, and he does not remember anything that has happened to him for a long time past. At least, he wants me to believe so, and I shall never ask.

"He has had some terrible shock, and I fear it might tax his poor brain if he were to try to recall it. Sister Agatha, who is a good creature and a born nurse, tells me that he wanted her to tell me what they were, but she would only cross herself, and say she would never tell. That the ravings of the sick were the secrets of God, and that if a nurse through her vocation should hear them, she should respect her trust.

"She is a sweet, good soul, and the next day, when she saw I was troubled, she opened up the subject my poor dear raved about, added, 'I can tell you this much, my dear. That it was not about anything which he has done wrong himself, and you, as his wife to be, have no cause to be concerned. He has not forgotten you or what he owes to you. His fear was of great and terrible things, which no mortal can treat of.'

"I do believe the dear soul thought I might be jealous lest my poor dear should have fallen in love with any other girl. The idea of my being jealous about Jonathan! And yet, my dear, let me whisper, I felt a thrill of joy through me when I knew that no other woman was a cause for trouble. I am now sitting by his bedside, where I can see his face while he sleeps. He is waking!

"When he woke he asked me for his coat, as he wanted to get something from the pocket. I asked Sister Agatha, and she brought all his things. I saw amongst them was his notebook, and was going to ask him to let me look at it, for I knew that I might find some clue to his trouble, but I suppose he must have seen my wish in my eyes, for he sent me over to the window, saying he wanted to be quite alone for a moment.

"Then he called me back, and he said to me very solemnly, 'Wilhelmina', I knew then that he was in deadly earnest, for he has never called me by that name since he asked me to marry him, 'You know, dear, my ideas of the trust between husband and wife. There should be no secret, no concealment. I have had a great shock, and when I try to think of what it is I feel my head spin round, and I do not know if it was real of the dreaming of a madman. You know I had brain fever, and that is to be mad. The secret is here, and I do not want to know it. I want to take up my life here, with our marriage.' For, my dear, we had decided to be married as soon as the formalities are complete. 'Are you willing, Wilhelmina, to share my ignorance? Here is the book. Take it and keep it, read it if you will, but never let me know unless, indeed, some solemn duty should come upon me to go back to the bitter hours, asleep or awake, sane or mad, recorded here.' He fell back exhausted, and I put the book under his pillow, and kissed him. I have asked Sister Agatha to beg the Superior to let our wedding be this afternoon, and am waiting her reply . . ."

"She has come and told me that the Chaplain of the English mission church has been sent for. We are to be married in an hour, or as soon after as Jonathan awakes."

"Lucy, the time has come and gone. I feel very solemn, but very, very happy. Jonathan woke a little after the hour, and all was ready, and he sat up in bed, propped up with pillows. He answered his 'I will' firmly and strong. I could hardly speak. My heart was so full that even those words seemed to choke me.

"The dear sisters were so kind. Please, God, I shall never, never forget them, nor the grave and sweet responsibilities I have taken upon me. I must tell you of my wedding present. When the chaplain and the sisters had left me alone with my husband—oh, Lucy, it is the first time I have written the words 'my husband'—left me alone with my husband, I took the book from under his pillow, and wrapped it up in white paper, and tied it with a little bit of pale blue ribbon which was round my neck, and sealed it over the knot with sealing wax, and for my seal I used my wedding ring. Then I kissed it and showed it to my husband, and told him that I would keep it so, and then it would be an outward and visible sign for us all our lives that we trusted each other, that I would never open it unless it were for his own dear sake or for the sake of some stern duty. Then he took my hand in his, and oh, Lucy, it was the first time he took *his wife's* hand, and said that it was the dearest thing in all the wide world, and that he would go through all the past again to win it, if need be. The poor dear meant to have said a part of the past, but he cannot think of time yet, and I shall not wonder if at first he mixes up not only the month, but the year.

"Well, my dear, what could I say? I could only tell him that I was the happiest woman in all the wide world, and that I had nothing to give him except myself, my life, and my trust, and that with these went my love and duty for all the days of my life. And, my dear, when he kissed me, and drew me to him with his poor weak hands, it was like a solemn pledge between us.

"Lucy dear, do you know why I tell you all this? It is not only because it is all sweet to me, but because you have been, and are, very dear to me. It was my privilege to be your friend and guide when you came from the schoolroom to prepare for the world of life. I want you to see now, and with the eyes of a very happy wife, whither duty has led me, so that in your own married life you too may be all happy, as I am. My dear, please Almighty God, your life may be all it promises, a long day of sunshine, with no harsh wind, no forgetting duty, no distrust. I must not wish you no pain, for that can never be, but I do hope you will be always as happy as I am now. Goodbye, my dear. I shall post this at once, and perhaps, write you very soon again. I must stop, for Jonathan is waking. I must attend my husband!

"Your ever-loving

Mina Harker."

LETTER, LUCY WESTENRA TO MINA HARKER.

Whitby, 30 August.

"*My dearest Mina,*

"Oceans of love and millions of kisses, and may you soon be in your own home with your husband. I wish you were coming home soon enough to stay with us here. The strong air would soon restore Jonathan. It has quite restored me. I have an appetite like a cormorant, am full of life, and sleep well. You will be glad to know that I have quite given up walking in my sleep. I think I have not stirred out of my bed for a week, that is when I once got into it at night. Arthur says I am getting fat. By the way, I forgot to tell you that Arthur is here. We have such walks and drives, and rides, and rowing, and tennis, and fishing together, and I love him more than ever. He *tells* me that he loves me more, but I doubt that, for at first he told me that he couldn't love me more than he did then. But this is nonsense. There he is, calling to me. So no more just at present from your loving,

"Lucy.

"P.S.—Mother sends her love. She seems better, poor dear.

"P.P.S.—We are to be married on 28 September."

DR. SEWARD'S DIARY

20 August.—The case of Renfield grows even more interesting. He has now so far quieted that there are spells of cessation from his passion. For the first week after his attack he was perpetually violent. Then one night, just as the moon rose, he grew quiet, and kept murmuring to himself. "Now I can wait. Now I can wait."

The attendant came to tell me, so I ran down at once to have a look at him. He was still in the strait waistcoat and in the padded room, but the suffused look had gone from his face, and his eyes had something of their old pleading. I might almost say, cringing, softness. I was satisfied with his present condition, and directed him to be relieved. The attendants hesitated, but finally carried out my wishes without protest.

It was a strange thing that the patient had humour enough to see their distrust, for, coming close to me, he said in a whisper, all the while looking furtively at them, "They think I could hurt you! Fancy *me* hurting *you!* The fools!"

It was soothing, somehow, to the feelings to find myself disassociated even in the mind of this poor madman from the others, but all the same I do not follow his thought. Am I to take it that I have anything in common with him, so that we are, as it were, to stand together. Or has he to gain from me some good so stupendous that my well being is needful to Him? I must find out later on. Tonight he will not speak. Even the offer of a kitten or even a full-grown cat will not tempt him.

He will only say, "I don't take any stock in cats. I have more to think of now, and I can wait. I can wait."

After a while I left him. The attendant tells me that he was quiet until just before dawn, and that then he began to get uneasy, and at length violent, until at last he fell into a paroxysm which exhausted him so that he swooned into a sort of coma.

. . . Three nights has the same thing happened, violent all day then quiet from moonrise to sunrise. I wish I could get some clue to the cause. It would almost seem as if there was some influence which came and went. Happy thought! We shall tonight play sane wits against mad ones. He escaped before without our help. Tonight he shall escape with it. We shall give him a chance, and have the men ready to follow in case they are required.

23 August.—"The expected always happens." How well Disraeli knew life. Our bird when he found the cage open would not fly, so all our subtle arrangements were for nought. At any rate, we have proved one thing, that the spells of quietness last a reasonable time. We shall in future be able to ease his bonds for a few hours each day. I have given orders to the night attendant merely to shut him in the padded room, when once he is quiet, until the hour before sunrise. The poor soul's body will enjoy the relief even if his mind cannot appreciate it. Hark! The unexpected again! I am called. The patient has once more escaped.

Later.—Another night adventure. Renfield artfully waited until the attendant was entering the room to inspect. Then he dashed out past him and flew down the passage. I sent word for the attendants to follow. Again he went into the grounds of the deserted house, and we found him in the same place, pressed against the old chapel door. When he saw me he became furious, and had not the attendants seized him in time, he would have tried to kill me. As we were holding him a strange thing happened. He suddenly redoubled his efforts, and then as suddenly grew calm. I looked round instinctively, but could see nothing. Then I caught the patient's eye and followed it, but could trace nothing as it looked into the moonlight sky, except a big bat, which was flapping its silent and ghostly way to the west. Bats usually wheel about, but this one seemed to go straight on, as if it knew where it was bound for or had some intention of its own.

The patient grew calmer every instant, and presently said, "You needn't tie me. I shall go quietly!" Without trouble, we came back to the house. I feel there is something ominous in his calm, and shall not forget this night.

LUCY WESTENRA'S DIARY

Hillingham, 24 August.—I must imitate Mina, and keep writing things down. Then we can have long talks when we do meet. I wonder when it will be. I wish she were with me again, for I feel so unhappy. Last night

I seemed to be dreaming again just as I was at Whitby. Perhaps it is the change of air, or getting home again. It is all dark and horrid to me, for I can remember nothing. But I am full of vague fear, and I feel so weak and worn out. When Arthur came to lunch he looked quite grieved when he saw me, and I hadn't the spirit to try to be cheerful. I wonder if I could sleep in mother's room tonight. I shall make an excuse to try.

25 August.—Another bad night. Mother did not seem to take to my proposal. She seems not too well herself, and doubtless she fears to worry me. I tried to keep awake, and succeeded for a while, but when the clock struck twelve it waked me from a doze, so I must have been falling asleep. There was a sort of scratching or flapping at the window, but I did not mind it, and as I remember no more, I suppose I must have fallen asleep. More bad dreams. I wish I could remember them. This morning I am horribly weak. My face is ghastly pale, and my throat pains me. It must be something wrong with my lungs, for I don't seem to be getting air enough. I shall try to cheer up when Arthur comes, or else I know he will be miserable to see me so.

LETTER, ARTHUR TO DR. SEWARD

"Albemarle Hotel,

31 August

"My dear Jack,

"I want you to do me a favour. Lucy is ill, that is she has no special disease, but she looks awful, and is getting worse every day. I have asked her if there is any cause, I not dare to ask her mother, for to disturb the poor lady's mind about her daughter in her present state of health would be fatal. Mrs. Westenra has confided to me that her doom is spoken, disease of the heart, though poor Lucy does not know it yet. I am sure that there is something preying on my dear girl's mind. I am almost distracted when I think of her. To look at her gives me a pang. I told her I should ask you to see her, and though she demurred at first, I know why, old fellow, she finally consented. It will be a painful task for you, I know, old friend, but it is for her sake, and I must not hesitate to ask, or you to act. You are to come to lunch at Hillingham tomorrow, two o'clock, so as not to arouse any suspicion in Mrs. Westenra, and after lunch Lucy will take an opportunity of being alone with you. I am filled with anxiety, and want to consult with you alone as soon as I can after you have seen her. Do not fail!

"Arthur."

TELEGRAM, ARTHUR HOLMWOOD TO SEWARD

1 September

"Am summoned to see my father, who is worse. Am writing. Write me fully by tonight's post to Ring. Wire me if necessary."

LETTER FROM DR. SEWARD TO ARTHUR HOLMWOOD

2 September

"My dear old fellow,

"With regard to Miss Westenra's health I hasten to let you know at once that in my opinion there is not any functional disturbance or any malady that I know of. At the same time, I am not by any means satisfied with her appearance. She is woefully different from what she was when I saw her last. Of course you must bear in mind that I did not have full opportunity of examination such as I should wish. Our very friendship makes a little difficulty which not even medical science or custom can bridge over. I had better tell you exactly what happened, leaving you to draw, in a measure, your own conclusions. I shall then say what I have done and propose doing.

"I found Miss Westenra in seemingly gay spirits. Her mother was present, and in a few seconds I made up my mind that she was trying all she knew to mislead her mother and prevent her from being anxious. I have no doubt she guesses, if she does not know, what need of caution there is.

"We lunched alone, and as we all exerted ourselves to be cheerful, we got, as some kind of reward for our labours, some real cheerfulness amongst us. Then Mrs. Westenra went to lie down, and Lucy was left with me. We went into her boudoir, and till we got there her gaiety remained, for the servants were coming and going.

"As soon as the door was closed, however, the mask fell from her face, and she sank down into a chair with a great sigh, and hid her eyes with her hand. When I saw that her high spirits had failed, I at once took advantage of her reaction to make a diagnosis.

"She said to me very sweetly, 'I cannot tell you how I loathe talking about myself.' I reminded her that a doctor's confidence was sacred, but that you were grievously anxious about her. She caught on to my meaning at once, and settled that matter in a word. 'Tell Arthur everything you choose. I do not care for myself, but for him!' So I am quite free.

"I could easily see that she was somewhat bloodless, but I could not see the usual anemic signs, and by the chance, I was able to test the actual quality of her blood, for in opening a window which was stiff a cord gave way, and she cut her hand slightly with broken glass. It was a slight matter in itself, but it gave me an evident chance, and I secured a few drops of the blood and have analysed them.

"The qualitative analysis give a quite normal condition, and shows, I should infer, in itself a vigorous state of health. In other physical matters I was quite satisfied that there is no need for anxiety, but as there must be a cause somewhere, I have come to the conclusion that it must be something mental.

"She complains of difficulty breathing satisfactorily at times, and of heavy, lethargic sleep, with dreams that frighten her, but regarding which she can remember nothing. She says that as a child, she used to walk in her sleep, and that when in Whitby the habit came back, and that once she walked out in the night and went to East Cliff, where Miss Murray found her. But she assures me that of late the habit has not returned.

"I am in doubt, and so have done the best thing I know of. I have written to my old friend and master, Professor Van Helsing, of Amsterdam, who knows as much about obscure diseases as any one in the world. I have asked him to come over, and as you told me that all things were to be at your charge, I have mentioned to him who you are and your relations to Miss Westenra. This, my dear fellow, is in obedience to your wishes, for I am only too proud and happy to do anything I can for her.

"Van Helsing would, I know, do anything for me for a personal reason, so no matter on what ground he comes, we must accept his wishes. He is a seemingly arbitrary man, this is because he knows what he is talking about better than any one else. He is a philosopher and a metaphysician, and one of the most advanced scientists of his day, and he has, I believe, an absolutely open mind. This, with an iron nerve, a temper of the ice-brook, and indomitable resolution, self-command, and toleration exalted from virtues to blessings, and the kindliest and truest heart that beats, these form his equipment for the noble work that he is doing for mankind, work both in theory and practice, for his views are as wide as his all-embracing sympathy. I tell you these facts that you may know why I have such confidence in him. I have asked him to come at once. I shall see Miss Westenra tomorrow again. She is to meet me at the Stores, so that I may not alarm her mother by too early a repetition of my call.

"Yours always."

John Seward

LETTER, ABRAHAM VAN HELSING, MD, DPH, D. LIT, ETC, ETC, TO DR. SEWARD

2 September.

"My good Friend,

"When I received your letter I am already coming to you. By good fortune I can leave just at once, without wrong to any of those who have trusted me. Were fortune other, then it were bad for those who have trusted, for I come to my friend when he call me to aid those he holds dear. Tell your friend that when that time you suck from my wound so swiftly the poison of the gangrene from that knife that our other friend, too nervous, let slip, you did more for him when he wants my aids and you call for them than all his great fortune could do. But it is pleasure added to do for him, your friend, it is to you that I come. Have near at hand, and please it so arrange that we may see the young lady not too late on tomorrow, for it is likely that I may have to return here that night. But if need be I shall come again in three days, and stay longer if it must. Till then goodbye, my friend John.

"Van Helsing."

LETTER, DR. SEWARD TO HON. ARTHUR HOLMWOOD

3 September

"My dear Art,

"Van Helsing has come and gone. He came on with me to Hillingham, and found that, by Lucy's discretion, her mother was lunching out, so that we were alone with her.

"Van Helsing made a very careful examination of the patient. He is to report to me, and I shall advise you, for of course I was not present all the time. He is, I fear, much concerned, but says he must think. When I told him of our friendship and how you trust to me in the matter, he said, 'You must tell him all you think. Tell him what I think, if you can guess it, if you will. Nay, I am not jesting. This is no jest, but life and death, perhaps more.' I asked what he meant by that, for he was very serious. This was when we had come back to town, and he was having a cup of tea before starting on his return to Amsterdam. He would not give me any further clue. You must not be angry with me, Art, because his very reticence means that all his brains are working for her good. He will speak plainly enough when the time comes, be sure. So I told him I would simply write an account of our visit, just as if I were doing a descriptive special article for *The Daily Telegraph*. He seemed not to notice, but remarked that the smuts[96] of London were not quite so bad as they used to be when he was a student here. I am to get his report tomorrow if he can possibly make it. In any case I am to have a letter.

"Well, as to the visit, Lucy was more cheerful than on the day I first saw her, and certainly looked better. She had lost something of the ghastly look that so upset you, and her breathing was normal. She

---

96 Smog.

was very sweet to the Professor (as she always is), and tried to make him feel at ease, though I could see the poor girl was making a hard struggle for it.

"I believe Van Helsing saw it, too, for I saw the quick look under his bushy brows that I knew of old. Then he began to chat of all things except ourselves and diseases and with such an infinite geniality that I could see poor Lucy's pretense of animation merge into reality. Then, without any seeming change, he brought the conversation gently round to his visit, and suavely said,

"'My dear young miss, I have the so great pleasure because you are so much beloved. That is much, my dear, even were there that which I do not see. They told me you were down in the spirit, and that you were of a ghastly pale. To them I say "Pouf!"' And he snapped his fingers at me and went on. 'But you and I shall show them how wrong they are. How can he,' and he pointed at me with the same look and gesture as that with which he pointed me out in his class, on, or rather after, a particular occasion which he never fails to remind me of, 'know anything of a young ladies? He has his madmen to play with, and to bring them back to happiness, and to those that love them. It is much to do, and, oh, but there are rewards in that we can bestow such happiness. But the young ladies! He has no wife nor daughter, and the young do not tell themselves to the young, but to the old, like me, who have known so many sorrows and the causes of them. So, my dear, we will send him away to smoke the cigarette in the garden, whiles you and I have little talk all to ourselves.' I took the hint, and strolled about, and presently the professor came to the window and called me in. He looked grave, but said, 'I have made careful examination, but there is no functional cause. With you I agree that there has been much blood lost, it has been but is not. But the conditions of her are in no way anemic. I have asked her to send me her maid, that I may ask just one or two questions, that so I may not chance to miss nothing. I know well what she will say. And yet there is cause. There is always cause for everything. I must go back home and think. You must send me the telegram every day, and if there be cause I shall come again. The disease, for not to be well is a disease, interest me, and the sweet, young dear, she interest me too. She charm me, and for her, if not for you or disease, I come.'

"As I tell you, he would not say a word more, even when we were alone. And so now, Art, you know all I know. I shall keep stern watch. I trust your poor father is rallying. It must be a terrible thing to you, my dear old fellow, to be placed in such a position between two people who are both so dear to you. I know your idea of duty to your father, and you are right to stick to it. But if need be, I shall send you word to come at once to Lucy, so do not be over-anxious unless you hear from me."

DR. SEWARD'S DIARY

4 September.—Zoophagous patient still keeps up our interest in him. He had only one outburst and that was yesterday at an unusual time. Just before the stroke of noon he began to grow restless. The attendant knew the symptoms, and at once summoned aid. Fortunately the men came at a run, and were just in time, for at the stroke of noon he became so violent that it took all their strength to hold him. In about five minutes, however, he began to get more quiet, and finally sank into a sort of melancholy, in which state he has remained up to now. The attendant tells me that his screams whilst in the paroxysm were really appalling. I found my hands full when I got in, attending to some of the other patients who were frightened by him. Indeed, I can quite understand the effect, for the sounds disturbed even me, though I was some distance away. It is now after the dinner hour of the asylum, and as yet my patient sits in a corner brooding, with a dull, sullen, woe-begone look in his face, which seems rather to indicate than to show something directly. I cannot quite understand it.

Later.—Another change in my patient. At five o'clock I looked in on him, and found him seemingly as happy and contented as he used to be. He was catching flies and eating them, and was keeping note of his capture by making nailmarks on the edge of the door between the ridges of padding. When he saw me, he came over and apologized for his bad conduct, and asked me in a very humble, cringing way to be led back to his own room, and to have his notebook again. I thought it well to humour him, so he is back in his room with the window open. He has the sugar of his tea spread out on the window sill, and is reaping quite a harvest of flies. He is not now eating them, but putting them into a box, as of old, and is already examining the corners of his room to find a spider. I tried to get him to talk about the past few days, for any clue to his thoughts would be of immense help to me, but he would not rise. For a moment or two he looked very sad, and said in a sort of far away voice, as though saying it rather to himself than to me.

"All over! All over! He has deserted me. No hope for me now unless I do it myself!" Then suddenly turning to me in a resolute way, he said, "Doctor, won't you be very good to me and let me have a little more sugar? I think it would be very good for me."

"And the flies?" I said.

"Yes! The flies like it, too, and I like the flies, therefore I like it." And there are people who know so little as to think that madmen do not argue. I procured him a double supply, and left him as happy a man as, I suppose, any in the world. I wish I could fathom his mind.

Midnight.—Another change in him. I had been to see Miss Westenra, whom I found much better, and had just returned, and was standing at our own gate looking at the sunset, when once more I heard him yelling. As his room is on this side of the house, I could hear it better than in the morning. It was a shock to me to turn from the wonderful smoky beauty of a sunset over London, with its lurid lights and inky shadows and all the marvellous tints that come on foul clouds even as on foul water, and to realize all the grim sternness of my own cold stone building, with its wealth of breathing misery, and my own desolate heart to endure it all. I reached him just as the sun was going down, and from his window saw the red disc sink. As it sank he became less and less frenzied, and just as it dipped he slid from the hands that held him, an inert mass, on the floor. It is wonderful, however, what intellectual recuperative power lunatics have, for within a few minutes he stood up quite calmly and looked around him. I signalled to the attendants not to hold him, for I was anxious to see what he would do. He went straight over to the window and brushed out the crumbs of sugar. Then he took his fly box, and emptied it outside, and threw away the box. Then he shut the window, and crossing over, sat down on his bed. All this surprised me, so I asked him, "Are you going to keep flies any more?"

"No," said he. "I am sick of all that rubbish!" He certainly is a wonderfully interesting study. I wish I could get some glimpse of his mind or of the cause of his sudden passion. Stop. There may be a clue after all, if we can find why today his paroxysms came on at high noon and at sunset. Can it be that there is a malign influence of the sun at periods which affects certain natures, as at times the moon does others? We shall see.

TELEGRAM. SEWARD, LONDON, TO VAN HELSING, AMSTERDAM

"*4 September.*—Patient still better today."

TELEGRAM, SEWARD, LONDON, TO
VAN HELSING, AMSTERDAM

"*5 September.*—Patient greatly improved. Good appetite, sleeps naturally, good spirits, colour coming back."

TELEGRAM, SEWARD, LONDON, TO
VAN HELSING, AMSTERDAM

"*6 September.*—Terrible change for the worse. Come at once. Do not lose an hour. I hold over telegram to Holmwood till have seen you."

ஒ CHAPTER 10 ஐ

LETTER, DR. SEWARD TO HON. ARTHUR HOLMWOOD

6 September

"*My dear Art,*

"My news today is not so good. Lucy this morning had gone back a bit. There is, however, one good thing which has arisen from it. Mrs. Westenra was naturally anxious concerning Lucy, and has consulted me professionally about her. I took advantage of the opportunity, and told her that my old master, Van Helsing, the great specialist, was coming to stay with me, and that I would put her in his charge conjointly with myself. So now we can come and go without alarming her unduly, for a shock to her would mean sudden death, and this, in Lucy's weak condition, might be disastrous to her. We are hedged in with difficulties, all of us, my poor fellow, but, please God, we shall come through them all right. If any need I shall write, so that, if you do not hear from me, take it for granted that I am simply waiting for news, In haste,

"*Yours ever,*"

John Seward

DR. SEWARD'S DIARY

7 September.—The first thing Van Helsing said to me when we met at Liverpool Street was, "Have you said anything to our young friend, to lover of her?"

"No," I said. "I waited till I had seen you, as I said in my telegram. I wrote him a letter simply telling him that you were coming, as Miss Westenra was not so well, and that I should let him know if need be."

"Right, my friend," he said. "Quite right! Better he not know as yet. Perhaps he will never know. I pray so, but if it be needed, then he shall know all. And, my good friend John, let me caution you. You deal with the madmen. All men are mad in some way or the other, and inasmuch as you deal discreetly with your madmen, so deal with God's madmen too, the rest of the world. You tell not your madmen what you do nor why you do it. You tell them not what you think. So you shall keep knowledge in its place, where it may rest, where it may gather its kind around it and breed. You and I shall keep as yet what we know here, and here." He touched me on the heart and on the forehead, and then touched himself the same way. "I have for myself thoughts at the present. Later I shall unfold to you."

"Why not now?" I asked. "It may do some good. We may arrive at some decision." He looked at me and said, "My friend John, when the corn is grown, even before it has ripened, while the milk of its mother earth is in him, and the sunshine has not yet begun to paint him with his gold, the husbandman he pull the ear and rub him between his rough hands, and blow away the green chaff, and say to you, 'Look! He's good corn, he will make a good crop when the time comes.'"

I did not see the application and told him so. For reply he reached over and took my ear in his hand and pulled it playfully, as he used long ago to do at lectures, and said, "The good husbandman tell you so then because he knows, but not till then. But you do not find the good husbandman dig up his planted corn to see if he grow. That is for the children who play at husbandry, and not for those who take it as of the work of their life. See you now, friend John? I have sown my corn, and Nature has her work to do in making it sprout, if he sprout at all, there's some promise, and I wait till the ear begins to swell." He broke off, for he evidently saw that I understood. Then he went on gravely, "You were always a careful student, and your case book was ever more full than the rest. And I trust that good habit have not fail. Remember, my friend, that knowledge is stronger than memory, and we should not trust the weaker. Even if you have not kept the good practice, let me tell you that this case of our dear miss is one that may be, mind, I say may be, of such interest to us and others that all the rest may not make him kick the beam, as your people say. Take then good note of it. Nothing is too small. I counsel you, put down in record even your doubts and surmises. Hereafter it may be of interest to you to see how true you guess. We learn from failure, not from success!"

When I described Lucy's symptoms, the same as before, but infinitely more marked, he looked very grave, but said nothing. He took with him a bag in which were many instruments and drugs, "the ghastly paraphernalia of our beneficial trade," as he once called, in one of his lectures, the equipment of a professor of the healing craft.

When we were shown in, Mrs. Westenra met us. She was alarmed, but not nearly so much as I expected to find her. Nature in one of her beneficent moods has ordained that even death has some antidote to its own terrors. Here, in a case where any shock may prove fatal, matters are so ordered that, from some cause or other, the things not personal, even the terrible change in her daughter to whom she is so attached, do not seem to reach her. It is something like the way dame Nature gathers round a foreign body an envelope of some insensitive tissue which can protect from evil that which it would otherwise harm by contact. If this be an ordered selfishness, then we should pause before we condemn any one for the vice of egoism, for there may be deeper root for its causes than we have knowledge of.

I used my knowledge of this phase of spiritual pathology, and set down a rule that she should not be present with Lucy, or think of her illness more than was absolutely required. She assented readily, so readily that I saw again the hand of Nature fighting for life. Van Helsing and I were shown up to Lucy's room. If I was shocked when I saw her yesterday, I was horrified when I saw her today.

She was ghastly, chalkily pale. The red seemed to have gone even from her lips and gums, and the bones of her face stood out prominently. Her breathing was painful to see or hear. Van Helsing's face grew set as marble, and his eyebrows converged till they almost touched over his nose. Lucy lay motionless, and did not seem to have strength to speak, so for a while we were all silent. Then Van Helsing beckoned to me, and we went gently out of the room. The instant we had closed the door he stepped quickly along the passage to the next door, which was open. Then he pulled me quickly in with him and closed the door. "My god!" he said. "This is dreadful. There is not time to be lost. She will die for sheer want of blood to keep the heart's action as it should be. There must be a transfusion of blood at once. Is it you or me?"

"I am younger and stronger, Professor. It must be me."

"Then get ready at once. I will bring up my bag. I am prepared."

I went downstairs with him, and as we were going there was a knock at the hall door. When we reached the hall, the maid had just opened the door, and Arthur was stepping quickly in. He rushed up to me, saying in an eager whisper,

"Jack, I was so anxious. I read between the lines of your letter, and have been in an agony. The dad was better, so I ran down here to see for myself. Is not that gentleman Dr. Van Helsing? I am so thankful to you, sir, for coming."

When first the Professor's eye had lit upon him, he had been angry at his interruption at such a time, but now, as he took in his stalwart proportions and recognized the strong young manhood which seemed to emanate from him, his eyes gleamed. Without a pause he said to him as he held out his hand,

"Sir, you have come in time. You are the lover of our dear miss. She is bad, very, very bad. Nay, my child, do not go like that." For he suddenly grew pale and sat down in a chair almost fainting. "You are to help her. You can do more than any that live, and your courage is your best help."

"What can I do?" asked Arthur hoarsely. "Tell me, and I shall do it. My life is hers, and I would give the last drop of blood in my body for her."

The Professor has a strongly humorous side, and I could from old knowledge detect a trace of its origin in his answer.

"My young sir, I do not ask so much as that, not the last!"

"What shall I do?" There was fire in his eyes, and his open nostrils quivered with intent. Van Helsing slapped him on the shoulder.

"Come!" he said. "You are a man, and it is a man we want. You are better than me, better than my friend John." Arthur looked bewildered, and the Professor went on by explaining in a kindly way.

"Young miss is bad, very bad. She wants blood, and blood she must have or die. My friend John and I have consulted, and we are about to perform what we call transfusion of blood, to transfer from full veins of one to the empty veins which pine for him. John was to give his blood, as he is the more young and strong than me."—Here Arthur took my hand and wrung it hard in silence.—"But now you are here, you are more good than us, old or young, who toil much in the world of thought. Our nerves are not so calm and our blood so bright than yours!"

Arthur turned to him and said, "If you only knew how gladly I would die for her you would understand . . ." He stopped with a sort of choke in his voice.

"Good boy!" said Van Helsing. "In the not-so-far-off you will be happy that you have done all for her you love. Come now and be silent. You shall kiss her once before it is done, but then you must go, and you must leave at my sign. Say no word to Madame. You know how it is with her. There must be no shock, any knowledge of this would be one. Come!"

We all went up to Lucy's room. Arthur by direction remained outside. Lucy turned her head and looked at us, but said nothing. She was not asleep, but she was simply too weak to make the effort. Her eyes spoke to us, that was all.

Van Helsing took some things from his bag and laid them on a little table out of sight. Then he mixed a narcotic, and coming over to the bed, said cheerily, "Now, little miss, here is your medicine. Drink it off, like a good child. See, I lift you so that to swallow is easy. Yes." She had made the effort with success.

It astonished me how long the drug took to act. This, in fact, marked the extent of her weakness. The time seemed endless until sleep began to flicker in her eyelids. At last, however, the narcotic began to manifest its potency, and she fell into a deep sleep. When the Professor was satisfied, he called Arthur into the room, and bade him strip off his coat. Then he added, "You may take that one little kiss whiles I bring over the table. Friend John, help to me!" So neither of us looked whilst he bent over her.

Van Helsing, turning to me, said, "He is so young and strong, and of blood so pure that we need not defibrinate it."

Then with swiftness, but with absolute method, Van Helsing performed the operation. As the transfusion went on, something like life seemed to come back to poor Lucy's cheeks, and through Arthur's growing pallor the joy of his face seemed absolutely to shine. After a bit I began to grow anxious, for the loss of blood was telling on Arthur, strong man as he was. It gave me an idea of what a terrible strain Lucy's system must have undergone that what weakened Arthur only partially restored her.

But the Professor's face was set, and he stood watch in hand, and with his eyes fixed now on the patient and now on Arthur. I could hear my own heart beat. Presently, he said in a soft voice, "Do not stir an instant. It is enough. You attend him. I will look to her."

When all was over, I could see how much Arthur was weakened. I dressed the wound and took his arm to bring him away, when Van Helsing spoke without turning round, the man seems to have eyes in the back of his head, "The brave lover, I think, deserve another kiss, which he shall have presently." And as he had now finished his operation, he adjusted the pillow to the patient's head. As he did so the narrow black velvet band which she seems always to wear round her throat, buckled with an old diamond buckle which her lover had given her, was dragged a little up, and showed a red mark on her throat.

Arthur did not notice it, but I could hear the deep hiss of indrawn breath which is one of Van Helsing's ways of betraying emotion. He said nothing at the moment, but turned to me, saying, "Now take down our brave young lover, give him of the port wine, and let him lie down a while. He must then go home and rest, sleep much and eat much, that he may be recruited of what he has so given to his love. He must not stay here. Hold a moment! I may take it, sir, that you are anxious of result. Then bring it with you, that in all ways the operation is successful. You have saved her life this time, and you can go home and rest easy in mind that all that can be is. I shall tell her all when she is well. She shall love you none the less for what you have done. Goodbye."

When Arthur had gone I went back to the room. Lucy was sleeping gently, but her breathing was stronger. I could see the counterpane move as her breast heaved. By the bedside sat Van Helsing, looking at her intently. The velvet band again covered the red mark. I asked the Professor in a whisper, "What do you make of that mark on her throat?"

"What do you make of it?"

"I have not examined it yet," I answered, and then and there proceeded to loose the band. Just over the external jugular vein there were two punctures, not large, but not wholesome looking. There was no sign of disease, but the edges were white and worn looking, as if by some trituration. It at once occurred to me that that this wound, or whatever it was, might be the means of that manifest loss of blood. But I abandoned the idea as soon as it formed, for such a thing could not be. The whole bed would have been drenched to a scarlet with the blood which the girl must have lost to leave such a pallor as she had before the transfusion.

"Well?" said Van Helsing.

"Well," said I. "I can make nothing of it."

The Professor stood up. "I must go back to Amsterdam tonight," he said "There are books and things there which I want. You must remain here all night, and you must not let your sight pass from her."

"Shall I have a nurse?" I asked.

"We are the best nurses, you and I. You keep watch all night. See that she is well fed, and that nothing disturbs her. You must not sleep all the night. Later on we can sleep, you and I. I shall be back as soon as possible. And then we may begin."

"May begin?" I said. "What on earth do you mean?"

"We shall see!" he answered, as he hurried out. He came back a moment later and put his head inside the door and said with a warning finger held up, "Remember, she is your charge. If you leave her, and harm befall, you shall not sleep easy hereafter!"

DR. SEWARD'S DIARY—CONTINUED

8 September.—I sat up all night with Lucy. The opiate worked itself off towards dusk, and she waked naturally. She looked a different being from what she had been before the operation. Her spirits even were good, and she was full of a happy vivacity, but I could see evidences of the absolute prostration which she had undergone. When I told Mrs. Westenra that Dr. Van Helsing had directed that I should sit up with her, she almost pooh-poohed the idea, pointing out her daughter's renewed strength and excellent spirits. I was firm, however, and made preparations for my long vigil. When her maid had prepared her for the night I came in, having in the meantime had supper, and took a seat by the bedside.

She did not in any way make objection, but looked at me gratefully whenever I caught her eye. After a long spell she seemed sinking off to sleep, but with an effort seemed to pull herself together and shook it off. It was apparent that she did not want to sleep, so I tackled the subject at once.

"You do not want to sleep?"

"No. I am afraid."

"Afraid to go to sleep! Why so? It is the boon we all crave for."

"Ah, not if you were like me, if sleep was to you a presage of horror!"

"A presage of horror! What on earth do you mean?"

"I don't know. Oh, I don't know. And that is what is so terrible. All this weakness comes to me in sleep, until I dread the very thought."

"But, my dear girl, you may sleep tonight. I am here watching you, and I can promise that nothing will happen."

"Ah, I can trust you!" she said.

I seized the opportunity, and said, "I promise that if I see any evidence of bad dreams I will wake you at once."

"You will? Oh, will you really? How good you are to me. Then I will sleep!" And almost at the word she gave a deep sigh of relief, and sank back, asleep.

All night long I watched by her. She never stirred, but slept on and on in a deep, tranquil, life-giving, health-giving sleep. Her lips were slightly parted, and her breast rose and fell with the regularity of a pendulum. There was a smile on her face, and it was evident that no bad dreams had come to disturb her peace of mind.

In the early morning her maid came, and I left her in her care and took myself back home, for I was anxious about many things. I sent a short wire to Van Helsing and to Arthur, telling them of the excellent result of the operation. My own work, with its manifold arrears, took me all day to clear off. It was dark when I was able to inquire about my zoophagous patient. The report was good. He had been quite quiet for the past day and night. A telegram came from Van Helsing at Amsterdam whilst I was at dinner, suggesting that I should be at Hillingham tonight, as it might be well to be at hand, and stating that he was leaving by the night mail and would join me early in the morning.

9 September.—I was pretty tired and worn out when I got to Hilling-ham. For two nights I had hardly had a wink of sleep, and my brain was beginning to feel that numbness which marks cerebral exhaustion. Lucy was up and in cheerful spirits. When she shook hands with me she looked sharply in my face and said,

"No sitting up tonight for you. You are worn out. I am quite well again. Indeed, I am, and if there is to be any sitting up, it is I who will sit up with you."

I would not argue the point, but went and had my supper. Lucy came with me, and, enlivened by her charming presence, I made an excellent meal, and had a couple of glasses of the more than excellent port. Then Lucy took me upstairs, and showed me a room next her own, where a cozy fire was burning.

"Now," she said. "You must stay here. I shall leave this door open and my door too. You can lie on the sofa for I know that nothing would induce any of you doctors to go to bed whilst there is a patient above the horizon. If I want anything I shall call out, and you can come to me at once."

I could not but acquiesce, for I was dog tired, and could not have sat up had I tried. So, on her renewing her promise to call me if she should want anything, I lay on the sofa, and forgot all about everything.

LUCY WESTENRA'S DIARY

9 September.—I feel so happy tonight. I have been so miserably weak, that to be able to think and move about is like feeling sunshine after a long spell of east wind out of a steel sky. Somehow Arthur feels very, very close to me. I seem to feel his presence warm about me. I suppose it is that sick-ness and weakness are selfish things and turn our inner eyes and sympathy on ourselves, whilst health and strength give love rein, and in thought and feeling he can wander where he wills. I know where my thoughts are. If only Arthur knew! My dear, my dear, your ears must tingle as you sleep, as mine do waking. Oh, the blissful rest of last night! How I slept, with that dear, good Dr. Seward watching me. And tonight I shall not fear to sleep, since he is close at hand and within call. Thank everybody for being so good to me. Thank God! Goodnight Arthur.

DR. SEWARD'S DIARY

10 September.—I was conscious of the Professor's hand on my head, and started awake all in a second. That is one of the things that we learn in an asylum, at any rate.

"And how is our patient?"

"Well, when I left her, or rather when she left me," I answered.

"Come, let us see," he said. And together we went into the room.

The blind was down, and I went over to raise it gently, whilst Van Helsing stepped, with his soft, cat-like tread, over to the bed.

As I raised the blind, and the morning sunlight flooded the room, I heard the Professor's low hiss of inspiration, and knowing its rarity, a deadly fear shot through my heart. As I passed over he moved back, and his exclamation of horror, "Gott in Himmel!"[97] needed no enforcement from his agonized face. He raised his hand and pointed to the bed, and his iron face was drawn and ashen white. I felt my knees begin to tremble.

There on the bed, seemingly in a swoon, lay poor Lucy, more horribly white and wan-looking than ever. Even the lips were white, and the gums seemed to have shrunken back from the teeth, as we sometimes see in a corpse after a prolonged illness.

Van Helsing raised his foot to stamp in anger, but the instinct of his life and all the long years of habit stood to him, and he put it down again softly.

"Quick!" he said. "Bring the brandy."

I flew to the dining room, and returned with the decanter. He wetted the poor white lips with it, and together we rubbed palm and wrist and heart. He felt her heart, and after a few moments of agonizing suspense said,

"It is not too late. It beats, though but feebly. All our work is undone. We must begin again. There is no young Arthur here now. I have to call on you yourself this time, friend John." As he spoke, he was dipping into his bag, and producing the instruments of transfusion. I had taken off my coat and rolled up my shirt sleeve. There was no possibility of an opiate just at present, and no need of one; and so, without a moment's delay, we began the operation.

After a time, it did not seem a short time either, for the draining away of one's blood, no matter how willingly it be given, is a terrible feeling, Van

97 God in Heaven (German).

Helsing held up a warning finger. "Do not stir," he said. "But I fear that with growing strength she may wake, and that would make danger, oh, so much danger. But I shall precaution take. I shall give hypodermic injection of morphia." He proceeded then, swiftly and deftly, to carry out his intent.

The effect on Lucy was not bad, for the faint seemed to merge subtly into the narcotic sleep. It was with a feeling of personal pride that I could see a faint tinge of colour steal back into the pallid cheeks and lips. No man knows, till he experiences it, what it is to feel his own lifeblood drawn away into the veins of the woman he loves.

The Professor watched me critically. "That will do," he said. "Already?" I remonstrated. "You took a great deal more from Art." To which he smiled a sad sort of smile as he replied,

"He is her lover, her *fiancé*. You have work, much work to do for her and for others, and the present will suffice."

When we stopped the operation, he attended to Lucy, whilst I applied digital pressure to my own incision. I laid down, while I waited his leisure to attend to me, for I felt faint and a little sick. By and by he bound up my wound, and sent me downstairs to get a glass of wine for myself. As I was leaving the room, he came after me, and half whispered.

"Mind, nothing must be said of this. If our young lover should turn up unexpected, as before, no word to him. It would at once frighten him and enjealous him, too. There must be none. So!"

When I came back he looked at me carefully, and then said, "You are not much the worse. Go into the room, and lie on your sofa, and rest awhile, then have much breakfast and come here to me."

I followed out his orders, for I knew how right and wise they were. I had done my part, and now my next duty was to keep up my strength. I felt very weak, and in the weakness lost something of the amazement at what had occurred. I fell asleep on the sofa, however, wondering over and over again how Lucy had made such a retrograde movement, and how she could have been drained of so much blood with no sign any where to show for it. I think I must have continued my wonder in my dreams, for, sleeping and waking my thoughts always came back to the little punctures in her throat and the ragged, exhausted appearance of their edges, tiny though they were.

Lucy slept well into the day, and when she woke she was fairly well and strong, though not nearly so much so as the day before. When Van Helsing had seen her, he went out for a walk, leaving me in charge, with strict injunctions that I was not to leave her for a moment. I could hear his voice in the hall, asking the way to the nearest telegraph office.

Lucy chatted with me freely, and seemed quite unconscious that anything had happened. I tried to keep her amused and interested. When her mother came up to see her, she did not seem to notice any change whatever, but said to me gratefully,

"We owe you so much, Dr. Seward, for all you have done, but you really must now take care not to overwork yourself. You are looking pale yourself. You want a wife to nurse and look after you a bit, that you do!" As she spoke, Lucy turned crimson, though it was only momentarily, for her poor wasted veins could not stand for long an unwonted drain to the head. The reaction came in excessive pallor as she turned imploring eyes on me. I smiled and nodded, and laid my finger on my lips. With a sigh, she sank back amid her pillows.

Van Helsing returned in a couple of hours, and presently said to me: "Now you go home, and eat much and drink enough. Make yourself strong. I stay here tonight, and I shall sit up with little miss myself. You and I must watch the case, and we must have none other to know. I have grave reasons. No, do not ask me. Think what you will. Do not fear to think even the most not-improbable. Goodnight."

In the hall two of the maids came to me, and asked if they or either of them might not sit up with Miss Lucy. They implored me to let them, and when I said it was Dr. Van Helsing's wish that either he or I should sit up, they asked me quite piteously to intercede with the 'foreign gentleman'. I was much touched by their kindness. Perhaps it is because I am weak at present, and perhaps because it was on Lucy's account, that their devotion was manifested. For over and over again have I seen similar instances of woman's kindness. I got back here in time for a late dinner, went my rounds, all well, and set this down whilst waiting for sleep. It is coming.

11 September.—This afternoon I went over to Hillingham. Found Van Helsing in excellent spirits, and Lucy much better. Shortly after I had arrived, a big parcel from abroad came for the Professor. He opened it with much impressment, assumed, of course, and showed a great bundle of white flowers.

"These are for you, Miss Lucy," he said.

"For me? Oh, Dr. Van Helsing!"

"Yes, my dear, but not for you to play with. These are medicines." Here Lucy made a wry face. "Nay, but they are not to take in a decoction or in nauseous form, so you need not snub that so charming nose, or I shall point out to my friend Arthur what woes he may have to endure in seeing so much beauty that he so loves so much distort. Aha, my pretty miss, that bring the so nice nose all straight again. This is medicinal, but you do not know how. I put him in your window, I make pretty wreath, and hang him round your neck, so you sleep well. Oh, yes! They, like the lotus flower, make your trouble forgotten. It smell so like the waters of Lethe, and of that fountain of youth that the Conquistadores sought for in the Floridas, and find him all too late."

Whilst he was speaking, Lucy had been examining the flowers and smelling them. Now she threw them down saying, with half laughter, and half disgust,

"Oh, Professor, I believe you are only putting up a joke on me. Why, these flowers are only common garlic."

To my surprise, Van Helsing rose up and said with all his sternness, his iron jaw set and his bushy eyebrows meeting,

"No trifling with me! I never jest! There is grim purpose in what I do, and I warn you that you do not thwart me. Take care, for the sake of others if not for your own." Then seeing poor Lucy scared, as she might well be, he went on more gently, "Oh, little miss, my dear, do not fear me. I only do for your good, but there is much virtue to you in those so common flowers. See, I place them myself in your room. I make myself the wreath that you are to wear. But hush! No telling to others that make so inquisitive questions. We must obey, and silence is a part of obedience, and obedience is to bring you strong and well into loving arms that wait for you. Now sit still a while. Come with me, friend John, and you shall help me deck the room with my garlic, which is all the way from Haarlem, where my friend Vanderpool raise herb in his glass houses all the year. I had to telegraph yesterday, or they would not have been here."

We went into the room, taking the flowers with us. The Professor's actions were certainly odd and not to be found in any pharmacopeia that I ever heard of. First he fastened up the windows and latched them securely. Next, taking a handful of the flowers, he rubbed them all over the sashes, as though to ensure that every whiff of air that might get in would be laden with the garlic smell. Then with the wisp he rubbed all over the jamb of the door, above, below, and at each side, and round the fireplace in the same way. It all seemed grotesque to me, and presently I said, "Well, Professor, I know you always have a reason for what you do, but this certainly puzzles me. It is well we have no sceptic here, or he would say that you were working some spell to keep out an evil spirit."

"Perhaps I am!" he answered quietly as he began to make the wreath which Lucy was to wear round her neck.

We then waited whilst Lucy made her toilet for the night, and when she was in bed he came and himself fixed the wreath of garlic round her neck. The last words he said to her were,

"Take care you do not disturb it, and even if the room feel close, do not tonight open the window or the door."

"I promise," said Lucy. "And thank you both a thousand times for all your kindness to me! Oh, what have I done to be blessed with such friends?"

As we left the house in my fly,[98] which was waiting, Van Helsing said, "Tonight I can sleep in peace, and sleep I want, two nights of travel, much reading in the day between, and much anxiety on the day to follow, and a night to sit up, without to wink. Tomorrow in the morning early you call for me, and we come together to see our pretty miss, so much more strong for my 'spell' which I have work. Ho, ho!"

He seemed so confident that I, remembering my own confidence two nights before and with the baneful result, felt awe and vague terror. It must have been my weakness that made me hesitate to tell it to my friend, but I felt it all the more, like unshed tears.

ꙮ CHAPTER 11 ꙮ
LUCY WESTENRA'S DIARY

12 September.—How good they all are to me. I quite love that dear Dr. Van Helsing. I wonder why he was so anxious about these flowers. He positively frightened me, he was so fierce. And yet he must have been right, for I feel comfort from them already. Somehow, I do not dread being alone tonight, and I can go to sleep without fear. I shall not mind any flapping outside the window. Oh, the terrible struggle that I have had against sleep so often of late, the pain of sleeplessness, or the pain of the fear of sleep, and with such unknown horrors as it has for me! How blessed are some people, whose lives have no fears, no dreads, to whom sleep is a blessing that comes nightly, and brings nothing but sweet dreams. Well, here I am tonight, hoping for sleep, and lying like Ophelia in the play, with 'virgin crants and maiden strewments.' I never liked garlic before, but tonight it is delightful! There is peace in its smell. I feel sleep coming already. Goodnight, everybody.

DR. SEWARD'S DIARY

13 September.—Called at the Berkeley and found Van Helsing, as usual, up to time. The carriage ordered from the hotel was waiting. The Professor took his bag, which he always brings with him now.

---

98 One-horse carriage.

Let all be put down exactly. Van Helsing and I arrived at Hillingham at eight o'clock. It was a lovely morning. The bright sunshine and all the fresh feeling of early autumn seemed like the completion of nature's annual work. The leaves were turning to all kinds of beautiful colours, but had not yet begun to drop from the trees. When we entered we met Mrs. Westenra coming out of the morning room. She is always an early riser. She greeted us warmly and said,

"You will be glad to know that Lucy is better. The dear child is still asleep. I looked into her room and saw her, but did not go in, lest I should disturb her." The Professor smiled, and looked quite jubilant. He rubbed his hands together, and said, "Aha! I thought I had diagnosed the case. My treatment is working."

To which she replied, "You must not take all the credit to yourself, doctor. Lucy's state this morning is due in part to me."

"How do you mean, ma'am?" asked the Professor.

"Well, I was anxious about the dear child in the night, and went into her room. She was sleeping soundly, so soundly that even my coming did not wake her. But the room was awfully stuffy. There were a lot of those horrible, strong-smelling flowers about everywhere, and she had actually a bunch of them round her neck. I feared that the heavy odour would be too much for the dear child in her weak state, so I took them all away and opened a bit of the window to let in a little fresh air. You will be pleased with her, I am sure."

She moved off into her boudoir, where she usually breakfasted early. As she had spoken, I watched the Professor's face, and saw it turn ashen grey. He had been able to retain his self-command whilst the poor lady was present, for he knew her state and how mischievous a shock would be. He actually smiled on her as he held open the door for her to pass into her room. But the instant she had disappeared he pulled me, suddenly and forcibly, into the dining room and closed the door.

Then, for the first time in my life, I saw Van Helsing break down. He raised his hands over his head in a sort of mute despair, and then beat his palms together in a helpless way. Finally he sat down on a chair, and putting his hands before his face, began to sob, with loud, dry sobs that seemed to come from the very racking of his heart.

Then he raised his arms again, as though appealing to the whole universe. "God! God! God!" he said. "What have we done, what has this poor thing done, that we are so sore beset? Is there fate amongst us still, send down from the pagan world of old, that such things must be, and in such way? This poor mother, all unknowing, and all for the best as she think, does such thing as lose her daughter body and soul, and we must not tell her, we must not even warn her, or she die, then both die. Oh, how we are beset! How are all the powers of the devils against us!"

Suddenly he jumped to his feet. "Come," he said, "come, we must see and act. Devils or no devils, or all the devils at once, it matters not. We must fight him all the same." He went to the hall door for his bag, and together we went up to Lucy's room.

Once again I drew up the blind, whilst Van Helsing went towards the bed. This time he did not start as he looked on the poor face with the same awful, waxen pallor as before. He wore a look of stern sadness and infinite pity.

"As I expected," he murmured, with that hissing inspiration of his which meant so much. Without a word he went and locked the door, and then began to set out on the little table the instruments for yet another operation of transfusion of blood. I had long ago recognized the necessity, and begun to take off my coat, but he stopped me with a warning hand. "No!" he said. "Today you must operate. I shall provide. You are weakened already." As he spoke he took off his coat and rolled up his shirtsleeve.

Again the operation. Again the narcotic. Again some return of colour to the ashy cheeks, and the regular breathing of healthy sleep. This time I watched whilst Van Helsing recruited himself and rested.

Presently he took an opportunity of telling Mrs. Westenra that she must not remove anything from Lucy's room without consulting him. That the flowers were of medicinal value, and that the breathing of their odour was a part of the system of cure. Then he took over the care of the case himself, saying that he would watch this night and the next, and would send me word when to come.

After another hour Lucy waked from her sleep, fresh and bright and seemingly not much the worse for her terrible ordeal.

What does it all mean? I am beginning to wonder if my long habit of life amongst the insane is beginning to tell upon my own brain.

LUCY WESTENRA'S DIARY

17 September.—Four days and nights of peace. I am getting so strong again that I hardly know myself. It is as if I had passed through some long nightmare, and had just awakened to see the beautiful sunshine and feel the fresh air of the morning around me. I have a dim half remembrance of long, anxious times of waiting and fearing, darkness in which there was not even the pain of hope to make present distress more poignant. And then long spells of oblivion, and the rising back to life as a diver coming up through a great press of water. Since, however, Dr. Van Helsing has been with me, all this bad dreaming seems to have passed away. The noises that used to frighten me out of my wits, the flapping against the windows, the distant voices which seemed so close to me, the harsh sounds that came from I know not where and commanded me to do I know not what, have all ceased. I go to bed now without any fear of sleep. I do not even try to keep awake. I have grown quite fond of the garlic, and a boxful arrives for me every day from Haarlem. Tonight Dr. Van Helsing is going away, as he has to be for a day in Amsterdam. But I need not be watched. I am well enough to be left alone.

Thank God for Mother's sake, and dear Arthur's, and for all our friends who have been so kind! I shall not even feel the change, for last night Dr. Van Helsing slept in his chair a lot of the time. I found him asleep twice when I awoke. But I did not fear to go to sleep again, although the boughs or bats or something flapped almost angrily against the window panes.

The Pall Mall Gazette

18 September.

THE ESCAPED WOLF PERILOUS ADVENTURE OF OUR INTERVIEWER

Interview With The Keeper In The Zoological Gardens

After many inquiries and almost as many refusals, and perpetually using the words 'PALL MALL GAZETTE' as a sort of talisman, I managed to find the keeper of the section of the Zoological Gardens in which the wolf department is included. Thomas Bilder lives in one of the cottages in the enclosure behind the elephant house, and was just sitting down to his tea when I found him. Thomas and his wife are hospitable folk, elderly, and without children, and if the specimen I enjoyed of their hospitality be of the average kind, their lives must be pretty comfortable. The keeper would not enter on what he called business until the supper was over, and we were all satisfied. Then when the table was cleared, and he had lit his pipe, he said,

"Now, Sir, you can go on and arsk me what you want. You'll excoose me refoosin' to talk of perfeshunal subjucts afore meals. I gives the wolves and the jackals and the hyenas in all our section their tea afore I begins to arsk them questions."

"How do you mean, ask them questions?" I queried, wishful to get him into a talkative humor.

"'Ittin' of them over the 'ead with a pole is one way. Scratchin' of their ears in another, when gents as is flush wants a bit of a show-orf to their gals. I don't so much mind the fust, the 'ittin of the pole part afore I chucks in their dinner, but I waits till they've 'ad their sherry and kawffee, so to speak, afore I tries on with the ear scratchin'. Mind you," he added philosophically, "there's a deal of the same nature in us as in them theer animiles. Here's you a-comin' and arskin' of me questions about my business, and I that grump-like that only for your bloomin' 'arf-quid I'd 'a' seen you blowed fust 'fore I'd answer. Not even when you arsked me sarcastic like if I'd like you to arsk the Superintendent if you might arsk me questions. Without offence did I tell yer to go to 'ell?"

"You did."

"An' when you said you'd report me for usin' obscene language that was 'ittin' me over the 'ead. But the 'arf-quid made that all right. I weren't a-goin' to fight, so I waited for the food, and did with my 'owl as the wolves and lions and tigers does. But, lor' love yer 'art, now that the old 'ooman has stuck a chunk of her tea-cake in me, an' rinsed me out with her bloomin' old teapot, and I've lit hup, you may scratch my ears for all you're worth, and won't even get a growl out of me. Drive along with your questions. I know what yer a-comin' at, that 'ere escaped wolf."

"Exactly. I want you to give me your view of it. Just tell me how it happened, and when I know the facts I'll get you to say what you consider was the cause of it, and how you think the whole affair will end."

"All right, guv'nor. This 'ere is about the 'ole story. That 'ere wolf what we called Bersicker was one of three grey ones that came from Nor-way to Jamrach's, which we bought off him four years ago. He was a nice well-behaved wolf, that never gave no trouble to talk of. I'm more surprised at 'im for wantin' to get out nor any other animile in the place. But, there, you can't trust wolves no more nor women."

"Don't you mind him, Sir!" broke in Mrs. Tom, with a cheery laugh. "'E's got mindin' the animiles so long that blest if he ain't like a old wolf 'isself! But there ain't no 'arm in 'im."

"Well, Sir, it was about two hours after feedin' yesterday when I first hear my disturbance. I was makin' up a litter in the monkey house for a young puma which is ill. But when I heard the yelpin' and 'owlin' I kem away straight. There was Bersicker a-tearin' like a mad thing at the bars as if he wanted to get out. There wasn't much people about that day, and close at hand was only one man, a tall, thin chap, with a 'ook nose and a pointed beard, with a few white hairs runnin' through it. He had a 'ard, cold look and red eyes, and I took a sort of mislike to him, for it seemed as if it was 'im as they was hirritated at. He 'ad white kid gloves on 'is 'ands, and he pointed out the animiles to me and says, 'Keeper, these wolves seem upset at something.'

"'Maybe it's you,' says I, for I did not like the airs as he give 'isself. He didn't get angry, as I 'oped he would, but he smiled a kind of insolent smile, with a mouth full of white, sharp teeth. 'Oh no, they wouldn't like me,' 'e says.

"'Ow yes, they would,' says I, a-imitatin' of him. 'They always like a bone or two to clean their teeth on about tea time, which you 'as a bagful.'

"Well, it was a odd thing, but when the animiles see us a-talkin' they lay down, and when I went over to Bersicker he let me stroke his ears same as ever. That there man kem over, and blessed but if he didn't put in his hand and stroke the old wolf's ears too!

"'Tyke care,' says I. 'Bersicker is quick.'

"'Never mind,' he says. I'm used to 'em!'

"'Are you in the business yourself?' I says, tyking off my 'at, for a man what trades in wolves, anceterer, is a good friend to keepers.

"'Nom,' says he, 'not exactly in the business, but I 'ave made pets of several.' And with that he lifts his 'at as perlite as a lord, and walks away. Old Bersicker kep' a-lookin' arter 'im till 'e was out of sight, and then went and lay down in a corner and wouldn't come hout the 'ole hevening. Well, larst night, so soon as the moon was hup, the wolves here all began a-'owling. There warn't nothing for them to 'owl at. There warn't no one near, except some one that was evidently a-callin' a dog somewheres out back of the gardings in the Park road. Once or twice I went out to see that all was right, and it was, and then the 'owling stopped. Just before twelve o'clock I just took a look round afore turnin' in, an', bust me, but when I kem opposite to old Bersicker's cage I see the rails broken and twisted about and the cage empty. And that's all I know for certing."

"Did any one else see anything?"

"One of our gard'ners was a-comin' 'ome about that time from a 'armony, when he sees a big grey dog comin' out through the garding 'edges. At least, so he says, but I don't give much for it myself, for if he did 'e never said a word about it to his missis when 'e got 'ome, and it was only after the escape of the wolf was made known, and we had been up all night a-huntin' of the Park for Bersicker, that he remembered seein' anything. My own belief was that the 'armony 'ad got into his 'ead."

"Now, Mr. Bilder, can you account in any way for the escape of the wolf?"

"Well, Sir," he said, with a suspicious sort of modesty, "I think I can, but I don't know as 'ow you'd be satisfied with the theory."

"Certainly I shall. If a man like you, who knows the animals from experience, can't hazard a good guess at any rate, who is even to try?"

"Well then, Sir, I accounts for it this way. It seems to me that 'ere wolf escaped—simply because he wanted to get out."

From the hearty way that both Thomas and his wife laughed at the joke I could see that it had done service before, and that the whole explanation was simply an elaborate sell. I couldn't cope in badinage with the worthy Thomas, but I thought I knew a surer way to his heart, so I said, "Now, Mr. Bilder, we'll consider that first half-sovereign worked off, and this brother of his is waiting to be claimed when you've told me what you think will happen."

"Right y'are, Sir," he said briskly. "Ye'll excoose me, I know, for a-chaffin' of ye, but the old woman here winked at me, which was as much as telling me to go on."

"Well, I never!" said the old lady.

"My opinion is this: that 'ere wolf is a'idin' of, somewheres. The gard'ner wot didn't remember said he was a-gallopin' northward faster than a horse could go, but I don't believe him, for, yer see, Sir, wolves don't gallop no more nor dogs does, they not bein' built that way. Wolves is fine things in a storybook, and I dessay when they gets in packs and does be chivyin' somethin' that's more afeared than they is they can make a devil of a noise and chop it up, what-ever it is. But, Lor' bless you, in real life a wolf is only a low creature, not half so clever or bold as a good dog, and not half a quarter so much fight in 'im. This one ain't been used to fightin' or even to providin' for hisself, and more like he's somewhere round the Park a'hidin' an' a'shiverin' of, and if he thinks at all, wonderin' where he is to get his breakfast from. Or maybe he's got down some area and is in a coal cellar. My eye, won't some cook get a rum start when she sees his green eyes a-shinin' at her out of the dark! If he can't get food he's bound to look for it, and mayhap he may chance to light on a butcher's shop in time. If he doesn't, and some nursemaid goes out walkin' or orf with a soldier, leavin' of the hinfant in the perambulator—well, then I shouldn't be surprised if the census is one babby the less. That's all."

I was handing him the half-sovereign, when something came bobbing up against the window, and Mr. Bilder's face doubled its natural length with surprise.

"God bless me!" he said. "If there ain't old Bersicker come back by 'isself!"

He went to the door and opened it, a most unnecessary proceeding it seemed to me. I have always thought that a wild animal never looks so well as when some obstacle of pronounced durability is between us. A personal experience has intensified rather than di-minished that idea.

After all, however, there is nothing like custom, for neither Bilder nor his wife thought any more of the wolf than I should of a dog. The animal itself was a peaceful and well-behaved as that father of all picture-wolves, Red Riding Hood's quondam[99] friend, whilst moving her confidence in masquerade.

The whole scene was a unutterable mixture of comedy and pathos. The wicked wolf that for a half a day had paralyzed London and set all the children in town shivering in their shoes, was there in a sort of penitent mood, and was received and petted like a sort of vulpine prodigal son. Old Bilder examined him all over with most tender solicitude, and when he had finished with his penitent said,

"There, I knew the poor old chap would get into some kind of trouble. Didn't I say it all along? Here's his head all cut and full of broken glass. 'E's been a-gettin' over some bloomin' wall or other. It's a shyme that people are allowed to top their walls with broken bottles. This 'ere's what comes of it. Come along, Bersicker."

He took the wolf and locked him up in a cage, with a piece of meat that satisfied, in quantity at any rate, the elementary conditions of the fatted calf, and went off to report.

I came off too, to report the only exclusive information that is given today regarding the strange escapade at the Zoo.

DR. SEWARD'S DIARY

17 September.—I was engaged after dinner in my study posting up my books, which, through press of other work and the many visits to Lucy, had fallen sadly into arrear. Suddenly the door was burst open, and in rushed my patient, with his face distorted with passion. I was thunderstruck, for such a thing as a patient getting of his own accord into the Superintendent's study is almost unknown.

Without an instant's notice he made straight at me. He had a dinner knife in his hand, and as I saw he was dangerous, I tried to keep the table between us. He was too quick and too strong for me, however, for before I could get my balance he had struck at me and cut my left wrist rather severely.

Before he could strike again, however, I got in my right hand and he was sprawling on his back on the floor. My wrist bled freely, and quite a little pool trickled on to the carpet. I saw that my friend was not intent on further

99 Former.

effort, and occupied myself binding up my wrist, keeping a wary eye on the prostrate figure all the time. When the attendants rushed in, and we turned our attention to him, his employment positively sickened me. He was lying on his belly on the floor licking up, like a dog, the blood which had fallen from my wounded wrist. He was easily secured, and to my surprise, went with the attendants quite placidly, simply repeating over and over again, "The blood is the life! The blood is the life!"

I cannot afford to lose blood just at present. I have lost too much of late for my physical good, and then the prolonged strain of Lucy's illness and its horrible phases is telling on me. I am over excited and weary, and I need rest, rest, rest. Happily Van Helsing has not summoned me, so I need not forego my sleep. Tonight I could not well do without it.

TELEGRAM, VAN HELSING, ANTWERP, TO SEWARD, CARFAX

(Sent to Carfax, Sussex, as no county given, delivered late by twenty-two hours.)

17 September.—Do not fail to be at Hillingham tonight. If not watching all the time, frequently visit and see that flowers are as placed, very important, do not fail. Shall be with you as soon as possible after arrival.

DR. SEWARD'S DIARY

18 September.—Just off train to London. The arrival of Van Helsing's telegram filled me with dismay. A whole night lost, and I know by bitter experience what may happen in a night. Of course it is possible that all may be well, but what may have happened? Surely there is some horrible doom hanging over us that every possible accident should thwart us in all we try to do. I shall take this cylinder with me, and then I can complete my entry on Lucy's phonograph.

MEMORANDUM LEFT BY LUCY WESTENRA

17 September, Night.—I write this and leave it to be seen, so that no one may by any chance get into trouble through me. This is an exact record of what took place tonight. I feel I am dying of weakness, and have barely strength to write, but it must be done if I die in the doing.

I went to bed as usual, taking care that the flowers were placed as Dr. Van Helsing directed, and soon fell asleep.

I was waked by the flapping at the window, which had begun after that sleep-walking on the cliff at Whitby when Mina saved me, and which now I know so well. I was not afraid, but I did wish that Dr. Seward was in the next room, as Dr. Van Helsing said he would be, so that I might have called him. I tried to sleep, but I could not. Then there came to me the old fear of sleep, and I determined to keep awake. Perversely sleep would try to come then when I did not want it. So, as I feared to be alone, I opened my door and called out, "Is there anybody there?" There was no answer. I was afraid to wake mother, and so closed my door again. Then outside in the shrubbery I heard a sort of howl like a dog's, but more fierce and deeper. I went to the window and looked out, but could see nothing, except a big bat, which had evidently been buffeting its wings against the window. So I went back to bed again, but determined not to go to sleep. Presently the door opened, and mother looked in. Seeing by my moving that I was not asleep, she came in and sat by me. She said to me even more sweetly and softly than her wont,

"I was uneasy about you, darling, and came in to see that you were all right."

I feared she might catch cold sitting there, and asked her to come in and sleep with me, so she came into bed, and lay down beside me. She did not take off her dressing gown, for she said she would only stay a while and then go back to her own bed. As she lay there in my arms, and I in hers the flapping and buffeting came to the window again. She was startled and a little frightened, and cried out, "What is that?"

I tried to pacify her, and at last succeeded, and she lay quiet. But I could hear her poor dear heart still beating terribly. After a while there was the howl again out in the shrubbery, and shortly after there was a crash at the window, and a lot of broken glass was hurled on the floor. The window blind blew back with the wind that rushed in, and in the aperture of the broken panes there was the head of a great, gaunt grey wolf.

Mother cried out in a fright, and struggled up into a sitting posture, and clutched wildly at anything that would help her. Amongst other things, she clutched the wreath of flowers that Dr. Van Helsing insisted on my wearing round my neck, and tore it away from me. For a second or two she sat up, pointing at the wolf, and there was a strange and horrible gurgling in her throat. Then she fell over, as if struck with lightning, and her head hit my forehead and made me dizzy for a moment or two.

The room and all round seemed to spin round. I kept my eyes fixed on the window, but the wolf drew his head back, and a whole myriad of little specks seems to come blowing in through the broken window, and wheeling and circling round like the pillar of dust that travellers describe when there is a simoom[100] in the desert. I tried to stir, but there was some spell upon me, and dear Mother's poor body, which seemed to grow cold already, for her dear heart had ceased to beat, weighed me down, and I remembered no more for a while.

The time did not seem long, but very, very awful, till I recovered consciousness again. Somewhere near, a passing bell was tolling. The dogs all round the neighbourhood were howling, and in our shrubbery, seemingly just outside, a nightingale was singing. I was dazed and stupid with pain and terror and weakness, but the sound of the nightingale seemed like the voice of my dead mother come back to comfort me. The sounds seemed to have awakened the maids, too, for I could hear their bare feet pattering outside my door. I called to them, and they came in, and when they saw what had happened, and what it was that lay over me on the bed, they screamed out. The wind rushed in through the broken window, and the door slammed to. They lifted off the body of my dear mother, and laid her, covered up with a sheet, on the bed after I had got up. They were all so frightened and nervous that I directed them to go to the dining room and each have a glass of wine. The door flew open for an instant and closed again. The maids shrieked, and then went in a body to the dining room, and I laid what flowers I had on my dear mother's breast. When they were there I remembered what Dr. Van Helsing had told me, but I didn't like to remove them, and besides, I would have some of the servants to sit up with me now. I was surprised that the maids did not come back. I called them, but got no answer, so I went to the dining room to look for them.

My heart sank when I saw what had happened. They all four lay helpless on the floor, breathing heavily. The decanter of sherry was on the table half full, but there was a queer, acrid smell about. I was suspicious, and examined the decanter. It smelt of laudanum,[101] and looking on the sideboard, I found that the bottle which Mother's doctor uses for her—oh! did use—was empty. What am I to do? What am I to do? I am back in the room with Mother. I cannot leave her, and I am alone, save for the sleeping servants,

---

100 Wind storm.
101 Opium.

whom some one has drugged. Alone with the dead! I dare not go out, for I can hear the low howl of the wolf through the broken window.

The air seems full of specks, floating and circling in the draught from the window, and the lights burn blue and dim. What am I to do? God shield me from harm this night! I shall hide this paper in my breast, where they shall find it when they come to lay me out. My dear mother gone! It is time that I go too. Goodbye, dear Arthur, if I should not survive this night. God keep you, dear, and God help me!

ⅎ CHAPTER 12 Ⅎ
DR. SEWARD'S DIARY

18 September.—I drove at once to Hillingham and arrived early. Keeping my cab at the gate, I went up the avenue alone. I knocked gently and rang as quietly as possible, for I feared to disturb Lucy or her mother, and hoped to only bring a servant to the door. After a while, finding no response, I knocked and rang again, still no answer. I cursed the laziness of the servants that they should lie abed at such an hour, for it was now ten o'clock, and so rang and knocked again, but more impatiently, but still without response. Hitherto I had blamed only the servants, but now a terrible fear began to assail me. Was this desolation but another link in the chain of doom which seemed drawing tight round us? Was it indeed a house of death to which I had come, too late? I know that minutes, even seconds of delay, might mean hours of danger to Lucy, if she had had again one of those frightful relapses, and I went round the house to try if I could find by chance an entry anywhere.

I could find no means of ingress. Every window and door was fastened and locked, and I returned baffled to the porch. As I did so, I heard the rapid pit-pat of a swiftly driven horse's feet. They stopped at the gate, and a few seconds later I met Van Helsing running up the avenue. When he saw me, he gasped out, "Then it was you, and just arrived. How is she? Are we too late? Did you not get my telegram?"

I answered as quickly and coherently as I could that I had only got his telegram early in the morning, and had not a minute in coming here, and that I could not make any one in the house hear me. He paused and raised his hat as he said solemnly, "Then I fear we are too late. God's will be done!"

With his usual recuperative energy, he went on, "Come. If there be no way open to get in, we must make one. Time is all in all to us now."

We went round to the back of the house, where there was a kitchen window. The Professor took a small surgical saw from his case, and handing it to me, pointed to the iron bars which guarded the window. I attacked them at once and had very soon cut through three of them. Then with a long, thin knife we pushed back the fastening of the sashes and opened the window. I helped the Professor in, and followed him. There was no one in the kitchen or in the servants' rooms, which were close at hand. We tried all the rooms as we went along, and in the dining room, dimly lit by rays of light through the shutters, found four servant women lying on the floor. There was no need to think them dead, for their stertorous breathing and the acrid smell of laudanum in the room left no doubt as to their condition.

Van Helsing and I looked at each other, and as we moved away he said, "We can attend to them later." Then we ascended to Lucy's room. For an instant or two we paused at the door to listen, but there was no sound that we could hear. With white faces and trembling hands, we opened the door gently, and entered the room.

How shall I describe what we saw? On the bed lay two women, Lucy and her mother. The latter lay farthest in, and she was covered with a white sheet, the edge of which had been blown back by the drought through the broken window, showing the drawn, white, face, with a look of terror fixed upon it. By her side lay Lucy, with face white and still more drawn. The flowers which had been round her neck we found upon her mother's bosom, and her throat was bare, showing the two little wounds which we had noticed before, but looking horribly white and mangled. Without a word the Professor bent over the bed, his head almost touching poor Lucy's breast. Then he gave a quick turn of his head, as of one who listens, and leaping to his feet, he cried out to me, "It is not yet too late! Quick! Quick! Bring the brandy!"

I flew downstairs and returned with it, taking care to smell and taste it, lest it, too, were drugged like the decanter of sherry which I found on the table. The maids were still breathing, but more restlessly, and I fancied that the narcotic was wearing off. I did not stay to make sure, but returned to Van Helsing. He rubbed the brandy, as on another occasion, on her lips and gums and on her wrists and the palms of her hands. He said to me, "I can do this, all that can be at the present. You go wake those maids. Flick them in the face with a wet towel, and flick them hard. Make them get heat and fire and a warm bath. This poor soul is nearly as cold as that beside her. She will need be heated before we can do anything more."

I went at once, and found little difficulty in waking three of the women. The fourth was only a young girl, and the drug had evidently affected her more strongly so I lifted her on the sofa and let her sleep.

The others were dazed at first, but as remembrance came back to them they cried and sobbed in a hysterical manner. I was stern with them, however, and would not let them talk. I told them that one life was bad enough to lose, and if they delayed they would sacrifice Miss Lucy. So, sobbing and crying they went about their way, half clad as they were, and prepared fire and water. Fortunately, the kitchen and boiler fires were still alive, and there was no lack of hot water. We got a bath and carried Lucy out as she was and placed her in it. Whilst we were busy chafing her limbs there was a knock at the hall door. One of the maids ran off, hurried on some more clothes, and opened it. Then she returned and whispered to us that there was a gentleman who had come with a message from Mr. Holmwood. I bade her simply tell him that he must wait, for we could see no one now. She went away with the message, and, engrossed with our work, I clean forgot all about him.

I never saw in all my experience the Professor work in such deadly earnest. I knew, as he knew, that it was a stand-up fight with death, and in a pause told him so. He answered me in a way that I did not understand, but with the sternest look that his face could wear.

"If that were all, I would stop here where we are now, and let her fade away into peace, for I see no light in life over her horizon." He went on with his work with, if possible, renewed and more frenzied vigour.

Presently we both began to be conscious that the heat was beginning to be of some effect. Lucy's heart beat a trifle more audibly to the stethoscope, and her lungs had a perceptible movement. Van Helsing's face almost beamed, and as we lifted her from the bath and rolled her in a hot sheet to dry her he said to me, "The first gain is ours! Check to the King!"

We took Lucy into another room, which had by now been prepared, and laid her in bed and forced a few drops of brandy down her throat. I noticed that Van Helsing tied a soft silk handkerchief round her throat. She was still unconscious, and was quite as bad as, if not worse than, we had ever seen her.

Van Helsing called in one of the women, and told her to stay with her and not to take her eyes off her till we returned, and then beckoned me out of the room.

"We must consult as to what is to be done," he said as we descended the stairs. In the hall he opened the dining room door, and we passed in, he closing the door carefully behind him. The shutters had been opened, but the blinds were already down, with that obedience to the etiquette of death which the British woman of the lower classes always rigidly observes. The room was, therefore, dimly dark. It was, however, light enough for our purposes. Van Helsing's sternness was somewhat relieved by a look of perplexity. He was evidently torturing his mind about something, so I waited for an instant, and he spoke.

"What are we to do now? Where are we to turn for help? We must have another transfusion of blood, and that soon, or that poor girl's life won't be worth an hour's purchase. You are exhausted already. I am exhausted too. I fear to trust those women, even if they would have courage to submit. What are we to do for some one who will open his veins for her?"

"What's the matter with me, anyhow?"

The voice came from the sofa across the room, and its tones brought relief and joy to my heart, for they were those of Quincey Morris.

Van Helsing started angrily at the first sound, but his face softened and a glad look came into his eyes as I cried out, "Quincey Morris!" and rushed towards him with outstretched hands.

"What brought you here?" I cried as our hands met.

"I guess Art is the cause."

He handed me a telegram.—'Have not heard from Seward for three days, and am terribly anxious. Cannot leave. Father still in same condition. Send me word how Lucy is. Do not delay.—Holmwood.'

"I think I came just in the nick of time. You know you have only to tell me what to do."

Van Helsing strode forward, and took his hand, looking him straight in the eyes as he said, "A brave man's blood is the best thing on this earth when a woman is in trouble. You're a man and no mistake. Well, the devil may work against us for all he's worth, but God sends us men when we want them."

Once again we went through that ghastly operation. I have not the heart to go through with the details. Lucy had got a terrible shock and it told on her more than before, for though plenty of blood went into her veins, her body did not respond to the treatment as well as on the other occasions. Her struggle back into life was something frightful to see and hear. However, the action of both heart and lungs improved, and Van Helsing made a sub-cutaneous injection of morphia, as before, and with good effect. Her faint became a profound slumber. The Professor watched whilst I went downstairs with Quincey Morris, and sent one of the maids to pay off one of the cabmen who were waiting.

I left Quincey lying down after having a glass of wine, and told the cook to get ready a good breakfast. Then a thought struck me, and I went back to the room where Lucy now was. When I came softly in, I found Van Helsing with a sheet or two of note paper in his hand. He had evidently read it, and was thinking it over as he sat with his hand to his brow. There was a look of grim satisfaction in his face, as of one who has had a doubt solved. He handed me the paper saying only, "It dropped from Lucy's breast when we carried her to the bath."

When I had read it, I stood looking at the Professor, and after a pause asked him, "In God's name, what does it all mean? Was she, or is she, mad, or what sort of horrible danger is it?" I was so bewildered that I did not know what to say more. Van Helsing put out his hand and took the paper, saying,

"Do not trouble about it now. Forget it for the present. You shall know and understand it all in good time, but it will be later. And now what is it that you came to me to say?" This brought me back to fact, and I was all myself again.

"I came to speak about the certificate of death. If we do not act properly and wisely, there may be an inquest, and that paper would have to be produced. I am in hopes that we need have no inquest, for if we had it would surely kill poor Lucy, if nothing else did. I know, and you know, and the other doctor who attended her knows, that Mrs. Westenra had disease of the heart, and we can certify that she died of it. Let us fill up the certificate at once, and I shall take it myself to the registrar and go on to the undertaker."

"Good, oh my friend John! Well thought of! Truly Miss Lucy, if she be sad in the foes that beset her, is at least happy in the friends that love her. One, two, three, all open their veins for her, besides one old man. Ah, yes, I know, friend John. I am not blind! I love you all the more for it! Now go."

In the hall I met Quincey Morris, with a telegram for Arthur telling him that Mrs. Westenra was dead, that Lucy also had been ill, but was now going on better, and that Van Helsing and I were with her. I told him where I was going, and he hurried me out, but as I was going said,

"When you come back, Jack, may I have two words with you all to ourselves?" I nodded in reply and went out. I found no difficulty about the registration, and arranged with the local undertaker to come up in the evening to measure for the coffin and to make arrangements.

When I got back Quincey was waiting for me. I told him I would see him as soon as I knew about Lucy, and went up to her room. She was still sleeping, and the Professor seemingly had not moved from his seat at her side. From his putting his finger to his lips, I gathered that he expected her to wake before long and was afraid of fore-stalling nature. So I went down to Quincey and took him into the breakfast room, where the blinds were not drawn down, and which was a little more cheerful, or rather less cheerless, than the other rooms.

When we were alone, he said to me, "Jack Seward, I don't want to shove myself in anywhere where I've no right to be, but this is no ordinary case.

You know I loved that girl and wanted to marry her, but although that's all past and gone, I can't help feeling anxious about her all the same. What is it that's wrong with her? The Dutchman, and a fine old fellow he is, I can see that, said that time you two came into the room, that you must have another transfusion of blood, and that both you and he were exhausted. Now I know well that you medical men speak in camera, and that a man must not expect to know what they consult about in private. But this is no common matter, and whatever it is, I have done my part. Is not that so?"

"That's so," I said, and he went on.

"I take it that both you and Van Helsing had done already what I did today. Is not that so?"

"That's so."

"And I guess Art was in it too. When I saw him four days ago down at his own place he looked queer. I have not seen anything pulled down so quick since I was on the Pampas and had a mare that I was fond of go to grass all in a night. One of those big bats that they call vampires had got at her in the night, and what with his gorge and the vein left open, there wasn't enough blood in her to let her stand up, and I had to put a bullet through her as she lay. Jack, if you may tell me without betraying confidence, Arthur was the first, is not that so?"

As he spoke the poor fellow looked terribly anxious. He was in a torture of suspense regarding the woman he loved, and his utter ignorance of the terrible mystery which seemed to surround her intensified his pain. His very heart was bleeding, and it took all the manhood of him, and there was a royal lot of it, too, to keep him from breaking down. I paused before answering, for I felt that I must not betray anything which the Professor wished kept secret, but already he knew so much, and guessed so much, that there could be no reason for not answering, so I answered in the same phrase.

"That's so."

"And how long has this been going on?"

"About ten days."

"Ten days! Then I guess, Jack Seward, that that poor pretty creature that we all love has had put into her veins within that time the blood of four strong men. Man alive, her whole body wouldn't hold it." Then coming close to me, he spoke in a fierce half-whisper. "What took it out?"

I shook my head. "That," I said, "is the crux. Van Helsing is simply frantic about it, and I am at my wits' end. I can't even hazard a guess. There has been a series of little circumstances which have thrown out all our calculations as to Lucy being properly watched. But these shall not occur again. Here we stay until all be well, or ill."

Quincey held out his hand. "Count me in," he said. "You and the Dutchman will tell me what to do, and I'll do it."

When she woke late in the afternoon, Lucy's first movement was to feel in her breast, and to my surprise, produced the paper which Van Helsing had given me to read. The careful Professor had replaced it where it had come from, lest on waking she should be alarmed. Her eyes then lit on Van Helsing and on me too, and gladdened. Then she looked round the room, and seeing where she was, shuddered. She gave a loud cry, and put her poor thin hands before her pale face.

We both understood what was meant, that she had realized to the full her mother's death. So we tried what we could to comfort her. Doubtless sympathy eased her somewhat, but she was very low in thought and spirit, and wept silently and weakly for a long time. We told her that either or both of us would now remain with her all the time, and that seemed to comfort her. Towards dusk she fell into a doze. Here a very odd thing occurred. Whilst still asleep she took the paper from her breast and tore it in two. Van Helsing stepped over and took the pieces from her. All the same, however, she went on with the action of tearing, as though the material were still in her hands. Finally she lifted her hands and opened them as though scattering the fragments. Van Helsing seemed surprised, and his brows gathered as if in thought, but he said nothing.

19 September.—All last night she slept fitfully, being always afraid to sleep, and something weaker when she woke from it. The Professor and I took in turns to watch, and we never left her for a moment unattended. Quincey Morris said nothing about his intention, but I knew that all night long he patrolled round and round the house.

When the day came, its searching light showed the ravages in poor Lucy's strength. She was hardly able to turn her head, and the little nourishment which she could take seemed to do her no good. At times she slept, and both Van Helsing and I noticed the difference in her, between sleeping and waking. Whilst asleep she looked stronger, although more haggard, and her breathing was softer. Her open mouth showed the pale gums drawn back from the teeth, which looked positively longer and sharper than usual. When she woke the softness of her eyes evidently changed the expression, for she looked her own self, although a dying one. In the afternoon she asked for Arthur, and we telegraphed for him. Quincey went off to meet him at the station.

When he arrived it was nearly six o'clock, and the sun was setting full and warm, and the red light streamed in through the window and gave more colour to the pale cheeks. When he saw her, Arthur was simply choking with emotion, and none of us could speak. In the hours that had passed, the fits of sleep, or the comatose condition that passed for it, had grown more frequent, so that the pauses when conversation was possible were shortened. Arthur's presence, however, seemed to act as a stimulant. She rallied a little, and spoke to him more brightly than she had done since we arrived. He too pulled himself together, and spoke as cheerily as he could, so that the best was made of everything.

It is now nearly one o'clock, and he and Van Helsing are sitting with her. I am to relieve them in a quarter of an hour, and I am entering this on Lucy's phonograph. Until six o'clock they are to try to rest. I fear that tomorrow will end our watching, for the shock has been too great. The poor child cannot rally. God help us all.

LETTER MINA HARKER TO LUCY WESTENRA

(Unopened by her)

17 September

My dearest Lucy,

"It seems an age since I heard from you, or indeed since I wrote. You will pardon me, I know, for all my faults when you have read all my budget of news. Well, I got my husband back all right. When we arrived at Exeter there was a carriage waiting for us, and in it, though he had an attack of gout, Mr. Hawkins. He took us to his house, where there were rooms for us all nice and comfortable, and we dined together. After dinner Mr. Hawkins said,

"'My dears, I want to drink your health and prosperity, and may every blessing attend you both. I know you both from children, and have, with love and pride, seen you grow up. Now I want you to make your home here with me. I have left to me neither chick nor child. All are gone, and in my will I have left you everything.' I cried, Lucy dear, as Jonathan and the old man clasped hands. Our evening was a very, very happy one.

"So here we are, installed in this beautiful old house, and from both my bedroom and the drawing room I can see the great elms of the cathedral close, with their great black stems standing out against the old yellow stone of the cathedral, and I can hear the rooks overhead cawing and cawing and chattering and chattering and gossiping all

363

FIRST BLOOD: BIRTH OF THE VAMPIRE

day, after the manner of rooks—and humans. I am busy, I need not tell you, arranging things and housekeeping. Jonathan and Mr. Hawkins are busy all day, for now that Jonathan is a partner, Mr. Hawkins wants to tell him all about the clients.

"How is your dear mother getting on? I wish I could run up to town for a day or two to see you, dear, but I dare not go yet, with so much on my shoulders, and Jonathan wants looking after still. He is beginning to put some flesh on his bones again, but he was terribly weakened by the long illness. Even now he sometimes starts out of his sleep in a sudden way and awakes all trembling until I can coax him back to his usual placidity. However, thank God, these occasions grow less frequent as the days go on, and they will in time pass away altogether, I trust. And now I have told you my news, let me ask yours. When are you to be married, and where, and who is to perform the ceremony, and what are you to wear, and is it to be a public or private wedding? Tell me all about it, dear, tell me all about everything, for there is nothing which interests you which will not be dear to me. Jonathan asks me to send his 'respectful duty', but I do not think that is good enough from the junior partner of the important firm Hawkins & Harker. And so, as you love me, and he loves me, and I love you with all the moods and tenses of the verb, I send you simply his 'love' instead. Goodbye, my dearest Lucy, and blessings on you.

"Yours,

"Mina Harker"

REPORT FROM PATRICK HENNESSEY, M.D., M.R.C.S.L.K., Q.C.P.I., ETC, ETC, TO JOHN SEWARD, M.D.

20 September

My dear Sir:

"In accordance with your wishes, I enclose report of the conditions of everything left in my charge. With regard to patient, Renfield, there is more to say. He has had another outbreak, which might have had a dreadful ending, but which, as it fortunately happened, was unattended with any unhappy results. This afternoon a carrier's cart with two men made a call at the empty house whose grounds abut on ours, the house to which, you will remember, the patient twice ran away. The men stopped at our gate to ask the porter their way, as they were strangers.

"I was myself looking out of the study window, having a smoke after dinner, and saw one of them come up to the house. As he passed the window of Renfield's room, the patient began to rate him from within, and called him all the foul names he could lay his tongue to. The man, who seemed a decent fellow enough, contented himself by telling him to 'shut up for a foul-mouthed beggar', whereon our man accused him of robbing him and wanting to murder him and said that he would hinder him if he were to swing for it. I opened the window and signed to the man not to notice, so he contented himself after looking the place over and making up his mind as to what kind of place he had got to by saying, 'Lor' bless yer, sir, I wouldn't mind what was said to me in a bloomin' madhouse. I pity ye and the guv'nor for havin' to live in the house with a wild beast like that.'

"Then he asked his way civilly enough, and I told him where the gate of the empty house was. He went away followed by threats and curses and revilings from our man. I went down to see if I could make out any cause for his anger, since he is usually such a well-behaved man, and except his violent fits nothing of the kind had ever occurred. I found him, to my astonishment, quite composed and most genial in his manner. I tried to get him to talk of the incident, but he blandly asked me questions as to what I meant, and led me to believe that he was completely oblivious of the affair. It was, I am sorry to say, however, only another instance of his cunning, for within half an hour I heard of him again. This time he had broken out through the window of his room, and was running down the avenue. I called to the attendants to follow me, and ran after him, for I feared he was intent on some mischief. My fear was justified when I saw the same cart which had passed before coming down the road, having on it some great wooden boxes. The men were wiping their foreheads, and were flushed in the face, as if with violent exercise. Before I could get up to him, the patient rushed at them, and pulling one of them off the cart, began to knock his head against the ground. If I had not seized him just at the moment, I believe he would have killed the man there and then. The other fellow jumped down and struck him over the head with the butt end of his heavy whip. It was a horrible blow, but he did not seem to mind it, but seized him also, and struggled with the three of us, pulling us to and fro as if we were kittens. You know I am no lightweight, and the others were both burly men. At first he was silent in his fighting, but as we began to master him, and the attendants were putting a strait waistcoat on him, he began to shout, 'I'll frustrate them! They shan't rob me! They shan't murder me by inches! I'll fight for my Lord and Master!' and all sorts of similar incoherent ravings. It was with very considerable difficulty that they got him back to the house and put him in the padded room. One of the attendants, Hardy, had a finger broken. However, I set it all right, and he is going on well.

"The two carriers were at first loud in their threats of actions for damages, and promised to rain all the penalties of the law on us. Their threats were, however, mingled with some sort of indirect apology for the defeat of the two of them by a feeble madman. They said that if it had not been for the way their strength had been spent in carrying and raising the heavy boxes to the cart they would have made short work of him. They gave as another reason for their defeat the extraordinary state of drouth[102] to which they had been reduced by the dusty nature of their occupation and the reprehensible distance from the scene of their labors of any place of public entertainment. I quite understood their drift, and after a stiff glass of strong grog, or rather more of the same, and with each a sovereign in hand, they made light of the attack, and swore that they would encounter a worse madman any day for the pleasure of meeting so 'bloomin' good a bloke' as your correspondent. I took their names and addresses, in case they might be needed. They are as follows: Jack Smollet, of Dudding's Rents, King George's Road, Great Walworth, and Thomas Snelling, Peter Farley's Row, Guide Court, Bethnal Green. They are both in the employment of Harris & Sons, Moving and Shipment Company, Orange Master's Yard, Soho.

"I shall report to you any matter of interest occurring here, and shall wire you at once if there is anything of importance.

"Believe me, dear Sir,

"*Yours faithfully,*

"*Patrick Hennessey.*"

---

102 Thirst (Scottish).

LETTER, MINA HARKER TO LUCY WESTENRA

(Unopened by her)

18 September

"My dearest Lucy,

"Such a sad blow has befallen us. Mr. Hawkins has died very suddenly. Some may not think it so sad for us, but we had both come to so love him that it really seems as though we had lost a father. I never knew either father or mother, so that the dear old man's death is a real blow to me. Jonathan is greatly distressed. It is not only that he feels sorrow, deep sorrow, for the dear, good man who has befriended him all his life, and now at the end has treated him like his own son and left him a fortune which to people of our modest bringing up is wealth beyond the dream of avarice, but Jonathan feels it on another account. He says the amount of responsibility which it puts upon him makes him nervous. He begins to doubt himself. I try to cheer him up, and my belief in *him* helps *him* to have a belief in himself. But it is here that the grave shock that he experienced tells upon him the most. Oh, it is too hard that a sweet, simple, noble, strong nature such as his, a nature which enabled him by our dear, good friend's aid to rise from clerk to master in a few years, should be so injured that the very essence of its strength is gone. Forgive me, dear, if I worry you with my troubles in the midst of your own happiness, but Lucy dear, I must tell someone, for the strain of keeping up a brave and cheerful appearance to Jonathan tries me, and I have no one here that I can confide in. I dread coming up to London, as we must do that day after tomorrow, for poor Mr. Hawkins left in his will that he was to be buried in the grave with his father. As there are no relations at all, Jonathan will have to be chief mourner. I shall try to run over to see you, dearest, if only for a few minutes. Forgive me for troubling you. With all blessings,

"Your loving

"Mina Harker"

DR. SEWARD'S DIARY

20 September.—Only resolution and habit can let me make an entry to-night. I am too miserable, too low spirited, too sick of the world and all in it, including life itself, that I would not care if I heard this moment the flapping of the wings of the angel of death. And he has been flapping those grim wings to some purpose of late, Lucy's mother and Arthur's father, and now . . . Let me get on with my work.

I duly relieved Van Helsing in his watch over Lucy. We wanted Arthur to go to rest also, but he refused at first. It was only when I told him that we should want him to help us during the day, and that we must not all break down for want of rest, lest Lucy should suffer, that he agreed to go.

Van Helsing was very kind to him. "Come, my child," he said. "Come with me. You are sick and weak, and have had much sorrow and much mental pain, as well as that tax on your strength that we know of. You must not be alone, for to be alone is to be full of fears and alarms. Come to the drawing room, where there is a big fire, and there are two sofas. You shall lie on one, and I on the other, and our sympathy will be comfort to each other, even though we do not speak, and even if we sleep."

Arthur went off with him, casting back a longing look on Lucy's face, which lay in her pillow, almost whiter than the lawn. She lay quite still, and I looked around the room to see that all was as it should be. I could see that the Professor had carried out in this room, as in the other, his purpose of using the garlic. The whole of the window sashes reeked with it, and round Lucy's neck, over the silk handkerchief which Van Helsing made her keep on, was a rough chaplet of the same odorous flowers.

Lucy was breathing somewhat stertorously, and her face was at its worst, for the open mouth showed the pale gums. Her teeth, in the dim, uncertain light, seemed longer and sharper than they had been in the morning. In particular, by some trick of the light, the canine teeth looked longer and sharper than the rest.

I sat down beside her, and presently she moved uneasily. At the same moment there came a sort of dull flapping or buffeting at the window. I went over to it softly, and peeped out by the corner of the blind. There was a full moonlight, and I could see that the noise was made by a great bat, which wheeled around, doubtless attracted by the light, although so dim, and every now and again struck the window with its wings. When I came back to my seat, I found that Lucy had moved slightly, and had torn away the garlic flowers from her throat. I replaced them as well as I could, and sat watching her.

Presently she woke, and I gave her food, as Van Helsing had prescribed. She took but a little, and that languidly. There did not seem to be with her now the unconscious struggle for life and strength that had hitherto so marked her illness. It struck me as curious that the moment she became conscious she pressed the garlic flowers close to her. It was certainly odd that whenever she got into that lethargic state, with the stertorous breathing, she put the flowers from her, but that when she waked she clutched them close. There was no possibility of making any mistake about this, for in the long hours that followed, she had many spells of sleeping and waking and repeated both actions many times.

At six o'clock Van Helsing came to relieve me. Arthur had then fallen into a doze, and he mercifully let him sleep on. When he saw Lucy's face I could hear the hissing indraw of breath, and he said to me in a sharp whisper. "Draw up the blind. I want light!" Then he bent down, and, with his face almost touching Lucy's, examined her carefully. He removed the flowers and lifted the silk handkerchief from her throat. As he did so he started back and I could hear his ejaculation, "Mein Gott!" as it was smothered in his throat. I bent over and looked, too, and as I noticed some queer chill came over me. The wounds on the throat had absolutely disappeared.

For fully five minutes Van Helsing stood looking at her, with his face at its sternest. Then he turned to me and said calmly, "She is dying. It will not be long now. It will be much difference, mark me, whether she dies conscious or in her sleep. Wake that poor boy, and let him come and see the last. He trusts us, and we have promised him."

I went to the dining room and waked him. He was dazed for a moment, but when he saw the sunlight streaming in through the edges of the shutters he thought he was late, and expressed his fear. I assured him that Lucy was still asleep, but told him as gently as I could that both Van Helsing and I feared that the end was near. He covered his face with his hands, and slid down on his knees by the sofa, where he remained, perhaps a minute, with his head buried, praying, whilst his shoulders shook with grief. I took him by the hand and raised him up. "Come," I said, "my dear old fellow, summon all your fortitude. It will be best and easiest for *her*."

When we came into Lucy's room I could see that Van Helsing had, with his usual forethought, been putting matters straight and making everything look as pleasing as possible. He had even brushed Lucy's hair, so that it lay on the pillow in its usual sunny ripples. When we came into the room she opened her eyes, and seeing him, whispered softly, "Arthur! Oh, my love, I am so glad you have come!"

He was stooping to kiss her, when Van Helsing motioned him back. "No," he whispered, "not yet! Hold her hand, it will comfort her more."

So Arthur took her hand and knelt beside her, and she looked her best, with all the soft lines matching the angelic beauty of her eyes. Then gradually her eyes closed, and she sank to sleep. For a little bit her breast heaved softly, and her breath came and went like a tired child's.

And then insensibly there came the strange change which I had noticed in the night. Her breathing grew stertorous, the mouth opened, and the pale gums, drawn back, made the teeth look longer and sharper than ever. In a sort of sleep-waking, vague, unconscious way she opened her eyes, which were now dull and hard at once, and said in a soft, voluptuous voice, such as I had never heard from her lips, "Arthur! Oh, my love, I am so glad you have come! Kiss me!"

Arthur bent eagerly over to kiss her, but at that instant Van Helsing, who, like me, had been startled by her voice, swooped upon him, and catching him by the neck with both hands, dragged him back with a fury of strength which I never thought he could have possessed, and actually hurled him almost across the room.

"Not on your life!" he said, "not for your living soul and hers!" And he stood between them like a lion at bay.

Arthur was so taken aback that he did not for a moment know what to do or say, and before any impulse of violence could seize him he realized the place and the occasion, and stood silent, waiting.

I kept my eyes fixed on Lucy, as did Van Helsing, and we saw a spasm as of rage flit like a shadow over her face. The sharp teeth clamped together. Then her eyes closed, and she breathed heavily.

Very shortly after she opened her eyes in all their softness, and putting out her poor, pale, thin hand, took Van Helsing's great brown one, drawing it close to her, she kissed it. "My true friend," she said, in a faint voice, but with untellable pathos, "My true friend, and his! Oh, guard him, and give me peace!"

"I swear it!" he said solemnly, kneeling beside her and holding up his hand, as one who registers an oath. Then he turned to Arthur, and said to him, "Come, my child, take her hand in yours, and kiss her on the forehead, and only once."

Their eyes met instead of their lips, and so they parted. Lucy's eyes closed, and Van Helsing, who had been watching closely, took Arthur's arm, and drew him away.

And then Lucy's breathing became stertorous again, and all at once it ceased.

"It is all over," said Van Helsing. "She is dead!"

I took Arthur by the arm, and led him away to the drawing room, where he sat down, and covered his face with his hands, sobbing in a way that nearly broke me down to see.

I went back to the room, and found Van Helsing looking at poor Lucy, and his face was sterner than ever. Some change had come over her body. Death had given back part of her beauty, for her brow and cheeks had recovered some of their flowing lines. Even the lips had lost their deadly pallor. It was as if the blood, no longer needed for the working of the heart, had gone to make the harshness of death as little rude as might be.

> "We thought her dying whilst she slept,
> and sleeping when she died."

I stood beside Van Helsing, and said, "Ah well, poor girl, there is peace for her at last. It is the end!"

He turned to me, and said with grave solemnity, "Not so, alas! Not so. It is only the beginning!"

When I asked him what he meant, he only shook his head and answered, "We can do nothing as yet. Wait and see."

ℬ CHAPTER 13 ℭ

DR. SEWARD'S DIARY—CONT.

The funeral was arranged for the next succeeding day, so that Lucy and her mother might be buried together. I attended to all the ghastly formalities, and the urbane undertaker proved that his staff was afflicted, or blessed, with something of his own obsequious suavity. Even the woman who performed the last offices for the dead remarked to me, in a confidential, brother-professional way, when she had come out from the death chamber,

"She makes a very beautiful corpse, sir. It's quite a privilege to attend on her. It's not too much to say that she will do credit to our establishment!"

I noticed that Van Helsing never kept far away. This was possible from the disordered state of things in the household. There were no relatives at hand, and as Arthur had to be back the next day to attend at his father's funeral, we were unable to notify any one who should have been bidden. Under the circumstances, Van Helsing and I took it upon ourselves to examine papers, etc. He insisted upon looking over Lucy's papers himself. I asked him why, for I feared that he, being a foreigner, might not be quite aware of English legal requirements, and so might in ignorance make some unnecessary trouble.

He answered me, "I know, I know. You forget that I am a lawyer as well as a doctor. But this is not altogether for the law. You knew that, when you avoided the coroner. I have more than him to avoid. There may be papers more, such as this."

As he spoke he took from his pocket book the memorandum which had been in Lucy's breast, and which she had torn in her sleep.

"When you find anything of the solicitor who is for the late Mrs. Westenra, seal all her papers, and write him tonight. For me, I watch here in the room and in Miss Lucy's old room all night, and I myself search for what may be. It is not well that her very thoughts go into the hands of strangers."

I went on with my part of the work, and in another half hour had found the name and address of Mrs. Westenra's solicitor and had written to him. All the poor lady's papers were in order. Explicit directions regarding the place of burial were given. I had hardly sealed the letter, when, to my surprise, Van Helsing walked into the room, saying,

"Can I help you friend John? I am free, and if I may, my service is to you."

"Have you got what you looked for?" I asked.

To which he replied, "I did not look for any specific thing. I only hoped to find, and find I have, all that there was, only some letters and a few memoranda, and a diary new begun. But I have them here, and we shall for the present say nothing of them. I shall see that poor lad tomorrow evening, and, with his sanction, I shall use some."

When we had finished the work in hand, he said to me, "And now, friend John, I think we may to bed. We want sleep, both you and I, and rest to recuperate. Tomorrow we shall have much to do, but for the tonight there is no need of us. Alas!"

Before turning in we went to look at poor Lucy. The undertaker had certainly done his work well, for the room was turned into a small *chapelle ardente*.[103] There was a wilderness of beautiful white flowers, and death was made as little repulsive as might be. The end of the winding sheet was laid over the face. When the Professor bent over and turned it gently back, we both started at the beauty before us. The tall wax candles showing a sufficient light to note it well. All Lucy's loveliness had come back to her in death, and the hours that had passed, instead of leaving traces of 'decay's effacing fingers', had but restored the beauty of life, till positively I could not believe my eyes that I was looking at a corpse.

The Professor looked sternly grave. He had not loved her as I had, and there was no need for tears in his eyes. He said to me, "Remain till I return,"

103 Chapel to mourn the dead.

and left the room. He came back with a handful of wild garlic from the box waiting in the hall, but which had not been opened, and placed the flowers amongst the others on and around the bed. Then he took from his neck, inside his collar, a little gold crucifix, and placed it over the mouth. He restored the sheet to its place, and we came away.

I was undressing in my own room, when, with a premonitory tap at the door, he entered, and at once began to speak.

"Tomorrow I want you to bring me, before night, a set of post-mortem knives."

"Must we make an autopsy?" I asked.

"Yes and no. I want to operate, but not what you think. Let me tell you now, but not a word to another. I want to cut off her head and take out her heart. Ah! You a surgeon, and so shocked! You, whom I have seen with no tremble of hand or heart, do operations of life and death that make the rest shudder. Oh, but I must not forget, my dear friend John, that you loved her, and I have not forgotten it for is I that shall operate, and you must not help. I would like to do it tonight, but for Arthur I must not. He will be free after his father's funeral tomorrow, and he will want to see her, to see *it*. Then, when she is coffined ready for the next day, you and I shall come when all sleep. We shall unscrew the coffin lid, and shall do our operation, and then replace all, so that none know, save we alone."

"But why do it at all? The girl is dead. Why mutilate her poor body without need? And if there is no necessity for a post-mortem and nothing to gain by it, no good to her, to us, to science, to human knowledge, why do it? Without such it is monstrous."

For answer he put his hand on my shoulder, and said, with infinite tenderness, "Friend John, I pity your poor bleeding heart, and I love you the more because it does so bleed. If I could, I would take on myself the burden that you do bear. But there are things that you know not, but that you shall know, and bless me for knowing, though they are not pleasant things. John, my child, you have been my friend now many years, and yet did you ever know me to do any without good cause? I may err, I am but man, but I believe in all I do. Was it not for these causes that you send for me when the great trouble came? Yes! Were you not amazed, nay horrified, when I would not let Arthur kiss his love, though she was dying, and snatched him away by all my strength? Yes! And yet you saw how she thanked me, with her so beautiful dying eyes, her voice, too, so weak, and she kiss my rough old hand and bless me? Yes! And did you not hear me swear promise to her, that so she closed her eyes grateful? Yes!

"Well, I have good reason now for all I want to do. You have for many years trust me. You have believe me weeks past, when there be things so strange that you might have well doubt. Believe me yet a little, friend John. If you trust me not, then I must tell what I think, and that is not perhaps well. And if I work, as work I shall, no matter trust or no trust, without my friend trust in me, I work with heavy heart and feel oh so lonely when I want all help and courage that may be!" He paused a moment and went on solemnly, "Friend John, there are strange and terrible days before us. Let us not be two, but one, that so we work to a good end. Will you not have faith in me?"

I took his hand, and promised him. I held my door open as he went away, and watched him go to his room and close the door. As I stood without moving, I saw one of the maids pass silently along the passage, she had her back to me, so did not see me, and go into the room where Lucy lay. The sight touched me. Devotion is so rare, and we are so grateful to those who show it unasked to those we love. Here was a poor girl putting aside the terrors which she naturally had of death to go watch alone by the bier of the mistress whom she loved, so that the poor clay might not be lonely till laid to eternal rest.

I must have slept long and soundly, for it was broad daylight when Van Helsing waked me by coming into my room. He came over to my bedside and said, "You need not trouble about the knives. We shall not do it."

"Why not?" I asked. For his solemnity of the night before had greatly impressed me.

"Because," he said sternly, "it is too late, or too early. See!" Here he held up the little golden crucifix.

"This was stolen in the night."

"How stolen," I asked in wonder, "since you have it now?"

"Because I get it back from the worthless wretch who stole it, from the woman who robbed the dead and the living. Her punishment will surely come, but not through me. She knew not altogether what she did, and thus unknowing, she only stole. Now we must wait." He went away on the word, leaving me with a new mystery to think of, a new puzzle to grapple with.

The forenoon was a dreary time, but at noon the solicitor came, Mr. Marquand, of Wholeman, Sons, Marquand & Lidderdale. He was very genial and very appreciative of what we had done, and took off our hands all cares as to details. During lunch he told us that Mrs. Westenra had for some time expected sudden death from her heart, and had put her affairs in absolute order. He informed us that, with the exception of a certain entailed property of Lucy's father which now, in default of direct issue, went back to a distant branch of the family, the whole estate, real and personal, was left absolutely to Arthur Holmwood. When he had told us so much he went on,

"Frankly we did our best to prevent such a testamentary disposition, and pointed out certain contingencies that might leave her daughter either penniless or not so free as she should be to act regarding a matrimonial alliance. Indeed, we pressed the matter so far that we almost came into collision, for she asked us if we were or were not prepared to carry out her wishes. Of course, we had then no alternative but to accept. We were right in principle, and ninety-nine times out of a hundred we should have proved, by the logic of events, the accuracy of our judgment.

"Frankly, however, I must admit that in this case any other form of disposition would have rendered impossible the carrying out of her wishes. For by her predeceasing her daughter the latter would have come into possession of the property, and, even had she only survived her mother by five minutes, her property would, in case there were no will, and a will was a practical impossibility in such a case, have been treated at her decease as under intestacy. In which case Lord Godalming, though so dear a friend, would have had no claim in the world. And the inheritors, being remote, would not be likely to abandon their just rights, for sentimental reasons regarding an entire stranger. I assure you, my dear sirs, I am rejoiced at the result, perfectly rejoiced."

He was a good fellow, but his rejoicing at the one little part, in which he was officially interested, of so great a tragedy, was an object-lesson in the limitations of sympathetic understanding.

He did not remain long, but said he would look in later in the day and see Lord Godalming. His coming, however, had been a certain comfort to us, since it assured us that we should not have to dread hostile criticism as to any of our acts. Arthur was expected at five o'clock, so a little before that time we visited the death chamber. It was so in very truth, for now both mother and daughter lay in it. The undertaker, true to his craft, had made the best display he could of his goods, and there was a mortuary air about the place that lowered our spirits at once.

Van Helsing ordered the former arrangement to be adhered to, explaining that, as Lord Godalming was coming very soon, it would be less harrowing to his feelings to see all that was left of his *fiancée* quite alone.

The undertaker seemed shocked at his own stupidity and exerted himself to restore things to the condition in which we left them the night before, so that when Arthur came such shocks to his feelings as we could avoid were saved.

Poor fellow! He looked desperately sad and broken. Even his stalwart manhood seemed to have shrunk somewhat under the strain of his much-tried emotions. He had, I knew, been very genuinely and devotedly attached to his father, and to lose him, and at such a time, was a bitter blow to him.

With me he was warm as ever, and to Van Helsing he was sweetly courteous. But I could not help seeing that there was some constraint with him. The professor noticed it too, and motioned me to bring him upstairs. I did so, and left him at the door of the room, as I felt he would like to be quite alone with her, but he took my arm and led me in, saying huskily,

"You loved her too, old fellow. She told me all about it, and there was no friend had a closer place in her heart than you. I don't know how to thank you for all you have done for her. I can't think yet . . ."

Here he suddenly broke down, and threw his arms round my shoulders and laid his head on my breast, crying, "Oh, Jack! Jack! What shall I do? The whole of life seems gone from me all at once, and there is nothing in the wide world for me to live for."

I comforted him as well as I could. In such cases men do not need much expression. A grip of the hand, the tightening of an arm over the shoulder, a sob in unison, are expressions of sympathy dear to a man's heart. I stood still and silent till his sobs died away, and then I said softly to him, "Come and look at her."

Together we moved over to the bed, and I lifted the lawn from her face. God! How beautiful she was. Every hour seemed to be enhancing her loveliness. It frightened and amazed me somewhat. And as for Arthur, he fell to trembling, and finally was shaken with doubt as with an ague. At last, after a long pause, he said to me in a faint whisper, "Jack, is she really dead?"

I assured him sadly that it was so, and went on to suggest, for I felt that such a horrible doubt should not have life for a moment longer than I could help, that it often happened that after death faces become softened and even resolved into their youthful beauty, that this was especially so when death had been preceded by any acute or prolonged suffering. I seemed to quite do away with any doubt, and after kneeling beside the couch for a while and looking at her lovingly and long, he turned aside. I told him that that must be goodbye, as the coffin had to be prepared, so he went back and took her dead hand in his and kissed it, and bent over and kissed her forehead. He came away, fondly looking back over his shoulder at her as he came.

I left him in the drawing room, and told Van Helsing that he had said goodbye, so the latter went to the kitchen to tell the undertaker's men to proceed with the preparations and to screw up the coffin. When he came out of the room again I told him of Arthur's question, and he replied, "I am not surprised. Just now I doubted for a moment myself!"

We all dined together, and I could see that poor Art was trying to make the best of things. Van Helsing had been silent all dinner time, but when we had lit our cigars he said, "Lord . . ." but Arthur interrupted him.

"No, no, not that, for God's sake! Not yet at any rate. Forgive me, sir. I did not mean to speak offensively. It is only because my loss is so recent."

The Professor answered very sweetly, "I only used that name because I was in doubt. I must not call you 'Mr.' and I have grown to love you, yes, my dear boy, to love you, as Arthur."

Arthur held out his hand, and took the old man's warmly. "Call me what you will," he said. "I hope I may always have the title of a friend. And let me say that I am at a loss for words to thank you for your goodness to my poor dear." He paused a moment, and went on, "I know that she understood your goodness even better than I do. And if I was rude or in any way wanting at that time you acted so, you remember"—the Professor nodded—"you must forgive me."

He answered with a grave kindness, "I know it was hard for you to quite trust me then, for to trust such violence needs to understand, and I take it that you do not, that you cannot, trust me now, for you do not yet understand. And there may be more times when I shall want you to trust when you cannot, and may not, and must not yet understand. But the time will come when your trust shall be whole and complete in me, and when you shall understand as though the sunlight himself shone through. Then you shall bless me from first to last for your own sake, and for the sake of others, and for her dear sake to whom I swore to protect."

"And indeed, indeed, sir," said Arthur warmly. "I shall in all ways trust you. I know and believe you have a very noble heart, and you are Jack's friend, and you were hers. You shall do what you like."

The Professor cleared his throat a couple of times, as though about to speak, and finally said, "May I ask you something now?"

"Certainly."

"You know that Mrs. Westenra left you all her property?"

"No, poor dear. I never thought of it."

"And as it is all yours, you have a right to deal with it as you will. I want you to give me permission to read all Miss Lucy's papers and letters. Believe me, it is no idle curiosity. I have a motive of which, be sure, she would have approved. I have them all here. I took them before we knew that all was yours, so that no strange hand might touch them, no strange eye look through words into her soul. I shall keep them, if I may. Even you may not see them yet, but I shall keep them safe. No word shall be lost, and in the good time I shall give them back to you. It is a hard thing that I ask, but you will do it, will you not, for Lucy's sake?"

Arthur spoke out heartily, like his old self, "Dr. Van Helsing, you may do what you will. I feel that in saying this I am doing what my dear one would have approved. I shall not trouble you with questions till the time comes."

The old Professor stood up as he said solemnly, "And you are right. There will be pain for us all, but it will not be all pain, nor will this pain be the last. We and you too, you most of all, dear boy, will have to pass through the bitter water before we reach the sweet. But we must be brave of heart and unselfish, and do our duty, and all will be well!"

I slept on a sofa in Arthur's room that night. Van Helsing did not go to bed at all. He went to and fro, as if patroling the house, and was never out of sight of the room where Lucy lay in her coffin, strewn with the wild garlic flowers, which sent through the odour of lily and rose, a heavy, overpowering smell into the night.

MINA HARKER'S JOURNAL

22 September.—In the train to Exeter. Jonathan sleeping. It seems only yesterday that the last entry was made, and yet how much between then, in Whitby and all the world before me, Jonathan away and no news of him, and now, married to Jonathan, Jonathan a solicitor, a partner, rich, master of his business, Mr. Hawkins dead and buried, and Jonathan with another attack that may harm him. Some day he may ask me about it. Down it all goes. I am rusty in my shorthand, see what unexpected prosperity does for us, so it may be as well to freshen it up again with an exercise anyhow.

The service was very simple and very solemn. There were only ourselves and the servants there, one or two old friends of his from Exeter, his London agent, and a gentleman representing Sir John Paxton, the President of the Incorporated Law Society. Jonathan and I stood hand in hand, and we felt that our best and dearest friend was gone from us.

We came back to town quietly, taking a bus to Hyde Park Corner. Jonathan thought it would interest me to go into the Row for a while, so we sat down. But there were very few people there, and it was sad-looking and desolate to see so many empty chairs. It made us think of the empty chair at home. So we got up and walked down Piccadilly. Jonathan was holding me by the arm, the way he used to in the old days before I went to school. I felt it very improper, for you can't go on for some years teaching etiquette and decorum to other girls without the pedantry of it biting into yourself a bit. But it was Jonathan, and he was my husband, and we didn't know anybody who saw us, and we didn't care if they did, so on we walked. I was looking at a very beautiful girl, in a big cart-wheel hat, sitting in a victoria[104] outside

---

104 Carriage.

Guiliano's, when I felt Jonathan clutch my arm so tight that he hurt me, and he said under his breath, "My God!"

I am always anxious about Jonathan, for I fear that some nervous fit may upset him again. So I turned to him quickly, and asked him what it was that disturbed him.

He was very pale, and his eyes seemed bulging out as, half in terror and half in amazement, he gazed at a tall, thin man, with a beaky nose and black moustache and pointed beard, who was also observing the pretty girl. He was looking at her so hard that he did not see either of us, and so I had a good view of him. His face was not a good face. It was hard, and cruel, and sensual, and big white teeth, that looked all the whiter because his lips were so red, were pointed like an animal's. Jonathan kept staring at him, till I was afraid he would notice. I feared he might take it ill, he looked so fierce and nasty. I asked Jonathan why he was disturbed, and he answered, evidently thinking that I knew as much about it as he did, "Do you see who it is?"

"No, dear," I said. "I don't know him, who is it?" His answer seemed to shock and thrill me, for it was said as if he did not know that it was me, Mina, to whom he was speaking. "It is the man himself!"

The poor dear was evidently terrified at something, very greatly terrified. I do believe that if he had not had me to lean on and to support him he would have sunk down. He kept staring. A man came out of the shop with a small parcel, and gave it to the lady, who then drove off. The dark man kept his eyes fixed on her, and when the carriage moved up Piccadilly he followed in the same direction, and hailed a hansom. Jonathan kept looking after him, and said, as if to himself,

"I believe it is the Count, but he has grown young. My God, if this be so! Oh, my God! My God! If only I knew! If only I knew!" He was distressing himself so much that I feared to keep his mind on the subject by asking him any questions, so I remained silent. I drew away quietly, and he, holding my arm, came easily. We walked a little further, and then went in and sat for a while in the Green Park. It was a hot day for autumn, and there was a comfortable seat in a shady place. After a few minutes' staring at nothing, Jonathan's eyes closed, and he went quickly into a sleep, with his head on my shoulder. I thought it was the best thing for him, so did not disturb him. In about twenty minutes he woke up, and said to me quite cheerfully,

"Why, Mina, have I been asleep! Oh, do forgive me for being so rude. Come, and we'll have a cup of tea somewhere."

He had evidently forgotten all about the dark stranger, as in his illness he had forgotten all that this episode had reminded him of. I don't like this lapsing into forgetfulness. It may make or continue some injury to the brain. I must not ask him, for fear I shall do more harm than good, but I must somehow learn the facts of his journey abroad. The time is come, I fear, when I must open the parcel, and know what is written. Oh, Jonathan, you will, I know, forgive me if I do wrong, but it is for your own dear sake.

Later.—A sad homecoming in every way, the house empty of the dear soul who was so good to us. Jonathan still pale and dizzy under a slight relapse of his malady, and now a telegram from Van Helsing, whoever he may be. "You will be grieved to hear that Mrs. Westenra died five days ago, and that Lucy died the day before yesterday. They were both buried today."

Oh, what a wealth of sorrow in a few words! Poor Mrs. Westenra! Poor Lucy! Gone, gone, never to return to us! And poor, poor Arthur, to have lost such a sweetness out of his life! God help us all to bear our troubles.

DR. SEWARD'S DIARY

22 September.—It is all over. Arthur has gone back to Ring, and has taken Quincey Morris with him. What a fine fellow is Quincey! I believe in my heart of hearts that he suffered as much about Lucy's death as any of us, but he bore himself through it like a moral Viking. If America can go on breeding men like that, she will be a power in the world indeed. Van Helsing is lying down, having a rest preparatory to his journey. He goes to Amsterdam tonight, but says he returns tomorrow night, that he only wants to make some arrangements which can only be made personally. He is to stop with me then, if he can. He says he has work to do in London which may take him some time. Poor old fellow! I fear that the strain of the past week has broken down even his iron strength. All the time of the burial he was, I could see, putting some terrible restraint on himself. When it was all over, we were standing beside Arthur, who, poor fellow, was speaking of his part in the operation where his blood had been transfused to his Lucy's veins. I could see Van Helsing's face grow white and purple by turns. Arthur was saying that he felt since then as if they two had been really married, and that she was his wife in the sight of God. None of us said a word of the other operations, and none of us ever shall. Arthur and Quincey went away together to the station, and Van Helsing and I came on here. The moment we were alone in the carriage he gave way to a regular fit of hysterics. He has denied to me since that it was hysterics, and insisted that it was only his sense of humor asserting itself under very terrible conditions. He laughed till he cried, and I had to draw down the blinds lest any one should see us and misjudge. And then he cried, till he laughed again, and laughed and cried together, just as a woman does. I tried to be stern with him, as one is to a woman under the circumstances, but it had no effect. Men and women are so different in manifestations of nervous strength or weakness! Then when his face grew grave and stern again I asked him why his mirth, and why at such a time. His reply was in a way characteristic of him, for it was logical and forceful and mysterious. He said,

"Ah, you don't comprehend, friend John. Do not think that I am not sad, though I laugh. See, I have cried even when the laugh did choke me. But no more think that I am all sorry when I cry, for the laugh he come just the same. Keep it always with you that laughter who knock at your door and say, 'May I come in?' is not true laughter. No! He is a king, and he come when and how he like. He ask no person, he choose no time of suitability. He say, 'I am here.' Behold, in example I grieve my heart out for that so sweet young girl. I give my blood for her, though I am old and worn. I give my time, my skill, my sleep. I let my other sufferers want that she may have all. And yet I can laugh at her very grave, laugh when the clay from the spade of the sexton drop upon her coffin and say 'Thud, thud!' to my heart, till it send back the blood from my cheek. My heart bleed for that poor boy, that dear boy, so of the age of mine own boy had I been so blessed that he live, and with his hair and eyes the same.

"There, you know now why I love him so. And yet when he say things that touch my husband-heart to the quick, and make my father-heart yearn to him as to no other man, not even you, friend John, for we are more level in experiences than father and son, yet even at such a moment King Laugh he come to me and shout and bellow in my ear, 'Here I am! Here I am!' till the blood come dance back and bring some of the sunshine that he carry with him to my cheek. Oh, friend John, it is a strange world, a sad world, a world full of miseries, and woes, and troubles. And yet when King Laugh come, he make them all dance to the tune he play. Bleeding hearts, and dry bones of the churchyard, and tears that burn as they fall, all dance together to the music that he make with that smileless mouth of him. And believe me, friend John, that he is good to come, and kind. Ah, we men and women are like ropes drawn tight with strain that pull us different ways. Then tears come, and like the rain on the ropes, they brace us up, until perhaps the strain become too great, and we break. But King Laugh he come like the sunshine, and he ease off the strain again, and we bear to go on with our labor, what it may be."

I did not like to wound him by pretending not to see his idea, but as I did not yet understand the cause of his laughter, I asked him. As he answered me his face grew stern, and he said in quite a different tone,

"Oh, it was the grim irony of it all, this so lovely lady garlanded with flowers, that looked so fair as life, till one by one we wondered if she were truly dead, she laid in that so fine marble house in that lonely churchyard, where rest so many of her kin, laid there with the mother who loved her, and whom she loved, and that sacred bell going 'Toll! Toll! Toll!' so sad and slow, and those holy men, with the white garments of the angel, pretending to read books, and yet all the time their eyes never on the page, and all of us with the bowed head. And all for what? She is dead, so! Is it not?"

"Well, for the life of me, Professor," I said, "I can't see anything to laugh at in all that. Why, your expression makes it a harder puzzle than before. But even if the burial service was comic, what about poor Art and his trouble? Why his heart was simply breaking."

"Just so. Said he not that the transfusion of his blood to her veins had made her truly his bride?"

"Yes, and it was a sweet and comforting idea for him."

"Quite so. But there was a difficulty, friend John. If so that, then what about the others? Ho, ho! Then this so sweet maid is a polyandrist, and me, with my poor wife dead to me, but alive by Church's law, though no wits, all gone, even I, who am faithful husband to this now-no-wife, am bigamist."

"I don't see where the joke comes in there either!" I said, and I did not feel particularly pleased with him for saying such things. He laid his hand on my arm, and said,

"Friend John, forgive me if I pain. I showed not my feeling to others when it would wound, but only to you, my old friend, whom I can trust. If you could have looked into my heart then when I want to laugh, if you could have done so when the laugh arrived, if you could do so now, when King Laugh have pack up his crown, and all that is to him, for he go far, far away from me, and for a long, long time, maybe you would perhaps pity me the most of all."

I was touched by the tenderness of his tone, and asked why.

"Because I know!"

And now we are all scattered, and for many a long day loneliness will sit over our roofs with brooding wings. Lucy lies in the tomb of her kin, a lordly death house in a lonely churchyard, away from teeming London, where the air is fresh, and the sun rises over Hampstead Hill, and where wild flowers grow of their own accord.

So I can finish this diary, and God only knows if I shall ever begin another. If I do, or if I even open this again, it will be to deal with different people and different themes, for here at the end, where the romance of my life is told, ere I go back to take up the thread of my life-work, I say sadly and without hope, "FINIS".

The Westminster Gazette

25 September

A HAMPSTEAD MYSTERY

The neighborhood of Hampstead is just at present exercised with a series of events which seem to run on lines parallel to those of what was known to the writers of headlines as "The Kensington Horror," or "The Stabbing Woman," or "The Woman in Black." During the past two or three days several cases have occurred of young children straying from home or neglecting to return from their playing on the Heath. In all these cases the children were too young to give any properly intelligible account of themselves, but the consensus of their excuses is that they had been with a "bloofer lady.[105]" It has always been late in the evening when they have been missed, and on two occasions the children have not been found until early in the following morning. It is generally supposed in the neighbor-hood that, as the first child missed gave as his reason for being away that a "bloofer lady" had asked him to come for a walk, the others had picked up the phrase and used it as occasion served. This is the more natural as the favourite game of the little ones at present is luring each other away by wiles. A correspondent writes us that to see some of the tiny tots pretending to be the "bloofer lady" is supremely funny. Some of our caricaturists might, he says, take a lesson in the irony of grotesque by comparing the reality and the picture. It is only in accordance with general principles of human nature that the "bloofer lady" should be the popular role at these *al fresco* performances. Our correspondent naively says that even Ellen Terry could not be so winningly attractive as some of these grubby-faced little children pretend, and even imagine themselves, to be.

There is, however, possibly a serious side to the question, for some of the children, indeed all who have been missed at night, have been slightly torn or wounded in the throat. The wounds seem such as might be made by a rat or a small dog, and although of not much importance individually, would tend to show that whatever animal inflicts them has a system or method of its own. The police of the

---

105 Beautiful lady.

division have been instructed to keep a sharp lookout for straying children, especially when very young, in and around Hampstead Heath, and for any stray dog which may be about.

The Westminster Gazette,

25 September
✦ Extra Special ✦

THE HAMPSTEAD HORROR
ANOTHER CHILD INJURED
The "Bloofer Lady"

We have just received intelligence that another child, missed last night, was only discovered late in the morning under a furze bush at the Shooter's Hill side of Hampstead Heath, which is perhaps, less frequented than the other parts. It has the same tiny wound in the throat as has been noticed in other cases. It was terribly weak, and looked quite emaciated. It too, when partially restored, had the common story to tell of being lured away by the "bloofer lady".

ೕ CHAPTER 14 ೕ

MINA HARKER'S JOURNAL

23 September.—Jonathan is better after a bad night. I am so glad that he has plenty of work to do, for that keeps his mind off the terrible things, and oh, I am rejoiced that he is not now weighed down with the responsibility of his new position. I knew he would be true to himself, and now how proud I am to see my Jonathan rising to the height of his advancement and keeping pace in all ways with the duties that come upon him. He will be away all day till late, for he said he could not lunch at home. My household work is done, so I shall take his foreign journal, and lock myself up in my room and read it.

24 September.—I hadn't the heart to write last night, that terrible record of Jonathan's upset me so. Poor dear! How he must have suffered, whether it be true or only imagination. I wonder if there is any truth in it at all. Did he get his brain fever, and then write all those terrible things, or had he some cause for it all? I suppose I shall never know, for I dare not open the subject to him. And yet that man we saw yesterday! He seemed quite certain of him, poor fellow! I suppose it was the funeral upset him and sent his mind back on some train of thought.

He believes it all himself. I remember how on our wedding day he said "Unless some solemn duty come upon me to go back to the bitter hours, asleep or awake, mad or sane . . ." There seems to be through it all some thread of continuity. That fearful Count was coming to London. If it should be, and he came to London, with its teeming millions . . . There may be a solemn duty, and if it come we must not shrink from it. I shall be prepared. I shall get my typewriter this very hour and begin transcribing. Then we shall be ready for other eyes if required. And if it be wanted, then, perhaps, if I am ready, poor Jonathan may not be upset, for I can speak for him and never let him be troubled or worried with it at all. If ever Jonathan quite gets over the nervousness he may want to tell me of it all, and I can ask him questions and find out things, and see how I may comfort him.

LETTER, VAN HELSING TO MRS. HARKER

24 September, (Confidence)

"Dear Madam,

"I pray you to pardon my writing, in that I am so far friend as that I sent to you sad news of Miss Lucy Westenra's death. By the kindness of Lord Godalming, I am empowered to read her letters and papers, for I am deeply concerned about certain matters vitally important. In them I find some letters from you, which show how great friends you were and how you love her. Oh, Madam Mina, by that love, I implore you, help me. It is for others' good that I ask, to redress great wrong, and to lift much and terrible troubles, that may be more great than you can know. May it be that I see you? You can trust me. I am friend of Dr. John Seward and of Lord Godalming (that was Arthur of Miss Lucy). I must keep it private for the present from all. I should come to Exeter to see you at once if you tell me I am privilege to come, and where and when. I implore your pardon, Madam. I have read your letters to poor Lucy, and know how good you are and how your husband suffer. So I pray you, if it may be, enlighten him not, least it may harm. Again your pardon, and forgive me.

"Van Helsing"

TELEGRAM, MRS. HARKER TO VAN HELSING

25 September.—Come today by quarter past ten train if you can catch it. Can see you any time you call. *"Wilhelmina Harker"*

MINA HARKER'S JOURNAL

25 September.—I cannot help feeling terribly excited as the time draws near for the visit of Dr. Van Helsing, for somehow I expect that it will throw some light upon Jonathan's sad experience, and as he attended poor dear Lucy in her last illness, he can tell me all about her. That is the reason of his coming. It is concerning Lucy and her sleep-walking, and not about Jonathan. Then I shall never know the real truth now! How silly I am. That awful journal gets hold of my imagination and tinges everything with something of its own colour. Of course it is about Lucy. That habit came back to the poor dear, and that awful night on the cliff must have made her ill. I had almost forgotten in my own affairs how ill she was afterwards. She must have told him of her sleep-walking adventure on the cliff, and that I knew all about it, and now he wants me to tell him what I know, so that he may understand. I hope I did right in not saying anything of it to Mrs. Westenra. I should never forgive myself if any act of mine, were it even a negative one, brought harm on poor dear Lucy. I hope too, Dr. Van Helsing will not blame me. I have had so much trouble and anxiety of late that I feel I cannot bear more just at present.

I suppose a cry does us all good at times, clears the air as other rain does. Perhaps it was reading the journal yesterday that upset me, and then Jonathan went away this morning to stay away from me a whole day and night, the first time we have been parted since our marriage. I do hope the dear fellow will take care of himself, and that nothing will occur to upset him. It is two o'clock, and the doctor will be here soon now. I shall say nothing of Jonathan's journal unless he asks me. I am so glad I have typewritten out my own journal, so that, in case he asks about Lucy, I can hand it to him. It will save much questioning.

Later.—He has come and gone. Oh, what a strange meeting, and how it all makes my head whirl round. I feel like one in a dream. Can it be all possible, or even a part of it? If I had not read Jonathan's journal first, I should never have accepted even a possibility. Poor, poor, dear Jonathan! How he must have suffered. Please the good God, all this may not upset him again. I shall try to save him from it. But it may be even a consolation and a help to him, terrible though it be and awful in its consequences, to know for certain that his eyes and ears and brain did not deceive him, and that it is all true. It may be that it is the doubt which haunts him, that when the doubt is removed, no matter which, waking or dreaming, may prove the truth, he will be more satisfied and better able to bear the shock. Dr. Van Helsing must be a good man as well as a clever one if he is Arthur's friend and Dr. Seward's, and if they brought him all the way from Holland to look after Lucy. I feel from having seen him that he is good and kind and of a noble nature. When he comes tomorrow I shall ask him about Jonathan. And then, please God, all this sorrow and anxiety may lead to a good end. I used to think I would like to practice interviewing. Jonathan's friend on "The Exeter News" told him that memory is everything in such work, that you must be able to put down exactly almost every word spoken, even if you had to refine some of it afterwards. Here was a rare interview. I shall try to record it *verbatim*.

It was half-past two o'clock when the knock came. I took my courage *a deux mains*[106] and waited. In a few minutes Mary opened the door, and announced "Dr. Van Helsing".

I rose and bowed, and he came towards me, a man of medium weight, strongly built, with his shoulders set back over a broad, deep chest and a neck well balanced on the trunk as the head is on the neck. The poise of the head strikes me at once as indicative of thought and power. The head is noble, well-sized, broad, and large behind the ears. The face, clean-shaven, shows a hard, square chin, a large resolute, mobile mouth, a good-sized nose, rather straight, but with quick, sensitive nostrils, that seem to broaden as the big bushy brows come down and the mouth tightens. The forehead is broad and fine, rising at first almost straight and then sloping back above two bumps or ridges wide apart, such a forehead that the reddish hair cannot possibly tumble over it, but falls naturally back and to the sides. Big, dark blue eyes are set widely apart, and are quick and tender or stern with the man's moods. He said to me,

"Mrs. Harker, is it not?" I bowed assent.

---

106 In both hands (French).

"That was Miss Mina Murray?" Again I assented.

"It is Mina Murray that I came to see that was friend of that poor dear child Lucy Westenra. Madam Mina, it is on account of the dead that I come."

"Sir," I said, "you could have no better claim on me than that you were a friend and helper of Lucy Westenra." And I held out my hand. He took it and said tenderly,

"Oh, Madam Mina, I know that the friend of that poor little girl must be good, but I had yet to learn . . ." He finished his speech with a courtly bow. I asked him what it was that he wanted to see me about, so he at once began.

"I have read your letters to Miss Lucy. Forgive me, but I had to begin to inquire somewhere, and there was none to ask. I know that you were with her at Whitby. She sometimes kept a diary, you need not look surprised, Madam Mina. It was begun after you had left, and was an imitation of you, and in that diary she traces by inference certain things to a sleep-walking in which she puts down that you saved her. In great perplexity then I come to you, and ask you out of your so much kindness to tell me all of it that you can remember."

"I can tell you, I think, Dr. Van Helsing, all about it."

"Ah, then you have good memory for facts, for details? It is not always so with young ladies."

"No, doctor, but I wrote it all down at the time. I can show it to you if you like."

"Oh, Madam Mina, I well be grateful. You will do me much favour."

I could not resist the temptation of mystifying him a bit, I suppose it is some taste of the original apple that remains still in our mouths, so I handed him the shorthand diary. He took it with a grateful bow, and said, "May I read it?"

"If you wish," I answered as demurely as I could. He opened it, and for an instant his face fell. Then he stood up and bowed.

"Oh, you so clever woman!" he said. "I knew long that Mr. Jonathan was a man of much thankfulness, but see, his wife have all the good things. And will you not so much honour me and so help me as to read it for me? Alas! I know not the shorthand."

By this time my little joke was over, and I was almost ashamed. So I took the typewritten copy from my work basket and handed it to him.

"Forgive me," I said. "I could not help it, but I had been thinking that it was of dear Lucy that you wished to ask, and so that you might not have time to wait, not on my account, but because I know your time must be precious, I have written it out on the typewriter for you."

He took it and his eyes glistened. "You are so good," he said. "And may I read it now? I may want to ask you some things when I have read."

"By all means," I said, "read it over whilst I order lunch, and then you can ask me questions whilst we eat."

He bowed and settled himself in a chair with his back to the light, and became so absorbed in the papers, whilst I went to see after lunch chiefly in order that he might not be disturbed. When I came back, I found him walking hurriedly up and down the room, his face all ablaze with excitement. He rushed up to me and took me by both hands.

"Oh, Madam Mina," he said, "how can I say what I owe to you? This paper is as sunshine. It opens the gate to me. I am dazed, I am dazzled, with so much light, and yet clouds roll in behind the light every time. But that you do not, cannot comprehend. Oh, but I am grateful to you, you so clever woman. Madame," he said this very solemnly, "if ever Abraham Van Helsing can do anything for you or yours, I trust you will let me know. It will be pleasure and delight if I may serve you as a friend, as a friend, but all I have ever learned, all I can ever do, shall be for you and those you love. There are darknesses in life, and there are lights. You are one of the lights. You will have a happy life and a good life, and your husband will be blessed in you."

"But, doctor, you praise me too much, and you do not know me."

"Not know you, I, who am old, and who have studied all my life men and women, I who have made my specialty the brain and all that belongs to him and all that follow from him! And I have read your diary that you have so goodly written for me, and which breathes out truth in every line. I, who have read your so sweet letter to poor Lucy of your marriage and your trust, not know you! Oh, Madam Mina, good women tell all their lives, and by day and by hour and by minute, such things that angels can read. And we men who wish to know have in us something of angels' eyes. Your husband is noble nature, and you are noble too, for you trust, and trust cannot be where there is mean nature. And your husband, tell me of him. Is he quite well? Is all that fever gone, and is he strong and hearty?"

I saw here an opening to ask him about Jonathan, so I said, "He was almost recovered, but he has been greatly upset by Mr. Hawkins death."

He interrupted, "Oh, yes. I know. I know. I have read your last two letters."

I went on, "I suppose this upset him, for when we were in town on Thursday last he had a sort of shock."

"A shock, and after brain fever so soon! That is not good. What kind of shock was it?"

"He thought he saw some one who recalled something terrible, something which led to his brain fever." And here the whole thing seemed to overwhelm me in a rush. The pity for Jonathan, the horror which he experienced, the whole fearful mystery of his diary, and the fear that has been brooding over me ever since, all came in a tumult. I suppose I was hysterical, for I threw myself on my knees and held up my hands to him, and implored him to make my husband well again. He took my hands and raised me up, and made me sit on the sofa, and sat by me. He held my hand in his, and said to me with, oh, such infinite sweetness,

"My life is a barren and lonely one, and so full of work that I have not had much time for friendships, but since I have been summoned to here by my friend John Seward I have known so many good people and seen such nobility that I feel more than ever, and it has grown with my advancing years, the loneliness of my life. Believe me, then, that I come here full of respect for you, and you have given me hope, hope, not in what I am seeking of, but that there are good women still left to make life happy, good women, whose lives and whose truths may make good lesson for the children that are to be. I am glad, glad, that I may here be of some use to you. For if your husband suffer, he suffer within the range of my study and experience. I promise you that I will gladly do *all* for him that I can, all to make his life strong and manly, and your life a happy one. Now you must eat. You are overwrought and perhaps over-anxious. Husband Jonathan would not like to see you so pale, and what he like not where he love, is not to his good. Therefore for his sake you must eat and smile. You have told me about Lucy, and so now we shall not speak of it, lest it distress. I shall stay in Exeter tonight, for I want to think much over what you have told me, and when I have thought I will ask you questions, if I may. And then too, you will tell me of husband Jonathan's trouble so far as you can, but not yet. You must eat now, afterwards you shall tell me all."

After lunch, when we went back to the drawing room, he said to me, "And now tell me all about him."

When it came to speaking to this great learned man, I began to fear that he would think me a weak fool, and Jonathan a madman, that journal is all so strange, and I hesitated to go on. But he was so sweet and kind, and he had promised to help, and I trusted him, so I said,

"Dr. Van Helsing, what I have to tell you is so queer that you must not laugh at me or at my husband. I have been since yesterday in a sort of fever of doubt. You must be kind to me, and not think me foolish that I have even half believed some very strange things."

He reassured me by his manner as well as his words when he said, "Oh, my dear, if you only know how strange is the matter regarding which I am here, it is you who would laugh. I have learned not to think little of any one's belief, no matter how strange it may be. I have tried to keep an open mind, and it is not the ordinary things of life that could close it, but the strange things, the extraordinary things, the things that make one doubt if they be mad or sane."

"Thank you, thank you a thousand times! You have taken a weight off my mind. If you will let me, I shall give you a paper to read. It is long, but I have typewritten it out. It will tell you my trouble and Jonathan's. It is the copy of his journal when abroad, and all that happened. I dare not say anything of it. You will read for yourself and judge. And then when I see you, perhaps, you will be very kind and tell me what you think."

"I promise," he said as I gave him the papers. "I shall in the morning, as soon as I can, come to see you and your husband, if I may."

"Jonathan will be here at half-past eleven, and you must come to lunch with us and see him then. You could catch the quick 3:34 train, which will leave you at Paddington before eight." He was surprised at my knowledge of the trains offhand, but he does not know that I have made up all the trains to and from Exeter, so that I may help Jonathan in case he is in a hurry.

So he took the papers with him and went away, and I sit here thinking, thinking I don't know what.

LETTER (BY HAND), VAN HELSING TO MRS. HARKER

25 September, 6 o'clock

"Dear Madam Mina,

"I have read your husband's so wonderful diary. You may sleep without doubt. Strange and terrible as it is, it is *true*! I will pledge my life on it. It may be worse for others, but for him and you there is no dread. He is a noble fellow, and let me tell you from experience of men, that one who would do as he did in going down that wall and to that room, aye, and going a second time, is not one to be injured in permanence by a shock. His brain and his heart are all right, this I swear, before I have even seen him, so be at rest. I shall have much to ask him of other things. I am blessed that today I come to see you, for I have learn all at once so much that again I am dazzled, dazzled more than ever, and I must think.

"Yours the most faithful,

"Abraham Van Helsing."

LETTER, MRS. HARKER TO VAN HELSING

25 September, 6:30 P.M.

"My dear Dr. Van Helsing,

"A thousand thanks for your kind letter, which has taken a great weight off my mind. And yet, if it be true, what terrible things there are in the world, and what an awful thing if that man, that monster, be really in London! I fear to think. I have this moment, whilst writing, had a wire from Jonathan, saying that he leaves by the 6:25 tonight from Launceston and will be here at 10:18, so that I shall have no fear tonight. Will you, therefore, instead of lunching with us, please come to breakfast at eight o'clock, if this be not too early for you? You can get away, if you are in a hurry, by the 10:30 train, which will bring you to Paddington by 2:35. Do not answer this, as I shall take it that, if I do not hear, you will come to breakfast.

"Believe me,

"Your faithful and grateful friend,

"Mina Harker."

JONATHAN HARKER'S JOURNAL

26 September.—I thought never to write in this diary again, but the time has come. When I got home last night Mina had supper ready, and when we had supped she told me of Van Helsing's visit, and of her having given him the two diaries copied out, and of how anxious she has been about me. She showed me in the doctor's letter that all I wrote down was true. It seems to have made a new man of me. It was the doubt as to the reality of the whole thing that knocked me over. I felt impotent, and in the dark, and distrustful. But, now that I *know*, I am not afraid, even of the Count. He has succeeded after all, then, in his design in getting to London, and it was he I saw. He has got younger, and how? Van Helsing is the man to unmask him and hunt him out, if he is anything like what Mina says. We sat late, and talked it over. Mina is dressing, and I shall call at the hotel in a few minutes and bring him over.

He was, I think, surprised to see me. When I came into the room where he was, and introduced myself, he took me by the shoulder, and turned my face round to the light, and said, after a sharp scrutiny,

"But Madam Mina told me you were ill, that you had had a shock."

It was so funny to hear my wife called 'Madam Mina' by this kindly, strong-faced old man. I smiled, and said, "I *was* ill, I *have* had a shock, but you have cured me already."

"And how?"

"By your letter to Mina last night. I was in doubt, and then everything took a hue of unreality, and I did not know what to trust, even the evidence of my own senses. Not knowing what to trust, I did not know what to do, and so had only to keep on working in what had hitherto been the groove of my life. The groove ceased to avail me, and I mistrusted myself. Doctor, you don't know what it is to doubt everything, even yourself. No, you don't, you couldn't with eyebrows like yours."

He seemed pleased, and laughed as he said, "So! You are a physiogno-mist. I learn more here with each hour. I am with so much pleasure coming to you to breakfast, and, oh, sir, you will pardon praise from an old man, but you are blessed in your wife."

I would listen to him go on praising Mina for a day, so I simply nodded and stood silent.

"She is one of God's women, fashioned by His own hand to show us men and other women that there is a heaven where we can enter, and that its light can be here on earth. So true, so sweet, so noble, so little an egoist, and that, let me tell you, is much in this age, so sceptical and selfish. And you, sir . . . I have read all the letters to poor Miss Lucy, and some of them speak of you, so I know you since some days from the knowing of others, but I have seen your true self since last night. You will give me your hand, will you not? And let us be friends for all our lives."

We shook hands, and he was so earnest and so kind that it made me quite choky.

"And now," he said, "may I ask you for some more help? I have a great task to do, and at the beginning it is to know. You can help me here. Can you tell me what went before your going to Transylvania? Later on I may ask more help, and of a different kind, but at first this will do."

"Look here, Sir," I said, "does what you have to do concern the Count?"

"It does," he said solemnly.

"Then I am with you heart and soul. As you go by the 10:30 train, you will not have time to read them, but I shall get the bundle of papers. You can take them with you and read them in the train."

After breakfast I saw him to the station. When we were parting he said, "Perhaps you will come to town if I send for you, and take Madam Mina too."

"We shall both come when you will," I said.

I had got him the morning papers and the London papers of the previous night, and while we were talking at the carriage window, waiting for the train to start, he was turning them over. His eyes suddenly seemed to catch something in one of them, "The Westminster Gazette", I knew it by the colour, and he grew quite white. He read something intently, groaning to himself, "Mein Gott! Mein Gott! So soon! So soon!" I do not think he remembered me at the moment. Just then the whistle blew, and the train moved off. This recalled him to himself, and he leaned out of the window and waved his hand, calling out, "Love to Madam Mina. I shall write so soon as ever I can."

DR. SEWARD'S DIARY

26 September.—Truly there is no such thing as finality. Not a week since I said "Finis," and yet here I am starting fresh again, or rather going on with the record. Until this afternoon I had no cause to think of what is done. Renfield had become, to all intents, as sane as he ever was. He was already well ahead with his fly business, and he had just started in the spider line also, so he had not been of any trouble to me. I had a letter from Arthur, written on Sunday, and from it I gather that he is bearing up wonderfully well. Quincey Morris is with him, and that is much of a help, for he himself is a bubbling well of good spirits. Quincey wrote me a line too, and from him I hear that Arthur is beginning to recover something of his old buoyancy, so as to them all my mind is at rest. As for myself, I was settling down to my work with the enthusiasm which I used to have for it, so that I might fairly have said that the wound which poor Lucy left on me was becoming cicatrised.

Everything is, however, now reopened, and what is to be the end God only knows. I have an idea that Van Helsing thinks he knows, too, but he will only let out enough at a time to whet curiosity. He went to Exeter yesterday, and stayed there all night. Today he came back, and almost bounded into the room at about half-past five o'clock, and thrust last night's "Westminster Gazette" into my hand.

"What do you think of that?" he asked as he stood back and folded his arms.

I looked over the paper, for I really did not know what he meant, but he took it from me and pointed out a paragraph about children being decoyed away at Hampstead. It did not convey much to me, until I reached a passage where it described small puncture wounds on their throats. An idea struck me, and I looked up.

"Well?" he said.

"It is like poor Lucy's."

"And what do you make of it?"

"Simply that there is some cause in common. Whatever it was that injured her has injured them." I did not quite understand his answer.

"That is true indirectly, but not directly."

"How do you mean, Professor?" I asked. I was a little inclined to take his seriousness lightly, for, after all, four days of rest and freedom from burning, harrowing, anxiety does help to restore one's spirits, but when I saw his face, it sobered me. Never, even in the midst of our despair about poor Lucy, had he looked more stern.

"Tell me!" I said. "I can hazard no opinion. I do not know what to think, and I have no data on which to found a conjecture."

"Do you mean to tell me, friend John, that you have no suspicion as to what poor Lucy died of, not after all the hints given, not only by events, but by me?"

"Of nervous prostration following a great loss or waste of blood."

"And how was the blood lost or wasted?" I shook my head.

He stepped over and sat down beside me, and went on, "You are a clever man, friend John. You reason well, and your wit is bold, but you are too prejudiced. You do not let your eyes see nor your ears hear, and that which is outside your daily life is not of account to you. Do you not think that there are things which you cannot understand, and yet which are, that some people see things that others cannot? But there are things old and new which must not be contemplated by men's eyes, because they know, or think they know, some things which other men have told them. Ah, it is the fault of our science that it wants to explain all, and if it explain not, then it says there is nothing to explain. But yet we see around us every day the growth of new beliefs, which think themselves new, and which are yet but the old, which pretend to be young, like the fine ladies at the opera. I suppose now you do not believe in corporeal transference. No? Nor in materialization. No? Nor in astral bodies. No? Nor in the reading of thought. No? Nor in hypnotism . . ."

"Yes," I said. "Charcot has proved that pretty well."

He smiled as he went on, "Then you are satisfied as to it. Yes? And of course then you understand how it act, and can follow the mind of the great Charcot, alas that he is no more, into the very soul of the patient that he influence. No? Then, friend John, am I to take it that you simply accept fact, and are satisfied to let from premise to conclusion be a blank? No? Then tell me, for I am a student of the brain, how you accept hypnotism and reject the thought reading. Let me tell you, my friend, that there are things done today in electrical science which would have been deemed unholy by the very man who discovered electricity, who would themselves not so long before been burned as wizards. There are always mysteries in life. Why was it that Methuselah lived nine hundred years, and 'Old Parr' one hundred and sixty-nine, and yet that poor Lucy, with four men's blood in her poor veins, could not live even one day? For, had she live one more day, we could save her. Do you know all the mystery of life and death? Do you know the altogether of comparative anatomy and can say wherefore the qualities of brutes are in some men, and not in others? Can you tell me why, when other spiders die small and soon, that one great spider lived for centuries in the tower of the old Spanish church and grew and grew, till, on descending, he could drink the oil of all the church lamps? Can you tell me why in the Pampas, ay and elsewhere, there are bats that come out at night and open the veins of cattle and horses and suck dry their veins, how in some islands of the Western seas there are bats which hang on the trees all day, and those who have seen describe as like giant nuts or pods, and that when the sailors sleep on the deck, because that it is hot, flit down on them and then, and then in the morning are found dead men, white as even Miss Lucy was?"

"Good God, Professor!" I said, starting up. "Do you mean to tell me that Lucy was bitten by such a bat, and that such a thing is here in London in the nineteenth century?"

He waved his hand for silence, and went on, "Can you tell me why the tortoise lives more long than generations of men, why the elephant goes on and on till he have sees dynasties, and why the parrot never die only of bite of cat of dog or other complaint? Can you tell me why men believe in all ages and places that there are men and women who cannot die? We all know, because science has vouched for the fact, that there have been toads shut up in rocks for thousands of years, shut in one so small hole that only hold him since the youth of the world. Can you tell me how the Indian fakir can make himself to die and have been buried, and his grave sealed and corn sowed on it, and the corn reaped and be cut and sown and reaped and cut again, and then men come and take away the unbroken seal and that there lie the Indian fakir, not dead, but that rise up and walk amongst them as before?"

Here I interrupted him. I was getting bewildered. He so crowded on my mind his list of nature's eccentricities and possible impossibilities that my imagination was getting fired. I had a dim idea that he was teaching me some lesson, as long ago he used to do in his study at Amsterdam. But he used them to tell me the thing, so that I could have the object of thought in mind all the time. But now I was without his help, yet I wanted to follow him, so I said,

"Professor, let me be your pet student again. Tell me the thesis, so that I may apply your knowledge as you go on. At present I am going in my mind from point to point as a madman, and not a sane one, follows an idea. I feel like a novice lumbering through a bog in a midst, jumping from one tussock to another in the mere blind effort to move on without knowing where I am going."

"That is a good image," he said. "Well, I shall tell you. My thesis is this, I want you to believe."

"To believe what?"

"To believe in things that you cannot. Let me illustrate. I heard once of an American who so defined faith, 'that faculty which enables us to believe things which we know to be untrue.' For one, I follow that man. He meant that we shall have an open mind, and not let a little bit of truth check the rush of the big truth, like a small rock does a railway truck. We get the small truth first. Good! We keep him, and we value him, but all the same we must not let him think himself all the truth in the universe."

"Then you want me not to let some previous conviction inure the receptivity of my mind with regard to some strange matter. Do I read your lesson aright?"

"Ah, you are my favourite pupil still. It is worth to teach you. Now that you are willing to understand, you have taken the first step to understand. You think then that those so small holes in the children's throats were made by the same that made the holes in Miss Lucy?"

"I suppose so."

He stood up and said solemnly, "Then you are wrong. Oh, would it were so! But alas! No. It is worse, far, far worse."

"In God's name, Professor Van Helsing, what do you mean?" I cried.

He threw himself with a despairing gesture into a chair, and placed his elbows on the table, covering his face with his hands as he spoke.

"They were made by Miss Lucy!"

℘ CHAPTER 15 ℀
DR. SEWARD'S DIARY—CONT.

For a while sheer anger mastered me. It was as if he had during her life struck Lucy on the face. I smote the table hard and rose up as I said to him, "Dr. Van Helsing, are you mad?"

He raised his head and looked at me, and somehow the tenderness of his face calmed me at once. "Would I were!" he said. "Madness were easy to bear compared with truth like this. Oh, my friend, why, think you, did I go so far round, why take so long to tell so simple a thing? Was it because I hate you and have hated you all my life? Was it because I wished to give you pain? Was it that I wanted, now so late, revenge for that time when you saved my life, and from a fearful death? Ah no!"

"Forgive me," said I.

He went on, "My friend, it was because I wished to be gentle in the breaking to you, for I know you have loved that so sweet lady. But even yet I do not expect you to believe. It is so hard to accept at once any abstract truth, that we may doubt such to be possible when we have always believed the 'no' of it. It is more hard still to accept so sad a concrete truth, and of such a one as Miss Lucy. Tonight I go to prove it. Dare you come with me?"

This staggered me. A man does not like to prove such a truth, Byron excepted from the category, jealousy.

"And prove the very truth he most abhorred."

He saw my hesitation, and spoke, "The logic is simple, no madman's logic this time, jumping from tussock to tussock in a misty bog. If it not be true, then proof will be relief. At worst it will not harm. If it be true! Ah, there is the dread. Yet every dread should help my cause, for in it is some need of belief. Come, I tell you what I propose. First, that we go off now and see that child in the hospital. Dr. Vincent, of the North Hospital, where the papers say the child is, is a friend of mine, and I think of yours since you were in class at Amsterdam. He will let two scientists see his case, if he will not let two friends. We shall tell him nothing, but only that we wish to learn. And then . . ."

"And then?"

He took a key from his pocket and held it up. "And then we spend the night, you and I, in the churchyard where Lucy lies. This is the key that lock the tomb. I had it from the coffin man to give to Arthur."

My heart sank within me, for I felt that there was some fearful ordeal before us. I could do nothing, however, so I plucked up what heart I could and said that we had better hasten, as the afternoon was passing.

We found the child awake. It had had a sleep and taken some food, and altogether was going on well. Dr. Vincent took the bandage from its throat, and showed us the punctures. There was no mistaking the similarity to those which had been on Lucy's throat. They were smaller, and the edges looked fresher, that was all. We asked Vincent to what he attributed them, and he replied that it must have been a bite of some animal, perhaps a rat, but for his own part, he was inclined to think it was one of the bats which are so numerous on the northern heights of London. "Out of so many harmless ones," he said, "there may be some wild specimen from the South of a more malignant species. Some sailor may have brought one home, and it managed to escape, or even from the Zoological Gardens a young one may have got loose, or one be bred there from a vampire. These things do occur, you, know. Only ten days ago a wolf got out, and was, I believe, traced up in this direction. For a week after, the children were playing nothing but Red Riding Hood on the Heath and in every alley in the place until this 'bloofer lady' scare came along, since then it has been quite a gala time with them. Even this poor little mite, when he woke up today, asked the nurse if he might go away. When she asked him why he wanted to go, he said he wanted to play with the 'bloofer lady'."

"I hope," said Van Helsing, "that when you are sending the child home you will caution its parents to keep strict watch over it. These fancies to stray are most dangerous, and if the child were to remain out another night, it would probably be fatal. But in any case I suppose you will not let it away for some days?"

"Certainly not, not for a week at least, longer if the wound is not healed."

Our visit to the hospital took more time than we had reckoned on, and the sun had dipped before we came out. When Van Helsing saw how dark it was, he said,

"There is not hurry. It is more late than I thought. Come, let us seek somewhere that we may eat, and then we shall go on our way."

We dined at 'Jack Straw's Castle' along with a little crowd of bicyclists and others who were genially noisy. About ten o'clock we started from the inn. It was then very dark, and the scattered lamps made the darkness greater when we were once outside their individual radius. The Professor had evidently noted the road we were to go, for he went on unhesitatingly, but, as for me, I was in quite a mixup as to locality. As we went further, we met fewer and fewer people, till at last we were somewhat surprised when we met even the patrol of horse police going their usual suburban round. At last we reached the wall of the churchyard, which we climbed over. With some little difficulty, for it was very dark, and the whole place seemed so strange to us, we found the Westenra tomb. The Professor took the key, opened the creaky door, and standing back, politely, but quite unconsciously, motioned me to precede him. There was a delicious irony in the offer, in the courtliness of giving preference on such a ghastly occasion. My companion followed me quickly, and cautiously drew the door to, after carefully ascertaining that the lock was a falling, and not a spring one. In the latter case we should have been in a bad plight. Then he fumbled in his bag, and taking out a matchbox and a piece of candle, proceeded to make a light. The tomb in the daytime, and when wreathed with fresh flowers, had looked grim and gruesome enough, but now, some days afterwards, when the flowers hung lank and dead, their whites turning to rust and their greens to browns, when the spider and the beetle had resumed their accustomed dominance, when the time-discoloured stone, and dust-encrusted mortar, and rusty, dank iron, and tarnished brass, and clouded silver-plating gave back the feeble glimmer of a candle, the effect was more miserable and sordid than could have been imagined. It conveyed irresistibly the idea that life, animal life, was not the only thing which could pass away.

Van Helsing went about his work systematically. Holding his candle so that he could read the coffin plates, and so holding it that the sperm dropped in white patches which congealed as they touched the metal, he made assurance of Lucy's coffin. Another search in his bag, and he took out a turnscrew.

"What are you going to do?" I asked.

"To open the coffin. You shall yet be convinced."

Straightway he began taking out the screws, and finally lifted off the lid, showing the casing of lead beneath. The sight was almost too much for me. It seemed to be as much an affront to the dead as it would have been to have stripped off her clothing in her sleep whilst living. I actually took hold of his hand to stop him.

He only said, "You shall see," and again fumbling in his bag took out a tiny fret saw. Striking the turnscrew through the lead with a swift downward stab, which made me wince, he made a small hole, which was, however, big enough to admit the point of the saw. I had expected a rush of gas from the week-old corpse. We doctors, who have had to study our dangers, have to become accustomed to such things, and I drew back towards the door. But the Professor never stopped for a moment. He sawed down a couple of feet along one side of the lead coffin, and then across, and down the other side. Taking the edge of the loose flange, he bent it back towards the foot of the coffin, and holding up the candle into the aperture, motioned to me to look.

I drew near and looked. The coffin was empty. It was certainly a surprise to me, and gave me a considerable shock, but Van Helsing was unmoved. He was now more sure than ever of his ground, and so emboldened to proceed in his task. "Are you satisfied now, friend John?" he asked.

I felt all the dogged argumentativeness of my nature awake within me as I answered him, "I am satisfied that Lucy's body is not in that coffin, but that only proves one thing."

"And what is that, friend John?"

"That it is not there."

"That is good logic," he said, "so far as it goes. But how do you, how can you, account for it not being there?"

"Perhaps a body-snatcher," I suggested. "Some of the undertaker's people may have stolen it." I felt that I was speaking folly, and yet it was the only real cause which I could suggest.

The Professor sighed. "Ah well!" he said, "we must have more proof. Come with me."

He put on the coffin lid again, gathered up all his things and placed them in the bag, blew out the light, and placed the candle also in the bag. We opened the door, and went out. Behind us he closed the door and locked it. He handed me the key, saying, "Will you keep it? You had better be assured."

I laughed, it was not a very cheerful laugh, I am bound to say, as I motioned him to keep it. "A key is nothing," I said, "there are many duplicates, and anyhow it is not difficult to pick a lock of this kind."

He said nothing, but put the key in his pocket. Then he told me to watch at one side of the churchyard whilst he would watch at the other.

I took up my place behind a yew tree, and I saw his dark figure move until the intervening headstones and trees hid it from my sight.

It was a lonely vigil. Just after I had taken my place I heard a distant clock strike twelve, and in time came one and two. I was chilled and unnerved, and angry with the Professor for taking me on such an errand and with myself for coming. I was too cold and too sleepy to be keenly observant, and not sleepy enough to betray my trust, so altogether I had a dreary, miserable time.

Suddenly, as I turned round, I thought I saw something like a white streak, moving between two dark yew trees at the side of the churchyard farthest from the tomb. At the same time a dark mass moved from the Professor's side of the ground, and hurriedly went towards it. Then I too moved, but I had to go round headstones and railed-off tombs, and I stumbled over graves. The sky was overcast, and somewhere far off an early cock crew. A little ways off, beyond a line of scattered juniper trees, which marked the pathway to the church, a white dim figure flitted in the direction of the tomb. The tomb itself was hidden by trees, and I could not see where the figure had disappeared. I heard the rustle of actual movement where I had first seen the white figure, and coming over, found the Professor holding in his arms a tiny child. When he saw me he held it out to me, and said, "Are you satisfied now?"

"No," I said, in a way that I felt was aggressive.

"Do you not see the child?"

"Yes, it is a child, but who brought it here? And is it wounded?"

"We shall see," said the Professor, and with one impulse we took our way out of the churchyard, he carrying the sleeping child.

When we had got some little distance away, we went into a clump of trees, and struck a match, and looked at the child's throat. It was without a scratch or scar of any kind.

"Was I right?" I asked triumphantly.

"We were just in time," said the Professor thankfully.

We had now to decide what we were to do with the child, and so consulted about it. If we were to take it to a police station we should have to give some account of our movements during the night. At least, we should have had to make some statement as to how we had come to find the child. So finally we decided that we would take it to the Heath, and when we heard a policeman coming, would leave it where he could not fail to find it. We would then seek our way home as quickly as we could. All fell out well. At the edge of Hampstead Heath we heard a policeman's heavy tramp, and laying the child on the pathway, we waited and watched until he saw it as he flashed his lantern to and fro. We heard his exclamation of astonishment, and then we went away silently. By good chance we got a cab near the 'Spainiards,' and drove to town.

I cannot sleep, so I make this entry. But I must try to get a few hours' sleep, as Van Helsing is to call for me at noon. He insists that I go with him on another expedition.

27 September.—It was two o'clock before we found a suitable opportunity for our attempt. The funeral held at noon was all completed, and the last stragglers of the mourners had taken themselves lazily away, when, looking carefully from behind a clump of alder trees, we saw the sexton lock the gate after him. We knew that we were safe till morning did we desire it, but the Professor told me that we should not want more than an hour at most. Again I felt that horrid sense of the reality of things, in which any effort of imagination seemed out of place, and I realized distinctly the perils of the law which we were incurring in our unhallowed work. Besides, I felt it was all so useless. Outrageous as it was to open a leaden coffin, to see if a woman dead nearly a week were really dead, it now seemed the height of folly to open the tomb again, when we knew, from the evidence of our own eyesight, that the coffin was empty. I shrugged my shoulders, however, and rested silent, for Van Helsing had a way of going on his own road, no matter who remonstrated. He took the key, opened the vault, and again courteously motioned me to precede. The place was not so gruesome as last night, but oh, how unutterably mean looking when the sunshine streamed in. Van Helsing walked over to Lucy's coffin, and I followed. He bent over and again forced back the leaden flange, and a shock of surprise and dismay shot through me.

There lay Lucy, seemingly just as we had seen her the night before her funeral. She was, if possible, more radiantly beautiful than ever, and I could not believe that she was dead. The lips were red, nay redder than before, and on the cheeks was a delicate bloom.

"Is this a juggle?" I said to him.

"Are you convinced now?" said the Professor, in response, and as he spoke he put over his hand, and in a way that made me shudder, pulled back the dead lips and showed the white teeth. "See," he went on, "they are even sharper than before. With this and this," and he touched one of the canine teeth and that below it, "the little children can be bitten. Are you of belief now, friend John?"

Once more argumentative hostility woke within me. I *could* not accept such an overwhelming idea as he suggested. So, with an attempt to argue of which I was even at the moment ashamed, I said, "She may have been placed here since last night."

"Indeed? That is so, and by whom?"

"I do not know. Someone has done it."

"And yet she has been dead one week. Most peoples in that time would not look so."

I had no answer for this, so was silent. Van Helsing did not seem to notice my silence. At any rate, he showed neither chagrin nor triumph. He was looking intently at the face of the dead woman, raising the eyelids and looking at the eyes, and once more opening the lips and examining the teeth. Then he turned to me and said,

"Here, there is one thing which is different from all recorded. Here is some dual life that is not as the common. She was bitten by the vampire when she was in a trance, sleep-walking, oh, you start. You do not know that, friend John, but you shall know it later, and in trance could he best come to take more blood. In trance she dies, and in trance she is UnDead, too. So it is that she differ from all other. Usually when the UnDead sleep at home," as he spoke he made a comprehensive sweep of his arm to designate what to a vampire was 'home', "their face show what they are, but this so sweet that was when she not UnDead she go back to the nothings of the common dead. There is no malign there, see, and so it make hard that I must kill her in her sleep."

This turned my blood cold, and it began to dawn upon me that I was accepting Van Helsing's theories. But if she were really dead, what was there of terror in the idea of killing her?

He looked up at me, and evidently saw the change in my face, for he said almost joyously, "Ah, you believe now?"

I answered, "Do not press me too hard all at once. I am willing to accept. How will you do this bloody work?"

"I shall cut off her head and fill her mouth with garlic, and I shall drive a stake through her body."

It made me shudder to think of so mutilating the body of the woman whom I had loved. And yet the feeling was not so strong as I had expected. I was, in fact, beginning to shudder at the presence of this being, this Un-Dead, as Van Helsing called it, and to loathe it. Is it possible that love is all subjective, or all objective?

I waited a considerable time for Van Helsing to begin, but he stood as if wrapped in thought. Presently he closed the catch of his bag with a snap, and said,

"I have been thinking, and have made up my mind as to what is best. If I did simply follow my inclining I would do now, at this moment, what is to be done. But there are other things to follow, and things that are thousand times more difficult in that them we do not know. This is simple. She have yet no life taken, though that is of time, and to act now would be to take danger from her forever. But then we may have to want Arthur, and how shall we tell him of this? If you, who saw the wounds on Lucy's throat, and saw the wounds so similar on the child's at the hospital, if you, who saw the coffin empty last night and full today with a woman who have not change only to be more rose and more beautiful in a whole week, after she die, if you know of this and know of the white figure last night that brought the child to the churchyard, and yet of your own senses you did not believe, how then, can I expect Arthur, who know none of those things, to believe?

"He doubted me when I took him from her kiss when she was dying. I know he has forgiven me because in some mistaken idea I have done things that prevent him say goodbye as he ought, and he may think that in some more mistaken idea this woman was buried alive, and that in most mistake of all we have killed her. He will then argue back that it is we, mistaken ones, that have killed her by our ideas, and so he will be much unhappy always. Yet he never can be sure, and that is the worst of all. And he will sometimes think that she he loved was buried alive, and that will paint his dreams with horrors of what she must have suffered, and again, he will think that we may be right, and that his so beloved was, after all, an Un-Dead. No! I told him once, and since then I learn much. Now, since I know it is all true, a hundred thousand times more do I know that he must pass through the bitter waters to reach the sweet. He, poor fellow, must have one hour that will make the very face of heaven grow black to him, then we can act for good all round and send him peace. My mind is made up. Let us go. You return home for tonight to your asylum, and see that all be well. As for me, I shall spend the night here in this churchyard in my own way. Tomorrow night you will come to me to the Berkeley Hotel at ten of the clock. I shall send for Arthur to come too, and also that so fine young man of America that gave his blood. Later we shall all have work to do. I come with you so far as Piccadilly and there dine, for I must be back here before the sun set."

So we locked the tomb and came away, and got over the wall of the churchyard, which was not much of a task, and drove back to Piccadilly.

NOTE LEFT BY VAN HELSING IN HIS PORTMANTEAU, BERKELEY HOTEL DIRECTED TO JOHN SEWARD, M. D.
(Not Delivered)

27 September

"Friend John,

"I write this in case anything should happen. I go alone to watch in that churchyard. It pleases me that the UnDead, Miss Lucy, shall not leave tonight, that so on the morrow night she may be more eager. Therefore I shall fix some things she like not, garlic and a crucifix, and so seal up the door of the tomb. She is young as UnDead, and will heed. Moreover, these are only to prevent her coming out. They may not prevail on her wanting to get in, for then the UnDead is desperate, and must find the line of least resistance, whatsoever it may be. I shall be at hand all the night from sunset till after sunrise, and if there be aught that may be learned I shall learn it. For Miss Lucy or from her, I have no fear, but that other to whom is there that she is UnDead, he have not the power to seek her tomb and find shelter. He is cunning, as I know from Mr. Jonathan and from the way that all along he have fooled us when he played with us for Miss Lucy's life, and we lost, and in many ways the UnDead are strong. He have always the strength in his hand of twenty men, even we four who gave our strength to Miss Lucy it also is all to him. Besides, he can summon his wolf and I know not what. So if it be that he came thither on this night he shall find me. But none other shall, until it be too late. But it may be that he will not attempt the place. There is no reason why he should. His hunting ground is more full of game than the churchyard where the UnDead woman sleeps, and the one old man watch.

"Therefore I write this in case . . . Take the papers that are with this, the diaries of Harker and the rest, and read them, and then find this great UnDead, and cut off his head and burn his heart or drive a stake through it, so that the world may rest from him.

"If it be so, farewell.

"Van Helsing."

DR. SEWARD'S DIARY

28 September.—It is wonderful what a good night's sleep will do for one. Yesterday I was almost willing to accept Van Helsing's monstrous ideas, but now they seem to start out lurid before me as outrages on common sense. I have no doubt that he believes it all. I wonder if his mind can have become in any way unhinged. Surely there must be *some* rational explanation of all these mysterious things. Is it possible that the Professor can have done it himself? He is so abnormally clever that if he went off his head he would carry out his intent with regard to some fixed idea in a wonderful way. I am loathe to think it, and indeed it would be almost as great a marvel as the other to find that Van Helsing was mad, but anyhow I shall watch him carefully. I may get some light on the mystery.

29 September.—Last night, at a little before ten o'clock, Arthur and Quincey came into Van Helsing's room. He told us all what he wanted us to do, but especially addressing himself to Arthur, as if all our wills were centred in his. He began by saying that he hoped we would all come with him too, "for," he said, "there is a grave duty to be done there. You were doubtless surprised at my letter?" This query was directly addressed to Lord Godalming.

"I was. It rather upset me for a bit. There has been so much trouble around my house of late that I could do without any more. I have been curious, too, as to what you mean.

"Quincey and I talked it over, but the more we talked, the more puzzled we got, till now I can say for myself that I'm about up a tree as to any meaning about anything."

"Me too," said Quincey Morris laconically.

"Oh," said the Professor, "then you are nearer the beginning, both of you, than friend John here, who has to go a long way back before he can even get so far as to begin."

It was evident that he recognized my return to my old doubting frame of mind without my saying a word. Then, turning to the other two, he said with intense gravity,

"I want your permission to do what I think good this night. It is, I know, much to ask, and when you know what it is I propose to do you will know, and only then how much. Therefore may I ask that you promise me in the dark, so that afterwards, though you may be angry with me for a time, I must not disguise from myself the possibility that such may be, you shall not blame yourselves for anything."

"That's frank anyhow," broke in Quincey. "I'll answer for the Professor. I don't quite see his drift, but I swear he's honest, and that's good enough for me."

"I thank you, Sir," said Van Helsing proudly. "I have done myself the honour of counting you one trusting friend, and such endorsement is dear to me." He held out a hand, which Quincey took.

Then Arthur spoke out, "Dr. Van Helsing, I don't quite like to 'buy a pig in a poke', as they say in Scotland, and if it be anything in which my honour as a gentleman or my faith as a Christian is concerned, I cannot make such a promise. If you can assure me that what you intend does not violate either of these two, then I give my consent at once, though for the life of me, I cannot understand what you are driving at."

"I accept your limitation," said Van Helsing, "and all I ask of you is that if you feel it necessary to condemn any act of mine, you will first consider it well and be satisfied that it does not violate your reservations."

"Agreed!" said Arthur. "That is only fair. And now that the *pourparlers*[107] are over, may I ask what it is we are to do?"

"I want you to come with me, and to come in secret, to the churchyard at Kingstead."

Arthur's face fell as he said in an amazed sort of way,

"Where poor Lucy is buried?"

The Professor bowed.

Arthur went on, "And when there?"

"To enter the tomb!"

Arthur stood up. "Professor, are you in earnest, or is it some monstrous joke? Pardon me, I see that you are in earnest." He sat down again, but I

---

107 Preliminary conference.

could see that he sat firmly and proudly, as one who is on his dignity. There was silence until he asked again, "And when in the tomb?"

"To open the coffin."

"This is too much!" he said, angrily rising again. "I am willing to be patient in all things that are reasonable, but in this, this desecration of the grave, of one who . . ." He fairly choked with indignation.

The Professor looked pityingly at him. "If I could spare you one pang, my poor friend," he said, "God knows I would. But this night our feet must tread in thorny paths, or later, and for ever, the feet you love must walk in paths of flame!"

Arthur looked up with set white face and said, "Take care, sir, take care!"

"Would it not be well to hear what I have to say?" said Van Helsing. "And then you will at least know the limit of my purpose. Shall I go on?"

"That's fair enough," broke in Morris.

After a pause Van Helsing went on, evidently with an effort, "Miss Lucy is dead, is it not so? Yes! Then there can be no wrong to her. But if she be not dead . . ."

Arthur jumped to his feet, "Good God!" he cried. "What do you mean? Has there been any mistake, has she been buried alive?" He groaned in anguish that not even hope could soften.

"I did not say she was alive, my child. I did not think it. I go no further than to say that she might be UnDead."

"UnDead! Not alive! What do you mean? Is this all a nightmare, or what is it?"

"There are mysteries which men can only guess at, which age by age they may solve only in part. Believe me, we are now on the verge of one. But I have not done. May I cut off the head of dead Miss Lucy?"

"Heavens and earth, no!" cried Arthur in a storm of passion. "Not for the wide world will I consent to any mutilation of her dead body. Dr. Van Helsing, you try me too far. What have I done to you that you should torture me so? What did that poor, sweet girl do that you should want to cast such dishonour on her grave? Are you mad, that you speak of such things, or am I mad to listen to them? Don't dare think more of such a desecration. I shall not give my consent to anything you do. I have a duty to do in protecting her grave from outrage, and by God, I shall do it!"

Van Helsing rose up from where he had all the time been seated, and said, gravely and sternly, "My Lord Godalming, I too, have a duty to do, a duty to others, a duty to you, a duty to the dead, and by God, I shall do it! All I ask you now is that you come with me, that you look and listen, and if when later I make the same request you do not be more eager for its fulfillment even than I am, then, I shall do my duty, whatever it may seem to me. And then, to follow your Lordship's wishes I shall hold myself at your disposal to render an account to you, when and where you will." His voice broke a little, and he went on with a voice full of pity.

"But I beseech you, do not go forth in anger with me. In a long life of acts which were often not pleasant to do, and which sometimes did wring my heart, I have never had so heavy a task as now. Believe me that if the time comes for you to change your mind towards me, one look from you will wipe away all this so sad hour, for I would do what a man can to save you from sorrow. Just think. For why should I give myself so much labor and so much of sorrow? I have come here from my own land to do what I can of good, at the first to please my friend John, and then to help a sweet young lady, whom too, I come to love. For her, I am ashamed to say so much, but I say it in kindness, I gave what you gave, the blood of my veins. I gave it, I who was not, like you, her lover, but only her physician and her friend. I gave her my nights and days, before death, after death, and if my death can do her good even now, when she is the dead UnDead, she shall have it freely." He said this with a very grave, sweet pride, and Arthur was much affected by it.

He took the old man's hand and said in a broken voice, "Oh, it is hard to think of it, and I cannot understand, but at least I shall go with you and wait."

ಣ CHAPTER 16 ೫

DR. SEWARD'S DIARY—CONT.

It was just a quarter before twelve o'clock when we got into the church-yard over the low wall. The night was dark with occasional gleams of moonlight between the dents of the heavy clouds that scudded across the sky. We all kept somehow close together, with Van Helsing slightly in front as he led the way. When we had come close to the tomb I looked well at Arthur, for I feared the proximity to a place laden with so sorrowful a memory would upset him, but he bore himself well. I took it that the very mystery of the proceeding was in some way a counteractant to his grief. The Professor unlocked the door, and seeing a natural hesitation amongst us for various reasons, solved the difficulty by entering first himself. The rest of us followed, and he closed the door. He then lit a dark lantern and pointed to a coffin. Arthur stepped forward hesitatingly. Van Helsing said to me, "You were with me here yesterday. Was the body of Miss Lucy in that coffin?"

"It was."

The Professor turned to the rest saying, "You hear, and yet there is no one who does not believe with me."

He took his screwdriver and again took off the lid of the coffin. Arthur looked on, very pale but silent. When the lid was removed he stepped forward. He evidently did not know that there was a leaden coffin, or at any rate, had not thought of it. When he saw the rent in the lead, the blood rushed to his face for an instant, but as quickly fell away again, so that he remained of a ghastly whiteness. He was still silent. Van Helsing forced back the leaden flange, and we all looked in and recoiled.

The coffin was empty!

For several minutes no one spoke a word. The silence was broken by Quincey Morris, "Professor, I answered for you. Your word is all I want. I wouldn't ask such a thing ordinarily, I wouldn't so dishonour you as to imply a doubt, but this is a mystery that goes beyond any honour or dishonour. Is this your doing?"

"I swear to you by all that I hold sacred that I have not removed or touched her. What happened was this. Two nights ago my friend Seward and I came here, with good purpose, believe me. I opened that coffin, which was then sealed up, and we found it as now, empty. We then waited, and saw something white come through the trees. The next day we came here in daytime and she lay there. Did she not, friend John?

"Yes."

"That night we were just in time. One more so small child was missing, and we find it, thank God, unharmed amongst the graves. Yesterday I came here before sundown, for at sundown the UnDead can move. I waited here all night till the sun rose, but I saw nothing. It was most probable that it was because I had laid over the clamps of those doors garlic, which the UnDead cannot bear, and other things which they shun. Last night there was no exodus, so tonight before the sundown I took away my garlic and other things. And so it is we find this coffin empty. But bear with me. So far there is much that is strange. Wait you with me outside, unseen and unheard, and things much stranger are yet to be. So," here he shut the dark slide of his lantern, "now to the outside." He opened the door, and we filed out, he coming last and locking the door behind him.

Oh! But it seemed fresh and pure in the night air after the terror of that vault. How sweet it was to see the clouds race by, and the passing gleams of the moonlight between the scudding clouds crossing and passing, like the gladness and sorrow of a man's life. How sweet it was to breathe the fresh air, that had no taint of death and decay. How humanizing to see the red lighting of the sky beyond the hill, and to hear far away the muffled roar that marks the life of a great city. Each in his own way was solemn and overcome. Arthur was silent, and was, I could see, striving to grasp the purpose and the inner meaning of the mystery. I was myself tolerably patient, and half inclined again to throw aside doubt and to accept Van Helsing's conclusions. Quincey Morris was phlegmatic in the way of a man who accepts all things, and accepts them in the spirit of cool bravery, with hazard of all he has at stake. Not being able to smoke, he cut himself a good-sized plug of tobacco and began to chew. As to Van Helsing, he was employed in a definite way. First he took from his bag a mass of what looked like thin, wafer-like biscuit, which was carefully rolled up in a white napkin. Next he took out a double handful of some whitish stuff, like dough or putty. He crumbled the wafer up fine and worked it into the mass between his hands. This he then took, and rolling it into thin strips, began to lay them into the crevices between the door and its setting in the tomb. I was somewhat puzzled at this, and being close, asked him what it was that he was doing. Arthur and Quincey drew near also, as they too were curious.

He answered, "I am closing the tomb so that the UnDead may not enter."
"And is that stuff you have there going to do it?"
"It is."
"What is that which you are using?" This time the question was by Arthur. Van Helsing reverently lifted his hat as he answered.
"The Host. I brought it from Amsterdam. I have an Indulgence."
It was an answer that appalled the most sceptical of us, and we felt individually that in the presence of such earnest purpose as the Professor's, a purpose which could thus use the to him most sacred of things, it was impossible to distrust. In respectful silence we took the places assigned to us close round the tomb, but hidden from the sight of any one approaching. I pitied the others, especially Arthur. I had myself been apprenticed by my former visits to this watching horror, and yet I, who had up to an hour ago repudiated the proofs, felt my heart sink within me. Never did tombs look so ghastly white. Never did cypress, or yew, or juniper so seem the embodiment of funeral gloom. Never did tree or grass wave or rustle so ominously. Never did bough creak so mysteriously, and never did the far-away howling of dogs send such a woeful presage through the night.

There was a long spell of silence, big, aching, void, and then from the Professor a keen "S-s-s-s!" He pointed, and far down the avenue of yews we saw a white figure advance, a dim white figure, which held something dark at its breast. The figure stopped, and at the moment a ray of moonlight fell upon the masses of driving clouds, and showed in startling prominence a dark-haired woman, dressed in the cerements of the grave. We could not see the face, for it was bent down over what we saw to be a fair-haired child.

There was a pause and a sharp little cry, such as a child gives in sleep, or a dog as it lies before the fire and dreams. We were starting forward, but the Professor's warning hand, seen by us as he stood behind a yew tree, kept us back. And then as we looked the white figure moved forwards again. It was now near enough for us to see clearly, and the moonlight still held. My own heart grew cold as ice, and I could hear the gasp of Arthur, as we recognized the features of Lucy Westenra. Lucy Westenra, but yet how changed. The sweetness was turned to adamantine, heartless cruelty, and the purity to voluptuous wantonness.

Van Helsing stepped out, and obedient to his gesture, we all advanced too. The four of us ranged in a line before the door of the tomb. Van Helsing raised his lantern and drew the slide. By the concentrated light that fell on Lucy's face we could see that the lips were crimson with fresh blood, and that the stream had trickled over her chin and stained the purity of her lawn death-robe.

We shuddered with horror. I could see by the tremulous light that even Van Helsing's iron nerve had failed. Arthur was next to me, and if I had not seized his arm and held him up, he would have fallen.

When Lucy, I call the thing that was before us Lucy because it bore her shape, saw us she drew back with an angry snarl, such as a cat gives when taken unawares, then her eyes ranged over us. Lucy's eyes in form and colour, but Lucy's eyes unclean and full of hell fire, instead of the pure, gentle orbs we knew. At that moment the remnant of my love passed into hate and loathing. Had she then to be killed, I could have done it with savage delight. As she looked, her eyes blazed with unholy light, and the face became wreathed with a voluptuous smile. Oh, God, how it made me shudder to see it! With a careless motion, she flung to the ground, callous as a devil, the child that up to now she had clutched strenuously to her breast, growling over it as a dog growls over a bone. The child gave a sharp cry, and lay there moaning. There was a cold-bloodedness in the act which wrung a groan from Arthur. When she advanced to him with outstretched arms and a wanton smile he fell back and hid his face in his hands.

She still advanced, however, and with a languorous, voluptuous grace, said, "Come to me, Arthur. Leave these others and come to me. My arms are hungry for you. Come, and we can rest together. Come, my husband, come!"

There was something diabolically sweet in her tones, something of the tinkling of glass when struck, which rang through the brains even of us who heard the words addressed to another.

As for Arthur, he seemed under a spell, moving his hands from his face, he opened wide his arms. She was leaping for them, when Van Helsing sprang forward and held between them his little golden crucifix. She recoiled from it, and, with a suddenly distorted face, full of rage, dashed past him as if to enter the tomb.

When within a foot or two of the door, however, she stopped, as if arrested by some irresistible force. Then she turned, and her face was shown in the clear burst of moonlight and by the lamp, which had now no quiver from Van Helsing's nerves. Never did I see such baffled malice on a face, and never, I trust, shall such ever be seen again by mortal eyes. The beautiful colour became livid, the eyes seemed to throw out sparks of hell fire, the brows were wrinkled as though the folds of flesh were the coils of Medusa's snakes, and the lovely, blood-stained mouth grew to an open square, as in the passion masks of the Greeks and Japanese. If ever a face meant death, if looks could kill, we saw it at that moment.

And so for full half a minute, which seemed an eternity, she remained between the lifted crucifix and the sacred closing of her means of entry.

Van Helsing broke the silence by asking Arthur, "Answer me, oh my friend! Am I to proceed in my work?"

"Do as you will, friend. Do as you will. There can be no horror like this ever any more." And he groaned in spirit.

Quincey and I simultaneously moved towards him, and took his arms. We could hear the click of the closing lantern as Van Helsing held it down. Coming close to the tomb, he began to remove from the chinks some of the sacred emblem which he had placed there. We all looked on with horrified amazement as we saw, when he stood back, the woman, with a corporeal body as real at that moment as our own, pass through the interstice where scarce a knife blade could have gone. We all felt a glad sense of relief when we saw the Professor calmly restoring the strings of putty to the edges of the door.

When this was done, he lifted the child and said, "Come now, my friends. We can do no more till tomorrow. There is a funeral at noon, so here we shall all come before long after that. The friends of the dead will all be gone by two, and when the sexton locks the gate we shall remain. Then there is more to do, but not like this of tonight. As for this little one, he is not much harmed, and by tomorrow night he shall be well. We shall leave him where the police will find him, as on the other night, and then to home."

Coming close to Arthur, he said, "My friend Arthur, you have had a sore trial, but after, when you look back, you will see how it was necessary. You are now in the bitter waters, my child. By this time tomorrow you will, please God, have passed them, and have drunk of the sweet waters. So do not mourn over-much. Till then I shall not ask you to forgive me."

Arthur and Quincey came home with me, and we tried to cheer each other on the way. We had left behind the child in safety, and were tired. So we all slept with more or less reality of sleep.

29 September, night.—A little before twelve o'clock we three, Arthur, Quincey Morris, and myself, called for the Professor. It was odd to notice that by common consent we had all put on black clothes. Of course, Arthur wore black, for he was in deep mourning, but the rest of us wore it by instinct. We got to the graveyard by half-past one, and strolled about, keeping out of official observation, so that when the gravediggers had completed their task and the sexton, under the belief that every one had gone, had locked the gate, we had the place all to ourselves. Van Helsing, instead of his little black bag, had with him a long leather one, something like a cricketing bag. It was manifestly of fair weight.

When we were alone and had heard the last of the footsteps die out up the road, we silently, and as if by ordered intention, followed the Professor to the tomb. He unlocked the door, and we entered, closing it behind us. Then he took from his bag the lantern, which he lit, and also two wax candles, which, when lighted, he stuck by melting their own ends, on other coffins, so that they might give light sufficient to work by. When he again lifted the lid off Lucy's coffin we all looked, Arthur trembling like an aspen, and saw that the corpse lay there in all its death beauty. But there was no love in my own heart, nothing but loathing for the foul Thing which had taken Lucy's shape without her soul. I could see even Arthur's face grow hard as he looked. Presently he said to Van Helsing, "Is this really Lucy's body, or only a demon in her shape?"

"It is her body, and yet not it. But wait a while, and you shall see her as she was, and is."

She seemed like a nightmare of Lucy as she lay there, the pointed teeth, the blood stained, voluptuous mouth, which made one shudder to see, the whole carnal and unspirited appearance, seeming like a devilish mockery of Lucy's sweet purity. Van Helsing, with his usual methodicalness, began taking the various contents from his bag and placing them ready for use. First he took out a soldering iron and some plumbing solder, and then small oil lamp, which gave out, when lit in a corner of the tomb, gas which burned at a fierce heat with a blue flame, then his operating knives, which he placed to hand, and last a round wooden stake, some two and a half or three inches thick and about three feet long. One end of it was hardened by charring in the fire, and was sharpened to a fine point. With this stake came a heavy hammer, such as in households is used in the coal cellar for breaking the lumps. To me, a doctor's preparations for work of any kind are stimulating and bracing, but the effect of these things on both Arthur and Quincey was to cause them a sort of consternation. They both, however, kept their courage, and remained silent and quiet.

When all was ready, Van Helsing said, "Before we do anything, let me tell you this. It is out of the lore and experience of the ancients and of all those who have studied the powers of the UnDead. When they become such, there comes with the change the curse of immortality. They cannot die, but must go on age after age adding new victims and multiplying the evils of the world. For all that die from the preying of the Undead become themselves Undead, and prey on their kind. And so the circle goes on ever widening, like as the ripples from a stone thrown in the water. Friend Arthur, if you had met that kiss which you know of before poor Lucy die, or again, last night when you open your arms to her, you would in time, when you had died, have become *nosferatu*, as they call it in Eastern Europe, and would for all time make more of those Un-Deads that so have filled us with horror. The career of this so unhappy dear lady is but just begun. Those children whose blood she sucked are not as yet so much the worse, but if she lives on, UnDead, more and more they lose their blood and by her power over them they come to her, and so she draw their blood with that so wicked mouth. But if she die in truth, then all cease. The tiny wounds of the throats disappear, and they go back to their play unknowing ever of what has been. But of the most blessed of all, when this now UnDead be made to rest as true dead, then the soul of the poor lady whom we love shall again be free. Instead of working wickedness by night and growing more debased in the assimilating of it by day, she shall take her place with the other Angels. So that, my friend, it will be a blessed hand for her that shall strike the blow that sets her free. To this I am willing, but is there none amongst us who has a better right? Will it be no joy to think of hereafter in the silence of the night when sleep is not, 'It was my hand that sent her to the stars. It was the hand of him that loved her best, the hand that of all she would herself have chosen, had it been to her to choose?' Tell me if there be such a one amongst us?"

We all looked at Arthur. He saw too, what we all did, the infinite kindness which suggested that his should be the hand which would restore Lucy to us as a holy, and not an unholy, memory. He stepped forward and said bravely, though his hand trembled, and his face was as pale as snow, "My true friend, from the bottom of my broken heart I thank you. Tell me what I am to do, and I shall not falter!"

Van Helsing laid a hand on his shoulder, and said, "Brave lad! A moment's courage, and it is done. This stake must be driven through her. It well be a fearful ordeal, be not deceived in that, but it will be only a short time, and you will then rejoice more than your pain was great. From this grim tomb you will emerge as though you tread on air. But you must not falter when once you have begun. Only think that we, your true friends, are round you, and that we pray for you all the time."

"Go on," said Arthur hoarsely. "Tell me what I am to do."

"Take this stake in your left hand, ready to place to the point over the heart, and the hammer in your right. Then when we begin our prayer for the dead, I shall read him, I have here the book, and the others shall follow, strike in God's name, that so all may be well with the dead that we love and that the UnDead pass away."

Arthur took the stake and the hammer, and when once his mind was set on action his hands never trembled nor even quivered. Van Helsing opened his missal and began to read, and Quincey and I followed as well as we could.

Arthur placed the point over the heart, and as I looked I could see its dint in the white flesh. Then he struck with all his might.

The thing in the coffin writhed, and a hideous, blood-curdling screech came from the opened red lips. The body shook and quivered and twisted in wild contortions. The sharp white teeth champed together till the lips were cut, and the mouth was smeared with a crimson foam. But Arthur never faltered. He looked like a figure of Thor as his untrembling arm rose and fell, driving deeper and deeper the mercy-bearing stake, whilst the blood from the pierced heart welled and spurted up around it. His face was set, and high duty seemed to shine through it. The sight of it gave us courage so that our voices seemed to ring through the little vault.

And then the writhing and quivering of the body became less, and the teeth seemed to champ, and the face to quiver. Finally it lay still. The terrible task was over.

The hammer fell from Arthur's hand. He reeled and would have fallen had we not caught him. The great drops of sweat sprang from his forehead, and his breath came in broken gasps. It had indeed been an awful strain on him, and had he not been forced to his task by more than human considerations he could never have gone through with it. For a few minutes we were so taken up with him that we did not look towards the coffin. When we did, however, a murmur of startled surprise ran from one to the other of us. We gazed so eagerly that Arthur rose, for he had been seated on the ground, and came and looked too, and then a glad strange light broke over his face and dispelled altogether the gloom of horror that lay upon it.

There, in the coffin lay no longer the foul Thing that we had so dreaded and grown to hate that the work of her destruction was yielded as a privilege to the one best entitled to it, but Lucy as we had seen her in life, with her face of unequalled sweetness and purity. True that there were there, as we had seen them in life, the traces of care and pain and waste. But these were all dear to us, for they marked her truth to what we knew. One and all we felt that the holy calm that lay like sunshine over the wasted face and form was only an earthly token and symbol of the calm that was to reign for ever.

Van Helsing came and laid his hand on Arthur's shoulder, and said to him, "And now, Arthur my friend, dear lad, am I not forgiven?"

The reaction of the terrible strain came as he took the old man's hand in his, and raising it to his lips, pressed it, and said, "Forgiven! God bless you that you have given my dear one her soul again, and me peace." He put his hands on the Professor's shoulder, and laying his head on his breast, cried for a while silently, whilst we stood unmoving.

When he raised his head Van Helsing said to him, "And now, my child, you may kiss her. Kiss her dead lips if you will, as she would have you to, if for her to choose. For she is not a grinning devil now, not any more a foul Thing for all eternity. No longer she is the devil's UnDead. She is God's true dead, whose soul is with Him!"

Arthur bent and kissed her, and then we sent him and Quincey out of the tomb. The Professor and I sawed the top off the stake, leaving the point of it in the body. Then we cut off the head and filled the mouth with garlic. We soldered up the leaden coffin, screwed on the coffin lid, and gathering up our belongings, came away. When the Professor locked the door he gave the key to Arthur.

Outside the air was sweet, the sun shone, and the birds sang, and it seemed as if all nature were tuned to a different pitch. There was gladness and mirth and peace everywhere, for we were at rest ourselves on one account, and we were glad, though it was with a tempered joy.

Before we moved away Van Helsing said, "Now, my friends, one step of our work is done, one the most harrowing to ourselves. But there remains a greater task: to find out the author of all this our sorrow and to stamp him out. I have clues which we can follow, but it is a long task, and a difficult one, and there is danger in it, and pain. Shall you not all help me? We have learned to believe, all of us, is it not so? And since so, do we not see our duty? Yes! And do we not promise to go on to the bitter end?"

Each in turn, we took his hand, and the promise was made. Then said the Professor as we moved off, "Two nights hence you shall meet with me and dine together at seven of the clock with friend John. I shall entreat two others, two that you know not as yet, and I shall be ready to all our work show and our plans unfold. Friend John, you come with me home, for I have much to consult you about, and you can help me. Tonight I leave for Amsterdam, but shall return tomorrow night. And then begins our great quest. But first I shall have much to say, so that you may know what to do and to dread. Then our promise shall be made to each other anew. For there is a terrible task before us, and once our feet are on the ploughshare we must not draw back."

ᴓ CHAPTER 17 ᴔ

DR. SEWARD'S DIARY—CONT.

When we arrived at the Berkely Hotel, Van Helsing found a telegram waiting for him.

"Am coming up by train. Jonathan at Whitby. Important news. *Mina Harker.*"

The Professor was delighted. "Ah, that wonderful Madam Mina," he said, "pearl among women! She arrive, but I cannot stay. She must go to your house, friend John. You must meet her at the station. Telegraph her *en route* so that she may be prepared."

When the wire was dispatched he had a cup of tea. Over it he told me of a diary kept by Jonathan Harker when abroad, and gave me a typewritten copy of it, as also of Mrs. Harker's diary at Whitby. "Take these," he said, "and study them well. When I have returned you will be master of all the facts, and we can then better enter on our inquisition. Keep them safe, for there is in them much of treasure. You will need all your faith, even you who have had such an experience as that of today. What is here told," he laid his hand heavily and gravely on the packet of papers as he spoke, "may be the beginning of the end to you and me and many another, or it may sound the knell of the UnDead who walk the earth. Read all, I pray you, with the open mind, and if you can add in any way to the story here told do so, for it is all important. You have kept a diary of all these so strange things, is it not so? Yes! Then we shall go through all these together when we meet." He then made ready for his departure and shortly drove off to Liverpool Street. I took my way to Paddington, where I arrived about fifteen minutes before the train came in.

The crowd melted away, after the bustling fashion common to arrival platforms, and I was beginning to feel uneasy, lest I might miss my guest, when a sweet-faced, dainty looking girl stepped up to me, and after a quick glance said, "Dr. Seward, is it not?"

"And you are Mrs. Harker!" I answered at once, whereupon she held out her hand.

"I knew you from the description of poor dear Lucy, but . . ." She stopped suddenly, and a quick blush overspread her face.

The blush that rose to my own cheeks somehow set us both at ease, for it was a tacit answer to her own. I got her luggage, which included a type-writer, and we took the Underground to Fenchurch Street, after I had sent a wire to my housekeeper to have a sitting room and a bedroom prepared at once for Mrs. Harker.

In due time we arrived. She knew, of course, that the place was a lunatic asylum, but I could see that she was unable to repress a shudder when we entered.

She told me that, if she might, she would come presently to my study, as she had much to say. So here I am finishing my entry in my phonograph diary whilst I await her. As yet I have not had the chance of looking at the papers which Van Helsing left with me, though they lie open before me. I must get her interested in something, so that I may have an opportunity of reading them. She does not know how precious time is, or what a task we have in hand. I must be careful not to frighten her. Here she is!

MINA HARKER'S JOURNAL

29 September.—After I had tidied myself, I went down to Dr. Seward's study. At the door I paused a moment, for I thought I heard him talking with some one. As, however, he had pressed me to be quick, I knocked at the door, and on his calling out, "Come in," I entered.

To my intense surprise, there was no one with him. He was quite alone, and on the table opposite him was what I knew at once from the description to be a phonograph. I had never seen one, and was much interested.

"I hope I did not keep you waiting," I said, "but I stayed at the door as I heard you talking, and thought there was someone with you."

"Oh," he replied with a smile, "I was only entering my diary."

"Your diary?" I asked him in surprise.

"Yes," he answered. "I keep it in this." As he spoke he laid his hand on the phonograph. I felt quite excited over it, and blurted out, "Why, this beats even shorthand! May I hear it say something?"

"Certainly," he replied with alacrity, and stood up to put it in train for speaking. Then he paused, and a troubled look overspread his face.

"The fact is," he began awkwardly, "I only keep my diary in it, and as it is entirely, almost entirely, about my cases it may be awkward, that is, I mean . . ." He stopped, and I tried to help him out of his embarrassment.

"You helped to attend dear Lucy at the end. Let me hear how she died, for all that I know of her, I shall be very grateful. She was very, very dear to me."

To my surprise, he answered, with a horrorstruck look in his face, "Tell you of her death? Not for the wide world!"

"Why not?" I asked, for some grave, terrible feeling was coming over me.

Again he paused, and I could see that he was trying to invent an excuse. At length, he stammered out, "You see, I do not know how to pick out any particular part of the diary."

Even while he was speaking an idea dawned upon him, and he said with unconscious simplicity, in a different voice, and with the naivete of a child, "that's quite true, upon my honour. Honest Indian!"

I could not but smile, at which he grimaced. "I gave myself away that time!" he said. "But do you know that, although I have kept the diary for months past, it never once struck me how I was going to find any particular part of it in case I wanted to look it up?"

By this time my mind was made up that the diary of a doctor who attended Lucy might have something to add to the sum of our knowledge of that terrible Being, and I said boldly, "Then, Dr. Seward, you had better let me copy it out for you on my typewriter."

He grew to a positively deathly pallor as he said, "No! No! No! For all the world. I wouldn't let you know that terrible story!"

Then it was terrible. My intuition was right! For a moment, I thought, and as my eyes ranged the room, unconsciously looking for something or some opportunity to aid me, they lit on a great batch of typewriting on the table. His eyes caught the look in mine, and without his thinking, followed their direction. As they saw the parcel he realized my meaning.

"You do not know me," I said. "When you have read those papers, my own diary and my husband's also, which I have typed, you will know me better. I have not faltered in giving every thought of my own heart in this cause. But, of course, you do not know me, yet, and I must not expect you to trust me so far."

He is certainly a man of noble nature. Poor dear Lucy was right about him. He stood up and opened a large drawer, in which were arranged in order a number of hollow cylinders of metal covered with dark wax, and said,

"You are quite right. I did not trust you because I did not know you. But I know you now, and let me say that I should have known you long ago. I know that Lucy told you of me. She told me of you too. May I make the only atonement in my power? Take the cylinders and hear them. The first half-dozen of them are personal to me, and they will not horrify you. Then you will know me better. Dinner will by then be ready. In the meantime I shall read over some of these documents, and shall be better able to understand certain things."

He carried the phonograph himself up to my sitting room and adjusted it for me. Now I shall learn something pleasant, I am sure. For it will tell me the other side of a true love episode of which I know one side already.

DR. SEWARD'S DIARY

29 September.—I was so absorbed in that wonderful diary of Jonathan Harker and that other of his wife that I let the time run on without thinking. Mrs. Harker was not down when the maid came to announce dinner, so I said, "She is possibly tired. Let dinner wait an hour," and I went on with my work. I had just finished Mrs. Harker's diary, when she came in. She looked sweetly pretty, but very sad, and her eyes were flushed with crying. This somehow moved me much. Of late I have had cause for tears, God knows! But the relief of them was denied me, and now the sight of those sweet eyes, brightened by recent tears, went straight to my heart. So I said as gently as I could, "I greatly fear I have distressed you."

"Oh, no, not distressed me," she replied. "But I have been more touched than I can say by your grief. That is a wonderful machine, but it is cruelly true. It told me, in its very tones, the anguish of your heart. It was like a soul crying out to Almighty God. No one must hear them spoken ever again! See, I have tried to be useful. I have copied out the words on my typewriter, and none other need now hear your heart beat, as I did."

"No one need ever know, shall ever know," I said in a low voice. She laid her hand on mine and said very gravely, "Ah, but they must!"

"Must! But why?" I asked.

"Because it is a part of the terrible story, a part of poor Lucy's death and all that led to it. Because in the struggle which we have before us to rid the earth of this terrible monster we must have all the knowledge and all the help which we can get. I think that the cylinders which you gave me contained more than you intended me to know. But I can see that there are in your record many lights to this dark mystery. You will let me help, will you not? I know all up to a certain point, and I see already, though your diary only took me to 7 September, how poor Lucy was beset, and how her terrible doom was being wrought out. Jonathan and I have been working day and night since Professor Van Helsing saw us. He is gone to Whitby to get more information, and he will be here tomorrow to help us. We need have no secrets amongst us. Working together and with absolute trust, we can surely be stronger than if some of us were in the dark."

She looked at me so appealingly, and at the same time manifested such courage and resolution in her bearing, that I gave in at once to her wishes. "You shall," I said, "do as you like in the matter. God forgive me if I do wrong! There are terrible things yet to learn of, but if you have so far traveled on the road to poor Lucy's death, you will not be content, I know, to remain in the dark. Nay, the end, the very end, may give you a gleam of peace. Come, there is dinner. We must keep one another strong for what is before us. We have a cruel and dreadful task. When you have eaten you shall learn the rest, and I shall answer any questions you ask, if there be anything which you do not understand, though it was apparent to us who were present."

MINA HARKER'S JOURNAL

29 September.—After dinner I came with Dr. Seward to his study. He brought back the phonograph from my room, and I took a chair, and arranged the phonograph so that I could touch it without getting up, and showed me how to stop it in case I should want to pause. Then he very thoughtfully took a chair, with his back to me, so that I might be as free as possible, and began to read. I put the forked metal to my ears and listened.

When the terrible story of Lucy's death, and all that followed, was done, I lay back in my chair powerless. Fortunately I am not of a fainting disposition. When Dr. Seward saw me he jumped up with a horrified exclamation, and hurriedly taking a case bottle from the cupboard, gave me some brandy, which in a few minutes somewhat restored me. My brain was all in a whirl, and only that there came through all the multitude of horrors, the holy ray of light that my dear Lucy was at last at peace, I do not think I could have borne it without making a scene. It is all so wild and mysterious, and strange that if I had not known Jonathan's experience in Transylvania I could not have believed. As it was, I didn't know what to believe, and so got out of my difficulty by attending to something else. I took the cover off my typewriter, and said to Dr. Seward,

"Let me write this all out now. We must be ready for Dr. Van Helsing when he comes. I have sent a telegram to Jonathan to come on here when he arrives in London from Whitby. In this matter dates are everything, and

I think that if we get all of our material ready, and have every item put in chronological order, we shall have done much.

"You tell me that Lord Godalming and Mr. Morris are coming too. Let us be able to tell them when they come."

He accordingly set the phonograph at a slow pace, and I began to type-write from the beginning of the seventeenth cylinder. I used manifold, and so took three copies of the diary, just as I had done with the rest. It was late when I got through, but Dr. Seward went about his work of going his round of the patients. When he had finished he came back and sat near me, reading, so that I did not feel too lonely whilst I worked. How good and thoughtful he is. The world seems full of good men, even if there are monsters in it.

Before I left him I remembered what Jonathan put in his diary of the Professor's perturbation at reading something in an evening paper at the station at Exeter, so, seeing that Dr. Seward keeps his newspapers, I borrowed the files of 'The Westminster Gazette' and 'The Pall Mall Gazette' and took them to my room. I remember how much the 'Dailygraph' and 'The Whitby Gazette', of which I had made cuttings, had helped us to understand the terrible events at Whitby when Count Dracula landed, so I shall look through the evening papers since then, and perhaps I shall get some new light. I am not sleepy, and the work will help to keep me quiet.

DR. SEWARD'S DIARY

30 September.—Mr. Harker arrived at nine o'clock. He got his wife's wire just before starting. He is uncommonly clever, if one can judge from his face, and full of energy. If this journal be true, and judging by one's own wonderful experiences, it must be, he is also a man of great nerve. That going down to the vault a second time was a remarkable piece of daring. After reading his account of it I was prepared to meet a good specimen of manhood, but hardly the quiet, businesslike gentleman who came here today.

Later.—After lunch Harker and his wife went back to their own room, and as I passed a while ago I heard the click of the typewriter. They are hard at it. Mrs. Harker says that they are knitting together in chronological order every scrap of evidence they have. Harker has got the letters between the consignee of the boxes at Whitby and the carriers in London who took charge of them. He is now reading his wife's transcript of my diary. I wonder what they make out of it. Here it is . . .

Strange that it never struck me that the very next house might be the Count's hiding place! Goodness knows that we had enough clues from the conduct of the patient Renfield! The bundle of letters relating to the purchase of the house were with the transcript. Oh, if we had only had them earlier we might have saved poor Lucy! Stop! That way madness lies! Harker has gone back, and is again collecting material. He says that by dinner time they will be able to show a whole connected narrative. He thinks that in the meantime I should see Renfield, as hitherto he has been a sort of index to the coming and going of the Count. I hardly see this yet, but when I get at the dates I suppose I shall. What a good thing that Mrs. Harker put my cylinders into type! We never could have found the dates otherwise.

I found Renfield sitting placidly in his room with his hands folded, smiling benignly. At the moment he seemed as sane as any one I ever saw. I sat down and talked with him on a lot of subjects, all of which he treated naturally. He then, of his own accord, spoke of going home, a subject he has never mentioned to my knowledge during his sojourn here. In fact, he spoke quite confidently of getting his discharge at once. I believe that, had I not had the chat with Harker and read the letters and the dates of his outbursts, I should have been prepared to sign for him after a brief time of observation. As it is, I am darkly suspicious. All those out-breaks were in some way linked with the proximity of the Count. What then does this absolute content mean? Can it be that his instinct is satisfied as to the vampire's ultimate triumph? Stay. He is himself zoophagous, and in his wild ravings outside the chapel door of the deserted house he always spoke of 'master'. This all seems confirmation of our idea. However, after a while I came away. My friend is just a little too sane at present to make it safe to probe him too deep with questions. He might begin to think, and then . . . So I came away. I mistrust these quiet moods of his, so I have given the attendant a hint to look closely after him, and to have a strait waistcoat ready in case of need.

JONATHAN HARKER'S JOURNAL

29 September, in train to London.—When I received Mr. Billington's courteous message that he would give me any information in his power I thought it best to go down to Whitby and make, on the spot, such inquiries as I wanted. It was now my object to trace that horrid cargo of the Count's to its place in London. Later, we may be able to deal with it. Billington junior, a nice lad, met me at the station, and brought me to his father's house, where they had decided that I must spend the night. They are hospitable, with true Yorkshire hospitality, give a guest everything and leave him to do as he likes. They all knew that I was busy, and that my stay was short, and Mr. Billington had ready in his office all the papers concerning the consignment of boxes. It gave me almost a turn to see again one of the letters which I had seen on the Count's table before I knew of his diabolical plans. Everything had been carefully thought out, and done systematically and with precision. He seemed to have been prepared for every obstacle which might be placed by accident in the way of his intentions being carried out. To use an Americanism, he had 'taken no chances', and the absolute accuracy with which his instructions were fulfilled was simply the logical result of his care. I saw the invoice, and took note of it. 'Fifty cases of common earth, to be used for experimental purposes'. Also the copy of the letter to Carter Paterson, and their reply. Of both these I got copies. This was all the information Mr. Billington could give me, so I went down to the port and saw the coastguards, the Customs Officers and the harbour master, who kindly put me in communication with the men who had actually received the boxes. Their tally was exact with the list, and they had nothing to add to the simple description 'fifty cases of common earth', except that the boxes were 'main and mortal heavy', and that shifting them was dry work. One of them added that it was hard lines that there wasn't any gentleman 'such like as like yourself, squire', to show some sort of appreciation of their efforts in a liquid form. Another put in a rider that the thirst then generated was such that even the time which had elapsed had not completely allayed it. Needless to add, I took care before leaving to lift, forever and adequately, this source of reproach.

30 September.—The station master was good enough to give me a line to his old companion the station master at King's Cross, so that when I arrived there in the morning I was able to ask him about the arrival of the boxes. He, too put me at once in communication with the proper officials, and I saw that their tally was correct with the original invoice. The opportunities of acquiring an abnormal thirst had been here limited. A noble use of them had, however, been made, and again I was compelled to deal with the result in *ex post facto* manner.

From thence I went to Carter Paterson's central office, where I met with the utmost courtesy. They looked up the transaction in their day book and letter book, and at once telephoned to their King's Cross office for more details. By good fortune, the men who did the teaming were waiting for work, and the official at once sent them over, sending also by one of them the waybill and all the papers connected with the delivery of the boxes at Carfax. Here again I found the tally agreeing exactly. The carriers' men were able to supplement the paucity of the written words with a few more details. These were, I shortly found, connected almost solely with the dusty nature of the job, and the consequent thirst engendered in the operators. On my affording an opportunity, through the medium of the currency of the realm, of the allaying, at a later period, this beneficial evil, one of the men remarked,

"That 'ere 'ouse, guv'nor, is the rummiest I ever was in. Blyme! But it ain't been touched sence a hundred years. There was dust that thick in the place that you might have slep' on it without 'urtin' of yer bones. An' the place was that neglected that yer might 'ave smelled ole Jerusalem in it. But the old chapel, that took the cike, that did! Me and my mate, we thort we wouldn't never git out quick enough. Lor', I wouldn't take less nor a quid a moment to stay there arter dark."

Having been in the house, I could well believe him, but if he knew what I know, he would, I think have raised his terms.

Of one thing I am now satisfied. That *all* those boxes which arrived at Whitby from Varna in the *Demeter* were safely deposited in the old chapel at Carfax. There should be fifty of them there, unless any have since been removed, as from Dr. Seward's diary I fear.

Later.—Mina and I have worked all day, and we have put all the papers into order.

MINA HARKER'S JOURNAL

30 September.—I am so glad that I hardly know how to contain myself. It is, I suppose, the reaction from the haunting fear which I have had, that this terrible affair and the reopening of his old wound might act detrimentally on Jonathan. I saw him leave for Whitby with as brave a face as could, but I was sick with apprehension. The effort has, however, done him good. He was never so resolute, never so strong, never so full of volcanic energy, as at present. It is just as that dear, good Professor Van Helsing said, he is true grit, and he improves under strain that would kill a weaker nature. He came back full of life and hope and determination. We have got everything in order for tonight. I feel myself quite wild with excitement. I suppose one ought to pity anything so hunted as the Count. That is just it. This thing is not human, not even a beast. To read Dr. Seward's account of poor Lucy's death, and what followed, is enough to dry up the springs of pity in one's heart.

Later.—Lord Godalming and Mr. Morris arrived earlier than we expected. Dr. Seward was out on business, and had taken Jonathan with him, so I had to see them. It was to me a painful meeting, for it brought back all poor dear Lucy's hopes of only a few months ago. Of course they had heard Lucy speak of me, and it seemed that Dr. Van Helsing, too, had been quite 'blowing my trumpet', as Mr. Morris expressed it. Poor fellows, neither of them is aware that I know all about the proposals they made to Lucy. They did not quite know what to say or do, as they were ignorant of the amount of my knowledge. So they had to keep on neutral subjects. However, I thought the matter over, and came to the conclusion that the best thing I could do would be to post them on affairs right up to date. I knew from Dr. Seward's diary that they had been at Lucy's death, her real death, and that I need not fear to betray any secret before the time. So I told them, as well as I could, that I had read all the papers and diaries, and that my husband and I, having typewritten them, had just finished putting them in order. I gave them each a copy to read in the library. When Lord Godalming got his and turned it over, it does make a pretty good pile, he said, "Did you write all this, Mrs. Harker?"

I nodded, and he went on.

"I don't quite see the drift of it, but you people are all so good and kind, and have been working so earnestly and so energetically, that all I can do is to accept your ideas blindfold and try to help you. I have had one lesson already in accepting facts that should make a man humble to the last hour of his life. Besides, I know you loved my Lucy . . ."

Here he turned away and covered his face with his hands. I could hear the tears in his voice. Mr. Morris, with instinctive delicacy, just laid a hand for a moment on his shoulder, and then walked quietly out of the room. I suppose there is something in a woman's nature that makes a man free to break down before her and express his feelings on the tender or emotional side without feeling it derogatory to his manhood. For when Lord Godalming found himself alone with me he sat down on the sofa and gave way utterly and openly. I sat down beside him and took his hand. I hope he didn't think it forward of me, and that if he ever thinks of it afterwards he never will have such a thought. There I wrong him. I *know* he never will. He is too true a gentleman. I said to him, for I could see that his heart was breaking, "I loved dear Lucy, and I know what she was to you, and what you were to her. She and I were like sisters, and now she is gone, will you not let me be like a sister to you in your trouble? I know what sorrows you have had, though I cannot measure the depth of them. If sympathy and pity can help in your affliction, won't you let me be of some little service, for Lucy's sake?"

In an instant the poor dear fellow was overwhelmed with grief. It seemed to me that all that he had of late been suffering in silence found a vent at once. He grew quite hysterical, and raising his open hands, beat his palms together in a perfect agony of grief. He stood up and then sat down again, and the tears rained down his cheeks. I felt an infinite pity for him, and opened my arms unthinkingly. With a sob he laid his head on my shoulder and cried like a wearied child, whilst he shook with emotion.

We women have something of the mother in us that makes us rise above smaller matters when the mother spirit is invoked. I felt this big sorrowing man's head resting on me, as though it were that of a baby that some day may lie on my bosom, and I stroked his hair as though he were my own child. I never thought at the time how strange it all was.

After a little bit his sobs ceased, and he raised himself with an apology, though he made no disguise of his emotion. He told me that for days and nights past, weary days and sleepless nights, he had been unable to speak with any one, as a man must speak in his time of sorrow. There was no woman whose sympathy could be given to him, or with whom, owing to the terrible circumstance with which his sorrow was surrounded, he could speak freely.

"I know now how I suffered," he said, as he dried his eyes, "but I do not know even yet, and none other can ever know, how much your sweet sympathy has been to me today. I shall know better in time, and believe me that, though I am not ungrateful now, my gratitude will grow with my understanding. You will let me be like a brother, will you not, for all our lives, for dear Lucy's sake?"

"For dear Lucy's sake," I said as we clasped hands. "Ay, and for your own sake," he added, "for if a man's esteem and gratitude are ever worth the winning, you have won mine today. If ever the future should bring to you a time when you need a man's help, believe me, you will not call in vain. God grant that no such time may ever come to you to break the sunshine of your life, but if it should ever come, promise me that you will let me know."

He was so earnest, and his sorrow was so fresh, that I felt it would comfort him, so I said, "I promise."

As I came along the corridor I saw Mr. Morris looking out of a window. He turned as he heard my footsteps. "How is Art?" he said. Then noticing my red eyes, he went on, "Ah, I see you have been comforting him. Poor old fellow! He needs it. No one but a woman can help a man when he is in trouble of the heart, and he had no one to comfort him."

He bore his own trouble so bravely that my heart bled for him. I saw the manuscript in his hand, and I knew that when he read it he would realize how much I knew, so I said to him, "I wish I could comfort all who suffer from the heart. Will you let me be your friend, and will you come to me for comfort if you need it? You will know later why I speak."

He saw that I was in earnest, and stooping, took my hand, and raising it to his lips, kissed it. It seemed but poor comfort to so brave and unselfish a soul, and impulsively I bent over and kissed him. The tears rose in his eyes, and there was a momentary choking in his throat. He said quite calmly, "Little girl, you will never forget that true hearted kindness, so long as ever you live!" Then he went into the study to his friend.

"Little girl!" The very words he had used to Lucy, and, oh, but he proved himself a friend.

ℬ CHAPTER 18 ℛ

DR. SEWARD'S DIARY

30 September.—I got home at five o'clock, and found that Godalming and Morris had not only arrived, but had already studied the transcript of the various diaries and letters which Harker had not yet returned from his visit to the carriers' men, of whom Dr. Hennessey had written to me. Mrs. Harker gave us a cup of tea, and I can honestly say that, for the first time since I have lived in it, this old house seemed like *home.* When we had finished, Mrs. Harker said,

"Dr. Seward, may I ask a favour? I want to see your patient, Mr. Renfield. Do let me see him. What you have said of him in your diary interests me so much!"

She looked so appealing and so pretty that I could not refuse her, and there was no possible reason why I should, so I took her with me. When I went into the room, I told the man that a lady would like to see him, to which he simply answered, "Why?"

"She is going through the house, and wants to see every one in it," I answered.

"Oh, very well," he said, "let her come in, by all means, but just wait a minute till I tidy up the place."

His method of tidying was peculiar, he simply swallowed all the flies and spiders in the boxes before I could stop him. It was quite evident that he feared, or was jealous of, some interference. When he had got through his disgusting task, he said cheerfully, "Let the lady come in," and sat down on the edge of his bed with his head down, but with his eyelids raised so that he could see her as she entered. For a moment I thought that he might have some homicidal intent. I remembered how quiet he had been just before he attacked me in my own study, and I took care to stand where I could seize him at once if he attempted to make a spring at her.

She came into the room with an easy gracefulness which would at once command the respect of any lunatic, for easiness is one of the qualities mad people most respect. She walked over to him, smiling pleasantly, and held out her hand.

"Good evening, Mr. Renfield," said she. "You see, I know you, for Dr. Seward has told me of you." He made no immediate reply, but eyed her all over intently with a set frown on his face. This look gave way to one of wonder, which merged in doubt, then to my intense astonishment he said, "You're not the girl the doctor wanted to marry, are you? You can't be, you know, for she's dead."

Mrs. Harker smiled sweetly as she replied, "Oh no! I have a husband of my own, to whom I was married before I ever saw Dr. Seward, or he me. I am Mrs. Harker."

"Then what are you doing here?"

"My husband and I are staying on a visit with Dr. Seward."

"Then don't stay."

"But why not?"

I thought that this style of conversation might not be pleasant to Mrs. Harker, any more than it was to me, so I joined in, "How did you know I wanted to marry anyone?"

His reply was simply contemptuous, given in a pause in which he turned his eyes from Mrs. Harker to me, instantly turning them back again, "What an asinine question!"

"I don't see that at all, Mr. Renfield," said Mrs. Harker, at once championing me.

He replied to her with as much courtesy and respect as he had shown contempt to me, "You will, of course, understand, Mrs. Harker, that when a man is so loved and honoured as our host is, everything regarding him is of interest in our little community. Dr. Seward is loved not only by his household and his friends, but even by his patients, who, being some of them hardly in mental equilibrium, are apt to distort causes and effects. Since I myself have been an inmate of a lunatic asylum, I cannot but notice that the sophistic tendencies of some of its inmates lean towards the errors of *non causae* and *ignoratio elenche*.[108]"

I positively opened my eyes at this new development. Here was my own pet lunatic, the most pronounced of his type that I had ever met with, talking elemental philosophy, and with the manner of a polished gentleman. I

---

108 Respectively, 'there is no reason' and 'ignorance of the charge' (Latin).

wonder if it was Mrs. Harker's presence which had touched some chord in his memory. If this new phase was spontaneous, or in any way due to her unconscious influence, she must have some rare gift or power.

We continued to talk for some time, and seeing that he was seemingly quite reasonable, she ventured, looking at me questioningly as she began, to lead him to his favourite topic. I was again astonished, for he addressed himself to the question with the impartiality of the completest sanity. He even took himself as an example when he mentioned certain things.

"Why, I myself am an instance of a man who had a strange belief. Indeed, it was no wonder that my friends were alarmed, and insisted on my being put under control. I used to fancy that life was a positive and perpetual entity, and that by consuming a multitude of live things, no matter how low in the scale of creation, one might indefinitely prolong life. At times I held the belief so strongly that I actually tried to take human life. The doctor here will bear me out that on one occasion I tried to kill him for the purpose of strengthening my vital powers by the assimilation with my own body of his life through the medium of his blood, relying of course, upon the Scriptural phrase, 'For the blood is the life.' Though, indeed, the vendor of a certain nostrum has vulgarized the truism to the very point of contempt. Isn't that true, doctor?"

I nodded assent, for I was so amazed that I hardly knew what to either think or say, it was hard to imagine that I had seen him eat up his spiders and flies not five minutes before. Looking at my watch, I saw that I should go to the station to meet Van Helsing, so I told Mrs. Harker that it was time to leave.

She came at once, after saying pleasantly to Mr. Renfield, "Goodbye, and I hope I may see you often, under auspices pleasanter to yourself."

To which, to my astonishment, he replied, "Goodbye, my dear. I pray God I may never see your sweet face again. May He bless and keep you!"

When I went to the station to meet Van Helsing I left the boys behind me. Poor Art seemed more cheerful than he has been since Lucy first took ill, and Quincey is more like his own bright self than he has been for many a long day.

Van Helsing stepped from the carriage with the eager nimbleness of a boy. He saw me at once, and rushed up to me, saying, "Ah, friend John, how goes all? Well? So! I have been busy, for I come here to stay if need be. All affairs are settled with me, and I have much to tell. Madam Mina is with you? Yes. And her so fine husband? And Arthur and my friend Quincey, they are with you, too? Good!"

As I drove to the house I told him of what had passed, and of how my own diary had come to be of some use through Mrs. Harker's suggestion, at which the Professor interrupted me.

"Ah, that wonderful Madam Mina! She has man's brain, a brain that a man should have were he much gifted, and a woman's heart. The good God fashioned her for a purpose, believe me, when He made that so good combination. Friend John, up to now fortune has made that woman of help to us, after tonight she must not have to do with this so terrible affair. It is not good that she run a risk so great. We men are determined, nay, are we not pledged, to destroy this monster? But it is no part for a woman. Even if she be not harmed, her heart may fail her in so much and so many horrors and hereafter she may suffer, both in waking, from her nerves, and in sleep, from her dreams. And, besides, she is young woman and not so long married, there may be other things to think of some time, if not now. You tell me she has wrote all, then she must consult with us, but tomorrow she say goodbye to this work, and we go alone."

I agreed heartily with him, and then I told him what we had found in his absence, that the house which Dracula had bought was the very next one to my own. He was amazed, and a great concern seemed to come on him.

"Oh that we had known it before!" he said, "for then we might have reached him in time to save poor Lucy. However, 'the milk that is spilt cries not out afterwards,' as you say. We shall not think of that, but go on our way to the end." Then he fell into a silence that lasted till we entered my own gateway. Before we went to prepare for dinner he said to Mrs. Harker, "I am told, Madam Mina, by my friend John that you and your husband have put up in exact order all things that have been, up to this moment."

"Not up to this moment, Professor," she said impulsively, "but up to this morning."

"But why not up to now? We have seen hitherto how good light all the little things have made. We have told our secrets, and yet no one who has told is the worse for it."

Mrs. Harker began to blush, and taking a paper from her pockets, she said, "Dr. Van Helsing, will you read this, and tell me if it must go in. It is my record of today. I too have seen the need of putting down at present everything, however trivial, but there is little in this except what is personal. Must it go in?"

The Professor read it over gravely, and handed it back, saying, "It need not go in if you do not wish it, but I pray that it may. It can but make your husband love you the more, and all us, your friends, more honour you, as well as more esteem and love." She took it back with another blush and a bright smile.

And so now, up to this very hour, all the records we have are complete and in order. The Professor took away one copy to study after dinner, and before our meeting, which is fixed for nine o'clock. The rest of us have already read everything, so when we meet in the study we shall all be informed as to facts, and can arrange our plan of battle with this terrible and mysterious enemy.

MINA HARKER'S JOURNAL

30 September.—When we met in Dr. Seward's study two hours after dinner, which had been at six o'clock, we unconsciously formed a sort of board or committee. Professor Van Helsing took the head of the table, to which Dr. Seward motioned him as he came into the room. He made me sit next to him on his right, and asked me to act as secretary. Jonathan sat next to me. Opposite us were Lord Godalming, Dr. Seward, and Mr. Morris, Lord Godalming being next the Professor, and Dr. Seward in the centre.

The Professor said, "I may, I suppose, take it that we are all acquainted with the facts that are in these papers." We all expressed assent, and he went on, "Then it were, I think, good that I tell you something of the kind of enemy with which we have to deal. I shall then make known to you something of the history of this man, which has been ascertained for me. So we then can discuss how we shall act, and can take our measure according.

"There are such beings as vampires, some of us have evidence that they exist. Even had we not the proof of our own unhappy experience, the teachings and the records of the past give proof enough for sane peoples. I admit that at the first I was sceptic. Were it not that through long years I have trained myself to keep an open mind, I could not have believed until such time as that fact thunder on my ear. 'See! See! I prove, I prove.' Alas! Had I known at first what now I know, nay, had I even guess at him, one so precious life had been spared to many of us who did love her. But that is gone, and we must so work, that other poor souls perish not, whilst we can save. The *nosferatu* do not die like the bee when he sting once. He is only stronger, and being stronger, have yet more power to work evil. This vampire which is amongst us is of himself so strong in person as twenty men, he is of cunning more than mortal, for his cunning be the growth of ages, he have still the aids of necromancy, which is, as his etymology imply, the divination by the dead, and all the dead that he can come nigh to are for him at command; he is brute, and more than brute; he is devil in callous, and the heart of him is not; he can, within his range, direct the elements, the storm, the fog, the thunder; he can command all the meaner things, the rat, and the owl, and the bat, the moth, and the fox, and the wolf, he can grow and become small; and he can at times vanish and come unknown. How then are we to begin our strike to destroy him? How shall we find his where, and having found it, how can we destroy? My friends, this is much, it is a terrible task that we undertake, and there may be consequence to make the brave shudder. For if we fail in this our fight he must surely win, and then where end we? Life is nothings, I heed him not. But to fail here, is not mere life or death. It is that we become as him, that we henceforward become foul things of the night like him, without heart or conscience, preying on the bodies and the souls of those we love best. To us forever are the gates of heaven shut, for who shall open them to us again? We go on for all time abhorred by all, a blot on the face of God's sunshine, an arrow in the side of Him who died for man. But we are face to face with duty, and in such case must we shrink? For me, I say no, but then I am old, and life, with his sunshine, his fair places, his song of birds, his music and his love, lie far behind. You others are young. Some have seen sorrow, but there are fair days yet in store. What say you?"

Whilst he was speaking, Jonathan had taken my hand. I feared, oh so much, that the appalling nature of our danger was overcoming him when I saw his hand stretch out, but it was life to me to feel its touch, so strong, so self reliant, so resolute. A brave man's hand can speak for itself, it does not even need a woman's love to hear its music.

When the Professor had done speaking my husband looked in my eyes, and I in his, there was no need for speaking between us.

"I answer for Mina and myself," he said.

"Count me in, Professor," said Mr. Quincey Morris, laconically as usual.

"I am with you," said Lord Godalming, "for Lucy's sake, if for no other reason."

Dr. Seward simply nodded.

The Professor stood up and, after laying his golden crucifix on the table, held out his hand on either side. I took his right hand, and Lord Godalming his left, Jonathan held my right with his left and stretched across to Mr. Morris. So as we all took hands our solemn compact was made. I felt my heart icy cold, but it did not even occur to me to draw back. We resumed our places, and Dr. Van Helsing went on with a sort of cheerfulness which showed that the serious work had begun. It was to be taken as gravely, and in as businesslike a way, as any other transaction of life.

"Well, you know what we have to contend against, but we too, are not without strength. We have on our side power of combination, a power denied to the vampire kind, we have sources of science, we are free to act and think, and the hours of the day and the night are ours equally. In fact, so far as our powers extend, they are unfettered, and we are free to use them. We have self devotion in a cause and an end to achieve which is not a selfish one. These things are much.

"Now let us see how far the general powers arrayed against us are restrict, and how the individual cannot. In fine, let us consider the limitations of the vampire in general, and of this one in particular.

"All we have to go upon are traditions and superstitions. These do not at the first appear much, when the matter is one of life and death, nay of more than either life or death. Yet must we be satisfied, in the first place because we have to be, no other means is at our control, and secondly, because, after all these things, tradition and superstition, are everything. Does not the belief in vampires rest for others, though not, alas! for us, on them? A year ago which of us would have received such a possibility, in the midst of our scientific, sceptical, matter-of-fact nineteenth century? We even scouted a belief that we saw justified under our very eyes. Take it, then, that the vampire, and the belief in his limitations and his cure, rest for the moment on the same base. For, let me tell you, he is known everywhere that men have been. In old Greece, in old Rome, he flourish in Germany all over, in France, in India, even in the Chermosese, and in China, so far from us in all ways, there even is he, and the peoples for him at this day. He have follow the wake of the berserker Icelander, the devil-begotten Hun, the Slav, the Saxon, the Magyar.

"So far, then, we have all we may act upon, and let me tell you that very much of the beliefs are justified by what we have seen in our own so un-happy experience. The vampire live on, and cannot die by mere passing of the time, he can flourish when that he can fatten on the blood of the living. Even more, we have seen amongst us that he can even grow younger, that his vital faculties grow strenuous, and seem as though they refresh them-selves when his special pabulum is plenty.

"But he cannot flourish without this diet, he eat not as others. Even friend Jonathan, who lived with him for weeks, did never see him eat, never! He throws no shadow, he make in the mirror no reflect, as again Jonathan observe. He has the strength of many of his hand, witness again Jonathan when he shut the door against the wolves, and when he help him from the diligence too. He can transform himself to wolf, as we gather from the ship arrival in Whitby, when he tear open the dog, he can be as bat, as Madam Mina saw him on the window at Whitby, and as friend John saw him fly from this so near house, and as my friend Quincey saw him at the window of Miss Lucy.

"He can come in mist which he create, that noble ship's captain proved him of this, but, from what we know, the distance he can make this mist is limited, and it can only be round himself.

"He come on moonlight rays as elemental dust, as again Jonathan saw those sisters in the castle of Dracula. He become so small, we ourselves saw Miss Lucy, ere she was at peace, slip through a hairbreadth space at the tomb door. He can, when once he find his way, come out from anything or into anything, no matter how close it be bound or even fused up with fire, solder you call it. He can see in the dark, no small power this, in a world which is one half shut from the light. Ah, but hear me through.

"He can do all these things, yet he is not free. Nay, he is even more prisoner than the slave of the galley, than the madman in his cell. He cannot go where he lists, he who is not of nature has yet to obey some of nature's laws, why we know not. He may not enter anywhere at the first, unless there be some one of the household who bid him to come, though afterwards he can come as he please. His power ceases, as does that of all evil things, at the coming of the day.

"Only at certain times can he have limited freedom. If he be not at the place whither he is bound, he can only change himself at noon or at exact sunrise or sunset. These things we are told, and in this record of ours we have proof by inference. Thus, whereas he can do as he will within his limit, when he have his earth-home, his coffin-home, his hell-home, the place unhallowed, as we saw when he went to the grave of the suicide at Whitby, still at other time he can only change when the time come. It is said, too, that he can only pass running water at the slack or the flood of the tide. Then there are things which so afflict him that he has no power, as the garlic that we know of, and as for things sacred, as this symbol, my crucifix, that was amongst us even now when we resolve, to them he is nothing, but in their presence he take his place far off and silent with respect. There are others, too, which I shall tell you of, lest in our seeking we may need them.

"The branch of wild rose on his coffin keep him that he move not from it, a sacred bullet fired into the coffin kill him so that he be true dead, and as for the stake through him, we know already of its peace, or the cut off head that giveth rest. We have seen it with our eyes.

"Thus when we find the habitation of this man-that-was, we can confine him to his coffin and destroy him, if we obey what we know. But he is clever. I have asked my friend Arminius, of Buda-Pesth University, to make his record, and from all the means that are, he tell me of what he has been. He must, indeed, have been that Voivode Dracula who won his name against the Turk, over the great river on the very frontier of Turkeyland. If it be so, then was he no common man, for in that time, and for centuries after, he was spoken of as the cleverest and the most cunning, as well as the bravest of the sons of the 'land beyond the forest.' That mighty brain and that iron resolution went with him to his grave, and are even now arrayed against us. The Draculas were, says Arminius, a great and noble race, though now and again were scions who were held by their coevals to have had dealings with the Evil One. They learned his secrets in the Scholomance, amongst the mountains over Lake Hermanstadt, where the devil claims the tenth scholar as his due. In the records are such words as 'stregoica' witch, 'ordog' and 'pokol' Satan and hell, and in one manuscript this very Dracula is spoken of as 'wampyr,' which we all understand too well. There have been from the loins of this very one great men and good women, and their graves make sacred the earth where alone this foulness can dwell. For it is not the least of its terrors that this evil thing is rooted deep in all good, in soil barren of holy memories it cannot rest."

Whilst they were talking Mr. Morris was looking steadily at the window, and he now got up quietly, and went out of the room. There was a little pause, and then the Professor went on.

"And now we must settle what we do. We have here much data, and we must proceed to lay out our campaign. We know from the inquiry of Jonathan that from the castle to Whitby came fifty boxes of earth, all of which were delivered at Carfax, we also know that at least some of these boxes have been removed. It seems to me, that our first step should be to ascertain whether all the rest remain in the house beyond that wall where we look today, or whether any more have been removed. If the latter, we must trace . . ."

Here we were interrupted in a very startling way. Outside the house came the sound of a pistol shot, the glass of the window was shattered with a bullet, which ricochetting from the top of the embrasure, struck the far wall of the room. I am afraid I am at heart a coward, for I shrieked out. The men all jumped to their feet, Lord Godalming flew over to the window and threw up the sash. As he did so we heard Mr. Morris' voice without, "Sorry! I fear I have alarmed you. I shall come in and tell you about it."

A minute later he came in and said, "It was an idiotic thing of me to do, and I ask your pardon, Mrs. Harker, most sincerely, I fear I must have frightened you terribly. But the fact is that whilst the Professor was talking there came a big bat and sat on the window sill. I have got such a horror of the damned brutes from recent events that I cannot stand them, and I went out to have a shot, as I have been doing of late of evenings, whenever I have seen one. You used to laugh at me for it then, Art."

"Did you hit it?" asked Dr. Van Helsing.

"I don't know, I fancy not, for it flew away into the wood." Without saying any more he took his seat, and the Professor began to resume his statement.

"We must trace each of these boxes, and when we are ready, we must either capture or kill this monster in his lair, or we must, so to speak, sterilize the earth, so that no more he can seek safety in it. Thus in the end we may find him in his form of man between the hours of noon and sunset, and so engage with him when he is at his most weak.

"And now for you, Madam Mina, this night is the end until all be well. You are too precious to us to have such risk. When we part tonight, you no more must question. We shall tell you all in good time. We are men and are able to bear, but you must be our star and our hope, and we shall act all the more free that you are not in the danger, such as we are."

All the men, even Jonathan, seemed relieved, but it did not seem to me good that they should brave danger and, perhaps lessen their safety, strength being the best safety, through care of me, but their minds were made up, and though it was a bitter pill for me to swallow, I could say nothing, save to accept their chivalrous care of me.

Mr. Morris resumed the discussion, "As there is no time to lose, I vote we have a look at his house right now. Time is everything with him, and swift action on our part may save another victim."

I own that my heart began to fail me when the time for action came so close, but I did not say anything, for I had a greater fear that if I appeared as a drag or a hindrance to their work, they might even leave me out of their counsels altogether. They have now gone off to Carfax, with means to get into the house.

Manlike, they had told me to go to bed and sleep, as if a woman can sleep when those she loves are in danger! I shall lie down, and pretend to sleep, lest Jonathan have added anxiety about me when he returns.

DR. SEWARD'S DIARY

1 October, 4 a.m.—Just as we were about to leave the house, an urgent message was brought to me from Renfield to know if I would see him at once, as he had something of the utmost importance to say to me. I told the messenger to say that I would attend to his wishes in the morning, I was busy just at the moment.

The attendant added, "He seems very importunate, sir. I have never seen him so eager. I don't know but what, if you don't see him soon, he will have one of his violent fits." I knew the man would not have said this without some cause, so I said, "All right, I'll go now," and I asked the others to wait a few minutes for me, as I had to go and see my patient.

"Take me with you, friend John," said the Professor. "His case in your diary interest me much, and it had bearing, too, now and again on *our* case. I should much like to see him, and especial when his mind is disturbed."

"May I come also?" asked Lord Godalming.

"Me too?" said Quincey Morris. "May I come?" said Harker. I nodded, and we all went down the passage together.

We found him in a state of considerable excitement, but far more rational in his speech and manner than I had ever seen him. There was an unusual understanding of himself, which was unlike anything I had ever met with in a lunatic, and he took it for granted that his reasons would prevail with others entirely sane. We all five went into the room, but none of the others at first said anything. His request was that I would at once release him from the asylum and send him home. This he backed up with arguments regarding his complete recovery, and adduced his own existing sanity.

"I appeal to your friends," he said, "they will, perhaps, not mind sitting in judgement on my case. By the way, you have not introduced me."

I was so much astonished, that the oddness of introducing a madman in an asylum did not strike me at the moment, and besides, there was a certain dignity in the man's manner, so much of the habit of equality, that I at once made the introduction, "Lord Godalming, Professor Van Helsing, Mr. Quincey Morris, of Texas, Mr. Jonathan Harker, Mr. Renfield."

He shook hands with each of them, saying in turn, "Lord Godalming, I had the honour of seconding your father at the Windham; I grieve to know, by your holding the title, that he is no more. He was a man loved and honoured by all who knew him, and in his youth was, I have heard, the inventor of a burnt rum punch, much patronized on Derby night. Mr. Morris, you should be proud of your great state. Its reception into the Union was a precedent which may have far-reaching effects hereafter, when the Pole and the Tropics may hold alliance to the Stars and Stripes. The power of Treaty may yet prove a vast engine of enlargement, when the Monroe doctrine takes its true place as a political fable. What shall any man say of his pleasure at meeting Van Helsing? Sir, I make no apology for dropping all forms of conventional prefix. When an individual has revolutionized therapeutics by his discovery of the continuous evolution of brain matter, conventional forms are unfitting, since they would seem to limit him to one of a class. You, gentlemen, who by nationality, by heredity, or by the possession of natural gifts, are fitted to hold your respective places in the moving world, I take to witness that I am as sane as at least the majority of men who are in full possession of their liberties. And I am sure that you, Dr. Seward, humanitarian and medico-jurist as well as scientist, will deem it a moral duty to deal with me as one to be considered as under exceptional circumstances." He made this last appeal with a courtly air of conviction which was not without its own charm.

I think we were all staggered. For my own part, I was under the conviction, despite my knowledge of the man's character and history, that his reason had been restored, and I felt under a strong impulse to tell him that I was satisfied as to his sanity, and would see about the necessary formalities for his release in the morning. I thought it better to wait, however, before making so grave a statement, for of old I knew the sudden changes to which this particular patient was liable. So I contented myself with making a general statement that he appeared to be improving very rapidly, that I would have a longer chat with him in the morning, and would then see what I could do in the direction of meeting his wishes.

This did not at all satisfy him, for he said quickly, "But I fear, Dr. Seward, that you hardly apprehend my wish. I desire to go at once, here, now, this very hour, this very moment, if I may. Time presses, and in our implied agreement with the old scytheman it is of the essence of the contract. I am sure it is only necessary to put before so admirable a practitioner as Dr. Seward so simple, yet so momentous a wish, to ensure its fulfilment."

He looked at me keenly, and seeing the negative in my face, turned to the others, and scrutinized them closely. Not meeting any sufficient response, he went on, "Is it possible that I have erred in my supposition?"

"You have," I said frankly, but at the same time, as I felt, brutally.

There was a considerable pause, and then he said slowly, "Then I suppose I must only shift my ground of request. Let me ask for this concession, boon, privilege, what you will. I am content to implore in such a case, not on personal grounds, but for the sake of others. I am not at liberty to give you the whole of my reasons, but you may, I assure you, take it from me that they are good ones, sound and unselfish, and spring from the highest sense of duty.

"Could you look, sir, into my heart, you would approve to the full the sentiments which animate me. Nay, more, you would count me amongst the best and truest of your friends."

Again he looked at us all keenly. I had a growing conviction that this sudden change of his entire intellectual method was but yet another phase of his madness, and so determined to let him go on a little longer, knowing from experience that he would, like all lunatics, give himself away in the end. Van Helsing was gazing at him with a look of utmost intensity, his bushy eyebrows almost meeting with the fixed concentration of his look. He said to Renfield in a tone which did not surprise me at the time, but only when I thought of it afterwards, for it was as of one addressing an equal, "Can you not tell frankly your real reason for wishing to be free tonight? I will undertake that if you will satisfy even me, a stranger, without prejudice, and with the habit of keeping an open mind, Dr. Seward will give you, at his own risk and on his own responsibility, the privilege you seek."

He shook his head sadly, and with a look of poignant regret on his face. The Professor went on, "Come, sir, bethink yourself. You claim the privilege of reason in the highest degree, since you seek to impress us with your complete reasonableness. You do this, whose sanity we have reason to doubt, since you are not yet released from medical treatment for this very defect. If you will not help us in our effort to choose the wisest course, how can we perform the duty which you yourself put upon us? Be wise, and help us, and if we can we shall aid you to achieve your wish."

He still shook his head as he said, "Dr. Van Helsing, I have nothing to say. Your argument is complete, and if I were free to speak I should not hesitate a moment, but I am not my own master in the matter. I can only ask you to trust me. If I am refused, the responsibility does not rest with me."

I thought it was now time to end the scene, which was becoming too comically grave, so I went towards the door, simply saying, "Come, my friends, we have work to do. Goodnight."

As, however, I got near the door, a new change came over the patient. He moved towards me so quickly that for the moment I feared that he was about to make another homicidal attack. My fears, however, were groundless, for he held up his two hands imploringly, and made his petition in a moving manner. As he saw that the very excess of his emotion was militating against him, by restoring us more to our old relations, he became still more demonstrative. I glanced at Van Helsing, and saw my conviction reflected in his eyes, so I became a little more fixed in my manner, if not more stern, and motioned to him that his efforts were unavailing. I had previously seen something of the same constantly growing excitement in him when he had to make some request of which at the time he had thought much, such for instance, as when he wanted a cat, and I was prepared to see the collapse into the same sullen acquiescence on this occasion.

My expectation was not realized, for when he found that his appeal would not be successful, he got into quite a frantic condition. He threw himself on his knees, and held up his hands, wringing them in plaintive supplication, and poured forth a torrent of entreaty, with the tears rolling down his cheeks, and his whole face and form expressive of the deepest emotion.

"Let me entreat you, Dr. Seward, oh, let me implore you, to let me out of this house at once. Send me away how you will and where you will, send keepers with me with whips and chains, let them take me in a strait waistcoat, manacled and leg-ironed, even to gaol, but let me go out of this. You don't know what you do by keeping me here. I am speaking from the depths of my heart, of my very soul. You don't know whom you wrong, or how, and I may not tell. Woe is me! I may not tell. By all you hold sacred, by all you hold dear, by your love that is lost, by your hope that lives, for the sake of the Almighty, take me out of this and save my soul from guilt! Can't you hear me, man? Can't you understand? Will you never learn? Don't you know that I am sane and earnest now, that I am no lunatic in a mad fit, but a sane man fighting for his soul? Oh, hear me! Hear me! Let me go, let me go, let me go!"

I thought that the longer this went on the wilder he would get, and so would bring on a fit, so I took him by the hand and raised him up.

"Come," I said sternly, "no more of this, we have had quite enough already. Get to your bed and try to behave more discreetly."

He suddenly stopped and looked at me intently for several moments. Then, without a word, he rose and moving over, sat down on the side of the bed. The collapse had come, as on former occasions, just as I had expected.

When I was leaving the room, last of our party, he said to me in a quiet, well-bred voice, "You will, I trust, Dr. Seward, do me the justice to bear in mind, later on, that I did what I could to convince you tonight."

℘ CHAPTER 19 ℃
JONATHAN HARKER'S JOURNAL

1 October, 5 a.m.—I went with the party to the search with an easy mind, for I think I never saw Mina so absolutely strong and well. I am so glad that she consented to hold back and let us men do the work. Somehow, it was a dread to me that she was in this fearful business at all, but now that her work is done, and that it is due to her energy and brains and foresight that the whole story is put together in such a way that every point tells, she may well feel that her part is finished, and that she can henceforth leave the rest to us. We were, I think, all a little upset by the scene with Mr. Renfield. When we came away from his room we were silent till we got back to the study.

Then Mr. Morris said to Dr. Seward, "Say, Jack, if that man wasn't attempting a bluff, he is about the sanest lunatic I ever saw. I'm not sure, but I believe that he had some serious purpose, and if he had, it was pretty rough on him not to get a chance."

Lord Godalming and I were silent, but Dr. Van Helsing added, "Friend John, you know more lunatics than I do, and I'm glad of it, for I fear that if it had been to me to decide I would before that last hysterical outburst have given him free. But we live and learn, and in our present task we must take no chance, as my friend Quincey would say. All is best as they are."

Dr. Seward seemed to answer them both in a dreamy kind of way, "I don't know but that I agree with you. If that man had been an ordinary lunatic I would have taken my chance of trusting him, but he seems so mixed up with the Count in an indexy kind of way that I am afraid of doing anything wrong by helping his fads. I can't forget how he prayed with almost equal fervor for a cat, and then tried to tear my throat out with his teeth. Besides, he called the Count 'lord and master', and he may want to get out to help him in some diabolical way. That horrid thing has the wolves and the rats and his own kind to help him, so I suppose he isn't above trying to use a respectable lunatic. He certainly did seem earnest, though. I only hope we have done what is best. These things, in conjunction with the wild work we have in hand, help to unnerve a man."

The Professor stepped over, and laying his hand on his shoulder, said in his grave, kindly way, "Friend John, have no fear. We are trying to do our duty in a very sad and terrible case, we can only do as we deem best. What else have we to hope for, except the pity of the good God?"

Lord Godalming had slipped away for a few minutes, but now he returned. He held up a little silver whistle as he remarked, "That old place may be full of rats, and if so, I've got an antidote on call."

Having passed the wall, we took our way to the house, taking care to keep in the shadows of the trees on the lawn when the moonlight shone out. When we got to the porch the Professor opened his bag and took out a lot of things, which he laid on the step, sorting them into four little groups, evidently one for each. Then he spoke.

"My friends, we are going into a terrible danger, and we need arms of many kinds. Our enemy is not merely spiritual. Remember that he has the strength of twenty men, and that, though our necks or our windpipes are of the common kind, and therefore breakable or crushable, his are not amenable to mere strength. A stronger man, or a body of men more strong in all than him, can at certain times hold him, but they cannot hurt him as we can be hurt by him. We must, therefore, guard ourselves from his touch. Keep this near your heart." As he spoke he lifted a little silver crucifix and held it out to me, I being nearest to him, "put these flowers round your neck," here he handed to me a wreath of withered garlic blossoms, "for other enemies more mundane, this revolver and this knife, and for aid in all, these so small electric lamps, which you can fasten to your breast, and for all, and above all at the last, this, which we must not desecrate needless."

This was a portion of Sacred Wafer, which he put in an envelope and handed to me. Each of the others was similarly equipped.

"Now," he said, "friend John, where are the skeleton keys? If so that we can open the door, we need not break house by the window, as before at Miss Lucy's."

Dr. Seward tried one or two skeleton keys, his mechanical dexterity as a surgeon standing him in good stead. Presently he got one to suit, after a little play back and forward the bolt yielded, and with a rusty clang, shot back. We pressed on the door, the rusty hinges creaked, and it slowly opened. It was startlingly like the image conveyed to me in Dr. Seward's diary of the opening of Miss Westenra's tomb, I fancy that the same idea seemed to strike the others, for with one accord they shrank back. The Professor was the first to move forward, and stepped into the open door.

"*In manus tuas, Domine!*"[109] he said, crossing himself as he passed over the threshold. We closed the door behind us, lest when we should have lit our lamps we should possibly attract attention from the road. The Professor carefully tried the lock, lest we might not be able to open it from within should we be in a hurry making our exit. Then we all lit our lamps and proceeded on our search.

The light from the tiny lamps fell in all sorts of odd forms, as the rays crossed each other, or the opacity of our bodies threw great shadows. I could not for my life get away from the feeling that there was someone else amongst us. I suppose it was the recollection, so powerfully brought home to me by the grim surroundings, of that terrible experience in Transylvania. I think the feeling was common to us all, for I noticed that the others kept looking over their shoulders at every sound and every new shadow, just as I felt myself doing.

The whole place was thick with dust. The floor was seemingly inches deep, except where there were recent footsteps, in which on holding down my lamp I could see marks of hobnails where the dust was cracked. The walls were fluffy and heavy with dust, and in the corners were masses of spider's webs, whereon the dust had gathered till they looked like old tattered rags as the weight had torn them partly down. On a table in the hall was a great bunch of keys, with a time-yellowed label on each. They had been used several times, for on the table were several similar rents in the blanket of dust, similar to that exposed when the Professor lifted them.

He turned to me and said, "You know this place, Jonathan. You have copied maps of it, and you know it at least more than we do. Which is the way to the chapel?"

---

109 Into thy hand, O Lord! (Latin).

I had an idea of its direction, though on my former visit I had not been able to get admission to it, so I led the way, and after a few wrong turnings found myself opposite a low, arched oaken door, ribbed with iron bands.

"This is the spot," said the Professor as he turned his lamp on a small map of the house, copied from the file of my original correspondence regarding the purchase. With a little trouble we found the key on the bunch and opened the door. We were prepared for some unpleasantness, for as we were opening the door a faint, malodorous air seemed to exhale through the gaps, but none of us ever expected such an odour as we encountered. None of the others had met the Count at all at close quarters, and when I had seen him he was either in the fasting stage of his existence in his rooms or, when he was bloated with fresh blood, in a ruined building open to the air, but here the place was small and close, and the long disuse had made the air stagnant and foul. There was an earthy smell, as of some dry miasma, which came through the fouler air. But as to the odour itself, how shall I describe it? It was not alone that it was composed of all the ills of mortality and with the pungent, acrid smell of blood, but it seemed as though corruption had become itself corrupt. Faugh! It sickens me to think of it. Every breath exhaled by that monster seemed to have clung to the place and intensified its loathsomeness.

Under ordinary circumstances such a stench would have brought our enterprise to an end, but this was no ordinary case, and the high and terrible purpose in which we were involved gave us a strength which rose above merely physical considerations. After the involuntary shrinking consequent on the first nauseous whiff, we one and all set about our work as though that loathsome place were a garden of roses.

We made an accurate examination of the place, the Professor saying as we began, "The first thing is to see how many of the boxes are left, we must then examine every hole and corner and cranny and see if we cannot get some clue as to what has become of the rest."

A glance was sufficient to show how many remained, for the great earth chests were bulky, and there was no mistaking them.

There were only twenty-nine left out of the fifty! Once I got a fright, for, seeing Lord Godalming suddenly turn and look out of the vaulted door into the dark passage beyond, I looked too, and for an instant my heart stood still. Somewhere, looking out from the shadow, I seemed to see the high lights of the Count's evil face, the ridge of the nose, the red eyes, the red lips, the awful pallor. It was only for a moment, for, as Lord Godalming said, "I thought I saw a face, but it was only the shadows," and resumed his inquiry, I turned my lamp in the direction, and stepped into the passage. There was no sign of anyone, and as there were no corners, no doors, no aperture of any kind, but only the solid walls of the passage, there could be no hiding place even for *him*. I took it that fear had helped imagination, and said nothing.

A few minutes later I saw Morris step suddenly back from a corner, which he was examining. We all followed his movements with our eyes, for undoubtedly some nervousness was growing on us, and we saw a whole mass of phosphorescence, which twinkled like stars. We all instinctively drew back. The whole place was becoming alive with rats.

For a moment or two we stood appalled, all save Lord Godalming, who was seemingly prepared for such an emergency. Rushing over to the great iron-bound oaken door, which Dr. Seward had described from the outside, and which I had seen myself, he turned the key in the lock, drew the huge bolts, and swung the door open. Then, taking his little silver whistle from his pocket, he blew a low, shrill call. It was answered from behind Dr. Seward's house by the yelping of dogs, and after about a minute three terriers came dashing round the corner of the house. Unconsciously we had all moved towards the door, and as we moved I noticed that the dust had been much disturbed. The boxes which had been taken out had been brought this way. But even in the minute that had elapsed the number of the rats had vastly increased. They seemed to swarm over the place all at once, till the lamplight, shining on their moving dark bodies and glittering, baleful eyes, made the place look like a bank of earth set with fireflies. The dogs dashed on, but at the threshold suddenly stopped and snarled, and then, simultaneously lifting their noses, began to howl in most lugubrious fashion. The rats were multiplying in thousands, and we moved out.

Lord Godalming lifted one of the dogs, and carrying him in, placed him on the floor. The instant his feet touched the ground he seemed to recover his courage, and rushed at his natural enemies. They fled before him so fast that before he had shaken the life out of a score, the other dogs, who had by now been lifted in the same manner, had but small prey ere the whole mass had vanished.

With their going it seemed as if some evil presence had departed, for the dogs frisked about and barked merrily as they made sudden darts at their prostrate foes, and turned them over and over and tossed them in the air with vicious shakes. We all seemed to find our spirits rise. Whether it was the purifying of the deadly atmosphere by the opening of the chapel door, or the relief which we experienced by finding ourselves in the open I know not, but most certainly the shadow of dread seemed to slip from us like a robe, and the occasion of our coming lost something of its grim significance, though we did not slacken a whit in our resolution. We closed the outer door and barred and locked it, and bringing the dogs with us, began our search of the house. We found nothing throughout except dust in extraordinary proportions, and all untouched save for my own footsteps when I had made my first visit. Never once did the dogs exhibit any symptom of uneasiness, and even when we returned to the chapel they frisked about as though they had been rabbit hunting in a summer wood.

The morning was quickening in the east when we emerged from the front. Dr. Van Helsing had taken the key of the hall door from the bunch, and locked the door in orthodox fashion, putting the key into his pocket when he had done.

"So far," he said, "our night has been eminently successful. No harm has come to us such as I feared might be and yet we have ascertained how many boxes are missing. More than all do I rejoice that this, our first, and perhaps our most difficult and dangerous, step has been accomplished without the bringing thereinto our most sweet Madam Mina or troubling her waking or sleeping thoughts with sights and sounds and smells of horror which she might never forget. One lesson, too, we have learned, if it be allowable to argue *a particulari*, that the brute beasts which are to the Count's command are yet themselves not amenable to his spiritual power, for look, these rats that would come to his call, just as from his castle top he summon the wolves to your going and to that poor mother's cry, though they come to him, they run pell-mell from the so little dogs of my friend Arthur. We have other matters before us, other dangers, other fears, and that monster . . . He has not used his power over the brute world for the only or the last time tonight. So be it that he has gone elsewhere. Good! It has given us opportunity to cry 'check' in some ways in this chess game, which we play for the stake of human souls. And now let us go home. The dawn is close at hand, and we have reason to be content with our first night's work. It may be ordained that we have many nights and days to follow, if full of peril, but we must go on, and from no danger shall we shrink."

The house was silent when we got back, save for some poor creature who was screaming away in one of the distant wards, and a low, moaning sound from Renfield's room. The poor wretch was doubtless torturing himself, after the manner of the insane, with needless thoughts of pain.

I came tiptoe into our own room, and found Mina asleep, breathing so softly that I had to put my ear down to hear it. She looks paler than usual. I hope the meeting tonight has not upset her. I am truly thankful that she is to be left out of our future work, and even of our deliberations. It is too great a strain for a woman to bear. I did not think so at first, but I know better now. Therefore I am glad that it is settled. There may be things which would frighten her to hear, and yet to conceal them from her might be worse than to tell her if once she suspected that there was any concealment. Henceforth our work is to be a sealed book to her, till at least such time as we can tell her that all is finished, and the earth free from a monster of the nether world. I daresay it will be difficult to begin to keep silence after such confidence as ours, but I must be resolute, and tomorrow I shall keep dark over tonight's doings, and shall refuse to speak of anything that has happened. I rest on the sofa, so as not to disturb her.

1 October, later.—I suppose it was natural that we should have all overslept ourselves, for the day was a busy one, and the night had no rest at all. Even Mina must have felt its exhaustion, for though I slept till the sun was high, I was awake before her, and had to call two or three times before she awoke. Indeed, she was so sound asleep that for a few seconds she did not recognize me, but looked at me with a sort of blank terror, as one looks who has been waked out of a bad dream. She complained a little of being tired, and I let her rest till later in the day. We now know of twenty-one boxes having been removed, and if it be that several were taken in any of these removals we may be able to trace them all. Such will, of course, immensely simplify our labor, and the sooner the matter is attended to the better. I shall look up Thomas Snelling today.

DR. SEWARD'S DIARY

1 October.—It was towards noon when I was awakened by the Professor walking into my room. He was more jolly and cheerful than usual, and it is quite evident that last night's work has helped to take some of the brooding weight off his mind.

After going over the adventure of the night he suddenly said, "Your patient interests me much. May it be that with you I visit him this morning? Or if that you are too occupy, I can go alone if it may be. It is a new experience to me to find a lunatic who talk philosophy, and reason so sound."

I had some work to do which pressed, so I told him that if he would go alone I would be glad, as then I should not have to keep him waiting, so I called an attendant and gave him the necessary instructions. Before the Professor left the room I cautioned him against getting any false impression from my patient.

"But," he answered, "I want him to talk of himself and of his delusion as to consuming live things. He said to Madam Mina, as I see in your diary of yesterday, that he had once had such a belief. Why do you smile, friend John?"

"Excuse me," I said, "but the answer is here." I laid my hand on the typewritten matter. "When our sane and learned lunatic made that very statement of how he *used* to consume life, his mouth was actually nauseous with the flies and spiders which he had eaten just before Mrs. Harker entered the room."

Van Helsing smiled in turn. "Good!" he said. "Your memory is true, friend John. I should have remembered. And yet it is this very obliquity of thought and memory which makes mental disease such a fascinating study. Perhaps I may gain more knowledge out of the folly of this madman than I shall from the teaching of the most wise. Who knows?"

I went on with my work, and before long was through that in hand. It seemed that the time had been very short indeed, but there was Van Helsing back in the study.

"Do I interrupt?" he asked politely as he stood at the door.

"Not at all," I answered. "Come in. My work is finished, and I am free. I can go with you now, if you like."

"It is needless, I have seen him!"

"Well?"

"I fear that he does not appraise me at much. Our interview was short. When I entered his room he was sitting on a stool in the centre, with his elbows on his knees, and his face was the picture of sullen discontent. I spoke to him as cheerfully as I could, and with such a measure of respect as I could assume. He made no reply whatever. 'Don't you know me?' I asked. His answer was not reassuring: 'I know you well enough; you are the old fool Van Helsing. I wish you would take yourself and your idiotic brain theories somewhere else. Damn all thick-headed Dutchmen!' Not a word more would he say, but sat in his implacable sullenness as indifferent to me as though I had not been in the room at all. Thus departed for this time my chance of much learning from this so clever lunatic, so I shall go, if I may, and cheer myself with a few happy words with that sweet soul Madam Mina. Friend John, it does rejoice me unspeakable that she is no more to be pained, no more to be worried with our terrible things. Though we shall much miss her help, it is better so."

"I agree with you with all my heart," I answered earnestly, for I did not want him to weaken in this matter. "Mrs. Harker is better out of it. Things are quite bad enough for us, all men of the world, and who have been in many tight places in our time, but it is no place for a woman, and if she had remained in touch with the affair, it would in time infallibly have wrecked her."

So Van Helsing has gone to confer with Mrs. Harker and Harker, Quincey and Art are all out following up the clues as to the earth boxes. I shall finish my round of work and we shall meet tonight.

MINA HARKER'S JOURNAL

1 October.—It is strange to me to be kept in the dark as I am today, after Jonathan's full confidence for so many years, to see him manifestly avoid certain matters, and those the most vital of all. This morning I slept late after the fatigues of yesterday, and though Jonathan was late too, he was the earlier. He spoke to me before he went out, never more sweetly or tenderly, but he never mentioned a word of what had happened in the visit to the Count's house. And yet he must have known how terribly anxious I was. Poor dear fellow! I suppose it must have distressed him even more than it did me. They all agreed that it was best that I should not be drawn further into this awful work, and I acquiesced. But to think that he keeps anything from me! And now I am crying like a silly fool, when I *know* it comes from my husband's great love and from the good, good wishes of those other strong men.

That has done me good. Well, some day Jonathan will tell me all. And lest it should ever be that he should think for a moment that I kept anything from him, I still keep my journal as usual. Then if he has feared of my trust I shall show it to him, with every thought of my heart put down for his dear eyes to read. I feel strangely sad and low-spirited today. I suppose it is the reaction from the terrible excitement.

Last night I went to bed when the men had gone, simply because they told me to. I didn't feel sleepy, and I did feel full of devouring anxiety. I kept thinking over everything that has been ever since Jonathan came to see me in London, and it all seems like a horrible tragedy, with fate pressing on relentlessly to some destined end. Everything that one does seems, no matter how right it may be, to bring on the very thing which is most to be deplored. If I hadn't gone to Whitby, perhaps poor dear Lucy would be with us now. She hadn't taken to visiting the churchyard till I came, and if she hadn't come there in the day time with me she wouldn't have walked in her sleep. And if she hadn't gone there at night and asleep, that monster couldn't have destroyed her as he did. Oh, why did I ever go to Whitby? There now, crying again! I wonder what has come over me today. I must hide it from Jonathan, for if he knew that I had been crying twice in one morning . . . I, who never cried on my own account, and whom he has never caused to shed a tear, the dear fellow would fret his heart out. I shall put a bold face on, and if I do feel weepy, he shall never see it. I suppose it is just one of the lessons that we poor women have to learn . . .

I can't quite remember how I fell asleep last night. I remember hearing the sudden barking of the dogs and a lot of queer sounds, like praying on a very tumultuous scale, from Mr. Renfield's room, which is somewhere under this. And then there was silence over everything, silence so profound that it startled me, and I got up and looked out of the window. All was dark and silent, the black shadows thrown by the moonlight seeming full of a silent mystery of their own. Not a thing seemed to be stirring, but all to be grim and fixed as death or fate, so that a thin streak of white mist, that crept with almost imperceptible slowness across the grass towards the house, seemed to have a sentience and a vitality of its own. I think that the digression of my thoughts must have done me good, for when I got back to bed I found a lethargy creeping over me. I lay a while, but could not quite sleep, so I got out and looked out of the window again. The mist was spreading, and was now close up to the house, so that I could see it lying thick against the wall, as though it were stealing up to the windows. The poor man was more loud than ever, and though I could not distinguish a word he said, I could in some way recognize in his tones some passionate entreaty on his part. Then there was the sound of a struggle, and I knew that the attendants were dealing with him. I was so frightened that I crept into bed, and pulled the clothes over my head, putting my fingers in my ears. I was not then a bit sleepy, at least so I thought, but I must have fallen asleep, for except dreams, I do not remember anything until the morning, when Jonathan woke me. I think that it took me an effort and a little time to realize where I was, and that it was Jonathan who was bending over me. My dream was very peculiar, and was almost typical of the way that waking thoughts become merged in, or continued in, dreams.

I thought that I was asleep, and waiting for Jonathan to come back. I was very anxious about him, and I was powerless to act, my feet, and my hands, and my brain were weighted, so that nothing could proceed at the usual pace. And so I slept uneasily and thought. Then it began to dawn upon me that the air was heavy, and dank, and cold. I put back the clothes from my face, and found, to my surprise, that all was dim around. The gaslight which I had left lit for Jonathan, but turned down, came only like a tiny red spark through the fog, which had evidently grown thicker and poured into the room. Then it occurred to me that I had shut the window before I had come to bed. I would have got out to make certain on the point, but some leaden lethargy seemed to chain my limbs and even my will. I lay still and endured, that was all. I closed my eyes, but could still see through my eyelids. (It is wonderful what tricks our dreams play us, and how conveniently we can imagine.) The mist grew thicker and thicker and I could see now how it came in, for I could see it like smoke, or with the white energy of boiling water, pouring in, not through the window, but through the joinings of the door. It got thicker and thicker, till it seemed as if it became concentrated into a sort of pillar of cloud in the room, through the top of which I could see the light of the gas shining like a red eye. Things began to whirl through my brain just as the cloudy column was now whirling in the room, and through it all came the scriptural words "a pillar of cloud by day and of fire by night." Was it indeed such spiritual guidance that was coming to me in my sleep? But the pillar was composed of both the day and the night guiding, for the fire was in the red eye, which at the thought got a new fascination for me, till, as I looked, the fire divided, and seemed to shine on me through the fog like two red eyes, such as Lucy told me of in her momentary mental wandering when, on the cliff, the dying sunlight struck the windows of St. Mary's Church. Suddenly the horror burst upon me that it was thus that Jonathan had seen those awful women growing into reality through the whirling mist in the moonlight, and in my dream I must have fainted, for all became black darkness. The last conscious effort which imagination made was to show me a livid white face bending over me out of the mist.

I must be careful of such dreams, for they would unseat one's reason if there were too much of them. I would get Dr. Van Helsing or Dr. Seward to prescribe something for me which would make me sleep, only that I fear to alarm them. Such a dream at the present time would become woven into their fears for me. Tonight I shall strive hard to sleep naturally. If I do not, I shall tomorrow night get them to give me a dose of chloral, that cannot hurt me for once, and it will give me a good night's sleep. Last night tired me more than if I had not slept at all.

2 October 10 p.m.—Last night I slept, but did not dream. I must have slept soundly, for I was not waked by Jonathan coming to bed, but the sleep has not refreshed me, for today I feel terribly weak and spiritless. I spent all yesterday trying to read, or lying down dozing. In the afternoon, Mr. Renfield asked if he might see me. Poor man, he was very gentle, and when I came away he kissed my hand and bade God bless me. Some way it affected me much. I am crying when I think of him. This is a new weakness, of which I must be careful. Jonathan would be miserable if he knew I had been crying. He and the others were out till dinner time, and they all came in tired. I did what I could to brighten them up, and I suppose that the effort did me good, for I forgot how tired I was. After dinner they sent me to bed, and all went off to smoke together, as they said, but I knew that they wanted to tell each other of what had occurred to each during the day. I could see from Jonathan's manner that he had something important to communicate. I was not so sleepy as I should have been, so before they went I asked Dr. Seward to give me a little opiate of some kind, as I had not slept well the night before. He very kindly made me up a sleeping draught, which he gave to me, telling me that it would do me no harm, as it was very mild . . . I have taken it, and am waiting for sleep, which still keeps aloof. I hope I have not done wrong, for as sleep begins to flirt with me, a new fear comes: that I may have been foolish in thus depriving myself of the power of waking. I might want it. Here comes sleep. Goodnight.

℘ CHAPTER 20 ℘
JONATHAN HARKER'S JOURNAL

1 October, evening.—I found Thomas Snelling in his house at Bethnal Green, but unhappily he was not in a condition to remember anything. The very prospect of beer which my expected coming had opened to him had proved too much, and he had begun too early on his expected debauch. I learned, however, from his wife, who seemed a decent, poor soul, that he was only the assistant of Smollet, who of the two mates was the responsible person. So off I drove to Walworth, and found Mr. Joseph Smollet at home and in his shirtsleeves, taking a late tea out of a saucer. He is a decent, intelligent fellow, distinctly a good, reliable type of workman, and with a headpiece of his own. He remembered all about the incident of the boxes, and from a wonderful dog-eared notebook, which he produced from some mysterious receptacle about the seat of his trousers, and which had hieroglyphical entries in thick, half-obliterated pencil, he gave me the destinations of the boxes. There were, he said, six in the cartload which he took from Carfax and left at 197 Chicksand Street, Mile End New Town, and another six which he deposited at Jamaica Lane, Bermondsey. If then the Count meant to scatter these ghastly refuges of his over London, these places were chosen as the first of delivery, so that later he might distribute more fully. The systematic manner in which this was done made me think that he could not mean to confine himself to two sides of London. He was now fixed on the far east on the northern shore, on the east of the southern shore, and on the south. The north and west were surely never meant to be left out of his diabolical scheme, let alone the City itself and the very heart of fashionable London in the south-west and west. I went back to Smollet, and asked him if he could tell us if any other boxes had been taken from Carfax.

He replied, "Well guv'nor, you've treated me very 'an'some", I had given him half a sovereign, "an I'll tell yer all I know. I heard a man by the name of Bloxam say four nights ago in the 'Are an' 'Ounds, in Pincher's Alley, as 'ow he an' his mate 'ad 'ad a rare dusty job in a old 'ouse at Purfleet. There ain't a many such jobs as this 'ere, an' I'm thinkin' that maybe Sam Bloxam could tell ye summut."

I asked if he could tell me where to find him. I told him that if he could get me the address it would be worth another half sovereign to him. So he gulped down the rest of his tea and stood up, saying that he was going to begin the search then and there.

At the door he stopped, and said, "Look 'ere, guv'nor, there ain't no sense in me a keepin' you 'ere. I may find Sam soon, or I mayn't, but anyhow he ain't like to be in a way to tell ye much tonight. Sam is a rare one when he starts on the booze. If you can give me a envelope with a stamp on it, and put yer address on it, I'll find out where Sam is to be found and post it ye tonight. But ye'd better be up arter 'im soon in the mornin', never mind the booze the night afore."

This was all practical, so one of the children went off with a penny to buy an envelope and a sheet of paper, and to keep the change. When she came back, I addressed the envelope and stamped it, and when Smollet had again faithfully promised to post the address when found, I took my way to home. We're on the track anyhow. I am tired tonight, and I want to sleep. Mina is fast asleep, and looks a little too pale. Her eyes look as though she had been crying. Poor dear, I've no doubt it frets her to be kept in the dark, and it may make her doubly anxious about me and the others. But it is best as it is. It is better to be disappointed and worried in such a way now than to have her nerve broken. The doctors were quite right to insist on her being kept out of this dreadful business. I must be firm, for on me this particular burden of silence must rest. I shall not ever enter on the subject with her under any circumstances. Indeed, It may not be a hard task, after all, for she herself has become reticent on the subject, and has not spoken of the Count or his doings ever since we told her of our decision.

2 October, evening—A long and trying and exciting day. By the first post I got my directed envelope with a dirty scrap of paper enclosed, on which was written with a carpenter's pencil in a sprawling hand, "Sam Bloxam, Korkrans, 4 Poters Cort, Bartel Street, Walworth. Arsk for the depite."

I got the letter in bed, and rose without waking Mina. She looked heavy and sleepy and pale, and far from well. I determined not to wake her, but that when I should return from this new search, I would arrange for her going back to Exeter. I think she would be happier in our own home, with her daily tasks to interest her, than in being here amongst us and in ignorance. I only saw Dr. Seward for a moment, and told him where I was off to, promising to come back and tell the rest so soon as I should have found out anything. I drove to Walworth and found, with some difficulty, Potter's Court. Mr. Smollet's spelling misled me, as I asked for Poter's Court instead of Potter's Court. However, when I had found the court, I had no difficulty in discovering Corcoran's lodging house.

When I asked the man who came to the door for the "depite," he shook his head, and said, "I dunno 'im. There ain't no such a person 'ere. I never 'eard of 'im in all my bloomin' days. Don't believe there ain't nobody of that kind livin' 'ere or anywheres."

I took out Smollet's letter, and as I read it it seemed to me that the lesson of the spelling of the name of the court might guide me. "What are you?" I asked.

"I'm the depity," he answered.

I saw at once that I was on the right track. Phonetic spelling had again misled me. A half crown tip put the deputy's knowledge at my disposal, and I learned that Mr. Bloxam, who had slept off the remains of his beer on the previous night at Corcoran's, had left for his work at Poplar at five o'clock that morning. He could not tell me where the place of work was situated, but he had a vague idea that it was some kind of a "new-fangled ware'us," and with this slender clue I had to start for Poplar. It was twelve o'clock before I got any satisfactory hint of such a building, and this I got at a coffee shop, where some workmen were having their dinner. One of them suggested that there was being erected at Cross Angel Street a new "cold storage" building, and as this suited the condition of a "new-fangled ware'us," I at once drove to it. An interview with a surly gatekeeper and a surlier foreman, both of whom were appeased with the coin of the realm, put me on the track of Bloxam. He was sent for on my suggestion that I was willing to pay his days wages to his foreman for the privilege of asking him a few questions on a private matter. He was a smart enough fellow, though rough of speech and bearing. When I had promised to pay for his information and given him an earnest, he told me that he had made two journeys between Carfax and a house in Piccadilly, and had taken from this house to the latter nine great boxes, "main heavy ones," with a horse and cart hired by him for this purpose.

I asked him if he could tell me the number of the house in Piccadilly, to which he replied, "Well, guv'nor, I forgits the number, but it was only a few door from a big white church, or somethink of the kind, not long built. It was a dusty old 'ouse, too, though nothin' to the dustiness of the 'ouse we tooked the bloomin' boxes from."

"How did you get in if both houses were empty?"

"There was the old party what engaged me a waitin' in the 'ouse at Purfleet. He 'elped me to lift the boxes and put them in the dray. Curse me, but he was the strongest chap I ever struck, an' him a old feller, with a white moustache, one that thin you would think he couldn't throw a shadder."

How this phrase thrilled through me!

"Why, 'e took up 'is end o' the boxes like they was pounds of tea, and me a puffin' an' a blowin' afore I could upend mine anyhow, an' I'm no chicken, neither."

"How did you get into the house in Piccadilly?" I asked.

"He was there too. He must 'a started off and got there afore me, for when I rung of the bell he kem an' opened the door 'isself an' 'elped me carry the boxes into the 'all."

"The whole nine?" I asked.

"Yus, there was five in the first load an' four in the second. It was main dry work, an' I don't so well remember 'ow I got 'ome."

I interrupted him, "Were the boxes left in the hall?"

"Yus, it was a big 'all, an' there was nothin' else in it."

I made one more attempt to further matters. "You didn't have any key?"

"Never used no key nor nothink. The old gent, he opened the door 'isself an' shut it again when I druv off. I don't remember the last time, but that was the beer."

"And you can't remember the number of the house?"

"No, sir. But ye needn't have no difficulty about that. It's a 'igh 'un with a stone front with a bow on it, an' 'igh steps up to the door. I know them steps, 'avin' 'ad to carry the boxes up with three loafers what come round to earn a copper. The old gent give them shillin's, an' they seein' they got so much, they wanted more. But 'e took one of them by the shoulder and was like to throw 'im down the steps, till the lot of them went away cussin'."

I thought that with this description I could find the house, so having paid my friend for his information, I started off for Piccadilly. I had gained a new painful experience. The Count could, it was evident, handle the earth boxes himself. If so, time was precious, for now that he had achieved a certain amount of distribution, he could, by choosing his own time, complete the task unobserved. At Piccadilly Circus I discharged my cab, and walked westward. Beyond the Junior Constitutional I came across the house described and was satisfied that this was the next of the lairs arranged by Dracula. The house looked as though it had been long untenanted. The windows were encrusted with dust, and the shutters were up. All the framework was black with time, and from the iron the paint had mostly scaled away. It was evident that up to lately there had been a large notice board in front of the balcony. It had, however, been roughly torn away, the uprights which had supported it still remaining. Behind the rails of the balcony I saw there were some loose boards, whose raw edges looked white. I would have given a good deal to have been able to see the notice board intact, as it would, perhaps, have given some clue to the ownership of the house. I remembered my experience of the investigation and purchase of Carfax, and I could not but feel that if I could find the former owner there might be some means discovered of gaining access to the house.

There was at present nothing to be learned from the Piccadilly side, and nothing could be done, so I went around to the back to see if anything could be gathered from this quarter. The mews were active, the Piccadilly houses being mostly in occupation. I asked one or two of the grooms and helpers whom I saw around if they could tell me anything about the empty house. One of them said that he heard it had lately been taken, but he couldn't say from whom. He told me, however, that up to very lately there had been a notice board of "For Sale" up, and that perhaps Mitchell, Sons, & Candy the house agents could tell me something, as he thought he remembered seeing the name of that firm on the board. I did not wish to seem too eager, or to let my informant know or guess too much, so thanking him in the usual manner, I strolled away. It was now growing dusk, and the autumn night was closing in, so I did not lose any time. Having learned the address of Mitchell, Sons, & Candy from a directory at the Berkeley, I was soon at their office in Sackville Street.

The gentleman who saw me was particularly suave in manner, but uncommunicative in equal proportion. Having once told me that the Piccadilly house, which throughout our interview he called a "mansion," was sold, he considered my business as concluded. When I asked who had purchased it, he opened his eyes a thought wider, and paused a few seconds before replying, "It is sold, sir."

"Pardon me," I said, with equal politeness, "but I have a special reason for wishing to know who purchased it."

Again he paused longer, and raised his eyebrows still more. "It is sold, sir," was again his laconic reply.

"Surely," I said, "you do not mind letting me know so much."

"But I do mind," he answered. "The affairs of their clients are absolutely safe in the hands of Mitchell, Sons, & Candy."

This was manifestly a prig of the first water, and there was no use arguing with him. I thought I had best meet him on his own ground, so I said, "Your clients, sir, are happy in having so resolute a guardian of their confidence. I am myself a professional man."

Here I handed him my card. "In this instance I am not prompted by curiosity, I act on the part of Lord Godalming, who wishes to know something of the property which was, he understood, lately for sale."

These words put a different complexion on affairs. He said, "I would like to oblige you if I could, Mr. Harker, and especially would I like to oblige his lordship. We once carried out a small matter of renting some chambers for him when he was the honourable Arthur Holmwood. If you will let me have his lordship's address I will consult the House on the subject, and will, in any case, communicate with his lordship by tonight's post. It will be a pleasure if we can so far deviate from our rules as to give the required information to his lordship."

I wanted to secure a friend, and not to make an enemy, so I thanked him, gave the address at Dr. Seward's and came away. It was now dark, and I was tired and hungry. I got a cup of tea at the Aerated Bread Company and came down to Purfleet by the next train.

I found all the others at home. Mina was looking tired and pale, but she made a gallant effort to be bright and cheerful. It wrung my heart to think that I had had to keep anything from her and so caused her inquietude. Thank God, this will be the last night of her looking on at our conferences, and feeling the sting of our not showing our confidence. It took all my courage to hold to the wise resolution of keeping her out of our grim task. She seems somehow more reconciled, or else the very subject seems to have become repugnant to her, for when any accidental allusion is made she actually shudders. I am glad we made our resolution in time, as with such a feeling as this, our growing knowledge would be torture to her.

I could not tell the others of the day's discovery till we were alone, so after dinner, followed by a little music to save appearances even amongst ourselves, I took Mina to her room and left her to go to bed. The dear girl was more affectionate with me than ever, and clung to me as though she would detain me, but there was much to be talked of and I came away. Thank God, the ceasing of telling things has made no difference between us.

When I came down again I found the others all gathered round the fire in the study. In the train I had written my diary so far, and simply read it off to them as the best means of letting them get abreast of my own information.

When I had finished Van Helsing said, "This has been a great day's work, friend Jonathan. Doubtless we are on the track of the missing boxes. If we find them all in that house, then our work is near the end. But if there be some missing, we must search until we find them. Then shall we make our final *coup*, and hunt the wretch to his real death."

We all sat silent awhile and all at once Mr. Morris spoke, "Say! How are we going to get into that house?"

"We got into the other," answered Lord Godalming quickly.

"But, Art, this is different. We broke house at Carfax, but we had night and a walled park to protect us. It will be a mighty different thing to commit burglary in Piccadilly, either by day or night. I confess I don't see how we are going to get in unless that agency duck can find us a key of some sort."

Lord Godalming's brows contracted, and he stood up and walked about the room. By-and-by he stopped and said, turning from one to another of us, "Quincey's head is level. This burglary business is getting serious. We got off once all right, but we have now a rare job on hand. Unless we can find the Count's key basket."

As nothing could well be done before morning, and as it would be at least advisable to wait till Lord Godalming should hear from Mitchell's, we decided not to take any active step before breakfast time. For a good while we sat and smoked, discussing the matter in its various lights and bearings. I took the opportunity of bringing this diary right up to the moment. I am very sleepy and shall go to bed . . .

Just a line. Mina sleeps soundly and her breathing is regular. Her forehead is puckered up into little wrinkles, as though she thinks even in her sleep. She is still too pale, but does not look so haggard as she did this morning. Tomorrow will, I hope, mend all this. She will be herself at home in Exeter. Oh, but I am sleepy!

DR. SEWARD'S DIARY

1 October.—I am puzzled afresh about Renfield. His moods change so rapidly that I find it difficult to keep touch of them, and as they always mean something more than his own well-being, they form a more than interesting study. This morning, when I went to see him after his repulse of Van Helsing, his manner was that of a man commanding destiny. He was, in fact, commanding destiny, subjectively. He did not really care for any of the things of mere earth, he was in the clouds and looked down on all the weaknesses and wants of us poor mortals.

I thought I would improve the occasion and learn something, so I asked him, "What about the flies these times?"

He smiled on me in quite a superior sort of way, such a smile as would have become the face of Malvolio, as he answered me, "The fly, my dear sir, has one striking feature. It's wings are typical of the aerial powers of the psychic faculties. The ancients did well when they typified the soul as a butterfly!"

I thought I would push his analogy to its utmost logically, so I said quickly, "Oh, it is a soul you are after now, is it?"

His madness foiled his reason, and a puzzled look spread over his face as, shaking his head with a decision which I had but seldom seen in him.

He said, "Oh, no, oh no! I want no souls. Life is all I want." Here he brightened up. "I am pretty indifferent about it at present. Life is all right. I have all I want. You must get a new patient, doctor, if you wish to study zoophagy!"

This puzzled me a little, so I drew him on. "Then you command life. You are a god, I suppose?"

He smiled with an ineffably benign superiority. "Oh no! Far be it from me to arrogate to myself the attributes of the Deity. I am not even concerned in His especially spiritual doings. If I may state my intellectual position I am, so far as concerns things purely terrestrial, somewhat in the position which Enoch occupied spiritually!"

This was a poser to me. I could not at the moment recall Enoch's appositeness, so I had to ask a simple question, though I felt that by so doing I was lowering myself in the eyes of the lunatic. "And why with Enoch?"

"Because he walked with God."

I could not see the analogy, but did not like to admit it, so I harked back to what he had denied. "So you don't care about life and you don't want souls. Why not?" I put my question quickly and somewhat sternly, on purpose to disconcert him.

The effort succeeded, for an instant he unconsciously relapsed into his old servile manner, bent low before me, and actually fawned upon me as he replied. "I don't want any souls, indeed, indeed! I don't. I couldn't use them if I had them. They would be no manner of use to me. I couldn't eat them or . . ."

He suddenly stopped and the old cunning look spread over his face, like a wind sweep on the surface of the water.

"And doctor, as to life, what is it after all? When you've got all you require, and you know that you will never want, that is all. I have friends, good friends, like you, Dr. Seward." This was said with a leer of inexpressible cunning. "I know that I shall never lack the means of life!"

I think that through the cloudiness of his insanity he saw some antagonism in me, for he at once fell back on the last refuge of such as he, a dogged silence. After a short time I saw that for the present it was useless to speak to him. He was sulky, and so I came away.

Later in the day he sent for me. Ordinarily I would not have come without special reason, but just at present I am so interested in him that I would gladly make an effort. Besides, I am glad to have anything to help pass the time. Harker is out, following up clues, and so are Lord Godalming and Quincey. Van Helsing sits in my study poring over the record prepared by the Harkers. He seems to think that by accurate knowledge of all details he will light up on some clue. He does not wish to be disturbed in the work, without cause. I would have taken him with me to see the patient, only I thought that after his last repulse he might not care to go again. There was also another reason. Renfield might not speak so freely before a third person as when he and I were alone.

I found him sitting in the middle of the floor on his stool, a pose which is generally indicative of some mental energy on his part. When I came in, he said at once, as though the question had been waiting on his lips. "What about souls?"

It was evident then that my surmise had been correct. Unconscious cerebration was doing its work, even with the lunatic. I determined to have the matter out.

"What about them yourself?" I asked.

He did not reply for a moment but looked all around him, and up and down, as though he expected to find some inspiration for an answer.

"I don't want any souls!" he said in a feeble, apologetic way. The matter seemed preying on his mind, and so I determined to use it, to "be cruel only to be kind." So I said, "You like life, and you want life?"

"Oh yes! But that is all right. You needn't worry about that!"

"But," I asked, "how are we to get the life without getting the soul also?"

This seemed to puzzle him, so I followed it up, "A nice time you'll have some time when you're flying out here, with the souls of thousands of flies and spiders and birds and cats buzzing and twittering and moaning all around you. You've got their lives, you know, and you must put up with their souls!"

Something seemed to affect his imagination, for he put his fingers to his ears and shut his eyes, screwing them up tightly just as a small boy does when his face is being soaped. There was something pathetic in it that touched me. It also gave me a lesson, for it seemed that before me was a child, only a child, though the features were worn, and the stubble on the jaws was white. It was evident that he was undergoing some process of mental disturbance, and knowing how his past moods had interpreted things seemingly foreign to himself, I thought I would enter into his mind as well as I could and go with him.

The first step was to restore confidence, so I asked him, speaking pretty loud so that he would hear me through his closed ears, "Would you like some sugar to get your flies around again?"

He seemed to wake up all at once, and shook his head. With a laugh he replied, "Not much! Flies are poor things, after all!" After a pause he added, "But I don't want their souls buzzing round me, all the same."

"Or spiders?" I went on.

"Blow spiders! What's the use of spiders? There isn't anything in them to eat or . . ." He stopped suddenly as though reminded of a forbidden topic.

"So, so!" I thought to myself, "this is the second time he has suddenly stopped at the word 'drink'. What does it mean?"

Renfield seemed himself aware of having made a lapse, for he hurried on, as though to distract my attention from it, "I don't take any stock at all in such matters. 'Rats and mice and such small deer,' as Shakespeare has it, 'chicken feed of the larder' they might be called. I'm past all that sort of nonsense. You might as well ask a man to eat molecules with a pair of chopsticks, as to try to interest me about the less carnivora, when I know of what is before me."

"I see," I said. "You want big things that you can make your teeth meet in? How would you like to breakfast on an elephant?"

"What ridiculous nonsense you are talking?" He was getting too wide awake, so I thought I would press him hard.

"I wonder," I said reflectively, "what an elephant's soul is like!"

The effect I desired was obtained, for he at once fell from his high-horse and became a child again.

"I don't want an elephant's soul, or any soul at all!" he said. For a few moments he sat despondently. Suddenly he jumped to his feet, with his eyes blazing and all the signs of intense cerebral excitement. "To hell with you and your souls!" he shouted. "Why do you plague me about souls? Haven't I got enough to worry, and pain, to distract me already, without thinking of souls?"

He looked so hostile that I thought he was in for another homicidal fit, so I blew my whistle.

The instant, however, that I did so he became calm, and said apologetically, "Forgive me, Doctor. I forgot myself. You do not need any help. I am so worried in my mind that I am apt to be irritable. If you only knew the problem I have to face, and that I am working out, you would pity, and tolerate, and pardon me. Pray do not put me in a strait waistcoat. I want to think and I cannot think freely when my body is confined. I am sure you will understand!"

He had evidently self-control, so when the attendants came I told them not to mind, and they withdrew. Renfield watched them go. When the door was closed he said with considerable dignity and sweetness, "Dr. Seward, you have been very considerate towards me. Believe me that I am very, very grateful to you!"

I thought it well to leave him in this mood, and so I came away. There is certainly something to ponder over in this man's state. Several points seem to make what the American interviewer calls "a story," if one could only get them in proper order. Here they are:

Will not mention "drinking."

Fears the thought of being burdened with the "soul" of anything.

Has no dread of wanting "life" in the future.

Despises the meaner forms of life altogether, though he dreads being haunted by their souls.

Logically all these things point one way! He has assurance of some kind that he will acquire some higher life.

He dreads the consequence, the burden of a soul. Then it is a human life he looks to!

And the assurance . . .?

Merciful God! The Count has been to him, and there is some new scheme of terror afoot!

Later.—I went after my round to Van Helsing and told him my suspicion. He grew very grave, and after thinking the matter over for a while asked me to take him to Renfield. I did so. As we came to the door we heard the lunatic within singing gaily, as he used to do in the time which now seems so long ago.

When we entered we saw with amazement that he had spread out his sugar as of old. The flies, lethargic with the autumn, were beginning to buzz into the room. We tried to make him talk of the subject of our previous conversation, but he would not attend. He went on with his singing, just as though we had not been present. He had got a scrap of paper and was folding it into a notebook. We had to come away as ignorant as we went in.

His is a curious case indeed. We must watch him tonight.

LETTER, MITCHELL, SONS & CANDY TO LORD GODALMING.

"1 October.

"My Lord,

"We are at all times only too happy to meet your wishes. We beg, with regard to the desire of your Lordship, expressed by Mr. Harker on your behalf, to supply the following information concerning the sale and purchase of No. 347, Piccadilly. The original vendors are the executors of the late Mr. Archibald Winter-Suffield. The purchaser is a foreign nobleman, Count de Ville, who effected the purchase himself paying the purchase money in notes 'over the counter,' if your Lordship will pardon us using so vulgar an expression. Beyond this we know nothing whatever of him.

"We are, my Lord,

"Your Lordship's humble servants,

"Mitchell, Sons & Candy."

DR. SEWARD'S DIARY

2 October.—I placed a man in the corridor last night, and told him to make an accurate note of any sound he might hear from Renfield's room, and gave him instructions that if there should be anything strange he was to call me. After dinner, when we had all gathered round the fire in the study, Mrs. Harker having gone to bed, we discussed the attempts and discoveries of the day. Harker was the only one who had any result, and we are in great hopes that his clue may be an important one.

Before going to bed I went round to the patient's room and looked in through the observation trap. He was sleeping soundly, his heart rose and fell with regular respiration.

This morning the man on duty reported to me that a little after midnight he was restless and kept saying his prayers somewhat loudly. I asked him if that was all. He replied that it was all he heard. There was something about his manner, so suspicious that I asked him point blank if he had been asleep.

He denied sleep, but admitted to having "dozed" for a while. It is too bad that men cannot be trusted unless they are watched.

Today Harker is out following up his clue, and Art and Quincey are looking after horses. Godalming thinks that it will be well to have horses always in readiness, for when we get the information which we seek there will be no time to lose. We must sterilize all the imported earth between sunrise and sunset. We shall thus catch the Count at his weakest, and without a refuge to fly to. Van Helsing is off to the British Museum looking up some authorities on ancient medicine. The old physicians took account of things which their followers do not accept, and the Professor is searching for witch and demon cures which may be useful to us later.

I sometimes think we must be all mad and that we shall wake to sanity in strait waistcoats.

Later.—We have met again. We seem at last to be on the track, and our work of tomorrow may be the beginning of the end. I wonder if Renfield's quiet has anything to do with this. His moods have so followed the doings of the Count, that the coming destruction of the monster may be carried to him some subtle way. If we could only get some hint as to what passed in his mind, between the time of my argument with him today and his resumption of fly-catching, it might afford us a valuable clue. He is now seemingly quiet for a spell . . . Is he? That wild yell seemed to come from his room . . .

The attendant came bursting into my room and told me that Renfield had somehow met with some accident. He had heard him yell, and when he went to him found him lying on his face on the floor, all covered with blood. I must go at once . . .

ᔆᴑ CHAPTER 21 ᔆᴚ
DR. SEWARD'S DIARY

3 October.—Let me put down with exactness all that happened, as well as I can remember, since last I made an entry. Not a detail that I can recall must be forgotten. In all calmness I must proceed.

When I came to Renfield's room I found him lying on the floor on his left side in a glittering pool of blood. When I went to move him, it became at once apparent that he had received some terrible injuries. There seemed none of the unity of purpose between the parts of the body which marks even lethargic sanity. As the face was exposed I could see that it was horribly bruised, as though it had been beaten against the floor. Indeed it was from the face wounds that the pool of blood originated.

The attendant who was kneeling beside the body said to me as we turned him over, "I think, sir, his back is broken. See, both his right arm and leg and the whole side of his face are paralysed." How such a thing could have happened puzzled the attendant beyond measure. He seemed quite bewildered, and his brows were gathered in as he said, "I can't understand the two things. He could mark his face like that by beating his own head on the floor. I saw a young woman do it once at the Eversfield Asylum before anyone could lay hands on her. And I suppose he might have broken his neck by falling out of bed, if he got in an awkward kink. But for the life of me I can't imagine how the two things occurred. If his back was broke, he couldn't beat his head, and if his face was like that before the fall out of bed, there would be marks of it."

I said to him, "Go to Dr. Van Helsing, and ask him to kindly come here at once. I want him without an instant's delay."

The man ran off, and within a few minutes the Professor, in his dressing gown and slippers, appeared. When he saw Renfield on the ground, he looked keenly at him a moment, and then turned to me. I think he recognized my thought in my eyes, for he said very quietly, manifestly for the ears of the attendant, "Ah, a sad accident! He will need very careful watching, and much attention. I shall stay with you myself, but I shall first dress myself. If you will remain I shall in a few minutes join you."

The patient was now breathing stertorously and it was easy to see that he had suffered some terrible injury.

Van Helsing returned with extraordinary celerity, bearing with him a surgical case. He had evidently been thinking and had his mind made up, for almost before he looked at the patient, he whispered to me, "Send the attendant away. We must be alone with him when he becomes conscious, after the operation."

I said, "I think that will do now, Simmons. We have done all that we can at present. You had better go your round, and Dr. Van Helsing will operate. Let me know instantly if there be anything unusual anywhere."

The man withdrew, and we went into a strict examination of the patient. The wounds of the face were superficial. The real injury was a depressed fracture of the skull, extending right up through the motor area.

The Professor thought a moment and said, "We must reduce the pressure and get back to normal conditions, as far as can be. The rapidity of the suffusion shows the terrible nature of his injury. The whole motor area seems affected. The suffusion of the brain will increase quickly, so we must trephine at once or it may be too late."

As he was speaking there was a soft tapping at the door. I went over and opened it and found in the corridor without, Arthur and Quincey in pajamas and slippers; the former spoke, "I heard your man call up Dr. Van Helsing and tell him of an accident. So I woke Quincey or rather called for him as he was not asleep. Things are moving too quickly and too strangely for sound sleep for any of us these times. I've been thinking that tomorrow night will not see things as they have been. We'll have to look back, and forward a little more than we have done. May we come in?"

I nodded, and held the door open till they had entered, then I closed it again. When Quincey saw the attitude and state of the patient, and noted the horrible pool on the floor, he said softly, "My God! What has happened to him? Poor, poor devil!"

I told him briefly, and added that we expected he would recover consciousness after the operation, for a short time, at all events. He went at once and sat down on the edge of the bed, with Godalming beside him. We all watched in patience.

"We shall wait," said Van Helsing, "just long enough to fix the best spot for trephining, so that we may most quickly and perfectly remove the blood clot, for it is evident that the haemorrhage is increasing."

The minutes during which we waited passed with fearful slowness. I had a horrible sinking in my heart, and from Van Helsing's face I gathered that he felt some fear or apprehension as to what was to come. I dreaded the words Renfield might speak. I was positively afraid to think. But the conviction of what was coming was on me, as I have read of men who have heard the death watch. The poor man's breathing came in uncertain gasps. Each instant he seemed as though he would open his eyes and speak, but then would follow a prolonged stertorous breath, and he would relapse into a more fixed insensibility. Inured as I was to sick beds and death, this suspense grew and grew upon me. I could almost hear the beating of my own heart, and the blood surging through my temples sounded like blows from a hammer. The silence finally became agonizing. I looked at my companions, one after another, and saw from their flushed faces and damp brows that they were enduring equal torture. There was a nervous suspense over us all, as though overhead some dread bell would peal out powerfully when we should least expect it.

At last there came a time when it was evident that the patient was sinking fast. He might die at any moment. I looked up at the Professor and caught his eyes fixed on mine. His face was sternly set as he spoke, "There is no time to lose. His words may be worth many lives. I have been thinking so, as I stood here. It may be there is a soul at stake! We shall operate just above the ear."

Without another word he made the operation. For a few moments the breathing continued to be stertorous. Then there came a breath so prolonged that it seemed as though it would tear open his chest. Suddenly his eyes opened, and became fixed in a wild, helpless stare. This was continued for a few moments, then it was softened into a glad surprise, and from his lips came a sigh of relief. He moved convulsively, and as he did so, said, "I'll be quiet, Doctor. Tell them to take off the strait waistcoat. I have had a terrible dream, and it has left me so weak that I cannot move. What's wrong with my face? It feels all swollen, and it smarts dreadfully."

He tried to turn his head, but even with the effort his eyes seemed to grow glassy again so I gently put it back. Then Van Helsing said in a quiet grave tone, "Tell us your dream, Mr. Renfield."

As he heard the voice his face brightened, through its mutilation, and he said, "That is Dr. Van Helsing. How good it is of you to be here. Give me some water, my lips are dry, and I shall try to tell you. I dreamed . . ."

He stopped and seemed fainting. I called quietly to Quincey, "The brandy, it is in my study, quick!" He flew and returned with a glass, the decanter of brandy and a carafe of water. We moistened the parched lips, and the patient quickly revived.

It seemed, however, that his poor injured brain had been working in the interval, for when he was quite conscious, he looked at me piercingly with an agonized confusion which I shall never forget, and said, "I must not deceive myself. It was no dream, but all a grim reality." Then his eyes roved round the room. As they caught sight of the two figures sitting patiently on the edge of the bed he went on, "If I were not sure already, I would know from them."

For an instant his eyes closed, not with pain or sleep but voluntarily, as though he were bringing all his faculties to bear. When he opened them he said, hurriedly, and with more energy than he had yet displayed, "Quick, Doctor, quick, I am dying! I feel that I have but a few minutes, and then I must go back to death, or worse! Wet my lips with brandy again. I have something that I must say before I die. Or before my poor crushed brain dies anyhow. Thank you! It was that night after you left me, when I implored you to let me go away. I couldn't speak then, for I felt my tongue was tied. But I was as sane then, except in that way, as I am now. I was in an agony of despair for a long time after you left me, it seemed hours. Then there came a sudden peace to me. My brain seemed to become cool again, and I realized where I was. I heard the dogs bark behind our house, but not where He was!"

As he spoke, Van Helsing's eyes never blinked, but his hand came out and met mine and gripped it hard. He did not, however, betray himself. He nodded slightly and said, "Go on," in a low voice.

Renfield proceeded. "He came up to the window in the mist, as I had seen him often before, but he was solid then, not a ghost, and his eyes were fierce like a man's when angry. He was laughing with his red mouth, the sharp white teeth glinted in the moonlight when he turned to look back over the belt of trees, to where the dogs were barking. I wouldn't ask him to come in at first, though I knew he wanted to, just as he had wanted all along. Then he began promising me things, not in words but by doing them."

He was interrupted by a word from the Professor, "How?"

"By making them happen. Just as he used to send in the flies when the sun was shining. Great big fat ones with steel and sapphire on their wings. And big moths, in the night, with skull and cross-bones on their backs."

Van Helsing nodded to him as he whispered to me unconsciously, "The *Acherontia Atropos of the Sphinges*, what you call the 'Death's-head Moth'?"

The patient went on without stopping, "Then he began to whisper. 'Rats, rats, rats! Hundreds, thousands, millions of them, and every one a life. And dogs to eat them, and cats too. All lives! All red blood, with years of life in it, and not merely buzzing flies!' I laughed at him, for I wanted to see what he could do. Then the dogs howled, away beyond the dark trees in His house. He beckoned me to the window. I got up and looked out, and He raised his hands, and seemed to call out without using any words. A dark mass spread over the grass, coming on like the shape of a flame of fire. And then He moved the mist to the right and left, and I could see that there were thousands of rats with their eyes blazing red, like His only smaller. He held up his hand, and they all stopped, and I thought he seemed to be saying, 'All these lives will I give you, ay, and many more and greater, through countless ages, if you will fall down and worship me!' And then a red cloud, like the colour of blood, seemed to close over my eyes, and before I knew what I was doing, I found myself opening the sash and saying to Him, 'Come in, Lord and Master!' The rats were all gone, but He slid into the room through the sash, though it was only open an inch wide, just as the Moon herself has often come in through the tiniest crack and has stood before me in all her size and splendour."

His voice was weaker, so I moistened his lips with the brandy again, and he continued, but it seemed as though his memory had gone on working in the interval for his story was further advanced. I was about to call him back to the point, but Van Helsing whispered to me, "Let him go on. Do not interrupt him. He cannot go back, and maybe could not proceed at all if once he lost the thread of his thought."

He proceeded, "All day I waited to hear from him, but he did not send me anything, not even a blowfly, and when the moon got up I was pretty angry with him. When he did slide in through the window, though it was shut, and did not even knock, I got mad with him. He sneered at me, and his white face looked out of the mist with his red eyes gleaming, and he went on as though he owned the whole place, and I was no one. He didn't even smell the same as he went by me. I couldn't hold him. I thought that, somehow, Mrs. Harker had come into the room."

The two men sitting on the bed stood up and came over, standing behind him so that he could not see them, but where they could hear better. They were both silent, but the Professor started and quivered. His face, however, grew grimmer and sterner still. Renfield went on without noticing, "When Mrs. Harker came in to see me this afternoon she wasn't the same. It was like tea after the teapot has been watered." Here we all moved, but no one said a word.

He went on, "I didn't know that she was here till she spoke, and she didn't look the same. I don't care for the pale people. I like them with lots of blood in them, and hers all seemed to have run out. I didn't think of it at the time, but when she went away I began to think, and it made me mad to know that He had been taking the life out of her." I could feel that the rest quivered, as I did; but we remained otherwise still. "So when He came tonight I was ready for Him. I saw the mist stealing in, and I grabbed it tight. I had heard that madmen have unnatural strength. And as I knew I was a madman, at times anyhow, I resolved to use my power. Ay, and He felt it too, for He had to come out of the mist to struggle with me. I held tight, and I thought I was going to win, for I didn't mean Him to take any more of her life, till I saw His eyes. They burned into me, and my strength became like water. He slipped through it, and when I tried to cling to Him, He raised me up and flung me down. There was a red cloud before me, and a noise like thunder, and the mist seemed to steal away under the door."

His voice was becoming fainter and his breath more stertorous. Van Helsing stood up instinctively.

"We know the worst now," he said. "He is here, and we know his purpose. It may not be too late. Let us be armed, the same as we were the other night, but lose no time, there is not an instant to spare."

There was no need to put our fear, nay our conviction, into words, we shared them in common. We all hurried and took from our rooms the same things that we had when we entered the Count's house. The Professor had his ready, and as we met in the corridor he pointed to them significantly as he said, "They never leave me, and they shall not till this unhappy business is over. Be wise also, my friends. It is no common enemy that we deal with

Alas! Alas! That dear Madam Mina should suffer!" He stopped, his voice was breaking, and I do not know if rage or terror predominated in my own heart.

Outside the Harkers' door we paused. Art and Quincey held back, and the latter said, "Should we disturb her?"

"We must," said Van Helsing grimly. "If the door be locked, I shall break it in."

"May it not frighten her terribly? It is unusual to break into a lady's room!"

Van Helsing said solemnly, "You are always right. But this is life and death. All chambers are alike to the doctor. And even were they not they are all as one to me tonight. Friend John, when I turn the handle, if the door does not open, do you put your shoulder down and shove; and you too, my friends. Now!"

He turned the handle as he spoke, but the door did not yield. We threw ourselves against it. With a crash it burst open, and we almost fell headlong into the room. The Professor did actually fall, and I saw across him as he gathered himself up from hands and knees. What I saw appalled me. I felt my hair rise like bristles on the back of my neck, and my heart seemed to stand still.

The moonlight was so bright that through the thick yellow blind the room was light enough to see. On the bed beside the window lay Jonathan Harker, his face flushed and breathing heavily as though in a stupor. Kneeling on the near edge of the bed facing outwards was the white-clad figure of his wife. By her side stood a tall, thin man, clad in black. His face was turned from us, but the instant we saw we all recognized the Count, in every way, even to the scar on his forehead. With his left hand he held both Mrs. Harker's hands, keeping them away with her arms at full tension. His right hand gripped her by the back of the neck, forcing her face down on his bosom. Her white nightdress was smeared with blood, and a thin stream trickled down the man's bare chest which was shown by his torn-open dress. The attitude of the two had a terrible resemblance to a child forcing a kitten's nose into a saucer of milk to compel it to drink. As we burst into the room, the Count turned his face, and the hellish look that I had heard described seemed to leap into it. His eyes flamed red with devilish passion. The great nostrils of the white aquiline nose opened wide and quivered at the edge, and the white sharp teeth, behind the full lips of the blood dripping mouth, clamped together like those of a wild beast. With a wrench, which threw his victim back upon the bed as though hurled from a height, he turned and sprang at us. But by this time the Professor had gained his feet, and was holding towards him the envelope which contained the Sacred Wafer. The Count suddenly stopped, just as poor Lucy had done outside the tomb, and cowered back. Further and further back he cowered, as we, lifting our crucifixes, advanced. The moonlight suddenly failed, as a great black cloud sailed across the sky. And when the gaslight sprang up under Quincey's match, we saw nothing but a faint vapour. This, as we looked, trailed under the door, which with the recoil from its bursting open, had swung back to its old position. Van Helsing, Art, and I moved forward to Mrs. Harker, who by this time had drawn her breath and with it had given a scream so wild, so ear-piercing, so despairing that it seems to me now that it will ring in my ears till my dying day. For a few seconds she lay in her helpless attitude and disarray. Her face was ghastly, with a pallor which was accentuated by the blood which smeared her lips and cheeks and chin. From her throat trickled a thin stream of blood. Her eyes were mad with terror. Then she put before her face her poor crushed hands, which bore on their whiteness the red mark of the Count's terrible grip, and from behind them came a low desolate wail which made the terrible scream seem only the quick expression of an endless grief. Van Helsing stepped forward and drew the coverlet gently over her body, whilst Art, after looking at her face for an instant despairingly, ran out of the room.

Van Helsing whispered to me, "Jonathan is in a stupor such as we know the Vampire can produce. We can do nothing with poor Madam Mina for a few moments till she recovers herself. I must wake him!"

He dipped the end of a towel in cold water and with it began to flick him on the face, his wife all the while holding her face between her hands and sobbing in a way that was heart breaking to hear. I raised the blind, and looked out of the window. There was much moonshine, and as I looked I could see Quincey Morris run across the lawn and hide himself in the shadow of a great yew tree. It puzzled me to think why he was doing this. But at the instant I heard Harker's quick exclamation as he woke to partial consciousness, and turned to the bed. On his face, as there might well be, was a look of wild amazement. He seemed dazed for a few seconds, and then full consciousness seemed to burst upon him all at once, and he started up.

His wife was aroused by the quick movement, and turned to him with her arms stretched out, as though to embrace him. Instantly, however, she drew them in again, and putting her elbows together, held her hands before her face, and shuddered till the bed beneath her shook.

"In God's name what does this mean?" Harker cried out. "Dr. Seward, Dr. Van Helsing, what is it? What has happened? What is wrong? Mina, dear what is it? What does that blood mean? My God, my God! Has it come to this!" And, raising himself to his knees, he beat his hands wildly together. "Good God help us! Help her! Oh, help her!"

With a quick movement he jumped from bed, and began to pull on his clothes, all the man in him awake at the need for instant exertion. "What has happened? Tell me all about it!" he cried without pausing. "Dr. Van Helsing, you love Mina, I know. Oh, do something to save her. It cannot have gone too far yet. Guard her while I look for *him*!"

His wife, through her terror and horror and distress, saw some sure danger to him. Instantly forgetting her own grief, she seized hold of him and cried out.

"No! No! Jonathan, you must not leave me. I have suffered enough tonight, God knows, without the dread of his harming you. You must stay with me. Stay with these friends who will watch over you!" Her expression became frantic as she spoke. And, he yielding to her, she pulled him down sitting on the bedside, and clung to him fiercely.

Van Helsing and I tried to calm them both. The Professor held up his golden crucifix, and said with wonderful calmness, "Do not fear, my dear. We are here, and whilst this is close to you no foul thing can approach. You are safe for tonight, and we must be calm and take counsel together."

She shuddered and was silent, holding down her head on her husband's breast. When she raised it, his white nightrobe was stained with blood where her lips had touched, and where the thin open wound in the neck had sent forth drops. The instant she saw it she drew back, with a low wail, and whispered, amidst choking sobs.

"Unclean, unclean! I must touch him or kiss him no more. Oh, that it should be that it is I who am now his worst enemy, and whom he may have most cause to fear."

To this he spoke out resolutely, "Nonsense, Mina. It is a shame to me to hear such a word. I would not hear it of you. And I shall not hear it from you. May God judge me by my deserts, and punish me with more bitter suffering than even this hour, if by any act or will of mine anything ever come between us!"

He put out his arms and folded her to his breast. And for a while she lay there sobbing. He looked at us over her bowed head, with eyes that blinked damply above his quivering nostrils. His mouth was set as steel.

After a while her sobs became less frequent and more faint, and then he said to me, speaking with a studied calmness which I felt tried his nervous power to the utmost.

"And now, Dr. Seward, tell me all about it. Too well I know the broad fact. Tell me all that has been."

I told him exactly what had happened and he listened with seeming impassiveness, but his nostrils twitched and his eyes blazed as I told how the ruthless hands of the Count had held his wife in that terrible and horrid position, with her mouth to the open wound in his breast. It interested me, even at that moment, to see that whilst the face of white set passion worked convulsively over the bowed head, the hands tenderly and lovingly stroked the ruffled hair. Just as I had finished, Quincey and Godalming knocked at the door. They entered in obedience to our summons. Van Helsing looked at me questioningly. I understood him to mean if we were to take advantage of their coming to divert if possible the thoughts of the unhappy husband and wife from each other and from themselves. So on nodding acquiescence to him he asked them what they had seen or done. To which Lord Godalming answered.

"I could not see him anywhere in the passage, or in any of our rooms. I looked in the study but, though he had been there, he had gone. He had, however . . ." He stopped suddenly, looking at the poor drooping figure on the bed.

Van Helsing said gravely, "Go on, friend Arthur. We want here no more concealments. Our hope now is in knowing all. Tell freely!"

So Art went on, "He had been there, and though it could only have been for a few seconds, he made rare hay of the place. All the manuscript had been burned, and the blue flames were flickering amongst the white ashes. The cylinders of your phonograph too were thrown on the fire, and the wax had helped the flames."

Here I interrupted. "Thank God there is the other copy in the safe!"

His face lit for a moment, but fell again as he went on. "I ran downstairs then, but could see no sign of him. I looked into Renfield's room, but there was no trace there except . . ." Again he paused.

"Go on," said Harker hoarsely. So he bowed his head and moistening his lips with his tongue, added, "except that the poor fellow is dead."

Mrs. Harker raised her head, looking from one to the other of us she said solemnly, "God's will be done!"

I could not but feel that Art was keeping back something. But, as I took it that it was with a purpose, I said nothing.

Van Helsing turned to Morris and asked, "And you, friend Quincey, have you any to tell?"

"A little," he answered. "It may be much eventually, but at present I can't say. I thought it well to know if possible where the Count would go when he left the house. I did not see him, but I saw a bat rise from Renfield's window, and flap westward. I expected to see him in some shape go back to Carfax, but he evidently sought some other lair. He will not be back tonight, for the sky is reddening in the east, and the dawn is close. We must work tomorrow!"

He said the latter words through his shut teeth. For a space of perhaps a couple of minutes there was silence, and I could fancy that I could hear the sound of our hearts beating.

Then Van Helsing said, placing his hand tenderly on Mrs. Harker's head, "And now, Madam Mina, poor dear, dear, Madam Mina, tell us exactly what happened. God knows that I do not want that you be pained, but it is need that we know all. For now more than ever has all work to be done quick and sharp, and in deadly earnest. The day is close to us that must end all, if it may be so, and now is the chance that we may live and learn."

The poor dear lady shivered, and I could see the tension of her nerves as she clasped her husband closer to her and bent her head lower and lower still on his breast. Then she raised her head proudly, and held out one hand to Van Helsing who took it in his, and after stooping and kissing it reverently, held it fast. The other hand was locked in that of her husband, who held his other arm thrown round her protectingly. After a pause in which she was evidently ordering her thoughts, she began.

"I took the sleeping draught which you had so kindly given me, but for a long time it did not act. I seemed to become more wakeful, and myriads of horrible fancies began to crowd in upon my mind. All of them connected with death, and vampires, with blood, and pain, and trouble." Her husband involuntarily groaned as she turned to him and said lovingly, "Do not fret, dear. You must be brave and strong, and help me through the horrible task. If you only knew what an effort it is to me to tell of this fearful thing at all, you would understand how much I need your help. Well, I saw I must try to help the medicine to its work with my will, if it was to do me any good, so I resolutely set myself to sleep. Sure enough sleep must soon have come to me, for I remember no more. Jonathan coming in had not waked me, for he lay by my side when next I remember. There was in the room the same thin white mist that I had before noticed. But I forget now if you know of this. You will find it in my diary which I shall show you later. I felt the same vague terror which had come to me before and the same sense of some presence. I turned to wake Jonathan, but found that he slept so soundly that it seemed as if it was he who had taken the sleeping draught, and not I. I tried, but I could not wake him. This caused me a great fear, and I looked around terrified. Then indeed, my heart sank within me. Beside the bed, as if he had stepped out of the mist, or rather as if the mist had turned into his figure, for it had entirely disappeared, stood a tall, thin man, all in black. I knew him at once from the description of the others. The waxen face, the high aquiline nose, on which the light fell in a thin white line, the parted red lips, with the sharp white teeth showing between, and the red eyes that I had seemed to see in the sunset on the windows of St. Mary's Church at

Whitby. I knew, too, the red scar on his forehead where Jonathan had struck him. For an instant my heart stood still, and I would have screamed out, only that I was paralyzed. In the pause he spoke in a sort of keen, cutting whisper, pointing as he spoke to Jonathan.

"'Silence! If you make a sound I shall take him and dash his brains out before your very eyes.' I was appalled and was too bewildered to do or say anything. With a mocking smile, he placed one hand upon my shoulder and, holding me tight, bared my throat with the other, saying as he did so, 'First, a little refreshment to reward my exertions. You may as well be quiet. It is not the first time, or the second, that your veins have appeased my thirst!' I was bewildered, and strangely enough, I did not want to hinder him. I suppose it is a part of the horrible curse that such is, when his touch is on his victim. And oh, my God, my God, pity me! He placed his reeking lips upon my throat!" Her husband groaned again. She clasped his hand harder, and looked at him pityingly, as if he were the injured one, and went on.

"I felt my strength fading away, and I was in a half swoon. How long this horrible thing lasted I know not, but it seemed that a long time must have passed before he took his foul, awful, sneering mouth away. I saw it drip with the fresh blood!" The remembrance seemed for a while to overpower her, and she drooped and would have sunk down but for her husband's sustaining arm. With a great effort she recovered herself and went on.

"Then he spoke to me mockingly, 'And so you, like the others, would play your brains against mine. You would help these men to hunt me and frustrate me in my design! You know now, and they know in part already, and will know in full before long, what it is to cross my path. They should have kept their energies for use closer to home. Whilst they played wits against me, against me who commanded nations, and intrigued for them, and fought for them, hundreds of years before they were born, I was countermining them. And you, their best beloved one, are now to me, flesh of my flesh, blood of my blood, kin of my kin, my bountiful wine-press for a while, and shall be later on my companion and my helper. You shall be avenged in turn, for not one of them but shall minister to your needs. But as yet you are to be punished for what you have done. You have aided in thwarting me. Now you shall come to my call. When my brain says "Come!" to you, you shall cross land or sea to do my bidding. And to that end this!'

"With that he pulled open his shirt, and with his long sharp nails opened a vein in his breast. When the blood began to spurt out, he took my hands in one of his, holding them tight, and with the other seized my neck and pressed my mouth to the wound, so that I must either suffocate or swallow some to the . . . Oh, my God! My God! What have I done? What have I done to deserve such a fate, I who have tried to walk in meekness and righteousness all my days. God pity me! Look down on a poor soul in worse than mortal peril. And in mercy pity those to whom she is dear!" Then she began to rub her lips as though to cleanse them from pollution.

As she was telling her terrible story, the eastern sky began to quicken, and everything became more and more clear. Harker was still and quiet; but over his face, as the awful narrative went on, came a grey look which deepened and deepened in the morning light, till when the first red streak of the coming dawn shot up, the flesh stood darkly out against the whitening hair.

We have arranged that one of us is to stay within call of the unhappy pair till we can meet together and arrange about taking action.

Of this I am sure. The sun rises today on no more miserable house in all the great round of its daily course.

&o CHAPTER 22 ca
JONATHAN HARKER'S JOURNAL

3 October.—As I must do something or go mad, I write this diary. It is now six o'clock, and we are to meet in the study in half an hour and take something to eat, for Dr. Van Helsing and Dr. Seward are agreed that if we do not eat we cannot work our best. Our best will be, God knows, required today. I must keep writing at every chance, for I dare not stop to think. All, big and little, must go down. Perhaps at the end the little things may teach us most. The teaching, big or little, could not have landed Mina or me anywhere worse than we are today. However, we must trust and hope. Poor Mina told me just now, with the tears running down her dear cheeks, that it is in trouble and trial that our faith is tested. That we must keep on trusting, and that God will aid us up to the end. The end! Oh my God! What end? . . . To work! To work!

When Dr. Van Helsing and Dr. Seward had come back from seeing poor Renfield, we went gravely into what was to be done. First, Dr. Seward told us that when he and Dr. Van Helsing had gone down to the room below they had found Renfield lying on the floor, all in a heap. His face was all bruised and crushed in, and the bones of the neck were broken.

Dr. Seward asked the attendant who was on duty in the passage if he had heard anything. He said that he had been sitting down, he confessed to half dozing, when he heard loud voices in the room, and then Renfield had called out loudly several times, "God! God! God!" After that there was a sound of falling, and when he entered the room he found him lying on the floor, face down, just as the doctors had seen him. Van Helsing asked if he had heard "voices" or "a voice," and he said he could not say. That at first it had seemed to him as if there were two, but as there was no one in the room it could have been only one. He could swear to it, if required, that the word "God" was spoken by the patient.

Dr. Seward said to us, when we were alone, that he did not wish to go into the matter. The question of an inquest had to be considered, and it would never do to put forward the truth, as no one would believe it. As it was, he thought that on the attendant's evidence he could give a certificate of death by misadventure in falling from bed. In case the coroner should demand it, there would be a formal inquest, necessarily to the same result.

When the question began to be discussed as to what should be our next step, the very first thing we decided was that Mina should be in full confidence. That nothing of any sort, no matter how painful, should be kept from her. She herself agreed as to its wisdom, and it was pitiful to see her so brave and yet so sorrowful, and in such a depth of despair.

"There must be no concealment," she said. "Alas! We have had too much already. And besides there is nothing in all the world that can give me more pain than I have already endured, than I suffer now! Whatever may happen, it must be of new hope or of new courage to me!"

Van Helsing was looking at her fixedly as she spoke, and said, suddenly but quietly, "But dear Madam Mina, are you not afraid. Not for yourself, but for others from yourself, after what has happened?"

Her face grew set in its lines, but her eyes shone with the devotion of a martyr as she answered, "Ah no! For my mind is made up!"

"To what?" he asked gently, whilst we were all very still, for each in our own way we had a sort of vague idea of what she meant.

Her answer came with direct simplicity, as though she was simply stating a fact, "Because if I find in myself, and I shall watch keenly for it, a sign of harm to any that I love, I shall die!"

"You would not kill yourself?" he asked, hoarsely.

"I would. If there were no friend who loved me, who would save me such a pain, and so desperate an effort!" She looked at him meaningly as she spoke.

He was sitting down, but now he rose and came close to her and put his hand on her head as he said solemnly. "My child, there is such an one if it were for your good. For myself I could hold it in my account with God to find such an euthanasia for you, even at this moment if it were best. Nay, were it safe! But my child . . ."

For a moment he seemed choked, and a great sob rose in his throat. He gulped it down and went on, "There are here some who would stand between you and death. You must not die. You must not die by any hand, but least of all your own. Until the other, who has fouled your sweet life, is true dead you must not die. For if he is still with the quick Undead, your death would make you even as he is. No, you must live! You must struggle and strive to live, though death would seem a boon unspeakable. You must fight Death himself, though he come to you in pain or in joy. By the day, or the night, in safety or in peril! On your living soul I charge you that you do not die. Nay, nor think of death, till this great evil be past."

The poor dear grew white as death, and shook and shivered, as I have seen a quicksand shake and shiver at the incoming of the tide. We were all silent. We could do nothing. At length she grew more calm and turning to him said sweetly, but oh so sorrowfully, as she held out her hand, "I promise you, my dear friend, that if God will let me live, I shall strive to do so. Till, if it may be in His good time, this horror may have passed away from me."

She was so good and brave that we all felt that our hearts were strengthened to work and endure for her, and we began to discuss what we were to do. I told her that she was to have all the papers in the safe, and all the papers or diaries and phonographs we might hereafter use, and was to keep the record as she had done before. She was pleased with the prospect of anything to do, if "pleased" could be used in connection with so grim an interest.

As usual Van Helsing had thought ahead of everyone else, and was prepared with an exact ordering of our work.

"It is perhaps well," he said, "that at our meeting after our visit to Carfax we decided not to do anything with the earth boxes that lay there. Had we done so, the Count must have guessed our purpose, and would doubtless have taken measures in advance to frustrate such an effort with regard to the others. But now he does not know our intentions. Nay, more, in all probability, he does not know that such a power exists to us as can sterilize his lairs, so that he cannot use them as of old.

"We are now so much further advanced in our knowledge as to their disposition that, when we have examined the house in Piccadilly, we may track the very last of them. Today then, is ours, and in it rests our hope. The sun that rose on our sorrow this morning guards us in its course. Until it sets tonight, that monster must retain whatever form he now has. He is confined within the limitations of his earthly envelope. He cannot melt into thin air nor disappear through cracks or chinks or crannies. If he go through a doorway, he must open the door like a mortal. And so we have this day to hunt out all his lairs and sterilize them. So we shall, if we have not yet catch him and destroy him, drive him to bay in some place where the catching and the destroying shall be, in time, sure."

Here I started up for I could not contain myself at the thought that the minutes and seconds so preciously laden with Mina's life and happiness were flying from us, since whilst we talked action was impossible. But Van Helsing held up his hand warningly.

"Nay, friend Jonathan," he said, "in this, the quickest way home is the longest way, so your proverb say. We shall all act and act with desperate quick, when the time has come. But think, in all probable the key of the situation is in that house in Piccadilly. The Count may have many houses which he has bought. Of them he will have deeds of purchase, keys and other things. He will have paper that he write on. He will have his book of cheques. There are many belongings that he must have somewhere. Why not in this place so central, so quiet, where he come and go by the front or the back at all hours, when in the very vast of the traffic there is none to notice. We shall go there and search that house. And when we learn what it holds, then we do what our friend Arthur call, in his phrases of hunt 'stop the earths' and so we run down our old fox, so? Is it not?"

"Then let us come at once," I cried, "we are wasting the precious, precious time!"

The Professor did not move, but simply said, "And how are we to get into that house in Piccadilly?"

"Any way!" I cried. "We shall break in if need be."

"And your police? Where will they be, and what will they say?"

I was staggered, but I knew that if he wished to delay he had a good reason for it. So I said, as quietly as I could, "Don't wait more than need be. You know, I am sure, what torture I am in."

"Ah, my child, that I do. And indeed there is no wish of me to add to your anguish. But just think, what can we do, until all the world be at movement. Then will come our time. I have thought and thought, and it seems to me that the simplest way is the best of all. Now we wish to get into the house, but we have no key. Is it not so?" I nodded.

"Now suppose that you were, in truth, the owner of that house, and could not still get in. And think there was to you no conscience of the house-breaker, what would you do?"

"I should get a respectable locksmith, and set him to work to pick the lock for me."

"And your police, they would interfere, would they not?"

"Oh no! Not if they knew the man was properly employed."

"Then," he looked at me as keenly as he spoke, "all that is in doubt is the conscience of the employer, and the belief of your policemen as to whether or not that employer has a good conscience or a bad one. Your police must indeed be zealous men and clever, oh so clever, in reading the heart, that they trouble themselves in such matter. No, no, my friend Jonathan, you go take the lock off a hundred empty houses in this your London, or of any city in the world, and if you do it as such things are rightly done, and at the time such things are rightly done, no one will interfere. I have read of a gentleman who owned a so fine house in London, and when he went for months of summer to Switzerland and lock up his house, some burglar come and broke window at back and got in. Then he went and made open the shutters in front and walk out and in through the door, before the very eyes of the police. Then he have an auction in that house, and advertise it, and put up big notice. And when the day come he sell off by a great auctioneer all the goods of that other man who own them. Then he go to a builder, and he sell him that house, making an agreement that he pull it down and take all away within a certain time. And your police and other authority help him all they can. And when that owner come back from his holiday in Switzerland he find only an empty hole where his house had been. This was all done *en régle*,[110] and in our work we shall be *en régle* too. We shall not go so early that the policemen who have then little to think of, shall deem it strange. But we shall go after ten o'clock, when there are many about, and such things would be done were we indeed owners of the house."

I could not but see how right he was and the terrible despair of Mina's face became relaxed in thought. There was hope in such good counsel.

Van Helsing went on, "When once within that house we may find more clues. At any rate some of us can remain there whilst the rest find the other places where there be more earth boxes, at Bermondsey and Mile End."

Lord Godalming stood up. "I can be of some use here," he said. "I shall wire to my people to have horses and carriages where they will be most convenient."

"Look here, old fellow," said Morris, "it is a capital idea to have all ready in case we want to go horse backing, but don't you think that one of your snappy carriages with its heraldic adornments in a byway of Walworth or Mile End would attract too much attention for our purpose? It seems to me that we ought to take cabs when we go south or east. And even leave them somewhere near the neighbourhood we are going to."

"Friend Quincey is right!" said the Professor. "His head is what you call in plane with the horizon. It is a difficult thing that we go to do, and we do not want no peoples to watch us if so it may."

Mina took a growing interest in everything and I was rejoiced to see that the exigency of affairs was helping her to forget for a time the terrible experience of the night. She was very, very pale, almost ghastly, and so thin that her lips were drawn away, showing her teeth in somewhat of

---

110 According to rule (French).

prominence. I did not mention this last, lest it should give her needless pain, but it made my blood run cold in my veins to think of what had occurred with poor Lucy when the Count had sucked her blood. As yet there was no sign of the teeth growing sharper, but the time as yet was short, and there was time for fear.

When we came to the discussion of the sequence of our efforts and of the disposition of our forces, there were new sources of doubt. It was finally agreed that before starting for Piccadilly we should destroy the Count's lair close at hand. In case he should find it out too soon, we should thus be still ahead of him in our work of destruction. And his presence in his purely material shape, and at his weakest, might give us some new clue.

As to the disposal of forces, it was suggested by the Professor that, after our visit to Carfax, we should all enter the house in Piccadilly. That the two doctors and I should remain there, whilst Lord Godalming and Quincey found the lairs at Walworth and Mile End and destroyed them. It was possible, if not likely, the Professor urged, that the Count might appear in Piccadilly during the day, and that if so we might be able to cope with him then and there. At any rate, we might be able to follow him in force. To this plan I strenuously objected, and so far as my going was concerned, for I said that I intended to stay and protect Mina. I thought that my mind was made up on the subject, but Mina would not listen to my objection. She said that there might be some law matter in which I could be useful. That amongst the Count's papers might be some clue which I could understand out of my experience in Transylvania. And that, as it was, all the strength we could muster was required to cope with the Count's extraordinary power. I had to give in, for Mina's resolution was fixed. She said that it was the last hope for her that we should all work together.

"As for me," she said, "I have no fear. Things have been as bad as they can be. And whatever may happen must have in it some element of hope or comfort. Go, my husband! God can, if He wishes it, guard me as well alone as with any one present."

So I started up crying out, "Then in God's name let us come at once, for we are losing time. The Count may come to Piccadilly earlier than we think."

"Not so!" said Van Helsing, holding up his hand.

"But why?" I asked.

"Do you forget," he said, with actually a smile, "that last night he banqueted heavily, and will sleep late?"

Did I forget! Shall I ever . . . can I ever! Can any of us ever forget that terrible scene! Mina struggled hard to keep her brave countenance, but the pain overmastered her and she put her hands before her face, and shuddered whilst she moaned. Van Helsing had not intended to recall her frightful experience. He had simply lost sight of her and her part in the affair in his intellectual effort.

When it struck him what he said, he was horrified at his thoughtlessness and tried to comfort her.

"Oh, Madam Mina," he said, "dear, dear, Madam Mina, alas! That I of all who so reverence you should have said anything so forgetful. These stupid old lips of mine and this stupid old head do not deserve so, but you will forget it, will you not?" He bent low beside her as he spoke.

She took his hand, and looking at him through her tears, said hoarsely, "No, I shall not forget, for it is well that I remember. And with it I have so much in memory of you that is sweet, that I take it all together. Now, you must all be going soon. Breakfast is ready, and we must all eat that we may be strong."

Breakfast was a strange meal to us all. We tried to be cheerful and encourage each other, and Mina was the brightest and most cheerful of us. When it was over, Van Helsing stood up and said, "Now, my dear friends, we go forth to our terrible enterprise. Are we all armed, as we were on that night when first we visited our enemy's lair. Armed against ghostly as well as carnal attack?"

We all assured him.

"Then it is well. Now, Madam Mina, you are in any case *quite* safe here until the sunset. And before then we shall return . . . if . . . We shall return! But before we go let me see you armed against personal attack. I have myself, since you came down, prepared your chamber by the placing of things of which we know, so that He may not enter. Now let me guard yourself. On your forehead I touch this piece of Sacred Wafer in the name of the Father, the Son, and . . ."

There was a fearful scream which almost froze our hearts to hear. As he had placed the Wafer on Mina's forehead, it had seared it . . . had burned into the flesh as though it had been a piece of white-hot metal. My poor darling's brain had told her the significance of the fact as quickly as her nerves received the pain of it, and the two so overwhelmed her that her overwrought nature had its voice in that dreadful scream.

But the words to her thought came quickly. The echo of the scream had not ceased to ring on the air when there came the reaction, and she sank on her knees on the floor in an agony of abasement. Pulling her beautiful hair over her face, as the leper of old his mantle, she wailed out.

"Unclean! Unclean! Even the Almighty shuns my polluted flesh! I must bear this mark of shame upon my forehead until the Judgement Day."

They all paused. I had thrown myself beside her in an agony of helpless grief, and putting my arms around held her tight. For a few minutes our sorrowful hearts beat together, whilst the friends around us turned away their eyes that ran tears silently. Then Van Helsing turned and said gravely. So gravely that I could not help feeling that he was in some way inspired, and was stating things outside himself.

"It may be that you may have to bear that mark till God himself see fit, as He most surely shall, on the Judgement Day, to redress all wrongs of the earth and of His children that He has placed thereon. And oh, Madam Mina, my dear, my dear, may we who love you be there to see, when that red scar, the sign of God's knowledge of what has been, shall pass away, and leave your forehead as pure as the heart we know. For so surely as we live, that scar shall pass away when God sees right to lift the burden that is hard upon us. Till then we bear our Cross, as His Son did in obedience to His Will. It may be that we are chosen instruments of His good pleasure, and that we ascend to His bidding as that other through stripes and shame. Through tears and blood. Through doubts and fear, and all that makes the difference between God and man."

There was hope in his words, and comfort. And they made for resignation. Mina and I both felt so, and simultaneously we each took one of the old man's hands and bent over and kissed it. Then without a word we all knelt down together, and all holding hands, swore to be true to each other. We men pledged ourselves to raise the veil of sorrow from the head of her whom, each in his own way, we loved. And we prayed for help and guidance in the terrible task which lay before us. It was then time to start. So I said farewell to Mina, a parting which neither of us shall forget to our dying day, and we set out.

To one thing I have made up my mind. If we find out that Mina must be a vampire in the end, then she shall not go into that unknown and terrible land alone. I suppose it is thus that in old times one vampire meant many. Just as their hideous bodies could only rest in sacred earth, so the holiest love was the recruiting sergeant for their ghastly ranks.

We entered Carfax without trouble and found all things the same as on the first occasion. It was hard to believe that amongst so prosaic surroundings of neglect and dust and decay there was any ground for such fear as already we knew. Had not our minds been made up, and had there not been terrible memories to spur us on, we could hardly have proceeded with our task. We found no papers, or any sign of use in the house. And in the old chapel the great boxes looked just as we had seen them last.

Dr. Van Helsing said to us solemnly as we stood before him, "And now, my friends, we have a duty here to do. We must sterilize this earth, so sacred of holy memories, that he has brought from a far distant land for such fell use. He has chosen this earth because it has been holy. Thus we defeat him with his own weapon, for we make it more holy still. It was sanctified to such use of man, now we sanctify it to God."

As he spoke he took from his bag a screwdriver and a wrench, and very soon the top of one of the cases was thrown open. The earth smelled musty and close, but we did not somehow seem to mind, for our attention was concentrated on the Professor. Taking from his box a piece of the Sacred Wafer he laid it reverently on the earth, and then shutting down the lid began to screw it home, we aiding him as he worked.

One by one we treated in the same way each of the great boxes, and left them as we had found them to all appearance. But in each was a portion of the Host. When we closed the door behind us, the Professor said solemnly, "So much is already done. It may be that with all the others we can be so successful, then the sunset of this evening may shine of Madam Mina's forehead all white as ivory and with no stain!"

As we passed across the lawn on our way to the station to catch our train we could see the front of the asylum. I looked eagerly, and in the window of my own room saw Mina. I waved my hand to her, and nodded to tell that our work there was successfully accomplished. She nodded in reply to show that she understood. The last I saw, she was waving her hand in farewell. It was with a heavy heart that we sought the station and just caught the train, which was steaming in as we reached the platform. I have written this in the train.

Piccadilly, 12:30 o'clock.—Just before we reached Fenchurch Street Lord Godalming said to me, "Quincey and I will find a locksmith. You had better not come with us in case there should be any difficulty. For under the circumstances it wouldn't seem so bad for us to break into an empty house. But you are a solicitor and the Incorporated Law Society might tell you that you should have known better."

I demurred as to my not sharing any danger even of odium, but he went on, "Besides, it will attract less attention if there are not too many of us. My title will make it all right with the locksmith, and with any policeman that may come along. You had better go with Jack and the Professor and stay in the Green Park. Somewhere in sight of the house, and when you see the door opened and the smith has gone away, do you all come across. We shall be on the lookout for you, and shall let you in."

"The advice is good!" said Van Helsing, so we said no more. Godalming and Morris hurried off in a cab, we following in another. At the corner of Arlington Street our contingent got out and strolled into the Green Park. My heart beat as I saw the house on which so much of our hope was centred, looming up grim and silent in its deserted condition amongst its more lively and spruce-looking neighbours. We sat down on a bench within good view, and began to smoke cigars so as to attract as little attention as possible. The minutes seemed to pass with leaden feet as we waited for the coming of the others.

At length we saw a four-wheeler drive up. Out of it, in leisurely fashion, got Lord Godalming and Morris. And down from the box descended a thick-set working man with his rush-woven basket of tools. Morris paid the cabman, who touched his hat and drove away. Together the two ascended the steps, and Lord Godalming pointed out what he wanted done. The workman took off his coat leisurely and hung it on one of the spikes of the rail, saying something to a policeman who just then sauntered along. The policeman nodded acquiescence, and the man kneeling down placed his bag beside him. After searching through it, he took out a selection of tools which he proceeded to lay beside him in orderly fashion. Then he stood up, looked in the keyhole, blew into it, and turning to his employers, made some remark. Lord Godalming smiled, and the man lifted a good sized bunch of keys. Selecting one of them, he began to probe the lock, as if feeling his way with it. After fumbling about for a bit he tried a second, and then a third. All at once the door opened under a slight push from him, and he and the two others entered the hall. We sat still. My own cigar burnt furiously, but Van Helsing's went cold altogether. We waited patiently as we saw the workman come out and bring his bag. Then he held the door partly open, steadying it with his knees, whilst he fitted a key to the lock. This he finally handed to Lord Godalming, who took out his purse and gave him something. The man touched his hat, took his bag, put on his coat and departed. Not a soul took the slightest notice of the whole transaction.

When the man had fairly gone, we three crossed the street and knocked at the door. It was immediately opened by Quincey Morris, beside whom stood Lord Godalming lighting a cigar.

"The place smells so vilely," said the latter as we came in. It did indeed smell vilely. Like the old chapel at Carfax. And with our previous experience it was plain to us that the Count had been using the place pretty freely. We moved to explore the house, all keeping together in case of attack, for we knew we had a strong and wily enemy to deal with, and as yet we did not know whether the Count might not be in the house.

In the dining room, which lay at the back of the hall, we found eight boxes of earth. Eight boxes only out of the nine which we sought! Our work was not over, and would never be until we should have found the missing box.

First we opened the shutters of the window which looked out across a narrow stone flagged yard at the blank face of a stable, pointed to look like the front of a miniature house. There were no windows in it, so we were not afraid of being overlooked. We did not lose any time in examining the chests. With the tools which we had brought with us we opened them, one by one, and treated them as we had treated those others in the old chapel. It was evident to us that the Count was not at present in the house, and we proceeded to search for any of his effects.

After a cursory glance at the rest of the rooms, from basement to attic, we came to the conclusion that the dining room contained any effects which might belong to the Count. And so we proceeded to minutely examine them. They lay in a sort of orderly disorder on the great dining room table.

There were title deeds of the Piccadilly house in a great bundle, deeds of the purchase of the houses at Mile End and Bermondsey, notepaper, envelopes, and pens and ink. All were covered up in thin wrapping paper to keep them from the dust. There were also a clothes brush, a brush and comb, and a jug and basin. The latter containing dirty water which was reddened as if with blood. Last of all was a little heap of keys of all sorts and sizes, probably those belonging to the other houses.

When we had examined this last find, Lord Godalming and Quincey Morris taking accurate notes of the various addresses of the houses in the East and the South, took with them the keys in a great bunch, and set out to destroy the boxes in these places. The rest of us are, with what patience we can, waiting their return, or the coming of the Count.

℘ CHAPTER 23 ℅
DR. SEWARD'S DIARY

3 October.—The time seemed terribly long whilst we were waiting for the coming of Godalming and Quincey Morris. The Professor tried to keep our minds active by using them all the time. I could see his beneficent purpose, by the side glances which he threw from time to time at Harker. The poor fellow is overwhelmed in a misery that is appalling to see. Last night he was a frank, happy-looking man, with strong, youthful face, full of energy, and with dark brown hair. Today he is a drawn, haggard old man, whose white hair matches well with the hollow burning eyes and grief-written lines of his face. His energy is still intact. In fact, he is like a living flame. This may yet be his salvation, for if all go well, it will tide him over the despairing period. He will then, in a kind of way, wake again to the realities of life. Poor fellow, I thought my own trouble was bad enough, but his . . . !

The Professor knows this well enough, and is doing his best to keep his mind active. What he has been saying was, under the circumstances, of absorbing interest. So well as I can remember, here it is:

"I have studied, over and over again since they came into my hands, all the papers relating to this monster, and the more I have studied, the greater seems the necessity to utterly stamp him out. All through there are signs of his advance. Not only of his power, but of his knowledge of it. As I learned from the researches of my friend Arminius of Buda-Pesth, he was in life a most wonderful man. Soldier, statesman, and alchemist—which latter was the highest development of the science knowledge of his time. He had a mighty brain, a learning beyond compare, and a heart that knew no fear and no remorse. He dared even to attend the Scholomance, and there was no branch of knowledge of his time that he did not essay.

"Well, in him the brain powers survived the physical death. Though it would seem that memory was not all complete. In some faculties of mind he has been, and is, only a child. But he is growing, and some things that were childish at the first are now of man's stature. He is experimenting, and doing it well. And if it had not been that we have crossed his path he would be yet, he may be yet if we fail, the father or furtherer of a new order of beings, whose road must lead through Death, not Life."

Harker groaned and said, "And this is all arrayed against my darling! But how is he experimenting? The knowledge may help us to defeat him!"

"He has all along, since his coming, been trying his power, slowly but surely. That big child-brain of his is working. Well for us, it is as yet a child-brain. For had he dared, at the first, to attempt certain things he would long ago have been beyond our power. However, he means to succeed, and a man who has centuries before him can afford to wait and to go slow. *Festina lente*[III] may well be his motto."

"I fail to understand," said Harker wearily. "Oh, do be more plain to me! Perhaps grief and trouble are dulling my brain."

The Professor laid his hand tenderly on his shoulder as he spoke, "Ah, my child, I will be plain. Do you not see how, of late, this monster has been creeping into knowledge experimentally. How he has been making use of the zoophagous patient to effect his entry into friend John's home. For your Vampire, though in all afterwards he can come when and how he will, must at the first make entry only when asked thereto by an inmate. But these are not his most important experiments. Do we not see how at the first all these so great boxes were moved by others. He knew not then but that must be so. But all the time that so great child-brain of his was growing, and he began to consider whether he might not himself move the box. So he began

III Hasten slowly (Latin).

to help. And then, when he found that this be all right, he try to move them all alone. And so he progress, and he scatter these graves of him. And none but he know where they are hidden.

"He may have intend to bury them deep in the ground. So that only he use them in the night, or at such time as he can change his form, they do him equal well, and none may know these are his hiding place! But, my child, do not despair, this knowledge came to him just too late! Already all of his lairs but one be sterilize as for him. And before the sunset this shall be so. Then he have no place where he can move and hide. I delayed this morning that so we might be sure. Is there not more at stake for us than for him? Then why not be more careful than him? By my clock it is one hour and already, if all be well, friend Arthur and Quincey are on their way to us. Today is our day, and we must go sure, if slow, and lose no chance. See! There are five of us when those absent ones return."

Whilst we were speaking we were startled by a knock at the hall door, the double postman's knock of the telegraph boy. We all moved out to the hall with one impulse, and Van Helsing, holding up his hand to us to keep silence, stepped to the door and opened it. The boy handed in a dispatch. The Professor closed the door again, and after looking at the direction, opened it and read aloud.

"Look out for D. He has just now, 12:45, come from Carfax hurriedly and hastened towards the South. He seems to be going the round and may want to see you: Mina."

There was a pause, broken by Jonathan Harker's voice, "Now, God be thanked, we shall soon meet!"

Van Helsing turned to him quickly and said, "God will act in His own way and time. Do not fear, and do not rejoice as yet. For what we wish for at the moment may be our own undoings."

"I care for nothing now," he answered hotly, "except to wipe out this brute from the face of creation. I would sell my soul to do it!"

"Oh, hush, hush, my child!" said Van Helsing. "God does not purchase souls in this wise, and the Devil, though he may purchase, does not keep faith. But God is merciful and just, and knows your pain and your devotion to that dear Madam Mina. Think you, how her pain would be doubled, did she but hear your wild words. Do not fear any of us, we are all devoted to this cause, and today shall see the end. The time is coming for action. To-day this Vampire is limit to the powers of man, and till sunset he may not change. It will take him time to arrive here, see it is twenty minutes past one, and there are yet some times before he can hither come, be he never so quick. What we must hope for is that my Lord Arthur and Quincey arrive first."

About half an hour after we had received Mrs. Harker's telegram, there came a quiet, resolute knock at the hall door. It was just an ordinary knock, such as is given hourly by thousands of gentlemen, but it made the Professor's heart and mine beat loudly. We looked at each other, and together moved out into the hall. We each held ready to use our various armaments, the spiritual in the left hand, the mortal in the right. Van Helsing pulled back the latch, and holding the door half open, stood back, having both hands ready for action. The gladness of our hearts must have shown upon our faces when on the step, close to the door, we saw Lord Godalming and Quincey Morris. They came quickly in and closed the door behind them, the former saying, as they moved along the hall:

"It is all right. We found both places. Six boxes in each and we destroyed them all."

"Destroyed?" asked the Professor.

"For him!" We were silent for a minute, and then Quincey said, "There's nothing to do but to wait here. If, however, he doesn't turn up by five o'clock, we must start off. For it won't do to leave Mrs. Harker alone after sunset."

"He will be here before long now," said Van Helsing, who had been consulting his pocketbook. "*Nota bene*, in Madam's telegram he went south from Carfax. That means he went to cross the river, and he could only do so at slack of tide, which should be something before one o'clock. That he went south has a meaning for us. He is as yet only suspicious, and he went from Carfax first to the place where he would suspect interference least. You must have been at Bermondsey only a short time before him. That he is not here already shows that he went to Mile End next. This took him some time, for he would then have to be carried over the river in some way. Believe me, my friends, we shall not have long to wait now. We should have ready some plan of attack, so that we may throw away no chance. Hush, there is no time now. Have all your arms! Be ready!" He held up a warning hand as he spoke, for we all could hear a key softly inserted in the lock of the hall door.

I could not but admire, even at such a moment, the way in which a dominant spirit asserted itself. In all our hunting parties and adventures in different parts of the world, Quincey Morris had always been the one to arrange the plan of action, and Arthur and I had been accustomed to obey him implicitly. Now, the old habit seemed to be renewed instinctively. With a swift glance around the room, he at once laid out our plan of attack, and without speaking a word, with a gesture, placed us each in position. Van Helsing, Harker, and I were just behind the door, so that when it was opened the Professor could guard it whilst we two stepped between the incomer and the door. Godalming behind and Quincey in front stood just out of sight ready to move in front of the window. We waited in a suspense that made the seconds pass with nightmare slowness. The slow, careful steps came along the hall. The Count was evidently prepared for some surprise, at least he feared it.

Suddenly with a single bound he leaped into the room. Winning a way past us before any of us could raise a hand to stay him. There was something so pantherlike in the movement, something so unhuman, that it seemed to sober us all from the shock of his coming. The first to act was Harker, who with a quick movement, threw himself before the door leading into the room in the front of the house. As the Count saw us, a horrible sort of snarl passed over his face, showing the eyeteeth long and pointed. But the evil smile as quickly passed into a cold stare of lion-like disdain. His expression again changed as, with a single impulse, we all advanced upon him. It was a pity that we had not some better organized plan of attack, for even at the moment I wondered what we were to do. I did not myself know whether our lethal weapons would avail us anything.

Harker evidently meant to try the matter, for he had ready his great Kukri knife and made a fierce and sudden cut at him. The blow was a powerful one; only the diabolical quickness of the Count's leap back saved him. A second less and the trenchant blade had shorn through his heart. As it was, the point just cut the cloth of his coat, making a wide gap whence a bundle of bank notes and a stream of gold fell out. The expression of the Count's face was so hellish, that for a moment I feared for Harker, though I saw him throw the terrible knife aloft again for another stroke. Instinctively I moved forward with a protective impulse, holding the Crucifix and Wafer in my left hand. I felt a mighty power fly along my arm, and it was without surprise that I saw the monster cower back before a similar movement made spontaneously by each one of us. It would be impossible to describe the expression of hate and baffled malignity, of anger and hellish rage, which came over the Count's face. His waxen hue became greenish-yellow by the contrast of his burning eyes, and the red scar on the forehead showed on the pallid skin like a palpitating wound. The next instant, with a sinuous dive he swept under Harker's arm, ere his blow could fall, and grasping a handful of the money from the floor, dashed across the room, threw himself at the window. Amid the crash and glitter of the falling glass, he tumbled into the flagged area below. Through the sound of the shivering glass I could hear the "ting" of the gold, as some of the sovereigns fell on the flagging.

We ran over and saw him spring unhurt from the ground. He, rushing up the steps, crossed the flagged yard, and pushed open the stable door. There he turned and spoke to us.

"You think to baffle me, you with your pale faces all in a row, like sheep in a butcher's. You shall be sorry yet, each one of you! You think you have left me without a place to rest, but I have more. My revenge is just begun! I spread it over centuries, and time is on my side. Your girls that you all love are mine already. And through them you and others shall yet be mine, my creatures, to do my bidding and to be my jackals when I want to feed. Bah!"

With a contemptuous sneer, he passed quickly through the door, and we heard the rusty bolt creak as he fastened it behind him. A door beyond opened and shut. The first of us to speak was the Professor. Realizing the difficulty of following him through the stable, we moved toward the hall.

"We have learnt something . . . much! Notwithstanding his brave words, he fears us. He fears time, he fears want! For if not, why he hurry so? His very tone betray him, or my ears deceive. Why take that money? You follow quick. You are hunters of the wild beast, and understand it so. For me, I make sure that nothing here may be of use to him, if so that he returns."

As he spoke he put the money remaining in his pocket, took the title deeds in the bundle as Harker had left them, and swept the remaining things into the open fireplace, where he set fire to them with a match.

Godalming and Morris had rushed out into the yard, and Harker had lowered himself from the window to follow the Count. He had, however, bolted the stable door, and by the time they had forced it open there was no sign of him. Van Helsing and I tried to make inquiry at the back of the house. But the mews was deserted and no one had seen him depart.

It was now late in the afternoon, and sunset was not far off. We had to recognize that our game was up. With heavy hearts we agreed with the Professor when he said, "Let us go back to Madam Mina. Poor, poor dear Madam Mina. All we can do just now is done, and we can there, at least, protect her. But we need not despair. There is but one more earth box, and we must try to find it. When that is done all may yet be well."

I could see that he spoke as bravely as he could to comfort Harker. The poor fellow was quite broken down, now and again he gave a low groan which he could not suppress. He was thinking of his wife.

With sad hearts we came back to my house, where we found Mrs. Harker waiting us, with an appearance of cheerfulness which did honour to her bravery and unselfishness. When she saw our faces, her own became as pale as death. For a second or two her eyes were closed as if she were in secret prayer.

And then she said cheerfully, "I can never thank you all enough. Oh, my poor darling!"

As she spoke, she took her husband's grey head in her hands and kissed it.

"Lay your poor head here and rest it. All will yet be well, dear! God will protect us if He so will it in His good intent." The poor fellow groaned. There was no place for words in his sublime misery.

We had a sort of perfunctory supper together, and I think it cheered us all up somewhat. It was, perhaps, the mere animal heat of food to hungry people, for none of us had eaten anything since breakfast, or the sense of companionship may have helped us, but anyhow we were all less miserable, and saw the morrow as not altogether without hope.

True to our promise, we told Mrs. Harker everything which had passed. And although she grew snowy white at times when danger had seemed to threaten her husband, and red at others when his devotion to her was manifested, she listened bravely and with calmness. When we came to the part where Harker had rushed at the Count so recklessly, she clung to her husband's arm, and held it tight as though her clinging could protect him from any harm that might come. She said nothing, however, till the narration was all done, and matters had been brought up to the present time.

Then without letting go her husband's hand she stood up amongst us and spoke. Oh, that I could give any idea of the scene. Of that sweet, sweet, good, good woman in all the radiant beauty of her youth and animation, with the red scar on her forehead, of which she was conscious, and which we saw with grinding of our teeth, remembering whence and how it came. Her loving kindness against our grim hate. Her tender faith against all our fears and doubting. And we, knowing that so far as symbols went, she with all her goodness and purity and faith, was outcast from God.

"Jonathan," she said, and the word sounded like music on her lips it was so full of love and tenderness, "Jonathan dear, and you all my true, true friends, I want you to bear something in mind through all this dreadful time. I know that you must fight. That you must destroy even as you destroyed the false Lucy so that the true Lucy might live hereafter. But it is not a work of hate. That poor soul who has wrought all this misery is the saddest case of all. Just think what will be his joy when he, too, is destroyed in his worser part that his better part may have spiritual immortality. You must be pitiful to him, too, though it may not hold your hands from his destruction."

As she spoke I could see her husband's face darken and draw together, as though the passion in him were shriveling his being to its core. Instinctively the clasp on his wife's hand grew closer, till his knuckles looked white. She did not flinch from the pain which I knew she must have suffered, but looked at him with eyes that were more appealing than ever.

As she stopped speaking he leaped to his feet, almost tearing his hand from hers as he spoke.

"May God give him into my hand just for long enough to destroy that earthly life of him which we are aiming at. If beyond it I could send his soul forever and ever to burning hell I would do it!"

"Oh, hush! Oh, hush in the name of the good God. Don't say such things, Jonathan, my husband, or you will crush me with fear and horror. Just think, my dear . . . I have been thinking all this long, long day of it . . . that . . . perhaps . . . some day . . . I, too, may need such pity, and that some other like you, and with equal cause for anger, may deny it to me! Oh, my husband! My husband, indeed I would have spared you such a thought had there been another way. But I pray that God may not have treasured your wild words, except as the heart-broken wail of a very loving and sorely stricken man. Oh, God, let these poor white hairs go in evidence of what he has suffered, who all his life has done no wrong, and on whom so many sorrows have come."

We men were all in tears now. There was no resisting them, and we wept openly. She wept, too, to see that her sweeter counsels had prevailed. Her husband flung himself on his knees beside her, and putting his arms round her, hid his face in the folds of her dress. Van Helsing beckoned to us and we stole out of the room, leaving the two loving hearts alone with their God.

Before they retired the Professor fixed up the room against any coming of the Vampire, and assured Mrs. Harker that she might rest in peace. She tried to school herself to the belief, and manifestly for her husband's sake, tried to seem content. It was a brave struggle, and was, I think and believe, not without its reward. Van Helsing had placed at hand a bell which either of them was to sound in case of any emergency. When they had retired, Quincey, Godalming, and I arranged that we should sit up, dividing the night between us, and watch over the safety of the poor stricken lady. The first watch falls to Quincey, so the rest of us shall be off to bed as soon as we can.

Godalming has already turned in, for his is the second watch. Now that my work is done I, too, shall go to bed.

JONATHAN HARKER'S JOURNAL

3-4 October, close to midnight.—I thought yesterday would never end. There was over me a yearning for sleep, in some sort of blind belief that to wake would be to find things changed, and that any change must now be for the better. Before we parted, we discussed what our next step was to be, but we could arrive at no result. All we knew was that one earth box remained, and that the Count alone knew where it was. If he chooses to lie hidden, he may baffle us for years. And in the meantime, the thought is too horrible, I dare not think of it even now. This I know, that if ever there was a woman who was all perfection, that one is my poor wronged darling. I loved her a thousand times more for her sweet pity of last night, a pity that made my own hate of the monster seem despicable. Surely God will not permit the world to be the poorer by the loss of such a creature. This is hope to me. We are all drifting reefwards now, and faith is our only anchor. Thank God! Mina is sleeping, and sleeping without dreams. I fear what her dreams might be like, with such terrible memories to ground them in. She has not been so calm, within my seeing, since the sunset. Then, for a while, there came over her face a repose which was like spring after the blasts of March. I thought at the time that it was the softness of the red sunset on her face, but somehow now I think it has a deeper meaning. I am not sleepy myself, though I am weary . . . weary to death. However, I must try to sleep. For there is tomorrow to think of, and there is no rest for me until . . .

Later—I must have fallen asleep, for I was awakened by Mina, who was sitting up in bed, with a startled look on her face. I could see easily, for we did not leave the room in darkness. She had placed a warning hand over my mouth, and now she whispered in my ear, "Hush! There is someone in the corridor!" I got up softly, and crossing the room, gently opened the door.

Just outside, stretched on a mattress, lay Mr. Morris, wide awake. He raised a warning hand for silence as he whispered to me, "Hush! Go back to bed. It is all right. One of us will be here all night. We don't mean to take any chances!"

His look and gesture forbade discussion, so I came back and told Mina. She sighed and positively a shadow of a smile stole over her poor, pale face as she put her arms round me and said softly, "Oh, thank God for good brave men!" With a sigh she sank back again to sleep. I write this now as I am not sleepy, though I must try again.

4 October, morning.—Once again during the night I was wakened by Mina. This time we had all had a good sleep, for the grey of the coming dawn was making the windows into sharp oblongs, and the gas flame was like a speck rather than a disc of light.

She said to me hurriedly, "Go, call the Professor. I want to see him at once."

"Why?" I asked.

"I have an idea. I suppose it must have come in the night, and matured without my knowing it. He must hypnotize me before the dawn, and then I shall be able to speak. Go quick, dearest, the time is getting close."

I went to the door. Dr. Seward was resting on the mattress, and seeing me, he sprang to his feet.

"Is anything wrong?" he asked, in alarm.

"No," I replied. "But Mina wants to see Dr. Van Helsing at once."

"I will go," he said, and hurried into the Professor's room.

Two or three minutes later Van Helsing was in the room in his dressing gown, and Mr. Morris and Lord Godalming were with Dr. Seward at the door asking questions. When the Professor saw Mina a smile, a positive smile ousted the anxiety of his face.

He rubbed his hands as he said, "Oh, my dear Madam Mina, this is indeed a change. See! Friend Jonathan, we have got our dear Madam Mina, as of old, back to us today!" Then turning to her, he said cheerfully, "And what am I to do for you? For at this hour you do not want me for nothing."

"I want you to hypnotize me!" she said. "Do it before the dawn, for I feel that then I can speak, and speak freely. Be quick, for the time is short!" Without a word he motioned her to sit up in bed.

Looking fixedly at her, he commenced to make passes in front of her, from over the top of her head downward, with each hand in turn. Mina gazed at him fixedly for a few minutes, during which my own heart beat like a trip hammer, for I felt that some crisis was at hand. Gradually her eyes closed, and she sat, stock still. Only by the gentle heaving of her bosom could one know that she was alive. The Professor made a few more passes and then stopped, and I could see that his forehead was covered with great beads of perspiration. Mina opened her eyes, but she did not seem the same woman. There was a far-away look in her eyes, and her voice had a sad dreaminess which was new to me. Raising his hand to impose silence, the Professor motioned to me to bring the others in. They came on tiptoe, closing the door behind them, and stood at the foot of the bed, looking on. Mina appeared not to see them. The stillness was broken by Van Helsing's voice speaking in a low level tone which would not break the current of her thoughts.

"Where are you?" The answer came in a neutral way.

"I do not know. Sleep has no place it can call its own." For several minutes there was silence. Mina sat rigid, and the Professor stood staring at her fixedly.

The rest of us hardly dared to breathe. The room was growing lighter. Without taking his eyes from Mina's face, Dr. Van Helsing motioned me to pull up the blind. I did so, and the day seemed just upon us. A red streak shot up, and a rosy light seemed to diffuse itself through the room. On the instant the Professor spoke again.

"Where are you now?"

The answer came dreamily, but with intention. It were as though she were interpreting something. I have heard her use the same tone when reading her shorthand notes.

"I do not know. It is all strange to me!"

"What do you see?"

"I can see nothing. It is all dark."

"What do you hear?" I could detect the strain in the Professor's patient voice.

"The lapping of water. It is gurgling by, and little waves leap. I can hear them on the outside."

"Then you are on a ship?'"

We all looked at each other, trying to glean something each from the other. We were afraid to think.

The answer came quick, "Oh, yes!"

"What else do you hear?"

"The sound of men stamping overhead as they run about. There is the creaking of a chain, and the loud tinkle as the check of the capstan falls into the ratchet."

"What are you doing?"

"I am still, oh so still. It is like death!" The voice faded away into a deep breath as of one sleeping, and the open eyes closed again.

By this time the sun had risen, and we were all in the full light of day. Dr. Van Helsing placed his hands on Mina's shoulders, and laid her head down softly on her pillow. She lay like a sleeping child for a few moments, and then, with a long sigh, awoke and stared in wonder to see us all around her.

"Have I been talking in my sleep?" was all she said. She seemed, however, to know the situation without telling, though she was eager to know what she had told. The Professor repeated the conversation, and she said, "Then there is not a moment to lose. It may not be yet too late!"

Mr. Morris and Lord Godalming started for the door but the Professor's calm voice called them back.

"Stay, my friends. That ship, wherever it was, was weighing anchor at the moment in your so great Port of London. Which of them is it that you seek? God be thanked that we have once again a clue, though whither it may lead us we know not. We have been blind somewhat. Blind after the manner of men, since we can look back we see what we might have seen looking forward if we had been able to see what we might have seen! Alas, but that sentence is a puddle, is it not? We can know now what was in the Count's mind, when he seize that money, though Jonathan's so fierce knife put him in the danger that even he dread. He meant escape. Hear me, ESCAPE! He saw that with but one earth box left, and a pack of men following like dogs after a fox, this London was no place for him. He have take his last earth box on board a ship, and he leave the land. He think to escape, but no! We follow him. Tally Ho! As friend Arthur would say when he put on his red frock! Our old fox is wily. Oh! So wily, and we must follow with wile. I, too, am wily and I think his mind in a little while. In meantime we may rest and in peace, for there are between us which he do not want to pass, and which he could not if he would. Unless the ship were to touch the land, and then only at full or slack tide. See, and the sun is just rose, and all day to sunset is us. Let us take bath, and dress, and have breakfast which we all need, and which we can eat comfortably since he be not in the same land with us."

Mina looked at him appealingly as she asked, "But why need we seek him further, when he is gone away from us?"

He took her hand and patted it as he replied, "Ask me nothing as yet. When we have breakfast, then I answer all questions." He would say no more, and we separated to dress.

After breakfast Mina repeated her question. He looked at her gravely for a minute and then said sorrowfully, "Because my dear, dear Madam Mina, now more than ever must we find him even if we have to follow him to the jaws of Hell!"

She grew paler as she asked faintly, "Why?"

"Because," he answered solemnly, "he can live for centuries, and you are but mortal woman. Time is now to be dreaded, since once he put that mark upon your throat."

I was just in time to catch her as she fell forward in a faint.

℘ CHAPTER 24 ℘
DR. SEWARD'S PHONOGRAPH DIARY

Spoken By Van Helsing

This to Jonathan Harker.

You are to stay with your dear Madam Mina. We shall go to make our search, if I can call it so, for it is not search but knowing, and we seek confirmation only. But do you stay and take care of her today. This is your best and most holiest office. This day nothing can find him here.

Let me tell you that so you will know what we four know already, for I have tell them. He, our enemy, have gone away. He have gone back to his Castle in Transylvania. I know it so well, as if a great hand of fire wrote it on the wall. He have prepare for this in some way, and that last earth box was ready to ship somewheres. For this he took the money. For this he hurry at the last, lest we catch him before the sun go down. It was his last hope, save that he might hide in the tomb that he think poor Miss Lucy, being as he thought like him, keep open to him. But there was not of time. When that fail he make straight for his last resource, his last earth-work I might say did I wish *double entente*. He is clever, oh so clever! He know that his game here was finish. And so he decide he go back home. He find ship going by the route he came, and he go in it.

We go off now to find what ship, and whither bound. When we have discover that, we come back and tell you all. Then we will comfort you and poor Madam Mina with new hope. For it will be hope when you think it over, that all is not lost. This very creature that we pursue, he take hundreds of years to get so far as London. And yet in one day, when we know of the disposal of him we drive him out. He is finite, though he is powerful to do much harm and suffers not as we do. But we are strong, each in our purpose, and we are all more strong together. Take heart afresh, dear husband of Madam Mina. This battle is but begun and in the end we shall win. So sure as that God sits on high to watch over His children. Therefore be of much comfort till we return.

Van Helsing.

JONATHAN HARKER'S JOURNAL

4 October.—When I read to Mina, Van Helsing's message in the phonograph, the poor girl brightened up considerably. Already the certainty that the Count is out of the country has given her comfort. And comfort is strength to her. For my own part, now that his horrible danger is not face to face with us, it seems almost impossible to believe in it. Even my own terrible experiences in Castle Dracula seem like a long forgotten dream. Here in the crisp autumn air in the bright sunlight.

Alas! How can I disbelieve! In the midst of my thought my eye fell on the red scar on my poor darling's white forehead. Whilst that lasts, there can be no disbelief. Mina and I fear to be idle, so we have been over all the diaries again and again. Somehow, although the reality seem greater each

time, the pain and the fear seem less. There is something of a guiding purpose manifest throughout, which is comforting. Mina says that perhaps we
are the instruments of ultimate good. It may be! I shall try to think as she
does. We have never spoken to each other yet of the future. It is better to
wait till we see the Professor and the others after their investigations.

The day is running by more quickly than I ever thought a day could run
for me again. It is now three o'clock.

MINA HARKER'S JOURNAL

5 October, 5 p.m.—Our meeting for report. Present: Professor Van Helsing, Lord Godalming, Dr. Seward, Mr. Quincey Morris, Jonathan Harker,
Mina Harker.

Dr. Van Helsing described what steps were taken during the day to discover on what boat and whither bound Count Dracula made his escape.

"As I knew that he wanted to get back to Transylvania, I felt sure that he
must go by the Danube mouth, or by somewhere in the Black Sea, since by
that way he come. It was a dreary blank that was before us. *Omne ignotum
pro magnifico*;[112] and so with heavy hearts we start to find what ships leave
for the Black Sea last night. He was in sailing ship, since Madam Mina tell
of sails being set. These not so important as to go in your list of the shipping in the *Times*, and so we go, by suggestion of Lord Godalming, to your
Lloyd's, where are note of all ships that sail, however so small. There we find
that only one Black Sea bound ship go out with the tide. She is the *Czarina Catherine*, and she sail from Doolittle's Wharf for Varna, and thence
to other ports and up the Danube. 'So!' said I, 'this is the ship whereon is
the Count.' So off we go to Doolittle's Wharf, and there we find a man
in an office. From him we inquire of the goings of the *Czarina Catherine*.
He swear much, and he red face and loud of voice, but he good fellow all
the same. And when Quincey give him something from his pocket which
crackle as he roll it up, and put it in a so small bag which he have hid deep in
his clothing, he still better fellow and humble servant to us. He come with
us, and ask many men who are rough and hot. These be better fellows too
when they have been no more thirsty. They say much of blood and bloom,
and of others which I comprehend not, though I guess what they mean. But
nevertheless they tell us all things which we want to know.

"They make known to us among them, how last afternoon at about five
o'clock comes a man so hurry. A tall man, thin and pale, with high nose

112 That which is not known is enchanting (Latin).

and teeth so white, and eyes that seem to be burning. That he be all in black, except that he have a hat of straw which suit not him or the time. That he scatter his money in making quick inquiry as to what ship sails for the Black Sea and for where. Some took him to the office and then to the ship, where he will not go aboard but halt at shore end of gangplank, and ask that the captain come to him. The captain come, when told that he will be pay well, and though he swear much at the first he agree to term. Then the thin man go and some one tell him where horse and cart can be hired. He go there and soon he come again, himself driving cart on which a great box. This he himself lift down, though it take several to put it on truck for the ship. He give much talk to captain as to how and where his box is to be place. But the captain like it not and swear at him in many tongues, and tell him that if he like he can come and see where it shall be. But he say 'no,' that he come not yet, for that he have much to do. Whereupon the captain tell him that he had better be quick, with blood, for that his ship will leave the place, of blood, before the turn of the tide, with blood. Then the thin man smile and say that of course he must go when he think fit, but he will be surprise if he go quite so soon. The captain swear again, polyglot, and the thin man make him bow, and thank him, and say that he will so far intrude on his kindness as to come aboard before the sailing. Final the captain, more red than ever, and in more tongues, tell him that he doesn't want no Frenchmen, with bloom upon them and also with blood, in his ship, with blood on her also. And so, after asking where he might purchase ship forms, he departed.

"No one knew where he went 'or bloomin' well cared' as they said, for they had something else to think of, well with blood again. For it soon became apparent to all that the *Czarina Catherine* would not sail as was expected. A thin mist began to creep up from the river, and it grew, and grew. Till soon a dense fog enveloped the ship and all around her. The captain swore polyglot, very polyglot, polyglot with bloom and blood, but he could do nothing. The water rose and rose, and he began to fear that he would lose the tide altogether. He was in no friendly mood, when just at full tide, the thin man came up the gangplank again and asked to see where his box had been stowed. Then the captain replied that he wished that he and his box, old and with much bloom and blood, were in hell. But the thin man did not be offend, and went down with the mate and saw where it was place, and came up and stood awhile on deck in fog. He must have come off by himself, for none notice him. Indeed they thought not of him, for soon the fog begin to melt away, and all was clear again. My friends of the thirst and the language that was of bloom and blood laughed, as they told how the captain's swears exceeded even his usual polyglot, and was more than ever full of picturesque, when on questioning other mariners who were on movement up and down the river that hour, he found that few of them had seen any of fog at all, except where it lay round the wharf. However, the ship went out on the ebb tide, and was doubtless by morning far down the river mouth. She was then, when they told us, well out to sea.

"And so, my dear Madam Mina, it is that we have to rest for a time, for our enemy is on the sea, with the fog at his command, on his way to the Danube mouth. To sail a ship takes time, go she never so quick. And when we start to go on land more quick, and we meet him there. Our best hope is to come on him when in the box between sunrise and sunset. For then he can make no struggle, and we may deal with him as we should. There are days for us, in which we can make ready our plan. We know all about where he go. For we have seen the owner of the ship, who have shown us invoices and all papers that can be. The box we seek is to be landed in Varna, and to be given to an agent, one Ristics who will there present his credentials. And so our merchant friend will have done his part. When he ask if there be any wrong, for that so, he can telegraph and have inquiry made at Varna, we say 'no,' for what is to be done is not for police or of the customs. It must be done by us alone and in our own way."

When Dr. Van Helsing had done speaking, I asked him if he were certain that the Count had remained on board the ship. He replied, "We have the best proof of that, your own evidence, when in the hypnotic trance this morning."

I asked him again if it were really necessary that they should pursue the Count, for oh! I dread Jonathan leaving me, and I know that he would surely go if the others went. He answered in growing passion, at first quietly. As he went on, however, he grew more angry and more forceful, till in the end we could not but see wherein was at least some of that personal dominance which made him so long a master amongst men.

"Yes, it is necessary, necessary, necessary! For your sake in the first, and then for the sake of humanity. This monster has done much harm already, in the narrow scope where he find himself, and in the short time when as yet he was only as a body groping his so small measure in darkness and not knowing. All this have I told these others. You, my dear Madam Mina, will learn it in the phonograph of my friend John, or in that of your husband. I have told them how the measure of leaving his own barren land, barren of peoples, and coming to a new land where life of man teems till they are like the multitude of standing corn, was the work of centuries. Were another of the Undead, like him, to try to do what he has done, perhaps not all the centuries of the world that have been, or that will be, could aid him. With this one, all the forces of nature that are occult and deep and strong must have worked together in some wonderous way. The very place, where he have been alive, Undead for all these centuries, is full of strangeness of the geologic and chemical world. There are deep caverns and fissures that reach none know whither. There have been volcanoes, some of whose openings still send out waters of strange properties, and gases that kill or make to vivify. Doubtless, there is something magnetic or electric in some of these combinations of occult forces which work for physical life in strange way, and in himself were from the first some great qualities. In a hard and warlike time he was celebrate that he have more iron nerve, more subtle brain, more braver heart, than any man. In him some vital principle have in strange way found their utmost. And as his body keep strong and grow and thrive, so his brain grow too. All this without that diabolic aid which is surely to him. For it have to yield to the powers that come from, and are, symbolic of good. And now this is what he is to us. He have infect you, oh forgive me, my dear, that I must say such, but it is for good of you that I speak. He infect you in such wise, that even if he do no more, you have only to live, to live in your own old, sweet way, and so in time, death, which is of man's common lot and with God's sanction, shall make you like to him. This must not be! We have sworn together that it must not. Thus are we ministers of God's own wish. That the world, and men for whom His Son die, will not be given over to monsters, whose very existence would defame Him. He have allowed us to redeem one soul already, and we go out as the old knights of the Cross to redeem more. Like them we shall travel towards the sunrise. And like them, if we fall, we fall in good cause."

He paused and I said, "But will not the Count take his rebuff wisely? Since he has been driven from England, will he not avoid it, as a tiger does the village from which he has been hunted?"

"Aha!" he said, "your simile of the tiger good, for me, and I shall adopt him. Your maneater, as they of India call the tiger who has once tasted blood of the human, care no more for the other prey, but prowl unceasing till he get him. This that we hunt from our village is a tiger, too, a maneater, and he never cease to prowl. Nay, in himself he is not one to retire and stay afar. In his life, his living life, he go over the Turkey frontier and attack his enemy on his own ground. He be beaten back, but did he stay? No! He come again, and again, and again. Look at his persistence and endurance. With the child-brain that was to him he have long since conceive the idea of coming to a great city. What does he do? He find out the place of all the world most of promise for him. Then he deliberately set himself down to prepare for the task. He find in patience just how is his strength, and what are his powers. He study new tongues. He learn new social life, new environment of old ways, the politics, the law, the finance, the science, the habit of a new land and a new people who have come to be since he was.

His glimpse that he have had, whet his appetite only and enkeen his desire. Nay, it help him to grow as to his brain. For it all prove to him how right he was at the first in his surmises. He have done this alone, all alone! From a ruin tomb in a forgotten land. What more may he not do when the greater world of thought is open to him. He that can smile at death, as we know him. Who can flourish in the midst of diseases that kill off whole peoples. Oh! If such an one was to come from God, and not the Devil, what a force for good might he not be in this old world of ours. But we are pledged to set the world free. Our toil must be in silence, and our efforts all in secret. For in this enlightened age, when men believe not even what they see, the doubting of wise men would be his greatest strength. It would be at once his sheath and his armor, and his weapons to destroy us, his enemies, who are willing to peril even our own souls for the safety of one we love. For the good of mankind, and for the honour and glory of God."

After a general discussion it was determined that for tonight nothing be definitely settled. That we should all sleep on the facts, and try to think out the proper conclusions. Tomorrow, at breakfast, we are to meet again, and after making our conclusions known to one another, we shall decide on some definite cause of action . . .

I feel a wonderful peace and rest tonight. It is as if some haunting presence were removed from me. Perhaps . . .

My surmise was not finished, could not be, for I caught sight in the mirror of the red mark upon my forehead, and I knew that I was still unclean.

DR. SEWARD'S DIARY

5 October.—We all arose early, and I think that sleep did much for each and all of us. When we met at early breakfast there was more general cheerfulness than any of us had ever expected to experience again.

It is really wonderful how much resilience there is in human nature. Let any obstructing cause, no matter what, be removed in any way, even by death, and we fly back to first principles of hope and enjoyment. More than once as we sat around the table, my eyes opened in wonder whether the whole of the past days had not been a dream. It was only when I caught sight of the red blotch on Mrs. Harker's forehead that I was brought back to reality. Even now, when I am gravely revolving the matter, it is almost impossible to realize that the cause of all our trouble is still existent. Even Mrs. Harker seems to lose sight of her trouble for whole spells. It is only now and again, when something recalls it to her mind, that she thinks of her terrible scar. We are to meet here in my study in half an hour and decide on our course of action. I see only one immediate difficulty, I know it by instinct rather than reason. We shall all have to speak frankly. And yet I fear that in some mysterious way poor Mrs. Harker's tongue is tied. I *know* that she forms conclusions of her own, and from all that has been I can guess how brilliant and how true they must be. But she will not, or cannot, give them utterance. I have mentioned this to Van Helsing, and he and I are to talk it over when we are alone. I suppose it is some of that horrid poison which has got into her veins beginning to work. The Count had his own purposes when he gave her what Van Helsing called "the Vampire's baptism of blood." Well, there may be a poison that distills itself out of good things. In an age when the existence of ptomaines[113] is a mystery we should not wonder at anything! One thing I know, that if my instinct be true regarding poor Mrs. Harker's silences, then there is a terrible difficulty, an unknown danger, in the work before us. The same power that compels her silence may compel her speech. I dare not think further, for so I should in my thoughts dishonour a noble woman!

Later.—When the Professor came in, we talked over the state of things. I could see that he had something on his mind, which he wanted to say, but felt some hesitancy about broaching the subject. After beating about the bush a little, he said, "Friend John, there is something that you and I must talk of alone, just at the first at any rate. Later, we may have to take the others into our confidence."

Then he stopped, so I waited. He went on, "Madam Mina, our poor, dear Madam Mina is changing."

A cold shiver ran through me to find my worst fears thus endorsed. Van Helsing continued.

"With the sad experience of Miss Lucy, we must this time be warned before things go too far. Our task is now in reality more difficult than ever, and this new trouble makes every hour of the direst importance. I can see the characteristics of the vampire coming in her face. It is now but very, very slight. But it is to be seen if we have eyes to notice without prejudge. Her teeth are sharper, and at times her eyes are more hard. But these are not all, there is to her the silence now often, as so it was with Miss Lucy. She did not speak, even when she wrote that which she wished to be known later. Now my fear is this. If it be that she can, by our hypnotic trance, tell what the Count see and hear, is it not more true that he who have hypnotize

---

113 Poison found in decaying plants and animals.

her first, and who have drink of her very blood and make her drink of his, should if he will, compel her mind to disclose to him that which she know?"

I nodded acquiescence. He went on, "Then, what we must do is to prevent this. We must keep her ignorant of our intent, and so she cannot tell what she know not. This is a painful task! Oh, so painful that it heartbreak me to think of it, but it must be. When today we meet, I must tell her that for reason which we will not to speak she must not more be of our council, but be simply guarded by us."

He wiped his forehead, which had broken out in profuse perspiration at the thought of the pain which he might have to inflict upon the poor soul already so tortured. I knew that it would be some sort of comfort to him if I told him that I also had come to the same conclusion. For at any rate it would take away the pain of doubt. I told him, and the effect was as I expected.

It is now close to the time of our general gathering. Van Helsing has gone away to prepare for the meeting, and his painful part of it. I really believe his purpose is to be able to pray alone.

Later.—At the very outset of our meeting a great personal relief was experienced by both Van Helsing and myself. Mrs. Harker had sent a message by her husband to say that she would not join us at present, as she thought it better that we should be free to discuss our movements without her presence to embarrass us. The Professor and I looked at each other for an instant, and somehow we both seemed relieved. For my own part, I thought that if Mrs. Harker realized the danger herself, it was much pain as well as much danger averted. Under the circumstances we agreed, by a questioning look and answer, with finger on lip, to preserve silence in our suspicions, until we should have been able to confer alone again. We went at once into our Plan of Campaign.

Van Helsing roughly put the facts before us first, "*The Czarina Catherine* left the Thames yesterday morning. It will take her at the quickest speed she has ever made at least three weeks to reach Varna. But we can travel overland to the same place in three days. Now, if we allow for two days less for the ship's voyage, owing to such weather influences as we know that the Count can bring to bear, and if we allow a whole day and night for any delays which may occur to us, then we have a margin of nearly two weeks.

"Thus, in order to be quite safe, we must leave here on 17th at latest. Then we shall at any rate be in Varna a day before the ship arrives, and able to make such preparations as may be necessary. Of course we shall all go armed, armed against evil things, spiritual as well as physical."

Here Quincey Morris added, "I understand that the Count comes from a wolf country, and it may be that he shall get there before us. I propose that we add Winchesters to our armament. I have a kind of belief in a Winchester when there is any trouble of that sort around. Do you remember, Art, when we had the pack after us at Tobolsk? What wouldn't we have given then for a repeater apiece!"

"Good!" said Van Helsing, "Winchesters it shall be. Quincey's head is level at times, but most so when there is to hunt, metaphor be more dishonour to science than wolves be of danger to man. In the meantime we can do nothing here. And as I think that Varna is not familiar to any of us, why not go there more soon? It is as long to wait here as there. Tonight and tomorrow we can get ready, and then if all be well, we four can set out on our journey."

"We four?" said Harker interrogatively, looking from one to another of us.

"Of course!" answered the Professor quickly. "You must remain to take care of your so sweet wife!"

Harker was silent for awhile and then said in a hollow voice, "Let us talk of that part of it in the morning. I want to consult with Mina."

I thought that now was the time for Van Helsing to warn him not to disclose our plan to her, but he took no notice. I looked at him significantly and coughed. For answer he put his finger to his lips and turned away.

JONATHAN HARKER'S JOURNAL

5 October, afternoon.—For some time after our meeting this morning I could not think. The new phases of things leave my mind in a state of wonder which allows no room for active thought. Mina's determination not to take any part in the discussion set me thinking. And as I could not argue the matter with her, I could only guess. I am as far as ever from a solution now. The way the others received it, too puzzled me. The last time we talked of the subject we agreed that there was to be no more concealment of anything amongst us. Mina is sleeping now, calmly and sweetly like a little child. Her lips are curved and her face beams with happiness. Thank God, there are such moments still for her.

Later.—How strange it all is. I sat watching Mina's happy sleep, and I came as near to being happy myself as I suppose I shall ever be. As the evening drew on, and the earth took its shadows from the sun sinking lower, the silence of the room grew more and more solemn to me.

All at once Mina opened her eyes, and looking at me tenderly said, "Jonathan, I want you to promise me something on your word of honour. A promise made to me, but made holily in God's hearing, and not to be broken though I should go down on my knees and implore you with bitter tears. Quick, you must make it to me at once."

"Mina," I said, "a promise like that, I cannot make at once. I may have no right to make it."

"But, dear one," she said, with such spiritual intensity that her eyes were like pole stars, "it is I who wish it. And it is not for myself. You can ask Dr. Van Helsing if I am not right. If he disagrees you may do as you will. Nay, more if you all agree, later you are absolved from the promise."

"I promise!" I said, and for a moment she looked supremely happy. Though to me all happiness for her was denied by the red scar on her forehead.

She said, "Promise me that you will not tell me anything of the plans formed for the campaign against the Count. Not by word, or inference, or implication, not at any time whilst this remains to me!" And she solemnly pointed to the scar. I saw that she was in earnest, and said solemnly, "I promise!" and as I said it I felt that from that instant a door had been shut between us.

Later, midnight.—Mina has been bright and cheerful all the evening. So much so that all the rest seemed to take courage, as if infected somewhat with her gaiety. As a result even I myself felt as if the pall of gloom which weighs us down were somewhat lifted. We all retired early. Mina is now sleeping like a little child. It is wonderful thing that her faculty of sleep remains to her in the midst of her terrible trouble. Thank God for it, for then at least she can forget her care. Perhaps her example may affect me as her gaiety did tonight. I shall try it. Oh! For a dreamless sleep.

6 October, morning.—Another surprise. Mina woke me early, about the same time as yesterday, and asked me to bring Dr. Van Helsing. I thought that it was another occasion for hypnotism, and without question went for the Professor. He had evidently expected some such call, for I found him dressed in his room. His door was ajar, so that he could hear the opening of the door of our room. He came at once. As he passed into the room, he asked Mina if the others might come, too.

"No," she said quite simply, "it will not be necessary. You can tell them just as well. I must go with you on your journey."

Dr. Van Helsing was as startled as I was. After a moment's pause he asked, "But why?"

"You must take me with you. I am safer with you, and you shall be safer, too."

"But why, dear Madam Mina? You know that your safety is our solemnest duty. We go into danger, to which you are, or may be, more liable than any of us from . . . from circumstances . . . things that have been." He paused embarrassed.

As she replied, she raised her finger and pointed to her forehead. "I know. That is why I must go. I can tell you now, whilst the sun is coming up. I may not be able again. I know that when the Count wills me I must go. I know that if he tells me to come in secret, I must by wile. By any device to hoodwink, even Jonathan." God saw the look that she turned on me as she spoke, and if there be indeed a Recording Angel that look is noted to her ever-lasting honour. I could only clasp her hand. I could not speak. My emotion was too great for even the relief of tears.

She went on. "You men are brave and strong. You are strong in your numbers, for you can defy that which would break down the human endurance of one who had to guard alone. Besides, I may be of service, since you can hypnotize me and so learn that which even I myself do not know."

Dr. Van Helsing said gravely, "Madam Mina, you are, as always, most wise. You shall with us come. And together we shall do that which we go forth to achieve."

When he had spoken, Mina's long spell of silence made me look at her. She had fallen back on her pillow asleep. She did not even wake when I had pulled up the blind and let in the sunlight which flooded the room. Van Helsing motioned to me to come with him quietly. We went to his room, and within a minute Lord Godalming, Dr. Seward, and Mr. Morris were with us also.

He told them what Mina had said, and went on. "In the morning we shall leave for Varna. We have now to deal with a new factor, Madam Mina. Oh, but her soul is true. It is to her an agony to tell us so much as she has done. But it is most right, and we are warned in time. There must be no chance lost, and in Varna we must be ready to act the instant when that ship arrives."

"What shall we do exactly?" asked Mr. Morris laconically.

The Professor paused before replying, "We shall at the first board that ship. Then, when we have identified the box, we shall place a branch of the wild rose on it. This we shall fasten, for when it is there none can emerge, so that at least says the superstition. And to superstition must we trust at the first. It was man's faith in the early, and it have its root in faith still. Then, when we get the opportunity that we seek, when none are near to see, we shall open the box, and . . . and all will be well."

"I shall not wait for any opportunity," said Morris. "When I see the box I shall open it and destroy the monster, though there were a thousand men looking on, and if I am to be wiped out for it the next moment!" I grasped his hand instinctively and found it as firm as a piece of steel. I think he understood my look. I hope he did.

"Good boy," said Dr. Van Helsing. "Brave boy. Quincey is all man. God bless him for it. My child, believe me none of us shall lag behind or pause from any fear. I do but say what we may do . . . what we must do. But, indeed, indeed we cannot say what we may do. There are so many things which may happen, and their ways and their ends are so various that until the moment we may not say. We shall all be armed, in all ways. And when the time for the end has come, our effort shall not be lack. Now let us today put all our affairs in order. Let all things which touch on others dear to us, and who on us depend, be complete. For none of us can tell what, or when, or how, the end may be. As for me, my own affairs are regulate, and as I have nothing else to do, I shall go make arrangements for the travel. I shall have all tickets and so forth for our journey."

There was nothing further to be said, and we parted. I shall now settle up all my affairs of earth, and be ready for whatever may come.

Later.—It is done. My will is made, and all complete. Mina if she survive is my sole heir. If it should not be so, then the others who have been so good to us shall have remainder.

It is now drawing towards the sunset. Mina's uneasiness calls my attention to it. I am sure that there is something on her mind which the time of exact sunset will reveal. These occasions are becoming harrowing times for us all. For each sunrise and sunset opens up some new danger, some new pain, which however, may in God's will be means to a good end. I write all these things in the diary since my darling must not hear them now. But if it may be that she can see them again, they shall be ready. She is calling to me.

⅋ CHAPTER 25 ⅏
DR. SEWARD'S DIARY

11 October, Evening.—Jonathan Harker has asked me to note this, as he says he is hardly equal to the task, and he wants an exact record kept.

I think that none of us were surprised when we were asked to see Mrs. Harker a little before the time of sunset. We have of late come to understand that sunrise and sunset are to her times of peculiar freedom. When her old self can be manifest without any controlling force subduing or restraining her, or inciting her to action. This mood or condition begins some half hour or more before actual sunrise or sunset, and lasts till either the sun is high, or whilst the clouds are still aglow with the rays streaming above the horizon. At first there is a sort of negative condition, as if some tie were loosened, and then the absolute freedom quickly follows. When, however, the freedom ceases the change back or relapse comes quickly, preceded only by a spell of warning silence.

Tonight, when we met, she was somewhat constrained, and bore all the signs of an internal struggle. I put it down myself to her making a violent effort at the earliest instant she could do so.

A very few minutes, however, gave her complete control of herself. Then, motioning her husband to sit beside her on the sofa where she was half reclining, she made the rest of us bring chairs up close.

Taking her husband's hand in hers, she began, "We are all here together in freedom, for perhaps the last time! I know that you will always be with me to the end." This was to her husband whose hand had, as we could see, tightened upon her. "In the morning we go out upon our task, and God alone knows what may be in store for any of us. You are going to be so good to me to take me with you. I know that all that brave earnest men can do for a poor weak woman, whose soul perhaps is lost, no, no, not yet, but is at any rate at stake, you will do. But you must remember that I am not as you are. There is a poison in my blood, in my soul, which may destroy me, which must destroy me, unless some relief comes to us. Oh, my friends, you know as well as I do, that my soul is at stake. And though I know there is one way out for me, you must not and I must not take it!" She looked appealingly to us all in turn, beginning and ending with her husband.

"What is that way?" asked Van Helsing in a hoarse voice. "What is that way, which we must not, may not, take?"

"That I may die now, either by my own hand or that of another, before the greater evil is entirely wrought. I know, and you know, that were I once dead you could and would set free my immortal spirit, even as you did my poor Lucy's. Were death, or the fear of death, the only thing that stood in the way I would not shrink to die here now, amidst the friends who love me. But death is not all. I cannot believe that to die in such a case, when there is hope before us and a bitter task to be done, is God's will. Therefore, I on my part, give up here the certainty of eternal rest, and go out into the dark where may be the blackest things that the world or the nether world holds!"

We were all silent, for we knew instinctively that this was only a prelude. The faces of the others were set, and Harker's grew ashen grey. Perhaps, he guessed better than any of us what was coming.

She continued, "This is what I can give into the hotch-pot.[114]" I could not but note the quaint legal phrase which she used in such a place, and with all seriousness. "What will each of you give? Your lives I know," she went on quickly, "that is easy for brave men. Your lives are God's, and you can give them back to Him, but what will you give to me?" She looked again questioningly, but this time avoided her husband's face. Quincey seemed to understand, he nodded, and her face lit up. "Then I shall tell you plainly what I want, for there must be no doubtful matter in this connection between us now. You must promise me, one and all, even you, my beloved husband, that should the time come, you will kill me."

"What is that time?" The voice was Quincey's, but it was low and strained.

"When you shall be convinced that I am so changed that it is better that I die that I may live. When I am thus dead in the flesh, then you will, without a moment's delay, drive a stake through me and cut off my head, or do whatever else may be wanting to give me rest!"

Quincey was the first to rise after the pause. He knelt down before her and taking her hand in his said solemnly, "I'm only a rough fellow, who hasn't, perhaps, lived as a man should to win such a distinction, but I swear to you by all that I hold sacred and dear that, should the time ever come, I shall not flinch from the duty that you have set us. And I promise you, too, that I shall make all certain, for if I am only doubtful I shall take it that the time has come!"

"My true friend!" was all she could say amid her fast-falling tears, as bending over, she kissed his hand.

"I swear the same, my dear Madam Mina!" said Van Helsing. "And I!" said Lord Godalming, each of them in turn kneeling to her to take the oath. I followed, myself.

Then her husband turned to her wan-eyed and with a greenish pallor which subdued the snowy whiteness of his hair, and asked, "And must I, too, make such a promise, oh, my wife?"

"You too, my dearest," she said, with infinite yearning of pity in her voice and eyes. "You must not shrink. You are nearest and dearest and all the world to me. Our souls are knit into one, for all life and all time. Think, dear, that there have been times when brave men have killed their wives and their womenkind, to keep them from falling into the hands of the enemy. Their hands did not falter any the more because those that they loved implored them to slay them. It is men's duty towards those whom they love, in such times of sore trial! And oh, my dear, if it is to be that I must meet death at any hand, let it be at the hand of him that loves me best. Dr. Van Helsing, I have not forgotten your mercy in poor Lucy's case to him who

114 Property to be divided.

loved." She stopped with a flying blush, and changed her phrase, "to him who had best right to give her peace. If that time shall come again, I look to you to make it a happy memory of my husband's life that it was his loving hand which set me free from the awful thrall upon me."

"Again I swear!" came the Professor's resonant voice.

Mrs. Harker smiled, positively smiled, as with a sigh of relief she leaned back and said, "And now one word of warning, a warning which you must never forget. This time, if it ever come, may come quickly and unexpectedly, and in such case you must lose no time in using your opportunity. At such a time I myself might be . . . nay! If the time ever come, *shall be*, leagued with your enemy against you.

"One more request," she became very solemn as she said this, "it is not vital and necessary like the other, but I want you to do one thing for me, if you will."

We all acquiesced, but no one spoke. There was no need to speak.

"I want you to read the Burial Service." She was interrupted by a deep groan from her husband. Taking his hand in hers, she held it over her heart, and continued. "You must read it over me some day. Whatever may be the issue of all this fearful state of things, it will be a sweet thought to all or some of us. You, my dearest, will I hope read it, for then it will be in your voice in my memory forever, come what may!"

"But oh, my dear one," he pleaded, "death is afar off from you."

"Nay," she said, holding up a warning hand. "I am deeper in death at this moment than if the weight of an earthly grave lay heavy upon me!"

"Oh, my wife, must I read it?" he said, before he began.

"It would comfort me, my husband!" was all she said, and he began to read when she had got the book ready.

How can I, how could anyone, tell of that strange scene, its solemnity, its gloom, its sadness, its horror, and withal, its sweetness. Even a sceptic, who can see nothing but a travesty of bitter truth in anything holy or emotional, would have been melted to the heart had he seen that little group of loving and devoted friends kneeling round that stricken and sorrowing lady; or heard the tender passion of her husband's voice, as in tones so broken and emotional that often he had to pause, he read the simple and beautiful service from the Burial of the Dead. I cannot go on . . . words . . . and v-voices . . . f-fail m-me!

She was right in her instinct. Strange as it was, bizarre as it may hereafter seem even to us who felt its potent influence at the time, it comforted us much. And the silence, which showed Mrs. Harker's coming relapse from her freedom of soul, did not seem so full of despair to any of us as we had dreaded.

JONATHAN HARKER'S JOURNAL

15 October, Varna.—We left Charing Cross on the morning of the 12th, got to Paris the same night, and took the places secured for us in the Orient Express. We traveled night and day, arriving here at about five o'clock. Lord Godalming went to the Consulate to see if any telegram had arrived for him, whilst the rest of us came on to this hotel, "the Odessus." The journey may have had incidents. I was, however, too eager to get on, to care for them. Until the *Czarina Catherine* comes into port there will be no interest for me in anything in the wide world. Thank God! Mina is well, and looks to be getting stronger. Her colour is coming back. She sleeps a great deal. Throughout the journey she slept nearly all the time. Before sunrise and sunset, however, she is very wakeful and alert. And it has become a habit for Van Helsing to hypnotize her at such times. At first, some effort was needed, and he had to make many passes. But now, she seems to yield at once, as if by habit, and scarcely any action is needed. He seems to have power at these particular moments to simply will, and her thoughts obey him. He always asks her what she can see and hear.

She answers to the first, "Nothing, all is dark."

And to the second, "I can hear the waves lapping against the ship, and the water rushing by. Canvas and cordage strain and masts and yards creak. The wind is high . . . I can hear it in the shrouds, and the bow throws back the foam."

It is evident that the *Czarina Catherine* is still at sea, hastening on her way to Varna. Lord Godalming has just returned. He had four telegrams, one each day since we started, and all to the same effect. That the *Czarina Catherine* had not been reported to Lloyd's from anywhere. He had arranged before leaving London that his agent should send him every day a telegram saying if the ship had been reported. He was to have a message even if she were not reported, so that he might be sure that there was a watch being kept at the other end of the wire.

We had dinner and went to bed early. Tomorrow we are to see the Vice Consul, and to arrange, if we can, about getting on board the ship as soon as she arrives. Van Helsing says that our chance will be to get on the boat between sunrise and sunset. The Count, even if he takes the form of a bat, cannot cross the running water of his own volition, and so cannot leave the ship. As he dare not change to man's form without suspicion, which he evidently wishes to avoid, he must remain in the box. If, then, we can come on board after sunrise, he is at our mercy, for we can open the box and make sure of him, as we did of poor Lucy, before he wakes. What mercy he shall get from us all will not count for much. We think that we shall not have much trouble with officials or the seamen. Thank God! This is the country where bribery can do anything, and we are well supplied with money. We have only to make sure that the ship cannot come into port between sunset and sunrise without our being warned, and we shall be safe. Judge Money-bag will settle this case, I think!

16 October.—Mina's report still the same. Lapping waves and rushing water, darkness and favouring winds. We are evidently in good time, and when we hear of the *Czarina Catherine* we shall be ready. As she must pass the Dardanelles we are sure to have some report.

17 October.—Everything is pretty well fixed now, I think, to welcome the Count on his return from his tour. Godalming told the shippers that he fancied that the box sent aboard might contain something stolen from a friend of his, and got a half consent that he might open it at his own risk. The owner gave him a paper telling the Captain to give him every facility in doing whatever he chose on board the ship, and also a similar authorization to his agent at Varna. We have seen the agent, who was much impressed with Godalming's kindly manner to him, and we are all satisfied that whatever he can do to aid our wishes will be done.

We have already arranged what to do in case we get the box open. If the Count is there, Van Helsing and Seward will cut off his head at once and drive a stake through his heart. Morris and Godalming and I shall prevent interference, even if we have to use the arms which we shall have ready. The Professor says that if we can so treat the Count's body, it will soon after fall into dust. In such case there would be no evidence against us, in case any suspicion of murder were aroused. But even if it were not, we should stand or fall by our act, and perhaps some day this very script may be evidence to come between some of us and a rope. For myself, I should take the chance only too thankfully if it were to come. We mean to leave no stone unturned to carry out our intent. We have arranged with certain officials that the instant the *Czarina Catherine* is seen, we are to be informed by a special messenger.

24 October.—A whole week of waiting. Daily telegrams to Godalming, but only the same story. "Not yet reported." Mina's morning and evening hypnotic answer is unvaried. Lapping waves, rushing water, and creaking masts.

TELEGRAM, OCTOBER 24TH RUFUS SMITH, LLOYD'S, LONDON, TO LORD GODALMING, CARE OF H. B. M. VICE CONSUL, VARNA

"*Czarina Catherine* reported this morning from Dardanelles."

DR. SEWARD'S DIARY

25 October.—How I miss my phonograph! To write a diary with a pen is irksome to me! But Van Helsing says I must. We were all wild with excitement yesterday when Godalming got his telegram from Lloyd's. I know now what men feel in battle when the call to action is heard. Mrs. Harker, alone of our party, did not show any signs of emotion. After all, it is not strange that she did not, for we took special care not to let her know anything about it, and we all tried not to show any excitement when we were in her presence. In old days she would, I am sure, have noticed, no matter how we might have tried to conceal it. But in this way she is greatly changed during the past three weeks. The lethargy grows upon her, and though she seems strong and well, and is getting back some of her colour, Van Helsing and I are not satisfied. We talk of her often. We have not, however, said a word to the others. It would break poor Harker's heart, certainly his nerve, if he knew that we had even a suspicion on the subject. Van Helsing examines, he tells me, her teeth very carefully, whilst she is in the hypnotic condition, for he says that so long as they do not begin to sharpen there is no active danger of a change in her. If this change should come, it would be necessary to take steps! We both know what those steps would have to be, though we do not mention our thoughts to each other. We should neither of us shrink from the task, awful though it be to contemplate. "Euthanasia" is an excellent and a comforting word! I am grateful to whoever invented it.

It is only about 24 hours' sail from the Dardanelles to here, at the rate the *Czarina Catherine* has come from London. She should therefore arrive some time in the morning, but as she cannot possibly get in before noon, we are all about to retire early. We shall get up at one o'clock, so as to be ready.

25 October, Noon.—No news yet of the ship's arrival. Mrs. Harker's hypnotic report this morning was the same as usual, so it is possible that we may get news at any moment. We men are all in a fever of excitement, except Harker, who is calm. His hands are cold as ice, and an hour ago I found him whetting the edge of the great Ghoorka knife which he now always carries with him. It will be a bad lookout for the Count if the edge of that "Kukri" ever touches his throat, driven by that stern, ice-cold hand!

Van Helsing and I were a little alarmed about Mrs. Harker today. About noon she got into a sort of lethargy which we did not like. Although we kept silence to the others, we were neither of us happy about it. She had been restless all the morning, so that we were at first glad to know that she was sleeping. When, however, her husband mentioned casually that she was sleeping so soundly that he could not wake her, we went to her room to see for ourselves. She was breathing naturally and looked so well and peaceful that we agreed that the sleep was better for her than anything else. Poor girl, she has so much to forget that it is no wonder that sleep, if it brings oblivion to her, does her good.

Later.—Our opinion was justified, for when after a refreshing sleep of some hours she woke up, she seemed brighter and better than she had been for days. At sunset she made the usual hypnotic report. Wherever he may be in the Black Sea, the Count is hurrying to his destination. To his doom, I trust!

26 October.—Another day and no tidings of the *Czarina Catherine.* She ought to be here by now. That she is still journeying *somewhere* is apparent, for Mrs. Harker's hypnotic report at sunrise was still the same. It is possible that the vessel may be lying by, at times, for fog. Some of the steamers which came in last evening reported patches of fog both to north and south of the port. We must continue our watching, as the ship may now be signalled any moment.

27 October, Noon.—Most strange. No news yet of the ship we wait for. Mrs. Harker reported last night and this morning as usual. "Lapping waves and rushing water," though she added that "the waves were very faint." The telegrams from London have been the same, "no further report." Van Helsing is terribly anxious, and told me just now that he fears the Count is escaping us.

He added significantly, "I did not like that lethargy of Madam Mina's. Souls and memories can do strange things during trance." I was about to ask him more, but Harker just then came in, and he held up a warning hand. We must try tonight at sunset to make her speak more fully when in her hypnotic state.

28 OCTOBER.—TELEGRAM. RUFUS SMITH, LONDON, TO LORD GODALMING, CARE H. B. M. VICE CONSUL, VARNA

"*Czarina Catherine* reported entering Galatz at one o'clock today."

DR. SEWARD'S DIARY

28 October.—When the telegram came announcing the arrival in Galatz I do not think it was such a shock to any of us as might have been expected. True, we did not know whence, or how, or when, the bolt would come. But I think we all expected that something strange would happen. The day of arrival at Varna made us individually satisfied that things would not be just as we had expected. We only waited to learn where the change would occur. None the less, however, it was a surprise. I suppose that nature works on such a hopeful basis that we believe against ourselves that things will be as they ought to be, not as we should know that they will be. Transcendentalism is a beacon to the angels, even if it be a will-o'-the-wisp to man. Van Helsing raised his hand over his head for a moment, as though in remonstrance with the Almighty. But he said not a word, and in a few seconds stood up with his face sternly set.

Lord Godalming grew very pale, and sat breathing heavily. I was myself half stunned and looked in wonder at one after another. Quincey Morris tightened his belt with that quick movement which I knew so well. In our old wandering days it meant "action." Mrs. Harker grew ghastly white, so that the scar on her forehead seemed to burn, but she folded her hands meekly and looked up in prayer. Harker smiled, actually smiled, the dark, bitter smile of one who is without hope, but at the same time his action belied his words, for his hands instinctively sought the hilt of the great Kukri knife and rested there.

"When does the next train start for Galatz?" said Van Helsing to us generally.

"At 6:30 tomorrow morning!" We all started, for the answer came from Mrs. Harker.

"How on earth do you know?" said Art.

"You forget, or perhaps you do not know, though Jonathan does and so does Dr. Van Helsing, that I am the train fiend. At home in Exeter I always used to make up the time tables, so as to be helpful to my husband. I found it so useful sometimes, that I always make a study of the time tables now. I knew that if anything were to take us to Castle Dracula we should go by

Galatz, or at any rate through Bucharest, so I learned the times very carefully. Unhappily there are not many to learn, as the only train tomorrow
leaves as I say."

"Wonderful woman!" murmured the Professor.

"Can't we get a special?" asked Lord Godalming.

Van Helsing shook his head, "I fear not. This land is very different from
yours or mine. Even if we did have a special, it would probably not arrive
as soon as our regular train. Moreover, we have something to prepare. We
must think. Now let us organize. You, friend Arthur, go to the train and
get the tickets and arrange that all be ready for us to go in the morning. Do
you, friend Jonathan, go to the agent of the ship and get from him letters
to the agent in Galatz, with authority to make a search of the ship just as it
was here. Quincey Morris, you see the Vice Consul, and get his aid with his
fellow in Galatz and all he can do to make our way smooth, so that no times
be lost when over the Danube. John will stay with Madam Mina and me,
and we shall consult. For so if time be long you may be delayed. And it will
not matter when the sun set, since I am here with Madam to make report."

"And I," said Mrs. Harker brightly, and more like her old self than she
had been for many a long day, "shall try to be of use in all ways, and shall
think and write for you as I used to do. Something is shifting from me in
some strange way, and I feel freer than I have been of late!"

The three younger men looked happier at the moment as they seemed
to realize the significance of her words. But Van Helsing and I, turning to
each other, met each a grave and troubled glance. We said nothing at the
time, however.

When the three men had gone out to their tasks Van Helsing asked Mrs.
Harker to look up the copy of the diaries and find him the part of Harker's
journal at the Castle. She went away to get it.

When the door was shut upon her he said to me, "We mean the same!
Speak out!"

"Here is some change. It is a hope that makes me sick, for it may deceive
us."

"Quite so. Do you know why I asked her to get the manuscript?"

"No!" said I, "unless it was to get an opportunity of seeing me alone."

"You are in part right, friend John, but only in part. I want to tell you
something. And oh, my friend, I am taking a great, a terrible, risk. But I
believe it is right. In the moment when Madam Mina said those words that
arrest both our understanding, an inspiration came to me. In the trance of
three days ago the Count sent her his spirit to read her mind. Or more like
he took her to see him in his earth box in the ship with water rushing, just
as it go free at rise and set of sun. He learn then that we are here, for she

have more to tell in her open life with eyes to see ears to hear than he, shut as he is, in his coffin box. Now he make his most effort to escape us. At present he want her not.

"He is sure with his so great knowledge that she will come at his call. But he cut her off, take her, as he can do, out of his own power, that so she come not to him. Ah! There I have hope that our man brains that have been of man so long and that have not lost the grace of God, will come higher than his child-brain that lie in his tomb for centuries, that grow not yet to our stature, and that do only work selfish and therefore small. Here comes Madam Mina. Not a word to her of her trance! She knows it not, and it would overwhelm her and make despair just when we want all her hope, all her courage, when most we want all her great brain which is trained like man's brain, but is of sweet woman and have a special power which the Count give her, and which he may not take away altogether, though he think not so. Hush! Let me speak, and you shall learn. Oh, John, my friend, we are in awful straits. I fear, as I never feared before. We can only trust the good God. Silence! Here she comes!"

I thought that the Professor was going to break down and have hysterics, just as he had when Lucy died, but with a great effort he controlled himself and was at perfect nervous poise when Mrs. Harker tripped into the room, bright and happy looking and, in the doing of work, seemingly forgetful of her misery. As she came in, she handed a number of sheets of typewriting to Van Helsing. He looked over them gravely, his face brightening up as he read.

Then holding the pages between his finger and thumb he said, "Friend John, to you with so much experience already, and you too, dear Madam Mina, that are young, here is a lesson. Do not fear ever to think. A half thought has been buzzing often in my brain, but I fear to let him loose his wings. Here now, with more knowledge, I go back to where that half thought come from and I find that he be no half thought at all. That be a whole thought, though so young that he is not yet strong to use his little wings. Nay, like the 'Ugly Duck' of my friend Hans Andersen, he be no duck thought at all, but a big swan thought that sail nobly on big wings, when the time come for him to try them. See I read here what Jonathan have written.

"That other of his race who, in a later age, again and again, brought his forces over The Great River into Turkey Land, who when he was beaten back, came again, and again, and again, though he had to come alone from the bloody field where his troops were being slaughtered, since he knew that he alone could ultimately triumph.

"What does this tell us? Not much? No! The Count's child thought see nothing, therefore he speak so free. Your man thought see nothing. My man thought see nothing, till just now. No! But there comes another word from some one who speak without thought because she, too, know not what it mean, what it *might* mean. Just as there are elements which rest, yet when in nature's course they move on their way and they touch, the pouf! And there comes a flash of light, heaven wide, that blind and kill and destroy some. But that show up all earth below for leagues and leagues. Is it not so? Well, I shall explain. To begin, have you ever study the philosophy of crime? 'Yes' and 'No.' You, John, yes, for it is a study of insanity. You, no, Madam Mina, for crime touch you not, not but once. Still, your mind works true, and argues not a *particulari ad universale*.[115] There is this peculiarity in criminals. It is so constant, in all countries and at all times, that even police, who know not much from philosophy, come to know it empirically, that it is. That is to be empiric. The criminal always work at one crime, that is the true criminal who seems predestinate to crime, and who will of none other. This criminal has not full man brain. He is clever and cunning and resourceful, but he be not of man stature as to brain. He be of child brain in much. Now this criminal of ours is predestinate to crime also. He, too, have child brain, and it is of the child to do what he have done. The little bird, the little fish, the little animal learn not by principle, but empirically. And when he learn to do, then there is to him the ground to start from to do more. 'Dos pou sto,' said Archimedes. 'Give me a fulcrum, and I shall move the world!' To do once, is the fulcrum whereby child brain become man brain. And until he have the purpose to do more, he continue to do the same again every time, just as he have done before! Oh, my dear, I see that your eyes are opened, and that to you the lightning flash show all the leagues," for Mrs. Harker began to clap her hands and her eyes sparkled.

He went on, "Now you shall speak. Tell us two dry men of science what you see with those so bright eyes." He took her hand and held it whilst he spoke. His finger and thumb closed on her pulse, as I thought instinctively and unconsciously, as she spoke.

"The Count is a criminal and of criminal type. Nordau and Lombroso would so classify him, and *qua* criminal he is of an imperfectly formed mind. Thus, in a difficulty he has to seek resource in habit. His past is a clue, and the one page of it that we know, and that from his own lips, tells that once before, when in what Mr. Morris would call a 'tight place,' he went back to his own country from the land he had tried to invade, and thence, without losing purpose, prepared himself for a new effort. He came again better equipped for his work, and won. So he came to London to invade a

---

115 From the particular to the general (Latin).

new land. He was beaten, and when all hope of success was lost, and his existence in danger, he fled back over the sea to his home. Just as formerly he had fled back over the Danube from Turkey Land."

"Good, good! Oh, you so clever lady!" said Van Helsing, enthusiastically, as he stooped and kissed her hand. A moment later he said to me, as calmly as though we had been having a sick room consultation, "Seventy-two only, and in all this excitement. I have hope."

Turning to her again, he said with keen expectation, "But go on. Go on! There is more to tell if you will. Be not afraid. John and I know. I do in any case, and shall tell you if you are right. Speak, without fear!"

"I will try to. But you will forgive me if I seem too egotistical."

"Nay! Fear not, you must be egotist, for it is of you that we think."

"Then, as he is criminal he is selfish. And as his intellect is small and his action is based on selfishness, he confines himself to one purpose. That purpose is remorseless. As he fled back over the Danube, leaving his forces to be cut to pieces, so now he is intent on being safe, careless of all. So his own selfishness frees my soul somewhat from the terrible power which he acquired over me on that dreadful night. I felt it! Oh, I felt it! Thank God, for His great mercy! My soul is freer than it has been since that awful hour. And all that haunts me is a fear lest in some trance or dream he may have used my knowledge for his ends."

The Professor stood up, "He has so used your mind, and by it he has left us here in Varna, whilst the ship that carried him rushed through enveloping fog up to Galatz, where, doubtless, he had made preparation for escaping from us. But his child mind only saw so far. And it may be that as ever is in God's Providence, the very thing that the evil doer most reckoned on for his selfish good, turns out to be his chiefest harm. The hunter is taken in his own snare, as the great Psalmist says. For now that he think he is free from every trace of us all, and that he has escaped us with so many hours to him, then his selfish child brain will whisper him to sleep. He think, too, that as he cut himself off from knowing your mind, there can be no knowledge of him to you. There is where he fail! That terrible baptism of blood which he give you makes you free to go to him in spirit, as you have as yet done in your times of freedom, when the sun rise and set. At such times you go by my volition and not by his. And this power to good of you and others, you have won from your suffering at his hands. This is now all more precious that he know it not, and to guard himself have even cut himself off from his knowledge of our where. We, however, are not selfish, and we believe that God is with us through all this blackness, and these many dark hours. We shall follow him, and we shall not flinch, even if we peril ourselves that we become like him. Friend John, this has been a great hour, and it have done much to advance us on our way. You must be scribe and write him all down, so that when the others return from their work you can give it to them, then they shall know as we do."

And so I have written it whilst we wait their return, and Mrs. Harker has written with the typewriter all since she brought the MS to us.

℘ CHAPTER 26 ℘
DR. SEWARD'S DIARY

29 October.—This is written in the train from Varna to Galatz. Last night we all assembled a little before the time of sunset. Each of us had done his work as well as he could, so far as thought, and endeavour, and opportunity go, we are prepared for the whole of our journey, and for our work when we get to Galatz. When the usual time came round Mrs. Harker prepared herself for her hypnotic effort, and after a longer and more serious effort on the part of Van Helsing than has been usually necessary, she sank into the trance. Usually she speaks on a hint, but this time the Professor had to ask her questions, and to ask them pretty resolutely, before we could learn anything. At last her answer came.

"I can see nothing. We are still. There are no waves lapping, but only a steady swirl of water softly running against the hawser[116]. I can hear men's voices calling, near and far, and the roll and creak of oars in the rowlocks. A gun is fired somewhere, the echo of it seems far away. There is tramping of feet overhead, and ropes and chains are dragged along. What is this? There is a gleam of light. I can feel the air blowing upon me."

Here she stopped. She had risen, as if impulsively, from where she lay on the sofa, and raised both her hands, palms upwards, as if lifting a weight. Van Helsing and I looked at each other with understanding. Quincey raised his eyebrows slightly and looked at her intently, whilst Harker's hand instinctively closed round the hilt of his Kukri. There was a long pause. We all knew that the time when she could speak was passing, but we felt that it was useless to say anything.

Suddenly she sat up, and as she opened her eyes said sweetly, "Would none of you like a cup of tea? You must all be so tired!"

We could only make her happy, and so acquiesced. She bustled off to get tea. When she had gone Van Helsing said, "You see, my friends. He is close to land. He has left his earth chest. But he has yet to get on shore. In the

---

116 Ship's cable.

night he may lie hidden somewhere, but if he be not carried on shore, or if the ship do not touch it, he cannot achieve the land. In such case he can, if it be in the night, change his form and jump or fly on shore, then, unless he be carried he cannot escape. And if he be carried, then the customs men may discover what the box contain. Thus, in fine, if he escape not on shore tonight, or before dawn, there will be the whole day lost to him. We may then arrive in time. For if he escape not at night we shall come on him in daytime, boxed up and at our mercy. For he dare not be his true self, awake and visible, lest he be discovered."

There was no more to be said, so we waited in patience until the dawn, at which time we might learn more from Mrs. Harker.

Early this morning we listened, with breathless anxiety, for her response in her trance. The hypnotic stage was even longer in coming than before, and when it came the time remaining until full sunrise was so short that we began to despair. Van Helsing seemed to throw his whole soul into the effort. At last, in obedience to his will she made reply.

"All is dark. I hear lapping water, level with me, and some creaking as of wood on wood." She paused, and the red sun shot up. We must wait till tonight.

And so it is that we are travelling towards Galatz in an agony of expectation. We are due to arrive between two and three in the morning. But already, at Bucharest, we are three hours late, so we cannot possibly get in till well after sunup. Thus we shall have two more hypnotic messages from Mrs. Harker! Either or both may possibly throw more light on what is happening.

Later.—Sunset has come and gone. Fortunately it came at a time when there was no distraction. For had it occurred whilst we were at a station, we might not have secured the necessary calm and isolation. Mrs. Harker yielded to the hypnotic influence even less readily than this morning. I am in fear that her power of reading the Count's sensations may die away, just when we want it most. It seems to me that her imagination is beginning to work. Whilst she has been in the trance hitherto she has confined herself to the simplest of facts. If this goes on it may ultimately mislead us. If I thought that the Count's power over her would die away equally with her power of knowledge it would be a happy thought. But I am afraid that it may not be so.

When she did speak, her words were enigmatical, "Something is going out. I can feel it pass me like a cold wind. I can hear, far off, confused sounds, as of men talking in strange tongues, fierce falling water, and the howling of wolves." She stopped and a shudder ran through her, increasing in intensity for a few seconds, till at the end, she shook as though in a palsy.

She said no more, even in answer to the Professor's imperative questioning. When she woke from the trance, she was cold, and exhausted, and languid, but her mind was all alert. She could not remember anything, but asked what she had said. When she was told, she pondered over it deeply for a long time and in silence.

30 October, 7 A.M.—We are near Galatz now, and I may not have time to write later. Sunrise this morning was anxiously looked for by us all. Knowing of the increasing difficulty of procuring the hypnotic trance, Van Helsing began his passes earlier than usual. They produced no effect, however, until the regular time, when she yielded with a still greater difficulty, only a minute before the sun rose. The Professor lost no time in his questioning.

Her answer came with equal quickness, "All is dark. I hear water swirling by, level with my ears, and the creaking of wood on wood. Cattle low far off. There is another sound, a queer one like . . ." She stopped and grew white, and whiter still.

"Go on, go on! Speak, I command you!" said Van Helsing in an agonized voice. At the same time there was despair in his eyes, for the risen sun was reddening even Mrs. Harker's pale face. She opened her eyes, and we all started as she said, sweetly and seemingly with the utmost unconcern.

"Oh, Professor, why ask me to do what you know I can't? I don't remember anything." Then, seeing the look of amazement on our faces, she said, turning from one to the other with a troubled look, "What have I said? What have I done? I know nothing, only that I was lying here, half asleep, and heard you say 'go on! speak, I command you!' It seemed so funny to hear you order me about, as if I were a bad child!"

"Oh, Madam Mina," he said, sadly, "it is proof, if proof be needed, of how I love and honour you, when a word for your good, spoken more earnest than ever, can seem so strange because it is to order her whom I am proud to obey!"

The whistles are sounding. We are nearing Galatz. We are on fire with anxiety and eagerness.

MINA HARKER'S JOURNAL

30 October.—Mr. Morris took me to the hotel where our rooms had been ordered by telegraph, he being the one who could best be spared, since he does not speak any foreign language. The forces were distributed much as they had been at Varna, except that Lord Godalming went to the Vice

Consul, as his rank might serve as an immediate guarantee of some sort to the official, we being in extreme hurry. Jonathan and the two doctors went to the shipping agent to learn particulars of the arrival of the *Czarina Catherine*.

Later.—Lord Godalming has returned. The Consul is away, and the Vice Consul sick. So the routine work has been attended to by a clerk. He was very obliging, and offered to do anything in his power.

JONATHAN HARKER'S JOURNAL

30 October.—At nine o'clock Dr. Van Helsing, Dr. Seward, and I called on Messrs. Mackenzie & Steinkoff, the agents of the London firm of Hapgood. They had received a wire from London, in answer to Lord Godalming's telegraphed request, asking them to show us any civility in their power. They were more than kind and courteous, and took us at once on board the *Czarina Catherine*, which lay at anchor out in the river harbor. There we saw the Captain, Donelson by name, who told us of his voyage. He said that in all his life he had never had so favourable a run.

"Man!" he said, "but it made us afeard, for we expect it that we should have to pay for it wi' some rare piece o' ill luck, so as to keep up the average. It's no canny[117] to run frae London to the Black Sea wi' a wind ahint[118] ye, as though the Deil himself were blawin' on yer sail for his ain purpose. An' a' the time we could no speer[119] a thing. Gin[120] we were nigh a ship, or a port, or a headland, a fog fell on us and travelled wi' us, till when after it had lifted and we looked out, the deil a thing could we see. We ran by Gibraltar wi' oot bein' able to signal. An' til we came to the Dardanelles and had to wait to get our permit to pass, we never were within hail o' aught. At first I inclined to slack off sail and beat about till the fog was lifted. But whiles, I thocht that if the Deil was minded to get us into the Black Sea quick, he was like to do it whether we would or no. If we had a quick voyage it would be no to our miscredit wi' the owners, or no hurt to our traffic, an' the Old Mon[121] who had served his ain purpose wad be decently grateful to us for no hinderin' him."

---

117 Not natural.
118 Behind.
119 See.
120 When.
121 Old man; the devil.

This mixture of simplicity and cunning, of superstition and commercial reasoning, aroused Van Helsing, who said, "Mine friend, that Devil is more clever than he is thought by some, and he know when he meet his match!"

The skipper was not displeased with the compliment, and went on, "When we got past the Bosphorus the men began to grumble. Some o' them, the Roumanians, came and asked me to heave overboard a big box which had been put on board by a queer lookin' old man just before we had started frae London. I had seen them speer at the fellow, and put out their twa fingers when they saw him, to guard them against the evil eye. Man! but the supersteetion of foreigners is pairfectly rideeculous! I sent them aboot their business pretty quick, but as just after a fog closed in on us I felt a wee bit as they did anent[122] something, though I wouldn't say it was again the big box. Well, on we went, and as the fog didn't let up for five days I joost let the wind carry us, for if the Deil wanted to get somewheres, well, he would fetch it up a'reet. An' if he didn't, well, we'd keep a sharp lookout anyhow. Sure eneuch, we had a fair way and deep water all the time. And two days ago, when the mornin' sun came through the fog, we found ourselves just in the river opposite Galatz. The Roumanians were wild, and wanted me right or wrong to take out the box and fling it in the river. I had to argy wi' them aboot it wi' a handspike. An' when the last o' them rose off the deck wi' his head in his hand, I had convinced them that, evil eye or no evil eye, the property and the trust of my owners were better in my hands than in the river Danube. They had, mind ye, taken the box on the deck ready to fling in, and as it was marked Galatz via Varna, I thocht I'd let it lie till we discharged in the port an' get rid o't althegither. We didn't do much clearin' that day, an' had to remain the nicht at anchor. But in the mornin', braw an' airly, an hour before sunup, a man came aboard wi' an order, written to him from England, to receive a box marked for one Count Dracula. Sure eneuch the matter was one ready to his hand. He had his papers a' reet, an' glad I was to be rid o' the dam' thing, for I was beginnin' masel' to feel uneasy at it. If the Deil did have any luggage aboord the ship, I'm thinkin' it was nane ither than that same!"

"What was the name of the man who took it?" asked Dr. Van Helsing with restrained eagerness.

"I'll be tellin' ye quick!" he answered, and stepping down to his cabin, produced a receipt signed "Immanuel Hildesheim." Burgen-strasse 16 was the address. We found out that this was all the Captain knew, so with thanks we came away.

We found Hildesheim in his office, a Hebrew of rather the Adelphi Theatre type, with a nose like a sheep, and a fez. His arguments were pointed

122 About.

with specie,[123] we doing the punctuation, and with a little bargaining he told us what he knew. This turned out to be simple but important. He had received a letter from Mr. de Ville of London, telling him to receive, if possible before sunrise so as to avoid customs, a box which would arrive at Galatz in the *Czarina Catherine*. This he was to give in charge to a certain Petrof Skinsky, who dealt with the Slovaks who traded down the river to the port. He had been paid for his work by an English bank note, which had been duly cashed for gold at the Danube International Bank. When Skinsky had come to him, he had taken him to the ship and handed over the box, so as to save porterage. That was all he knew.

We then sought for Skinsky, but were unable to find him. One of his neighbors, who did not seem to bear him any affection, said that he had gone away two days before, no one knew whither. This was corroborated by his landlord, who had received by messenger the key of the house together with the rent due, in English money. This had been between ten and eleven o'clock last night. We were at a standstill again.

Whilst we were talking one came running and breathlessly gasped out that the body of Skinsky had been found inside the wall of the churchyard of St. Peter, and that the throat had been torn open as if by some wild animal. Those we had been speaking with ran off to see the horror, the women crying out. "This is the work of a Slovak!" We hurried away lest we should have been in some way drawn into the affair, and so detained.

As we came home we could arrive at no definite conclusion. We were all convinced that the box was on its way, by water, to somewhere, but where that might be we would have to discover. With heavy hearts we came home to the hotel to Mina.

When we met together, the first thing was to consult as to taking Mina again into our confidence. Things are getting desperate, and it is at least a chance, though a hazardous one. As a preliminary step, I was released from my promise to her.

MINA HARKER'S JOURNAL

30 October, evening.—They were so tired and worn out and dispirited that there was nothing to be done till they had some rest, so I asked them all to lie down for half an hour whilst I should enter everything up to the moment. I feel so grateful to the man who invented the "Traveller's" typewriter,

---

123 Coins.

and to Mr. Morris for getting this one for me. I should have felt quite astray doing the work if I had to write with a pen . . .

It is all done. Poor dear, dear Jonathan, what he must have suffered, what he must be suffering now. He lies on the sofa hardly seeming to breathe, and his whole body appears in collapse. His brows are knit. His face is drawn with pain. Poor fellow, maybe he is thinking, and I can see his face all wrinkled up with the concentration of his thoughts. Oh! if I could only help at all. I shall do what I can.

I have asked Dr. Van Helsing, and he has got me all the papers that I have not yet seen. Whilst they are resting, I shall go over all carefully, and perhaps I may arrive at some conclusion. I shall try to follow the Professor's example, and think without prejudice on the facts before me . . .

I do believe that under God's providence I have made a discovery. I shall get the maps and look over them.

I am more than ever sure that I am right. My new conclusion is ready, so I shall get our party together and read it. They can judge it. It is well to be accurate, and every minute is precious.

MINA HARKER'S MEMORANDUM

(Entered In Her Journal)

GROUND OF INQUIRY.—
COUNT DRACULA'S PROBLEM IS TO GET BACK TO HIS OWN PLACE.

(a) He must be *brought back* by some one. This is evident; for had he power to move himself as he wished he could go either as man, or wolf, or bat, or in some other way. He evidently fears discovery or interference, in the state of helplessness in which he must be, confined as he is between dawn and sunset in his wooden box.

(b) *How is he to be taken?*—Here a process of exclusions may help us. By road, by rail, by water?

1. *By Road.*—There are endless difficulties, especially in leaving the city.

(x) There are people. And people are curious, and investigate. A hint, a surmise, a doubt as to what might be in the box, would destroy him.

(y) There are, or there may be, customs and octroi[124] officers to pass.

(z) His pursuers might follow. This is his highest fear. And in order to prevent his being betrayed he has repelled, so far as he can, even his victim, me!

2. *By Rail.*—There is no one in charge of the box. It would have to take its chance of being delayed, and delay would be fatal, with enemies on the track. True, he might escape at night. But what would he be, if left in a strange place with no refuge that he could fly to? This is not what he intends, and he does not mean to risk it.

3. *By Water.*—Here is the safest way, in one respect, but with most danger in another. On the water he is powerless except at night. Even then he can only summon fog and storm and snow and his wolves. But were he wrecked, the living water would engulf him, helpless, and he would indeed be lost. He could have the vessel drive to land, but if it were unfriendly land, wherein he was not free to move, his position would still be desperate.

We know from the record that he was on the water, so what we have to do is to ascertain what water.

The first thing is to realize exactly what he has done as yet. We may, then, get a light on what his task is to be.

Firstly.—We must differentiate between what he did in London as part of his general plan of action, when he was pressed for moments and had to arrange as best he could.

Secondly.—We must see, as well as we can surmise it from the facts we know of, what he has done here.

As to the first, he evidently intended to arrive at Galatz, and sent invoice to Varna to deceive us lest we should ascertain his means of exit from England. His immediate and sole purpose then was to escape. The proof of this, is the letter of instructions sent to Immanuel Hildesheim to clear and take away the box *before sunrise.* There is also the instruction to Petrof Skinsky. These we must only guess at, but there must have been some letter or message, since Skinsky came to Hildesheim.

---

124 Tax.

That, so far, his plans were successful we know. The *Czarina Catherine* made a phenomenally quick journey. So much so that Captain Donelson's suspicions were aroused. But his superstition united with his canniness played the Count's game for him, and he ran with his favouring wind through fogs and all till he brought up blindfold at Galatz. That the Count's arrangements were well made, has been proved. Hildesheim cleared the box, took it off, and gave it to Skinsky. Skinsky took it, and here we lose the trail. We only know that the box is somewhere on the water, moving along. The customs and the octroi, if there be any, have been avoided.

Now we come to what the Count must have done after his arrival, *on land*, at Galatz.

The box was given to Skinsky before sunrise. At sunrise the Count could appear in his own form. Here, we ask why Skinsky was chosen at all to aid in the work? In my husband's diary, Skinsky is mentioned as dealing with the Slovaks who trade down the river to the port. And the man's remark, that the murder was the work of a Slovak, showed the general feeling against his class. The Count wanted isolation.

My surmise is this, that in London the Count decided to get back to his castle by water, as the most safe and secret way. He was brought from the castle by Szgany, and probably they delivered their cargo to Slovaks who took the boxes to Varna, for there they were shipped to London. Thus the Count had knowledge of the persons who could arrange this service. When the box was on land, before sunrise or after sunset, he came out from his box, met Skinsky and instructed him what to do as to arranging the carriage of the box up some river. When this was done, and he knew that all was in train, he blotted out his traces, as he thought, by murdering his agent.

I have examined the map and find that the river most suitable for the Slovaks to have ascended is either the Pruth or the Sereth. I read in the typescript that in my trance I heard cows low and water swirling level with my ears and the creaking of wood. The Count in his box, then, was on a river in an open boat, propelled probably either by oars or poles, for the banks are near and it is working against stream. There would be no such if floating down stream.

Of course it may not be either the Sereth or the Pruth, but we may possibly investigate further. Now of these two, the Pruth is the more easily navigated, but the Sereth is, at Fundu, joined by the Bistritza which runs up round the Borgo Pass. The loop it makes is manifestly as close to Dracula's castle as can be got by water.

MINA HARKER'S JOURNAL—CONTINUED

When I had done reading, Jonathan took me in his arms and kissed me. The others kept shaking me by both hands, and Dr. Van Helsing said, "Our dear Madam Mina is once more our teacher. Her eyes have been where we were blinded. Now we are on the track once again, and this time we may succeed. Our enemy is at his most helpless. And if we can come on him by day, on the water, our task will be over. He has a start, but he is powerless to hasten, as he may not leave this box lest those who carry him may suspect. For them to suspect would be to prompt them to throw him in the stream where he perish. This he knows, and will not. Now men, to our Council of War, for here and now, we must plan what each and all shall do."

"I shall get a steam launch and follow him," said Lord Godalming.

"And I, horses to follow on the bank lest by chance he land," said Mr. Morris.

"Good!" said the Professor, "both good. But neither must go alone. There must be force to overcome force if need be. The Slovak is strong and rough, and he carries rude arms." All the men smiled, for amongst them they carried a small arsenal.

Said Mr. Morris, "I have brought some Winchesters. They are pretty handy in a crowd, and there may be wolves. The Count, if you remember, took some other precautions. He made some requisitions on others that Mrs. Harker could not quite hear or understand. We must be ready at all points."

Dr. Seward said, "I think I had better go with Quincey. We have been accustomed to hunt together, and we two, well armed, will be a match for whatever may come along. You must not be alone, Art. It may be necessary to fight the Slovaks, and a chance thrust, for I don't suppose these fellows carry guns, would undo all our plans. There must be no chances, this time. We shall not rest until the Count's head and body have been separated, and we are sure that he cannot reincarnate."

He looked at Jonathan as he spoke, and Jonathan looked at me. I could see that the poor dear was torn about in his mind. Of course he wanted to be with me. But then the boat service would, most likely, be the one which would destroy the . . . the . . . Vampire. (Why did I hesitate to write the word?)

He was silent awhile, and during his silence Dr. Van Helsing spoke, "Friend Jonathan, this is to you for twice reasons. First, because you are young and brave and can fight, and all energies may be needed at the last. And again that it is your right to destroy him. That, which has wrought such woe to you and yours. Be not afraid for Madam Mina. She will be my care, if I may. I am old. My legs are not so quick to run as once. And I am not used to ride so long or to pursue as need be, or to fight with lethal weapons. But I can be of other service. I can fight in other way. And I can die, if need be, as well as younger men. Now let me say that what I would is this. While you, my Lord Godalming and friend Jonathan go in your so swift little steamboat up the river, and whilst John and Quincey guard the bank where perchance he might be landed, I will take Madam Mina right into the heart of the enemy's country. Whilst the old fox is tied in his box, floating on the running stream whence he cannot escape to land, where he dares not raise the lid of his coffin box lest his Slovak carriers should in fear leave him to perish, we shall go in the track where Jonathan went, from Bistritz over the Borgo, and find our way to the Castle of Dracula. Here, Madam Mina's hypnotic power will surely help, and we shall find our way, all dark and unknown otherwise, after the first sunrise when we are near that fateful place. There is much to be done, and other places to be made sanctify, so that that nest of vipers be obliterated."

Here Jonathan interrupted him hotly, "Do you mean to say, Professor Van Helsing, that you would bring Mina, in her sad case and tainted as she is with that devil's illness, right into the jaws of his deathtrap? Not for the world! Not for Heaven or Hell!"

He became almost speechless for a minute, and then went on, "Do you know what the place is? Have you seen that awful den of hellish infamy, with the very moonlight alive with grisly shapes, and every speck of dust that whirls in the wind a devouring monster in embryo? Have you felt the Vampire's lips upon your throat?"

Here he turned to me, and as his eyes lit on my forehead he threw up his arms with a cry, "Oh, my God, what have we done to have this terror upon us?" and he sank down on the sofa in a collapse of misery.

The Professor's voice, as he spoke in clear, sweet tones, which seemed to vibrate in the air, calmed us all.

"Oh, my friend, it is because I would save Madam Mina from that awful place that I would go. God forbid that I should take her into that place. There is work, wild work, to be done before that place can be purify. Remember that we are in terrible straits. If the Count escape us this time, and he is strong and subtle and cunning, he may choose to sleep him for a century, and then in time our dear one," he took my hand, "would come to him to keep him company, and would be as those others that you, Jonathan, saw. You have told us of their gloating lips. You heard their ribald laugh as they clutched the moving bag that the Count threw to them. You shudder, and well may it be. Forgive me that I make you so much pain, but it is necessary. My friend, is it not a dire need for that which I am giving, possibly my life? If it were that any one went into that place to stay, it is I who would have to go to keep them company."

"Do as you will," said Jonathan, with a sob that shook him all over, "we are in the hands of God!"

Later.—Oh, it did me good to see the way that these brave men worked. How can women help loving men when they are so earnest, and so true, and so brave! And, too, it made me think of the wonderful power of money! What can it not do when basely used. I felt so thankful that Lord Godalming is rich, and both he and Mr. Morris, who also has plenty of money, are willing to spend it so freely. For if they did not, our little expedition could not start, either so promptly or so well equipped, as it will within another hour. It is not three hours since it was arranged what part each of us was to do. And now Lord Godalming and Jonathan have a lovely steam launch, with steam up ready to start at a moment's notice. Dr. Seward and Mr. Morris have half a dozen good horses, well appointed. We have all the maps and appliances of various kinds that can be had. Professor Van Helsing and I are to leave by the 11:40 train tonight for Veresti, where we are to get a carriage to drive to the Borgo Pass. We are bringing a good deal of ready money, as we are to buy a carriage and horses. We shall drive ourselves, for we have no one whom we can trust in the matter. The Professor knows something of a great many languages, so we shall get on all right. We have all got arms, even for me a large bore revolver. Jonathan would not be happy unless I was armed like the rest. Alas! I cannot carry one arm that the rest do, the scar on my forehead forbids that. Dear Dr. Van Helsing comforts me by telling me that I am fully armed as there may be wolves. The weather is getting colder every hour, and there are snow flurries which come and go as warnings.

Later.—It took all my courage to say goodbye to my darling. We may never meet again. Courage, Mina! The Professor is looking at you keenly. His look is a warning. There must be no tears now, unless it may be that God will let them fall in gladness.

JONATHAN HARKER'S JOURNAL

30 October, night.—I am writing this in the light from the furnace door of the steam launch. Lord Godalming is firing up. He is an experienced hand at the work, as he has had for years a launch of his own on the Thames, and another on the Norfolk Broads. Regarding our plans, we finally decided that Mina's guess was correct, and that if any waterway was chosen for the Count's escape back to his Castle, the Sereth and then the Bistritza at its junction, would be the one. We took it, that somewhere about the 47th degree, north latitude, would be the place chosen for crossing the country between the river and the Carpathians. We have no fear in running at good speed up the river at night. There is plenty of water, and the banks are wide enough apart to make steaming, even in the dark, easy enough. Lord Godalming tells me to sleep for a while, as it is enough for the present for one to be on watch. But I cannot sleep, how can I with the terrible danger hanging over my darling, and her going out into that awful place . . .

My only comfort is that we are in the hands of God. Only for that faith it would be easier to die than to live, and so be quit of all the trouble. Mr. Morris and Dr. Seward were off on their long ride before we started. They are to keep up the right bank, far enough off to get on higher lands where they can see a good stretch of river and avoid the following of its curves. They have, for the first stages, two men to ride and lead their spare horses, four in all, so as not to excite curiosity. When they dismiss the men, which shall be shortly, they shall themselves look after the horses. It may be necessary for us to join forces. If so they can mount our whole party. One of the saddles has a moveable horn, and can be easily adapted for Mina, if required.

It is a wild adventure we are on. Here, as we are rushing along through the darkness, with the cold from the river seeming to rise up and strike us, with all the mysterious voices of the night around us, it all comes home. We seem to be drifting into unknown places and unknown ways. Into a whole world of dark and dreadful things. Godalming is shutting the furnace door . . .

31 October.—Still hurrying along. The day has come, and Godalming is sleeping. I am on watch. The morning is bitterly cold, the furnace heat is grateful, though we have heavy fur coats. As yet we have passed only a few open boats, but none of them had on board any box or package of anything like the size of the one we seek. The men were scared every time we turned our electric lamp on them, and fell on their knees and prayed.

1 November, evening.—No news all day. We have found nothing of the kind we seek. We have now passed into the Bistritza, and if we are wrong in our surmise our chance is gone. We have overhauled every boat, big and little. Early this morning, one crew took us for a Government boat, and treated us accordingly. We saw in this a way of smoothing matters, so at Fundu, where the Bistritza runs into the Sereth, we got a Roumanian flag which we now fly conspicuously. With every boat which we have overhauled since then this trick has succeeded. We have had every deference shown to us, and not once any objection to whatever we chose to ask or do. Some of the Slovaks tell us that a big boat passed them, going at more than usual speed as she had a double crew on board. This was before they came to Fundu, so they could not tell us whether the boat turned into the Bistritza or continued on up the Sereth. At Fundu we could not hear of any such boat, so she must have passed there in the night. I am feeling very sleepy. The cold is perhaps beginning to tell upon me, and nature must have rest some time. Godalming insists that he shall keep the first watch. God bless him for all his goodness to poor dear Mina and me.

2 November, morning.—It is broad daylight. That good fellow would not wake me. He says it would have been a sin to, for I slept peacefully and was forgetting my trouble. It seems brutally selfish to me to have slept so long, and let him watch all night, but he was quite right. I am a new man this morning. And, as I sit here and watch him sleeping, I can do all that is necessary both as to minding the engine, steering, and keeping watch. I can feel that my strength and energy are coming back to me. I wonder where Mina is now, and Van Helsing. They should have got to Veresti about noon on Wednesday. It would take them some time to get the carriage and horses. So if they had started and travelled hard, they would be about now at the Borgo Pass. God guide and help them! I am afraid to think what may happen. If we could only go faster. But we cannot. The engines are throbbing and doing their utmost. I wonder how Dr. Seward and Mr. Morris are getting on. There seem to be endless streams running down the mountains into this river, but as none of them are very large, at present, at all events, though they are doubtless terrible in winter and when the snow melts, the horsemen may not have met much obstruction. I hope that before we get to Strasba we may see them. For if by that time we have not overtaken the Count, it may be necessary to take counsel together what to do next.

DR. SEWARD'S DIARY

2 November.—Three days on the road. No news, and no time to write it if there had been, for every moment is precious. We have had only the rest needful for the horses. But we are both bearing it wonderfully. Those adventurous days of ours are turning up useful. We must push on. We shall never feel happy till we get the launch in sight again.

3 November.—We heard at Fundu that the launch had gone up the Bistritza. I wish it wasn't so cold. There are signs of snow coming. And if it falls heavy it will stop us. In such case we must get a sledge and go on, Russian fashion.

4 November.—Today we heard of the launch having been detained by an accident when trying to force a way up the rapids. The Slovak boats get up all right, by aid of a rope and steering with knowledge. Some went up only a few hours before. Godalming is an amateur fitter[125] himself, and evidently it was he who put the launch in trim again.

Finally, they got up the rapids all right, with local help, and are off on the chase afresh. I fear that the boat is not any better for the accident, the peasantry tell us that after she got upon smooth water again, she kept stopping every now and again so long as she was in sight. We must push on harder than ever. Our help may be wanted soon.

MINA HARKER'S JOURNAL

31 October.—Arrived at Veresti at noon. The Professor tells me that this morning at dawn he could hardly hypnotize me at all, and that all I could say was, "dark and quiet." He is off now buying a carriage and horses. He says that he will later on try to buy additional horses, so that we may be able to change them on the way. We have something more than 70 miles before us. The country is lovely, and most interesting. If only we were under different conditions, how delightful it would be to see it all. If Jonathan and I were driving through it alone what a pleasure it would be. To stop and see people, and learn something of their life, and to fill our minds and memories with all the colour and picturesqueness of the whole wild, beautiful country and the quaint people! But, alas!

---

125 Steam engine repairman.

Later.—Dr. Van Helsing has returned. He has got the carriage and horses. We are to have some dinner, and to start in an hour. The landlady is putting us up a huge basket of provisions. It seems enough for a company of soldiers. The Professor encourages her, and whispers to me that it may be a week before we can get any food again. He has been shopping too, and has sent home such a wonderful lot of fur coats and wraps, and all sorts of warm things. There will not be any chance of our being cold.

We shall soon be off. I am afraid to think what may happen to us. We are truly in the hands of God. He alone knows what may be, and I pray Him, with all the strength of my sad and humble soul, that He will watch over my beloved husband. That whatever may happen, Jonathan may know that I loved him and honoured him more than I can say, and that my latest and truest thought will be always for him.

ℬ CHAPTER 27 ℛ
MINA HARKER'S JOURNAL

1 November.—All day long we have travelled, and at a good speed. The horses seem to know that they are being kindly treated, for they go willingly their full stage at best speed. We have now had so many changes and find the same thing so constantly that we are encouraged to think that the journey will be an easy one. Dr. Van Helsing is laconic, he tells the farmers that he is hurrying to Bistritz, and pays them well to make the exchange of horses. We get hot soup, or coffee, or tea, and off we go. It is a lovely country. Full of beauties of all imaginable kinds, and the people are brave, and strong, and simple, and seem full of nice qualities. They are *very, very* superstitious. In the first house where we stopped, when the woman who served us saw the scar on my forehead, she crossed herself and put out two fingers towards me, to keep off the evil eye. I believe they went to the trouble of putting an extra amount of garlic into our food, and I can't abide garlic. Ever since then I have taken care not to take off my hat or veil, and so have escaped their suspicions. We are travelling fast, and as we have no driver with us to carry tales, we go ahead of scandal. But I daresay that fear of the evil eye will follow hard behind us all the way. The Professor seems tireless. All day he would not take any rest, though he made me sleep for a long spell. At sunset time he hypnotized me, and he says I answered as usual, "darkness, lapping water and creaking wood." So our enemy is still on the river. I am afraid to think of Jonathan, but somehow I have now no fear for him, or for myself. I write this whilst we wait in a farmhouse for the horses to be ready. Dr. Van Helsing is sleeping. Poor dear, he looks very tired and old and grey, but his mouth is set as firmly as a conqueror's. Even in his sleep he is intense with resolution. When we have well started I must make him rest whilst I drive. I shall tell him that we have days before us, and he must not break down when most of all his strength will be needed . . . All is ready. We are off shortly.

2 November, morning.—I was successful, and we took turns driving all night. Now the day is on us, bright though cold. There is a strange heaviness in the air. I say heaviness for want of a better word. I mean that it oppresses us both. It is very cold, and only our warm furs keep us comfortable. At dawn Van Helsing hypnotized me. He says I answered "darkness, creaking wood and roaring water," so the river is changing as they ascend. I do hope that my darling will not run any chance of danger, more than need be, but we are in God's hands.

2 November, night.—All day long driving. The country gets wilder as we go, and the great spurs of the Carpathians, which at Veresti seemed so far from us and so low on the horizon, now seem to gather round us and tower in front. We both seem in good spirits. I think we make an effort each to cheer the other, in the doing so we cheer ourselves. Dr. Van Helsing says that by morning we shall reach the Borgo Pass. The houses are very few here now, and the Professor says that the last horse we got will have to go on with us, as we may not be able to change. He got two in addition to the two we changed, so that now we have a rude four-in-hand. The dear horses are patient and good, and they give us no trouble. We are not worried with other travellers, and so even I can drive. We shall get to the Pass in daylight. We do not want to arrive before. So we take it easy, and have each a long rest in turn. Oh, what will tomorrow bring to us? We go to seek the place where my poor darling suffered so much. God grant that we may be guided aright, and that He will deign to watch over my husband and those dear to us both, and who are in such deadly peril. As for me, I am not worthy in His sight. Alas! I am unclean to His eyes, and shall be until He may deign to let me stand forth in His sight as one of those who have not incurred His wrath.

MEMORANDUM BY ABRAHAM VAN HELSING

4 November.—This to my old and true friend John Seward, M.D., of Purfleet, London, in case I may not see him. It may explain. It is morning, and I write by a fire which all the night I have kept alive, Madam Mina aiding me. It is cold, cold. So cold that the grey heavy sky is full of snow, which when it falls will settle for all winter as the ground is hardening to receive it. It seems to have affected Madam Mina. She has been so heavy of head all day that she was not like herself. She sleeps, and sleeps, and sleeps! She who is usual so alert, have done literally nothing all the day. She even have lost her appetite. She make no entry into her little diary, she who write so faithful at every pause. Something whisper to me that all is not well. However, tonight she is more *vif*[126]. Her long sleep all day have refresh and restore her, for now she is all sweet and bright as ever. At sunset I try to hypnotize her, but alas! with no effect. The power has grown less and less with each day, and tonight it fail me altogether. Well, God's will be done, whatever it may be, and whithersoever it may lead!

Now to the historical, for as Madam Mina write not in her stenography, I must, in my cumbrous old fashion, that so each day of us may not go unrecorded.

We got to the Borgo Pass just after sunrise yesterday morning. When I saw the signs of the dawn I got ready for the hypnotism. We stopped our carriage, and got down so that there might be no disturbance. I made a couch with furs, and Madam Mina, lying down, yield herself as usual, but more slow and more short time than ever, to the hypnotic sleep. As before, came the answer, "darkness and the swirling of water." Then she woke, bright and radiant and we go on our way and soon reach the Pass. At this time and place, she become all on fire with zeal. Some new guiding power be in her manifested, for she point to a road and say, "This is the way."

"How know you it?" I ask.

"Of course I know it," she answer, and with a pause, add, "Have not my Jonathan travelled it and wrote of his travel?"

At first I think somewhat strange, but soon I see that there be only one such byroad. It is used but little, and very different from the coach road from the Bukovina to Bistritz, which is more wide and hard, and more of use.

So we came down this road. When we meet other ways, not always were we sure that they were roads at all, for they be neglect and light snow have fallen, the horses know and they only. I give rein to them, and they go on so

126 Lively.

patient. By and by we find all the things which Jonathan have note in that wonderful diary of him. Then we go on for long, long hours and hours. At the first, I tell Madam Mina to sleep. She try, and she succeed. She sleep all the time, till at the last, I feel myself to suspicious grow, and attempt to wake her. But she sleep on, and I may not wake her though I try. I do not wish to try too hard lest I harm her. For I know that she have suffer much, and sleep at times be all-in-all to her. I think I drowse myself, for all of sudden I feel guilt, as though I have done something. I find myself bolt up, with the reins in my hand, and the good horses go along jog, jog, just as ever. I look down and find Madam Mina still asleep. It is now not far off sunset time, and over the snow the light of the sun flow in big yellow flood, so that we throw great long shadow on where the mountain rise so steep. For we are going up, and up, and all is oh so wild and rocky, as though it were the end of the world.

Then I arouse Madam Mina. This time she wake with not much trouble, and then I try to put her to hypnotic sleep. But she sleep not, being as though I were not. Still I try and try, till all at once I find her and myself in dark, so I look round, and find that the sun have gone down. Madam Mina laugh, and I turn and look at her. She is now quite awake, and look so well as I never saw her since that night at Carfax when we first enter the Count's house. I am amaze, and not at ease then. But she is so bright and tender and thoughtful for me that I forget all fear. I light a fire, for we have brought supply of wood with us, and she prepare food while I undo the horses and set them, tethered in shelter, to feed. Then when I return to the fire she have my supper ready. I go to help her, but she smile, and tell me that she have eat already. That she was so hungry that she would not wait. I like it not, and I have grave doubts. But I fear to affright her, and so I am silent of it. She help me and I eat alone, and then we wrap in fur and lie beside the fire, and I tell her to sleep while I watch. But presently I forget all of watching. And when I sudden remember that I watch, I find her lying quiet, but awake, and looking at me with so bright eyes. Once, twice more the same occur, and I get much sleep till before morning. When I wake I try to hypnotize her, but alas! though she shut her eyes obedient, she may not sleep. The sun rise up, and up, and up, and then sleep come to her too late, but so heavy that she will not wake. I have to lift her up, and place her sleeping in the carriage when I have harnessed the horses and made all ready. Madam still sleep, and she look in her sleep more healthy and more redder than before. And I like it not. And I am afraid, afraid, afraid! I am afraid of all things, even to think but I must go on my way. The stake we play for is life and death, or more than these, and we must not flinch.

5 November, morning.—Let me be accurate in everything, for though you and I have seen some strange things together, you may at the first think that I, Van Helsing, am mad. That the many horrors and the so long strain on nerves has at the last turn my brain.

All yesterday we travel, always getting closer to the mountains, and moving into a more and more wild and desert land. There are great, frowning precipices and much falling water, and Nature seem to have held sometime her carnival. Madam Mina still sleep and sleep. And though I did have hunger and appeased it, I could not waken her, even for food. I began to fear that the fatal spell of the place was upon her, tainted as she is with that Vampire baptism. "Well," said I to myself, "if it be that she sleep all the day, it shall also be that I do not sleep at night." As we travel on the rough road, for a road of an ancient and imperfect kind there was, I held down my head and slept.

Again I waked with a sense of guilt and of time passed, and found Madam Mina still sleeping, and the sun low down. But all was indeed changed. The frowning mountains seemed further away, and we were near the top of a steep rising hill, on summit of which was such a castle as Jonathan tell of in his diary. At once I exulted and feared. For now, for good or ill, the end was near.

I woke Madam Mina, and again tried to hypnotize her, but alas! unavailing till too late. Then, ere the great dark came upon us, for even after down sun the heavens reflected the gone sun on the snow, and all was for a time in a great twilight. I took out the horses and fed them in what shelter I could. Then I make a fire, and near it I make Madam Mina, now awake and more charming than ever, sit comfortable amid her rugs. I got ready food, but she would not eat, simply saying that she had not hunger. I did not press her, knowing her unavailingness. But I myself eat, for I must needs now be strong for all. Then, with the fear on me of what might be, I drew a ring so big for her comfort, round where Madam Mina sat. And over the ring I passed some of the wafer, and I broke it fine so that all was well guarded. She sat still all the time, so still as one dead. And she grew whiter and even whiter till the snow was not more pale, and no word she said. But when I drew near, she clung to me, and I could know that the poor soul shook her from head to feet with a tremor that was pain to feel.

I said to her presently, when she had grown more quiet, "Will you not come over to the fire?" for I wished to make a test of what she could. She rose obedient, but when she have made a step she stopped, and stood as one stricken.

"Why not go on?" I asked. She shook her head, and coming back, sat down in her place. Then, looking at me with open eyes, as of one waked from sleep, she said simply, "I cannot!" and remained silent. I rejoiced, for I knew that what she could not, none of those that we dreaded could. Though there might be danger to her body, yet her soul was safe!

Presently the horses began to scream, and tore at their tethers till I came to them and quieted them. When they did feel my hands on them, they whinnied low as in joy, and licked at my hands and were quiet for a time. Many times through the night did I come to them, till it arrive to the cold hour when all nature is at lowest, and every time my coming was with quiet of them. In the cold hour the fire began to die, and I was about stepping forth to replenish it, for now the snow came in flying sweeps and with it a chill mist. Even in the dark there was a light of some kind, as there ever is over snow, and it seemed as though the snow flurries and the wreaths of mist took shape as of women with trailing garments. All was in dead, grim silence only that the horses whinnied and cowered, as if in terror of the worst. I began to fear, horrible fears. But then came to me the sense of safety in that ring wherein I stood. I began too, to think that my imaginings were of the night, and the gloom, and the unrest that I have gone through, and all the terrible anxiety. It was as though my memories of all Jonathan's horrid experience were befooling me. For the snow flakes and the mist began to wheel and circle round, till I could get as though a shadowy glimpse of those women that would have kissed him. And then the horses cowered lower and lower, and moaned in terror as men do in pain. Even the madness of fright was not to them, so that they could break away. I feared for my dear Madam Mina when these weird figures drew near and circled round. I looked at her, but she sat calm, and smiled at me. When I would have stepped to the fire to replenish it, she caught me and held me back, and whispered, like a voice that one hears in a dream, so low it was.

"No! No! Do not go without. Here you are safe!"

I turned to her, and looking in her eyes said, "But you? It is for you that I fear!"

Whereat she laughed, a laugh low and unreal, and said, "Fear for *me*! Why fear for me? None safer in all the world from them than I am," and as I wondered at the meaning of her words, a puff of wind made the flame leap up, and I see the red scar on her forehead. Then, alas! I knew. Did I not, I would soon have learned, for the wheeling figures of mist and snow came closer, but keeping ever without the Holy circle. Then they began to materialize till, if God have not taken away my reason, for I saw it through my eyes. There were before me in actual flesh the same three women that Jonathan saw in the room, when they would have kissed his throat. I knew the swaying round forms, the bright hard eyes, the white teeth, the ruddy colour, the voluptuous lips. They smiled ever at poor dear Madam Mina.

And as their laugh came through the silence of the night, they twined their arms and pointed to her, and said in those so sweet tingling tones that Jonathan said were of the intolerable sweetness of the water glasses, "Come, sister. Come to us. Come!"

In fear I turned to my poor Madam Mina, and my heart with gladness leapt like flame. For oh! the terror in her sweet eyes, the repulsion, the horror, told a story to my heart that was all of hope. God be thanked she was not, yet, of them. I seized some of the firewood which was by me, and holding out some of the Wafer, advanced on them towards the fire. They drew back before me, and laughed their low horrid laugh. I fed the fire, and feared them not. For I knew that we were safe within the ring, which she could not leave no more than they could enter. The horses had ceased to moan, and lay still on the ground. The snow fell on them softly, and they grew whiter. I knew that there was for the poor beasts no more of terror.

And so we remained till the red of the dawn began to fall through the snow gloom. I was desolate and afraid, and full of woe and terror. But when that beautiful sun began to climb the horizon life was to me again. At the first coming of the dawn the horrid figures melted in the whirling mist and snow. The wreaths of transparent gloom moved away towards the castle, and were lost.

Instinctively, with the dawn coming, I turned to Madam Mina, intending to hypnotize her. But she lay in a deep and sudden sleep, from which I could not wake her. I tried to hypnotize through her sleep, but she made no response, none at all, and the day broke. I fear yet to stir. I have made my fire and have seen the horses, they are all dead. Today I have much to do here, and I keep waiting till the sun is up high. For there may be places where I must go, where that sunlight, though snow and mist obscure it, will be to me a safety.

I will strengthen me with breakfast, and then I will do my terrible work. Madam Mina still sleeps, and God be thanked! She is calm in her sleep . . .

JONATHAN HARKER'S JOURNAL

4 November, evening.—The accident to the launch has been a terrible thing for us. Only for it we should have overtaken the boat long ago, and by now my dear Mina would have been free. I fear to think of her, off on the wolds near that horrid place. We have got horses, and we follow on the track. I note this whilst Godalming is getting ready. We have our arms. The Szgany must look out if they mean to fight. Oh, if only Morris and Seward were with us. We must only hope! If I write no more Goodby Mina! God bless and keep you.

DR. SEWARD'S DIARY

5 November.—With the dawn we saw the body of Szgany before us dashing away from the river with their leiter wagon. They surrounded it in a cluster, and hurried along as though beset. The snow is falling lightly and there is a strange excitement in the air. It may be our own feelings, but the depression is strange. Far off I hear the howling of wolves. The snow brings them down from the mountains, and there are dangers to all of us, and from all sides. The horses are nearly ready, and we are soon off. We ride to death of some one. God alone knows who, or where, or what, or when, or how it may be . . .

DR. VAN HELSING'S MEMORANDUM

5 November, afternoon.—I am at least sane. Thank God for that mercy at all events, though the proving it has been dreadful. When I left Madam Mina sleeping within the Holy circle, I took my way to the castle. The blacksmith hammer which I took in the carriage from Veresti was useful, though the doors were all open I broke them off the rusty hinges, lest some ill intent or ill chance should close them, so that being entered I might not get out. Jonathan's bitter experience served me here. By memory of his diary I found my way to the old chapel, for I knew that here my work lay. The air was oppressive. It seemed as if there was some sulphurous fume, which at times made me dizzy. Either there was a roaring in my ears or I heard afar off the howl of wolves. Then I bethought me of my dear Madam Mina, and I was in terrible plight. The dilemma had me between his horns.

Her, I had not dare to take into this place, but left safe from the Vampire in that Holy circle. And yet even there would be the wolf! I resolve me that my work lay here, and that as to the wolves we must submit, if it were God's will. At any rate it was only death and freedom beyond. So did I choose for her. Had it but been for myself the choice had been easy, the maw of the wolf were better to rest in than the grave of the Vampire! So I make my choice to go on with my work.

I knew that there were at least three graves to find, graves that are inhab-it. So I search, and search, and I find one of them. She lay in her Vampire sleep, so full of life and voluptuous beauty that I shudder as though I have come to do murder. Ah, I doubt not that in the old time, when such things were, many a man who set forth to do such a task as mine, found at the last his heart fail him, and then his nerve. So he delay, and delay, and delay, till the mere beauty and the fascination of the wanton Undead have hypnotize him. And he remain on and on, till sunset come, and the Vampire sleep be over. Then the beautiful eyes of the fair woman open and look love, and the voluptuous mouth present to a kiss, and the man is weak. And there remain one more victim in the Vampire fold. One more to swell the grim and grisly ranks of the Undead! . . .

There is some fascination, surely, when I am moved by the mere presence of such an one, even lying as she lay in a tomb fretted with age and heavy with the dust of centuries, though there be that horrid odour such as the lairs of the Count have had. Yes, I was moved. I, Van Helsing, with all my purpose and with my motive for hate. I was moved to a yearning for delay which seemed to paralyze my faculties and to clog my very soul. It may have been that the need of natural sleep, and the strange oppression of the air were beginning to overcome me. Certain it was that I was lapsing into sleep, the open eyed sleep of one who yields to a sweet fascination, when there came through the snow-stilled air a long, low wail, so full of woe and pity that it woke me like the sound of a clarion. For it was the voice of my dear Madam Mina that I heard.

Then I braced myself again to my horrid task, and found by wrenching away tomb tops one other of the sisters, the other dark one. I dared not pause to look on her as I had on her sister, lest once more I should begin to be enthrall. But I go on searching until, presently, I find in a high great tomb as if made to one much beloved that other fair sister which, like Jona-than I had seen to gather herself out of the atoms of the mist. She was so fair to look on, so radiantly beautiful, so exquisitely voluptuous, that the very instinct of man in me, which calls some of my sex to love and to protect one of hers, made my head whirl with new emotion. But God be thanked, that soul wail of my dear Madam Mina had not died out of my ears. And, before the spell could be wrought further upon me, I had nerved myself to my wild work. By this time I had searched all the tombs in the chapel, so far as I could tell. And as there had been only three of these Undead phantoms around us in the night, I took it that there were no more of active Undead existent. There was one great tomb more lordly than all the rest. Huge it was, and nobly proportioned. On it was but one word.

DRACULA

This then was the Undead home of the King Vampire, to whom so many more were due. Its emptiness spoke eloquent to make certain what I knew. Before I began to restore these women to their dead selves through my awful work, I laid in Dracula's tomb some of the Wafer, and so banished him from it, Undead, for ever.

Then began my terrible task, and I dreaded it. Had it been but one, it had been easy, comparative. But three! To begin twice more after I had been through a deed of horror. For it was terrible with the sweet Miss Lucy, what would it not be with these strange ones who had survived through centuries, and who had been strengthened by the passing of the years. Who would, if they could, have fought for their foul lives . . .

Oh, my friend John, but it was butcher work. Had I not been nerved by thoughts of other dead, and of the living over whom hung such a pall of fear, I could not have gone on. I tremble and tremble even yet, though till all was over, God be thanked, my nerve did stand. Had I not seen the repose in the first place, and the gladness that stole over it just ere the final dissolution came, as realization that the soul had been won, I could not have gone further with my butchery. I could not have endured the horrid screeching as the stake drove home, the plunging of writhing form, and lips of bloody foam. I should have fled in terror and left my work undone. But it is over! And the poor souls, I can pity them now and weep, as I think of them placid each in her full sleep of death for a short moment ere fading. For, friend John, hardly had my knife severed the head of each, before the whole body began to melt away and crumble into its native dust, as though the death that should have come centuries ago had at last assert himself and say at once and loud, "I am here!"

Before I left the castle I so fixed its entrances that never more can the Count enter there Undead.

When I stepped into the circle where Madam Mina slept, she woke from her sleep and, seeing me, cried out in pain that I had endured too much.

"Come!" she said, "come away from this awful place! Let us go to meet my husband who is, I know, coming towards us." She was looking thin and pale and weak. But her eyes were pure and glowed with fervour. I was glad to see her paleness and her illness, for my mind was full of the fresh horror of that ruddy vampire sleep.

And so with trust and hope, and yet full of fear, we go eastward to meet our friends, and *him*, whom Madam Mina tell me that she *know* are coming to meet us.

MINA HARKER'S JOURNAL

6 November.—It was late in the afternoon when the Professor and I took our way towards the east whence I knew Jonathan was coming. We did not go fast, though the way was steeply downhill, for we had to take heavy rugs and wraps with us. We dared not face the possibility of being left without warmth in the cold and the snow. We had to take some of our provisions too, for we were in a perfect desolation, and so far as we could see through the snowfall, there was not even the sign of habitation. When we had gone about a mile, I was tired with the heavy walking and sat down to rest. Then we looked back and saw where the clear line of Dracula's castle cut the sky. For we were so deep under the hill whereon it was set that the angle of perspective of the Carpathian mountains was far below it. We saw it in all its grandeur, perched a thousand feet on the summit of a sheer precipice, and with seemingly a great gap between it and the steep of the adjacent mountain on any side. There was something wild and uncanny about the place. We could hear the distant howling of wolves. They were far off, but the sound, even though coming muffled through the deadening snowfall, was full of terror. I knew from the way Dr. Van Helsing was searching about that he was trying to seek some strategic point, where we would be less exposed in case of attack. The rough roadway still led downwards. We could trace it through the drifted snow.

In a little while the Professor signalled to me, so I got up and joined him. He had found a wonderful spot, a sort of natural hollow in a rock, with an entrance like a doorway between two boulders. He took me by the hand and drew me in.

"See!" he said, "here you will be in shelter. And if the wolves do come I can meet them one by one."

He brought in our furs, and made a snug nest for me, and got out some provisions and forced them upon me. But I could not eat, to even try to do so was repulsive to me, and much as I would have liked to please him, I could not bring myself to the attempt. He looked very sad, but did not reproach me. Taking his field glasses from the case, he stood on the top of the rock, and began to search the horizon.

Suddenly he called out, "Look! Madam Mina, look! Look!"

I sprang up and stood beside him on the rock. He handed me his glasses and pointed. The snow was now falling more heavily, and swirled about fiercely, for a high wind was beginning to blow. However, there were times when there were pauses between the snow flurries and I could see a long way round. From the height where we were it was possible to see a great distance. And far off, beyond the white waste of snow, I could see the river lying like a black ribbon in kinks and curls as it wound its way. Straight in front of us and not far off, in fact so near that I wondered we had not noticed before, came a group of mounted men hurrying along. In the midst of them was a cart, a long leiter wagon which swept from side to side, like a dog's tail wagging, with each stern inequality of the road. Outlined against the snow as they were, I could see from the men's clothes that they were peasants or gypsies of some kind.

On the cart was a great square chest. My heart leaped as I saw it, for I felt that the end was coming. The evening was now drawing close, and well I knew that at sunset the Thing, which was till then imprisoned there, would take new freedom and could in any of many forms elude pursuit. In fear I turned to the Professor. To my consternation, however, he was not there. An instant later, I saw him below me. Round the rock he had drawn a circle, such as we had found shelter in last night.

When he had completed it he stood beside me again saying, "At least you shall be safe here from *him*!" He took the glasses from me, and at the next lull of the snow swept the whole space below us. "See," he said, "they come quickly. They are flogging the horses, and galloping as hard as they can."

He paused and went on in a hollow voice, "They are racing for the sunset. We may be too late. God's will be done!" Down came another blinding rush of driving snow, and the whole landscape was blotted out. It soon passed, however, and once more his glasses were fixed on the plain.

Then came a sudden cry, "Look! Look! Look! See, two horsemen follow fast, coming up from the south. It must be Quincey and John. Take the glass. Look before the snow blots it all out!" I took it and looked. The two men might be Dr. Seward and Mr. Morris. I knew at all events that neither of them was Jonathan. At the same time I *knew* that Jonathan was not far off. Looking around I saw on the north side of the coming party two other men, riding at breakneck speed. One of them I knew was Jonathan, and the other I took, of course, to be Lord Godalming. They too, were pursuing the party with the cart. When I told the Professor he shouted in glee like a schoolboy, and after looking intently till a snow fall made sight impossible, he laid his Winchester rifle ready for use against the boulder at the opening of our shelter.

"They are all converging," he said. "When the time comes we shall have gypsies on all sides." I got out my revolver ready to hand, for whilst we were speaking the howling of wolves came louder and closer. When the snow storm abated a moment we looked again. It was strange to see the snow falling in such heavy flakes close to us, and beyond, the sun shining more and more brightly as it sank down towards the far mountain tops. Sweeping the glass all around us I could see here and there dots moving singly and in twos and threes and larger numbers. The wolves were gathering for their prey.

Every instant seemed an age whilst we waited. The wind came now in fierce bursts, and the snow was driven with fury as it swept upon us in circling eddies. At times we could not see an arm's length before us. But at others, as the hollow sounding wind swept by us, it seemed to clear the air space around us so that we could see afar off. We had of late been so accustomed to watch for sunrise and sunset, that we knew with fair accuracy when it would be. And we knew that before long the sun would set. It was hard to believe that by our watches it was less than an hour that we waited in that rocky shelter before the various bodies began to converge close upon us. The wind came now with fiercer and more bitter sweeps, and more steadily from the north. It seemingly had driven the snow clouds from us, for with only occasional bursts, the snow fell. We could distinguish clearly the individuals of each party, the pursued and the pursuers. Strangely enough those pursued did not seem to realize, or at least to care, that they were pursued. They seemed, however, to hasten with redoubled speed as the sun dropped lower and lower on the mountain tops.

Closer and closer they drew. The Professor and I crouched down behind our rock, and held our weapons ready. I could see that he was determined that they should not pass. One and all were quite unaware of our presence.

All at once two voices shouted out to "Halt!" One was my Jonathan's, raised in a high key of passion. The other Mr. Morris' strong resolute tone of quiet command. The gypsies may not have known the language, but there was no mistaking the tone, in whatever tongue the words were spoken. Instinctively they reined in, and at the instant Lord Godalming and Jonathan dashed up at one side and Dr. Seward and Mr. Morris on the other. The leader of the gypsies, a splendid looking fellow who sat his horse like a centaur, waved them back, and in a fierce voice gave to his companions some word to proceed. They lashed the horses which sprang forward. But the four men raised their Winchester rifles, and in an unmistakable way commanded them to stop. At the same moment Dr. Van Helsing and I rose behind the rock and pointed our weapons at them. Seeing that they were surrounded the men tightened their reins and drew up. The leader turned to them and gave a word at which every man of the gypsy party drew what weapon he carried, knife or pistol, and held himself in readiness to attack. Issue was joined in an instant.

The leader, with a quick movement of his rein, threw his horse out in front, and pointed first to the sun, now close down on the hill tops, and then to the castle, said something which I did not understand. For answer, all four men of our party threw themselves from their horses and dashed towards the cart. I should have felt terrible fear at seeing Jonathan in such danger, but that the ardor of battle must have been upon me as well as the rest of them. I felt no fear, but only a wild, surging desire to do something. Seeing the quick movement of our parties, the leader of the gypsies gave a command. His men instantly formed round the cart in a sort of undisciplined endeavour, each one shouldering and pushing the other in his eagerness to carry out the order.

In the midst of this I could see that Jonathan on one side of the ring of men, and Quincey on the other, were forcing a way to the cart. It was evident that they were bent on finishing their task before the sun should set. Nothing seemed to stop or even to hinder them. Neither the levelled weapons nor the flashing knives of the gypsies in front, nor the howling of the wolves behind, appeared to even attract their attention. Jonathan's impetuosity, and the manifest singleness of his purpose, seemed to overawe those in front of him. Instinctively they cowered aside and let him pass. In an instant he had jumped upon the cart, and with a strength which seemed incredible, raised the great box, and flung it over the wheel to the ground. In the meantime, Mr. Morris had had to use force to pass through his side of the ring of Szgany. All the time I had been breathlessly watching Jonathan I had, with the tail of my eye, seen him pressing desperately forward, and had seen the knives of the gypsies flash as he won a way through them, and they cut at him. He had parried with his great bowie knife, and at first I thought that he too had come through in safety. But as he sprang beside Jonathan, who had by now jumped from the cart, I could see that with his left hand he was clutching at his side, and that the blood was spurting through his fingers. He did not delay notwithstanding this, for as Jonathan, with desperate energy, attacked one end of the chest, attempting to prize off the lid with his great Kukri knife, he attacked the other frantically with his bowie. Under the efforts of both men the lid began to yield. The nails drew with a screeching sound, and the top of the box was thrown back.

By this time the gypsies, seeing themselves covered by the Winchesters, and at the mercy of Lord Godalming and Dr. Seward, had given in and made no further resistance. The sun was almost down on the mountain tops, and the shadows of the whole group fell upon the snow. I saw the Count lying within the box upon the earth, some of which the rude falling from the cart had scattered over him. He was deathly pale, just like a waxen image, and the red eyes glared with the horrible vindictive look which I knew so well.

As I looked, the eyes saw the sinking sun, and the look of hate in them turned to triumph.

But, on the instant, came the sweep and flash of Jonathan's great knife. I shrieked as I saw it shear through the throat. Whilst at the same moment Mr. Morris's bowie knife plunged into the heart.

It was like a miracle, but before our very eyes, and almost in the drawing of a breath, the whole body crumbled into dust and passed from our sight.

I shall be glad as long as I live that even in that moment of final dissolution, there was in the face a look of peace, such as I never could have imagined might have rested there.

The Castle of Dracula now stood out against the red sky, and every stone of its broken battlements was articulated against the light of the setting sun.

The gypsies, taking us as in some way the cause of the extraordinary disappearance of the dead man, turned, without a word, and rode away as if for their lives. Those who were unmounted jumped upon the leiter wagon and shouted to the horsemen not to desert them. The wolves, which had withdrawn to a safe distance, followed in their wake, leaving us alone.

Mr. Morris, who had sunk to the ground, leaned on his elbow, holding his hand pressed to his side. The blood still gushed through his fingers. I flew to him, for the Holy circle did not now keep me back; so did the two doctors. Jonathan knelt behind him and the wounded man laid back his head on his shoulder. With a sigh he took, with a feeble effort, my hand in that of his own which was unstained.

He must have seen the anguish of my heart in my face, for he smiled at me and said, "I am only too happy to have been of service! Oh, God!" he cried suddenly, struggling to a sitting posture and pointing to me. "It was worth for this to die! Look! Look!"

The sun was now right down upon the mountain top, and the red gleams fell upon my face, so that it was bathed in rosy light. With one impulse the men sank on their knees and a deep and earnest "Amen" broke from all as their eyes followed the pointing of his finger.

The dying man spoke, "Now God be thanked that all has not been in vain! See! The snow is not more stainless than her forehead! The curse has passed away!"

And, to our bitter grief, with a smile and in silence, he died, a gallant gentleman.

NOTE

Seven years ago we all went through the flames. And the happiness of some of us since then is, we think, well worth the pain we endured. It is an added joy to Mina and to me that our boy's birthday is the same day as that on which Quincey Morris died. His mother holds, I know, the secret belief that some of our brave friend's spirit has passed into him.

His bundle of names links all our little band of men together. But we call him Quincey.

In the summer of this year we made a journey to Transylvania, and went over the old ground which was, and is, to us so full of vivid and terrible memories. It was almost impossible to believe that the things which we had seen with our own eyes and heard with our own ears were living truths. Every trace of all that had been was blotted out. The castle stood as before, reared high above a waste of desolation.

When we got home we were talking of the old time, which we could all look back on without despair, for Godalming and Seward are both happily married. I took the papers from the safe where they had been ever since our return so long ago. We were struck with the fact, that in all the mass of material of which the record is composed, there is hardly one authentic document. Nothing but a mass of typewriting, except the later notebooks of Mina and Seward and myself, and Van Helsing's memorandum. We could hardly ask any one, even did we wish to, to accept these as proofs of so wild a story. Van Helsing summed it all up as he said, with our boy on his knee.

"We want no proofs. We ask none to believe us! This boy will some day know what a brave and gallant woman his mother is. Already he knows her sweetness and loving care. Later on he will understand how some men so loved her, that they did dare much for her sake."

Jonathan Harker